River Forth

Stirling

Dysart

Firth of Forth

Culross

Carriden
Blackness

Berecrofts

Carriden

Dirleton

Linlithgow

Corstorphine

Leith

Seton

Haddington

Torphichen

Edinburgh

Tranent

River Avon

Renfrew
Paisley

Roslin

Beltrees

SCOTLAND

0   10   20

Miles

Kilmarnock

Peebles

Biggar

Broughton

KINGDOM OF HUNGARY

Principality of Moldavia

KDM. OF GEORGIA

Caffa
(Genoese control)

Pr. of Wallachia

Black Sea

Danube

Trebizond

Principality of Serbia

Kerasous

Ragusa

OTTOMAN

Bosphorus

Emirate of the White Sheep Turks

Venice

Constantinople

SULTANATE

Salonika

ALBANIA

Bursa

Ankara

Corfu
(to Venice)

Phocoea

Smyrna

Emirate

of

Konya

Aleppo

Negroponte

Karaman

Antioch

SYRIA

Zante
(to Venice)

Athens

Alanya

Modon
(to Venice)

Rhodes

Nicosia

Famagusta

Beirut

Damascus

CYPRUS

Middle

Crete
(to Venice)

Sea

Jaffa

Jerusalem

Gaza

Damietta

Alexandria

EUROPE &
THE LEVANT

1468 ~ 1471

Cairo

Sinai
Pen.

Gulf
of Aqaba

MAMELUKE
SULTANATE

Tor

Nile

Red
Sea

EGYPT

The
Unicorn Hunt

The House of Niccolò

The
Unicorn Hunt

Dorothy Dunnett

ALFRED A. KNOPF   NEW YORK   1994

THIS IS A BORZOI BOOK
PUBLISHED BY ALFRED A. KNOPF, INC.

Copyright © 1993 by Dorothy Dunnett
Introduction copyright © 1994 by Judith Wilt

Library of Congress Cataloging-in-Publication Data
Dunnett, Dorothy.
The unicorn hunt / Dorothy Dunnett. — 1st ed.
p. cm.
ISBN 0-394-58628-X
1. Vander Poele, Nicholas (Fictitious character)—Fiction.
2. Fifteenth century—Fiction. 3. Bankers—Europe—Fiction. I. Title.
PR6054.U56U55 1994
823'.914—dc20 93-35692
CIP

Manufactured in the United States of America
FIRST AMERICAN EDITION

Characters

October, 1468 – February, 1471
(Those marked * are recorded in history)

Rulers
*England: King Edward IV, House of York, vying with *Henry VI,
    House of Lancaster
*Scotland: King James III
*France: King Louis XI
*Flanders: Duke Charles of Burgundy
*Pope: Paul II
*Venice: Doge Cristoforo Moro
*Milan: Duke Galeazzo-Maria Sforza
*Cyprus: King James de Lusignan (Zacco)
*Portugal: King Alfonso V
*Ottoman Empire: Sultan Mehmet II
*Mameluke Empire: Sultan Qayt Bey

House of Niccolò
(COUNTING-HOUSES IN VENICE AND BRUGES):
  Nicholas (Niccolò) de Fleury, master (formerly vander Poele)
  Gelis van Borselen, dame de Fleury, his wife
  Gregorio (Goro) of Asti, lawyer and manager
  Margot, Gregorio's mistress
  Julius of Bologna, notary and manager
  Cristoffels (Cefo), Venice management
  Tobias Beventini of Grado, physician
  Father Godscalc of Cologne, chaplain
  Father Moriz of Augsburg, chaplain and metallurgist
  John le Grant, engineer, Alexandria agent
  Diniz Vasquez, Bruges management
  Mathilde (Tilde) de Charetty, his wife
  Catherine de Charetty, her younger sister
  Henninc, dyeworks manager, Bruges
  Astorre (Syrus de Astariis) mercenary commander
  Thomas, deputy to Astorre
  Michael Crackbene, shipmaster

*John (Jannekin) Bonkle, agent in Scotland, bastard of the Provost of
    Trinity College, Edinburgh
Oliver Semple, Scottish land factor
Wilhelm of Hall, goldsmith
Bertuccio, agent in Florence
Achille, sub-agent, Alexandria
Govaerts of Brussels, steward
Ederic of Antwerp, manservant
Donat of Louvain, huntsman/groom
Dionigi, cook
Ochoa de Marchena, former shipmaster of the *Ghost/Doria*

Scotland
*James Stewart, (third of the name), King of Scotland
*Alexander (Sandy) Stewart, Duke of Albany, his brother
*Sir James (Jamie) Liddell of Halkerston, Albany's steward
*John Stewart, Earl of Mar, the King's younger brother
*Margaret Stewart (Bleezie Meg), the King's younger sister
*Mariota Darrauch, nurse to Margaret
*Mary Stewart, Countess of Arran, the King's elder sister
*Thomas Boyd, Earl of Arran, her husband
*Robert, Lord Boyd, father of Thomas
*James Stewart of Auchterhouse (Hearty James), half-uncle to King
    James
*John Stewart, Earl of Atholl, another half-uncle
*Margaret of Denmark, Norway, Vandalia etc., bride of King James
*Colin Campbell, 1st Earl of Argyll, Master of the Royal Household
*Archibald Whitelaw, Royal Secretary
*Andrew Stewart, Lord Avandale, Chancellor
*Patrick Graham, Bishop of St Andrews (nephew of Bishop Kennedy)
*James Hamilton of Cadzow, 1st Lord Hamilton
*Joneta Hamilton, his natural daughter
*Sir Robert Semple of Elliotstoun, sheriff of Renfrew
*William Semple his son, 'second cousin to Oliver Semple'
*Robert, Lord Fleming of Biggar
*Malcolm Fleming, his son
*John and David, his grandsons
Jordan de St Pol of Kilmirren, vicomte de Ribérac, merchant-magnate
    of Scotland and France
Simon de St Pol the Younger of Kilmirren, his son
Henry de St Pol, son of Simon's late wife Katelina, sister to Gelis van
    Borselen
Lucia, sister of Simon and mother of Diniz Vasquez
Matten, her maid
Isobella (Bel) of Cuthilgurdy, her neighbour
*Andro Wodman, 'escort of Bel'
*John Lamb, Leith merchant
*Thomas (Thom) Swift, Edinburgh merchant

*William of Berecrofts (Old Will), Canongate merchant
*Archibald of Berecrofts the Younger (Archie), his son
*Robin, son of Archie
*William Sinclair, Earl of Caithness and Orkney
*Elizabeth (Betha) Sinclair, his daughter, widow of Patrick Dunbar of
    Blantyre and Cumnock
*Catherine Sinclair, his daughter by another wife
*Euphemia (Phemie) Dunbar, Betha's cousin, daughter of George
    Dunbar, Earl of March, and of Orkney's sister
*Elizabeth, Prioress, Cistercian Priory, Haddington
*Dame Alisia Maitland, nun of the same priory
 Ada, priory servant
*William Roger (Whistle Willie), English musician
*Thomas Cochrane, master mason
*William Scheves, cleric, royal apothecary
*Archibald Crawford, Abbot of Holyrood
*Sir William Knollys, Preceptor in Scotland of the Order of the Knights
    Hospitaller of St John of Jerusalem
*John Gosyn of Kinloch, a chaplain of the Order
*David (Davie) Lindsay, 5th Earl of Crawford
*James (Jack) Lindsay, his cousin in the Tyrol
*George, second Lord Seton
*Edward Bonkle, Provost of Trinity College, Edinburgh
*Andrew Haliburton, merchant
*Cornelia, his wife, daughter of Catherine van der Goes
*Alexander Napier of Merchiston, merchant, vice-admiral of Scotland
*Gilbert of Edmonston, merchant of Leith
*Walter Bertram, merchant of Canongate
*Stephen Angus, agent, Canongate and Bruges
*John Brown, merchant of Leith
*John Lauder, burgess of Canongate
*Martin Gordon, merchant, Canongate and Leith
*William Touris, merchant of Canongate
*Matthew Auchinleck, goldsmith of Canongate

Flanders and the Duchy of Burgundy
*Charles, Duke of Burgundy and Brabant, Count of Flanders, Holland,
    Zeeland etc.
*Margaret of York, his wife and sister of King Edward IV
*Cecily Nevill, Duchess of York, mother of Duchess Margaret and King
    Edward
*Isabelle of Portugal, Dowager Duchess of Burgundy
*Anselm Adorne, merchant, nobleman, magistrate, of the Hôtel Jerusalem,
    Bruges
*Margriet van der Banck, his wife
*Anselm Sersanders, his nephew from Ghent
*Katelijne (Kathi) Sersanders, his niece
*Jan Adorne, law student, his oldest son

*Katelijne Adorne, his daughter, serving Duchess Cecily in England
*Maarten, divinity student, a younger son
*Lewisje, Antoon and Arnoud, youngest sons
  Emmelot, maid to Katelijne Sersanders
*Dr Andreas of Vesalia, physician in Bruges and Scotland
*Jehan Metteneye, host to Scots merchants in Bruges
*Daniel Colebrant, Bruges merchant
*Lambert van de Walle, merchant kinsman of Adorne
*Pieter Reyphin, merchant kinsman of van de Walle
*Antoine de Francqueville, chaplain to the Duke of Burgundy
*Audomaro, monk of St Nicholas, Furnes, his companion
*William Caxton, Governor of the English Nation at Bruges
*Henry van Borselen, seigneur of Veere, admiral to the Duke; 'uncle' of
      Gelis van Borselen
*Wolfaert van Borselen, his son
*Charlotte de Bourbon, daughter of the Count of Montpensier, Wolfaert's
      second wife
*Paul van Borselen, bastard son of Wolfaert
*Louis de Bruges, seigneur de Gruuthuse, merchant nobleman
*Marguerite van Borselen, his wife
*William Hugonet, Chancellor of the Duchy of Burgundy
*Michael Alighieri, merchant of Florence and Trebizond
*Nerio of Trebizond, exile, Burgundian court
*Hugo van der Goes, artist
*Colard Mansion, scribe and illustrator

Republic of Venice
*Marco Corner, merchant, sugar-grower in Cyprus
*Fiorenza of Naxos, his wife, sister of Valenza and Violante below
*Andrea Corner, his brother
*Catherine, his daughter, Queen of Cyprus
*Giovanni (Vanni) Loredano, deputy Bailie of Cyprus
*Valenza of Naxos his wife
*Caterino Zeno, merchant
*Violante of Naxos, his wife
*Paul Erizzo, Venetian Bailie in Negroponte
*Anne, his daughter
*Niccolò da Canale, Captain-General of the Sea
*Piero Bembo, merchant
*Family of Filippo Buonaccorsi of Murano
*Brother Lorenzo of Crete, steward and treasurer of the monastery of St
      Catherine's, Mount Sinai

Republic of Florence
*Piero de' Medici, head of the House of Medici
*Pierfrancesco de' Medici, his cousin
*Laudomia Acciajuoli, wife to Pierfrancesco
*Nicholai Giorgio de' Acciajuoli, Greek-Florentine cousin of Laudomia

*Bartolomeo Giorgio (Zorzi) his brother, alum merchant
*Benedetto Dei, Medici agent in Africa and the Levant
*Tommaso Portinari, Medici manager in Bruges
*Maria, his wife, daughter of Francesco Bandini Baroncelli
*Alessandra Macinghi negli Strozzi, merchant's widow
*Filippo Strozzi of Naples and Florence, her elder son
*Lorenzo di Matteo Strozzi of Naples, her younger son
*Antonia, his wife, sister of Maria Baroncelli above
*Caterina, daughter of Alessandra Strozzi
*Marco Parenti, silk merchant, husband of Caterina
*Mariotto Squarcialupi, Florentine consul in Cyprus and Alexandria
*Francesco Sassetti, Medici manager, Lyons
*Francesco Nori, recently of the Medici company, Lyons

The Duchy of the Tyrol
*Sigismond, Duke of Austria and Styria and Count of the Tyrol
*Eleanor Stewart, his wife, aunt to the King of Scotland
  Gertrude, mistress of the Duchess's ladies
*Antonio Cavalli, Venetian adviser to the Duke

The Vatachino Company and Associates: Genoese
*David de Salmeton, broker, merchant and agent
Martin, broker, merchant and agent
*Prospero Schiaffino de Camulio de' Medici, Genoese and Milanese
    agent
*Pietro de Persis, Genoese consul in Alexandria
*Tobias Lomellini, Treasurer of the Knights Hospitaller

Rome
*Pope Paul II
*Bessarion (John) of Trebizond, Cardinal Patriarch of Constantinople,
    Archbishop of Negroponte
*Father Ludovico de Severi da Bologna, Patriarch of Antioch
*Philibert Hugonet, doyen of St Vincent of Mâcon (brother of Chancellor
    Hugonet of Burgundy)

Mameluke Sultanate of Cairo and Alexandria
*Sultan Qayt Bey, Cairo
*Grand Emir the Dawadar Yachbak, Cairo
*Emir Madjlis, Master of Ceremonies, Cairo
*Katib Musa, of the imamate of Sankore, Timbuktu
  Abderrahman ibn Said, merchant of Timbuktu
*Katib al Sirr, the Clerk of the Secrets, Cairo
*Chief Dragoman, Cairo
*Cami Bey, Second Dragoman, Cairo

Cyprus
*King James de Lusignan (Zacco)

*Marietta of Patras, his mother (Cropnose)
*Jorgin, his servant
*Sir Rizzo di Marino, Sicilian chamberlain to the King
*Sor de Naves, Sicilian Constable of Cyprus
*Louis Perez Fabrice, Catalan Archbishop of Nicosia
*John Langstrother, former Grand Commander of Kolossi Castle of the
    Knights

Persia and Karamania
*Uzum Hasan, Turcoman prince of Persia
*Hadji Mehmet, his Chief Delegate
*Emir Kilidje Arslan II of Karamania

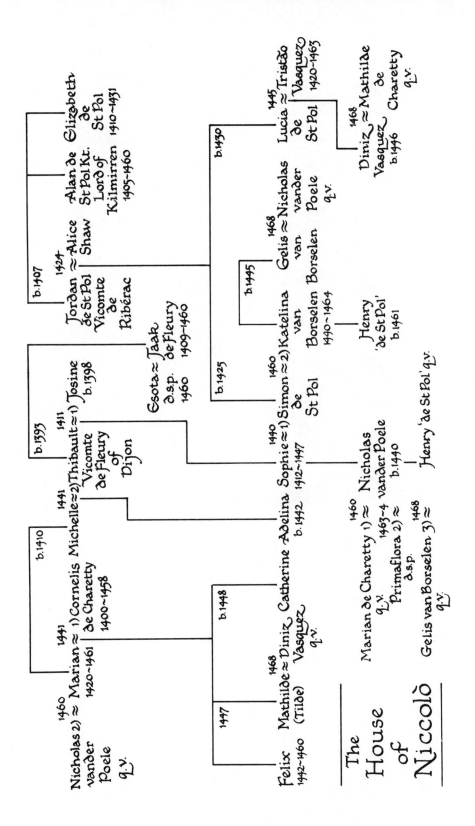

The
House
of
Niccolò

INTRODUCTION

THE ELEGANT WORKING out of designs historical and romantic, political and commercial, psychological and moral, over a multivolume novel is a Dorothy Dunnett specialty. In her first work in this genre, the six-volume "Lymond Chronicles," suspense was created and relieved in each volume, and over the whole set of volumes; the final, beautifully inevitable, romantic secret was disclosed on the very last page of the last volume. *The House of Niccolò* does the same.

The reader of *The Unicorn Hunt*, then, may wish to move directly to the narrative for a first experience of that pattern, with a reader's faith in an experienced author's caretaking; the novel itself briefly supplies the information you need to know from past novels, telling its own tale while completing and inaugurating others. What follows, as a sketch of the geopolitical and dramatic terrain unfolding in the volumes which precede *The Unicorn Hunt*, may be useful to read now, or at any point along the narrative, or after reading, as an indication of which stories of interest to this volume may be found most fully elaborated in which previous volume.

VOLUME I: *Niccolò Rising*

"From Venice to Cathay, from Seville to the Gold Coast of Africa, men anchored their ships and opened their ledgers and weighed one thing against another as if nothing would ever change." The first sentence of the first volume indicates the scope of this series, and the cultural and psychological dynamic of the story and its hero, whose private motto is "Change, change and adapt." It is the motto, too, of fifteenth-century Bruges, center of commerce and conduit of new ideas and technologies between the Islamic East and the Christian West, between the Latin South and the Celtic-Saxon North, haven of political refugees from the English Wars of the Roses, a site of muted conflict between trading giants Venice and Genoa and states in the making and on the take all around. Mrs. Dunnett has set her story in the fifteenth century, between Gutenberg and Columbus, between Donatello and Martin Luther, between the rise of mercantile culture and the fall of chivalry, as that age of receptivity to—addiction to—change called "the Renaissance" gathers its powers.

Her hero is a deceptively silly-looking, disastrously tactless eighteen-year-old dyeworks artisan named "Claes," who emerges by the end of the novel as the merchant-mathematician Nicholas vander Poele. Prodigiously gifted at numbers, and the material and social "engineering" skills that go with it, Nicholas has until now resisted the responsibility of his powers, his identity fractured by the enmity of both his mother's husband's family, the Scottish St Pols, who refuse to own him legitimate, and his maternal family, the Burgundian de Fleurys, who failed his mother and abused him and reduced him to serfdom as a child. He found refuge at age ten with his grandfather's in-laws, especially the Bruges widow Marian de Charetty, whose dyeing and broking business becomes the tool of Nicholas' desperate self-fashioning apart from the malice of his blood relatives.

Soon even public Bruges and the states beyond come to see the engineer under the artisan. The Charetty business expands to include a courier and intelligence service between Italian and Northern states, its bodyguard sharpened into a skilled mercenary force, its pawnbroking consolidated toward banking and commodities trading. And as the chameleon artificer of all this, Nicholas incurs the ambiguous interest of the Bruges patrician Anselm Adorne and the Greco-Florentine prince Nicholai Giorgio de' Acciajuoli, both of whom steer him toward a role in the rivalry between Venice, in whose interest Acciajuoli labors, and Genoa, original home of the Adorne family. This trading rivalry will erupt in different novels around different, always highly symbolic commodities: silk, sugar, glass, gold, and human beings. In this first novel the contested product is alum, the mineral that binds dyes to cloth, blood to the body, conspirators to a conspiracy—in this case, to keep secret the news of a newly found deposit of the mineral in the Papal States while Venice and her allies monopolize the current supply.

Acciajuoli and Adorne are father-mentor figures Nicholas can respect, resist, or join on roughly equal intellectual terms—whereas the powerful elder males of his blood, his mother's uncle, Jaak de Fleury, and his father's father, Jordan de Ribérac, steadily rip open wounds first inflicted in childhood. In direct conflict he is emotionally helpless before them. What he possesses superbly, however, are the indirect defenses of an "engineer." The Charetty business partners and others who hitch their wagons to his star—Astorre the mercenary leader, Julius the notary, Gregorio the lawyer, Tobias Beventini the physician, the Guinea slave Lopez—watch as a complex series of commodity and currency maneuvers by the apparently innocent Nicholas brings about the financial and political ruin of de Fleury and de Ribérac; and they nearly desert him for the conscienceless avenger he appears to be, especially after de Fleury dies in a fight with, though not directly at the hands of, his nephew.

The faith and love of Marian de Charetty make them rethink their view of this complicated personality. Marian, whose son was killed beside Nicholas in the Italian wars, and whose sister married into his family, is moved towards the end of the novel to suggest that Nicholas take her in marriage. It is to be platonic: her way of giving him standing, of displaying her trust in him and his management of the business, and of solacing him in his anguish. Once married, however, she longs despite herself for physical love, and Nicholas, who owes her everything, finds happiness also in making the marriage complete.

That marriage, however, sows the seeds of tragedy. The royally connected Katelina van Borselen, "characterful," intelligent, and hungry for experiences usually denied a genteel lady, has refused the vicious or vacuous suitors considered eligible, and seeks sexual initiation at the hands of the merry young artisan so popular with the kitchen wenches of Bruges. Against his better judgment, Nicholas is led to comply, for, however brusque her demands, she has just saved his life in one of the several episodes in which the St Pols try to destroy him. Two nights of genuine intimacy undermined by mismatched desires and miscommunicated intentions culminate in Katelina's solitary pregnancy. Unaware of this, Nicholas enters his marriage with Marian, and Katelina, alone, fatalistically marries the man in pursuit of her, the handsome, shrewd, and fatally self-centered Simon de St Pol, the man Nicholas claims is his father. Sickened at what she believes is Nicholas' ultimate revenge on his family—to illegitimately father its heir—Katelina becomes Nicholas' most determined enemy.

VOLUME II: *The Spring of the Ram*

Simon de St Pol, the overshadowed son of Jordan de Ribérac, husband of the bitter Katelina, father of the secretly illegitimate Henry, has clearly had his spirit poisoned long since by the powerful

and malignant de Ribérac, and is as much pitied as loathed by
Nicholas vander Poele, who sees in Simon something of his own
deracinated brilliance. Looking to find a sphere of activity where
Simon and Nicholas can no longer injure each other, Marian de
Charetty, now the wife of Nicholas, persuades her husband to
take up an exciting and dangerous project: to trade in Trebizond,
last outpost of the ancient empire of Byzantium.

It is less than a decade since Sultan Mehmet took Constantinople, and the several forces of Islam—Mehmet's Ottomans, Uzum
Hassan's Turcomans, Kushcadam's Egyptian Mamelukes—ring the
Christian outpost while delegates from the Greek Orthodox East,
led by the very earthy and autocratic Franciscan friar Ludovico de
Severi da Bologna, scour the Latin West for money and troops to
mount still another crusade. With Medici backing and Church
approval, Nicholas sets out for Trebizond to trade as Florentine consul, bringing his skilled mercenaries as a show of support from the
West—a show that will soon turn real as the Sultan moves against
the city more quickly than anyone had anticipated.

Nicholas' rival, and in some ways alter ego, is the gifted, charming,
and amoral Pagano Doria, trading for Genoa, gaming with Venice's
Nicholas in a series of brilliant pranks and tricks which include,
terribly, the seduction of the thirteen-year-old Catherine de Charetty,
one of Nicholas' two rebellious stepdaughters. Pagano, who is
secretly financed by Nicholas' enemy Simon de St Pol, has invited
the adolescent Catherine to challenge her stepfather, and no pleas or
arguments from Nicholas, her mother's officers, or the new figures
joining the Company—the priest Godscalc and the engineer John le
Grant—can sway her.

In Trebizond, Nicholas deploys his trading skills while he assesses
Byzantine culture, once spiritually and politically supreme, now
calcified in routine, crumbling in self-indulgence. Nicholas must
resist the Emperor David's languidly amorous overtures while he
takes the lead in preparing the city for, and then withstanding, the
siege of the Sultan. The city, however, is betrayed by its Emperor
and his scheming Chancellor, and Pagano Doria suffers his own fall,
killed by a black page whom he carelessly loved and then sold to the
Sultan. Nicholas has willed neither fall, yet has set in motion some
of the psychopolitical "engineering" which has triggered these
disasters, and he carries, with Father Godscalc's reflective help and
the more robust assistance of Tobie and le Grant, part of the moral
burden of them.

The burden weighs even during the triumphant trip back to
Venice with a rescued if still recalcitrant Catherine and a fortune

in silk, gold, alum, and Eastern manuscripts, the "golden fleece" which this Jason looks to lay at the feet of his beloved wife. A final skirmish with Simon, angry at the failure of his agent Doria, ends the novel abruptly, with news which destroys all the remaining dream of homecoming: Marian de Charetty, traveling through Burgundy in her husband's absence, has died.

VOLUME III: *Race of Scorpions*

Rich and courted, yet emotionally drained and subconsciously enraged, Nicholas seeks a new shape for his life after visiting his wife's grave, establishing his still-resentful stepdaughters in business for themselves, and allowing his associates to form the Trading Company and Bank of Niccolò in Venice. Determined to avoid the long arm of Venetian policy, attracted to the military life not precisely for its sanction of killing but for the "sensation of living through danger" it offers, Nicholas returns from Bruges to the war over Naples in which he had, years before, lost Marian's son Felix and contracted a marsh fever which revisits him in moments of stress. When he is kidnapped in mid-battle, he at first supposes it to be by order of his personal enemies, Simon and Katelina; but in fact it is Venice which wants him and his mercantile and military skills in another theater of war, Cyprus.

The brilliant and charismatic but erratic James de Lusignan and his Egyptian Mameluke allies have taken two-thirds of the sugar-rich island of Cyprus from his legitimate Lusignan sister, the clever and energetic Carlotta, and her allies, the Christian Knights of St. John and the Genoese, who hold the great commercial port of Famagusta. Sensing that, of the two Lusignan "scorpions," James holds the winning edge, Nicholas agrees to enter his service. He intends to design the game this time, not be its pawn, but he doesn't reckon with the enmity of Katelina, who comes to Rhodes to warn Carlotta against him, or the sudden presence of Simon's Portuguese brother-in-law Tristão Vasquez and Vasquez's naïve sixteen-year-old son Diniz, all three of whom do become pawns.

Nicholas is now the lover of Carlotta's courtesan, the beautiful Primaflora, whose games he also thinks he can control, and he recognizes a crisis of countermanipulations brewing between Katelina and Primaflora. Only at the end of the novel, after Katelina's love/hate for Nicholas has been manipulated to bring Tristão to his death and Diniz to captivity under James, after Nicholas and Katelina rediscover intimacy and establish the truth of their relationship, after a brilliant and deadly campaign waged by Nicholas for James has brought him to ultimate tragedy—the siege of Fama-gusta which he planned and executed has resulted, without his knowledge, in the death of Katelina and the near-death of Diniz, trapped in the starving city—only at the end does Nicholas fully admit even to himself that much of this has been planned or sanc-tioned by Primaflora, intent on securing her own future.

In the end, too, the determinedly rational Nicholas gives vent to his rage. Punishment for the pain of the complex desires and denials in his private and public history cannot be visited upon the complex and only half-guilty figures of his family or his trading and political rivals and clients. But in this novel, for the first time, he finds a person he can gladly kill, the unspeakably cruel Mame-luke Emir Tzani-bey al-Ablak, whom he fatally mutilates in single combat while James, unknown to him, has the Emir's four-hundred-man army massacred in a preemptive strike carrying all the glory and damnation of Renaissance kingship.

Like Pagano Doria, like Nicholas himself, Primaflora is a "mod-ern" type, a talented and alienated "self-made" person. Unlike the other two, Nicholas has the memory of family in which to ground a wary, half-reluctant, but genuine adult existence in the community. At the same time, however, he avoids close relationships: he has established the Bank of Niccolò as a company, not a family. But, resisting and insisting, the members of the company forge bonds of varying intimacy with Nicholas, especially the priest Godscalc and the physician Tobie, who alone at this point know the secret of Katelina's baby and carry the dying woman's written affirmation of Nicholas' paternity.

Nicholas' only true intimate, however, is a man of a different race entirely, the African who came to Bruges as a slave and was befriended by the servant Claes, who first communicated the secret of the alum deposit, who traveled with him to Trebizond to run the trading household, and to Cyprus to organize and under Nicholas reinvent the sugar industry there. His African name is as yet unknown, his Portuguese name is Lopez, his company name Loppe. Now a major figure in the company, and the family, he listens at the end of the novel as both Nicholas and his new rival, the broker of the mysterious Vatachino company, look to the Gold Coast of Africa as the next place of questing and testing.

VOLUME IV: *Scales of Gold*

For those who know the truth, the deaths of Katelina, Tristão, and Tzani-bey, the brutal forging of a new monarchy for Cyprus, even Nicholas' alienation from and reconciliation with young Diniz, have stemmed from honorable, even noble motives. But gossip in Europe, fed by de Ribérac and St Pol, puts a more sinister stamp on these events. Under financial attack by the Genoese firm of Vatachino, the Bank of Niccolò undertakes a commercial expedition to Africa, which young Diniz Vasquez joins partly as an act of faith in Nicholas, while Gelis van Borselen, Katelina's bitter and beautiful sister, joins to prove him the profit-mongering amoralist she believes him to be. They are accompanied by Diniz' mother's companion Bel of Cuthilgurdy, a valiant and razor-tongued Scottish matron who comes to guide the young man and woman and ends up dispensing wisdom and healing to all; by Father Godscalc, who desires to prove his own faith by taking the Cross through East Africa to the fabled Ethiopia of Prester John; and by Lopez, whose designs are the most complex of all. Through Madeira to the Gambia and into the interior they journey, facing and eventually outfacing the competition of the Vatachino and Simon de St Pol.

Like everyone but the Africans, both companies have underestimated even the size, let alone the cultural and religious complexity, of Africa: no travelers in this age can reach Ethiopia from the East, and the profits from the voyages of discovery and commerce recently begun by Prince Henry the Navigator are as yet mainly knowledge, and self-knowledge. There is gold in the Gambia, and there is a trade in black human beings which is, as Lopez is concerned to demonstrate, just beginning to take the shape that will constitute one of the supreme flaws of the civilization of the West. There is also, up the Joliba floodplain, the metropolis of Timbuktu, commercial and psychological "terminus," and Islamic cultural center, in which Diniz finds his manhood and Lopez regains his original identity as the jurist and scholar Umar; where Gelis consummates with Nicholas the supreme relationship of her life, hardly able as yet to distinguish whether its essence is love or hatred.

On this journey, Godscalc the Christian priest and Umar the Islamic scholar both function as soul friends to Nicholas, prodding him through extremities of activity and meditation that finally draw the sting, as it appears, from the old wounds of family. Certainly there is no doubt of the affection of Diniz for Nicholas, and surely there can be none about the passion of Katelina's sister Gelis, his lover. As the ships of the Bank of Niccolò return to Lisbon, to Venice and Bruges, success in commerce, friendship, and passion mitigates even the novel's first glimpse of Katelina's and Nicholas' four-year-old son Henry, molded by his putative father, Simon, in his own insecure, narcissistic, and violent image.

On the way to his marriage bed, the climax and reward of years of struggle, Nicholas is stunned by two blows which will undermine all the spiritual balance he has achieved in his African journey. He learns that Umar—his teacher, his other self—is dead in primitive battle, together with most of the gentle scholars of Timbuktu and their children. And on the heels of that news his bride Gelis, fierce, unreadable, looses the punishment she has prepared for him all these months: she tells him how she has deliberately conceived a child with Nicholas' enemy Simon, to duplicate in reverse—out of what hatred he cannot conceive—the tragedy of Katelina. As the novel closes, we know that he is planning to accept the child as his own, and that he is going to Scotland.

How Nicholas will be affected by the double betrayal—the involuntary death, the act of wilful cruelty—we do not know. There is a shield half in place, but Umar, who helped him create it, is gone. For Nicholas, religious institutions like political ones follow cultural patterns which may be rationally assessed; religious faith is simply another quantum in the minds of those he must analyze. His own spiritual experience, deeply guarded, has had to do with the intersection of mathematics and beauty, with the mind-cleansing horizons of sea and sky and now desert, and with the display in friend and foe alike of the compelling qualities of valor and joy and empathy. He may feel these have vanished. He is burdened, too, with something he cannot understand, a gift or a disability which teases his mind with unknown events, unknown places, thoughts that are not his. So far, his identity and his fortune have depended on the numerate skills of the marketplace. He does not know, nor do we, if he can face the new future—the conflict of person with person, kingdom with kingdom, faith with faith—with what he has now.

Judith Wilt
Boston, 1994

Part I

Open Season:
THE WAITING GAME

Chapter 1

ENRY HAD OFTEN considered killing his grandfather; there was so much of him, and Henry disliked all of it.

Today the impulse came back quite strongly when, sticking his head upside down through the casement, he discovered the old man himself riding over the Kilmirren drawbridge. He could see his big hat, and the pennants, and the baggage-mules, and the men in half-armour to protect what was in all the boxes. They hadn't sounded their trumpets, and below in the courtyard people were scampering in every direction, attempting to help with the horses or even running away. No one liked Henry's grandfather.

Monseigneur Jourdain, the servants called him. It meant Chamberpot. His real name was Jordan de St Pol, vicomte de Ribérac, and all this castle of Kilmirren was his, and the yards and trees and bothies that Henry looked down on, and the good farmlands and villages just beyond that Henry's father was supposed to look after. This was Monseigneur's Scottish castle, which he came to examine most years. The rest of the time he stayed in France.

Usually, everybody knew when to expect him. The message would come, and his father would curse, and then there would be a week when everyone was in a bad temper, trying to put things to rights. Then on the day, his father would stand in the doorway with Henry, his only son, at his side, and they would both welcome the old man as if they meant it. Fat Father Jordan was how his father referred to him.

Today, there had been no warning, which was terrible. No one knew better than Henry just how terrible it actually was. Henry set aside the hawk he had been feeding and, whirling down from his room, shoved open the door to his father's great chamber.

The bedcurtains were only half closed, so that he could see, with a pang of admiration and interest, what was happening behind them. Even now, in an emergency, he knew better than to interrupt. When it was finished (the signs were familiar) he said shrilly, 'Father! Father! Monseigneur is here!'

The first face to appear was the lady's. He had seen her before. She looked flushed, but didn't giggle like Beth or conceal herself with the sheet like the other one. This lady frowned at him, certainly, but bent and picked up her robe like an ordinary person. Like all his father's ladies, she was well set up as to the chest. Henry's friends all mentioned that, and the servants. They, too, were proud of his father. Henry used to wonder, now and then, if his mother had been flat in front like himself. She had died when Henry was three, but he didn't miss her. He didn't know why people thought he ought to miss her. He said, 'Father?' again, in case he had gone back to sleep.

'God's blood and bones,' said his father, and rolled over and pushed himself up.

Even angry, his father Simon was beautiful. Blond and blue-eyed and beautiful, and the finest jouster, the most splendid chevalier in the whole of Scotland. When Henry's grandfather was dead, Henry's father would be the lord of this castle and its grazing in the mid-west of Scotland. He would own his grandfather's castle in France, and his ships and his mills and his vineyards. His father would be Simon de St Pol, vicomte de Ribérac, and Henry would be his sole son and heir, and a knight, with ladies to bounce with in bed. Flattish ladies, to be truthful, for preference.

God smote Henry then in the back. Henry was nervous of God. At once he saw, with relief, that it was the door, flung crashing open, which had pushed him aside. Then the relief promptly died, for in the entrance stood Jordan de St Pol, vicomte de Ribérac, who was fatter than God and clean-shaven. Monseigneur Jourdain, his grandfather.

His grandfather said, 'Get rid of the bawd.'

'*Bawd!*' said the lady.

'I beg your pardon,' said his grandfather, looking at her. 'My lady, will you excuse us? And – Henry? I see your father is furthering your education?'

He didn't know what to say. 'Go!' muttered his father in no special direction.

'I should prefer to dress,' said the lady.

'Then pray do,' said Monseigneur. 'We see you don't mind an audience. I might even be more appreciative than a seven-year-old. Henry, I shall speak to you later.'

'Simon?' said the lady.

'I think you'd better dress in Henry's room,' said his father. 'Henry will show you the way. I apologise for the vicomte. Although he does not lodge in this wing, he seems to feel entitled to go where he pleases. Henry?'

Henry said, 'She can go somewhere else. I've got hawks in my room.'

'That, of course, must take precedence. So take her somewhere else, Henry,' said his grandfather. 'And then return to your room until I call for you.'

He took her somewhere else, but instead of returning to his room, he crept back to the half-open door, behind which his grandfather was haranguing his father. He could see them by holding the tapestry back just a little. If he were his father, he would knock him down. If his grandfather lifted a hand to his father he, Henry, would rush in and kill him. With the fire-tongs. With anything. He listened.

It was the old story. You would think that at last it didn't matter, whether the crops were sown a bit late or the hides not always cured to perfection or the smithwork patchy, or the peats left cut and lying too long. With the money from Madeira and the African voyage, they had enough to buy clothes with for years – even his silly aunt Lucia said so. And silver harness, and hawks, and jousting-armour. He had seen his father's new jousting-armour. You would think even his grandfather would be impressed, instead of threatening to get rid of Hugo and Steen, who had run the house and the land all the time his father was in Madeira and Flanders and Portugal. If Hugo and Steen were no good, why was his father being blamed for not staying in Flanders?

Flanders was a country far to the south, further south than England, across the Narrow Sea. Flanders was ruled by the Duke of Burgundy, the richest prince in the world. Henry had never been to Flanders.

'I cut short my visit to Bruges,' his grandfather said, 'because I bear a French title, and should be far from welcome at the Duke of Burgundy's wedding. But Kilmirren sends cargoes to Flanders. Why did you leave?'

Chamberpot Jordan. He occupied the only big chair like a throne. Everything about his father's father was big: his height, his width, the huge rolled hat on his head, the thick coat, the long robe, the solid boots. His hair was grey, and the whites of his eyes were yellow. He was old. He was over sixty years old and would live for ever, his father said, because he kept the accounts of the devil. His father had got out of bed and, without hurrying, had pulled on a gown without fastening it. His father had a narrow, ridged shape like Jesus. The old man said, 'You had a meeting with Nicholas.'

'Who?' said his father. He sat down on the platform-base of the bed and pulled on his slippers. Then he got up without an excuse and busied himself round the door of the privy. Henry felt hot. He knew who Nicholas was. Nicholas vander Poele, a wicked trades-man from Bruges who hated and cheated his father, if he could. But his father always won.

His father came back and sat down on the bed-base. 'Good. Are you comfortable?' said his grandfather. 'How unfortunate that we always seem to meet when your physique and intellect are both at their feeblest. I asked about your meeting with Nicholas. It was, as I remember, to determine the fate of two court cases. What was the outcome?'

His father laughed. The colour had come back to his skin. 'What do you think? He gave in. He promised not to take us to law over one ship, if we would agree not to contest possession of the other. We were lucky. He could have caused us some trouble.'

'So why didn't he?' the old man said.

His father had started to dress. Since Madeira, all his clothes were of silk. 'Who knows? Jellied in the brain from the African suns. He doesn't even claim us as kin any more. I wish he'd told me beforehand. I might have spared the mattress a little.'

The look that Henry feared had congealed upon his grandfather's face. His grandfather said, 'I am not sure what you mean.'

'I mean I got Gelis van Borselen under me,' his father said. 'Here, this summer. She made a little visit to Scotland six weeks before vander Poele married her. Now he's wedded my leavings. How's that?' He went on tying his points to his shirt. After a while, he looked up.

'Your late wife's sister,' said Grandfather Jordan reflectively. 'You seduced your sister by marriage, Gelis van Borselen of Veere, related to the rulers of Scotland and Burgundy? You raped her in advance of her wedding, because Nicholas vander Poele was her affianced husband?'

'Raped her!' his father said in mild protest. 'When did I ever need to do that? The girl was born with an itch, like her sister.'

The old man made a sound with his teeth, then resumed. 'In spite of which, she went back to Bruges. She *did* marry?'

'Of course she did!' his father said. 'He's settled half his fortune on her – half the gold he brought back from Africa. She'll be the richest woman in Flanders, and safe. He'd never know on the night. A well-trodden path, as they say, shows no prints.'

He smiled at the thought, and the smile broadened into a yawn. 'I've no complaints, and she won't soon forget it. She wanted to find out what her sister enjoyed, and she did.' He stopped smiling and flung up an arm. 'Damn you!' he exclaimed.

It was so quick, the movement of his grandfather's wrist, the pomander striking its target, the crash as the pierced silver ball fell to the floor, that Henry had no time to move. He heard his father cry out and saw the punch-mark on his brow where the skin began to turn bluish-red. Then his father roared, 'Damn you!' again.

It was why Henry was there, to protect him. He had his fists; he could kick. He jumped to his feet but failed to dash through the door, being arrested by the clutch of four arms, and silenced by a hardened hand over his mouth. The men had come from behind, and wore the livery, he saw, of his aunt.

They took him away. He struggled as much as he could but they lifted him up from the step and swept him down the stairs of the turnpike, while his father's sister Lucia – the spy! the traitor! – actually knelt at the door in his place.

Unwitnessed by Henry de St Pol, the vicomte de Ribérac remained seated inside the chamber and watched his cursing son clutch his bruised head.

'I should have done it before,' said his lordship. 'Your choice of language would disgrace a pig-gutter. The topic is distasteful enough as it is. Let us finish. You and the girl served each other. She married. Now the wedding is over, will it amuse her to tell vander Poele what has happened?'

'Christ!' said Simon de St Pol. 'How do I know? I hope not. I want to tell him myself. I'd like him to know whose lap she came to him from. I'd planned to tell him in Bruges, once they'd married, and we'd got our concessions.'

'But you didn't?' said the vicomte de Ribérac.

'No. Well, there was the threat of plague in the town. You didn't stay for the Burgundy wedding. After it, the Duke rode off to Holland, and his Duchess left on her tour. There was no one left.'

'Not even vander Poele?' Jordan de Ribérac said. 'He didn't go with his bride?'

'He could hardly go with the Duchess,' said Simon. 'He may have finished up in the suite of the Duke, but I couldn't reach him. I left. But don't worry, I'll tell him. I'll pick a moment he'll never forget.'

'You think so,' said his father. He got to his feet, drawing his sword. Crossing the floor, he lowered the tip and threaded the fallen pomander on the point of the steel, so that it hung on the blade like an apple. He lifted the weapon, viewing it from end to end. Then he raised his eyes to his son.

'How wrong you are. You will now listen to me. You will not boast to vander Poele that you have ravished his lady. You will ensure that his wife admits nothing. You will, if it pleases you, oppose him as much as you like in sport, or business, or chivalry, and you will prevail if you can. But you will not, you will *not* advertise your misconduct with a member of the van Borselen family. They are too powerful to offend.'

'Old Henry? Wolfaert?' said Simon. 'You expect them to take ship and challenge me?'

'I expect your trade – our trade – with Flanders to come to a halt. I remind you that Henry van Borselen, lord of Veere, is the grand-uncle of the unfortunate child who was present just now, and the uncle of Gelis van Borselen. I further remind you that Gelis van Borselen held royal office in Scotland: a Burgundian position of honour with the King's older sister. And lastly, although I am sure you would rank this the least, I should point out that there is someone who, if he knew, would certainly abandon his truce and take ship forthwith to challenge you.'

'Vander Poele?' his son said. 'You are trying to frighten me with the cuckold himself?'

'On the contrary,' said the vicomte. 'I said you would perceive it as the least of your worries. But I have given you other reasons enough. You will not broadcast this unfortunate conquest.'

'Or you will do what?' said Simon de St Pol. 'Run me through? Cease to settle my wine bills? What harm can you do to me now?'

The old man regarded him. Despite the weight of the sword, he had not allowed it to lower. He said, 'I could strike you again. And this time you might permit yourself to respond. Is that a threat, or merely a rash invitation? Only you know.'

'It is a rash invitation,' said Simon. Round the bruise, he had become very pale.

'I think,' said his father, 'that you understand yourself very little. But still. Let me summon my auxiliary arguments . . .'

Again, he had acted faster than Simon was prepared for. The sword whipped in his hand. The freed pomander sighed through the room and pushed the door-hanging clear of the door, striking something resistant but soft as it did so. A woman cried out.

'Oh,' said Jordan de Ribérac. His expression relaxed, by a fraction. He lowered the sword. He said, 'I fear, my dear, I have underrated both you and my grandson. Are you hurt? It was not, believe me, my intention.'

'Of course you meant it,' said his widowed daughter, rubbing her arm as she entered. 'I know you. You told Henry to bring that wench to my room, I know you did. You probably meant him to come back and listen. And if he heard what I heard, what is that wretched child going to believe of his mother and Gelis?' She turned to her brother. '*Gelis!* How could you?'

She had been beautiful once. She was still brilliantly blonde, with not a chain, a cuff, a sleeve, a fold of her veil out of place. She had cradled her arm and was glaring at them.

'Oh, come,' the vicomte said. 'It wasn't a shot from a bombard. Sit down. Simon will get you some wine. And why the fuss? The woman Gelis was eager, I hear. And Henry is no sheltered innocent: I give you my word as of today. I have to suppose that you know what was under discussion?'

He had returned to his chair. She sat on a chest-cushion while Simon, not unamused, found a pitcher. She snapped at him. 'Gelis van Borselen eager? After what you tried to do to us all in Madeira? I don't believe it. She loathed you.'

'That was the fascination,' her brother said. 'Really, you have no imagination. We quite astonished each other. But now I'm not supposed to bait vander Poele with it. I might as well not have taken the trouble.'

'For once,' his father said, 'I share your regret. Since it is too late for restraint, let me repeat myself. No one will learn from you what has happened. Lucia will forget what she has heard. As for vander Poele, his Bank is in Venice, and he and his bride are no doubt safely out of your way.'

'No. He's here,' Lucia said.

Her father's head turned. Even Simon forgot his grievance and looked at her. The vicomte said, 'Who is where? Be explicit.'

'Nicholas vander Poele is in Scotland,' his daughter said spitefully. 'He's been here for weeks. The King's sister got news at Dean Castle.'

'*Here?*' said de Ribérac.

One word was enough. In that tone, it always had been enough. She said, her voice high, 'Not in these parts. On the east coast. At Edinburgh. He has a bodyguard of armed men, but no wife.'

'Indeed? And why should that be?' her father remarked. 'Rich, newly wed, with a palatial banking house, a busy fleet, a small army, why should vander Poele choose to travel to Edinburgh by himself? Or no, with some strength, we are told. Simon, what do you think?'

'He can't have found out about Gelis and me?' Simon said.

'You sound less than pleased. I thought that was all you desired, that Nicholas should appreciate your singular – or was it your multiple coup?'

'Yes. Yes it is. But,' said Simon, 'I wanted to tell him myself.'

'Then in that case,' said the vicomte de Ribérac, 'let us take time, my dear impetuous boy, to find out what vander Poele may know, and what he may suspect, and of what he is ignorant, so that we may act as befits our best interests. You will remain at Kilmirren. I shall launch some enquiries. I may even, in time, visit Edinburgh.'

'If he knows –' Simon began.

His father regarded him with calm. 'If I meet him, and he knows, I should beware of his temper?'

Simon said, 'No. If he knows, don't tell him too much. I want to tell him myself.'

'I have that point, I think,' said his father.

Chapter 2

ON THE EAST COAST, naturally enough, everyone knew where Nicholas vander Poele was, except his acquaintance the Burgundian Envoy, who on that same afternoon in October 1468 was methodically sailing into the river-haven at Leith, the port of the King's great town of Edinburgh. As with the owner of Kilmirren Castle, Anselm Adorne arrived before he was expected.

The sail from Flanders had been achieved without incident, which had saddened the children – the young people – hoping for pirates. The autumn sun, resting on the broad waters of the Firth of Forth estuary, was acceptably warm for a region so barbarically northern, and the view to the south was famous from drawing and plan, and familiar even to Adorne, who had never seen it before.

The town of Edinburgh stood on its ridge, with the Castle Rock at the top and the houses of its inhabitants outlined on the inferior slope. Behind the Rock was a range of green treeless hills. Other outcrops, more abrupt, reared themselves between the shore and the town.

Close at hand was the mouth of the river Leith, timber-shored on each side, with some coasting vessels and a quantity of fishing-boats within a breakwater made of rough stobs and boulders. To left and right of the river stood a smoky collection of thatched cabins, kailyards, wood and stone warehouses, and a number of tallish houses of a more ambitious sort, with kilns and bakehouses and wooden sheds round about them.

Among them was a single church spire, a well-head in a puddle, and a circular wall with an assortment of new stone and timber buildings inside. The King's Wark, Anselm Adorne had been told. A royal enclave, in which the King's ordnance could be stored, and where the Court could stay when travelling. For this was the haven of Edinburgh. This was the greatest port in the kingdom.

The greatest port in the kingdom. Anselm Adorne thought of Sluys, the harbour of Bruges, with its well-equipped quays, its scores of tall masts, the fine buildings where princes might stay. He thought of the celebration when the Venetian galleys arrived: the flags, the music, the fireworks. Then he dismissed it all firmly from his mind. Sluys was one of the richest ports in the world, along with Venice and Genoa and Alexandria. It would be hard enough to prevent the children – the young people – from drawing comparisons. Scottish trade mattered to Bruges, and to Burgundy. The rulers of Scotland and Burgundy were related. One must not offend.

At the same time, one should not allow oneself to be ignored. It was known that he was coming, yet despite the great flag of Burgundy that floated over his head, bright with fine silks and bullion, no boat had put off to guide them up the estuary. The navigator taken aboard at Newcastle was familiar enough with the coast, but might well have balked at attempting the haven, with its notorious sandbar, condemning them to a day or even more in the roads.

As it was, he brought them in on the dregs of the tide, but the anchor came down without direction or guidance in a river-mouth as devoid of activity as a port with the plague. He wondered, fleetingly, if that were the explanation, although Dr Andreas, his physician, thought not. A great ship arriving was an event which, anywhere in the civilised world, commanded a crowded jetty, a customs boat, a fleet of business-seeking skiffs. And this was not merely a great ship, but an embassy from Burgundy. The royal officials should have appeared there on the jetty at the first sound of his trumpets, and should be aboard, with the fellow Lamb, his host, amongst them.

Instead, as the sails were stowed and the ship swung to her anchor, he could see nothing but a few old men watching him over their fishing-lines, and some curious faces peering out of the boats. He sent his chamberlain, who spoke Scots, to hail one of them. A calm man, Anselm Adorne showed no alarm, but wished, not for the first time, that all his companions were mature like himself, like his officers, like Andreas and Metteneye.

Twenty-four, of course, was not so youthful, except to an ambassador who was twenty years older. Anselm Sersanders his nephew (who was exactly that age) said, 'It can't be the plague, or they'd have warned us. And they wouldn't be sitting there.' Sersanders was intelligent, and reliable, and five feet six inches in height.

Katelijne his niece said, 'I expect it's dinner-time.' She too was small in the way that gadflies are small, with the hazel eyes and bark-coloured Sersanders hair mixed (her uncle was vain enough to know) with the comely looks of the Adorne doges of Genoa. Katelijne was fourteen and here to stay, because her parents were worn out with trying to keep pace with her. Anselm Adorne knew how they felt.

And Maarten, the last child in his company, although twenty and his own second son, was more of a child than the other two, because he had the sturdy good looks and the brains of Margriet, Anselm's dear wife, which would ensure him a plain, decent living in some branch of the Church, but never more. Anselm Adorne was a good father to all of his many children, but did not bestow his dearest love on this child. Who doubtless knew it.

'You always think it's dinner-time,' said his nephew, answering his sister.

'It would account for it, though,' said Adorne, returning to the present. 'I imagine our hosts went to eat, thinking we should be held in the roads till next tide. We *are* staying with Lamb, isn't that so?'

It was the case, of course. Lamb had the biggest house. He was a merchant, and used to putting up travellers, in the same way that Jehan Metteneye's own home in Bruges acted as hostelry for incoming traders; as Adorne's own palatial mansion did for others more princely. They would stay with Lamb, who would see they got to Edinburgh safely tomorrow. Meanwhile, they were stuck.

Or perhaps not. 'They're coming for us,' said Maarten, Adorne's son. 'Look, they're running.'

Three or four men of unprosperous appearance were hurrying down the bank of the river, intoning. A moment later, a boat had put off from the shore. A remarkably short time after that, the Burgundian embassy, its young and its officers were climbing the forestair to a large stone-built house whose owner was absent, and where the honours had been launched in his place by a courageously dignified wife with her head wrapped in Flemish-style linen.

Maister Lamb, she said, was *doun on the strand with the childer.* With the rest of his household. *They didna expect his lordship sae soon.* But she prayed that their lordships would enter, and the *burd would be spread so soon as the ovens were fired and the laddie came back frae the cook-house.*

Anyone living in Bruges was familiar with the Scots language. Born of generations of Bruges burgomasters and ducal officials, Anselm Adorne also knew all about civic disasters. Provided no insult was intended, it was always best to be lenient.

He said, 'There is no haste. We ate well on board, and need exercise rather than rest. Where is the strand? Perhaps your husband is on his way back? The young people and I might go to meet him?'

Surprisingly, the eyes of two of their host's kinsmen met. Their hostess herself seemed to hesitate. Then she said, 'Aweel now, I'm no certain sure.'

'Why?' said Anselm Adorne. He kept any sharpness out of his voice.

The woman looked at her household again, and seemed to make up her mind. 'Because . . .' she began. 'Because the King is there, that's the truth o' it. It's horse-sport and suchlike. Him and his siblings, they like to race on the sand, and you'll not keep a Leither at home while there's something to wager about, so all the port-folk are there, instead of minding their wark, and what's rightly due tae a guest. And John himself was commandit, and couldna say nay, or he'd have been here when ye came. Otherwise, I wouldna have tellt ye.'

'The King and his brothers are here? On the shore?'

She flushed. 'I hear they keep mair state in Burgundy. It's not that way with our King.'

'No,' said Anselm Adorne, smiling at her. 'I knew his brother in Flanders. But tell me: do you think we may go and watch him without causing offence?'

She bit her lip. She said, 'It's a rough crowd, Maister Adorne. John wad never forgie me gin ye came to ony hairm. And the King, forbye, would tak nae tent, or his gentlemen. When they're gone to their sport, commoners are meant tae turn a blind eye.'

Adorne said, 'He need not know we were there. You don't tell me that a crowd of Leith burghers and porters would cause harm to a group of visiting Flemings? But of course, if you think so . . .'

'Are you coming?' said his niece Katelijne from the doorway. 'See, Master Lamb's cousin is going to take Anselm and Maarten and me, and I expect you could come. He says there are lots of women there, and children, and a cook with a fire. I'm going.'

They went. Not with Andreas, who preferred to stay, or the other officers of the household, whom he left to see to the boxes. But Metteneye and Adorne went with the children – with the young people – picking their way east through the cabins, the poultry and fish-creels to the rough grazing that ran down to the sea, where cattle browsed through the whin, and geese hissed, and half a dozen middle-aged burghers in decent serge doublets swished through the grass with thick sticks, as if beating for hares. A ball rose in the air, and fell at Metteneye's feet. He bent to lift it, and was deterred by a shout.

Adorne said, 'They are playing a game. We are disturbing it.'

'I know the game. I have played it. They each hold a kolf, and are hitting a ball with it,' said his niece. 'But where is the target?'

'Us,' said her brother. 'Don't be silly: there isn't a target, they hit the ball into holes. Come on. You can't play. I thought you wanted to see the races.' And taking her by the arm, he dashed down the links to the beach, Maarten following, while Adorne and Metteneye followed at their own pace, looking about them.

The crowds on the edge of the beach were not like the burghers of Bruges. The men who, touched on the shoulder, gave way readily enough to the foreigners, were dressed in plain canvas or fustian, with their leather aprons on top, as if they had just left their boats or their spades or their workshops. By contrast, the inner circle of spectators wore the swords, the leather jerkins, the fine wool doublets and light cloaks of officers of the Crown, of guards, and of landed men of the Court, and even Katelijne did not thrust between them, but stood with the others and tried to see what they and the crowd were all watching. After a bit, she dropped on her knees and looked between their legs, lifting her hair out of the sand. Her brother said, '*Katelijne!*' but she was used to that.

She saw the beach, dry near at hand, and further away firm and shining and pocked like a ploughed field with hoof-marks. Beyond was the grey sea, and far beyond that, the pale shores and blue hills of the land on the other side of the estuary. Near at hand from the right came the sound of low drumming. She put her weight on her hands and peered forward, pushing someone's scabbard out of the way.

The beach was far longer than she had imagined. It ran glistening and yellow-grey into the distance, where a cloud of silvery spume announced the approach of a massed group of riders, vying with one another in and out of the surf. The drumming sound came from their hooves. The other roar, from behind, came from the frenzied throats of the waiting Leithers, laying off wagers. The riders came nearer.

They were not commoners. You could tell that from quite far away. First, the colours showed through the watery mist: crimson, azure and tawny, golden and black. Then the stuffs of the hats, the pourpoints, the gowns and the doublets: velvets, satins and taffetas, winking with jewels among the great dashes and drips of salt water. No one stopped them ruining their clothes, which surprised and then pleased her. She had thought Scotland was a poor country. Then she saw that they were children.

She revised her opinion in a moment: there were grown men and women among them; pretty women and handsome, high-coloured men. But the two leaders were barely fledged: boys of reddish hair and complexion, mounted on horses the like of which she had seen only once or twice even in Ghent; horses with the long-shafted bones, the dark muzzles and eyes of the Arab. The harness of both was of silver. Their whips working, the rivals glared and strained, their pale-rimmed eyes stark with endeavour. The younger, a boy of no more than her own age, was winning.

They were the only ones of their kind. Behind them, the horses were Flemish and the riders in their twenties and thirties, although she saw a boy she put at ten or eleven, and a red-haired girl-child on a pony. She got to her feet and stood beside her brother. The race hadn't quite finished.

Their uncle's voice said, 'Do you recognise the boy in the lead? Alexander? He lived at Veere until he was ten.'

Katelijne knew all about Veere in Holland. The lord of Veere was Henry van Borselen. His son had married a Scottish princess, and Alexander the princess's nephew had been sent to her household in Flanders for training.

Accordingly, the boy in front, if the same, was Alexander Stewart of Scotland, Duke of Albany, Admiral of Scotland, Earl of March, lord of Annandale and of Man. And the older boy striving to beat him must be – was, from his looks, his dress, his annoyance – the older brother of Duke Alexander. In other words, James, Third of the Name, monarch of Scotland. Katelijne said, 'No wonder they let him get his clothes wet.'

Alexander won the race. The King, flexing his whip, rode aside while older competitors, red and blue, green and black, clustered about him. After a moment he broke away from the group and, accompanied by the blue and the black, walked his horse to where others awaited him. They formed a company, and began to ride off. The men in blue and black came back again. Those who were left on the strand wheeled about, their horses tossing their heads. The man in black remained in one place, but replied smiling to the nobles and gentlewomen who curvetted about him. Alexander, cursing his excited horse, could be heard expressing an opinion.

Now that half the courtiers had gone, Katelijne could see and hear better. The prince spoke, and a man in green took out a whistle and played a a flourish of notes by way of comment. The man in black said, 'You don't really want to go on?' His voice was drowned by others opposing him. He added, with a certain patience, 'The horses are tired.' The smallest, the red-haired girl, was shrieking demands.

'Anselm?' said Katelijne. Behind, a man in burgher's dress had joined her uncle and Metteneye. It was almost certainly Master John Lamb, their host. Adorne was introducing Maarten. She said, 'Anselm?' again.

'Yes?' said her brother. He was drifting backwards and watching the strand. Play was being resumed. This time, the participants were lining up in two teams, four to a side, and people were scattering back to make room for them. The rest of the riders, dismounted, joined the spectators.

The wagering had started again. The teams were hopelessly uneven – children's teams, with the red-head and the boy of eleven in one, and Alexander of Albany in the other. The spaces were filled up by those who had already taken the greater part of the action – the men in red and green, black and blue. The eighth player was a handsome woman in velvet.

Katelijne said, 'You know why I'm here?'

Her brother grunted. He hadn't wanted her to be sent to Scotland. She knew that; but also accepted, without resentment, that she was a nuisance at home. And it was a privilege among Flemish families of rank to offer a child to serve a foreign princess. Her uncle Adorne had just left a daughter in England. Gelis van Borselen and her sister had both held positions in Scotland. All the same . . .

At last, her brother had taken the trouble to observe where she was looking. He said, 'The red-head? You think that brat is Albany's sister? The one you're coming to serve?'

'He called her Margaret,' Katelijne said. 'I was told she was eight. I was told she was bright and adventurous. I think I'm going home.'

Her uncle, approaching, had overheard. He said, 'No, you're not. You don't need her, but she needs someone like you.'

'If she survives. What are they trying to play?'

'Tzukanion,' her uncle said. He spoke rather slowly.

'What?' said her brother.

'It's a game horsemen play in the Orient. They use long switches like that, and a ball. Each team tries to push the ball over the other team's line.'

'How do you know?' said Katelijne. She wasn't jealous of his knowledge; just interested.

'From cousins. You ought to know. There have been a lot of

Adornes in the Levant,' her uncle said. 'And tales come to Bruges.' His face, normally composed, had become neutral, as if he were back at home, judging a dispute between traders. He added dryly, 'Your little lady will come to no harm. Two at least have played it before.'

Long ago, Katelijne had learned to trust her uncle Adorne, as had her brother. Watching now, she saw that he was right. Roaring, screaming and whacking, all eight amateur players of tzukanion were joyously slamming the ball. Two, however, were experts, sitting easily in the saddle, swaying and swooping to one side or the other, and connecting each time, stick to ball, with a sharp and satisfactory click. The athlete in red, and the acrobat, the actor in black.

She had no sooner distinguished it than one of them hit a lifting and powerful stroke which sent the ball whistling over their heads and beyond beach and crowd into acres of bushes. There was no possibility of recovering it.

As neat a way as any of ending the game. The air was filled with catcalls and laughter and the sound of coins changing hands. The angry shrilling of the child Margaret's voice halted them.

'They should stop her,' said Katelijne.

'In public,' said her uncle, 'it would be difficult.'

'Then they should find another ball quickly. Oh dear, but no. But no. Anselm, that wouldn't be fair.'

'What?' said her brother.

The man in black, facing inland, was pointing. The man in red, following his finger, turned his horse and began to trot up the beach and towards the rough grass of the links. He came close, so that for the first time they clearly saw his brown hair, his firm nose and jaw, and the set of his straight double-velvet-clad shoulders.

They recognised him. He saw them at the same time and, with a pleased smile, reined in beside them. The pleasure sprang as much from self-satisfaction, one might suspect, as from joy at the sight of his neighbours from Bruges.

'There you all are,' said Julius of Bologna, the handsomest manager of the Banco di Niccolò. 'We heard you were coming. Tedious, isn't it? We ought to be finished soon. Where are you staying? John Lamb's? I'll tell Nicholas.'

'Your Nicholas?' said Adorne civilly. 'Vander Poele? Is he here?' His niece Katelijne, below general notice, noted that he betrayed none of the amazement that her brother showed, or Master Metteneye, who nine years ago must have been acquainted with Nicholas, apprentice to the Charetty company, which – she had been told – employed Julius, too, as its lawyer.

The same Julius produced a casual grimace. 'Do you think I'd be here unless Nicholas was? That's him over there. Bonkle bought him a house, and he likes it. He's out of his mind. If you had what he has, would you come here to spend it?'

Adorne said, 'It depends. Perhaps Gelis wanted to come back to Scotland. A bride enjoys meeting old friends.'

Julius glanced over his shoulder. 'Oh Christ,' he said. 'He's gone and picked up a ball. Excuse me. We'll have to go on.' He pulled a face and, wheeling again, tipped his feathered red hat at them all. Then he spurred dashingly off.

Metteneye said, 'Those were rubies.' They were speaking, as always, in Flemish.

'They were not, certainly, sprays of honesty,' Adorne said. 'The man in black must be Nicholas. I thought him thicker. And certainly black is far from his usual choice. Or, indeed, his usual pocket. What ball? *Katelijne!*'

Katelijne had guessed what ball the riders were going for. Before even her uncle exclaimed, before Anselm her brother had moved, she had set off to scamper back through the sand to the links. The man in black, mounted, arrived just before her, scattering the few grazing heifers and causing the half-dozen foot-players to stumble aside from the hole over which they were poring. Two of them shouted, and one lifted his stick at the horse.

The man in black plucked it out of his grasp and broke it over his knee. Then, gathering his reins, he swept his own stick in a low, graceful arc, and settling it outside the ball, whipped it showily out of their reach, while the mare between his knees swerved and followed, in visibly perfect control. The ball, chipped into the air, fell ahead and was securely caught, with a smack, between the two open palms of Katelijne.

For a moment, she stood her ground as the rider swooped to her side and drew rein. She let him begin to lean down, before she lifted her palm and threw the ball back where it had come from, at the feet of the shouting, hurrying golfers.

They looked down at it, and at her. The man in black said in French, 'You would like to join in the game?' He was at least as old as her brother. His sleeve smelled of brine, and horse, and scent, and his doublet was made of plain black silk, sewn, embroidered and pleated. Under the brim of his hat, his eyes were as large as those of swan-seduced Leda in a painting she had not, when a child, comprehended.

'Isn't it over?' she said.

'Do you know,' he said, 'I fear that it is.' He had hardly shifted his gaze.

She whirled. Behind her back, the man in rubies, the man Julius in red, had ridden up and, bending, had scooped the ball again from its owners. Feet disputed, and voices. Then Julius, laughing, turned his horse, and with ease punted the ball across to the black rider again.

This time, she was on the wrong side to catch it. She picked up her skirts and ran forward none the less as the red rider thundered behind her, and the golfers, silent and dogged, pounded after. Ahead, the man with the whistle played a cadenza of notes with one hand and, when the black rider glanced over, beckoned. The black rider, his horse in motion, bent in a mist of cold scent to dispatch the ball in his direction.

The stick had just connected when his horse pecked, staggered, and all but threw him. The ball, knocked awry, flew instead towards the child Margaret.

The black rider, with a muted exclamation, righted himself. The golfer who had thrown the stick at his horse ran to his side, hooting with righteous joy, and squealed as Katelijne reached up and thrust her arm in his and held him tight. 'Long live the game. No quarter!' she called to the black rider. And ducked like he did as the ball, hit by the child, came hurtling back to the links.

It was stopped in mid-air by the club of another golfer.

The youth Albany jerked his stick upwards in rage and then lowered it sulkily. The golfing party, spreading out, lobbed the ball laughing to one another, to the cheers of the spectators. Katelijne chased panting among them, sometimes close enough to touch the ball herself, or even kick it. She glimpsed her brother, not quite taking part, but still grinning. The black rider, arriving without apparent effort, collected the ball, drew back his arm, and hit it sweetly out to the strand, to fall between the Prince and Princess of Scotland, who had not been smiling at all.

The girl got to it first. The boy said, 'Stop. You'll let the fools have it,' and, when she paid no attention, drove his spur into the flank of her pony, which reared. The child screamed. Ignoring her, the boy rescued the ball and struck it carefully and accurately towards the expert player in black. The girl, still screaming, drove her pony against her brother's fine-bred, magnificent Arab with such suddenness that, leaning low at the end of his stroke, he was flung from the saddle. His sister then bent down and began hitting him with her stick.

'Well, well,' said the man in black, and took careful aim. Katelijne, running towards the fallen youth, saw the practised stick hit the ball just as she caught Alexander's loose, distraught horse by the reins. This time, the ball went nowhere near golfers or riders. It simply flew over the beach and, far, far away, plummeted with a splash into the sea. Where, being made from the very best boxwood, it floated.

On the beach, there was a single, fierce moment filled with juvenile fury and adult approval. Then the child Margaret screamed, 'No!' and whipped her pony straight into the estuary.

Katelijne was nearest, with Albany's reins still in her grasp. She forked her skirts with one hand, put a foot in the stirrup and, springing into Albany's saddle, pushed the priceless mare into the sea. Behind her, she heard another horse following.

On the links and the beach, the spectators saw it, as did the golfers, leaning panting on their clubs, and the six remaining members of the tzukanion teams, wheeling and calling. Julius, in red, was the first to throw his horse forward, followed by Jamie Liddell of Halkerston, Albany's officer. The boy, the whistler in green and the young woman followed. The youth Alexander, sprawled on the sand, scowled at the rump of his child-sister's pony, veiled in spray and clogged with a load of wet velvet.

He sat up with a jerk as his own horse also entered the sea, ridden with frightening vehemence by a minute brown-haired girl. And then he scrambled to his feet as a horse more crudely powerful than either plunged into the water and followed, kicking up sand and water, spray and foam and finally sinking, like the rest, to swim into the pull of deep water. Three people, chasing a ball.

The tide was receding. It was the first thing anyone brought up in Flanders would notice. Adorne did so, and the silent group of his fellows: Sersanders had long since left them to race down to the shore. Had it not been so, one would simply have waited, and ball and child would both have come in.

As it was, the broad head of the pony and the bared red hair of the King's sister forging outwards rose and fell among the great waves of the estuary while the ball, the evil ball, lilted ahead, clearly visible but always retreating. For eight, she was an excellent rider, and full of Stewart valour – or obstinacy.

Pursuing, Katelijne bestowed frothing curses on both. They were now well out from the shore. The only advantage of that was the silence. As the shouting and the crash of the land-waves receded, she began to call at the head of each surge. 'Margaret! Hey!' cried Katelijne. 'They've found a ball! You're missing the game!'

One did not address princesses as 'Hey.' One did not allow one's future employer to drown. Katelijne said, 'All right, run away. You knew you couldn't win, anyway.'

She wasn't heard. Or perhaps she was: the round cheek bulged, as if a Stewart jaw had been set. The russet hair, too wet to whip in the wind, lay like leaves on the leaden pall of spoiled velvet. The girl didn't look round.

A voice in languid French said, 'Leave it to me.' The black rider, his horse swimming beside Katelijne's. Passing, he caught the mare's eye and hissed at her provocatively.

Katelijne said, 'Can you capture the ball?'

'If I must,' he remarked. 'I doubt if the dear creature can swim.'

'I can,' she said. He was already in front, the black velvet and the embroidery drenched; his hair, hatless now, cut curling and smart on the nape of his neck; his eyes, his pale, densely focused eyes on the child.

'I offer candles,' he said, without turning. The words barely reached her. Whatever he offered, he had given her no advice and no orders. She followed.

It was more difficult now, further out from the shore. The wind sliced the tops from the waves, and the waves themselves, curling high, sometimes bore her horse up and over in safety, but sometimes broke in her face while the horse struggled and snorted beneath her. Ahead, Margaret's mount was hardly swimming. The lady Margaret, whom she had come from Flanders to serve, and who was going to be served, whether they had been introduced to one another or not.

The wind brought a gust of sound from behind. Help belatedly on the way, it was to be supposed. A number of big men on big horses. Or a boat, even.

And they would be too late, for ahead there had come the wave which the pony was too slight and too scared to survive. The poor beast was no more, except as a turmoil three deep waves from the spot where the black rider's powerful gelding was swimming.

Katelijne saw the pony's head break water and sink. And saw, to one side, a red head rise and sink also. The pony was drowning. The child had left the saddle and was drowning as well.

Katelijne dragged her feet out of the stirrups and stopped. In a surge of water, the black rider had abandoned his horse. Freed, it began to swim back to the shore.

Katelijne wasted no time on trying to catch it, but concentrated on driving her own mount to the spot. It would have helped if it hadn't been an Arab and somewhat unused to water. She wondered what fool had brought it to Scotland. The man in black appeared, vanished and suddenly reappeared quite close beside her, a limp red head over his shoulder. He could swim. A billow of velvet floated up and then vanished, leaving a brief scrap of white in its place. A hand reached up to her, offering a knife.

'Cut your skirts off and take her. I'll lead Epyaxa.' His own doublet and pourpoint were gone, leaving him in black hose and shirt, like a tennis-player. He paddled, holding the reins, while she ripped off her half-gown and some of her linen. (*Epyaxa?*) The child, pulled up before her, was alive, but retching and weeping and calling for one Mariota.

Katelijne set about turning the mare and found the task taken from her, almost at once, by the swimmer. After that, he stayed by her side, his hand by the Arab's cheek-harness, his voice in its ear. The mare's ears were stark upright, as if she understood what she was being told. The language was Greek. Ahead, and approaching fast, was a splashing line of frantic chevaliers, the man in scarlet in front.

'Dear Julius,' said the swimmer below her. He rolled on his side and glanced up. 'Well, come on, sweetheart; use your knees and let's get to the shore. We did all the work. We might as well get all the credit.'

'Who did all the work?' said Katelijne.

'I, the irreproachable Knight Highmount, loved and feared by many. I did,' he said; and, reaching into his shirt, produced something and lobbed it towards her. She freed a hand and just caught it. It was the wooden ball. The child, who had stopped choking and was just howling, abruptly ceased doing either and took it.

'I offer candles,' said Katelijne.

'I'd prefer a percentage of your contract,' he said. 'But I dare say I shall get some good of it all. Here they are. Look exhausted.'

'I *am* exhausted,' she said tentatively. She had stopped trembling, she found.

'You couldn't do it again?'

Willing hands, reaching her, had taken the child and found a cloak for her shoulders. Soon, she was able to dismount and wade, the other riders splashing and shouting beside them. Someone took her arm, and she removed it.

'You'd need two other idiots,' she said. 'One to hit the ball out to sea, and the other to try to ride after it.'

The child was already on shore, and set at the feet of a square, kneeling nurse and a gentlewoman in the robes of a prioress. The child, struggling free, looked back and called to Katelijne. She said, 'I wasn't running away.' She was hugging the ball. Someone was trying to give her another one.

'You know, I saw that,' said Katelijne in answer. 'But there are easier ways of getting a ball.' She smiled, and the child, hoisted again, returned the smile over a retreating manservant's shoulder.

She had missed something: a gesture. The man beside her put up his hand and the spare ball, flung from nowhere, smacked into it. 'Well?' he said, and glanced suggestively out to sea.

She said, 'Well, why not? But shouldn't it be something more exciting? And I'm hungry. I'll race you to Master Lamb's house, if you like.'

He said, 'And that would be exciting? Once you wouldn't have thought so.'

She looked up. 'Upside down on our *hands*?' He was scanning the crowds, without listening.

Now that nothing but streaming cambric was left, she could see that, within his considerable frame, he was spare as a man in severe training might be. His hair, tamped down with water, was an indeterminate brown, but cut so well that it was already lifting round his temples and neck. His brow and cheekbones were broader than those of the men of her family, and his eyes wider set on either side of the slender bridge of his nose. Below that, his lips were as rounded and full as a woman's.

He said, 'You will know me again,' and she said quickly, 'I was afraid I might need to, Ser Niccolò.' She added, 'You think I'm Anselm Adorne's daughter.'

He said, 'Of course you are. But if you're not, how do you know who I am?'

'Doesn't everybody, even the horse?' said Katelijne. 'You're Nicholas vander Poele, and I'm Anselm Sersanders's sister. If I had a lisp, I couldn't say that.'

'Deserts would hire you. By my God and Creator . . . I saw your revered uncle, and Maarten and Metteneye. But what is your brother doing here? He isn't working in Scotland as well? *Julius!* Anselm Sersanders is here!'

'I know,' said the man in red. 'And the windmills. And the water-wheels, I have no doubt. If the rest of Bruges is coming over, we'd better tell the magistrates to board up the markets. Nicholas, you know you've caused mayhem and that poor lad is standing there, waiting to thank you?'

Indeed, on the shore, backed by his courtiers, the Duke of Albany was waiting to greet them; his blackened doublet and hose caked with sand; his braid and buttons protruding like baitworm.

Nevertheless, his chin high, his auburn hair blowing, the Prince knew the duty due to his blood. He allowed Katelijne to kiss his hand first. Although they were of the same age and he was praising her, there was no doubt that he was the King's brother, and she was merely the Flemish demoiselle appointed to his young sister's household. Then he turned to Nicholas vander Poele.

The words of gratitude he used were almost the same, but the tone was subtly different. Of course, a youth of fourteen spoke to a man of twenty-seven. Also, they knew one another. More: there was a relationship there, or one just beginning.

And now Katelijne's own family were around her, asking questions, hugging her anxiously. Her brother said, 'You're an imbecile, and Nicholas is even worse. I should have warned you. What was he trying to do just now? Get you to swim out again?'

There had been no relationship at all in the water: that was what she had found so agreeable. She said, 'Maybe. It was strenuous. You know. You feel, stopping, you could strangle a lion. He is restless.'

'He was born restless,' said her brother. 'He doesn't need any more stirring-up, and neither do you. Come on. We're promised hot malmsey and ginger, spices by courtesy of Nicholas. Aren't you cold?'

'I'm hungry,' she said. 'Race you back to the house on your hands?'

Then she said, 'Listen.'

'It's only the young gentlefolk,' said their host, Master Lamb, coming up. 'Whistle Willie – Master Roger, that is, and Master Jamie and the trumpet, that's Albany's pursuivant. You'll hear them later, gin my lord Duke has his way. Ye ken my young lord Alexander has elected to sup with us, of his own free motive will, sic an honour? You won't mislike an entertainment of seemly-like music?'

'It depends,' said Katelijne.

'A purist,' said her uncle, on her other side. 'But at least, my dear, you have, I think, decided not to go straight back to Flanders?'

Chapter 3

THE QUESTION WAS asked that night at Master Lamb's table: the question about Gelis van Borselen which, this time, would have to be answered. And it was Anselm Adorne once more who asked it, but this time directly of the girl's husband.

'So where, you fortunate man, is your charming wife Gelis?' asked Anselm Adorne, seating himself two places from Nicholas at Master Lamb's table shortly afterwards. Behind them, Albany's trumpeter let off a blast, and Julius, in the middle, began cheerfully to cut up his meat.

Julius, who had supervised (he felt) the upbringing of Nicholas, always enjoyed overhearing personal questions and especially this one, because of the slight variations in the answers Nicholas gave.

Nicholas was, naturally, wearing black. They were all freshly dressed – Adorne and his party from their sea-coffers, the Duke of Albany and his officers from the wardrobe at the King's Wark and Nicholas and himself from the clothes they kept over the river, where Nicholas had leased some convenient rooms in North Leith.

Since his departure from Bruges, Nicholas had elected to dress only in black, the most expensive dye in the world. And not only himself, but his page, his groom, his cook and his menservants had been put into black livery, and the select company of his men at arms wore black hats and black sleeves. Jannekin Bonkle, related to half the merchant colony of Bruges and Edinburgh, had organised it. It was, in its way, a gesture of unutterable flamboyance. Julius loved it.

Julius, of course, loved all that had happened since they left Bruges for Scotland. His wealth, the reputation of the Bank, and the respected name of the van Borselen family had ensured an honourable welcome from the young King's advisers for Gelis van

Borselen's husband. In return, Nicholas had not sought unreasonable privileges, and had not gone out of his way to court the child King or his brother. If Albany (sitting beyond Nicholas now) was seeking his company more and more, it was not Nicholas's fault. And the absence of a wife had proved no disadvantage.

As to that, Julius had not encouraged Nicholas to make this latest marriage, although the rest of the Bank had approved. Nicholas unshackled was thought to represent a challenge to normal society. Himself, he preferred Nicholas free. The happiest time of any lawyer's career could not offer more than the years Julius had spent managing the Banco di Niccolò in Venice. Gregorio, who had preceded him, would agree.

When Nicholas, back from Africa, had taken Gelis van Borselen to wife, the union had not been unexpected. She had followed him overseas; she had been compromised; she had powerful relatives. Nevertheless it had been a surprise when, the bridal night over, Gelis had dutifully followed the Duchess of Burgundy, while her husband had attached himself, after an unexplained absence, to the train of the Duke.

Then he had reappeared in Bruges with an entourage of new and highly trained followers, and had commanded Julius to come with him to Scotland.

The merits of such an expedition were reasonably obvious. The master of the Banco di Niccolò had not, as yet, visited the agency opened for him in Scotland, or studied how to exploit and protect it. Added to which, the fair Gelis van Borselen had once been an attendant of Mary, the King's married sister, and a bridal visit to Scotland should please her. Except, of course, that Nicholas had come to Scotland and Gelis had stayed at home.

'A pity,' explained vander Poele cordially now, between the laden dishes at Master Lamb's table in Leith. 'Did I not threaten her with divorce? But the Duchess had commanded her presence, and you don't have to remind a van Borselen how important the English may be to a Bank. Gelis went with the Duchess, for my sake. But I expect her to join me.'

His voice expressed simple confidence. Anselm Adorne said kindly, 'I am sure that she will. I expect she writes to you daily. You will have more news from Bruges than I do.'

'Not unless it's coming by pigeon,' Nicholas said. 'Ships are slow in bad weather. But I hope to hear from her soon.'

Julius continued to eat without catching anyone's eye. Ships from the south had been remarkably frequent that autumn. He himself dealt with the numberless packets which managed to find their way post-haste to Nicholas from Venice and Florence, Rome and Catalonia; the letter-bags arriving from Bruges with the familiar superscriptions of friends and colleagues and – over and over again – Gregorio's fierce legal script. Julius had read them all. And among them had been no message from Gelis van Borselen.

Albany, leaning forward, broke in. 'Can your wife swim? Who taught you?'

Of course, the King's brother knew Gelis from childhood. Nicholas said, 'My lord Admiral, I shall try her in water as soon as may be: up to the present I had not thought to ask. I was taught to swim by a black man. He is dead, but there are plenty of others.'

'You will teach me,' said Albany.

'Why, tonight, if you like,' Nicholas said. 'We can light a bonfire. Once you have learned, we can play tzukanion in the water.'

Albany's officer Liddell exclaimed, and Albany's voice rose, overriding others. Guests' faces turned, including that of Adorne's athletic niece Katelijne, her long, sticky hair in a caul. Beside her, Julius saw, were one or two sturdy figures he recognised from among the golfers. Adorne said, 'Is vander Poele drunk?'

'No,' said Julius. It was true, and untrue. Returned from the sea, they had all been served with spiced wine, as promised. All except Nicholas, who had been drunk on nothing but water since Bruges. Julius added, 'You know his style.'

'I knew his style, if you could call it that, at eighteen,' Adorne said. 'But nine years later, I expected maturity.'

'Surplus energy,' Julius said. 'He has a lot to spare, now the feud with Simon is over.'

'It is over?' said Adorne.

Nicholas was smiling, a danger sign. He appeared, however, to be listening to Will Roger, the man they all called Whistle Willie, who had come to lean, sent by Albany, at his shoulder. His green doublet was a mess. Julius turned his back. 'The feud?' he said to Adorne. 'Of course it's over. It finished in Bruges. Simon and Jordan are of no interest to Nicholas now. He doesn't even use the name vander Poele any more.'

'Why?' said Adorne.

'Because I thought it sounded vulgar,' Nicholas said. He *had* been listening. The whistler had gone.

Adorne said, 'It has earned more honours now than the name of St Pol. You know Simon is at Kilmirren?'

'And his father,' Nicholas said. He speared a fig and regarded it.

'The vicomte? How do you know?'

'It rained frogs in Kilmarnock, and the monks' wine in Paisley turned sour. The vicomte is undoubtedly there. In fact, I trust I shall meet him in Edinburgh. Cry the peace of the fair: we're all merchants, we ought to be friendly. You're here to patch up the Scots' trade in Bruges?'

'If I can. Why are you here, Nicholas?' said Anselm Adorne.

'Figs! Fegs, why kittle your belly with figs, when there's beef and ham and deer collops afore ye?' It was John Lamb, their host, half-risen and calling.

'Because I'm full of seawater. John, why am I here? Master Adorne has been asking.'

'To buy houses,' said Lamb, sitting down again and wiping his chin. It was a large one, and gleaming with bristles in the light of his best candelabra. His hat-shadow loomed on the painted wood ceiling. 'Ye ken this lad has bought yon fair little house with the orchard in the High Street of Edinburgh? Or the Bonkle family for him. And now do you ken what he has done? He's taken two of Old Berecrofts's tenements. Berecrofts, ye ken? Him who made a fortune from salt-pans and coalheughs? That's Robin, his grandson. Aye, well, Master Nicholas has got some good competent ground, and is building himself a stone house in the Canongate.'

'In the thick of the Abbot's merchant colony. I heard. So you are contemplating serious trading in Scotland?' Adorne said.

'Julius and Jannekin are,' vander Poele said. 'But I'm not here for that at all. I thought I was, but I'm not. Did you know the King is getting married?'

Everyone knew that the King, aged sixteen, was getting married to a Scandinavian child-bride of eleven. Half the Court was in Denmark concluding the deal for the dowry. The voice of Adorne's nephew said, 'Nicholas? You're going to do them a Burgundian wedding? Oh, my God!'

'They've *had* a Burgundian wedding,' said vander Poele. 'Her grace the late Queen Mother was Guelders-born, wasn't she? But I might contrive a fresh fancy or two.'

'Pissing wine,' ejaculated Sersanders. 'You didn't see what Nicholas led into —'

'Most of us did,' said his uncle. 'My lord Duke will think us uncouth. But I can recommend Nicholas to you. I have seldom met a more ingenious engineer. And when is the royal wedding?'

'Ask the wind and King Christian of Denmark,' said Jamie Liddell. 'He's got to get the money together. It's winter. Next year at this rate.'

'Time to practise the jousts,' said vander Poele thoughtfully. 'You know, my lord, that Master Adorne and Master Metteneye are both famous jousters? And young Sersanders. Does Maarten indulge?'

'Maarten is to take minor orders,' his father said. 'He will be at the Bishop's court at St Andrews. As for the rest of us, it is a long time since we first rode to the barriers, but we should be delighted, of course, to join in the sport. You have some fine exponents yourselves.'

'Simon de St Pol,' said Sersanders with malice. (*Young!*)

'And Master Julius and you, Master Nicholas,' said the Duke of Albany.

This time vander Poele laughed. He said, 'That would be sport indeed. No. I can hold my own on a battlefield, but I shouldn't waste Simon's time in the lists, either with him or against him. Are you disappointed?'

He spoke, Julius thought, to Sersanders beside him, but it was Adorne's dark-robed doctor beyond that who answered. Andreas said, 'Unthinking persons might accuse you of cowardice. You must not feel compelled, under pressure, to fight.'

'I shall quote you. *Cedere* rather than *contendere*,' Nicholas said pleasantly. Julius flushed. It had been an insulting remark. He wished that Tobie had come, and not this talkative Flemish physician with the fuzzy ash-coloured hair and large-featured face. The eyes in it were clear as two radishes. He went on talking while Nicholas smiled, with one dimple. He didn't know Nicholas.

'We have a mutual friend,' Dr Andreas was saying. 'The lord Nicholai Giorgio de' Acciajuoli told me that he stayed in this self-same house when in Scotland. You remember him? He has a wooden leg. You and he talked about Volos.'

'I remember him,' Nicholas said. 'He would have given me advice, I am sure, about this jousting matter.'

'I doubt it,' said the physician. 'He would have drunk only water, as you and I and the demoiselle Katelijne have been doing. So who taught Master Anselm's young lady sister to swim? The same black servant you mentioned?'

Julius groaned. Nicholas smiled in a meaningful way. Nicholas said, 'And if so, what else did he teach her? Anselm, why is your sister in Scotland?'

Julius kicked him under the table. The smile didn't waver. Sersanders said, 'What? Katelijne? She's going to that Cistercian foundation in Haddington where all the princesses are sent. Where Whistle Willie – where Will Roger teaches.'

'She's being sent to a *nunnery*?' Nicholas said.

Julius kicked him again. Dr Andreas said, 'I thought you would have known that.'

'He does,' Julius said. 'He needs another game of tzukanion. Or a swim, perhaps.' He felt like the Charetty notary once again, making excuses for Nicholas.

He was saying something to that effect when a horn blew in the darkness outside. Nicholas said, 'You were useless at excuses, *and* as a notary in Bruges. Anyway, you can't use your notarial seal in Scotland without being a priest. Godscalc's a priest. He could be a notary here, except that his handwriting is frankly appalling. That's the horn, and Albany's on his feet. Aren't you going?'

'What's the horn for?' Julius asked, rising because Albany did. No one answered. Everyone seemed to be leaving the house, so Julius went with them. He was relieved. Sometimes, in the company of Nicholas, the random fire became dangerous. It reminded him of a field manned by broken artillery.

Which was mad. He was trained. He could curb – he could always curb Nicholas.

The horn summoned them outside the house, but it was the whistle that led them all to the beach.

The house had been warm. Outside, the October moon lit the strand and silvered the waves as they crashed on the shore. The bonfire which burned on the sands was red and gold and enormous: in all the Lowlands, only the stackyards of Leith could have supplied it with timber.

The scores of people lolling, weaving, chorusing round the bonfire were also from Leith, Adorne's nephew Sersanders could see. Dogs yapped and bayed, and someone was playing the pipes to the merry patter of several drums. While the lords had been indoors, decorously eating from platters, the families who belonged here had brought out their food and a barrel of ale, and were continuing, in their own cheerful mode, the pleasures of the King's play.

Clouds of smuts, billows of heat swirled from the fire. Outside its range, the air was fresh but not piercing, although the sullen waters sounded cold. Sersanders began rather quickly to look about him for the youth Alexander, for Nicholas, and especially for Katelijne his sister.

They were with Will Roger on the other side of the fire. Sersanders saw the King's brother, secure within the sturdy group of his household, and the young women of title were there, laughing as well. They were harnessing dogs to the porters' ship-sleds and the young people were climbing aboard – his cousin Maarten, the Scots boy Robin, his own Katelijne. And Alexander, the heir to the throne. Older people strode about, lending a hand. He could hear the wagers being laid, and see the families leaving the fire to crowd round.

If the heir to the throne was to take part, surely the rest would be safe. His uncle Adorne, standing quietly behind, said, 'I don't think you could stop it. Maarten will take care of your sister. Don't you want to join in? You used to do things like that with Nicholas.'

He had, long ago, when he was twelve and Nicholas a sophisticated sixteen, an apprentice called Claes who knew every kitchenmaid and was the source of every inventive exploit in Bruges. Sersanders had known Julius too, partly as the Charetty lawyer who could chastise them both; partly as the young man who, off duty, was not averse to some adventure himself.

Today, he had exchanged hardly a word with Julius or with Nicholas vander Poele, once Claes, apart from that silly exchange about Katelijne. The camaraderie had gone. With his uncle, too, there had been a change in the old kindly relationship. Of course, wealth and power made men cold, even cruel. It wasn't surprising. Only he found himself thinking of the man by his surname this time. He was vander Poele: he was not a friend you called Claes. Sersanders said, 'At least they don't seem to be going to swim.'

He missed the first race, but joined the next one, and did quite well, with Maarten this time running beside him and yelling. They had a donkey race next, and then the pinners' men took them on at the tursing, which meant a race with a two-hundredweight load on your back. The professionals won that, but vander Poele and Julius led the laymen behind them, and vied with each other over the last hundred yards, using every dirty trick of toe and knee and shoulder anyone had ever heard of, accompanied by a stream of unquotable badinage. The boy Duke had tears streaming from his pale eyes, and Katelijne was white with delight and exertion.

Then Liddell said, 'Why don't we sing?'

So, as the moon shone on the sea, they settled round the red glowing mound of the fire, and the young gentlefolk sang, as Master Lamb had predicted. Now the families had begun to walk back through the sand to their cabins, and the artisans, for whom the day started at dawn, had with reluctance plodded back to the workshops. But many stayed, young men mostly, with a few elders hoping to catch a royal glance, plus a few who had snored themselves into their night's happy sleep. All the royal party was there, and the Flemings, even to Dr Andreas.

Anselm Sersanders was not a great man for music, although he had heard plenty of it in church and had a full student's repertoire of verses and rounds and choruses, dirty and clean. The Adornes, because of their family church, were painfully assiduous patrons, and Sersanders blamed his uncle for encouraging Katelijne's prejudices. She fidgeted now, consumed with impatience as the flasks were passed round and the songs roared out, to whistle and trumpet and drum, and the bagpipe wheezed now and then, until someone got up and threw it into the sea. Then Will Roger started making up verses.

His was one of the good voices; as it ought to be, since he'd come from England with the name of musician and stayed because, it seemed, he'd made himself popular with the Court. He was not one of nature's beauties, having a coarse face rather than an ascetic one, and a barrel chest and fingers like bolsters. But they were agile enough on a whistle, and the words he improvised were as neat as the measure he sang them to. Then he threw both across to James Liddell, and sang a descant while Jamie, no newcomer to the game, hummed and thought, and produced his own verse, and repeated it twice, with some help. Then Alexander made up a verse, not quite rhyming and losing the tune, but everyone chanted it after him, and Will Roger gave it its due before he turned to the girl Katelijne. He said, 'I think I have heard a sweet voice. Do you want to try it?'

'I need it higher,' she said, and drew breath, and began. The first line was a joke, developing an idea of Liddell's. The second was a parody of Will Roger's tentative start. The third and fourth were evolutions of both. The music was precisely Roger's throughout, except that at the end she changed the key down to minor, to prepare for lowering the range.

The applause and laughter had started by then, and almost drowned Roger's voice as it addressed her. 'Do it again. Keep it high. I'll adapt.' And when the shouting died, it revealed the two voices singing together, one high and one low, with the man improvising to the girl. They used the same words. At the end, they broke off, loudly acclaimed, and the versifying passed to other skittish, everyday voices.

Anselm Adorne said, 'She has a great gift. I think we have brought her to the right place.' His nephew glanced at him, and away.

Julius was singing. His voice was terrible and his verses didn't scan, but were fertile with waggish allusions. He had wandered off tune. Following him, Maarten (who had a good voice) said, 'I've lost the key. No, all right: I have it.'

Someone had quoted him the opening phrase at its original

pitch. The whistle, which had begun to give out the notes, promptly
stopped. The whistler looked round. 'Nicholas,' Julius replied to
the unspoken question. 'He carries keys in his head. Like a
housewife.' The fire shone on their red laughing faces.

Will Roger said, 'Go on, Maarten,' but didn't listen. At the end,
he applauded. He said, 'Why don't we try something more
complex? Nicholas-with-the-keys, can you give the little lady her
note? You can. Now let her sing her verse high, and make your
own words below her as I did. Or sing the same tune if you like.'

Adorne said, 'That's asking rather a lot. But inventing verse at
least will give our friend no pain.' The girl was singing, her face
full of mischief. Then vander Poele joined her, with unbroken
good humour.

Sersanders had heard him roar out the pithy songs they all knew,
and had known him improvise words. It was a skill that came to
him easily. The words he invented now were pointed rather than
coarse, but they rhymed and they scanned; and the notes were, to
begin with, the precise harmonies that Will Roger had used. The
girl, singing, faced him across the flickering fire. Then vander
Poele, without warning, moved into her tune, so that for a moment
they were singing in unison. Then the voices divided again. She
had taken the harmony, and left him with the original notes.

A moment later, the sound changed again. The whistle had
joined them. Will Roger, his fingers rippling, stood up. Katelijne,
her face rapt, also sprang to her feet and vander Poele, singing on
undisturbed, did the same. Roger dropped his hand away for a
moment. He said, 'Go on. Never mind the words. I'll keep the
tune.'

What followed lasted no longer than it took to empty a cup, and
very few round the fire listened closely, or knew what they were
hearing. The whistle held to its part and the girl to hers, leaving to
the other singer the freedom to find a third tune to weave about
them and, maliciously, some new lines of verse for the girl to reply
to. She did, changing her descant and forcing him to change his.
Then he altered his tempo as well and, while she kept the old pace,
began to double both the words and the notes, weaving faster and
faster about the core of the tune. She doubled too, but could not
quite match him. Then the whistle changed also, and became a
quotation.

The girl laughed from sheer excitement, and vander Poele
screwed his lips. But when she began to sing, he sang with her, and
went on singing when the whistle stopped altogether, and was
replaced by Will Roger's own rich voice, held well down. The

piece, though intricate, was not long, and ended quietly, with the three voices blended in unison.

Then Roger drew breath and said, 'My God, that's enough. Are we to work for you all night? A dance! A dance, your honours!' And, readily, the company scrambled to its feet while the trumpet lifted and flashed, and the drum began to thud out its measure.

Roger, whistle in hand, was not dancing, but had crossed to snare his two singers. The child Katelijne was there, but vander Poele had sprung off to join the light-hearted column, a comely noblewoman on either arm.

Julius, who had been late finding a partner, came and sat by Adorne and Sersanders and followed their gaze to the dancers. He said, 'Bravo, my good knight de Fleury. What was the last song they made up?'

'They weren't making it up. It was from the Divine Office. Tenebrae, darkness. *De Fleury*, you said?'

'His mother's family name,' Julius said. 'I told you. He decided at Bruges to bury the family feud; to forget he wanted Simon and Jordan to recognise him as one of their blood. So if he isn't St Pol, he isn't vander Poele either. That's how I understand it. The Duke's started calling him Nicol. You know they're going to roll barrels? Ten in a row, on the highway from Leith to Edinburgh? When the dancing finishes, we have to get torches.'

'Aren't you tired?' Adorne said.

'No. Well, a bit. But what a night! They're an energetic crowd, the Scots,' Julius said. 'It should suit M. de Fleury.'

Soon after the rolling of barrels, Jamie Liddell led his lord the King's brother to bed in the King's Wark at Leith, and Master Lamb was able at last to retire, and his weary Flemish guests with him. Quiet at last was bestowed on the strand and the river of Leith. Quiet, and soulful oblivion.

No one forded the river that night to Berecrofts's house in North Leith. Julius found a corner pallet with Lamb. Nicholas de Fleury, three months wed, was elsewhere; having lately had at his disposal the bed and the person of Beth, a minor laird's giggling daughter.

Chapter 4

THREE WEEKS AFTER that, Jordan de St Pol, vicomte de Ribérac, rode across Scotland to his house in the Cowgate of Edinburgh and from there made several calls. His last was to the Burgundian Envoy.

Anselm Adorne received him calmly in the large chamber of the merchant's house whose hospitality he now enjoyed in the High Street.

Like all Burgundian Flemings, Adorne traded with France despite everything. His eldest son spoke not only Italian and Flemish but the French of the professors of Paris. He himself knew the names of all the Scots of noble blood who had fought in France against England, and who had remained to serve sly, brilliant King Louis in return for fortunes and titles and territory. The d'Aubigny. The Monypenny. And de Ribérac. He knew, too, the campaign this elderly, gross man had conducted over the years to deflect the claims the apprentice Claes vander Poele might have tried to impose on his family. Nicholas, born of Simon's first wife, whom Simon repudiated.

Now Adorne said, 'I am glad to see you, my lord. Your fells and hides are among the best that we import. I hope we may count on you to help us settle this difference of opinion about the needs of Scots traders in Bruges. We are merchants, men of the world. Quarrels damage us all.'

'Then I must warn you,' said the fat man opposite, seated in the only large chair, a cup in his broad, beringed hand. 'The damage will be greater than you can imagine if our mutual acquaintance vander Poele gets his way. He is no friend to Genoa. He could close his business in Flanders tomorrow and retire to Venice, leaving Scotland to trade with the Hanse, or with Florence and Venice through England.'

'You think him so dangerous?' Adorne said. He was pleased, on the whole, that Sersanders and Metteneye were out. Neither would ever be a match for this elderly man, whose intelligence lived, shrewd as a fox, behind the pursed eyes, the many-chinned face, the giant bulk swathed in velvet. Adorne added, 'I heard that, in Bruges, he made an end to his dispute with your family. He has even changed his name from yours to his mother's. And I have heard him utter no threats since he came here.'

'You mistake me. Whatever his name, vander Poele could never be dangerous,' de Ribérac said. 'But disruptive, yes. Wilful, yes. Irresponsible, yes. If I were a lord of this country, I should encourage him to go back to Venice. I called at his house to tell him so, but he was not there.'

'He has been north, as I have, with the Court. In any case, he seldom uses his Edinburgh house, I am told. It suits him better to live down the hill, in the Canongate, in the Abbot of Holyrood's parish. He is building, and lavishly. Even if he were to leave, his agency would remain with a considerable presence.'

'Including men like Mick Crackbene?' said the fat man. 'I, of course, have no objection if vander Poele's clients have none. I should have thought he would have shrunk from employing him.'

'*Crackbene?*' said Adorne. The man was a seaman, a mercenary, equally serving a man and his enemies. Adorne said, 'I am surprised.'

'You didn't know? The bastard Bonkle, the fool Julius, and Crackbene, the professional turncoat. That is vander Poele's Scottish company. They will do what he wants. Suppose he turns the King's mind against trading with Bruges? Offers to bring his army here? Persuades Scotland to increase her support to the Yorkist side in this evil English war between kings? Might vander Poele – I am only suggesting it – become a danger to you?'

Shrewd as a fox. But de Ribérac was not dealing with Sersanders, or Metteneye. Anselm Adorne smiled, and said, 'How on earth should he, could he threaten me? I take no sides in the English war, unless you think it a commitment to have placed my daughter at Court. She serves the English King's mother. Perhaps I should balance my interest with some gesture to the Lancastrian side? Or is it hardly worth the trouble?'

The vicomte did not blink. He said, 'The King of Scotland is young.'

'The King of Scotland is sixteen. His advisers are not. The Court, as you must know, is better regulated than its lack of functionaries might suggest, although it has to contend with youthful exuberance. The rulers of this kingdom will not be influenced by an outsider. And his army, you must know, is fighting for the Duke of Burgundy on the borders of France. Captain Astorre will not lightly give up that contract, which in turn relies on the presence of the House of Niccolò in Bruges. I am not going to hurry vander Poele home, even for you. He is not at present even trading.'

'Then why is he here?' de Ribérac said. 'Apart, that is, from treating the place as a brothel? No wench, no lady, no burgher's daughter, I am told, is safe from his attentions.'

Anselm said coolly, 'Of that, I know nothing. He came here, I assume, to offer his services as a banker, a merchant, a dealer. He has been asked, I believe, to help direct the royal Christmas and wedding festivities.'

'I could understand it,' said the vicomte, 'were his own marriage not so very recent and so hastily consummated. His wife, they say, has left the Duchess's court for the country.'

'I have heard nothing of it,' said Adorne. This time, it was not quite the truth. According to Julius the lawyer, Nicholas had had enough of black girls, and now was bent on a little variety. Gelis (he had remarked) wasn't a nun. Nicholas and she seemed a good enough match: Julius hadn't heard that they'd tired of each other. They were, the Lord knew, the most pig-headed pair Julius had ever encountered, but if there had been anything wrong, Nicholas was the sort who would have gone back and settled it. Which he hadn't. Which meant there was nothing.

Adorne had listened and nodded, since nodding was cheap. To de Ribérac now he spoke mildly. 'I can only tell you what everyone knows: that vander Poele and his wife were already close long before marriage. Hence a parting such as this, beneficial to business, might be tolerated if not welcomed by both.'

'So they are still fond, you are saying? And this exhibition of lust is merely the result of a cruel deprivation? It is a theory,' de Ribérac said. 'I must bring Simon to Court, and see if he cannot advise vander Poele in his predicament. It is an area in which he is well qualified to a fault. And one of your sons is here? Maarten is now at St Andrews?'

The inquisition took a different course. Adorne bore it all with undisturbed candour. His son was indeed to study under the Bishop. His niece Katelijne was likewise happy in her royal post, so like that of her cousin in England – a symmetry which did not need again to be stressed. The conversation faded; the vicomte was rising when the door opened on Dr Andreas.

The two men had never met face to face. It was surprising, therefore, that the physician should halt on the threshold, and that the fat man should markedly pause before completing the movement that brought him upright. Adorne presented them to each other.

The vicomte's greeting was cursory. The doctor ventured to add a remark. 'You have a grandson, Diniz Vasquez, monseigneur?'

'According to Simon my son,' said Jordan de St Pol, 'I have several.' He began to walk to the door.

'No,' said Dr Andreas. 'By him, monseigneur, you have only one.'

The vicomte turned. 'You have private information? I am fascinated. Or I hear that you study the stars? Tell me more.'

'I know no more,' said Dr Andreas. 'But perhaps that is enough.'

'Well, certainly, it is good news,' said the vicomte reflectively. 'Indeed, you must inform Master Henry de St Pol, when he is older. He, too, will be relieved. Meanwhile, I suggest that other parts of the firmament might prove more rewarding than the area that shines on my family? We possess, I think, lustre enough. Sir Anselm?'

He left. Adorne closed the door and looked at his physician. Andreas, from Vesalia, served his household, and the Guild, and the Hospital of St John at Bruges. Adorne was not in awe of him as the Guild members were, although he respected his peculiar skills. Now he said, 'I think you will have to explain that exchange. You disturbed him.'

Andreas said, 'It was not my intention. Sometimes, a truth comes to the tongue and must be spoken. He did not question it. But the grandson's name is not Henry.'

'What is it?' said Adorne.

'I cannot tell. My lord, I came because of the vicomte. What did he ask of you? Your reasons for coming?'

One did not need special powers to divine that. All the same, Adorne thought it prudent to sit the man down and then to describe the encounter. He omitted nothing.

At the end: 'Ah,' said Dr Andreas, easing his well-covered shoulders. 'Yes, I see. And now, Monseigneur will have gone to fetch his son Simon to Court. Will you warn M. de Fleury?'

It took a moment's thought, even yet, to attribute the Burgundian name to the dimpled, rumbustious apprentice. Adorne said, 'Of what should I warn him? He knows St Pol and his father are here. The battle is over, and vander – and de Fleury ready to bury the

hatchet.' The conversation was fresh in his mind. Cry the peace of
the fair. We're all merchants: we ought to be friendly.

'You are right,' said Dr Andreas. 'There is no need to warn him:
he knows.'

The man who, day and night watched Anselm Adorne, slipped
down the slope of the High Street and through the fortified gate
that divided the burgh of Edinburgh from that of the Canongate.
On his left was the road that plunged downhill and northwards to
Leith. Ahead was the highway to Holyrood Abbey. Packed between
the two was the merchant colony presided over by the family
Berecrofts, among which was the house of the Banco di Niccolò;
two floors of it finished, the rest in the hands of the masons.

Julius its lawyer was there, as well as its master and patron.
'Well?' Julius said when the spy had gone off. 'You said Jordan
would try Adorne first. Now you know Simon will follow.'

'I am brilliant,' de Fleury said, being sick, for the moment, of
Julius. They had spent the last three weeks on the road with the
Court, hunting, shooting, riding, hawking and discussing, among
other things, the King's wedding and the country's financial wellbeing. In the evenings they had played games and danced.

M. de Fleury had won, without much trouble, a great deal at
cards and had achieved, without much trouble, a mild acclaim for
inventing new diversions of a socially acceptable kind. He was, it
was established, seldom unwilling to sing, and in private displayed
a gift for deadly and accurate mime which had come to the ears of
the King and his brother. On the other hand, he had not courted
royal attention. His business had been with the royal officials. He
and Julius had been intermittent guests in a very large household
which also held, at intervals, the Burgundian Envoy and his suite.
Anselm Adorne had had several exchanges, always pleasant, with
Nicholas de Fleury of Bruges.

The evening of licence at Leith had not been repeated. The
squires in whom reposed charge of the King and his siblings had
been smartly dealt with, and exercise on the shorelands curtailed.
It told Nicholas de Fleury what he already knew, that this was a
well-conducted court, of such a size that a handful of good men
could run it. Of all the other actors of that night, he had interest
only in Anselm Adorne. The girl Beth, he rather thought, had
gone back to her father.

Since then he had hardly been celibate, but had not as yet
managed to coax to his bed, or indeed anywhere, the particular
woman he was interested in. The problem pleased him. He found

it entertaining to compound his physical assets: to dress as always in black, with a jewel placed each day on his glove, or his hat, or his breast, all of them set in the heaviest gold like the deeply worked chain which crossed his shoulders. His sword of ceremony was Byzantine and inlaid, and old. The Emperor of Trebizond who had given it to him had been a degenerate and a fool, and his courtiers good for nothing but reclining in shadow, debating.

Nicholas de Fleury was not only far from a fool: he was an artist. Within his dress he moved with a magnificent freedom, as eloquent as if he wore nothing at all. He had been expertly taught and, moreover, had lately spent much of his time in a climate where clothes were an irrelevance. He had no doubt that the one lady he wanted would come to him in the end. By Christmas, perhaps. Certainly before January had ended: he couldn't wait longer than that. But first, among a thousand delicate tasks, he had to make this visit to Haddington. He thought he would make it soon, before Simon came to town. He supposed he should inform Julius now.

Julius was drinking claret, while waiting to be told what to think. Nicholas poured himself a cup of water and, when the builders' dirt rose to the surface, threw it, without speaking, at the opposite wall.

Seventeen miles to the east of Edinburgh the priory of Haddington, the fourth largest town in the kingdom of Scotland, lay by its river in autumnal farmlands packed with fat Cistercian sheep, grazed by handsome Cistercian cattle, ploughed into soft, rich furrows for healthy Cistercian grain and thoroughly planted with fruit trees and vegetables. The mill-wheels groaned; the bells chimed; the dogs barked; the carts rumbled away to the tan-pits, the weavers, the markets; and the Prioress and her twenty white-gowned nuns were to be seen as often outside the precinct walls among the vast army of lay workers and servants as inside at their devotions. The priory of Haddington was not only a wealthy landed estate, it was rural lodging, salon and nursery for eminent ladies.

Katelijne Sersanders approved. She had not quite believed that she would escape the kind of convent her cousins inhabited, wrapped in stillness and piety. Haddington, on the contrary, could afford the luxurious appointments of a court because it was a court: Margaret was not the first royal child to be reared there. The nuns were of gentle birth and hand-picked from sister houses. There was one from Waverley, England; and one from Cîteaux itself. And providing companionship for the élite of the kingdom were other ladies and children who, for one reason or another, had retired (or

almost retired) from the world, and could afford to pay for their
keep, or were important enough to have it paid for them.

The priory performed other duties as well. The high officers of
the kingdom and the burghs had been known to gather in its
capacious Great Chamber. Envoys and couriers lodged there; the
King would come to see his young kindred while hunting; the
finest tutors were paid to visit and give of their wisdom to the royal
infants in tutelage. There was therefore no shortage of entertainment or sport or, of course, work.

Katelijne Sersanders, royal attendant, had a buoyant if occasionally menacing relationship with the lady Margaret, aged eight, but
shared her tasks with several others, from the body-nurse Mariota
to the well-bred nun Alisia, who taught the child her letters and
manners, a little Latin and French, and some simple techniques of
embroidery.

On the whole, Katelijne preferred the two Sinclair cousins, so
unlike each other. Mistress Phemie Dunbar was an unmarried lady
of wry demeanour, privately devoted to poetry, and skilled in the
art of settling disputes without seeming to try. Her mother's niece
Dame Betha Sinclair had brought up one princess already, and was
the widowed mother of three extremely docile young girls who
sometimes flinched when she passed them, chiefly because of the
volume of her voice. On matters of deportment, Mistress Phemie
and Dame Betha were mentors unparalleled, both being the
daughters of earls.

Least of all, Katelijne enjoyed the days when the Prioress herself
chose to teach, although the lady Elizabeth was a powerful woman,
trading in her own right with Bruges, and equally ready, if she had
to, to man and command the fortalice she was building as a
precaution. As a precaution against England, their presently amiable neighbour over the Border.

Most of all, Katelijne relished her lessons with the musician,
Will Roger. It was best when Margaret wasn't present, and there
were only one or two boys and herself, with her maidservant
Emmelot chaperoning them, asleep (despite the noise) in the corner.
It was after one such hilarious afternoon that she glanced out to the
courtyard, Master Willie chatting beside her, and saw what new
arrival had emerged from the gatehouse.

He seemed to be expected. She saw the porter ushering him
across; the steward coming out to direct his men; the stablemen
hurrying to lead off the horses. The newcomer had two servants
with him and ten mounted men, all in black, and a burly companion
of unknown provenance, who remained at his side.

'Balls!' said Katelijne Sersanders.

'What?' said her tutor.

'Remember? Balls,' said the Princess's companion. 'And I still have his ballocks knife. Tell him. I'll get it.' She whirled, colliding with the collected person of Mistress Phemie, upon which she had the grace to blush.

Mistress Phemie, in her habitual dress of high-necked gown and neat wimple, gave no sign of alarm, her attention being diverted, in her turn, to the visitor. She said, 'What a beautiful man.'

Unlike her taste in poetry, Mistress Phemie's grasp of secular matters was shaky. Katelijne corrected her. 'He isn't. He just walks as if he is. It's my uncle's friend M. de Fleury. Did you know he was coming?'

'Of course,' said Mistress Phemie. Above her chastely bound jaw, her round copper eyes followed the newcomer. 'He brings godly news of the evangelisation of Africa; setting up the truth, as Athanasius says, as a light upon its miraculous candlestick. Also he knows how to value our wool in the boll compared with the heathenish throw-away prices offered for Catalan.'

'I thought,' said Will Roger, puzzled, 'that Catalan wool came from other Cistercian houses?'

Mistress Phemie's jaw prodded its wimple. 'I pray you,' she said, 'refrain from reminding our holy mother, the Prioress. She is a great lady, but details escape her.'

Will Roger was among those who, an hour-glass after that, gathered with nuns, prioress and household, guests and officers, to learn about the Land of the Blacks through the equally unreliable memory of Nicholas de Fleury. The music master, a virtuoso entertainer himself, admired the performance. Here was not a beautiful man, by God no. But here was a skilful one.

At the end, he joined in the applause. It was merited. 'Poor Father Godscalc!' they exclaimed. 'How terrible! How sad! And what can be done for the heathen?'

To which their visitor answered by shaking his head. 'Nothing. Indeed, I am told the tribes have since rebelled, and Timbuktu and its sinners destroyed within sight of redemption. One must weep. One must weep, even for blacks.'

Then he answered their questions until, after a while, the discussion insensibly had departed from the Joliba to matters of deep concern to thinking people, such as the margin for pricing their leeks and the means of obtaining better terms for their fells and even how to make a profit from coal. One of the nuns, subject to sudden enthusiasms, exclaimed, 'But we know, don't we, who could help there?' and subsided, eyes lowered, before the Prioress's quick frown. De Fleury, who had excellent manners, paid no attention.

To one or two, his manners perhaps were too striking. Will Roger, a silent spectator, was not surprised when Dame Betha crossed to sit beside him and, for once, lowered her voice. 'That man. What do you know of him?'

She knew, better than he, who de Fleury was. He knew what she was asking, but preferred to hedge. 'He can swim,' Roger said. 'And sing. And act, I suspect. Katelijne?'

She thought. She always thought. She said, 'He tells lies very well. He is angry. He is rich, and married to Gelis van Borselen, who is related to the young Scottish King and to other great families by marriage. He used to be an apprentice. He is not nice, but I like him.'

'You like everybody,' said Will Roger. She was right. It was anger. He said, 'Mistress Phemie, what about you?'

The round, copper eyes had become canopied. 'I don't know,' she said. 'Why is he here?'

Her charge had been listening. The lady Margaret made her red hair flounce with impatience. 'You've just heard. About sailing to Africa. About taking Christ to the black men. Ask him yourself.'

He was touring the room with the Prioress. He was meeting even the cooks. He was talking to Emmelot, who came from Liège, as he would find out to his cost. When he reached the King's fiery-haired little sister, the lady Margaret didn't ask about black men. She said, 'You haven't taught me or Sandy to swim.'

His doublet velvet was cut in two heights. He said, 'No, your grace, it's too cold. I'll teach you both football instead. Mistress Katelijne, I want my ballocks knife back.'

'Where?' said Katelijne, producing it point first in a considering way. Girls with brothers, Will Roger had noticed, were seldom easily flustered.

'After dark, in the dairy? No? Thank you.' He received the knife from her and turned. 'And Master Roger. I thought you wore green. Viva Savoia.'

'It was only a loan,' said Will Roger. 'You're not very inventive yourself. The same scent, even. I enjoyed the story of Barbaria in Afric. It would curdle milk.'

'That was the scent,' de Fleury said. 'I hear you're teaching music to everybody: pigs, bell-ringers, ploughmen. Crackbene here wants to learn. And who is the good maidservant Ada, whom, they tell me, you are training to sing to the pots?'

Roger considered the question. The good maidservant Ada was here; he could see her at the back of the room. She had got the baby out, and the wherewithal to feed it, and was applying one to the other with gusto. The child had a large round yellow head and so had Ada. She also had a remarkable chest-voice.

De Fleury, following his gaze, drew a melodious breath. It was, one had to admit, an impressive picture. Roger said, 'You're in luck: she usually has a head either side. The lady Mary sent her over, I'm told. Warm your bed in a trice, if you're staying.'

The breath emerged all at once as a snort. 'Why not?' said the other. 'I've been asked to stop overnight. With my former shipmaster: you know him? Crackbene, do you want your bed warmed? No, leave the subject: we've been summoned to Dame Elizabeth's parlour. What shall we talk about there?'

'Well, sir,' someone said. 'What about your precious wife, Gelis van Borselen?'

De Fleury wheeled. Dame Betha, adroitly risen, fell into step alongside him. She said, 'The lady de Fleury? I hear delightful news, Master Nicholas.'

The Fleming walked on. 'You know my wife Gelis?' he said.

She was passably young, for the mother of three and a widow. She was nosy. She said, 'Do I ken my own wean? Your lady served the King's sister Mary; I reared her. The Countess of Arran, that is.'

'And the Earl your father tutored the King. What finer mentors,' said Nicholas de Fleury, 'could any man desire for his wife!' He quickened his pace into the parlour.

If he thought the topic closed, he was wrong. The Prioress sat, and waved de Fleury to a place at her side. Dame Betha leaned over. 'Prioress, here is the husband of Gelis, and you and I have something to tell him.' She had small, well-shaped teeth of various colours, and a shrewd eye which she turned on Will Roger.

The musician looked at the ceiling. *Warm your bed in a trice.* He should have kept his mouth shut, or horn in it.

The Prioress said, 'Family news perhaps deserves better privacy.'

'But such exciting news,' urged Dame Betha. Short and bright-eyed and muscular, she wore the alert look of an excellent badger-hound. Roger assumed the badger had noticed it.

'Well. I have to congratulate you, M. de Fleury,' said the Prioress, giving way. 'The blessed outcome is, of course, in God's hands, but the news came today, and bears a date in early October. You will rejoice to know that your marriage is fruitful. In March or April next year, the lady de Fleury, God willing, will bear to you.'

Will Roger brought his gaze down. Impassioned faces surrounded him. The exceptions were, perhaps, the child Margaret who scowled, and the girl Katelijne who appeared merely thoughtful. The third exception was the prospective father himself whose face had lost life for a moment, as it had when he caught sight of Ada. It came to Will Roger, with shame, that he might have mistaken that look.

Then Nicholas de Fleury smiled, the crimson flooding down to his throat. He said, 'Shall I confess that I knew of her hopes? And now I know it is true: she is carrying. What can I say? I am speechless.'

'You knew!' said Katelijne, delighted. 'That is why she didn't come!'

'Of course,' he said, the dimples round as two nutshells. The nuns, exclaiming, were bringing fresh wine. The man called Michael Crackbene stared into his cup as if navigating.

Roger wondered why the detachment. Himself, he felt a sudden deep affection for the man-with-keys-in-his-head. He said, 'Well, you don't drink to this news in your wretched water. Here's to you, Nicholas de Fleury of Bruges, and to your first-born son or daughter to come!'

He watched de Fleury set his lips to the wine, unsure whether well-water might have been kinder. But the man emptied that cup and the next, and matched the best of them for the rest of the evening. And even leaving, he only stumbled a little.

Having a hard Scandinavian head, Michael Crackbene steered vander Poele to his bed in the guest-quarters.

He thought of him as vander Poele because he couldn't remember to call him de Fleury. He had no interest in using his first name. He recognised that this was why he, Crackbene, was here: because he was a practical man who took employment from whomever might offer it, and could sail from Newcastle to Leith with his eyes shut.

People called him a renegade, but he was not. He was always meticulous in ending one contract before he went to take up another. Vander Poele had laid hands on him once as a warning, but had still employed him again when it suited him. He respected the man. He also knew – it was nothing to him – that vander Poele had not heard from his wife since he set out for Scotland.

They had been given a room to themselves in the guest-wing. Crackbene got rid of the pages as ordered, and debated how far to undress his companion. Of the two of them, he himself had had far more to drink. But vander Poele, perched on the bed, unclasped his doublet and dragged off and dropped his own boots before thudding back on the pillow and staring up at the crucifix on the canopy. He said, 'What about Ada?'

Crackbene said, 'They all sleep over the kitchen. She has to get up to suckle the children. There's a shed with straw by the kiln where she'd meet you. Or here. She doesn't charge much.'

'Children?' vander Poele said. He turned his head.

'You're going to spew,' Crackbene said. There was a bowl by the window.

'Maybe. Shellfish,' said the other inexplicably.

'Shellfish? We didn't have any,' said Crackbene. 'Children. She wet-nurses. Sometimes it stops the next child from coming and sometimes it doesn't. One of the babies is hers. She'd be quite lively, I think, if you don't mind milk all over the place. Do you think you are up to it?'

'No. But I think you are,' vander Poele said.

Crackbene gave a rare laugh. He supposed it was obvious. He said, 'And you'd pay for it?'

'I'm generous. But I'll not pay for aborting a Viking. Find out before you start which child is hers, and how old it is, and take precautions accordingly. If she comes from Dean Castle, she's got friends.'

Crackbene had already lifted the latch of the door. He said, 'That's why she charges. You'll manage?'

'I'm sure both of us will,' vander Poele said.

It was just before dawn when Crackbene returned. He was not done, but the girl had to get back by sunrise. By then she'd fed the two gasping brats twice, regardless of anything he might be doing. The first time, she'd squealed out that she wasn't a *pourceau*. The second, he'd found a way of driving her gradually crazy. There was no doubt she needed a man. He had to stop at the door, he wanted so much to go back.

Vander Poele said, 'Don't light it. So, what?' He sounded as tired as if he had done it himself, after all.

Crackbene said, 'Worth every farthing. She's sworn to say she's no claim if she breeds. And by God, you were right. She'd have tried to blame her last child on me if it wasn't eighteen months old and black-headed. The father's the pig-man at Dean, but won't own it. Did you speak?'

'An accident of the soul. Of the wine. I left a ducat. Consider it doubled.'

'Why?' said Crackbene. 'Listen, I need a light. You don't know what state I'm in.'

He struck flint and relit the lamp on the way to the corner. When he got back vander Poele had rolled over to sleep, head on arms, like a stone; like a corpse on a beach. Crackbene crashed down beside him, and sighed, and opened his mouth to the first, glorious snore.

Chapter 5

EXT DAY, NATURALLY, a packet from Bruges arrived in the
Canongate, and M. de Fleury, having left Haddington at
dawn, received it with no delay whatever. He opened and
spread out all the pages, both those which were written in
clear, and those in trading code, which Julius and Jannekin could
read just as easily. Gregorio – who else? – had set down the news
he had already gathered in Haddington. That is, the theme was the
same. He read it for the variations.

> *Visited by the petty ills of first breeding, the lady Gelis van
> Borselen, dame de Fleury, had withdrawn for convenience to a
> convent. Her doctors had advised against visitors, and M. de
> Fleury should not hasten home.* Indeed, wrote Gregorio, *it was
> felt that the extra excitement might harm her.*

M. de Fleury framed soundless praise for Gregorio. His head
turned, from lack of sleep, and then settled immediately.

'I know what he means,' Julius said. 'My God, you had enough
premarital excitement between you, rumour said, to last you the
first ten years of official matrimony.' Julius, the perpetual bachelor,
had received this dynastic news with some lack of enthusiasm.
Jannekin Bonkle, on the contrary, had wrung his old playmate's
hand and assured him that his father would preside at the christening. Mick Crackbene, as Nicholas had cause to know, was quite
indifferent both to the event and to its implications.

Julius now leaned over the paper. 'My God, what did you pay
for that ring? Is that all Gregorio says?'

'Look,' said Nicholas de Fleury, showing the papers. It was all
that was personal. It preceded many pages of financial detail from
Venice and Bruges, plus the latest of the Signoria's demands that
he should either pay them or fight for them. The smith was on his

way, which was good. Of other family news there was nothing. Gregorio could not use a closed code, or Julius would instantly have suspected collusion.

Julius said, 'He's put four extra words on the back. *For God's sake, write.* We replied to all his last letters? Are the answers going astray?'

'Send the last one again,' Nicholas said. Gregorio's words were dug into the paper, in the way that happened when he was especially angry. Nicholas had no intention of writing. He said, 'Come on. I'll deal with this later. We have this tournament to arrange. And I want to see the Berecrofts family and settle this licence. And what about Simon, *membrum diaboli*?'

'He's coming to the tournament,' Julius said.

'Nobody has told him I'm not taking part?'

'You're really not?' Julius said. 'You aren't at all bad.'

'Thank you. I'll give you a little fight all of your own one of these days, when you're not feeling too well. I didn't leave Bruges, bloated with temporal possessions, to receive my final accounting in Scotland.'

'Of course,' said Julius. 'You won't want to risk anything now, with a family. It's a shame, in a way.'

The news of the family spread to Kilmirren.

It came to Lucia first, in her comfortable Vasquez hall by the park of the tower. She sat and screamed until Matten came rushing, and then showed her the letter from Diniz which, of course, Matten could not read. Then, without even accepting the restoring drink Matten had brought her, she ordered her hooded cloak and hurried across to Kilmirren Castle.

The rain was cold. The rain had never been cold in Madeira, or in Portugal where her late husband came from. Diniz, only half Portuguese, never seemed to notice the rain. Diniz had married a burgher's daughter in Bruges, and seemed enchanted with her. Diniz had been enchanted by Nicholas ever since the African voyage. And now this letter, with news that Diniz plainly thought wonderful.

'It is appalling,' said Lucia de St Pol, thrusting her father's chamberlain aside and bursting into her father's parlour. 'I am going to faint. What shall we do? I cannot believe it!'

From his great cushioned chair her great cushioned father surveyed her with astonishment. He said, 'You have my permission to faint. Indeed, you may throw a fit, provided you do it on the other side of that door. You may not have observed. I am occupied.'

He wasn't. He was as good as alone. The short, stout woman (who did rise to her feet) was that neighbour who was well-enough bred to act as Lucia's companion from time to time when she travelled. Bel of Cuthilgurdy had accompanied Lucia to her husband's villa in Portugal. The widow Bel, of sturdy constitution, had even travelled to Africa with Diniz, and Gelis, and vander Poele. Now she said, 'Monseigneur de Ribérac, the lassie's distracted. Mistress Lucia, come away in and sit down. What's to do?'

Lucia sat, her son's letter clenched in one hand. She said, 'Diniz says they're both pregnant.'

Her father stared at her. 'Now that,' he said, 'is indeed a matter for swooning with all imaginable diligence. Diniz *and* his wife?'

She loathed him. She had always loathed him. She understood how her grown son and her small nephew Henry hated him too. She said, her voice shaking, 'You joke. Read that. Read that letter. Tilde de Charetty is pregnant. Your great-grandchild will be the descendant of pawnbrokers. But I'll tell you something worse than that. *Gelis van Borselen is carrying.*'

The face of Bel of Cuthilgurdy, featureless as a flour-bag, became slowly illumined. The countenance of Jordan de Ribérac expressed simple enquiry. He said, 'And one should faint? I hardly think so. You have, as always, made a mistake, Lucia. Go away.'

'A mistake!' she said. 'It is here, in black and white. The girl has hidden herself in a convent. The birth is due, they say – of course – in March or in April. *A child!*'

'Anything else would have been surprising,' her father said. 'Mistress Cuthilgurdy, will you excuse us?'

'No!' said Lucia. Even Bel, sometimes, could help.

But Bel was standing. 'My hinny,' she said. 'A bairn still in the making is no threat to you, surely. Your father will know what to do. Calm yourself. There is no harm in childer.'

'And you know Henry?' Lucia said. It pleased her to see the other woman hesitate. Then, without replying, Bel kissed her firmly and left. The door closed.

Her father said, 'If you are in some female decline, you might like to think of taking the veil. It would be a relief to us all. I take it you think Gelis is bearing to Simon, and will tell Nicholas so? I doubt it. She would lose her marriage settlement as a result. I see no cause for concern.'

'There would be no cause for concern,' Lucia said, 'if every man thought as you do. But you expect Gelis to rear a bastard of Simon's? You expect Simon to leave a child of his in Nicholas's hands? You are content that Nicholas, knowing nothing, should be left in his ignorance?'

Her father sighed. Within the veined, pallid flesh, the eyes weighed her, studied her, chilled her as they had done all the years of her childhood.

'Suggest it to him, and your brother is dead. Who knows who sired this coming child? It may be your brother. It may be born of the marriage, in wedlock. Only the date of its birth will confirm it. And meantime vander Poele, as its parent, will protect it. Cease to concern yourself,' said her father kindly. 'Go and find something to embroider. A pillow for your first grandchild. And let us pray God that it owes nothing to you.'

'Simon will tell him,' she said.

'And earn the immortal enmity of the van Borselen? No. Simon will do nothing,' her father said. 'And you will do nothing. Or I shall see that you never leave Kilmirren again.'

'You can't!' she said. 'I have money now. I can go where I like!'

He looked at her. The door had opened, on what summons she didn't know, and two of her father's servants stood there. 'My daughter is sick,' said her father. 'Find a room for her, and send for a doctor.'

They were, as always, gentle, but held her tightly none the less. She screamed from the doorway, 'What if vander Poele knows?'

Her father paused. Then he said, 'If he does, then I imagine he would do almost anything to prevent your making it public. Think about it. I do not wish to be harsh. But you find yourself in all these difficulties only because you will not think.'

He watched her leave. There was no one at the door when Jordan de Ribérac, lifting his bulk, moved soft-footed down the stair and walked towards the block which held the apartments of Simon his son. The rain had stopped, and there was some activity – two jousters – in the tiltyard. He heard the raucous voice of his son's master-at-arms before he saw the fellow, encased in full armour with a lance in his fist. The figure at which he was roaring was short as an undented whistle and topped by a spray of plumes as tall as itself. Two red-faced grooms stood by with horses. De Ribérac walked past without speaking.

Simon was in the room off the yard where the castle arms were secured. The trestle table was littered with pieces of equipment, and Simon was pacing the straw, throwing remarks at the two or three men who sat motionless, arrested while cleaning them. He looked up at his father's shadow.

'Get out,' de Riberac said. The men left.

Simon said, 'This time, the girl is under the table.'

De Ribérac gave no sign that he heard. 'The child is wearing silver,' he said. The articles of armour on the table, of full size, were of niellated silver as well. He sat down. 'How did you pay for it?'

Simon pushed aside a sword and perched on the table. The hair that looked artificial in Lucia was fine-spun gold when framing her brother's face – his angelic face, with its arched brow and lethargic blue eyes. Simon said, 'Out of my share of the profits from Africa. There is enough left for my next meal. I am told you've dismissed my farm manager. Another economy?'

'I have engaged a replacement. You will meet him tomorrow. I have news. The woman Gelis van Borselen is to give birth in March or in April.' Deliberately, he had given no warning.

Simon responded in character. His gaze lost its focus and shifted. His lips parted; a touch of red appeared on each jaw. Then his eyes returned, full of slow wonder. 'Holy Mary!' he said in a whisper.

'It was not, unfortunately, the Annunciation,' said Jordan de Ribérac. 'All that can be said is that the child is not yours.'

'You don't know,' Simon said. The flush had deepened. His voice gained in strength. 'How do you know? If it's mine, it's due long before. In February. In the middle of February. She's lying.'

'It is not yours,' repeated de Ribérac. 'It is not yours, even if it were to emerge upon stroke of bell forty weeks past its begetting, with the name Kilmirren stamped on its forehead. The mother is a van Borselen. As you did not advertise your carnal connection, so you will not advertise its unfortunate outcome.'

'But . . .' said Simon gently. He got off the table.

'There are no buts. I have told you. She has not confessed to vander Poele: I am told he suspects nothing. Bruges believes the child to be born of the marriage. She has retreated, I am told, to a convent.'

'To hide! She must know it is mine!'

'Perhaps,' said the vicomte de Ribérac wearily, 'she is not yet sure herself who the father is or, you might think, the nuns would already have found a way to resolve her difficulty. The date of her accouchement, yes, would clarify matters, but shall we ever hear it? The sisters are remarkably skilled in deception.'

'It will look like me,' Simon said. 'Her child. Our child. And then be damned to all your precautions.'

'It may even sound like you,' said his father. 'In which case, you are right, I do not know why I am troubling to preserve you or your livelihood. Meanwhile, have I made myself clear? You have your heir. You have your legitimate, your undisputed son, Henry. *This child is not yours.* And you will do nothing, at any time in the future, to claim that it is.'

'Or?' said Simon.

'Or you will find yourself in isolation, without money, in a place far less pleasant than this. I mean it,' said his father. 'You do not doubt that I could do it?'

'Then you will have to do the same to Lucia,' said Simon viciously.

'So I have told her,' his father said.

He waited, but Simon, it seemed, had thought of nothing more to say. Jordan de Ribérac rose and left. Outside, he saw a glint of silver and heard his grandson's shrill voice. He remembered the tournament.

He knew how Simon's mind worked. He could not keep Simon at Kilmirren for ever. He had given him leave to attend. But that was when all his enquiries had indicated that vander Poele was not aware that Gelis van Borselen had deceived him.

Now it was not enough to think so: the vicomte de Ribérac had to be sure. He began to consider how to do so.

The tournament of the Unicorn which, although properly run, was not a candidate for the heraldic record-books, took place in the first week in December and on the first day of the Christmas festivities, when anyone bearing the name of Nicholas could expect a certain amount of vulgar attention.

Since Haddington, Nicholas de Fleury had himself been the source of most of the more strenuous activities in Edinburgh. The stands, staging and devices for such entertainments, as well as the tents and pavilions, were in the hands of the carpenters, masons, tent-makers, painters, carriers and purveyors who usually moved the Court from place to place with its plate, its clothes, its furniture and occasionally the glass for its windows.

None of this was on the scale of the Dukes of Burgundy, who required seventy-two carts to remove their possessions from one of their five splendid palaces to another, but there was a routine; and de Fleury knew by now all the Court officials and merchants involved, and most of the labourers. Half of them, it seemed to him, were working on his own house as well.

His role was to enhance the spectacle: to produce ideas within the capacity of the operators and the limits of the short time available and, tactfully, to supervise them. At the same time, necessarily, he continued to invent, direct and process the enterprises which were his reason for coming to Scotland. For a short period the tempo of his life, always impressive, accelerated to an extreme. To Julius, there were days when he seemed to be physically present everywhere from the monastery of the Abbot of Holyrood at the foot of the Canongate to the King's lodgings in the Castle at the top, and most of the houses between. The rest of his time he might be found beside the West Port in the grassy space at the foot of the Castle Rock where the lists were to be set up.

It was where Anselm Adorne found him, the day before the Eve of St Nicholas, standing below the flagpoles and talking forcefully, a sausage in one outflung hand and a stick in the other. His voice sounded menacing, but the faces around him were grinning. Adorne called, 'Don't you ever take a rest? I could share that sausage with you, if you had another.' De Fleury turned, smiling, and beckoned him over and pointed.

Adorne dismounted, and left his sweating horse for his groom to walk while he found his way to the tent where the brazier was, and sat on a box beside a half-unpacked basket of food. He poked into it.

It was true that he was hungry, having just spent an hour with Sersanders running at a makeshift tilt in the burgh common. In his day, Anselm Adorne had been a man of international reputation in the jousting field: he had taken the helm of one of the best of Duke Philip's bastards, and had broken lance with Jacques de Lalaing, fair as Paris, pious as Aeneas, wise as Ulysses, brave as Hector and dead these fifteen years past.

Before James, King of Scotland, and his brothers were born, Jacques de Lalaing, together with Simon his uncle and another, had challenged three Scottish knights to a contest *à outrance* in Stirling, and had prevailed, although the fight had been stopped. All Scotland knew that, and tomorrow would look to see what Burgundy had sent them this time.

The answer was himself, who was the age that Simon de Lalaing had been on that day. Himself and his kinsman Jehan Metteneye, whose family for generations had also carried off the prize in the White Bear Society, jousting in Bruges. And Sersanders his nephew, who was young and had no wife and no children.

But, of course, this was not a tournament to the death. It was a blunt-weaponed exercise, put together in haste and economy, to enable the young King and his younger brothers to shine.

They would not have to face Anselm Adorne. All that would concern him and his countryman Metteneye would be the contests of honour where they would be pitched, there was no doubt, against the best Scotland could offer. The very best being Simon de St Pol the Younger of Kilmirren, who had been born just a year after himself.

Then young de Fleury came into the tent and said, 'There's wine: look, help yourself,' and, sitting with a thud, poured for himself from a great vessel of water. For work, he had left aside the lynx, the wildcat, the sable that had opened the King's youthful eyes, and wore leather over plain serge. Black serge, cut finely like velvet, with a cap thrust to the back of his head.

Now that the African sun had been bleached from his skin, the sharpened bones were dramatically visible. The childhood softness had gone. With what had taken its place, he would have no difficulty in obtaining any woman he wished, Adorne guessed. You would not expect such a man to take his relief, as others did, from the common pool of commercial service. It was a pity. He had thought, once, of mentioning it; but not now.

Instead he said, 'A change from the Feast of St Nicholas as held by James, King of Cyprus, according to what you told us last night. Another James. Our young host was enchanted.' He paused. 'You must have known James of Cyprus quite well. What would you say of him?'

'Apart from the fact that he purloined one of my wives? Resourceful,' said the other. 'Except in matters of marriage and progeny. I should not encourage an unmarried monarch to make his acquaintance. I, of course, am immune. You know I have entered the fatherhood stakes?'

It was, indeed, why he had come, but not to be treated like this. Adorne said, 'You did me the honour to marry the lady your first wife in my chapel.'

'And, as you see, matrimony developed into a habit. Vehement medicine. Was there something you wanted to ask me?'

It was hard to form a reply. Young men changed. This was not the new-married boy who long ago had aroused his compassion. Adorne said, 'I wondered when you planned to go home. We could travel together. Unless you mean to join your wife before Christmas.'

'Do you recommend it?' said de Fleury. 'The doctors demur, but I am open to argument. I thought of waiting until after Twelfth Night.'

Adorne said, 'Dr Andreas would advise you. He has to stay, but he is experienced in matters of childbirth. You know he studied with Scheves in Louvain?'

'The same subjects?' said Nicholas de Fleury. It sounded casual. But he also had studied at Louvain, and it was not.

Adorne said, 'Yes. He has skills: I am not sure whether I believe in them. He had something to say, recently, about Jordan de Ribérac.'

'Most people have,' de Fleury said. He leaned over and refilled Adorne's cup.

'No. He spoke of descendants. He said he could see only one son of Simon's. And he said the name of the child was not Henry.'

De Fleury looked up. Then he put the cup carefully down and surveyed it. 'Poor Henry,' he said. 'Do you think someone ill-disposed is going to finish him off at the tournament? Who? It won't be me, I assure you. I am reconciled to the St Pols. In fact, on his invitation, I'm on my way to visit Simon at present. He has come to Edinburgh, and has taken up residence.'

'I am glad,' said Adorne. He felt profoundly uneasy. He rose. 'I've been keeping you. I shall, of course, be meeting him myself in the field. What should I suggest? That you encourage him to eat and drink unwisely between now and tomorrow?'

De Fleury got up as well. He said, 'I'm better than your Dr Andreas. I predict that you will win your course, and that the King and the prince will win theirs. You know I've put up the prize?'

'Do I want it?' said Adorne. He made his voice light. There was no point in pursuing what would not be caught.

'I shouldn't think so. A unicorn's horn I brought back from Africa. Genuine,' de Fleury said. 'And a sure guard against poison. Or perhaps we should let Simon win it?'

'Nicholas?' Adorne said. His hand on the tent-flap, he turned.

De Fleury, already half changed, looked up.

Before that look, there was nothing to say. Adorne said, 'The sausage was excellent.'

Kilmirren House was on Castle Hill, at the place where the upper end of the High Street began to climb the increasing slope to the Castle itself. The quickest way there from the tilting-ground was through the broad space of the Horse Market and up the steep dog-leg path to the High Street. And on the other side of that street was Simon's house. Jordan's house. The Edinburgh house of the St Pol of Kilmirren.

The Horse Market was, of course, always thronged. A wide, muddy space lined with houses, today it was full of heralds, competitors, workmen, horse-copers, drinkers and merchant friends and merchant competitors. To the left rose the black basalt rock of the Castle. On the right, among the private houses, the taverns, and the chapels was the house of St John and the opulent monastery of the Franciscans, whose buildings covered the rise which led towards the Port to the common. Tomorrow, after the joust, the Eve of St Nicholas Feast would be held in the monastery and he, Nicholas de Fleury, would be there. But there was a great deal to do before that.

He stopped and talked to perhaps twenty people on his way to the Bow. More, it might be. To Logan of Restalrig about his warehouse. To Gilbert of Edmonston about carts to meet the *Ghost* coming in. To a locksmith about keys; to a Broughton man about plants. To a courier.

To a fletcher about arrows, and a stone-mason about copings for chimneys. To a man from Blackness and another from Linlithgow. To a bailie, a tanner, a master gunner; to the unicorn-maker.

He was halfway there.

To a brewer, to a candle-maker, to the secretary of the Abbot of Holyrood. To a man from Tranent, and a fish-curer. To a man who sold parchment and a man from the King's chamber with news of a dog.

He was at the top of the Bow.

To a notary; to a man who made mattocks; to the priest of St Giles whom he had to turn downhill to meet. Talking, taking his leave, Nicholas de Fleury was watching the street. Most of the houses were known to him now. There was a handsome one opposite, with a red roof and mottoes. He crossed the road to walk uphill again. It was no distance now to his destination, his destiny.

His safe, crowded mind became blank.

There was a Ewe had three lambs; and one of them was black. The one was hanged, the other drowned; the third was lost, and never found.

Space. Half-heard echoes. And only one thought remaining, as always.

February.

He continued to walk, although he did not remember talking to anyone. He knocked at the door of Simon's house and was admitted, and the servant, smiling broadly, flung open a parlour door for him to walk through. He moved forward and stood in the doorway.

There was no one there but a woman who started up, her face full of pity and shock. She said, '*Oh, my bairn. What have they done to you?*'

Already, blurting the words, Bel of Cuthilgurdy recognised that it was a mistake beyond any redemption. She had looked to see, through whatever cloud, the brave and generous man who had brought them all safely from Africa, and found his schooling there, however marred by the loss of his mentor. She had attended his joyous wedding in Bruges and had hoped to find, despite all she had learned from Simon, from Jordan, from Lucia, that he was untouched by whatever had followed: that he did not know of it, or was already bringing his intelligence to work on a remedy.

Instead she saw a man whose height and frame, if attenuated, were the same, but whose dress and face were together a rebuff and a mask and an omen of danger. And behind those, the thing that occasioned her outburst.

She had never had from him the look he gave her as she ended. Then his face melted into a smile and she saw him relax. She felt she saw each muscle relax as if separately levered. She felt ill.

Nicholas de Fleury said, 'Mistress Bel! How are you? Lucia isn't with you?' And he stepped forward, still smiling, and embraced her.

She said, 'No, I'm stupid,' and releasing herself, sat down and blew her nose violently. 'Aye,' she said. And then, adopting exactly his manner, 'No. Lucia's at home. So is Jordan. But you couldna keep me away when I heard. How is the lass, Nicholas? How is Gelis?'

He looked down at her, smiling amiably still. 'Blooming,' he said. He had glanced round the room. She supposed he had never seen the inside of the house owned by the St Pol in Edinburgh which, since Jordan had bought it, was in the best site in town but not extravagant in its fittings. The parlour she sat in was decent, with a good timber ceiling, a few kists, a few stools, some canvas hangings and a board with some silver and pewter laid out on it. The house itself was of two storeys only, of white-plastered timber, and thatched. And well maintained. That too was the vicomte de Ribérac, not Simon. She realised now why the other had looked round the room. He was listening for footsteps.

He was adding something about Gelis. 'Blooming, but better without me, I am told. The birth is not till the spring.' He had glanced again at the door. He raised his brows. 'Simon asked me to call.'

'He's been out, with the laddie. He might bring Henry in.'

'Have I time to leave?' her guest said, in pretended alarm. He had known, it was obvious, that a confrontation with Henry was likely. Once, in Madeira, Simon had planned to take his son to the beheading of Nicholas, but Nicholas had failed to keep the appointment. He and Henry had not as yet met.

'Aye. Ye'll have heard about Henry,' Bel said. 'You'll try to have patience.' She could hear the footsteps now. A man's and a boy's. Nicholas didn't reply.

The door opened.

It was like Simon to push his son in first. As Nicholas de Fleury had done, the child stayed on the threshold, looking within. Against the darkness behind, he stood fair and straight as an angelic judge. The hair curling about the pure forehead was fine as gold floss and the eyes were of an extraordinary blue, saved from daintiness by the well-marked brows which drew together above them. Often as she had seen Henry de St Pol, future vicomte de Ribérac and lord of Kilmirren, Bel felt her throat catch at his beauty.

Then he turned and looked at the man who had married his dead mother's sister. In the look was hatred, and fear, and contempt. Bel drew in her breath.

Nicholas spoke. 'Henry? I have come to shake the hand of your father. I hear you are fighting tomorrow.'

'Who are you?' Henry said. His nose was taut.

'I think you know,' Nicholas said.

The boy walked forward and stood beside Bel. He said, 'I forget. Are you Claes vander Poele the apprentice?'

'I see you like fighting,' his visitor said.

'I don't mind fighting,' said Henry. 'But that's in the breeding. You're a timid man, my father says.'

'Henry,' said Bel. She put her hand on his shoulder. He shook it off.

'Henry!' echoed a man's voice reproachfully from the door. 'Did I ever say that? Surely not. Meester vander Poele has an *unbroken* record of conquest. My dear Nicholas,' said Simon de St Pol, coming in, 'I thought the time was ripe to seal our new amity. I'm told you have altered your name? Your mother's family must be overjoyed. Wine? A grandfather and a very young aunt, I believe?' He stood, his hand at the child's milky neck. One saw that they were dressed alike, man and boy, to the last detail of cap and shoulder-trim, and even of points.

'You know more than I do,' said Nicholas. 'I thought they were all dead.' He took the wine and nursed it without a tremor.

'I hope not,' said Simon. He had a beauty, still, that women would die for. 'Of all people, Thibault and Adelina de Fleury should dote on the coming child, should they not? Should we not raise a cup to it ourselves? Come, Bel. Henry, a taste of wine with some water. Now. A toast to the first child of Gelis van Borselen, whatever sort it may be.'

He drank. Bel said, 'To your child, Nicholas; its safe birth, and a fair life and long. Henry, take a big drink.'

Henry took a small drink. His father said, 'And I suppose you long for a son? I often wish I had a brother for Henry. Indeed there are times – aren't there, Henry? – when I wouldn't object if someone left me a changeling. But then of course I relent.'

Their guest said, 'I should be pleased to have a son in the very image of Henry.'

'You couldn't,' said Henry.

'No, I couldn't,' said his uncle by marriage.

She had come hoping to prevent this. Anger at the two men overwhelmed her. Then she collected herself and entering the conversation wrenched it, with steely determination, into civilised channels.

Simon listened more than he spoke. De Fleury humoured her with minor gossip about Father Godscalc's health and Gregorio's growing position in Bruges; and sustained rhapsodies about the longed-for child to be born to Lucia's son Diniz and his wife. All the news was second-hand and he spoke as if he were little involved.

Asked about his own business, he mentioned Captain Astorre and his army, on the verge of taking the field with Duke Charles. Henry came back to life all at once. He said, 'If I had an army, I'd lead it.'

De Fleury said, 'You could, if it were a unit like mine. Captain Astorre has been its captain for a long time, and has been in many great battles. He has an Englishman, Thomas, to help him, and a master physician called Tobias. But, of course, that is only one company. The Sire Louis de Gruuthuse – he's famous, he's been in Scotland – commands all the Burgundian armies, and the Duke himself often goes into battle. You're interested in war?'

'I'm going to lead armies,' said Henry. 'And be a knight and fight against other knights. And challenge them. You'd be afraid to do that. If your wife had a son, he'd be afraid to do that as well.'

'I fought a Saracen once,' said de Fleury thoughtfully. 'And I've taken part in big wars now and then. Everyone is afraid when they fight. But I'm not sure about single combat. If I want to put someone down, I often do it in ways that last longer. It can be quite satisfactory.'

'*Gentlemen* fight,' Henry said. 'Gentlemen marry ladies and have gentle sons.' He got up and went out.

'Returning to Gelis,' Simon remarked. His eyes were bright. 'Thinking of poor Gelis again, I ought to give you greetings from her former mistress. The lady Mary, you know? My near neighbour. Seventeen now and childless, poor lady. She wept to hear your wife is with child. March, isn't it due? Or even in April? Her husband thought it essential, like you, to get out of the country.'

'Thomas Boyd? So she misses him?'

'Cries for him all the time. No one else does. The marriage only took place because the Boyds had their hands on the King at the time. Now it's different. If I were Tom Boyd, I shouldn't have risked going to Denmark. A lot can happen in a few months. Or so they tell me. Do you hear from Bruges much?'

'Often enough,' Nicholas de Fleury said. He stirred with sudden decisiveness. 'I've stayed too long. The Scottish champion has to prepare for his triumph. I look forward to that. I've never seen you in the lists.'

'No,' said Simon. From outside, clearer now, came the sounds of a distant commotion.

'But you will win. You can have no doubts?' said de Fleury.

'No,' said Simon. The door burst open and he sprang to his feet. His son Henry appeared in the doorway.

'Father! He says –'

Bel de Cuthilgurdy got up. De Fleury stayed where he was.

A man appeared in the doorway. He said, 'It hasna came. I'm sorry. The siller, or else.'

'What?' said Bel.

'Never mind,' Simon said. 'Business. We'll talk of this later. Nicholas –'

'Na,' said the man, planting himself in the doorway. 'We'll talk of this now. You've arms ye havena paid for. Ye say ye have, but the proof hasna came. I warned ye. I've come tae take it all back – and' – as Simon made a threatening gesture – 'I should tell ye that I've half a dozen lads wi' me outside wha'll not only tak' your arms, Master Simon, but let your neighbours ken loud and clear why they're doing it. So?'

'I *have* paid for it,' Simon said. 'You scoundrel, you're trying to make me pay twice over. I'll not.'

'Then ye'll no fight the morn, will ye, Master Simon?' said the man, and jerked his head backwards. Through the doorway, men could be seen entering the house. Simon started forward, his hand on his sword.

'No,' said de Fleury. His arm, mysteriously interposed, stopped Simon from drawing. De Fleury said, 'It's a mistake. A day will clear it. But you don't want this made public. I'm not fighting tomorrow. Take my armour. I'll get it back when you've sorted this out.'

'Your armour?' said Simon.

'You'll find it will fit you. It was never quite right for me. It's by a good maker,' said de Fleury. 'At least, if you don't like it, you can back down, and you'll be no worse off.'

Simon turned. The man in the doorway said, 'That's sensible, sir. Indeed, I've got a bailie's man there just behind ye who would endorse what I've said. Nae proof of payment, ye've nae right tae the arms.'

Bel said, 'Simon, let them go. Settle it quietly later on. Nicholas will let ye see what he has, to be sure. If it's not to your taste, then don't take it.'

'You can't wear his armour!' said Henry. 'A workman's armour! Ours is silver!'

Simon turned. 'Yours will still be silver,' he said. From red he had become rather pale. He spoke to the younger man stiffly. 'It is a mistake, of course. I shall have it put right by tomorrow. In any case, I have friends who, I believe, could accommodate me. But if not, be sure I shall remember your very good offer.'

De Fleury said, 'You need only come and see it. If it doesn't fit, it doesn't fit. Or if it is unsuitable in other ways.'

He left, considerately, before the armour was actually carried out of the house. Simon bade him farewell in a distracted way and vanished indoors. The boy Henry, biting his lip, had said nothing at all.

Bel followed Nicholas de Fleury to the stairs. There she stopped. She said, 'That was good-hearted.'

'I thought so,' he said. 'But as Godscalc mentioned in Bruges, I am a fine young man, when it comes over me. Is the child beyond hope?'

'I see no one here beyond hope,' said the dame. 'Child or man.'

Chapter 6

REPRESENTATIVES OF great powers visiting the smaller duchies and kingdoms took pains, as a rule, to advise their train upon matters of conduct. As a niece of Anselm Adorne, Katelijne Sersanders knew that not all towns on earth possessed sufficient burghers of wealth to sustain a permanent jousting society; that not all princes could afford the expense of a tournament. Bruges had a rich middle class: Scotland, as yet, merely a mercantile community of moderate power. But of men of first rank, it had blood as blue and fighters as good as any the White Bear had seen. So Adorne would have told her, had there been need.

As it was, she sat without scoffing at noon on the Eve of St Nicholas, wrapped in her thickest cloak against the wind that scoured down upon her from the face of the Castle, and the smoke that swirled equally round her from the braziers and bonfires round the tiltground.

To one side, grafted on to the lower ledges of rock was the long pavilion, its canvas snapping and belching, which contained, packed like cards, the Princesses of the Court – Margaret ecstatic, Mary forlorn – with nuns, attendant noblewomen, and pages about them. Behind, in a turmoil of whipping headdresses, sat the other ladies of birth: the chevaliers' wives. And next, the men of renown who were too old or too young to take part, including the men of the Church: William Scheves, cleric and apothecary; Archibald, Abbot of Holyrood; Edward Bonkle, Provost of Trinity College; Bishop Patrick Graham of St Andrews with the Charterhouse abbot and her cousin Maarten sitting beside him. Not, of course, the King, who was taking part, with Alexander and small John his brothers.

After the black and the red came the riot of colour, of velvet and satin and fur, that represented the merchants. Old Berecrofts, but not Archie his son, who was to fight, as was young Napier. Stephen Angus, more often in Bruges than in Scotland. Haliburton and Gilbert of Edmonston, Lamb and Auchinleck.

Only the old faces were there. The rest were among the trampling horses at the edge of the field, a little apart from the gold-swagged tents of the King and the nobility, with their sons and brothers and nephews to act as esquires. John Brown was taking part, and Touris, and Lauder, and Bertram and Gordon, and Thom Swift, whose great house her uncle was occupying. And young Bonkle, and Crackbene, who had come to the convent, and the lawyer called Julius – they were all fighting, but not the head of the House of Niccolò who, her brother said, was not accustomed to jousting.

One wanted to think about that. She was interested. Herself, she was proud to see her uncle's banner flying from one of the crowd of side-tents by the chapel of Our Lady, and to know that he and Jehan Metteneye and her brother would be breaking a lance for the town. Not for Burgundy, although it had to appear so. For the town.

She knew a lot about tournaments. Ghent, Lille, Brussels, Bruges – she had got herself taken to most of them, one way or another. Also, she had a good memory. It surprised the nuns that she knew so many people in Scotland. They forgot, perhaps, that all the merchants in Scotland visited Bruges at one time or another, and some of them settled there. Also, most people sooner or later had cause to come to the priory. Her uncle held his meetings with the town magistrates there. She had got him to tell her about them.

She wondered if it was true what they said about Crackbene and Ada. She thought it would be interesting to see, when the combatants took the field, what ladies' favours they wore. It was a pity de Fleury the Bank wasn't parading. Her brother had asked for a scarf of hers, on the advice of their uncle, no doubt. Perhaps Ada had offered Crackbene a napkin?

Will Roger said, 'What are you sniggering about? Look at your music. We're almost ready to start.'

In the Burgundian tent it was calm, but the turmoil outside – the uneven noise of the crowd, the squeal and clatter of arms, the stamping of horses – came through clearly enough, and in spite of the brazier Anselm Sersanders felt cold and a little sick, as he always did before fighting. Even when the weapons were bated, as now, a gentleman in the lists must still represent his people, must show all he has of skill and grace and courtesy and, if possible, must win.

Across the heads of the men who were attiring him, he caught his uncle's swift smile and wished his armour were like that, well-fitting but not new, burnished but with the patina that came from many, many conflicts. They no longer used shields, but the Adorne chequer lay clearly embroidered across his uncle's surcoat and on the strong, fringed furnishing of his horse. Within the visorless helm, the high cheekbones and long lines of the family face looked like a drawing on silver. And the scarf which fell to his shoulder was a royal one, given by the King's younger sister, the lady Margaret.

Nicholas de Fleury's voice said, 'Yes, he looks very nice. So do you. Have you everything that you want?'

He leaned at the entrance to the tent, unarmed as the servants were, except for one exquisite dagger at the side of a sable-edged doublet. Sersanders couldn't see what the jewel was today. Behind him stretched the green grass of the lists, all one hundred and fifty yards of it, and a third as wide. On one long side facing the Rock stood the mass of the common spectators, the source of a constant roar and a powerful smell of food and humanity.

Opposite them was the long pavilion for the Court. Beside that, on a platform, was the dummy unicorn with its dummy damsel, small in the distance; and smaller still, the choir of live maiden attendants, among whom his sister Katelijne was undoubtedly the liveliest. He caught the glitter of trumpets, preparing to lift.

Sersanders said, 'I'll tell you later if I have a complaint.'

'Tell the good Knights of St John,' de Fleury said. He seemed to have time on his hands. 'I wouldn't dare question the programme. My contribution was the unicorn. And I dressed one of the dwarves. You know your Dr Andreas is there if you need him? The lances are buttoned, but some of our friends are exceptionally good. I like the scarf.' He was, unnervingly, using both dimples without actually smiling.

Whatever Nicholas de Fleury said, he had done rather more than dress a dwarf. Barring his uncle Adorne and himself, de Fleury must know more than anyone present about the protocol for a joust of mixed ranks. And the Burgundian party couldn't be applied to: the tournament, after all, was in its honour.

You would think, therefore, de Fleury would be busy. Instead, he was intruding, deliberately intruding, where he was unwelcome. Sersanders said evenly, 'The scarf? It's Katelijne's.'

'Well, at least she didn't give you a ball. The Medici would have hanged her. I suppose I should wish you good luck.'

'Against Simon?' said Sersanders briefly. 'You'll have to wait. That comes last, before the King takes on the winner and wins.'

'You've done this before. No, I was wishing you enduring good health and fortitude. You could smack Crackbene for me, if you get the chance.'

'I wonder why?' Sersanders rejoined in the same tone. He was momentarily amused, amid his resentment.

'You ought to know. Your sister's in the same holy retreat,' de Fleury said. The rebuke in his voice was a mockery. 'And the King's little sister, who didn't really want to give her kerchief to your uncle, did she? Such a cold country: even the late Pope sired a son here; anything for comfort. Oh, listen. They're going to start. Did I wish you good luck?'

The trumpets blew and the drums began. The waiting was over, and one Burgundian contestant was colder than ever. And angry.

'Thank you,' said Sersanders bitterly.

'It comes with the service,' said de Fleury, standing off from the doorway. He was already looking elsewhere. It had been an idle impulse, it was clear; arisen from God knew what wish for diversion. He went off and, rather surprisingly, joined a dark-haired young woman in green. Sersanders watched him, and then walked carefully outside to where his page stood by his stirrup.

Will Roger said, 'Now, my darlings. And if you get the A right, I'll kiss each one of you twice after supper.'

He liked training choirs. He liked it best, to tell the truth, when the voices came to him natural as they were born, welling out of big healthy bodies whose owners spent their days in the fresh air of the fields or the shore, and not bent double sewing in palaces. He had very little time for palaces. It was probably why he got on with young James so well. Everyone should remember his manners, but there was no need to crawl.

The well-born bitch with the simper was going to lose the beat again. Will Roger caught her eye, smiling, and rocked his head up and down. While a performance was in progress, there was nothing he wouldn't do to keep them singing and happy. Strip and turn somersaults. Fuck them there on the stage, as they sang. He heard, with disbelief, that all the voices, ending, were coming together, at the right tempo, with the right tone, in the right notes, and they were articulating precisely as he had taught them.

Tears welled into his eyes. He loved them so much he could die for them.

Nicholas ran up the steps of the stand and found a place beside his rich landlord Berecrofts just as the parade of contestants began.

Will of Berecrofts, who had sharp enough sight for his years, noticed that de Fleury's bonny young friend had moved off, in her turn, to the women's enclosure. He knew who she was. So did most people there. He said, 'As I was saying, I'm holding the price, but I'm no daft enough to wait on ye for aye. What did Hamilton think?'

The parade of contestants had begun, led by the King, with his two brothers riding behind under the banner of Scotland. Against a prodigious blaring and a loyal roar which seemed to contain some genuine affection, Nicholas shouted a reply. 'I have to see him again. I'll tell you by noon tomorrow.'

Berecrofts said, 'I'll sell if you don't come. Dod, it's purgatory on earth, all thon hooting and crying. I'd melt down the lot and mak' jugs o' them. Davie Lindsay's no lookin' sae weel.' The first ranks of knights were riding in, two by two. Among them, white cross on black robes, were the Knights Hospitaller of St John, led by their Preceptor. 'And Will Knollys is showing a belly. He'll be fair put to it to harry a Turk if they call him to Rhodes. Seton's got his auld harness out: he'll hae tae get the rest back from pawn for the wedding. And are those your men-at-arms?'

'There's to be a mock fight,' de Fleury said.

'I ken, I ken. And Master Julius, weel set up as usual. And the banner of Burgundy. Now that's what I call a feast for the een. Well horsed, well set up, well armed, the hale retinue. A fine-looking man, Master Anselm Adorne, and naebody's fool in the council-chamber. He's got a niece as mad as a peerie.'

'She's sitting down there, with the choir.'

'Oh glory be, so she is, and them about to break into yowls any minute. And here's the childer.'

There were twelve ponies in all, groomed and glistening with their riders straight-backed and white-faced within their miniature armour. They wore their fathers' colours, and a page behind each carried a pennant. Nicholas de Fleury's eyes had followed them in. He said, 'Robin rides well.'

'Aye, aye,' said Berecrofts. He viewed his grandson, but didn't put his thoughts into words. A good lad. A kind-hearted, well-mannered wee fellow. Unlike some. He said, 'Will ye look at yon arrogant little bastard? He'll drive his horse mad.'

'He can ride,' Nicholas said.

'And wants us to know it. Silver armour on a child of that age! I suppose his father'll be wearing the same. Two cockerels needing their necks wrung.'

De Fleury, watching the procession, didn't trouble to answer, thereby confirming an opinion William of Berecrofts had already formed. Nothing that happened in Bruges went unnoticed in Edinburgh, and the ill-will between vander Poele – now de Fleury – and the heir to Kilmirren was notorious.

And now they said the quarrel was over. Berecrofts supposed it might be. Wealth could heal many sores, including the canker of ignoble parentage. And for sure, since coming to Scotland, de Fleury had shown no hint of spite against Simon de St Pol or his father, even if he'd hardly bestirred himself to seek them. Instead he'd turned his hand to his own diverse concerns with unchancy efficiency and an edge of downright impatience which sometimes roused Berecrofts's own temper. Nicholas de Fleury. Not a bairn you would trust at your back.

He pulled his thoughts away. The children had passed, and the landed gentry were advancing again. And foremost among them rode the child Henry's father.

A sigh passed through the crowd.

Berecrofts gazed. Berecrofts stared. Berecrofts said, 'Christ God, St Pol of Kilmirren . . . What farmyard could afford a cockerel such as that!'

Julius turned, hearing the same long hiss of surprise, and so did Archie Berecrofts the Younger, riding down the lists at his side. Comfortable about his own appearance and future performance, Julius was always willing to study the efforts of other people who were less travelled, and had no shares in the Banco di Niccolò.

At first his view was obscured by the file of plumes tossing behind him. Then he saw, entering the lists behind them all, the mounted figure which had drawn the audible tribute. Archie, who like his father had nothing wrong with his sight, said, 'Christ God. Simon de St Pol of Kilmirren. Would you credit it?'

'No,' said Julius absently. They turned a corner and began to ride back up the long side of the lists, and he got a really good look.

The surcoat was Simon's own, that was obvious. But it couldn't hide what was beneath it. Unlike the King or his brother the Duke; unlike the handsomely clad and gallantly accoutred high nobles of Scotland, the heir to the lord of Kilmirren rode into the lists of Edinburgh that December day attired like an emperor. Attired in a carapace of a soft, flowing, powerful metal, engraved, damascened, embossed in silver and gold, with inserts of turquoise, of enamel, of mother of pearl such as had never been seen in the West; with cloth of gold edging and overlaying it and exquisite pinions of the rarest of birds falling from the jewelled spire of its helmet.

The glorious face within the helmet was both haughty and flushed, and the blue long-lashed gaze was directed ahead. Whatever fortune he had brought back from Africa, Simon de St Pol could not have found or paid for these arms. His purse stretched to silver, of the kind the brat Henry was wearing. Archie knew it, and all those folk in the stands. And behind them (Julius turned) the boy Henry's hectic cheeks and bright, wary eyes told that he, also, was torn between doubts and bright pride. Young Berecrofts said, 'What's the man thinking of? Look at King Jamie.'

There was no need to look, but Julius did. He said, 'I heard St Pol'd got two new suits.'

'Silver. He did. Showy enough, but they'd thole it. Not this.'

'What happened?' said Julius. Simon passed on the opposite side, his arms and shoulders encrusted with light. Beyond him was the stand, with Nicholas seated beside Archie's father. Archie's father was talking and so was everyone else. Nicholas was watching the field and saying nothing at all so far as Julius could see.

'What happened? Wha kens? The new armour got lost, and I expect he either had to borrow some or withdraw from the tournament. He asked me, but I didna have spares. He should have withdrawn.'

Julius supposed that he should. On the other hand, Simon was vain. He had tried to find something plainer, but perhaps had not tried very hard. Archie said, 'But where in the name of the wee man did that armour come from?'

Julius had nothing against Archie or even his cantankerous father but, after all, they were provincials. He said, 'Trebizond. It's one of the ceremonial suits of the last Emperor, David.' He didn't mention that, pawned, it had helped save the Bank a few years before. He did add casually, 'It belongs to Nicholas.'

'De Fleury lent it to him?'

'He must have done. I don't suppose,' said Julius virtuously, 'that he wants much made of it. At least it lets Simon take part.' He couldn't imagine why Nicholas had done such a thing, any more than he could work out why Nicholas wasn't fighting.

Except that, of course, Simon was one of the best jousters of his day. Simon was the man whom Scotland sent as her representative to all the elaborate tourneys in France and in Flanders. And although he had no great business head, it was true, he was always first in the field with a troop when the King's peace was threatened, which compensated for a lot of poor management. He was a King's champion, and decorative, and no coward, for tournaments were not designed as a rule to be harmless. The tilting-field was a training for war.

And so, if you considered the matter, it seemed that the long contention between Simon and Nicholas had actually ceased. By avoiding combat, Nicholas had already ceded superiority in the field. Now, in the loan of this armour, he had made a public gesture of friendship. It was not, of course, true tilting-armour: no one was ever expected to raise a lance or a sword against the late David Comnenos when he rode forth thus on parade. But the ornamentation, suicidal in battle, would not matter today, when every weapon was blunt and all the combat was for pleasure, *à plaisance*.

Archie said, 'I think they're both daft. Mind you, the suit's safe on St Pol. Very few here can touch him, and even if you thought you could dent it you wouldn't.'

'Even for the honour of Burgundy?' Julius said. 'I think you'll find Anselm Adorne has other views.' He felt suddenly extraordinarily cheerful. He said, 'You must agree, having Nicholas about does make things brisk.'

'So I've noticed,' said Archie of Berecrofts quite thoughtfully. He was looking at the King's sisters who, like the King, appeared less than enraptured by Simon de St Pol of Kilmirren. It reminded Julius of a further pleasure in store. The lady Mary, whose favourite attendant had been Gelis van Borselen, had asked that Gelis van Borselen's new husband should be presented to her after the tournament. The face of Nicholas, receiving the summons, had been the picture of flattered delight. Julius, seldom deceived, felt quite excited.

By the time the lists opened, everyone within earshot of Julius knew the origin of Kilmirren's borrowed armour, if not the circumstances of its borrowing. Anselm Adorne heard the story from Sersanders his nephew, just before they rode into the field. In fact he delayed his entry a little, because of it. He had known Nicholas for a long time, nearly as long as Julius. And Nicholas never did or said anything without a reason.

The tournament was well arranged, for a local affair, calling for no more than a token attendance from those knights and gentles within reach of Edinburgh. There were two men from England, and one from the island of Orkney. The preliminary bouts, on horse and later on foot, were hard fought, with snapped lances in the muddy turf and nose-blood seeping down bevelled swords, and swollen flesh squeezed, red and blue, between bone and armour.

The King's own guard took part, but their ardour couldn't

match the hard professionalism of the Knights of St John, behind which could be discerned a hint of contempt. Adorne himself was opposed to the Preceptor himself, stout Will Knollys, and tried to spin out the fight until Knollys could give in with honour. One of Maarten's brothers was destined for the Order; all the Adorne family supported their hospice in Bruges; Father John of Kinloch used to live there. But one did not wish to draw too much attention to that.

He drew to the side and watched, while his page fetched him a fresh lance and a drink. The men Nicholas had brought with him from Bruges had done well. He recognised none of them. The old Charetty company, to be sure, was away fighting for Duke Charles. He liked the ruddy, forthright look of young Archie, the boy Robin's father, who was well matched against Sersanders his nephew.

Adorne reflected, as he watched, on the shrewdness which had brought the Berecrofts family from their ancestral home in the west to the profitable estate they occupied on the edge of the Forth, and now the even more profitable sites they held in the Canongate and in Leith upon which, for a price, men like Nicholas were allowed to build houses. Some men made their fortunes in towns and then chose to establish themselves and their families in baronial mansions. He himself had investments outside Bruges, but he was, to the soul, a man of that town. A man of the town and the Duke's, and God forfend he should ever have to divide the two loyalties. He watched his nephew, his thoughts for the moment elsewhere.

Berecrofts was struck from his horse. The combat on foot was quite long: they were both short men, he and Sersanders, of equal reach and equable tempers. As Adorne expected, Sersanders won. He smiled, riding heated back to the tent.

The display continued. Dusk came early in December: already the shadow of the Rock was crawling over the tilting-ground although the sun glowed yellow beyond, and the wind was only beginning to bite. Adorne moved. It was not wise to allow himself to become cold because he would be the last, of course, unless his fellow envoy forgot protocol and won too many fights. Sometimes, using his weight, Jehan Metteneye could unseat him. He had seen few others who could, skilled though some of them were. Anselm Adorne flung his cloak temporarily over his shoulders.

He won his remaining courses, knocking out a grinning Jehan in the first. He had to work hardest against Lindsay and Liddell, who was young. He could see, watching the youth Albany, who had had the teaching of him.

The Mêlée he took no part in. It was during that – forty men striking, grunting, squelching in the mud under a greying sky – that the lad Bonkle, at his side, said, 'Have you heard the news, Ser Anselm?'

Anselm Adorne had known John Bonkle's double family, Scots and Flemish, since the days of Robert Bonkle, that wily old merchant burgess of Edinburgh. Sanders Bonkle, Robert's son, was a burgess of both Bruges and Edinburgh. Edward, the boy's natural father, had been well known to the Scots queen from Guelders, who had made him both famous and rich as Provost of the church and hospice she founded in Edinburgh. The lad himself, though a bastard, had been sent to a Scots university and learned his business at the side of his uncle in Middleberg and Bruges.

Adorne had been pleased, although he had not said so, when Jannekin Bonkle had been offered commissions by vander Poele . . . by Nicholas de Fleury, and finally agreed to represent him in Scotland. He knew, from Sanders his uncle, how he fared, and quite a lot of what he was doing. Now Anselm Adorne said, 'What news?'

'From the borders of Burgundy. The town of Liège has risen for France against the rule of the Duke, and has been attacked by the Duke's army and gutted, the buildings burned. Hundreds are killed, or drowned in the Meuse, or dead of cold in the forests.'

Adorne was silent. Charles, Duke of Burgundy, was his master: his father had served the same family. He said, 'I am sorry. Duke Charles has a heavy hand when he is angry.' A cry rang out from the stand. The news was spreading. Liège was a rich trading town, a town like his own. Everyone had friends there.

'So has the King of France,' Jannekin said. 'They say he secretly incited the rebellion, but when it happened, he was in the Duke's power. He agreed to the destruction of Liège and his men also took part. Your niece is comforting her maid.'

'De Fleury sent you to tell me?' said Adorne. It came to him that the men who obeyed the Duke's orders at Liège must have included the army leased him by Nicholas. Astorre was there, and Thomas, and perhaps even Tobias, their doctor. He added, 'He must be concerned for his company. And for what it had to do.'

'Nicholas de Fleury?' Bonkle said. He paused. 'He thought you should know.'

'Yes. Thank you,' said Anselm Adorne; and rode into the lists for the final bout. And immediately, as he had expected, the wave of comment lessened, for the slaughter at Liège had taken place far to the south, across the Narrow Sea, four weeks ago, and the culminating match in this contest – barring the token victory of the

King, barring the last charming pageant of the children – was between himself and Simon de St Pol of Kilmirren.

He wondered, admiring the grace of man and mount pacing towards him, whether Simon had come to regret the magnificent loan he had accepted, or whether it meant more to him that he should be here, a single glittering figure drawing four thousand pairs of eyes in the dwindling light, the Scottish champion. He thought the latter.

He wondered if Simon's father de Ribérac, expecting so much of his heir, found some balm in this, his son's one undoubted excellence, and remembered his own days of military glory, fighting in France. The old man was not here, but would learn of it. Sometimes Adorne wondered if much of Simon's violent, impatient, disordered career was not in itself a cry to, as much as against his dominant father. He watched the other man's face, before he closed his visor at the other end of the barrier, and saw confirmed what he had suspected: Simon would show by his fighting that he expected no quarter for his armour or himself. Then the drums rolled and the trumpets blared, and he drove his horse into a gallop.

There were three courses to run, and three lances to break, if he could. The horse pounding towards him on the opposite side of the barrier showed no fear; no intention of deviating, and the long, heavy shaft gripped in Simon's right glove pointed steadily at the heart of his cuirass. Adorne adjusted his plated grip very slightly, and moved his weight in the saddle in the way his horse knew. The horses drove together; the point of Simon's lance flashed towards him and then slid, diverted from the plate at his breast while his own point, with all the force of his shoulders and back and arms, struck Simon in the centre of the incrustations by his shoulder and, locking there, thrust him half out of the saddle.

Half, but not quite. The next moment Adorne was past, the lance dragged free and Simon had gone, his horse somehow responding to his command even as he began to bring the weight of his body back to the saddle and reclaim his stirrups. Then they reached the ends and turned and took lance for the second course. And this time, Simon would be angry. Which, reflected Anselm Adorne, was not necessarily a bad thing.

The buffets the second time were full and direct: Adorne met the point this time without turning his mount or his body, and aimed his own solely to unbalance. His lance broke. He felt the impact through his whole body, and saw Simon shudder, but they passed, neither dislodged.

He reached the other end and turned, glancing down to take the fresh lance being offered him. His memory gave him, in retrospect, the roar of the crowd at the moment of collision and his eyes showed him now the grinning, jostling faces, colour drained from their tunics, their jackets, their caps. In the stand, flushed by the brightening gold of the braziers, he glimpsed the confident face and red hair of the child Margaret whose scarf he wore, and further along, almost equally distinct, the intent face of Nicholas de Fleury, once vander Poele. Below, a drift of white on stout cushions, sat the retired singing maidens, Will Roger beside them. The musician had his hand on the shoulder of Adorne's niece Katelijne who, her face bent, was rocking Emmelot her maid in her arms. Emmelot, who came from Liège.

He had almost missed the trumpet. Adorne saw that St Pol was already coming at full gallop towards him. He drew himself together, and collecting his horse, threw it forward as well.

Everyone saw the hesitation. Julius, his courses satisfactorily completed, inserted himself beside Nicholas without removing his gaze from Adorne for an instant. He sat chanting, 'Come on. Come on. Are you dreaming?'

'Be quiet,' said Nicholas.

The collision occurred. For a moment, as the horse-cloths swirled, it was difficult to tell what had happened, except that both horses had stopped. Then it could be seen that Adorne was in the saddle, trying to control a plunging, curvetting horse, while the saddle of Simon's horse was empty. Nicholas stood, wrenching up Julius with him. Men ran on to the grass.

They were bending over the glimmering object of the smith's art that was Simon. They put their hands under his arms and lifted him to his feet. He stood.

Nicholas said, 'He isn't dead. What a pity.'

Below him, Katelijne lifted her head. She said, 'How can you say that?'

'It's quite easy,' Nicholas said. 'Oh look, now they're going to fight each other on foot. Sword, axe and mace. My money's on Adorne. Simon's shaken. Look, he's dropped a couple of rubies. No, his chin is bleeding. Help us, Lord, upon this erde That there be spilt no blood Herein. Simon's down.'

'He's lost his temper,' said Julius. 'Adorne counted on it. I must say he's good. I'm not taking your wager. It's a foregone conclusion. Simon loses.' He watched, with some irritation, as events proceeded to prove him right.

Adorne wasn't as fast, but he had a great deal of experience, a gift for tactics, and a level head. For the rest, they were two handsome men, fit and well made and skilled in their craft, so that the crowd rose to them both. They were both over forty, and breathed still like men half their age. Julius said, 'If it had been a proper fight, the lance would have finished him. Simon.'

'They've spoiled our day,' Nicholas said. 'Let's go. No, we have to stay for the King and the children.'

Adorne won, and was crowned with laurels and promised his unicorn horn at the banquet. The King ran his ceremonial course, auburn hair gleaming in the light of the fires. Adorne was duly unhorsed and went to kneel at the feet of the youth. The lists emptied, and the lines of mounted children took their places at either end, armed with their stout wooden swords for the Little Mêlée. Robin, Old Berecrofts's grandson, was among them. And John of Mar, the King's youngest brother. And Simon's son Henry, in silver armour.

Far behind him, the vanquished Simon de St Pol stood frowning in his gorgeous array and glared at the boy.

But for the glistening armour, as offensive as the far more extravagant attire of Kilmirren, young John of Mar would probably never have chosen to single out an opponent so junior. At first, no one noticed. Free entertainment was not to be scorned, but the main contests were over; attention on the common side of the field had relaxed, and some parties were leaving. No one had left from the stands. These were their children.

Now the silhouette of the Castle was black against the fading glow from the west, and the blue haze from the blood-bright braziers swam over the ground. Julius said, 'Poor little monkeys, they'll kill one another in the dark. My money's on Robin's team, unless they've been told to lose out to Mar. Nicholas?'

'My dear Julius,' Nicholas said. 'Children don't always do what they're told. They'll probably kill one another.'

'Stop that!' said Katelijne from below. Her fancily wreathed face, thrown upwards, was livid.

'And go to Purgatory. It'll be like Liège,' Nicholas continued thoughtfully. 'Astorre and Thomas in some expiatory field condemned to batter into chivalric shape a mob of unpractised young, speaking exclusively in the Scottish vernacular. Do they have jousting in Purgatory? I feel sure they do.'

'Listen. Stop talking,' said Will Roger suddenly.

'Why?' said Nicholas, stopping courteously.

Julius saw why.

In the field, the lines had engaged. For a few moments, in the dim light, the boys had fought as they had been trained, as a team, but now it had become a general struggle, of the kind to be seen outside any school, with screaming child battering at screaming child and blood running.

The King's brother John of Mar was not screaming. His arm raised, he was dealing blow after blow at the silver armour of the heir to Kilmirren, and matching words to the blows. The words, if you listened, came quite clearly.

'That for Chamberpot's grandson. That for what your family did to Liège. They're bastards. They're traitors and bastards. Aren't they? Say it! Your grandfather's a bastard!'

'He's not!' Henry screamed. His arm lifted and fell, his strokes glancing off the royal armour. He dropped his reins and took his sword in both hands.

'Yes, he is. I think he likes boys. I think he licks the French King's arse when he's asked. I think –'

The words broke off. A two-handed blow from the furious child caught him in the face, and then full in the chest-piece. John of Mar jerked free of the saddle and then, leaning forward, grasped the boy Henry round the waist and dragged him with a crash to the ground. He got up slowly, and panting. 'Go on,' said the King's brother. 'Get up. Say I'm wrong. Say your father's got so many women he doesn't know who you are. Who are you, Henry?'

At that point, Julius got to his feet without quite knowing why. He saw that the girl Katelijne had jumped up also, Will Roger beside her. Julius looked to see what Nicholas thought. Apparently Nicholas had no opinion: he sat without expression or movement, his gaze on the field. You couldn't even be sure he saw what was happening.

The boy Henry got up off the ground. He stood, his armour scored and scratched and dented, his whitened face dim in the twilight, and looked up at his royal tormentor. Henry said, 'I am Henry de St Pol of Kilmirren. My grandfather is not a bastard, and neither am I. But maybe you are.' And without warning, he rushed at the older boy.

It was possible that Mar, thickly plated, had fallen more heavily than he intended. It was certainly true that he was taken by surprise, and that the first blows, on his arms, must have numbed them. But the avenging fury that came at him then, raining blows from its sword, from its fists, kicking and shrieking, gave him no time to lift up his sword, and when he suddenly stumbled, caught on the wrong foot, he had no chance to recover. As a ball might demolish a building, the boy Henry flung himself at him and crashed with him to the ground. Then he rose and, standing over him kicked and battered and swore.

Mar struggled. He rolled over, gripping his sword. Henry kicked it out of his reach. The movement had dislodged Mar's conical helmet, with the royal crest and the plume. Henry swept the helmet aside and lifting his wooden sword with both hands, prepared to drive it point down into the prince's horrified face.

He got no further. A large hand gripped his arm, and another pinioned his shoulder. A hated voice said, 'But your grandfather *is* a bastard, my dear. Never fight for lost causes. Apologise to my lord of Mar.'

'No!' screamed Henry.

The hand, moving down, had torn the sword from him, and now taking his arm had twisted it high behind his back. It was pressed against cold fur. 'You didn't mean to hurt him, and you were only joking when you lifted your sword against him just now.'

Henry screamed, from pain this time.

'You see?' said Nicholas de Fleury to the faces about him; and increased his grip. The rest of the fighting had stopped. The men running on to the field were royal officials and barons, and Mar's own tutor and nurse. Julius was among them, and Katelijne and Roger the musician. The light from the braziers glistened on the silver armour, the golden hair of the angelic boy, and left in demoniac shadow the jet-clad figure of Nicholas de Fleury at his back.

'He apologises,' Nicholas said sweetly. His hand, squeezing, covered half the child Henry's face. 'Do you accept the apology, my lord?'

It was Secretary Whitelaw, moving forward, who said abruptly, 'He accepts,' cutting across the prince's angry protest. A calm man, tutor once to the young King himself, he touched Mar on the arm as he spoke. 'Childish brawls. Nothing more need be said. My lord of Mar, let me take you to my tent.'

They began to leave. The crowd opened. Nicholas de Fleury slackened his grip, both of the child's jaws and his arm. The boy Henry said hoarsely, 'He lied! I will never apologise!' and tore himself free. A dark young woman in green ran up and then, noticing the boy's hazy stare, touched de Fleury's arm quickly and stepped back. The child's hollow gaze followed her.

'You have just apologised,' Nicholas de Fleury said to him. 'Abjectly. And you'd better thank me for it.'

The thanks came at once. De Fleury's own dagger, snatched from the sheath, flashed up and stabbed through the air, Henry's fist on the hilt.

Katelijne cried out a warning. Julius hurled himself forward and stopped. For the second time, as in a dream, the powerful hand of de Fleury closed upon that of the boy and arrested fist and dagger together, tight and still at his waist. Then, looking down, he disengaged the dagger with care and smiling, sheathed it below the folds of his cloak. His dimples appeared, untrustworthy chasms in his shadowy face. He said, 'My poor, stupid child. If you don't calm down, you'll hurt somebody. Mistress Bel?'

It was the first time Julius had noticed the old woman standing near the front of the crowd. Her shapeless face was the same colour as Henry's. Nicholas looked at her. He said reflectively, 'I think you should take him away.'

Julius thought he was crazy, but the boy didn't protest at all. He stood as if he hadn't heard, and then, when the woman touched him, he moved. He was shaking. He looked back, once, at Nicholas, but Nicholas was already strolling away.

Julius caught up with him. 'That should earn you a few contracts at Court. My God, I thought he was going to kill Mar. A temper as weird as his father's. Should we go back to the stand and be thanked? Or we can be thanked at the banquet.'

'We?' said Nicholas. He was being congratulated already, by spectators crowding about as they walked from the field. The wench in green seemed to have gone. Behind, the Mêlée had come to some sort of conclusion, and heralds and trumpets were beginning the ritual, in the near-dark, of ending the tourney. A free space opened before them. De Fleury said, 'Why don't we vanish modestly for the present? Can we avoid Katelijne?'

'No,' said Adorne's niece, standing before them. Behind her was Andreas, Adorne's physician. She said, 'Can you walk?'

'I learned quite early,' Nicholas de Fleury said. 'Your singing was bearable. Do you mind?' He made to brush past.

'Because,' she said, 'the Hospitallers' house is quite close. Or the Greyfriars are nearer. But the banquet is there.'

She stood in the gloom with the doctor, looking at Nicholas. Julius said dismissively, 'Well, we'll see you at the banquet.' People were beginning to pass again, calling to them.

The girl Katelijne, saying something impatient, seized Nicholas by the cloak. With the other hand, as the boy had done, she pulled his knife from its sheath and slanted it to catch the remains of the light.

The blade was wet. She did not speak. Julius thought she had gone mad, like Henry. Then he saw that the blade was not only wet. It was red to the hilt.

'As you say,' Nicholas said. 'A temper as weird as his father's. What a pity you saw it. The house of the Hospitallers, yes, perhaps.'

'You mean the brat managed to – I'll kill him!' said Julius.

'Do. That would solve everything,' said Nicholas de Fleury, and began to laugh, until Andreas stopped him.

Chapter 7

T HAT NIGHT THE boy Henry left the tilting-ground no less swiftly, and through an agency no less efficient. Bel of Cuthilgurdy, sweeping the child from the field, looked for and found sympathetic bystanders to help her, and sensible hands to undo the boy's armour and then convey them both to the Castle Hill house. She did not try to find Simon, whose task must be to reach the King before or after the banquet and make his excuses for what his son had attempted against the King's brother. They reached the house without Henry having spoken a word.

There, she sent a request for milk and warm water, and took him alone to his chamber where she stripped him prosaically in the privy and wrapped him in the biggest towel she could find. She talked, now and then, telling him what to do, but the shaking continued, and his white, dirty face hardly changed. It wasn't until the steaming tub had been left that he spoke. He said, 'I killed him.'

Bel sat back on her heels, holding the towel crossed on his chest. She said, 'You thought you did.'

'No,' said Henry. It was shrill.

Bel said, 'He's just a man, Henry. If you'd killed him, he'd be dead.'

The boy wasn't even looking at her. 'But it went in,' he said. 'The knife went in. I killed him.'

'You meant to,' said Bel. Sorrow filled her. She said, 'Men can walk, even when badly hurt. You hurt him. But he wouldn't hurt you.'

'I killed him!' Henry screamed and, sobbing at last, fell into her arms.

Later, Simon arrived. Later, Simon strode to the bed and roused the child from the oblivion of exhaustion with a blow that shocked Henry gasping awake, to be followed by slap after slap on his face. When Bel caught Simon's arm, he turned on her.

'Lullabies! Possets! Embraces! You know best, don't you, what a murderer needs? There is the result of your cosseting. A son of mine fights his prince like a gutter-born bastard; profanes his name; compels his father to beg his King for clemency. What Court will accept him now? What society?'

'Ye silly loon,' Bel said. 'You're hitting a boy for defending your honour. Prince or no, John of Mar was in the wrong. The people who saw it think your son is a hero. Daft, but a hero.'

Paper-white, the boy's face didn't change. '*Defending my honour!*' said Simon.

'Aye. A non-existent item, we ken, but he's only a bairn. But since he's about the only one on your side, it doesna make much sense to blame him. He beat Mar; it's over; the King's overlooked it, I'm sure, and we'd all be the better of a good night's sleep.' She touched Simon's arm. 'Leave it. I'll stay. There'll be time in the morning.'

'He'll be gone in the morning,' said Simon. 'Do you think I want him in Scotland?'

In a flurry of movement, Henry plunged to the edge of the bed. His eyes were wild. Bel said, 'Well, *I* want him in Scotland. He can come to me, or to Lucia.'

'Really?' said Simon. 'Well, why don't you take him? See if you can train him to keep his place in a mêlée and refrain from chopping up princes who happen to rile him. I've been wasting my time.'

'No!' said Henry. He thudded down to the floor. His skin was so white, the red weals of Simon's blows could be counted, as well as the darker abrasions of the fight. He said, 'I killed him. The other boy's father.'

Simon stared at him. Bel said quickly, 'See, you've scared him out of his wits. Go on. Go to bed. Leave him to me.'

'You've killed who?' said Simon. Beneath his full attention, the boy began breathing deeply at last.

'The other boy's father. Claes,' said Henry. 'The man with the wife you got under you. The wife that's birthing my brother. Now he can't be a knight, can he, my brother? Now that baby won't have a father like I have?'

'Oh, my hinny!' said Bel, and found tears of heartbreak and laughter creeping down her cheeks.

Simon said, 'What is he saying?'

She could have lied. She could have pretended not to know. But Henry was not going to leave it. Bel said, 'He means he stabbed Nicholas de Fleury. He seems to have had several reasons.'

'Stabbed . . .' Simon stared at the boy. You could see the anger leaving him.

'I killed him,' said Henry.

'No,' said Bel. Simon looked at her. She said, 'He was hurt, I'm afraid, but not mortally. And he kept quiet about it. You owe Nicholas something this time.'

'Good God! Henry *stabbed Nicholas?*' Simon said. Surprise and pleasure dawned on his face. Henry's face, too, slowly lit up.

'You're pleased?' Bel said.

'Well,' said Simon. He looked at Henry. 'But not dead?'

Bel said, 'Your son would be in the Tolbooth if Nicholas de Fleury were dead.'

Henry said, 'The other boy wouldn't do that.'

Bel said, 'For Christ's sake . . . There *is* no other boy, Henry. Your father wants *you*, not a baby by anyone else. It's not even born yet.' She rounded on Simon. 'How could you do this to him?'

'What?' said Simon. He hadn't even been listening. He said, 'Should I get Henry away? Who else knows what he did?'

'No one who will tell. Don't worry,' said Bel with heavy irony. 'You and Henry are safe.'

'But de Fleury will want a price for his silence?'

'Such as money?' said Bel. 'Or maybe a good suit of armour? I think de Fleury, being normal, was willing to spare a silly young child. He took the blow, and he didn't cry murder. If you owe him a return, it's one of perpetual gratitude.'

'Yes,' said Simon absently. He regarded the boy, and then stretched out to ruffle his hair. 'So what have you to say for yourself? My God! Stabbing apprentices!'

'I didn't kill him,' said Henry. Relief filled the painful chasm in Bel's ample chest.

'Well, you tried,' Simon said. 'I've reared a monster. And now I suppose I've got to hide you at Kilmirren. I expect you'll try to stab the master-at-arms next, or your aunt Lucia. Did someone give you your supper?'

'He's had all he wants,' Bel said. 'We all need sleep.'

'I don't want her here,' Henry said, his shining eyes raised. 'Tell her to go away. This house is for men.'

'How ungallant,' said Simon. 'But I suppose there's something in it. I'll find a nice horse to take Mistress Bel home in the morning.'

'Why not tonight? There's a good moon,' said Bel.

'Now you're joking,' said Simon; and smiled at his son.

The Knights Hospitaller of the Order of St John of Jerusalem in Edinburgh were not entirely eager to open their doors that same evening to some wealthy foreigner stabbed by thieves in the High Riggs; but Nicholas de Fleury arrived escorted by none other than Dr Andreas, and on the powerful recommendation of the Burgundian Envoy himself.

For the sake of Anselm Adorne, Sir William Knollys gave room to the Fleming who, in his time, had been a considerable nuisance to the Order in the Levant. To those of his companions who objected, Sir William pointed out that the hospice had a free bed. It was understood that the cut was slight, and that Dr Andreas himself would patch it up and stay overnight. Having given the appropriate orders, Sir William left for the banquet taking with him the worst of the dissidents. He had never liked John of Kinloch.

As ever, the Greyfriars' hospitality was excellent, and the food and entertainment first class. The choir performed twice, and there were jesters and jugglers and mountebanks, followed by a short play. Accepting his prize, Simon de St Pol was subdued, it was noted, and left early, as well he might. The King and his brethren took cognisance. When the occasion had finally ended, the King's sister Mary, Countess of Arran, rode her palfrey downhill to the house of the Order, and there demanded to see the lady Gelis van Borselen's husband. With her was her friend and mentor of old, Dame Betha Sinclair from Haddington. And following her were the Burgundian Envoy and his niece. Adorne was wearing his unicorn's horn.

To do him justice, the nursing brother in charge was not happy to find a quartet of visitors about to ascend to his patient, but was not likely to prevail against a Sinclair, more royal than royalty. They proceeded to the sickroom together.

Katelijne, entering last, saw only the Princess's quivering back as she recited, without preamble or greeting, 'M. de Fleury, I am Mary of Scotland. The King wishes to thank you, and so do I, for saving the young lord, our brother.'

Adorne coughed. Katelijne, edging round into view, examined Nicholas de Fleury in his latest manifestation.

Not surprisingly, he was in bed. Lying back in bleached flax he looked as collected as he had in black damask, and was displaying a dimple. His underlids were the colour of slate. He said, 'You make too much of it, my lady. The child St Pol lacked a stern enough tutor: I supplied one.'

She sat down by the bed. 'The boy defended his father. His grace my brother did not behave as he should. But for you, there might have been a tragedy. And now, by way of reward, I hear you have been set upon and robbed. Tell me how you were attacked, and by whom. We shall catch them. They will suffer.' Her hands were clasped tightly together.

Katelijne saw de Fleury's eyes rest on them and then heard him embark, with easy calm, on the fiction she had already heard. A sudden onslaught, a cut, and some blood loss. He would be on his feet and home by tomorrow.

She was entranced by his skill, and longed to know his reasons for lying. To protect the son of Simon de St Pol? Nothing she had seen of him had suggested that order of sensibility – even if, as her uncle supposed, the long-standing feud was now over. And she doubted if that was the case. There was something in the face and the voice that suggested that a charge of murder against the son of Simon de St Pol was the least of what this extraordinary man really wanted. Then she saw his eyes on her, and closed her mind quickly.

Mary, half-Flemish princess of Scotland, clearly had no understanding of either the man or the real situation. Young, untried, of middling intelligence, she knew her duty, you would guess, and once had leaned upon and loved this man's wife, and so had been chosen as envoy to thank him for his intervention.

You could see, looking at her, how she must have dreaded the childhood exile imposed on her aunts, tied for life to ducal, royal husbands in far-away lands. You could see how she must have been overjoyed when the powerful family Boyd, close to the throne, ambitious to influence the King, swept aside all her international suitors and forced through her marriage to the adept, vigorous Tom who – when he came back from Denmark, from the wonderful scheme which would give the King land, money, a bride – would build her a palace in Scotland and make her fully wife, mother, and chatelaine among her own kindred and friends.

An innocent, to whom it seemed Gelis van Borselen had been mildly attached. An innocent who did not understand, it was apparent, why her husband's father Lord Boyd appeared rather less often at Court, or who did not hear the rumours which even Burgundians heard. Which especially Burgundians heard, since the man responsible for some of them was said to be Nicholas de Fleury.

Perhaps public opinion was wrong. Certainly, here, Nicholas de Fleury hadn't mentioned the Boyds. On the contrary, he was explaining, although not very energetically, how well his dear wife was bearing her pregnancy, and how it pained him to be far from her side. But – new to fatherhood – he understood that some young mothers craved privacy, and he had agreed, at her wish, not to leave his affairs until the glad time was near. In March or April, they thought. By March or April, of course, he would be in Bruges.

He spoke with unstinted frankness; and if he caught his breath once, the rest of the time he sounded like a man in full health.

Katelijne listened. This performance was less believable, by a long way. The Princess appeared to accept it; Dame Betha, proficient with daughters, was more likely to have reservations. Katelijne wondered what Whistle Willie would think, or Mistress Phemie, who was accomplished with words. They weren't naïve, and neither was M. de Fleury, whom you didn't trust even when singing. As Willie had said outright to him once, it took a knave to make cunts of his tonsils. She wasn't supposed to have overheard that.

She did not interrupt: it was not her place. The sickly conversation came to an end. The Princess, with tears in her eyes, stretched out her hand and laid it on that of de Fleury. He smiled gratefully, and she removed it and rose. She had no natural grace, and her reddish-brown hair and long face were unimproved by the geometry of pearled wire and veiling that surrounded them. Even with the canvas inside, you could count her ribs through her braided silk bodice. She said, 'What will you name the child when it arrives?'

Adorne turned a natural movement into an indolent one. Katelijne watched through her lashes until she saw de Fleury had started to smile. He said, 'Of course, the name will be Mary. If your grace would allow.'

The long-shafted face flushed a little. Mary Stewart said, 'Tell your wife we are pleased. And if a boy?'

This time, the answer was ready. 'If a boy, then it will bear a van Borselen name. Or like your cousin, aspire to Charles, for the Duke. We have not yet reached conclusions.'

'It is another reason why you should not delay your return,' said Mary Stewart, Countess of Arran. 'The choosing of names for their children is what a husband and wife must speak of together.'

Her eyes were damp. Dame Betha said, 'We are tiring M. de Fleury. Come, Katelijne.' And with a strong, freckled hand she shepherded the Princess from the room. With reluctance, Katelijne walked after them.

Anselm Adorne stayed behind.

'Yes?' said Nicholas de Fleury.

Adorne said, 'Are you in pain?'

'No,' said de Fleury.

'I see. There is something I have to say. I shall say it quickly. But for good luck, today I might have killed your reconciled friend, Simon de St Pol of Kilmirren. One of the spears given me at the barre was a war-lance. The coronal was missing.'

The face on the pillow was unaltered; incurious even. 'So you didn't use it?'

'I had it changed for another. But I might not have noticed.'

De Fleury said, 'I might not have stopped the skewering of John of Mar.'

Adorne said, 'We are talking of Simon, not his son.'

'You are,' said de Fleury.

Adorne looked at him, and then let his eyes travel down over the linen, stretched unblemished and motionless as a coffin-cover. This was not the desperate Claes of eighteen, smiling, raw from some deserved beating. And yet, in some way, it was.

Adorne said, 'Yes. You are a strong man. Nevertheless, I know what happened. Does Simon?'

'I have no idea,' de Fleury said.

'You haven't told him? You really don't wish the truth . . . the extent . . . the details to be known?'

'Not particularly,' de Fleury said. 'I shall employ myself out of town. The prize of the Court's attention is yours. Yours and Simon's. You have the boy Henry to thank for it.'

Adorne got up slowly. 'The butcher has abjured his axe? I salute you,' he said.

'Do you?' de Fleury remarked. 'I might as well have entered the tournament. If I'd had any armour.'

Three days later, he departed for Berecrofts, the comfortable Forthside estate of his landlord. No one saw him go, and no one knew therefore the manner of his conveyance, although the nursing brother in charge could have suggested that it was not on the back of a horse.

Julius, who had been required to arrange the matter with Andreas, had taken the occasion, yet again, to invite Nicholas to arraign Henry de St Pol for attempted murder – and had been met, yet again, with blank refusal. Dr Andreas, consulted, had been soothing. 'There is an actual wound, you are right, but he is recovering. You do not admire his Christian spirit? He absolves a child, forgives a former enemy?'

'It's unnatural,' Julius said. 'He must be losing his wits.'

'Or has plans he is not telling us? You would prefer that,' Andreas said, 'to finding him reduced or complaisant?'

'He usually has plans he doesn't tell you,' said Julius. He had brightened. He said, 'I'm sure you'll tell Berecrofts the same, and I don't blame you. But it wouldn't surprise me if the bastard – if M. de Fleury isn't a little more fit than we think. He's preparing some mischief for Simon.'

'In one respect you are right,' said Dr Andreas. 'He is a man who lays plans for himself, and for all those around him. I had been told of him, although not quite enough.'

'Oh, he's a cool one,' said Julius.

'You admire him,' said the doctor. 'You would do well to be afraid of him, too.'

Julius kept his face straight. He wished he had Tobie or someone to share the joke with. He would not have confessed even to Tobie the thread of uneasiness that he, too, sometimes experienced in the company of Nicholas de Fleury. And Dr Andreas kept his counsel, for he had struck a bargain with M. de Fleury. In return for his care, he had undertaken not to reveal the small margin there had been between life and death at the hand of this child. The dreadful irony of the attack he did not know.

Nicholas de Fleury, who did, set it aside, for he had to recover.

This had happened before, with another man's hand over the steel. He had survived that. He always survived. Now, as the clock beat its way through December, he forged his own return to health, admitting Andreas when he could not avoid it; deviating hardly at all from the dense, the convoluted programme he had come to Scotland expressly to follow.

In only one respect did it change: Julius and Crackbene and Bonkle to a lesser degree carried the messages and pursued the negotiations that he could not keep for himself. And, as he had predicted, his place at Court fell to others as his absence lengthened, and was further prolonged after Yule by a deep frost followed by a sudden, early blanket of snow.

Before that, the laird's house in the Regality of Broughton by the south bank of the Forth saw more activity than old Berecrofts or Archie his son could well remember. And when the old man retired to his Canongate house for the winter, the younger stayed on with Robin his son, to study this self-contained man, younger than himself, who – from bed, from chair and then from the desk in his chamber – ran a business that seemed to span the margins of the known world.

Often, when Julius arrived, frozen after the long ride from Edinburgh with a satchel full of ledgers and papers and maps, Archie would persuade him aside after the meetings to talk. There were other couriers too, some of them far-travelled, from Flanders, from Florence and once even from Spain. The Bank of Niccolò, led by a small group of experts, was now engaged, he understood, in reform and expansion after its patron's long absence in Africa.

How it proposed to expand in Scotland, Berecrofts the Younger was not as yet perfectly certain. He knew of a land transaction, now lapsed. He suspected promises of heavy loans. He was aware, because de Fleury had built his Canongate house on Berecrofts's property, that there was a secure room lined with timber and locked, and a double cook-house built of stone in an odd place. He had seen iron boxes which took four men to lift.

He knew that there was a ship due to dock after Twelfth Night which was rumoured to be carrying articles of the kind men described who had been to Rome and Florence, Venice and Bruges, Paris and Rhodes. He had glimpsed arriving by night local men whom he knew, but who did not seem to wish to be recognised.

The only traffic which had decreased, understandably, since Nicholas de Fleury retired to Berecrofts was that of the *dames pour amours*, the amorous ladies. Joneta Hamilton of Kinneil, who had come twice, had left the second time weeping, and had not returned, which was as well, considering her over-prominence on the day of the jousts.

The other feminine visitations, hardly more successful, involved not a woman but young Katelijne Sersanders, come from Haddington with a pack of nuns to visit – so the excuse ran – the nearby Cistercian priory at Emmanuel. The real reason for the first visit, Archie deduced, was winter boredom overlaid with curiosity, and the Princess Margaret her mistress came with her.

That time, less than a week after the stabbing, Andreas had refused to admit them, and Archie had to deal with the Princess's displeasure as best he could, and see them all off – or so he thought. He returned to the house to discover the girl Katelijne actually inside de Fleury's chamber, having been smuggled there by a conspiratorial Robin. He cuffed his son and would have cuffed the Burgundian Envoy's niece, had he had the courage. As it was, she looked up at him with those shrewd hazel eyes and said, nodding to the pillow-packed bed, 'Isn't he bored as well?'

'And if he were, what do you propose to do about it?' said the patient's dispassionate voice. Since arriving, he had shown no inclination to talk. Now he appeared to examine his visitor. 'Ah. The guardian, chief flower and matchless ornament of Haddington. And how is the lady Margaret?'

'Annoyed,' Katelijne said, going in. 'They said you were sleeping.'

'That was Dr Andreas,' said Archie of Berecrofts. He wished Andreas would come back. He hesitated.

The wounded man said, 'Didn't you hear her? She requires entertainment. Leave her. If I become rough, she'll scream. What is the Prioress saying?'

Archie left them, pushing Robin before him. Had he remained, he would have seen nothing of moment, except the gleam in the eye of the girl Katelijne, preparing to taunt and be taunted.

'She's moved Ada and the baby to the priory at Coldstream,' Katelijne said. She found a cup, filled it, laid it on the tray by the bed, pulled out and plumped up his pillows, checked the brazier and sat down on a stool with a book he had been reading.

'I've read that. I'll tell you in a moment the bits I don't like. Haddington? We're all learning to dance: the King's dancing-master comes out from Torphichen. Mistress Phemie has written a poem, and Will Roger has set it to music. There are three verses the Prioress doesn't know about. Dame Alisia is going to her family for Christmas, while the rest of us attend the Princesses at Court. Thomas Boyd won't be there: the Danish bride will be held up for months. His father has a very bad cold and a rash. We are all waiting for your ship with the cut velvet in it: if it doesn't come soon, the Prioress will attack you with a knife, and this time it will be fatal. As you probably know, your friend Kilmirren and Henry have both gone back home. That's a very nice lady, Mistress Bel.'

He was sitting up, now. 'You mean she played ball with you?'

'I mean she knows what Henry did, but hasn't told. So does Simon. And my uncle, of course.'

'And the King?' he said. There was no urgency in the question. He was well enough for that.

'Believed your story implicitly. He's rounded up all the Horse Market vagrants and released them after a thrashing. The better class of citizen would like to put you up for a civic award. What does Berecrofts think?'

'The same. That I resent being robbed, and am prepared to pay to be spoiled. So spoil me.'

'Pay me,' said Katelijne.

He considered her. He said, 'Open that casket, and take out the two largest objects inside.'

The two largest objects were a pack of playing cards and a jew's trump.

He said, 'I am now going to teach you a very coarse game. If you win, you get the trump. If you lose, you have to walk on your hands back to the priory.'

'On my horse's back?' she said, bargaining.

'Providing you dress as you were in the water.'

'And that's only worth a trump?'

'I could improve the offer. What would you do for a guittern?'

'I'll settle,' she said, 'for the trump.'

It was the twang of the little instrument, and the raised voices, that brought Berecrofts to the door half an hour later. The girl left, the right way up, with her servants. Later still, when the harm had been assessed and Andreas, returned from the sickbed, required an explanation, Archie had been defensive. 'All he wanted was news. He made her talk. She only stayed half an hour. Well, it brought him to life at least, didn't it?'

That much was true, and although it brought him a fever as well, he emerged his own man, primed and ready for all that had to be done, and done quickly. When next Katelijne arrived, this time with Will Roger as escort, de Fleury was in no want of news but, leaving his laden desk readily, engaged in an arrow-shower of chatter and badinage which this time was patently effortless. Katelijne, rising to combat, spoke faster and faster: it was the musician who slowed in the end, spent with laughter.

It was not a long ride to Emmanuel. Will Roger said, 'So what do you think?'

Two weeks before, de Fleury had dismissed Andreas his doctor. It was because of Andreas they had come. Katelijne said, 'Sometimes the nuns speak and think very slowly. Then I feel the way I think he is feeling.'

Will Roger grunted. Although he made no concessions, she knew that she was watched; and that he had drawn some conclusions. He would agree, no doubt, with her parents. He said, 'He should let his business alone for a while.'

'You would. He wouldn't,' Katelijne said. 'He's cramming everything in. I think he does intend to get back to his wife by the spring. I think the *Ghost* is coming to take him.'

'So anxious a father? You'd think he'd apply for reassurance to Andreas,' Roger said. 'Or is that why . . .?'

'That's why there is no Dr Andreas. Dr Andreas offered to study his stars.'

'And got sent away. Why? I would have listened. He hasn't offered to study *my* stars,' said Will Roger.

'You haven't got any stars. You were born in a whistle. You couldn't give me an A.'

'Yes I could,' said Will Roger, and made his tuning-fork chime. It began to snow while they were alternately singing and racing each other, but they hardly noticed, they were so entertained.

Christmas came. Simon of Kilmirren, returned to acceptance, spent the height of the season at Court with a much qualified wardrobe, and passed the rest of his time at Kilmirren, drilling Henry. Bel of Cuthilgurdy, being of a nature which (grimly) never imposed itself uninvited, filled her comfortable house with comfortable friends, and generated some moderate happiness. Lucia, passing between homesteads, took care to see neither Bel nor her brother.

The boy Henry did not appear at Court at all, having been beaten by Simon, the other boys claimed, and his armour sold off. The borrowed armour of Simon, the more reliable story ran, had been returned to de Fleury with an apology for the shortcomings of the Kilmirren armourer. And certainly, the Emperor of Trebizond would never have worn the suit the way it looked now.

Nicholas de Fleury, whose entire bureau was now divided between Berecrofts and the Canongate, considered returning to Edinburgh for a space, and then reconsidered.

Socially, he had lost his light hold on the royal brothers and sisters, and would not readily make it up in a matter of days. Nor was he anxious, just yet, to risk meeting Simon in Edinburgh. On every other level of business, his Scottish transactions had continued without much interruption.

As for his overseas trade, transmission had slackened in winter, and any message that did come was brought him directly by Bonkle or Crackbene. Julius was now with him most of the time. As he expected, there had been no word from Gelis. There had been no word about her either: sick or well; dead or alive. If she were dead, he would hear. But if the weather closed in, he could be cut off from Edinburgh.

If the weather closed in, his ship might be late, or might sink, which would be . . . inconvenient. As it was, she was due any day, with her recondite cargo. And she was to come to the port of

Blackness, not to Leith, for Nicholas wanted her near him, and Blackness was only four miles from Linlithgow. That, in the end, was why he stayed at Berecrofts. That, and because he knew the nature of the Scottish Court. He had devoted three months to studying it.

Julius had learned, now, that Nicholas was leaving in a few weeks for Flanders, without waiting for spring or Adorne's company. Failing to argue him out of this plan, Julius proposed to come with him. Naturally, he and Nicholas would be back, having made such an investment in Scotland. Julius was not fool enough to believe that marriage counted for much to a rich man, or indeed any other, but accepted that Nicholas had to consult with Astorre, renew his status with the Duke, and review his dealings with Venice and Alexandria. By that time, his child born, Nicholas could make sure of the next, and return.

Nicholas de Fleury was familiar with all these opinions of Julius, as indeed he should be, having implanted them. Nicholas de Fleury waited, unsleeping, vigilant, drinking water, and was rewarded, after a fashion.

The *Ghost* arrived a week after Twelfth Night. Michael Crackbene, blue with cold, brought the news on horseback from Blackness, and reported that the carts had come, and she was already unloading. She was being revictualled at the same time, and soon the new freight would be in place.

'Revictualled to leave? After three weeks' hard sailing from Sluys?' Julius exclaimed.

'She's watertight. I'm changing her crew. I know her,' Crackbene said. 'I know the sea in these parts as well.'

He gazed at Julius, whom he neither liked nor disliked. Julius, a natural opponent of tolerance, glared in return, then transferred his annoyance to the ship's owner. 'I thought you meant to sail on that ship.'

'I did. I do,' Nicholas said. 'But it has to be now, apparently, because of the weather. I have only three days, Mick calculates, to get out of the estuary and turn south in safety. Otherwise I could be stuck here till spring.'

'Then stay till spring,' Julius said. 'Astorre won't rot; Gregorio loves being in charge; Cristoffels seems to be managing; the Mamelukes haven't killed John so far as I know. You could drown getting to Bruges in this weather. Keep the *Ghost* at Blackness. Or send it back without you, if you're so keen to turn over your profit. Crackbene'll take her.'

Crackbene said nothing. That was why he had been hired.

Julius, too, had been brought here for a purpose. One kept one's temper with Julius, except when it was useful to lose it. And Julius had no suspicions. Julius would never imagine that, in the warmth of this room, anyone could be seized with such cold that he had to grip his hands together to still them.

Nicholas said, 'When I want a lecture, I'll ask for one. I'm sailing with Crackbene. As I've already told you, you can stay.'

'Not unless you do,' Julius said. 'Oh, come on. See sense. Leave in three days? With the Court waiting for you, and all your business going so well? Unless . . .' He paused. 'Nicholas? You've got the Hamilton girl into pup? Or one of the others?'

Crackbene's stare switched from the floor to the ceiling. Nicholas saw it. He realised that losing his temper was useless. Instead he said, hesitating, 'There are certain problems. If you could manage to stay –' He broke off. He felt marginally better. It was one of the functions of Julius, to make him feel better. Some, at least, of the time.

'I'm not staying!' said Julius with alarm. 'So when are we going?'

'Tomorrow. Or the next day. I don't know. Should I announce it?'

'I shouldn't,' said Julius. 'Slip away. Crackbene?'

'Slip away. Easy enough,' Crackbene said. 'I'm packed, anyway.'

It occurred to Julius that he was not. He asked other questions, but upon receiving minimal answers he retired presently, looking doubtful, to make lists. Crackbene sat on, having more to report and a letter, brought by the ship, to deliver.

It was addressed to Nicholas de Fleury in Gregorio's writing. There was no time now, to read it in privacy. Whatever it was. Rising, de Fleury broke with steady hands the seal of the packet and drew out the single page it contained. He read it once by the brazier, before holding it over the flames to catch fire. Then he set it down on the embers, and prodded it slowly and deliberately into ashes.

Crackbene said, 'You have blistered your hand.' Nicholas had forgotten he was there.

The blisters were nothing. The rod he had gripped as a poker was red from its point to his fingers. Like blood on a knife. He knew, breathing slowly, where he wanted to sheath it. He said, without turning, 'Shouldn't you go?' and heard Crackbene rise.

Crackbene said, 'You are going on with it?'

'Oh yes,' Nicholas said. He turned. 'Something made me angry, that was all. Nothing has changed.'

'So I see,' Crackbene said.

It was the season for hunting: the season when, tempted into the open, the chosen prey turned and twisted and fled, and the young and strong and handsome raced after, to kill.

It was the day, the cold day of Crackbene's visit to Berecrofts, when the child Henry, bored with Kilmirren, persuaded the young hunt-servant left by his father to take him out on his pony and, collecting a group of young people, well attended, to spend the brightest hours hunting small game with them in the snow. Their sport took them to the door of Bel of Cuthilgurdy, who invited them in and gave them what refreshment she had.

Since Edinburgh, she had not laid eyes on Henry. It had worried her. The gossip she heard of Simon's vanity-struck disordered household gave her no confidence in his understanding of the boy, or his ability to make a home for him. Yet the constant practice, the training in chivalry in all its aspects, the concentrated attention must at least restore the child's confidence; must make him at least feel secure. But it pained her, a little, that the boy had not come to see her.

And now here he was. Because, it seemed, Simon was in Edinburgh, and had been for some time. Jordan his grandfather, of course, was in France. So, alone in a household of servants with his nurse, his tutor, his master-at-arms, Henry had felt himself bored and neglected, and was in the process of seeking a remedy.

There were few chances to talk. He looked as beautiful as ever, and well; had grown a little; was boisterous and commanding in the presence of children and servants; less so with the older boys, who delivered sly pinches and blows when they were not devouring her food. He had brought them for the sake of his popularity, that was all. It was what she should have expected.

At the end, they all politely thanked her, including the servants outside, and Henry, taking his leave, submitted to two or three questions to which he gave careless answers.

She found the answers disturbing. She continued to find them disturbing all evening. After an uneasy night, she rose in the dark before dawn and rode out the short distance necessary to satisfy herself that she was wrong.

When, presently, she left home again with her maid it was daylight, and she was warmly clad for a long journey, and accompanied by a party of men from the Kilmirren estate and its farms. Some, like young Andro, she had known a long time. The rest included the new steward appointed by Jordan, and the man from the east coast, from Broughton, whom Simon himself had selected. They took dogs and spare horses and food. They also took weapons. It was by then a fine day: full morning, with the sun in her eyes, dazzling white from the hoof-printed snow.

It was a good morning for hunting. The same sun roused the King's Court at Edinburgh, where the Castle seethed with restless young men. It was a good morning for hunting and moreover the *Ghost*, this Flemish ship with the fabulous cargo, had arrived, they had learned, and was lying within easy reach at Blackness.

The King had already conferred with Alexander his brother, or possibly the other way round. By the time the sun had climbed in the sky, a royal hunting-party had left for a day's sport to the hills west of Edinburgh.

They planned to hunt. They planned to descend for food upon the King's Palace of Linlithgow. Before turning homewards to Edinburgh, they planned to ride across to Blackness and inspect the *Ghost* and its wonderful merchandise. Among those who accompanied the King were Anselm Adorne and Simon de St Pol of Kilmirren.

By midday, the royal party was close to Linlithgow, and Bel of Cuthilgurdy was eight hours away.

Nicholas de Fleury waited.

It was only the first stage, that was all. It was only the first knot in the snare, the first flick of the hook; the first hint of spin in the arrow. The first letting of blood not his own.

Chapter 8

ADORNE HAD BEEN to Linlithgow Palace before. The drawbridge thudded down in a sunlit cloud of snow speckled with dust and the hounds, brown and black and white, poured past the horses like salmon. Above the carved lintel, the scaffolding stood against the pellucid blue sky, marking the advance of the masonwork.

The new rooms were to be ready by the time the King's bride came from Denmark. Through the winter, James had ridden out now and then to look at them, but not to stay. No one stayed there at present but the artisans and the Master of Works and their cook and, some of the time, the Keeper of the Palace.

Even to pause here for noon dinner had meant sending off a train of wagons at dawn, with food and trestles and benches and barrels of ale, and dishes and pots for the kitchen, and cloths and buckets and braziers. There were supposed to be spits already provided, and charcoal, and logs to heat the stone rooms. A host of servants in thick hooded mantles had travelled the sixteen miles with the baggage, glumly packed between kegs.

It was as well they had sent something to eat, for the morning's hunting had been indifferent: a few score game birds and some hares, which had hardly diminished the Princes' energy, or that of Sersanders and Adorne's niece, for that matter. The countryside was white with last night's snow: even the loch above which the Palace perched was smooth as a blanket, and the air crackled with redeeming frost over the workmen's latrines. Beyond the entrance passage and portcullis, the inner yard of the building was stiff with mud. The Keeper stood in it waiting, cap in hand, his beard fixed in a block like winter fodder. He had just finished sneezing.

Anselm Adorne thought of the Great Hall as last he had seen it, a hundred feet long and thirty wide with unshuttered windows and bare walls and stone seats and a black fog of fumes from the hearth. And that had been in autumn. He wondered if the well froze. Maintaining a lofty Burgundian calm, he exchanged a silent flicker of woe with Jehan Metteneye.

Behind, the rest of the party, losing animation, had fallen pettishly quiet, in the way of those about to blame someone for something. Katelijne was among them, with the nuns and her mistress, young Margaret. Adorne could hear Mistress Phemie's encouraging voice, supported by the rich tones of Will Roger. He smiled.

The stables at least were prepared, and the hounds were led off. Adorne greeted the Keeper, and took his place of honour in the cold procession shedding mud and snow up the flight of stone steps to the hall. Andreas was behind him, and Scheves. He caught sight of Kilmirren, clad in a sober wool cloak and black cap, taking the steps two at a time.

Kilmirren was in favour today, having driven the game the King's way, and refrained from taking the best. Kilmirren, working hard since his son's joust, had devoted his time to pleasing the King, and no less to warmly befriending Adorne who, as it happened, felt no pressing need of his company. He usually passed him to his nephew, who talked to him about jousting.

Now Simon, having sprung to his side, produced an apology for their surroundings. 'Linlithgow is not the Princenhof, I'm afraid. But even the Duke of Burgundy's palaces are stripped in winter, and cold.'

'It is so everywhere,' Adorne said. 'When his grace the King and his mother lived here, I make no doubt it was handsome, and will be more magnificent still. We understand: we are dining alfresco.'

The Keeper had reached the top of the stairs with the King, followed by the King's two half-uncles with Alexander of Albany behind. Mantled in quilted pourpoints and jackets and furs, they looked from below like a press of cattle, jammed fast at the neck of a gate. Adorne heard upraised voices.

'The wagons holding the wine have overturned,' said Metteneye, who had exceptional hearing. 'And the water has frozen. They suggest boiling the snow.'

The voices above became louder, and the press slackened. The King had walked into the Great Hall, with the Keeper following. The hunting-party, including Adorne, ascended and entered behind him.

The Great Hall was as stark as before – worse, for the shutters, chimney-cope and embrasures were thick with debris and dust.

Only the rushes were fresh and, this time, there were whole tree-trunks on the distant great hearth, burning bright with blue flames. There were trestles and benches, and a cross-table on the dais by the fire for the King, but no cloths and no cushions. The boards were half empty and half set with pewter. More than one wagon, you would say, had overturned.

The King was addressing the Keeper of the Palace in a part-broken, furious voice. 'And the food? I suppose the wolves have taken the food? What is your office worth?'

The man, his face pallid, said, 'The food is here, your grace, and being cooked. You came — We did not expect your grace so soon.'

'I think you did not expect me at all,' said the King. 'Perhaps I, too, was to be overturned on my way? It is not unknown. It has happened before. So mark you, if I ride back to Edinburgh as I intend to, without wine, without food, there will be a reckoning. And you, sir, will be the first to pay it. There is not even ale?'

'Unless . . .' said the Keeper.

'There are other houses nearby,' said the King's half-uncle James. 'Where is Hayning? Where is Hamilton? There will be wine at Kinneil.'

'There is wine here,' said the Keeper. 'But it belongs to —'

Katelijne Sersanders, in her uncle's hearing, said, '*No!*' Her voice expressed tremulous ecstasy.

'— but it is part of the cargo of the *Ghost*. The ship of M. de Fleury. I gave leave, since the warehouse at Blackness is insecure. The merchandise is below, in the vaults.'

'Here?' said the King. 'We don't have to go to Blackness?'

'No. Here. But locked. M. de Fleury is due to bring the keys when your grace should have finished his repast.'

The King looked at his brother, and at his two sturdy uncles, who were smiling. The younger lord (Hearty James, he was nicknamed) said, 'He can be sent for, your grace. Meanwhile, we can no doubt find a locksmith.'

'Or a hammer,' said Albany. Colour blended once more with his freckles, and his sister Margaret tugged his arm, her eyes shining. 'What are we waiting for?'

Anselm Adorne stayed above, while the rest swept down the stairs to the courtyard and across to the steps of the cellars. Not quite all the rest: Metteneye remained at his side with the nuns, and Maarten his son with Bishop Patrick, and Knollys, the Precep-tor of the Knights of St John with a group of older barons and clerics. Will Roger, whistling silently, had also remained in the hall.

But the children were all out there, jostling through the mud. The young people. Adorne stood by the open window and watched them. The King and Alexander of Albany and the young men of birth capering about them. The rotund Margaret, their juvenile sister. His own nephew and niece, walking quickly. And James of Auchterhouse and John, Earl of Atholl, not yet thirty, representing avuncular seniority and restraint. From above, their hats strutted like partridges.

And the sober black cap of Kilmirren, who had held back at first. Of course, thought Adorne, he had reason to hesitate. In sparing Henry, Nicholas de Fleury had for the first time achieved some ascendancy over Kilmirren. But it seemed the comradeship of the young King counted more. In any event, Simon had gone.

In the half-emptied hall, Will Roger said cryptically, 'I doubt.'

'I'm afraid, so do I,' said Euphemia Dunbar. She smiled at Roger and turned the smile, deepening, towards Adorne beside him. The remorseless line of the wimple exposed the irregularity of her features in which her round eyes were set like bronze pennies.

Euphemia, the Earl of March's unmarried daughter, might not look like the rhymster of Haddington but, in his regular calls on his niece, Adorne had identified the authoress of the verse that now embellished the unholy alliance of Katelijne's invention and Will Roger's music. At Haddington the three had become friends, and Adorne was very content to have it so.

Now he went forward and, easing a bench, made a space for her to sit beside Metteneye. Roger perched on the table by Maarten. Adorne said, 'You think they will make too free with the wine.' He returned to the window.

'With more than the wine,' said Will Roger. 'There are fine things in that cargo, I hear.'

The Bishop, standing nearby, stopped gnawing his lips. 'I shall be interested to see them. M. de Fleury knows how to barter paste beads with negroes, but the lords of this country live as other lords do. Our merchants frequent Bruges. My royal uncle himself imported nothing but goods of the finest of workmanship.'

He was thirty-three and hasty of tongue: an uncertain shadow of the late Bishop James Kennedy his uncle. Adorne, watching, saw Roger's brows jump, and Maarten redden. He hesitated to intervene, for in some ways Patrick Graham was right to defend his family's culture. However suspect his political acumen, James Kennedy had been a fearless and vigorous man, which was why the young Albany had loved him; why Anselm Adorne had placed Maarten in the care of his nephew. Some men grew into their office. Some offices transcended the man.

All the same, diplomacy should not be forgotten. Adorne said, 'My lord, whatever his taste, the young man does not, I believe, mean to impute to this nation a dearth of civilised comforts, but seeks merely to keep them replenished. It is all we merchants offer to do.'

The Bishop grunted, shuffling. Adorne, his thoughts disturbed, averted his gaze to the distant descent to the cellars. As he did so, a row of barrels emerged, and began to traverse the yard in the direction of the kitchen, followed by a man rolling a vat, and others shouldering kegs. He said aloud, 'The wine has been found.'

Metteneye got up and joined him, followed by Roger. Metteneye said with approval, 'They mean to heat it.'

'Well, some of it,' said the musician. He leaned out, pulling his cloak tight about him. Outside, an odour of warm roasting beef had begun to temper the air to the north. Other smells stirred. The ovens, heated at last, had been loaded with food. From the direction of the cellars came an outburst of muffled laughter and some shouting, followed by the hollow blows of a mallet. It did not sound as if a locksmith had been found, or even sought for. Will Roger gave an exclamation, and strode out of the hall.

Everyone else stood at the windows, the Prioress and the Bishop taking the centre, their eyes fixed on the recess where the cellar steps lay, still in sunlight. A small crowd of workmen and grooms had gathered hesitantly in the yard, giving way from time to time as a liveried servant disappeared down the steps. One of them carried a crowbar.

Adorne said, 'This is a pity.' He could say no more. The King was there, with his uncles. It was not for a foreigner to interfere.

The first person to emerge was the lady Margaret, climbing the steps and marching over the mud. Her hat was still intact, tied on top of her furious red hair, but her cloak had been replaced by many ells of black and gold velvet, unrolled from the bale and tied by some means to her shoulders, from which it fell as a train into the occasional grasp of a page. It did not fall in the mud, because someone was walking beneath it. Adorne recognised, choking a little, the legs of his niece. Knollys said, 'The stupid young wench – the expense o't!'

'To whom?' said the Bishop. 'Perhaps you would care to go out and help her? Then again, who knows what will come next?'

What came next were three folding chairs, each of velvet-trimmed leather and tasselled, and each borne on liveried legs. After a pause, and a burst of louder laughter, a scroll appeared which, lengthening, turned out to be a long roll of arras succeeded by a close-stool and a hat-stand. There followed cushions, many of them, and a procession of stand- and field-beds and a mirror. And then pile upon pile of fine linen followed by heavy objects which appeared to be plate-chests. There were coffers, and trays, and a wall-clock; lecterns and sheets; a perfume-burner and a fine Turkish carpet. There emerged Will Roger, grim-faced, supervising the carriage of two objects no one recognised at all.

By then the King's sister had entered the Great Hall with her train, inevitably mired, dragging behind her. Katelijne said, 'They are unpacking it all.'

Her uncle said, in Flemish, 'We can do and say nothing. You have helped as much as you could.'

He watched, since observation at least was open to him. Eventually all the King's party had made their hilarious way back to the warm, the filthy Great Hall. And below dirtied glorious arras, upon blemished cushions of silk and velvet and leather, served on embroidered snagged linen, aided by dented exquisite silver and lit by ill-hung, precious candelabra, the banquet was served.

Nicholas arrived at the end, with his keys. Arrived, in person, in the centre of the Great Hall, without warning from gate-keeper or porter; without discreet interception by Argyll or by Whitelaw to prepare, to explain, to excuse what the Princes had done.

Anselm Adorne saw him enter and stand, his sable cloak held at one shoulder; his other hand, finely gloved, hanging idly between the black hem of his doublet and the gilded leather below.

Far down the table, Simon glanced up and saw him, and his face changed. Adorne, ceaselessly observant, saw Nicholas de Fleury's dense gaze rest on Kilmirren for a moment, then move. It travelled slowly over every part of the vast room, from the dishevelled tapestried walls to the broken Venetian glass, the smeared salvers and magnificent salt-cellars on the strewn tables; and then extended to the diners, their servants beside them, whose inconsequential chatter and laughter began slowly to dwindle, and then resurrected itself, vaguely, in gleeful whispers.

Adorne said, 'The wine. What was in the wine?' At the top table, the Princes lay back in their tasselled chairs while the elders about them sat up, and tried to recover their gravity.

The wine, warmed, had been spiced. With what, Adorne could not say, although he had tasted something like it before. He was conscious that even his head, legendary in Bruges, had been affected.

Metteneye said, 'Lamb's house in Leith. The same spices.'

The same spices, before the night on Leith strand. The same spices, supplied by de Fleury.

Perhaps he exclaimed. The altered eyes of the same Nicholas de Fleury met his and then passed beyond, with the same level, measuring gaze. He showed no horror or anger. You might have thought him indifferent, except that in the real world, no merchant, no banker would tolerate this scale of capricious behaviour. The statesmen about the King must realise that. The King, the young people, the people perennially young like Simon of Kilmirren perhaps took it for meekness. The humiliating meekness of Claes; of a small, subservient merchant, afraid of offending his betters.

A rustle ran through the room. And even as it ran, Nicholas said, 'My lord. I intrude. I see you have keys of your own.'

The King sat up. Finding an uncle's hand on his shoulder, he shook it off. He said, 'We did not expect you to make of the simple journey from Berecrofts a task as long as your travels in Asia. Did you expect us to await you all night?'

His voice was indignant. Nicholas, between the two arms of the trestles, did not advance any nearer. He said, 'The fault is mine, my lord King. I would have unpacked and furnished the Palace myself, had I known you wished to purchase so much.'

The King glanced at Bishop Graham, and away. He said, 'Purchased? We have merely ordered a view of your goods, many of which are damaged, or below those standards common to Scotland. We shall tell you, in due course, which if any we propose to keep for ourselves.'

'My lord is gracious,' said Nicholas.

'You have, I hope, no complaint?' said the King. Below the table, visibly, he received a kick from Alexander his brother. A rustle of laughter ran round the room.

'My lord King, on the contrary: I excuse myself,' Nicholas said. 'And would ask you, as a favour, to receive from me without charge all those items you have identified – all those items which are not entirely perfect. Would it please my lord to accept them in loving gauge gift from a servant?'

'He's gone crazy,' said Metteneye.

'Has he?' said Adorne. The subdued laughter had increased.

'Are you serious?' said John, Earl of Atholl, his manner ponderous. 'It is an offer of exceptional generosity.'

'Of course,' Nicholas said. 'Provided, of course, his grace can make use of them. Perhaps they are not to his taste.'

He did not look at Bishop Patrick, but the shaft had pricked its target, Adorne thought, his apprehension shot through with passing amusement. But apprehension was what, increasingly, he now felt. Nicholas de Fleury was not nowadays a subservient man, and if he courted humiliation, it was for a purpose. The result, for the moment, was a murmur of subdued derision: the expression of a contempt which had its roots in disappointment. They had wanted an explosion, all those spoiled young men and their companions. It would have salved any pangs of conscience they might feel, or would feel in the morning.

Adorne began to consider not only the morning, but the immediate future. The tapers burned now, and the shutters were closed against darkening skies full of snow. This well-dined company would never travel home safely tonight. He tried, discreetly, to catch the Bishop's eye, and found it unnecessary. The King said, 'Perhaps M. de Fleury has supped less well than we, and would join us at table. Unless the Master of Works thinks we have had pleasures enough, and should leave before nightfall?'

'I beg,' Nicholas said, 'that the King's grace would not dream of delaying his departure. Although there are plumdames and nuts just arrived, which I had hoped to tempt him into tasting, and, of course, the merchandise to select. Or if it would please him to stay, there are beds and pallets enough to serve most of his company. The blankets are still in the chests.'

'And all, of course, for sale at moderate prices, allowing for damage and use,' someone said, without troubling to whisper. De Fleury gave no sign of having heard that, or the laughter that followed it. Or of noticing the pleasure mixed with contempt on the face of Simon de St Pol, as he listened to the patronising voice of the Court, deciding to spend the night on M. de Fleury's new beds in the candlelit luxury of the King's half-built Palace of Linlithgow.

Kilmirren himself got up shortly, and moved to where a place had been cleared and set for de Fleury, while the new sweetmeats were served. He saw that Julius, the Bank's manager, had been recruited to unpack them. He had been on his way to Blackness, and did not appear to relish the task. Simon said, 'Does your Bank complete many such deals? I now see the need for your journey to Africa.'

'It had some advantages. Do you want to buy anything? I have a few bales of dun cramoisy; a compt board; a hood set. Or a fine silver stoup with twelve stops?'

Simon looked, hazily smiling, round the echoing room. 'Hitherto unused, I am sure. We are all well beyond the twelve stops except you. I have no doubt you feel yourself safer.' He looked round. 'What was it you said of wine, Dr Andreas? Makes man joyous, aids Nature in its course, and delays the onset of old age? Or was that marriage?'

'I should hesitate to pronounce on marriage,' Dr Andreas said, 'although I am somewhat interested in the wine. I suggested to the young ladies that they refrain from indulging.'

Behind him, Katelijne Sersanders was surveying them. The woman Euphemia sat beyond her. Simon, smiling at them, said, 'It is the heat of the fire. You noticed the fire?' They could not fail to have noticed. The hearth, big enough for three stone arcades, could and did burn whole tree-trunks. The blaze today contained something else.

It was Dr Andreas the alchemist who replied, while his unemotional gaze rested on Claes. 'Indeed, I observed something novel. The black stones, of which the late Pope Pius made mention. There is coal locally, and the King can afford it?'

'Others, too,' Simon said. 'Already, some of us burn it. Soon there will be more. You yourself had hoped, Claes, to appropriate coal-bearing land? But the Hamiltons, it seems, felt some misgivings.'

'The time ran out,' Nicholas said. 'I hear it went to somebody else.' He looked up enquiringly, as Simon drew breath.

'To me,' Simon said. 'To me, a friend. Does that not soften the blow? I paid a good deal, of course. But when I export, you may be sure I shall give you special rates. Joneta is pleased.'

'Joneta?' The voice was that of the Sersanders girl, Katelijne. Simon gave her another beguiling smile, answering. She was pretty.

'Joneta Hamilton of Kinneil. Sir James's natural daughter. She acted as my intermediary.' He smiled again, differently. 'I believe you tried to engage her interest, Claes? Once or twice? On the day of the tournament? She told me all about it.'

The eyes of the girl Katelijne switched between Claes and himself. The girl said unexpectedly, 'The King calls him Master Nicol de Fleury.'

'And I call him by his real name,' Simon said. 'I have advised the King to do the same. The King's grace, my dear Claes, has charmed us all, while you have been away, with his readiness to be advised. Have you told Claes yet, demoiselle, of your uncle? Of Sir Anselm Adorne?'

She flushed with pride, he observed. She said, 'It is for my uncle to mention it.'

'Am I to know?' said the man he was taunting. The man he couldn't completely expose as a lout, or he could do some damage. But then, Simon could inflict some damage, too. And as a target, Claes was . . . irresistible.

It was Anselm Adorne himself who came over, hearing his name. Claes rose, as he had not done for Simon. Adorne said quickly, 'I wished to tell you myself. For love of his cousin of Burgundy, the King has seen fit greatly to honour me. It is a token deserved by our country, not myself.'

'But, no doubt, is none the less welcome. Let me think,' Claes said. 'You have received sword, baldric and spurs, and been proclaimed Guardian of Scotland?'

Adorne winced. He said, 'I cannot apologise for what is no doing of mine. I have been created a knight, yes. And a councillor to the King. It is a nominal office.'

'But will bring its own rewards. In land, I trust?'

'In *coal-bearing* land?' Simon intervened jocularly. He didn't mind someone else baiting Claes, provided he had a share.

'It has yet to be decided,' Adorne said. Understandably, he sounded repressive. It would not look well if two Burgundians fell out in the royal presence. And Adorne was an able man, who had not failed to profit from the absence of Claes. As had Simon.

'Oh, dear. Well, don't mourn,' said the object of their attention. 'The God Mercury, protector of merchants, will compensate me. There is a move afoot, I hear, to dash outdoors and commit riotous enormities. I shall come, to have something to remember you by. And you, M. de St Pol? Or don't you like bloodshed by torchlight?'

'It depends who is shedding it,' Simon said, laughing. It drew no reply but a dimpling smile.

It had stopped snowing by then, but far off to the west, the steward's big horse had foundered and he had had to transfer to one much less powerful, while two of the husbandmen had dropped out. Bel rode still, with the Broughton man, and young Wodman. There were no spare horses now, and darkness was coming.

It was like another ride she remembered, for endurance, but that ride had been in terrible heat, not in cold, and she had been ill then, and was strong now, although sick with fear. And that ride she had survived because of one loving man, who had carried her in his arms. Because of Nicholas.

Later, much later, when it was full dark, and new-fallen snow lay glimmering over the shire from Linlithgow to the sea, the wine-warmed company of James of Scotland and his companions called for their hunt-servants, their horses and hounds and, assuming their furs and their boots, took up their weapons and rode out, laughing and calling, to commit the riotous enormities their pedlar had spoken of.

He rode with them, cloaked in sable-lined damask; his face white and black in the light of the flambeaux; his voice ringing. Euphemia Dunbar said, 'The wine was strong.'

'It is not the wildness of wine,' Adorne said, 'but, I am assured, an explosion of spirits induced by the end of the Kilmirren feud.'

'The end?' said Mistress Phemie. 'Well, of course you must know. Otherwise I should have felt some solicitude for him tonight.'

'For whom? For *Nicholas?*' exclaimed Anselm Adorne.

She looked at him with her wise, uncomely face, and made no reply. It was his niece who enlightened him. It was Katelijne who said, 'Don't you hear it? *His* voice; and the voice of the dogs?'

Man and woman, they both looked at her then; and Andreas, riding beside them. Her eyes, her over-bright eyes were lamps, and the chameleon expressions flickered over her face, quicker than thought. She said, 'I think this is to be the night of the duel. The duel that wasn't fought at the tournament.'

'And you want to interfere?' Adorne said.

She lifted her chin. 'There is no one to arbitrate.'

'Is one of them without honour?' Adorne said. 'Or a murderer? Dr Andreas?'

The physician said, 'I have no advice to give you. I gave M. de Fleury the same reply, early this evening, on a broader matter.'

'He asked you his fortune?' said the woman.

'He was apprehensive,' suggested Adorne.

The doctor looked at him. He said, 'Very few men feel no physical fear. He is one, or has become one.'

'Nicholas?' said Adorne.

'Oh, yes,' said Dr Andreas. 'He has many skills, developed through boyhood. It is unlikely that you or anyone else have ever understood the real man. Or, at least, anyone in his world now.'

Chapter 9

THE SNOW WAS DEEP for the hounds, but once over the rise north of Linlithgow, the land was flat, and all you had to do was make sure you stopped before you reached the long selvedge of mud by the estuary.

Not that it would matter if the young devils ran straight out into the water: the dubs were firm enough, and even the edge of the spring tide was freezing. It would give them a shock, that was all. And meanwhile, between the salt-pans to the right and the mouth of the good river Avon away to the left, they could beat the ground as much as they wanted, until they got cold. The master huntsman had in mind to get them all back to the Palace before three short of midnight, and himself into his new Flemish draw-bed with a cummer or two and a rug and a flask.

He blew his horn and signalled his men, once again, to ring the group with their torches and head them away from such snow-mounded dykes and rickles of stone as would spoil the legs of their horses. The ponds and burns were all safe: they were hard enough to bear a wain and four bullocks.

They looked well, his young men and women, you had to grant that. He had trained the best ones himself. Jamie the King, and Alexander, that used to cry himself Sandy until he came back from foreign parts with a Flemish saddle and an English style with a crossbow. And the royal wee red-head, Bleezie Meg, as the stable-boys had it, that nocked her arrow and drew her bit bow as stout as a man, when he could get her away from the nuns. Better advised than the uncles, at times, although he'd had the polishing of the two of them too.

He liked them all, and wished he could have found them better sport, but there was little good scent to be had in the snow, and the wolves had gone to ground, it would seem. All they had got was a score of dazzled fowl in a tree and a hare or two, and the clouds were beginning to draw over the moon. He was ready for them to give up, when they started to talk of calling in at Kinneil yonder, where the Hamiltons always had a few barrels of wine in the cellar, in the days when the Lady was living. And so they did, and were welcomed, although Lord James was away, and it was the lassie, Joneta, who did them the honours.

And when the daft idea of the boar came up, it was no surprise when Sim of Kilmirren went off with the lassie to look for it. Everyone kent that the Hamilton girl had been moonstruck over her bonnie Simon, and was again, it would seem. The master huntsman wished he had a cross-bolt for every lass who had offered Kilmirren a shot. He sighed, getting the dogs under control, and the horses kept moving until their lordships had had their drink and were ready to ride out again.

It pleased but didn't surprise Simon when Joneta put her arm inside his and, sheltered under his cloak, guided him across the crisp, crumpled snow of the yard to the outbuildings. If the boar was still there as she thought, he would bring back some helpers to tie it. Then, loosed a good distance off, it would give them some sort of a run.

Hamilton wouldn't mind. Simon was on good terms with James, Lord Hamilton, having bought some expensive land off him, and denied it to Claes. He had enjoyed telling Claes, who would appreciate this pause at Kinneil all the less for it. Not that Claes was, in any case, having the luckiest day in his life. Wherever he went, he drew stifled amusement.

And meanwhile, there was no hurry to look for the boar. As he recalled, there was a bakehouse nearby which was generally warm and often empty. Remembering, he let his palm winnow down Joneta's flank, pausing to diverge now and then. Amid the increasing haze of pleasure, he hoped Claes had seen them depart.

He almost wished Claes was here now, as Henry was present occasionally, stimulatingly – reprehensibly, he supposed – at Kilmirren. With Joneta held expertly against him, Simon opened the bakehouse door.

Warmth emerged, and rosy light, and the delicious smell of hot bread, and three men who seized his arms as his grip of Joneta loosened, and then stuffed a rag into his mouth, binding it before he could shout.

Joneta, instead of running for help, stood holding her throat. She had pulled his cloak with her. It lay on the ground, exposing his hunting-dagger and sword. Both were taken, and his hands wrenched behind him and tied. He kicked and fought, using his spurred boots until, with difficulty, they pulled them off. Then they bound his feet. He hurled his weight from one side to the other.

Fighting with lance and sword were his forte, but he was well trained in combat of other kinds. You couldn't go to war on the Borders without being able to hold your own with your fists. But against three in ambush at night, when off his guard and roused for a girl . . .

Joneta. He glared at her. He couldn't speak, but his eyes must have frightened her. She turned and ran, taking the cloak. From beginning to end, his assailants had paid no attention to her. They knew she wouldn't raise the alarm. She had known they would be there.

They carried him, then. Behind the booth was a door in the wall, and nothing there but scrub trees, heavy with snow. As he struggled, the sounds from Kinneil became less: the rumble of voices, the trampling and whinny of horses, the clank of buckets, of harness. The flambeaux in the yard became spots in the darkness, and the house a ghost, with threads of light round the shutters and smoke rising, grey upon black. All about him, as the woods fell behind, were glistening fields of snow, eerie and blue in the night; stretching as far as he could see.

They set him down in it, beside a single twisted juniper bush which, buffeted, scattered its snow. Separated from the warmth of other bodies, he felt the chill of the air through doublet and shirt; the snow he stood in soaked the stuff of his hose and spread the chill higher.

His captors, standing about, were unknown to him. The doubtful light of the yard had shown him three burly men dressed in leather, their caps pulled low, their weapons heavy and serviceable. Professional soldiers, he guessed. They had worked together, and in silence; and so knew one another. There was no obvious leader. And although he carried the marks of the fight – so did they – they had not used their swords. But, close to the house, that didn't mean much.

So what was this, and how could he save himself? His mind had been busy, all the time he was being carried. Since his African venture, some people thought he was rich. But if they had snatched him for ransom, he would have been put on a horse. Instead, he had been brought here, where a murdered man could lie undiscovered for weeks. Murdered by sword, a quick death. Or left to die in the cold of the snow, or the cold of the estuary. Who hated him enough to want either? Who would benefit from his death? Who was rich enough to employ three professionals, and yet so detached that he had no wish to see the dénouement himself?

Or herself. He had displeased a good many women in his time.

Joneta. Would her father do this? A rich baron, whom he hardly knew and had never offended? Hardly. Hamilton had sold him that land. And Joneta had helped take it from Claes which meant, surely, that Claes wasn't her partner in this. His, Simon's, death wouldn't help Claes. The only person who would benefit from Simon's death was Simon's son Henry. Standing there in the cold, he was struck by a pang. Henry. If he died, what would happen to Henry? That useless master-at-arms . . .

His captors had only stopped to catch their breath. He had to do something quickly. Simon dropped to his knees and flung back his head, as if choking. The gag was so tight that he retched. For a moment, air genuinely failed him. Then, roughly, the kerchief was dragged away and the cloth pulled out. He dropped his head, coughing. His nose and eyes streamed, and his skin tightened, freezing and seared. He said hoarsely, 'Who paid you? I will pay you ten times.' He used French. Mercenaries knew French.

The man who had pulled out the gag looked at him, and at the others, and smiled. The gag lay on the snow.

So the language meant something. 'Ten times. More. Send for it,' Simon said.

The man bent and picked up the gag. He had failed. He could shout. Simon inhaled with a shriek and choked as the cloth was rammed in again and the kerchief bound brutally round. He threshed, resisting, and found himself flung back full length in the snow, one man holding his shoulders, the other his feet. A length of rope was bound round his waist. The two men remained where they knelt, their hands holding him still. Then the third man got up and, stepping back, drew his sword with a whine from the scabbard.

Bitterly, in that last moment, Simon wished his father were here. Fat father Jordan, who had found it so easy to adopt a new country, to forget the Scottish estates of his forebears, his brother, his heir. To wring land and title and riches from France, coming home in old age to mock his only son; to revile him; to attempt to brand him a failure.

So now the vicomte de Ribérac would have no son to taunt, and no one to blame but himself. Jordan had left him unprotected in Scotland, to be killed by the men Jordan had offended. For Simon saw it all now. These assassins were sent by Jordan's enemies.

They understood French. They had not been tempted by money – of course not. Jordan's rivals were wealthy. Only the rich opposed Jordan. Their mistake was that they thought, killing Simon, to cause Simon's father a moment of sorrow.

Simon watched the sword coming down.

For a long time now, the road had been uncertain. Until the last fall of snow, the track of horses and carts had shown dark in the torchlight but after Torphichen, their last brief halt, the way had been pristine, and the directions given Bel by the resident agitated Brother of the Knights of St John had not been of the clearest.

The Preceptor of the Order was at Linlithgow Palace, five miles off, with the King. But the Flemish gentleman, M. Nicholas de Fleury, was not of the party, so far as the Hospitaller knew. So far as he knew, M. de Fleury was at home in his lodging at Berecrofts. Berecrofts, to the west of the Avon, and no more than half of an hour-glass away.

At this point the Brother suggested, his manner full of concern, that if the matter could wait till the morning, he was sure that beds could be found in the Preceptory. She supposed she looked mortally tired. She had not time to be tired, or cold, or hungry. She thanked him and, with her small, silent entourage, set out again.

Such was the warmth of Kinneil and the quality of its wines that the King lingered and might well have slept there, but for the loud, rallying voice of the master, enquiring if his grace was ready, for the horses would be taking a chill, not to mention himself?

So they roused, the young men and women, and were handed once more into their mantles and wandered off in groups, chaffing, to relieve themselves, and take a last swallow of wine. Adorne said, 'Where is de Fleury?'

His nephew did not know. It was Andreas the doctor who said, 'Did he come to Kinneil at all? I assumed he had gone home to resume packing at Berecrofts.'

The eyes of Katelijne turned to her uncle. Adorne said, 'I think it unlikely. What of our other friend? Who has seen Simon of Kilmirren?'

'I have,' said someone with a tinge of relish. Julius, once the volatile Charetty lawyer in Bruges, and still fond enough of his hunting to resent having to see to the *Ghost*. Julius said, 'He went off with the girl. Hamilton's by-blow. Joneta. Do you want me to look for them?'

'No,' said Adorne abruptly. He softened it. 'You have to go to

Blackness.' Katelijne, he saw, had slipped off. Julius took his leave. Adorne began to prepare for the resumed hunt, conscious of a sense of foreboding. It was unnecessary, his intelligence told him. The boar, on investigation, did not exist: the hunt would rely as before on the hounds picking up scents. It could not last long. The King would tire, and they would ride back to Linlithgow. When Metteneye came for him, he was ready. He was here representing a Duchy. That came first.

All the same, setting off, the torches streaming behind, he was anxious. The cold now was extreme: his breath sparkled white in the air; the dogs, casting about, seemed to find nothing. Then, by a twisted juniper bush, dark in the snow, they stopped, and milled about snuffling, and then suddenly sprang forward strongly. The horn blew. The blood rose high in his veins and he spurred forward, eager once more.

Joneta, alone, watched them go. She was still there when some steward knocked at the door, enquiring the way to Berecrofts on behalf of his mistress. She did not see him herself, but her door-keeper, reporting, said he seemed to serve a good family, but would not take the time to come in, or name or bring in his party.

She wondered, then, who was visiting Nicholas, but had long learned not to feel jealousy. It was enough that she stood there, and waited.

On the battlefield, one was taught to face death, and learned also a lesson far harder: to keep one's courage when death changed its mind, and blood and flesh, still in life, turned to jelly.

The sword whistled down upon Simon. It slashed through the bonds at his feet. The man with the sword said, in French, 'Rise,' and made a gesture. For a moment, shocked, Simon couldn't move. Then the other two, standing over him, gripped the ends of the rope round his waist and brought him staggering upright. He stood, his arms still pinioned behind him, attached by rope to a man on each side. Then the horses came up.

By now, he did not know what to think, or what to hope for. There were two horses only, brought by a fourth man who remained in the saddle. The man with the sword, sheathing it, mounted the second. Then each took an end of his rope. The remaining two stood back and studied him. He trembled with cold. The newcomer laughed. The man with the sword said briefly, '*Eh bien, monsieur* – run.'

There were cruelties one had heard of, practised in antiquity and since, whereby a man tied to two horses would be made to run until the horses, diverging, tore his body in two.

This was not yet like that. The rope, wound many times round his middle, simply tugged him to right or to left, depending on which rider pulled harder. And the gathering speed of the horses forced him to keep his feet, matching their pace, or else be towed through the snow, scouring through hidden brush, bumping shoulder and thigh against boulders, tumbling down hidden declivities.

He lost footing once, near the beginning, and suffered all that before he forced himself upright again. Then he tried to think of nothing but running, his breath fierce and hot through the gag, his lungs steadily drawing, his body adjusting its balance to the unnatural weight of his arms. Then the horses increased their pace to a canter.

Soon after that, his legs began to become heavy. His chest heaved, no longer under his perfect control. Lack of breath made his head sing; interrupted his concentration. He stumbled then, and was borne along twisting, his heels tossed on the ground, as he tried to regain his balance.

That time, the riders stayed wide apart. The next time it happened, they spurred ahead and together, so that he was brought funnelling after, full length on his face in the snow, and had to roll over and over to save his head and give himself purchase. Then, separating, the horsemen gave him the half-lift he needed, but at the price of a sudden harsh tug which straightened his coils and set him to spin as if drunk.

Throughout it all, they said nothing, and their faces, dim in the snow-light, were quite impassive. He looked at their faces when he could, for he had never in his life felt for anyone the hatred he felt for them, and for whoever was doing this. He began to feel, as his numb body weakened, that the sheer power of his hatred would uphold him, whatever they did; would scorch and shrivel them; would draw righteous cohorts to his aid. When they stopped, and he saw the sky to the north had turned red, he thought the Lord had come to his aid. A Judgement was being pronounced. The Lord's Judgement upon those assailing him. He lay in the snow, and did not realise at once that the coils of rope lay about him.

The men who had dropped them sat motionless, watching him. Then the swordsman stirred. He said, in French, 'So we leave. You make a fine rabbit.' They both smiled. And then, turning, they rode swiftly off.

He lay like lead in the snow. He did not have to move. The relief began to send him to sleep. The relief, and the quiet. The sound of hooves deadened and vanished. Behind, in another direction, dogs barked remotely. Ahead, the dim red sky flickered and there were sounds. What sounds they were, he couldn't be troubled to think. Then it came to him that he was succumbing to the very fate he had dreaded at the beginning. He had been brought here to die in the cold. Only they had exhausted him first.

So he would beat them. His legs were free. They had bound his mouth and his arms, but had forgotten to retie his legs. He could walk. He could find help if he knew where to go. Slowly, he forced himself up to his knees, his feet, and stood swaying. Below the red sky, the landscape lay like rose-coloured icing. It was empty. He could try to go back, there where now he could hear the same dogs barking clearly. Or he could walk towards the red sky, and over the shallow rise lying before him, for he knew now what he would find.

The salt-pans must be here. He had never seen them, but he had heard how the brine was brought from the estuary and cooked until reduced to dry salt. They said the fires never went out. He did not imagine there would be people: not here, at midnight in January. But the fires would be there, or their embers. Warmth, and shelter till morning. And then they would see, all of them. Then, if it took the rest of his life, he would find whoever had done this. He began to walk.

He had almost come to the rise when his laboured attention was distracted, again, by the barking of dogs. There was another sound mingled with it. He identified it. The sound of a horn.

The hunt. The King's hunt – horses, friends, rescue – all coming this way. Directly this way. Where there were no lairs, no trees, no game to be seen, or any tracks in the snow.

Except his own. *You make a fine rabbit*, his captor had said. They had dragged him and left him as you would stake out a goat, having given its scent to the wolves, or the hounds. The King's hounds, trained to kill whatever they chased. They weren't chasing the boar: their tongues would be raucous, excited. There probably wasn't a boar. The boar was probably Joneta's invention.

Joneta, who had, of purpose, retained his cloak.

He began to run, then.

At the same moment, grey with fatigue, Bel of Cuthilgurdy arrived at the purlieus of Berecrofts and demanded to be taken to Nicholas de Fleury.

Berecrofts the Younger, shocked and worried, had her admitted at once, with her companions. Robin, sent running, came back with servants, extra braziers, blankets, wine, and women offering comfort and bed. Bel refused the wine, but stood before the braziers and repeated, gratingly, her demand.

Archie said, 'He went to Linlithgow. The King is there, maybe you know? They've been hunting.'

He was a sturdy, plainspoken man. She liked him, and the child. She said, 'I was told M. de Fleury was here.'

'Perhaps he is on his way,' Archie said. 'I could gather men and send out to meet him. I see it is something important.'

A man came in; a man she knew and distrusted. The burly shipmaster who worked for Nicholas now: Michael Crackbene. He addressed her in his strange mixture of accents in which Scandinavian now prevailed. 'You have a message for M. de Fleury?' He ignored Archie. She realised that Nicholas had separate lodgings in this house, and that they included his staff and his office.

'I maun see him,' she said. 'It is private.'

He said, 'You do not come to see Simon of Kilmirren?'

'No,' she said. 'Why?'

'It is of no consequence,' he replied. 'M. de Fleury is expected. His ship sails in a few hours. When he comes, he will have no time to speak.'

'I willna keep him,' said Bel. 'But speak with him I must. Are ye sending to look?'

The man hesitated. Archie said, 'Yes, we're sending. Robin's gone to get lanterns and men. Your own two fellows are willing. We'll make sure he gets here.'

'I'll come with you,' said Bel. 'Since time is short, and it's late.'

The King followed the hounds, fuelled on an elixir of frost and wine and excitement. What they followed, no one knew: the dogs themselves scattered the slots. It hardly mattered. Above were the stars; below the rare glistening white of the snow. And about him were his friends.

Nicholas de Fleury was not there, nor Simon de St Pol – nor, presently, Anselm Adorne who, slipping away, had left to Metteneye the guest-mantle of Burgundy.

Simon was very tired, and the pans were not as near as he thought. The first sign was the vanishing of the snow – the deadly, kindly, cushioning snow. Slowly, the ground became black. When he fell, he fell upon rock, thorn, unamenable gravel. When he struggled to the height of the rise, it was blackness he saw spread before him, lit by tongues of sullen flame, glowing smoke, smouldering circles.

A naked man hatted with straw appeared in the distance, gazed, and moved on through the roseate dark as if blind. A spectral child followed, round of stomach, its hair on its shoulders. It looked at him, and continued to walk. Banners of vapour floated above sombre lattices made not of wicker, but fire. Beyond, he seemed to see a black meadow peopled by wraiths, men, women and children, stooping or upright, linked by yokes, holding tenuous shafts in their hands. Some were black; some red as blood, face, torso and limbs; some streaked, or white as himself. The red light glimmered through nets without fish and spotted the dark: red eyes glaring through silent black eyelets.

He did not want to go on. He slowed. He stopped. Now he drew a quick breath and turned.

A great hound, caught in silent mid-leap, was rising towards him. The shock, the close, warm odour paralysed him for a moment. Then Simon turned and hurtled down, towards Hell, for Hell could not be worse than a mastiff about to tear out his throat. The hound, with a snarl, followed after.

And now he was in the inferno, where heat and cold fought in the air, and his throat was choked with the stench of blood and sulphur. He raced, fell and raced, tricked by shadows, tripped by some strange arsenal of iron weapons, beset by fire-dust falling like stars, which sizzled into his hair and soaked doublet and pierced his chilled skin like gnats.

The hound followed, as if bewitched. Simon stumbled through a maze of undefined shapes, red and black, sloping and vertical, trying this way and that to escape, and saw three naked men standing watching him in a river of heat. His mouth was stopped, his arms lashed, his dress soaked and torn. He ran to their feet, and as soon as he did so they faded into the darkness behind them. And the hound followed him, and not them.

Behind the gag, his breath sobbed with exhaustion so that he did not even hear, until it was close, the uproar of the rest of the pack, and the horn, and the cracking of whips as men tried to control the King's hounds. The King's hounds, trained to kill, and set upon him by someone, through the bitter agency of his mistress Joneta.

Hatred saved him. He knew that justice would not. Only great power could have brought this about. Power and money; the capacity to bribe and to frighten. Someone of consequence had willed him to die, and he would not.

He turned. He forced himself to think. The hound was there, and the fading spiritous forms, but he was not in Hell; he was among the pan-houses of a salt-garden, and although their doors were shut and their denizens hostile, he would find shelter somehow. There, where a door was just closing. Where, if he used the last of his strength, he could hurl himself through, sending the timber shuddering back, even as the hound closed its teeth on his elbow and the heat struck him as fiercely.

For a moment he thought he had failed; had merely brought the beast into the furnace. He kicked, ramming the brute with his shoulder, and knew, although he hardly felt it, that its jaws had clenched deep in his flesh.

Then they opened. The wet, muscular body lifted. He heard a short whistle, of a special kind he had heard before, and the hound, releasing him entirely, swung its massive neck and stood, looking outwards. Then it bounded off.

He lay, gathering strength. The door, drifting back, came to rest by his leg. He moved his foot, and it continued to close. On the outside was painted the usual mark, bird or beast, which distinguished the salt-house of each master. This time the picture held three creatures: a stag and two ratchets.

The crest of St Pol.

He looked up. The only other man present, lightly dressed, leaned against the door till it shut, and then locked it.

'And so, Simon?' said Nicholas de Fleury.

Chapter 10

A SALT-HOUSE IS AS close to Hades as ignorant man could well devise; made of plastered wattle and shingle, it is divided into three rooms, of which the first is the fuel-store and the last an outlet for smoke and for drying.

In the centre room is the source of the heat: a floor furnace eight feet long and eight wide shaped of rock-salt and clay, and bearing above it on three immense hooks a lead rectangle full of brine from the estuary. In the lead receptacle, called the cauldron, the brine boils until it is reduced to white salt, which is then shovelled into cone baskets and cooled. In the same middle room is a bench, the blood-tub and the reserve tub of brine. It is hot enough to make the heart pound.

Simon de St Pol lay, his frayed clothes steaming, within a yard of the furnace in the middle room. He lay on his face, to which position he had been tossed, and felt the vibration, but nothing else, as his deadened arms were set free. Then the knot of his mouth-band was cut, and his dry tongue expelled the cloth and then sought to form words. He tried to roll on his back, placing his weight on one elbow, and was shocked into gasping with the pain of the savaging; with the pain of restored feeling in his body and limbs. But the measure of his anguish was as nothing to the measure of his amazed disbelief.

He blurted something incoherent out of that first emotion, and stopped. From it, he found the strength to thrust himself round and sit back on his heels. Anger rose and rose. He managed, finally, to repeat it with clarity as well as contempt. 'Who are you working for?'

'*Who am I working for?*' the other man repeated. Then he sighed. He had chosen to dispose himself along the powdery bench, his smeared hands round one uplifted knee. The fire, dully red, whispered and murmured in its kingly bed, and the broth of salt popped and puttered above it.

Simon said, 'Who? Whoever it is, he set the King's dogs on me. Or Joneta did. You arranged it.'

'You set your dog on me once,' said the man on the bench dreamily. He spoke as the thugs had, in native French. The tongue of Simon's first wife.

Simon frowned.

'And had me captured, beaten and bound by hands quite as ungentle, I fear. You've forgotten that, too.'

Venice. Now he remembered. And the dogs in Bruges. That had been over Mabelie. His fury rose again. 'You forced Joneta –'

'After what you did to her? She needed no forcing. Have you been roughly handled? Once, you stabbed me.'

'That!' That had been long ago. 'That was an accident.'

'So was the mastiff just now. Have you noticed the heat? Once, you set my house on fire. My house and Marian's.'

'I didn't,' said Simon shortly. 'Now I wish I had. What is this? A boy's list of grudges?' He stared at the other man, and slowly, outrage was added to anger. He said, 'There is no one behind this but you! My God, *you* perpetrated all this!'

'I am easily piqued,' Nicholas de Fleury observed. 'May I continue?'

'No!' Simon said. Now he knew, it was easy. And he was rested. Aching, but rested. He got to his feet.

'Sit down,' the other man said. Between his hands, conjured from air, was a hatchet. He added gently, 'I don't mind using this.'

'Against an unarmed man?' Simon said. He sat down again, temporarily, on the floor, which was sticky and yielding and left smears on his hose, now half dry. He had his eye on a shovel.

The mild voice replied, 'You fought an unarmed man, near enough, when you fought me, and Gregorio.'

'I wouldn't quarrel with that,' Simon said. 'So what else have I done?' He was listening for sounds. The hunt had been coming this way. Now he was safe from the dogs, they could get him out of the grip of this lunatic. He thought, now, he could hear them.

'Let me think,' said his captor. 'Apart from claiming my ship, and attempting to steal the patrimony of your nephew Diniz? What about a sin of omission? The cartel you sent me in Venice, offering to fight me for my life and my business? Then you ran away.'

Simon said irritably, 'Of course, the cat runs from the mouse. You would have found me in Madeira. You did find me in Bruges and in Edinburgh. You withdrew your case. Changed your name to de Fleury.'

'So I did,' the other man said. 'But then, I didn't know all the facts. I didn't know that you and my future wife were currently lovers. I do apologise,' the unhurried voice added. 'A boy's list of grudges.'

He knew.

'You owed me a girl,' Simon said. He said it to cover the depth of his surprise; the breathlessness of a slow and stunning delight. *De Fleury knew.* All these months, he had known about Gelis. *This* was why he had come to Scotland; had tricked him and trapped him and, hiring four bullies, was now bent on some puerile accounting.

Everything was explained. At once Simon was relieved of the unreasonable fear he had felt out there under the sky, among ghostly watchers. Tonight he was in the hands of an aggrieved amateur, not a soldier; not the deadly and furious magnates whom he imagined de Ribérac had angered. His situation was perilous, but retrievable. And rendering it almost sweet was the knowledge that the other man had learned what he had done to Gelis van Borselen, and she with him, and would never cease to imagine it.

He, Simon, had effected a masterstroke of the bedchamber worth all the sneers of a Jordan de Ribérac. A stroke which repaid, in one blow, all the pin-pricks he had suffered from Claes; all the fury his very existence had caused him. Which almost surpassed, in its life-long implications, the bludgeon-blow attempted this evening. For which, in due course, he, Simon, would extract life itself for payment.

Simon smiled; and the other man, seeing the smile, said slowly, 'Yes, of course. It had to be true.' Then, hearing something, he lifted his head.

Simon's lips parted. Clear through the walls came the barking of the mastiffs at last, swarming into the settlement, and the blare of the horn close at hand, and the cries of the hunt-servants, and the cracking of whips. Freedom. The King's party, and freedom. He made to move.

Stupidly, he had been slow. His assailant – the cuckold, his attacker – was soundlessly on his knees beside him, the axe at his throat. De Fleury said, 'I should prefer you not to call them.' Simon reared, and the blade bit his neck. He lay still. It didn't matter. Life and purpose had returned to his body. He was an expert. There would be other chances.

They stayed, without moving. They heard voices raised in

enquiry, and other voices, answering. They heard the thud of bodies as the hounds belaboured the walls and the doors. Simon lay, his clothes, once sodden with snow, now again soaked with his own perspiration, and watched sweat streak the other man's cheekbones from the darkened screws of his heavy, waterlogged hair; slide from his brows and his lashes down the thin channel of Jordan's incision.

His hand on the axe-shaft was wet, but when Simon stirred, it tightened instantly. 'No,' said the man he had cuckolded.

Then, suddenly, the sounds began to grow fainter. Simon heard laughter. He heard a man's voice distantly raised in a chant, and others joining, slurred with wine, and overlaid with diminished barking. He heard the nasal twang of a jew's trump.

Above him, the other man's breathing checked. An instant's distraction was all Simon needed. He flung himself to one side, and then whined with pain as his captor swung his axe high and brought down the flat of its blade on the stob of his gnawed, bloodied elbow. The weapon returned to its place at his throat, where it stayed until all sound had vanished, upon which the other man rose and stepped back. Throughout, he had never appeared less than calm.

Simon said, 'What are you going to do?' He sat, holding the weight of his forearm. His injury throbbed.

'Shed blood,' said his captor. He was tall, with a long reach and broad shoulders, but carried too little flesh, as might a man fighting a long campaign or recently ill. Something inconvenient strayed into Simon's mind. The other man, hooking the axe at his side, lifted a scoop by its ear and lowered it into a bucket.

He said, 'I promised the salt-master I'd look after the cauldron. You know that salt has to have blood? It has to be male blood: bull or buck or calf. Or human, of course. You add it thus to the brine, and it clarifies it. See.' And he lifted the scoop.

He seemed to be absorbed. At his waist, the axe glinted. For an instant, Simon was ready to lunge; and then the smallest swing of the dipper warned him what was going to happen. He rolled back and the dipper, correcting itself, swung back and over the cauldron, into which it delivered its cargo of gore.

Deliberately, the brine had been permitted to boil. Instead of seething, turgid and brown, the blood leaped on the surface in vivid splashes and gouts, and inflated into thin blemished spheres which burst in fine crimson spray on the walls and dripped from the roof and filled the foetid air of the salt-house with the iron-sharp odour which, rank and stale with age, rose from the compact dirt he had been sitting in. Simon, fast though he moved, found himself – arms, shirt, doublet – filmed with blood, and felt it slide through the sweat on his face.

The other man, streaked with gore, had hardly troubled to avoid it. He plied a long-handled paddle, still smiling; and then, taking a rake, revived the flames in the furnace below. His eyes in the flare were large and wet-lashed and ruddy. Simon looked at him, and felt a doubt, and dismissed it.

The other man said, 'I shall need to add coal soon. You can help me.'

'Coal?' Simon said. He moved back, inoffensively, and sat down.

'Small coal. Dross. It comes from the mines near Kinneil. It gives more heat than wood or straw for less bulk, so the salt is quicker to form. You saw the mark on the door? Hamilton, of course, holds Kinneil and Carriden under the abbot, but he has agreed to let me develop it. Salt and sugar and alum have a good deal in common. I have access to a brilliant engineer, and some experience from the flatlands elsewhere. It all comes down to hydraulics and drainage.'

'You don't need to tell me about coal,' Simon said. He spoke as if amused, but in fact was astonished and angry. Hamilton should have mentioned this.

'You mean your new Hamilton land in the west? But your Hamilton land has no coal,' his captor said. 'You thought it had, because I wanted to buy it.'

There was a silence. Simon said, 'That won't wear. I saw the reports.' Then he remembered who brought him the reports.

'Quite so,' said the man he had cuckolded. 'But that was Joneta's doing, for me. Her father sold you the land in good faith. As you remember, he himself made no claims for it. But it's worthless, of course. Stone. You might get some gorse for your Kilmirren herd. If you manage to keep your Kilmirren herd.'

Simon looked at him.

The other man met the look. He said, 'Did you think that was all? Did you think that all I would do is bribe your armourer and make you look foolish? Sleep with your mistress? Compel you to run in the snow, and hurt you a little? Do you really think that I, *I* of all people could not find just the way, just the fitting, flawless, appropriate way for Simon de St Pol to pay his debts to me?'

'My armourer . . . You're mad,' Simon said. He believed it.

'Beginning with your name. You saw the crest on the door.'

'It is not your name,' Simon said. He felt himself whiten.

'Need we go into all that again?' For the first time the other man rose and walked off and turned without cause. He said, 'Your wife was my mother, and she named me as your child. I believe her. I know you were fifteen and forced to marry. I know she was nearly twice your age. Still, I cannot excuse you for denouncing her, or me. If I choose, I will use the name of St Pol as well as de Fleury. How will you enjoy hearing me call you Father? I could do it, *Father*.'

And this was insupportable. Simon said, 'You will not.'

The other man said, 'How will you stop me?'

Simon showed his teeth. 'By force.'

'But I have the ascendancy,' his captor said. 'And the axe.'

'You would kill your father?' said Simon. He spoke with derision.

'You invited your daughter-in-law to your bed.'

It was time to stop this. Simon said, 'That's enough. You are not of my blood, or my father's. As for Gelis van Borselen, keep her if you are able. She is too lusty for me. My God, I barely escaped with my manhood. She has a habit . . .'

He waited.

'Yes?' said de Fleury.

'Shall I tell you?' said Simon.

'If you want to. I thought I knew all her habits,' said the other man.

Already perplexed, Simon found himself outraged. 'One would think —'

'I didn't care? Of course I don't. But I dislike trespassers. I have returned the courtesy, by the way, so far as flesh will allow. Your taste and mine sometimes differ. Ada, for example. I felt the love of a working mother would be better savoured by Crackbene.' There reappeared the punctual insult of the dimples. The man was still calm. He stood there, exuding an unnatural calm.

Simon said, 'I may, then, announce your wife's coming child to be mine?'

'Of course,' said the other. 'And I shall say, hand on heart, that so long as it is healthy, I should welcome any sister or brother born of my wife.'

Put into words it was loathsome. Only a sick man would think of it. 'No one would believe you,' said Simon.

'But they would repeat the story,' the other man said. 'And unless I let you, you couldn't really deny it. Because I hold the ultimate card. The denunciation of Henry.'

The words fell into silence. Simon heard them, his thoughts in disorder. Henry's guilt. The danger he had remembered and tried to thrust out of mind: the murderous stabbing of young Mar's preserver to which so many could attest – Adorne and his niece, Julius, Roger. The stabbing which de Fleury had not reported, Simon now saw, for this very reason. To hold against this moment the weapon, sharper than steel, which Henry – his heir, his jewel, his joy – had placed in the hand of his enemy.

Simon drew all his forces together, and spoke. 'I gather he was competent? If not quite competent enough?'

The other man's face showed no emotion. 'Competent enough to ensure that, if Gelis survives, her child will pass for mine and not yours. If, sadly, neither survives, I have other propositions to put to the family.'

The words shrank and boiled like chips of ice in the heat. Simon tried to retrieve them. 'If neither survives?'

'I am going to Bruges,' the other man said. 'And coming back. Whatever it is, I shall convey my family news to you, or your father.'

The chill this time was unmistakable. Simon said, '*That* is why you are going back?'

He stared at Nicholas de Fleury who he now saw and had to accept was not the Claes he had known and despised. Who had come to Scotland on a cool, well-designed mission of vengeance which was not new, but had found many targets over the years, as he now recognised, although its full malevolence had never, until now, been turned against Simon himself.

Except, of course, through the killing of Katelina, his wife. No one had ever proved that Nicholas caused the death of Katelina in Cyprus, but here was evidence at least that he was capable of it. Capable of killing Simon's second wife, and now his own; now Gelis van Borselen, who had spoiled the pure line of the House he was carefully creating.

Therefore Simon would meet hatred with guile. He would remove Henry from Scotland, so that no accusations could harm him. And then, or before then, he would exterminate Nicholas. Or he could be in thrall to a monster for life.

He broke the silence innocuously. 'You mean to come back to Scotland from Bruges?'

'To fill your place,' the other man said. 'You are planning to take Henry away? And go yourself? It might be wise; I may not be a comfortable neighbour. You know I hold the land next to Kilmirren?'

In the pan, the bubbling had died. Now, choking the liquid, beds of orange-brown salt were appearing, stained by the blood and the scum which no one had troubled to skim. Where it touched the hot lead of the pan, it lay, hissing.

Simon forgot both Katelina and Gelis. He said, 'There is no vacant land there.'

'There is Kilmirren itself, which Jordan owns, and you manage. There is also the land Kilmirren held under the bailery. Until your superior tired – didn't you know? – of your mismanagement. Now it is out of your hands, and I have it.'

'Sir Robert has let you . . .?'

It was impossible. The old man was wandering. His superior was the titular head of his family. Once, their combined ancestors had owned all the land they now shared. Then, as junior branch, Simon's forebears had settled and built their own dynasty in Kilmirren. Henry's pure line. Henry's heritage.

'Sir Robert of Elliotstoun has installed me. Or his son in his name, to be accurate. Don't you believe me? Semple, they call themselves now, not St Pol. Should I do the same? You noticed the sign on the door.'

Simon said, 'And this is all against me? You're mad. You have no interest in Scotland.'

'You don't think so?' said the other man. 'The King will buy – don't you think he will feel compelled to buy? – some of the rather fine objects he saw today, and perhaps favour me in other ways. He did cause damage, and I have been amazingly humble. And my ship also brought people. Singers, carvers, masons and painters. A master melter and jesters. A glassing-wright and a goldsmith.

'Forgive me, but I could dispose of you alone rather more cheaply. I suppose' – he paused – 'I simply prefer to work on a broad canvas. And, of course, there is Jordan.'

'This is devilment for its own sake,' Simon said.

'Perhaps,' his captor said. 'But it is not careless devilment. You may at least know, as you suffer, that I mean it.' And he rose to his feet.

There was no point, now, in asking what he was going to do. The door was locked. The other man had the key, and an axe, and would be ruthless. His eyes spoke for him.

Simon watched him, and thought. He would have to fight – he had always known that. But fight this time while keeping his temper, and goading the other man into losing his. Where was de Fleury weak?

Simon said, 'So, for whom are you amassing this power? You won't get another wife now. Who would marry you? Didn't you kill Marian de Charetty as well?'

'You're going to itemise my wives?' the other man said. 'Let me do it for you. My first wife brought me the Charetty company, but I didn't kill her. My second I gave away to Zacco of Cyprus, who is not renowned for keeping his mistresses, and indeed, I am told she is dead. My third you know about. Do you want to talk about Joneta?'

'If you like. Or about Gelis and David de Salmeton. You do know about that? He was much less discreet than I was, but I think the poor girl was starved for companionship. Except for one purpose, you don't care for young women, do you?' He said it, thinking aloud: even thinking about something and someone else. He hardly saw the small reaction, but it was there. Simon held his breath, his mind racing. Then he said, 'My father was right about Diniz. I suppose you realise that?'

'Better,' the other man said. His tone was approving. Instead of coming nearer he stooped and, lifting the rake, stepped up and began to draw it through the mixed liquid and cake of the cauldron. The salt began to pile up at the sides. He said, 'Yes, better. I could become annoyed about that. Your fat father Jordan branded Diniz his grandson a sodomite. With whom, I can't quite remember. With me? With David de Salmeton? Not with me. And as you were saying, David de Salmeton has orthodox tastes, if unwise ones.'

'But so do you,' Simon said. 'Some men enjoy mixing their pleasures, and find marriage convenient. Diniz has a wife and a child on the way, so there has been no open scandal. Until now, that is.'

The rake continued to pass up and down slowly. 'Well, go on,' the other man said.

'Letters came to the Castle from Bruges,' Simon said. 'From Tommaso Portinari to the King's brother of Albany. They mentioned Diniz and the Charetty company. And Gregorio, your lawyer in Bruges. You know his mistress Margot has left him?'

The rake moved without cease. 'So I believe,' its handler said.

Simon showed his surprise. 'A courier here? Ah, no. I see. The *Ghost* brought you a letter. So you have heard the news, too, about Diniz?'

The other man stood the rake upright and leaned on it. 'I should like you to tell me,' he said.

Simon said, 'About Diniz's lovers. There is no doubt at all that he has them. Men and boys. Mostly men, from the artisan class. He is a good-looking fellow, my nephew.'

'Go on,' the other man said. He threw the rake down and lifting a basket, wedged it into the grid over the salt. Then he stepped down and brought up the shovel. It was, discommodingly, the one on which Simon's eye had been fixed. Gripping it, de Fleury continued. 'So how did it become known? They all sang the news in the streets?'

'A letter,' said Simon quickly. 'A love letter. His wife found it, and almost miscarried.'

'An artisan who could write?' his captor said.

'A scholar,' said Simon.

'From Bruges. Someone living in the same town who still felt impelled to risk a love letter?'

'From outside Bruges. From his travels. He brought the letter back with him. From his travels in Africa. All those long days and nights of great heat. You know how it was, you and Gelis. She told me. I can imagine it. The soaked mattress and pillows, the sweating skin, the suffocation, the ecstasy. She told me. Diniz was desperate, too – didn't you notice? But he found relief where you'd least expect it. In whose arms? Can you guess?'

'You are going to tell me,' said the man he had cuckolded. He stood peaceably on the bench, without breathing.

'It was Umar. Umar your well-endowed negro,' Simon said. 'A magnificent fellow, as you know, and sensitive to other men's wants.'

'*Thank you,*' the other man said.

It emerged distorted for, as he spoke, he had the shovel already upraised. Before Simon could get out of the way, the full spadeful of scalding salt hit him in the face where he sat. The pain made him grunt and the shock sent him lurching aside, but his wits didn't leave him. Sprawling, he touched the rake, seized it, and was on his knees presenting it before the second steaming, winking block came flying towards him. It struck his neck and shoulder and tumbled and clung, a burning avalanche, a blistering poultice.

His searing anger hurt more. The young brute had the axe, and the key. But the axe was not a sword: it was short in haft and only deadly when close. Simon surged to his feet and drove the rake with both hands towards the other man's face. For a moment, it seemed he would reach it. Then his adversary saved himself abruptly, swerving sideways and back.

The fellow hadn't looked round. Being more cunning than once he was, he had committed to memory all the elements of their miniature, smoking arena; the greatest part of it taken up with the hooded bed of hot salt with its latticework of thick beams and hooks. To its right, on the deep, yielding floor of solidified scum, stood the round bath of warm brine and the tub and dipper of blood, occupying most of the space between cauldron and wall.

To its left was the bench his captor had chosen as seat and later as step to the cauldron. The basket he had prepared remained tossed on its side on the grid while the others hung still from the roof, gently jostling in the updraught of the duel.

On that wall, the left, were the pegs for the implements. Some still hung there: a pair of ladles, a scoop, a mallet, some bowls, a set of tongs. On the floor below them lay a hoe, and the corner between fire-hood and wall was stacked with forked sticks for porterage and spare hooked bars to join lattice to cauldron. In the front, between the firebox and the locked door lay a poker, and the bar to open the firedoor.

These were, all of them, the arms for this contest. As much as a trial of strength, this was an exercise in improvisation, in strategy. Simon laughed with battle excitement. I have this rake; and you have an axe. What comes next? Of course: something long-shafted. The hoe. His opponent needed the hoe.

Bending at the end of his swerve, the other man almost had it when Simon clawed it away with his rake. Then Simon swore. It had been a feint. The rake was what his opponent wanted and got, wrenching it free and hurling it hard out of reach, while Simon himself was sent crashing on to the ground. Then, before he could rise, he was flattened under the full impact of the other man's weight, as his adversary flung himself down.

For an instant, Simon experienced the power of heavy young muscle; heavier than his own, and more violent. For an instant, for the first time in their lives, the two were implexed flesh to flesh; stamped together body to wet, heated body. Then, like a brand-iron lifting, the younger man abruptly started away.

It was what Simon needed. The weight gone, he could breathe. He used his experience, twisting and kicking. And although de Fleury counter-attacked as one who had remembered quite distinctly what he was doing and why, the lapse had given Simon his chance; he fought himself free, disregarding blisters, bruises, the agony in his elbow. The glint of the other man's axe caught his eye and as he scrambled up, he snatched at it.

He barely touched it, but it was enough to divert its owner's gaze for an instant. Then Simon had the firebox bar concealed in his hand, and locked in the door of the furnace so that, when he sprang back and the other man followed him, the iron door, red with heat, caught his antagonist's shin and the fire leaped out, brilliant in the dim light. Simon's captor stumbled and swerved, his hair brushing the cones, and a mesh of shadows swayed over the ground as the single torch streamed. By then, Simon was where he wanted to be, with his back to the wall where the tools hung. He snatched down the shears and held them before him.

'Again!' the other man said. Since that bitter *Thank you* he had not spoken. Nine years ago they had fought, and Claes had survived because of Marian de Charetty. But Marian de Charetty was dead.

So what now would he do? Step back, it seemed, to recover. Step back, always watching, feeling his way past the tubs. Simon followed, then stopped. It was too crude an invitation altogether. Claes might, but Nicholas de Fleury wouldn't back himself into a trap. Now he was against the far wall.

The other man said, 'You were right not to come,' and pressed the wall with one shoulder. It gave. A broad door had been made in what now appeared to be only a partition between this and a third and last room in the pan-house. Inside the third room it was dark, but he could glimpse another bench, and a pile of pale cones and rectangular tablets, bedded on straw. The room was filled with pale smoke, and at the far end Simon perceived two small windows, very high, through which fresh snow was blowing. A drying chamber, and a vent from the furnace. The windows were too small to squeeze through.

If he had dashed forward, he would have been pushed through and cut down. For there, of course, must be hidden the sword and dagger de Fleury had worn in the Great Hall at Linlithgow.

He could still prevent him from lifting them. Clearing the tubs, Simon landed in front of the door, shears in one hand, iron bar in the other. The axe glittered in the other man's grasp and for a moment his one weapon parried Simon's two in a blaze of blue light. Then, still fighting, Simon's foe slammed the door shut behind him and stretched up a hand.

There was no sword in his grasp, nor a dagger. Instead, he held a faggot of straw: held it pressed to the single poor tallow candle until it burst into flame. Simon backed. The young man laughed, his face bright as a lamp. Then lifting himself to the edge of the tub, he reached up and touched the first hanging basket.

Light bloomed. Simon jumped forward, and the axe glittered, and the fire flamed in his face. Then the Fleming touched off the second, the third. The straw, brittle and old, dashed into fire, flashing and crackling and hazing the air with sparks and needles of flame. The cords above glowed. The pan-room, once sombre, became a blaze of carnival lamps, whirling and dancing; the salt hissed, naked and dry in the pan; the blood-glazed floor shifted and glittered.

The pan was iron, the furnace salt and clay, the walls and ceiling luted and safe. Only the tubs were vulnerable to fire, and the wooden shovels and scoops, and themselves. Simon tracked his tormentor between the swaying cornucopias of flame, the heat approaching and leaving his face, his hair hissing and smouldering as he ducked and stooped. The other man was moving as quickly, retreating. After the last basket, he tossed the burned-out faggot aside. Then the baskets started to fall, and lay flaring. The heat was beyond belief.

It had to be ended. And now Simon knew how to do it. He said, 'So you *were* Diniz's lover. I didn't know the negro had you as well.'

Upon which, with unforeseen accuracy, the other man hurled the axe at Simon's head.

Chapter 11

THE BLOW SHOULD have killed. At first, in the jumble of light, the perpetrator clearly assumed that it had. He stood motionless, his eyes wide, and then stumbled aside, his hand seeking the wall.

By that single, rash act, he had disarmed himself. And Simon, because of a single opportune movement, was alive. More, behind him, sunk in the wall, was the axe.

His chance had come, and would never be better. He exchanged the shears for the axe. The crackle of burning straw and the fizz of salt masked his steps; the chiaroscuro of light disguised the speed of his rush. He was upon his would-be killer, hatchet lifted, even as the other man turned, his eyes open again, his actor's face split, too, into shards of darkness and light: agony, disbelief, wonder.

Its last expression was one of profound purpose. The movement with which he struck up Simon's fist round the haft was so hard that the blade, losing power, barely sank to de Fleury's own half-naked shoulder where for a moment it fitted into the scar of another wound. Then de Fleury used all his advantage of strength to drag himself apart and to kick, the way men kick when fighting for life on a battlefield, before bending to scoop up something at his feet.

A double-hooked bar, lying half under the fireball of straw which had felled it. It came towards Simon, clawing, its bent iron smoking and red, and Simon struck at it with the cold iron he, too, still held in one hand, and then swung the axe as his opponent backed, fencing. Behind him was the wall hung with tools, but the axe would get to him first. Then the axe itself glared a warning and Simon, alerted, had time to spring to one side as a dazzle of fire hurtled down and a basket, burning free, burst into a fireball of flame at his feet. By which time Nicholas de Fleury was again armed.

Now, no one spoke. In the struggle that followed Simon used most of the objects in the room, and had them used against him. The two men fell, sometimes, into the kind of close-gripped combat Simon preferred to avoid, but he held his own, although he received no more inconsequential advantages.

It worried Simon that, holding an axe, he could not immediately prevail. But then, as he had, de Fleury used long-shafted weapons against him. They both bore bleeding gashes and livid burns on their half-naked bodies and sometimes he remembered that he, the elder by fifteen years, had run a long way that evening. And the truth was that the other man was more of a match than he would ever have thought to be possible. Then his mind began to turn on the key.

He intended to win, and would win. But he was facing a man of strong passions; a man who had already tried to kill him tonight. He did not mean to die at his hand.

It was then, just over half an hour before midnight, as the fires were dying and the glow from the furnace burned low, that he began to plan his last strategy. Soon even the candle would be spent. Already the walls and floor were in darkness as they stalked one another, breathing quickly; attacked and dodged in the red light from the king-bed of salt and the dull, crimson hood at its end, its rim flushed, arch as a bonnet, from the glow of the strip of live, burning coals underneath. For the grid covered all of the salt, but not all of the fire.

Perhaps the other man, too, realised that his strength was not inexhaustible. It was easier to believe than that he had been waiting, measuring time, judging the moment when Simon would flag. Simon felt the change in his movements: an alteration in pace; a steadier rhythm of breathing. He knew that it was time, and he had to act now.

He did, first, what his opponent had done, and threw the axe. He made it appear a mistake, so that instead of striking to kill, it flew towards the glowing cross-timbers of the pan and slid between them, its blade in the salt. It shone, satin-red.

And de Fleury, as he hoped, went after it. They met at the bench-step in collision, the side-plates of the pan searing their ankles and calves. Simon by then already had his grip on the other. He levered and threw. The man crashed on his side on the poles over the salt-pan, arms and legs thrusting. Their purpose was not to save himself, Simon found, but to bring Simon with him.

Wrestling was leverage. And this Fleming was an expert in leverage. So instead of one, both men struggled there, the red-hot pan full of salt just below them, the hook-heads searing into their bodies, their ripped shirts and hose darkening in the heat, the air burning its way to their lungs. And this time, neither would give way.

The handle of the axe was scorched and smoking. The Fleming reached it first and had grasped it when Simon stopped him, his hands round his waist, and began to draw him away. Perspiration poured down his body and face and turned to steam underneath him: only the leather of the other man's belt gave him the purchase he needed. Then, within the thickness of the belt, he felt something hard under his fingers. The key.

If he sought for it, he released his opponent to draw out the axe. He hesitated. The other man spoke: it emerged between a gasp and a cry. Somewhere else, the impasse would have merited laughter. The pain increased and Simon wanted to move, but wouldn't. The other man spoke again. He demanded a rebuttal to do with someone called Umar. He held the axe-handle still, his hand blistering.

Simon remembered that Umar was Loppe. He said, 'I don't need to give promises to a corpse. I'll tell the world about Loppe when you're dead.'

His attention must have lapsed from the pain. The other man ripped his belt free. Taking proper grip of the axe, the other man swept it out of the salt and held it, radiant, above Simon's head. Then Nicholas de Fleury brought it down, twice.

It burned through the air, as the sword had. As before, it didn't touch Simon. Instead, it sliced through the two timbers upon which the end of the salt-pan was carried. De Fleury cut them both short of the traverse beam below which they passed, and then himself gripped the traverse beam hard. Behind him, under the hood, the shortened beams dropped, carrying the pan-supports with them. And the end of the pan, supported on nothing, dropped with a crash into the coals. Something bright followed: the blade of the axe, its handle charred through and snapped with the impact.

De Fleury ignored it. He clung to the beam, his head down, his body sloping, his feet almost touching the flames. Simon, grasping nothing, began to roll down the slope to the trough and caught at his adversary. For a moment he half dragged him loose, and then redoubled his grasp as the other resisted. The blood drummed in Simon's ears. Neither spoke.

He heard another noise, separate from them both. He saw his captor open his eyes and knew he had heard it as well. Outside, someone beat on the door. Someone shouted. His throat parched and burning, Simon made to answer and stopped. He saw de Fleury lower his head. He was frowning.

Anselm Adorne's voice said, 'Nicholas. Open the door.'

This time, the other man didn't move. It was Simon who pushed, grimly levering himself up the grid, and then preparing for the sudden fast turn that would end it. The other man let him get within six inches of the belt before he seized his wrist and wrung it. Simon swore and flung himself back, so that he almost broke the man's remaining one-handed grip and saw him fight to retain it. Adorne's voice said, 'Simon?' and this time, it seemed best to answer.

'He has the key,' Simon said. It was an excuse, not a complaint. It was far from being a complaint. He did not, at this moment, want Anselm Adorne. He wanted time in which to kill the brute he was fighting. Otherwise he would be hostage to this man for life.

He heard Adorne say, 'Nicholas, stop. One of you, open the door. You cannot go on, now I am here.' His voice, without emotion, proclaimed a truth. The other man was a burgess of Bruges; Simon a Scot of reputation. It further proclaimed that he knew, or guessed, what was happening.

Nicholas de Fleury opened his hand. Simon, released, heaved himself painfully to the edge of the grid and let himself crash down in the red gloom to the bench, where he crouched. De Fleury had lifted a hand to his belt.

Simon said, 'Give me the key.' The smoke from the disturbed coals made him cough. He didn't want the key. He wanted a moment's respite, and then a throwing hold on the other man's arm.

You could see he, too, was tired. He dragged himself up and, freeing raw fingers, tunnelled down and drew out the key. It lay in the palm of his hand, and he looked at it. Then he tossed it into the heart of the fire.

'Does that suit you?' he said; and came, a dark figure, heeling over the edge as Simon had done, to collide with him on the bench and then, grimly, drag him again to the floor.

It was Simon's intention that only one of them would survive. He had made it clear enough; he knew the other recognised as much, as they locked limbs and wrestled, cheek to cheek and arm to arm, breathing in sobs. This time, the other didn't slacken or check. This time, their concentration was such that they had no space to notice the eddy of cold air that touched their inferno, or hear the door from the third room pushed wide, or realise who, smaller than either, had managed to squeeze through the high window. Then Katelijne's voice spoke, a quarter-octave higher than usual, and cutting. 'The Ambassador my uncle says, if one of you kills, he will see the other hang.' She stood, red-lit, her wet feet planted beside them. To move was to hit her.

Beaten by pulses, Simon stopped. The other, too, ceased to move, but did not free Simon; nor did Simon disengage. The agony of the lock continued for seconds. It came to Simon that he was not going to prevail. His strength, deliberately sapped at the beginning, was not enough to break the other man's grip in this bout. He could not kill; yet he must. Well, to begin with, he could maim; and the girl would have to look out or shift. He drew on all his powers and thrust.

A panful of warm foetid water slapped full into his face and another drenched his opponent. Unable to breathe, Simon relaxed his grasp, retching and choking, and felt his body released as the other man, too, caught his breath. The girl, grim-faced, had another scoop almost ready. Simon, gasping, rolled aside and rose on his good elbow. Beside him, the Fleming did the opposite, dropping his head on his arm. He was shaking with what might have started as laughter.

'The key,' said the girl.

De Fleury said, 'It is in the fire.' Simon found he was trembling too.

The girl threw down the scoop and stepped back into the firelight. Barefoot and stripped to her soot-besmeared small-clothes, she appeared as voluptuous as the wick of a lamp. She gave them both one searching look and then, scrambling about in the dark, found the tongs and the rake, and sprang with them up to the bench where she began, cricket-elbowed, to rummage into the fire.

Where the rake had been, the blades of the shears flickered once, red in the new flames.

Simon sat up by degrees. The other man lay on his face, breathing fast as if spent. The low fire, reflected from the roof, showed the pale triangle of shoulder and waist, scrawled over by dirt and scorchmarks and blood and patterned with fissures through which the flesh showed merely black. His own was the same. They were well matched. But the other had taken care to create his advantage. No one else had ever had Simon dragged running and tied between two horses, or hounded by dogs. For that alone, he deserved death.

Simon turned and, flinging himself full length, seized the shears and brought them round in a single red murderous swing.

The girl shrieked. The other man, obeying some instinct, threw himself over and away and then turned, crouching, his fingers touching the ground as the shearpoints sank thudding down where he had been. Simon tugged them out and then stopped, for the girl was standing between them again, and in her two hands was the door-key held fast in the claws of the tongs. Claws and door-key glowed red. She said, 'Give me the shears.'

Behind her, the younger man stood. He said, 'Give her them.'

Simon hesitated. The key was darkening. She was only a girl.

She was Adorne's niece, and a witness.

He said, 'There are other ways,' and flung the shears to the back of the room. The girl was so short that he and de Fleury stood eye to eye, even though she was placed between them. Then she had gone, running, to open the door.

The other man said, 'There are no other ways.'

'You have partners,' Simon said. 'And possessions. Berecrofts will regret sheltering you, my friend, before this night is over.'

'The night is over, for you,' the other man said, his voice strange, and stepped forward.

It was the last vindictive flare of their battle, and brief though it was, it lasted in its fury until fresh, cold, powerful hands pulled them apart and held them, still struggling, like beasts. Then Simon stood still and Anselm Adorne, slackening his grip, transformed it into one of light support. Opposite, young Sersanders kept a strong arm round de Fleury until he too was still. Then Adorne's nephew shifted his grasp, with no tenderness, to his arms. His eyes, scanning Simon, were bright with horrified anger, and his dress caked and glistening with snow. Behind, the open door was a luminous rectangle of swirling, feathery white. Nicholas de Fleury said, 'You wouldn't care to give us five more minutes alone? For the price of a ship?'

Adorne said, 'You are barking-drunk, both of you. So is half the Court. St Pol, take my cloak and go while I hold him. There are horses waiting outside. Can you manage to ride to Linlithgow?'

Simon said, 'He had me dragged here roped to two riders.' He had not meant to blurt it out. But the alternative, now, was to have the other man walk out scatheless to Berecrofts.

Nicholas de Fleury said, 'I felt he deserved it. Should we not tell the whole story? Should we not go back and complain to the parasol of authority together?' The girl had brought in a torch, quick as a firefly, and was lighting others. They made a sunken glare of de Fleury's face, the dimples black as charcoal, or scorchmarks. The cool response had come from a furnace.

Adorne spoke to Simon. 'Pay no attention. You can't. Go. I shall take care of this.'

'No,' the Fleming said.

'Do I need to explain?' Adorne said. He stood, cloakless now, experienced and, of course, admirable, as he had stood victor in the lists against Simon himself. He said, 'So far, no one knows of this but we five. Do you want the world to witness this feud? St Pol, go!' The girl, running about, was raking together all the lethal debris under their feet and throwing it, with efficiency, into the third room, where the snow was melting under the window.

'Let us go together,' de Fleury said. The girl looked at him, and shut the door.

Adorne said, 'So that you can attack him again?'

'Would you let me?' said de Fleury. 'I won't harm him.'

'I don't propose to let you try,' Adorne said.

'Then you'll have to follow us,' Nicholas de Fleury said; and, flinging Sersanders off, took a first step towards Simon. Adorne exclaimed and sprang forward. Someone – the girl – dragged at Simon's arm, pulling him towards the door, and thrusting her uncle's cloak into his arms. Simon looked back.

Adorne shouted 'Go!' The word ended in a gasp. From the door, Simon saw the three men struggling together. There was nothing he could do. Just now, there was no way he could get rid of this man. But there would be other times. And meanwhile, there was Berecrofts, where the Bank of Niccolò kept more than one ledger whose loss would be felt.

He took the cloak and found himself outside the door, in a blue-white world of thick falling snow. He found the three Adorne horses, drooping in a bare withy shelter, and mounting one stiffly, turned its face to the west. The place must have been full of people but he saw no one: only the night, and the white veils of snow, hung with the rose-coloured blooms of the salt-fires.

He would have seen, had he remained, a struggle as bitter as any that had taken place within the last hour, as two fresh men tried to contain a third for whom, at the moment, exhaustion did not exist, as he tried to enforce his will, without weapons.

Adorne and Sersanders, in turn, did not draw their swords. At first, after overcoming the disadvantage of surprise, it was enough to bring de Fleury down, and then block his way to the door. But after that, the ferocity of the fighting took them both by surprise, and twice he nearly escaped them. Once, breathless, Adorne tried to reason. 'Nicholas, why? You can do nothing. You'll be hanged if you kill him.'

And then Nicholas said, 'He's going to set fire to Berecrofts.'

'Simon?' Sersanders said. And he laughed.

Adorne would have known better. As it was, de Fleury kicked, and kicked again, and when he got to his knees, he had Adorne's sword in his hand, and the point of it at Adorne's throat. He said, 'Let me go, or come with me.' And Sersanders, crazily, took out his own sword and slashed.

De Fleury engaged it. He played with him, moving backwards all the way to the door. It was half open. De Fleury glanced once behind him; and then again, fighting still, at Adorne leaping towards him. The girl was almost on him as well. She was carrying something.

Adorne reached him. Sersanders, striking wildly, found his steel locked and wrenched out of his grasp. He staggered back. De Fleury took one step through the door and Adorne grasped him. De Fleury said, '*No!*'

It was apparent then that against three, he would lose. The girl was close; Sersanders had already scooped up his sword; Adorne's grip was unexpectedly fierce. Adorne's eyes, magistrate's eyes, seized and held his. Nicholas de Fleury said, 'I have a sword. I will use it.'

'Then you will have to,' said Anselm Adorne.

And so de Fleury, lifting his blade, struck him down.

Adorne sank to his knees. Sersanders shouted. Katelijne looked wildly at both and then caught the door as de Fleury thrust through it. She took a pace at his heels and hurled something.

She had carried a one-handled pan. She threw the contents, and drenched him. He had expected a douche of seawater. He had even had time to think, ludicrously, how cold it was going to be, racing outside in the snow to where, a long way off – too far off – he had hidden his horse and his weapons.

In a way he had been right. It was cold. He reached his mount stiff and dizzy and shivering. He was actually riding before he realised that he was drenched not in water, but blood.

No one followed him – or not at once. Behind, Katelijne dropped the pan in the snow and ran back indoors, where her brother knelt, and her uncle lay in his man's lifeblood, proper for salt.

His eyes were closed. She said, 'How bad is it?'

'He can't walk. Stay with him. I'm going to follow the bastard and kill him.'

Once, Anselm Sersanders had been a member of that insouciant, merry tribe of youngsters in Bruges which had admired the wildness of Claes. Now Sersanders was a grown man, with the family temper. Katelijne said, 'Our uncle will bleed to death. Bandages. Take off your shirt.' She had her gown already pulled down. Her shift, underneath, was too dirty.

Her brother, though hasty, was not without sense. He looked at her and then, silently, ripped up the cloth that she needed. She showed him what to do, and ran out. Before he had finished she was back, with an old woman and a boy.

In that spectral uninhabited place, it was uncanny. She said, 'I've paid them. They're all hiding, from fear. Mysie will stay with you and tend him and keep the fire going. The boy will run to Kinneil for help. I'll ride to Linlithgow.'

'I'll do that!' Sersanders said. He made to get up.

'No,' said Adorne, rousing stubbornly. His eyes, heavy but clear, turned from his nephew to his niece. 'She is right. Someone must stay here on guard. If Simon can be persuaded not to complain, we may contain this matter yet. If I am attacked again and die, two nations will feel the hurt of it. Is de Fleury not due to sail?'

'The *Ghost* is waiting,' said Katelijne. 'You aren't going to accuse him? With this wound?'

'He will pay,' said Adorne. 'I am not, I hope, the man to accept this without some response. But not a public one. My horse threw me, and I was cut by my dagger.'

Sersanders started to argue. Katelijne finished dressing and threw on her cloak, and took a torch from the wall. The boy and the old woman gazed at her. She knelt by her uncle.

He was sallow, and grooves of pain ran from his nose to each side of his mouth. She said, 'I shall be careful,' and kissed him; and walked out into the snow, to where only two horses waited. She took the better and, as Simon had done, turned its face to the west, which was not the way to Linlithgow. It was then just short of midnight, and she was as far behind Nicholas as Nicholas was behind Simon. She was also weeping.

At Berecrofts, Bel of Cuthilgurdy sat in silence while Michael Crackbene paced up and down. He had sworn only once, when the man sent to Kinneil returned half an hour before midnight to report that Nicholas de Fleury was not there, and Mistress Joneta had not seen him all evening. Just after midnight, the man he had sent to Blackness came back, cold and sullen, to report that he had failed to see Julius, and de Fleury had never been there. Also, that if de Fleury intended to sail on the *Ghost*, he had only a few hours left to join her.

Shortly after that, on the insistence of Berecrofts and his family, he sent out search parties, and joined one himself, as did the man Archie and Robin. De Fleury, the least inept of individuals, was unlikely to be in trouble. But the snow had begun again. He was mortal. And the old woman, who would not tell Crackbene her business, was grey with anxiety.

Half an hour after midnight, news of the dead man came in.

Berecrofts the Younger brought it himself, a calm, decent young man with his arm round his son. He spoke to Bel gently. 'We don't yet know who it is. The man who found him says he must be a stranger, to trust the ice on the Avon just there. Mind you, the plain is covered with snow. He may not even have known the river ran through it.'

Bel said, 'Can they reach him?'

'They've got ladders. They'll try.' He had his hand on her shoulder. He said, 'M. de Fleury would know not to cross. He knows the river. This is someone who doesn't live here.'

'So you'll go on searching?' Bel said.

'Oh, yes,' Berecrofts said. 'I don't know what he can be up to, but we'll find him. We have to get him to Bruges, don't we, no matter what?'

Just an hour before that, the King's hunting-party had returned to the Palace and found itself somewhat reduced. It was Will Roger, in the end, who forced upon their attention the fact that the Burgundian Envoy and his niece and nephew were missing, not to mention Simon de St Pol of Kilmirren and the provider of all their present comforts, the Fleming de Fleury.

Had they been less young and more tired, they might have done nothing. But the hounds were lively, the sport had been poor, and it was a fact (as Dr Andreas reminded them) that at the house of Kinneil there was a cloak of Kilmirren's which would give them a very good scent. They set off through the snow, and arrived at Kinneil just after midnight. The young lady of Kinneil, somewhat distracted, served them wine and let the hounds sniff at the cloak. Amazingly, when they set off, they picked up a trail right away. It led west. The physician Andreas said, 'St Pol is going to Berecrofts.'

Chapter 12

THE TROUBLE WAS, the snow covered the blood. Obviously, Katelijne had known that it would, but it was the best marker she could devise, and she hadn't expected the snow to continue so thickly. Also, as de Fleury rode on, the blood would dry and congeal. From his hair and shoulders, however, it should run off diluted, she judged. Like cinnabar sinking through alum; lac-flushed sugar; dragon's blood clotted with salt.

If you knew enough about dyes, could you cancel out red? Contradict it with some opposite colour? What made colour? Did light vibrate and form tones, just like music? Could you contradict harmony? Nicholas de Fleury might know.

She was following Nicholas de Fleury. She had to keep thinking about that, and about spurring her horse to keep the best pace it could through the snow, while she strained to see the few landmarks she knew. She had been twice to the priory at Emmanuel. She had ridden this way at least once with her small royal lady. She had a memory as tenacious as horse-glue. So they told her.

She was on the right route for Berecrofts – if Berecrofts was where Simon and M. de Fleury were both going. That was less than five miles from the salt-pans. If her guess was quite wrong, then Linlithgow was only three miles away, but in quite a different direction. She held her torch out, flaring and sizzling, and the snow, soft as wool, clogged her tears. She had travelled two miles when it lessened. The sky cleared. Presently she saw the snowfield ahead, lit by starlight and stamped like bookbinders' work with a long narrow design inked in black.

The design formed by four hooves of a horse. And to one side of it, and still fogged over with snow, an earlier, more confused track. One horseman, following another. And beside the clearer trail, as she raced across to it and then reined, a freckle of pink on the white. The blood of male gender in which Nicholas de Fleury was drenched. She choked unexpectedly.

She had formed no plan except to be a deterrent, a witness. She followed the two trails, riding faster as the clouds drew aside and the moon rose, blanching the document bearing her own growing palimpsest. When, half an hour after midnight, she saw the flat white plain of the Avon before her and a dark horseman upon it, she swallowed again, and then gazed beyond, over the river, to where Berecrofts lay. She saw its windows, minute in the distance, and pale smoke rising. It was intact. Of a second horseman, there was no sign at all.

She lifted her whip, and sent her horse galloping to the edge of the snow-covered river. Had she looked up, she would have glimpsed, far on her left, a haze of light over the ridge which told of the King's party approaching. Had she looked across, a little upriver, she would have noticed a cluster of torches moving on the far side of the Avon, as a man's body was carried compassionately out of the cold. Instead, she rode down to the horseman, who was motionless now. Who, perhaps, had been motionless ever since she first glimpsed him. In that light, no one could say.

The snow at his feet was sprinkled with lac and with dragon's blood. She didn't recognise the cloak he was wearing, but knew him before he slowly turned back his hood with the care of a man decorticating a wound. The profile beneath, half pallid, half crazed with blood, was that of Nicholas de Fleury, her uncle's attacker.

He did not look round, although he must have heard her horse in the quiet. Although he probably knew, from its step, that it didn't carry a man. Her chest shuddered, anger fighting with fear. She said, 'What is it?' and dismounted. He didn't answer, his gaze concentrated far ahead. Then she saw what he was looking at.

First, at a horse, hardly visible at first, since only its flank showed above an upheaval of white which represented a fissure, blocked with ice, in the river. Then, to one side, half concealed by the horse, the cloaked shoulder and averted cheek of its rider, made small and toy-like by distance. All the rest was under water. Because the cloak was so dark, the yellow hair showed, a chill point of light in the gloom.

Katelijne said, 'He'll die! Quick!'

'He is dead,' said de Fleury.

Her heart sickened. She said, 'Maybe he isn't. I don't weigh much. I'm going to try.'

Then, whatever paralysis de Fleury was in, he emerged from it.

Before she could run forward, he was at the edge of the flats and had dragged off his horse-cloth. He said, 'There is no point in your drowning for nothing.' She was so short, the snow half soaked her gown.

You couldn't tell where the river began. And the edges of course would have frozen. She found a stick and hurried forward, probing the snow. The stick thrust down and skidded on ice. She said, 'I'm on water now.'

'Then get off it,' de Fleury said. And when she didn't obey, he thrust past her, far too fast, reaching out towards the place, nearer now, where the bulk of the animal loomed. It was motionless. It must have broken its neck and then stuck, the water freezing about it. Or perhaps it was not very deep. It wouldn't have to be. Given time, the cold would kill quite efficiently.

But Simon de St Pol was not wholly in the water, and so might not yet be dead. What had made de Fleury think otherwise?

Under her feet, the ice creaked. She moved sideways and followed his footsteps, where he seemed to have found more solid footing. He was some way ahead. Then he said distinctly, 'Stay where you are, and lie down.' He moved quickly back as he spoke, but for him it was too late. The foothold he sought gave way with a splash and she saw he was half in the water and trying to pull himself up. The cracks ran back nearly to where she was lying, but not quite. She dragged the cloth from her shoulder and flung one end of it.

He caught it the second time and pulled himself out, only to have the ice give way again. The surfaces before her were shaking, the water creeping up grey over the snow and the snow tilting. She sidled, gripping the cloth and easing herself over the snow to a firmer place. Next she began, hand over hand, to pull herself closer to him. Then he said, 'No, go back. I'm in. I might as well stay.'

There was nothing to say. She stopped, but didn't go back. The cloth fell back as he released it. As she watched, her teeth in her lip, he slipped fully into the water and began breaking his way through to the clutter of ice round the horse. As he reached it, the pool widened and the horse started to sink, dragging the ice shards round and over the swimmer. The rider's body, too, started to slide until de Fleury, thrusting forward, somehow caught and held it, as once he had saved the King's little sister from harm.

For a moment they all stayed immobile: animal, rider and rescuer. Something swirled in the water. The horse rose as if resurrected; then crashed over and sank in a great luminous wave that washed over both heads, yellow and brown. For a moment, both vanished. Then the surface was broken again and de Fleury, gasping, flung an arm on the ice. Against his shoulder the fair head lay exposed, silent. But to climb out now, it was obvious, was impossible.

Then Katelijne saw the lights, flickering on the snow and ice all about her, and heard the baying of hounds, and voices shouting behind.

The lawyer Julius got to her first. Julius who, cantering wearily from the east into Kinneil, had raced on white-faced to find and join the King's party. He held her trembling in his arms and handed her back to Will Roger behind him, drawing her safely back to the shore, while they plied her with questions.

She must have told them, because they asked her over and over, that her uncle was safe – had been hurt in an accident – was in the care of her brother at Carriden. But while she was still on the ice, they moved past her, taking torches and ropes, accompanied by barking, pattering dogs. And from the far shore, at the same time, the cluster of lights she had not noticed separated and spread out and then coalesced into a party approaching from the other bank carrying more rope, and ladders. Katelijne stood watching and shivering.

When they threw the rope, de Fleury could not hold it. Then he wrapped it somehow around himself and the weight in his arms and found the will, she saw, to lift himself a little and push. It was the rope from the far bank, the Berecrofts bank he had chosen.

Now the opposite party was close, she could see that Robin was in the group, and his father, and the sailing-master called Crackbene. And two men, on either side of a woman. The woman who had come forward at the joust and taken the child Henry away. Bel of Cuthilgurdy.

Bel of Cuthilgurdy stood and looked at the rope, and what it was carrying, but did not come any nearer, for the ice could not bear it. Katelijne heard her speak. She said, 'What have you done?'

He is dead, de Fleury had said. And could not have known.

And the lawyer Julius, kneeling in his turn on the ice, said roughly, 'Tried to save the man's life. Nicholas? Is he dead?'

The two of them were out, now. Locked as in love or battle together, streaming with blood and with water, they lay still for a moment on the treacherous, snow-covered skin, as men came daintily forward to help them. Then Nicholas de Fleury stirred, and looked down, and after what seemed a long while, began slowly to separate himself, for the last time, from his burden.

The lawyer said again, 'Is he dead?'

'She is dead,' de Fleury said. 'It isn't Simon. It is Lucia, his sister.'

All about him, silence fell: a blanket of disbelief, bafflement, curiosity. Further off, the babble not only increased but suddenly acquired a new focus: a raised, angry voice shouting questions. Deaf with horror, Katelijne ignored it. Then she saw faces turn. Thus she witnessed the cause of the commotion, the shouting. Simon de St Pol, in life, bursting forward, and driving his horse straight through them all to the ice.

If they hadn't caught hold of his bridle he would have joined de Fleury there in the water and killed him. Even when they shouted explanations, he threw them off and tried to force his way onwards. He had arrived to find himself a ghost. First a ghost, then a man with a dead sister. And, of course, he was in no doubt who her murderer was.

He didn't want to hear reason. It took physical force to restrain him and compel him to listen, while they told him over and over. The lady had drowned, riding over the river. And de Fleury, finding her, had done all that a man could to retrieve her.

'It is true,' said Katelijne. Her voice, uplifted among the rest, seemed to have the greatest effect. It could be seen, now, that Simon himself was marked as if caught in a fight; the blaze of anger, retreating, seemed to leave him mortally weary, and the face he turned to Katelijne was stark.

He stopped speaking. The lawyer Julius, holding her arm, fell silent also. Then Simon said, 'How can I cross?' His voice was quiet. The tension slackened and the group, falling apart, began to move up the trampled white banks.

Julius said, 'I'm going too. I don't trust him. What happened?'

'They fought,' she said. 'M. de St Pol and M. de Fleury.' Walking, she told him a little. Her teeth were chattering.

'Wounded your uncle!' the lawyer said.

'He was trying to stop them. And M. de Fleury thought Berecrofts was in danger.'

'So it was just coincidence,' the lawyer Julius said. 'Nicholas riding to Berecrofts at the same time as Lucia. And Simon wasn't anywhere near – he had changed his mind and started back to Linlithgow.'

'I suppose so,' she said. 'Was M. de Fleury expecting to sail?'

The lawyer came to a halt. 'He ought to. Unless you're going to stop him. You've every right.'

'No,' she said. 'But it might be as well if he leaves quickly. If he can.'

A gentle man of good sense, Archie of Berecrofts had separated the

two who had died on his doorstep that night: the man lay on clean
straw in the barn, and the lady, wrapped in dry linen, had been
laid on the bed in his guest-chamber, tended by his good serving-
women, with his visitor, Mistress Bel, to close the eyes and comb
the over-bright hair and cross the helpless ringed hands on the
widow's breast.

Robin had helped, and the two men the woman had brought
with her. Robin had seen death before, as part of the family
wisdom: his grandmother and mother, and the infants which didn't
survive his own living siblings. Robin had been more shocked by
the living: by the blue-white skin and livid weals on the face of his
particular friend M. de Fleury as he leaned drenched on the
doorpost. And then the face of the lady Robin also liked, the
woman called Mistress Bel who, instead of saying soothing, comforting things, stood foursquare before M. de Fleury and said, 'For
this, I will have your account.'

Then Master Crackbene the sailor had elbowed past her, taking
the other man with him.

After that, even though all the servants were up, there was so
much to do that Robin had no time to feel tired: fires to bank up,
water to heat, messengers to get on their way, food and drink to be
brought from the kitchen. The Flemish doctor Andreas arrived;
then the Bishop of St Andrews himself with the dead lady's
brother. And then, finally, the lawyer called Julius, bringing
Robin's friend Katelijne, looking like girls did when in bed with a
pain. Robin yelled to bring his father but it was the lady Bel who
hurried forward and took the girl in her arms. After that, it got
quiet.

It was very quiet in the room where Lucia lay. The Bishop had
gone. Dr Andreas, finishing his work, stood soberly by the lamp
while Simon, entering, found his way to the bed and looked down
at the face of his sister. It was void of expression. You couldn't tell
how she had died. The reticence was uncharacteristic. Whether
you wanted to or not, you always knew Lucia's feelings.

He bent and kissed her. He had never liked her. On the other
hand, she had never been capable of making positive trouble.
Unlike others. He looked up.

'She drowned,' said Dr Andreas. 'The ice gave way, and it was
too cold to struggle. There are no other marks.'

'She was driven on to the ice,' Simon said.

The doctor looked at him. 'There is no proof of that,' Andreas
answered. After a moment, he bowed and left him alone.

Simon sat down, since he wanted to think and was finding it difficult. For the sake of appearances, he had borrowed a shirt and a doublet: underneath, the rest of his linen had stiffened and stuck to his skin. When the door opened on Nicholas de Fleury, he noticed that he, too, had changed, if only roughly. Out of respect, of course, for the dead. Simon said, 'Come and see. You must be so disappointed.'

The other man, moving slowly, closed the door. Simon watched him. Beneath the open doublet, the lawn, he must be as bone-weary as Simon was, with a heaviness worse than the pain of the abrasions and burns they both carried. And if Simon himself was exhausted, then the river must have brought his late antagonist to the extremes of fatigue.

And indeed, when de Fleury spoke he let the weariness show, as if there were no point in dissembling. He said, 'No. I am sorry.' He moved, stopping short of the bed.

Simon said, 'You thought it was me.'

'For a while.' His gaze brushed the bed. 'We both killed her.'

'We *both* . . .?' It wasn't worth vehemence. Simon said, 'I lured you to the salt-pans?'

'To Scotland. Why was she here?'

His voice remained low, and hardly intensified. Despite that someone outside had heard them. Before Simon could answer, the door opened again. And this time it was the interfering old woman. Lucia's helpmeet, nursemaid, companion. The old woman Bel, in her thick gown, with cloth all over her head.

Simon said, 'Excuse me. This is private.'

'I'm sure it ought to be,' said Bel of Cuthilgurdy, coming in. She shut the door and, walking forward, sat down at the foot of the bed, her face as ever shapeless, her eyes buttons, her body a sack full of homely, sensible vipers. She looked at Simon. 'So answer him. Why was she here?'

Simon could guess, he thought, why Lucia was here. He was going to debate that very point with de Fleury. He didn't want the old woman here. Neither, it appeared, did de Fleury, who turned. The skin of his face, like Simon's own, was oddly frayed and raw with abrasions. It would be hard to deny what had happened between them. De Fleury said, 'We had finished talking.'

'Then you can start again,' said the old woman.

Simon lifted his eyes from her face and met Nicholas de Fleury's full gaze. He looked as he had in the ice. Then de Fleury said, 'This is not the place. No.'

'Is it not?' said the woman. 'In the face of that puir feckless lass on the bed, is it not the place to ask what or who brought her here to her death? And if St Pol canna tell ye, I will.'

The lamp burned. On the far side of the bed, de Fleury touched a settle, and sat. To Simon, seldom fanciful, it seemed as if they were all in a painting: the still, porcelain corpse with a silent guardian at either hand and its faithful donor and friend at its feet. There should be angels, lilies, lap-dogs, swaddling-bands, trumpets.

The old woman had noticed the movement. She said, 'Aye, get ready.' Her eyes were fixed on de Fleury. 'She made that ride for the sake of her family; because she thought she could succour Kilmirren, and Henry, and maybe even both of you. And you are both here, but she isna.'

De Fleury looked up, as if she had compelled him. Simon remembered that these two had been a long time together in Africa. It wasn't possible to say what was in the old woman's gaze, although he had seen something like it in the assize court. He saw suddenly that she was an ally.

Then de Fleury said, 'Could you be quick?' and Simon moved.

The woman turned. 'Calm yourself, Simon,' she said. 'I ken the ship's there. So does he. Ye can both wait for this. There is one on the bed can none other.'

'So speak,' de Fleury said.

'What brought Lucia here?' said the woman. 'It's simple enough. Nicholas? You've cause to mind the day in the lists. The Prince insulted the lad, and Henry tried to use his bairn's might against him, and when you interfered, against you. I canna measure the courage it took, except by the damage it did him.'

She turned to Simon. 'Henry was let off one crime. For two, he would have been banished or worse, if Nicholas had reported it. But then, Simon, you let the boy see you were proud of him. He couldna brag to his friends, but he gave a fine account of it to his aunt at Kilmirren. How he'd all but killed the Bruges merchant de Fleury.'

Simon cursed. He said, 'When?'

'Yestreen. The day afore, it is, now. He came by me, and said something of it. I should have done something sooner. But when I went to the castle, Lucia'd left with her man. And they said she'd gone east, to M. de Fleury.'

She switched her gaze. De Fleury sat as if the icefield had entered the room. He said, 'I think you will have to say why.'

'Because she didna trust you,' said Bel. 'And she didna trust Simon not to goad you, once you were fit to mix with others again.

Matten's not a maid with much sense, but Lucia talked to her. Lucia knew that you'd meet, and one of you would kindle the other, until Nicholas would take the revenge he planned all along. Of course, he never meant to spare Henry.'

'You think that?' de Fleury said.

'She thought that,' said Mistress Bel. 'And that is all we are speaking of.'

'So she was coming to plead,' said de Fleury.

'Lucia? No, my fine gentleman, no,' said the woman. 'She was coming to threaten. She had something to bargain with. She had something to tell you, or thought she had. If you took against Henry, Lucia would denounce your wife and St Pol here as wantons, and your coming child as conceived in his bed.' She stared at de Fleury. 'But perhaps you kent that already?'

Between the flaws, his skin was dazzling white, like a face painted for carnival. He said, 'Ask Simon. Or count his scars, maybe.'

'He knew,' said Simon. It was painful to smile, but he didn't mind. Suddenly, his tiredness was lifting. 'I didn't tell him. Monseigneur was rather anxious no one should tell him.'

'But you wanted him to ken what you'd done,' said the woman. 'So ye did away with the vicomte's own orders. Ye made it possible for Lucia to get out of Kilmirren. As she did.'

She was supposed to be on his side. 'And so it's all my fault? Hardly,' said Simon. 'She had a fancy, and couldn't wait until daylight, and ran straight into the very person –'

'She ran straight into no one,' said the woman harshly. 'She lost her way. Her man called at Kinneil, and then tried to cross the Avon and drowned.' She glanced at the bed. 'Alone, she hadna much chance. She wasna a strong lassie, or bold. As for her fancy, she was right, was she not? You were at each other's throats.'

'Yes,' de Fleury said. He waited. Then he said, 'How long have you known?'

The woman studied him. 'About Gelis? I was told at Kilmirren.'

He waited again. Then he said, 'Why did you follow? You thought the news would unhinge me, and I would harm someone?'

'For all the good it did,' she said flatly.

Simon said, 'For all the good it did Lucia. He killed her.'

He was staring at de Fleury, but the old woman answered. 'Oh, you'd like tae think so, nae doubt. But for why? Any secret she had, you had also.'

'He thought it was me,' Simon said. 'He just said so. He drove her into the water.'

'And rescued her? Simon,' said the woman. 'The hounds drove her into the water. She wore an auld cloak of yours. The King's hounds followed after. A half-turn of the hour-glass before, and she would have been safe.'

'No, she wouldn't,' de Fleury said. Then he became very still.

'You hear?' said Simon.

'She wasn't touched,' the woman said. Her gaze was locked with de Fleury's.

'He knows how she died. He had a dog. There was a dog at the salt-pans.' Simon spoke across the bed this time. 'You thought it was me.'

'Even so,' the woman said. She was still watching the other. She spoke to him. 'Even so, would you kill?'

Simon sat. The walls were so thick that no sound came from outside the room. His sister lay waxen and white, while the three voices passed and passed over her, teasing out the strands that had led to her death. Teasing and twisting them into a cord with which to take sasine of this man's bodily housing, his neck.

The woman also wanted the truth, he saw that. She said again, 'Would you kill?'

De Fleury said, 'I get angry.' It was an affirmative.

'Tonight?' she said.

'Oh yes, tonight.'

'And in the future?' she said. 'More of this? And you, Simon?'

'You expect me to forgive him?' said Simon. 'I tell you over my sister's dead body. He'll hang.'

'He maybe will,' said Bel of Cuthilgurdy, 'but not for this crime, or any other this night. You've forgotten the whip hand he has. You've forgotten Henry.'

She heaved to her feet and her eyes, resting with compassion on the bed, lifted up with the same compassion to Simon himself. She said, 'Nicholas de Fleury is going to depart, and ye maun let him depart. His ship will sail, and ye maun let it sail. But before he goes he will tell us, I hope, that he is never going to come back to Scotland.' She turned. 'You will stay away. Do you hear?'

'I hear,' the other man said. 'But it is not a promise that I can keep. I am sorry.'

He rose with an effort. For a moment, approaching the bed, he leaned towards it. When Simon made a quick, hostile gesture, he stopped. 'Did you think I was going to kiss her? I thought her son Diniz should be told how she looked, that was all.' He stood motionless where he had stopped, his eyes open.

'Nicholas.' It was the woman, reminding him.

'I am going,' said de Fleury, and shivered.

Simon was no less tired, no less angry, and with a brother's responsibility for what had happened. He said, 'I say when he goes. And he doesn't go quite so easily.'

The woman looked at him. She said, 'It's his house.' As she spoke, as on cue, the door opened. Simon looked towards it in haste.

Hacked out of Scandinavian whalebone, the renegade sea captain Crackbene stood there. He said, 'Padrone, it is time.'

De Fleury moved then, pulling himself erect like a bow at the stretch and looking at the woman, and then at Simon himself. He said, 'I am sorry. I have to go to Bruges, where so many, many riotous delights may be had. Sadly, I also mean to come back. Unfinished business: profits in prospect. I do own a Bank.'

He had begun to walk towards Crackbene, who was watching him. De Fleury glanced at him and then back. He said, 'It may not be as bad as you think. It may be worse. At least, Mistress Bel, you have tried. Simon . . . I am sorry. I cannot wait for the funeral.'

'I would throw you out if you came,' Simon said.

De Fleury turned at the door. 'Like you threw me out of the salt-pan,' he said. Simon moved; but the woman had thrust out her arm as a barrier. Her eyes were bright as two silver sequins.

The door opened and shut. The lamp flared. Lucia de St Pol lay on her bier, and the woman Bel stood, her arm still outflung like a curse or a blessing, or perhaps just a silent appeal.

The first stage was over.

The *Ghost* sailed before dawn, carrying Nicholas de Fleury to Bruges. As a matter of record, a horse bore him from Berecrofts to Blackness, but he did not see the sails raised, being felled once aboard as by death.

The voyage was rough but unmarked by disaster. They were stayed for a week in the harbour at Berwick, awaiting the abatement of winds, and forbidden to step on dry land except to snatch water and victuals. Having himself issued this edict, Crackbene slipped ashore without notice, and reappeared a day later, morosely rolling a barrel of salmon.

Julius was outraged. 'Where has he been?'

'In the family colony,' Nicholas had said. 'There are Crackbenes all over Berwick. They call themselves Crabbes.'

It was true, so far as it went. There was no call to mention the priory at Coldstream, or Ada.

He was himself by that time, and it was some days since

Crackbene had brought him the letter addressed by Adorne. Unlike the others put early on board, inscribed to Adorne's fellow merchants and wife, to the Chancellor of Burgundy and the Duke, this had no chequered seal, and was hastily sewn. It contained three sentences only, written under evident stress at Kinneil:

For the sake of the town we both serve, I have attributed my wound to a mishap. I expect you to call on me in Bruges. I do not expect you to come back to Scotland.

'What does it matter to him?' Julius said. He had learned a little too much from Katelijne.

'I've no idea,' Nicholas said. 'He'll be home himself by the spring. I don't propose to let it upset our planning.'

It satisfied Julius, who did not always remember that planning occasionally failed. Circumstances arose. Nicholas himself had not spent the autumn, for example, entirely as he had intended. On the other hand, the one linchpin upon which all else depended was fixed. He would be arriving in February in Bruges.

He would be arriving in February in Bruges, to find out whether his marriage was fruitful.

Chapter 13

'*FOR GOD'S SAKE, WRITE*,' his manager had cried in dread and anger from Bruges to Nicholas de Fleury in Scotland. He couldn't say more, for fear that others might read it.

Alone of the company he, Gregorio of Asti, feared what Nicholas might be perpetrating in Scotland. For he, alone of the company, knew what Gelis had done. He had been there within earshot, when Gelis van Borselen, on her marriage bed, had informed her husband that she was pregnant by Simon.

If Nicholas was returning to Bruges, he was not coming thereto by chance. He was coming because his wife's child, announced for the spring, was due now.

He had been absent from Flanders for six months. In all that time, his letters to Bruges had dealt with nothing but business. In all that time, Gregorio had sent nothing private to Edinburgh except for one letter, dispatched by the *Ghost*, in which he had told Nicholas why Margot had left, who was to him what a wife might have been. And, of course, he had reported what all Bruges had learned by October: that Gelis van Borselen was expecting a child, and had retired to a place of retreat for her health.

So the months without Margot had passed, and Gregorio waited in the Hof Charetty–Niccolò, his home and his office in Bruges. The *Ghost* was coming, he knew; and Nicholas with her. The passage, he guessed, would be slow. The husband of Gelis must not seem to hurry too much, when the legitimate birth was so distant.

Because it was slow, the tidings of Lucia de St Pol's death came before it. The courier came from Kilmirren and brought letters for Diniz her son, and for her Vasquez brother by marriage, and for the van Borselen family because, twenty-five years before, Lucia had been maid of honour to Wolfaert's Scots first wife in Veere. The account said that Lucia had drowned in a river, by accident.

The letter had been written, Gregorio judged, by a clerk of Simon's and signed by him. Which meant that Simon at least was alive. It did not mention Nicholas de Fleury.

The news brought sadness, and a passing regret. To Diniz it meant more – after the loss of his father, Lucia was the only link with his happier childhood. But she had been a weak-natured, excitable woman, terrified of her father and hardly redeemed by her Portuguese marriage. After that, so far as Gregorio knew, she had done nothing that was not purely selfish. And Diniz, of course, had another protector and deity now.

After that, Gregorio counted the months and the days, and was unsurprised when news arrived that the roundship the *Ghost* had been sighted, and that Nicholas de Fleury would shortly be with them. It was the third week in February, and seven months and more had passed since his wedding.

There followed the hubbub that occurs in even the best-run establishment of bankers, dyers and merchants when the owner is about to descend on it. Gregorio handled it all, helped by Diniz Vasquez in mourning, whose pregnant wife Tilde was the step-daughter of Nicholas de Fleury. He even enjoyed the assistance of Tilde's unmarried young sister Catherine, currently attended by three different gallants.

One of them, who was related to Gelis, stopped calling. Nicholas, who had not been seen with his wife since their marriage, was not popular with her van Borselen kinsmen, who suspected that he had engineered her disappearance from society. No one dreamed that not even Nicholas knew where his wife of one half-night might be.

Public curiosity about the lady de Fleury's whereabouts had attained a lower and more forgiving level. It had been known for other brides to hide their qualms during pregnancy. They generally reappeared a year after the wedding accompanied by a babe with a full set of teeth. The babe, however, was expected to look like the husband.

Now that the prospective father was due to return, public curiosity (by the same token) revived. Merchants who invested in the House of Niccolò had good cause, of course, to call on Meester Gregorio, and relish a cup of his Portuguese wine, and establish that they would appreciate, presently, an interview with Meester Nicholas himself.

Rivals were worse. Tommaso Portinari, affluent, dashing, the Duke of Burgundy's chamberlain and manager of the Medici office in Bruges, announced his intention of riding to Sluys, the port of Bruges, and welcoming his old friend Claes in person. Diniz endorsed the idea, out of sheer inexperience and affection. 'Why don't we all go!'

Tommaso Portinari had been drunk throughout his last meeting with Nicholas de Fleury and might not therefore remember it. Unfortunately, Nicholas would.

Diniz Vasquez was a young, able man who should not have to meet the first onslaught of whatever the *Ghost* was to bring. Gregorio persuaded him to stay to welcome his patron at home. He persuaded everyone to stay except Tommaso. When he left for Sluys, Tommaso and his servants rode with him.

It was usual for the master of an important ship arriving in Sluys to invite on board those magnates who were waiting to welcome her. When the *Ghost* dropped her tattered sails in the harbour, mobbed by boats and with cannon speaking courteously from the castle, Crackbene himself came ashore in the lighter to bring Gregorio and the ducal chamberlain back to the vessel. Julius came with him.

Crackbene addressed Portinari. Julius seized Gregorio's arm. 'Well?'

'Well what? You have all my news. What about Nicholas?'

'Oh, he's gone off his head,' said Julius happily. 'You heard about Simon and Lucia? And young Henry did his utmost to murder him. We weren't allowed to write and tell you. Listen –'

'Lucia died,' said Gregorio sharply. 'We heard.'

'That's right. She drowned, after Nicholas and Simon tried to kill each other. And then Nicholas took a sword to Adorne.'

'*Adorne!* Why?'

'He was trying to stop them. Listen. We're to take Tommaso aboard, and Nicholas will butter him up, and then I've to keep him in talk so that Nicholas can have a word on the quiet with you. But I thought you'd better hear something beforehand. Scotland!' said Julius. 'You know what he used to be like in Bruges. But by God, Scotland has brought out the man in him.'

He turned away. Gregorio heard him address Portinari by his first name. Of course, they had known one another a long time. Crackbene said, 'We had a wager that Ser Tommaso would find his way here.' There was nothing in the large-blocked Scandinavian face except the marks of rough sailing and a certain hardness of scrutiny that in itself was not a bad augur.

Gregorio said something. He was not going to ask Crackbene for advice. Then he got into the skiff.

The *Ghost* was not a ship Gregorio had ever sailed in. He remained obdurately angry that Julius had been the preferred choice for Scotland, and not himself. He understood it, of course. Knowing nothing, Julius could not impede whatever Nicholas had set out to do. Whatever he had done.

The ducal chamberlain climbed aboard first, and Nicholas greeted him. Gregorio heard his voice, which was the same. At first sight he looked the same also, and the sombre magnificence of his dress manifested a style he had already adopted last autumn. Nicholas said, 'There is no need to frown. You are looking at two salt-pans and a coal mine. Tommaso tells me his staff has burst into flower and he's marrying.'

'When my lady mother —' began the Medici Bank's agent in Flanders.

'When his lady mother has found him a wife. It is much the best way, to leave it to mothers. Why don't you come in? The poop cabin has been scraped fairly clean, and we bought some wine from a keel in Newcastle, and Julius swears the pies have stopped moving.' His tone embodied no threat, no trace of recollection. Tommaso, innocently drunk last July, blurting out the news of the death of the African Umar, might have been forgiven, forgotten. Then again, he might not.

The Duke of Burgundy's chamberlain was given his due. But in a remarkably short time Tommaso Portinari was sunk in his seat, relating some long tale of triumph to Julius while Nicholas, on some excuse, was on deck. Gregorio joined him. He said, 'He'll have a very bad headache tomorrow.'

'God forgive me,' said Nicholas.

They were surrounded by seamen. The hatches off, unloading had already begun, and the lighters were assembling below on the water. Crackbene's voice came to them from the prow, but he did not look round or come over. The air was raw. Nicholas said, 'There is an empty cabin,' and leading the way there, closed the door and set his back to it. He said, 'Well?'

His eyes, cold and deep, completed the question. Gregorio said, 'I don't know what you have heard.'

'I've heard nothing since you wrote in October. How should I?' said the other man.

The gulls were screaming outside the casement: their shadows stirred in the cabin like vermin. *The bitch. The bitch.* Gregorio drew a steady breath. 'You know then that the lady —'

'My wife.'

'— that your wife retired from the Duchess's court to a convent. Or so she said. She didn't say where the convent was, either then or at any time afterwards. Not even her family knows where she is.

She did, however, send them a message to say she was well. That reached Veere in December.'

'Oh?' said Nicholas.

Gregorio looked up. He said, 'I didn't know when I wrote to you about Margot. It means, if you care, that she must have carried for seven months successfully. Otherwise she would have come back.'

The grey regard, which had been intense, changed in quality. The other man said, his voice lenient, 'Whom are you thinking of? Not my wife, surely. My wife and I invent much longer games. So you have heard nothing at all since December? No announcement?'

'Would you expect one?' Gregorio said.

The mild voice said, 'No. I wondered if you did. Now tell me about Margot.'

The winches squeaked, and from below came the thunder of barrels. Nowadays, no one spoke that name in Gregorio's hearing. He blocked her out of his thoughts, and dreamed of her nightly. He said, 'We disagreed.'

'You told her the exact situation? Yes, of course you did.'

'I told her what I heard,' Gregorio said.

'And she took my wife's part.'

'She took the coming child's part,' Gregorio said.

'It argues there is a child on the way,' said the other reflectively. 'Or at least that Margot's humanitarian impulses have found something or other to engage them. In other words, no one is dead, or not yet. You have made no effort to find them? No, you haven't.'

'I have tried,' said Gregorio.

'But not very hard. So I shall have to do it for you. Do you want Margot back, or shall I leave her wherever I find her?'

The enquiring face opposite blurred, and cramp seized his guts from sheer anger. Gregorio said, 'Keep your pain to yourself.'

'Do I show any?' the other man said in his composed voice. 'Such things demand a little self-knowledge, that is all. I recommend a spell in the desert.'

Gregorio said, 'Unfortunately, not having that advantage, I have to find my own way. I am not sure it isn't better than yours. Nicholas, what have you done?'

Nicholas moved away from the door and took up his stance against the bulkhead where he rested his back, one knee doubled. The woodwork was sweating a little with cold. He said, 'What did Julius tell you? Let me guess. Simon and I were conducting a running fight, and Lucia was the unfortunate victim? True enough in its way. She knew about Gelis, you see. Julius, you may be surprised to learn, does not.'

'And Adorne?' Gregorio said curtly.

'Ah. Anselm Adorne, the Scottish King's favourite counsellor. He has been created a knight, and given a chain with a unicorn on it. I was so jealous I stabbed him.'

'Is he badly hurt?' Gregorio said.

'He was hurt. He was also magnanimous. He isn't going to demand redress in Scotland, but he'll have something to say when he gets back to Bruges. Fortunately, I should be on my way back to Scotland by then.'

The shock was intolerable. Gregorio said, 'You can't go back!'

'To all these new Scottish projects?' said the other man. 'Of course I shall. I'm going to make you all even richer. Julius considers I ought to spend a few weeks in Bruges until – how did he put it? – the harvest is over, and it's time to start planting again. Then, of course, I must go back north to my other crops. Well now. What else can I tell you?'

'Nothing. Leave it,' said Gregorio. He walked to the door. 'I'm going back to Tommaso.'

'What did you expect?' Nicholas said. 'You know what you shouldn't know. That doesn't make you my confessor.'

Gregorio turned. He said, 'No. Your confessor thought he was your friend, but you haven't asked after him. If you are interested, Father Godscalc is still in your house, but not as strong as he was, and Tobie has left off his army doctoring to care for him. Tilde, too, is near the birth of her child, and Diniz is anxious about her. Catherine –' He broke off. 'Am I tiring you?'

'No. I am riveted. Tilde's sister Catherine? Not yet married?'

'No,' said Gregorio. He tried to recover his calm, in the face of a suspicion that his loss of calm had been what Nicholas at that moment had wanted. He said, 'She isn't married, but not for want of pursuit. Paul van Borselen and a young faun from Trebizond are only two of the suitors Diniz has had to deal with.'

'Indeed?' said Nicholas slowly. 'But not Jan Adorne?'

'Still away, studying law at Pavia. And just as well. Jan would be a fine suitor for Catherine, now that you've injured his father. What were you thinking of?'

'An old adage,' Nicholas said. 'If you are a peg, endure the knocking. If you are a mallet, strike.'

He had altered his negligent stance and stood balanced, as if the motion and sounds of the ship had again reclaimed his attention. He looked chilled. Gregorio said, 'Your family. What will you do? What will you do when you find them?'

He had spoken too abruptly. Nicholas looked at him. 'Why? You have a suggestion?'

Gregorio said, 'I don't know what you are thinking. You need someone who does.'

The concentrated gaze did not alter.

Gregorio said, 'Nicholas? At least you won't harm them?'

'I am unlikely to harm Margot,' Nicholas said.

'Your wife and the child.'

'You think there is a child? Well, what reassurance can I give you, other than the one you already have? My wife and I play a very long game.'

'So you believe you can find her?'

'Of course. I have a list – didn't I tell you? – of every convent which could conceivably shelter her. She has paid well to stay concealed. And she is not in want of money. As you have no doubt discovered, she has withdrawn from the Bank the whole sum she acquired on her marriage.'

'I know,' Gregorio said. The sum was immense – a single rash, magnificent gift bestowed by Nicholas on his bride. Its withdrawal had frightened and shocked him. He said, 'I cannot trace where it has gone.'

'No. It has been expertly done. That is, secrecy has been assured for so long as it matters.'

'And now you will search for them,' Gregorio said. He could hear the door of the master cabin open groggily.

'Now I shall wait,' Nicholas said. 'Not for long, for obvious reasons. But don't you think my wife will invite me to visit her soon? To show to me alone that her pregnancy is actually over? To prove to me alone that Simon's child has been born?'

'And if she doesn't send?' Gregorio said.

Nicholas considered. 'I should give her a week. Then I muster my men and we begin, one by one, to rout through every convent in Flanders. It may take some time. Unless, of course, you have an idea which way Margot went? It would spare blameless houses some harassment . . . Ah, Julius. You must be tired from talking so much. Can Tommaso still walk? Do you think we could induce him to go ashore now? Gregorio would be pleased to go with him.'

'Oh God,' Julius said. 'You've told him what you've been doing.' He grinned at Gregorio. 'I told you. The devil's own paymaster.'

Gregorio brushed past and walked out.

All winter, he had carried this abominable secret; had disputed with Margot over what should in fairness be done. In the end, she had left him for Gelis.

Throughout, he had been upheld by his knowledge of the moderate Nicholas of the past; by his belief in the mature Nicholas who had emerged from the anvil of Africa.

Throughout, he had built his hopes for the future on what Nicholas, given time, would have resolved.

And throughout, Margot – not he – had been right.

Chapter 14

I N SIX MONTHS, the Charetty–Niccolò mansion below the Tonlieu at Bruges had altered, as had its owner. It included, now, the adjacent building; and Gregorio had extended round both the solid fortified wall first begun by the Charetty daughters to keep Nicholas out. Now the two firms were one, but the precaution, after Liège, was a mark of Gregorio's unsleeping prudence.

The gates were open, waiting for Nicholas. Riding through with his trim cavalcade he saw the forecourt cleared now of its accretion of buildings. A new archway led to the back, where yards and stables and storerooms ought now to stand where the gardens and domestic offices used to be. His private accommodation had been moved to the other house. He had not altered his orders for that.

He hoped, remembering Scotland, that the builders' work was mostly over. After the vast, storm-lashed estuaries, the towns which straddled ravines, the keeps and lodges and cabins of grey stone and plaster and thatch, Bruges had appeared like a flat-bottomed toy, with its interlocking paved streets lined with red brick-patterned houses; its small-bridged canals ringing with the laughter of skaters. It was February, and cold.

Standing in the slush of the forecourt were groups of people: his outside staff, gathered to see him arrive. Their faces showed a kind of clouded vivacity. He had come back and his wife was not here, but was pregnant. He had come back, and Mistress Lucia was dead. Then he saw Lucia's son running over the yard – Diniz Vasquez, bronze of skin, dark and sturdy as his mother had been fragile and fair. A good man, who would run the Bruges office one day. One day, if it mattered.

He dismounted, and said what was fitting. Diniz looked up and said, 'I heard you tried to save her. Thank you.' His face was full of uneven colour, but he was not weeping.

Nicholas said, 'She should have lived to welcome her grandchild. How is it with Tilde?'

Diniz dropped one of his hands and half turned. 'She would like to see you; but not if you are busy. Have you time?'

'For Tilde? What does Tobie say?'

'Not much,' Diniz said. 'To rest and to wait. If you really have time, then – come and speak to her.'

Tilde lay in the chamber that had once been her mother's and his. The mound under the bedclothes was not as great as it should have been, and her sunk eyes were apprehensive, her brown hair coiled dull at her shoulders. Nicholas sat and took her hand in both of his. He was, after all, her step-father.

He said, 'In business, one makes a range of predictions, and then one plans for the worst. What has Tobie told you?'

'Nothing!' said Diniz.

Nicholas did not turn. 'Go away, Diniz,' he said. The girl's hand tightened in his. After a moment, Nicholas heard the door close.

He said, 'It is hard for men at such times. What did Tobie say?' He paused and then said, 'Come on. I've seen babies born.'

Her eyes, looking at his, suddenly brimmed. He released a hand and gave her his kerchief. She spoke, scrubbing it into wet corners. 'He says – he didn't want to say – I know its heartbeat is weak. I have to rest. I have to try to keep it.'

Nicholas took the cloth from her, tidied her cheeks, and took her hand again. 'You probably will. Are you very tired?'

Her face was narrow and pallid in illness, as her brother's had been. Only Catherine had their mother's red-brown hair and bright colour. Tilde said, 'The doctor says that is natural. He says I am not to worry: there will be others.'

His hands parted from hers. He said, 'That is what I wanted to hear. Of course, you want to give Diniz this baby. But there are many pearls on a string.'

'You have a child coming,' she said.

'*Inshallah*. If God wills,' he continued immediately. 'If not, I have you and Catherine. I haven't seen Gelis yet. Would you like her to come and stay with you, if she can?'

He saw, as he expected, a mixture of feelings. She said, 'If she can. But it might be unsafe. No, don't ask her. Have you seen Catherine yet?'

'Is she visible? I thought she had too many suitors. Which is she going to marry?'

'You have to tell her,' said Tilde. 'She will do whatever you say.'

She smiled at him shakily and then her brows, which had smoothed, drew strictly together. She said, 'Have you been sick, cousin Nicholas? I should be about my duties, to see you have food.'

'When your child has come, I shall demand it,' he said. Who had taught her to call him cousin Nicholas? He added, 'I'm not sick, and I shall eat when you do. Will you allow me to share your meals sometimes?'

She agreed, her eyes bright. He thought it might even be possible. At best, it would give him a respite from Godscalc and Tobie. All the time he had been speaking, a distant tapping had been increasing in volume. As he ended, there was a thud outside the door, a rattling latch, and Godscalc himself walked slowly in, followed by Tobias Beventini, physician.

Nicholas rose, with unconcealed distaste. 'Oh, I know,' he said. 'A pretty girl in bed somewhere, and who are the two most likely to find excuses to badger her?'

He addressed that to Tobie, who was shrewd enough, but whose initial perceptions would be medical. He wondered what they had been told, and if they had learned about Henry. A glance at Godscalc, fierce and silent, his weight on his stick, answered that question, and others. The vigorous German hulk of a man who had sought Prester John at his side had returned this blanched cripple, with one donation to God he was still determined to make. Nicholas turned to the priest and said, 'Father? You should sit.' The tone of his voice said three other things, as he meant.

Tobie said, 'What happened? Never mind. We heard you were with her. Are you cheering her up?'

He had just realised, Nicholas saw, that by joining him here he had debarred himself from all the sensitive topics. Gregorio had talked to them, he deduced, but not Julius, or he would sense anger and not just anxiety.

He said, 'Of course I'm not cheering her up: I want some advice about Scotland, and she's got a better brain than either of you. Unless she keeps it in her stomach, and you think facts and figures will upset it?'

Tobie sat on the opposite bed-step and looked at her, and at Nicholas. He said, 'What's new? You affect everyone's stomach. Go ahead.'

Nicholas delivered his talk. It was, in effect, a summary of his doings in Scotland. Julius knew it all, and Gregorio had the gist, but Tilde herself would take pride in telling Diniz her husband, and Catherine.

So far as it went, the account was perfectly accurate and, because indeed she had a good business head, he added to it specifics of costs and prices and outlay, ending with accurate figures of the profit to date, and impressive estimates of the income still to accrue, once he had returned to complete the whole project. He knew Gregorio, and could counter his arguments without having heard them.

In between, he clowned his way through a few true anecdotes and some not so true, and made Tilde smile and then break into real laughter. She asked questions: he answered them. Then he received, without appearing to, the unspoken message from Tobie and, rising, brought it all to an end. Hugging him, she whispered a message for Gelis. He realised that she had taken him to be afraid of, or revolted by pregnancy, and hence to have avoided his wife and herself. Now she knew differently. Soon she would begin to wonder why he *had* stayed away.

There were seven years between them. The age difference between Marian and himself had been nearly three times as great. He did not like being called cousin Nicholas.

It amused him then to walk through the house, noting the changes; to penetrate to the kitchens and charm the cooks and chat to the yardmen and porters. On the way, he came face to face with young Catherine, breathless from running and still wrapped in cold furs. Her cheek was fresh when he kissed it, and her eyes were brilliant blue.

He said, 'Gregorio and Diniz have commanded me. We'll talk later,' and squeezed her hand. It would be much later. Business had to come first, for there was not very much time, and he had to plan every moment accordingly. And, of course, he would be cornered by Godscalc and Tobie, who could not ask him in public what they most wanted to know. That would be the real inquisition, where they would demand answers and would, of course, get them. Of a sort.

So he went on, and found his way to the counting-house, big as a park, where he shook hands and greeted clerks and stopped once, to someone's terrified pleasure, to leaf through a ledger and comment. It was not difficult. It was different. It was different with every return. However long he had known these men and women, none of them now treated him as an old boyhood playmate, or would dare. Which was what he wanted.

Tobie had stayed with him, doctor's cap rolled in his fist, bald cranium pink with frustration. Tobias Beventini was of the same generation as Julius and Gregorio, but his snubbed pink face had always looked younger, until you examined the marks round the small mouth and pale eyes. Service with Astorre had left its scars: an army doctor lives in the field and suffers as soldiers do, and sometimes more. It was a hunger for knowledge that sent Tobie abroad with his scalpel and saw – that, and a repugnance for the easy life of the studio, such as his famous uncle in Pavia enjoyed.

Jan Adorne was a student in Pavia. Walking with Nicholas now, Tobie managed one interjection. 'You raised a sword to Adorne!'

And Nicholas said, 'He had a very good doctor.' Then the crowd about them claimed his attention again, until they reached the council-room at last, and their colleagues.

There was not enough room, even yet, for the luxury of a permanent table in the salon where the Charetty–Niccolò company met, and where it entertained its clients in Bruges. The Bank of Niccolò now employed thirty agents in the field, and had added eight clerks and factors to its already large staff in Venice, together with an under-manager for Cristoffels, who led the Venetian house.

It was obvious to all men of sense that Julius should not have been taken to Scotland, and that either he or Gregorio should be sent at once to operate the main Bank at Venice now that Nicholas de Fleury was back home in Bruges.

It was assumed he was going to stay. The commands streaming without cease from Scotland had seemed to herald – to confirm – the end of the sterile calm which had followed their African triumph. One ought, of course, to congratulate a man wealthy enough at twenty-eight to rusticate, if he chose, with his family. But the young padrone they thought they knew and had fostered – ablaze with ideas, theories, plans to force through new frontiers, to explode ancient barriers, tease and outwit former enemies – was the magnet they wanted to follow, even though few of them would admit it.

And only a few, of whom Gregorio was one, had taken time through the months to listen to Godscalc the priest when, thumping his stick with the claw-hand he had brought back from Africa, he would exclaim, 'But whom are you following? Do you know? The boy you once liked? Or the man who has come from nowhere and is going nowhere, but like a meteor will end in dead rock and dust, and you with him?'

'That was the man who went to Africa. I thought another came back,' said Gregorio the first time. But as the winter passed, and the commands came hurtling from Scotland in impersonal and increasing profusion, Gregorio had avoided the priest and those others who thought that men should not live by whim, but from conviction. And that Nicholas had no convictions.

Because it was true, in its way. It seemed that Nicholas had abjured whatever lessons the absent years and the desert had taught him, and had turned in their place to the pagan gods of men such as Crackbene, whom he had taken for pilot. And yet Gregorio, afraid though he was, understood, and could not condemn Nicholas outright. For the occupations of trade and of law were not, he felt, bad in themselves, and often drew others to greatness.

So the lawyer, overcast in mood, waited for Nicholas de Fleury in the council-room, and was joined by Julius (who would have been entertained by his misgivings) and by Godscalc, who slowly entered with Diniz and seated himself. Diniz was talking soberly of his mother. 'Once Tilde is delivered, I'll go to Scotland. With Nicholas, if he'll let me.'

'You should,' Julius said. 'That's the place to be, I've got to say. You know Nicholas. He can spot opportunities the way other men can find water. You wouldn't believe what he's doing.'

'Ask not the honey where swarmeth the bee,' said the man he was talking about, entering with extreme suddenness, as if travelling to the seat of a fire. He threw a heap of papers on the cloth-covered table the secretaries used and sat down in the single chair at the end of it. There were benches along either side. His five partners settled about him while he leafed through his papers.

Being warmer, he looked slightly less bleak, Gregorio thought, but his manner remained the reverse of intimate, and the loose sable velvet and the resplendent sleeves distanced him further. Gregorio saw again, on his skin, the fading scars and marks that once had been burns. Tobie's eyes had been fixed on them also. There was no need to speculate. Whatever had happened, Julius would tell them, in detail.

Gregorio set his papers, too, before him and listened, while Nicholas de Fleury addressed them briefly from where he sat, and called on him to speak. No time was being lost. Time was money. Time was not only money, but a black, unquantifiable space waiting to be filled by a summons from somewhere unknown. Gregorio shivered and, picking up the first of the documents, began to make his report.

He had forgotten how numerate Nicholas de Fleury was. Some of the questions, which descended like pricks of a measuring-compass whenever Gregorio paused, were answered by Diniz, flushed but ready; some by the others. Debate was allowed, if compressed. Three times, their interlocutor let them see he was out of temper.

The first time, Gregorio had presented the situation in Egypt and Syria, where the Bank's interests were controlled from the Venetian trading station at Alexandria. Their factor there was John le Grant, engineer and shipmaster. Nicholas had sent to have him recalled.

'And he is on his way home?' Nicholas said.

'With the Middle Sea about to go up in flames? I know you wanted it,' Gregorio said, 'but we might lose a ship, or he might never get back to Egypt, or he might lose the goodwill of this Sultan. I did pass on your order, but he sent to explain why he's staying.' He paused. 'He's right, I'm sure. You have to know the situation.'

'And you think I don't know the situation?' Nicholas said. His voice had not changed. He said, 'Whom did you send with the letter?'

'A Florentine captain. One of our men took it to Pisa.' He felt Tobie move.

Nicholas said, 'When this meeting is finished, I shall write you another, and you will send it south today. Four of my own men-at-arms will go with it. The situation will then be conducive to John le Grant obeying my orders, whether his opinion differs from mine or not. Perhaps you would bear that in mind for another time.'

'You will lose him,' said Godscalc. It was the first time he had spoken.

'Is he mine now?' Nicholas said; and dismissed the subject.

After that, Gregorio trod very carefully. But it was impossible to avoid mentioning the army and Captain Astorre, and what they had faced, compelled to fight for Burgundy in Liège.

Nicholas listened. 'He is a mercenary,' he said. 'He has chosen to fight other men's wars regardless of principle. Why balk now?'

'He thinks of Bruges as his town,' Gregorio said. 'A place with its own freedoms. He saw Liège as another such, maybe. Or perhaps it was just the treachery. The French were tricked into abetting the massacre. Even the Archers were sickened. You must have heard of it.'

'Yes, I heard of it,' Nicholas said. 'So, like John le Grant, Astorre would prefer to pick his own sphere of action? Is this a request to annul his contract with the Charetty company?'

'It is a request to see you,' Gregorio said. 'He is in camp at St Omer. It is not a matter of money. He will serve you anywhere else you care to send him.' Again, he paused. 'Venice is calling for mercenaries. The Senate has written to you twice.'

'To help when the Middle Sea goes up in flames. Now I remember. You have experienced,' Nicholas said, 'a certain amount of confusion, haven't you, while I have been away? It all seems perfectly simple. You should have sent Astorre to manage ships and keep books in Alexandria, and brought back John le Grant to lead the Burgundian army. What other dissatisfied friends do we have? Tobie?'

The doctor finished reflectively blowing his nose. He said, 'I agree with Astorre. If you want him to stay, you'll have to invent a whole new philosophy.'

'And you?' Nicholas said. Julius was smiling. Gregorio realised that this must be nothing new: that Nicholas had behaved in this way also in Scotland.

Tobie said, 'I like unwinding guts from trees. I don't need to stay with him or you.' It meant, Gregorio knew, that he intended to stay beside Godscalc, but he didn't suppose Nicholas realised it.

Nicholas said, 'When did I ever ask it? I thought you were doing something constructive with books, that is all. No doubt Astorre can make up his own mind.'

'You won't go to St Omer?' Diniz said. Below his dark skin he had paled. He said, 'Nicholas, I wouldn't do what Astorre and the rest had to do. Or I wouldn't promise anyone that I would do it twice.'

Nicholas gazed at him.

Diniz said, 'Duke Charles is not like Urbino. He is a ruthless man, and less able by far than his father. There are other wars.'

Nicholas said, 'But I want Astorre fighting for Burgundy. If I can, I shall go and see him. So, what next? The Vatachino?'

'Intensifying their competition, but we are watching them,' Gregorio said, with more confidence. Opposition, even from their most powerful rival, had never done more than stimulate Nicholas. He added, 'They've increased their agents, as we have, and added a third senior partner based, we think, in Genoa. They've also resorted to spoiling tactics: rumours that you're going to close down and retire; that you came back with less gold than you say; even that you bought some gold which later vanished.'

'Someone knows that we lost what the first roundship carried,' Nicholas said. 'That's interesting. It may even mean the Vatachino themselves were the pirates. It sounds, anyway, as if they're afraid of us.'

'I think the Vatachino bribed the crew and stole the gold,' Diniz said. 'You said you wanted to find it. We haven't tried very hard. I think we should get one of these men and beat the truth out of him. They tried to buy over Gregorio.'

'And John le Grant,' said Gregorio dryly.

Nicholas surveyed him. 'You think his resistance to bribery deserves more than a beakful of preen-oil? Of course he stayed. He doesn't like the Vatachino. He likes the Bank, and its ships, and his freedom to think up new toys. Of course you stayed; you have Margot to think of. Of the rest of you, Julius wouldn't leave, Godscalc couldn't, and Diniz is far too well off as he is. The Bank is thus protected against major defectors, and the other kind don't have access to ledgers.'

'Congratulations,' said Tobie. 'An eloquent dissertation on company loyalty. So we have the Vatachino sized up. What about our other competitors? Tell us about Simon de St Pol of Kilmirren, whose hand you shook so honestly here in the summer. Now we've got him and his father swearing they'll ruin the Bank. I'm a shareholder, and I want to know why.'

Gregorio said, 'Is the reason important? We know Simon's temper and it has not been – forgive me, Nicholas – the easiest of times, either, for a man separated from his wife. All we need to know is that the Bank is none the worse for what has happened, and Julius has assured me of that. There is nothing that Kilmirren can do to harm us in Scotland, from what I have heard.'

'And de Ribérac?' Tobie said. 'He's in Bruges. For God's sake, his daughter Lucia is dead, and it won't take him long to hear about your tussle with Simon – dockside gossip will spread it. Maybe the Bank is safe from Kilmirren the Younger, but the old man has influence.'

'He is in Bruges?' Nicholas said. He looked at Gregorio.

'Gregorio didn't know,' Tobie said. 'I found out today. He and the Vatachino are at one another's hearts and livers, I'm happy to tell you.'

'Tobie told me,' said Diniz. 'I shall have to go to de Ribérac. I'm his grandson. I thought – I hoped –'

'That I would go with you,' said Nicholas.

'You could tell him how it happened,' Julius said. 'His other brat of a grandson tried to kill you, and Lucia got herself drowned coming to beg you not to give Henry away. I'm sorry, Diniz, but that was what happened. And that's why you needn't be troubled about what Simon or his father can do to the Bank of Niccolò. I was there. I saw what Henry did. He walked up to Nicholas and pushed a knife into him up to the hilt. He meant to kill him all right.'

'He was spoiled,' Diniz said. He bit his lip. He said, 'Gregorio told us. He didn't say why.'

'A good enough reason for a child,' Nicholas said. 'Someone insulted his father.'

'You?' said Diniz. Tobie opened his mouth and then closed it, glancing at Godscalc.

'Did I insult him? No. It was another child, the King's brother. Henry lost his head in the lists and tried to deprive the poor prince of his eyes. He didn't like being stopped.'

Godscalc said, 'That was all? When you tried to restrain him, the child turned his attack upon you? And you were injured, but didn't report it?'

'And so, as you have heard, obtained a counterhold against the entire St Pol family. I hope you are reassured, Tobie. Your patron, as you see, will spare no pains to safeguard his shareholders . . . So is that all? Is everyone satisfied? Is there anything else that is urgent? Or, Diniz, might we now send for some food?'

No one demurred. Diniz left. Gregorio collected his papers and Tobie, bending, helped the big priest to rise. Julius said, strolling over, 'Well, Nicholas, you stood on some toes. So will you go to old man Jordan with Diniz? Go on. Now you can squeeze the brute for anything that you fancy.'

Gregorio caught the priest's eye. The priest said, 'The vicomte, of course, must be visited; but were you to ask me, it would be sufficient for Diniz to call in the morning. And alone, I should say. The death of a daughter – 'tis not a matter for strangers. As for Nicholas, I should appreciate a word in his ear.' He looked towards the chair.

'Yes?' Nicholas said. He stood, resting one arm on his chair-back. It was apparent he meant to remain there. Gregorio glanced at him, and went out, taking Julius with him. On the way he caught up with Tobie who, lingering, seemed to receive some sign from Godscalc, and left. The door closed.

'I am concerned for you,' Godscalc said.

'I know,' said Nicholas. On the other side of the door, the footsteps receded. Tobie had wanted to stay. He said, 'Come and sit in this chair. The back is better for you.'

'The master's chair?' the priest said. 'The chair of the lord who decides where and when we all go?' He moved towards it and lowered himself.

'You think I was hard?' Nicholas said. He left the end of the table and taking Gregorio's place on the long bench disposed himself along it, facing the priest across one uplifted knee, his wrist dangling. He saw Godscalc's glance caught by his rings.

Godscalc said, 'I think you are preoccupied.' He paused. 'This attack on you by the child. We were afraid, Tobie and I. We feared that the poor scrap had found out whose son he was.'

'No. You know it, and Tobie, and my wife. Diniz suspects, but I have told him he is mistaken. Three people know there is proof. That is all.'

'Gelis knows it!' said the priest. 'Since when?'

'It was unintentional. I rambled once, when I was sick. She knew, of course, that her sister and I had been lovers.'

'She didn't think Simon ought to be told?'

'There would have been no fun in that,' Nicholas said. 'Or rather, no point. Simon's range of understanding is small. He has one resource: physical violence. To appear twice a cuckold would merely drive him insane, and probably end in the death of the child. Better growing up wild than not growing.'

Godscalc looked at him. 'Better growing up to kill his own father? Nicholas, things are not as they were. We cannot lay on that child, all unknowing, a sin such as that. Sometime, you must tell him the truth.'

'Sometime,' Nicholas said. 'But not while Simon is alive. We spoke of this once.'

'Is that why you re-opened the quarrel?' Godscalc said. 'So that you can reclaim your son if you breed a dead child or children, or daughters? As you also said once, you have a fortune to leave, and your life is often at risk. Did you try to kill Simon?'

'I will not deny,' Nicholas said, 'that I am trying to punish him. Or that I did once try to kill him as Henry did me. But not in cold blood. Or not yet.'

'But why? You made peace,' Godscalc said.

'He broke it,' said Nicholas.

'And Gelis?' said Godscalc.

'What of her?' he said. He released his knee and turned, laying his arms on the table. His rings shone with absolute steadiness.

'Will you lay on her the strain of watching you pursue this ignoble duel? You have a young wife and family, and health and riches with which to sustain them. Can you not forgive this poor, silly man who has nothing but a boy who is not even his?'

'I have rendered him helpless,' Nicholas said. 'Julius was right. They can't harm me without harming Henry. My wife and my forthcoming child will have nothing to fear from Kilmirren. That I can swear to.'

'Nicholas?'

He looked up, still smiling.

The brown eyes frowned. The tonsure above was already shadowed with stubble, the tangled hair grey at each side. Godscalc said, 'Do you want this second child? This child Gelis will give you?'

Nicholas said, 'I want a family. I had none. Henry is seven. He will never be any man's son now but Simon's.'

'You want a family by Gelis?' Godscalc said.

'I have no other wife. And many bedfellows, but no serious mistress. Ask Julius.'

'There is seldom need,' Godscalc said. 'Answer me.'

'I thought I had. Yes, I want a family by Gelis,' said Nicholas. 'There is no cause for concern. I have new business in Scotland, that's all.' He saw, reflected in Godscalc's lined face, the weariness that had dogged him all day.

Godscalc said, 'When did you last make confession?'

'When did you last know whether I was telling the truth?' Nicholas said. The words were tired, too.

Godscalc fell silent. Then he shifted his bulk in his chair as if his limbs pained him. He said, 'Very well. I will not waste your time or mine. I have been entrusted with some information, to impart to you or not as I choose. You have not inspired me with confidence.'

'I know,' said Nicholas. If he could not be natural, he could be brief.

Godscalc said, 'Nor are you helping me now. It is your strongest card, we both know, that absence of personal pleading. Moreover, a priest, like a doctor, can recognise a man who is spending more of himself than he has. You will not trust me with the cause, whatever it is?'

'I conduct my own life,' Nicholas said.

'And you are managing so successfully?' Godscalc said. Then he looked down and, with a half-smile, lifted his twisted hand in the air. 'What right have I to say that? But for you, I should not be here.'

'We have carried each other. You have nothing to thank me for,' Nicholas said.

'No?' The priest let his palm fall on his lap as if it pained him. 'But you lock me out all the same. I have a message for the Nicholas who almost died for me once. I have a message from Gelis.'

By thud of drum, word passed through the Sahel and into the blood. The ground throbbed like this, and the temples, from the blood beating its way through the body. Nicholas moved. He said, 'Yes?'

Godscalc surely saw, but did not remark on it. He spoke dryly. 'As you know, your child was conceived far too early. To me, the responsibility and the blame are both yours, but the girl feels she was thoughtless, and has caused you embarrassment, perhaps anger. I am to find out how you feel, and act accordingly. That is, I know where she is and am empowered, if it seems wise, to tell you.'

'I knew it would be early,' Nicholas said. 'Is it born?'

'That I have not been told. But you will be able to see for yourself,' Godscalc said. 'Of course, you will be discreet. She does not want the world to know. I have told no one.'

'Not even Tobie?' he said.

'I have told no one. It is for you and for her to make what announcement you please. She will know by now you are here. I suggest you set out tomorrow. It will take you four hours to ride there, and I have had to promise that you will go alone. She has written the name of the convent.'

'Tomorrow?' said Nicholas.

'The day after your arrival. It is what she suggested. You are thinking of Diniz? I shall tell him some white lie, as priests can. He can meet de Ribérac and talk of his mother without you. He knows the circumstances of her death. Julius told him.'

'If you think so,' said Nicholas. He sat for a bit while Godscalc was trying to open his purse; then, leaning over, helped him politely.

The paper inside was from Gelis. It was much folded and creased, but the writing on it was bold and familiar with no trace of weakness; the first of hers he had seen since they parted. It contained only four lines: the address of a convent, and the bald directions for finding it. The covering letter was absent and, on reflection, he did not press to see it. He could imagine what it contained.

He did not have to set his men to harrying nunneries.

She had known that he would, and had invented this move to prevent it.

She had lodged the message with Godscalc, relying on Godscalc's understanding of Nicholas. Godscalc would never wittingly place her in danger.

And wittingly of course, neither he would.

Chapter 15

THE NUNS LIKED Mistress Margot, who was well mannered and handsome and kind, and had been thankful when she left her post with the lawyer in Bruges and came to help them with their difficult Lady.

Newly arrived, sore from her altercation with Gregorio, Margot deduced that the sisters had become a little flustered at first when Gelis van Borselen rode up with her servants and occupied all their guest-quarters, despite the extraordinary sum of money she deposited with them.

They felt a genuine sorrow, although they did not express it, that a lady so well born and wealthy should feel it incumbent to hide from her loved ones. When they learned that, at last, her dear husband was to be permitted to visit, they wept tears of joy.

Margot wept as well: tears of exhaustion and fear, which she kept to herself. She couldn't guess what was going to happen, for this time she knew Gregorio's instinct to be wrong. That is, Gregorio, whom she loved, was a lawyer and a temperate man, who thought other men were as he was, and who knew only one woman, herself.

She and Gregorio had been separated many times since first, long ago, they became lovers, but never by her will like this, and never as painfully. And if, because of the outcome, he did not want to take her back at the end, she had no hold over him. They were not man and wife.

Late one afternoon, the courier came to the convent to tell Dame Gelis the *Ghost* was in Sluys with her husband de Fleury on board. It meant, Margot comprehended, that Nicholas would be in his Bruges house by now. It meant that, if the priest thought it safe, Nicholas would have learned of his wife's invitation. It meant that tomorrow afternoon he could be here.

That night, Margot did not try to sleep. Lying alone in the darkness of her small chamber, she watched the line of gold under the door that told her Gelis, too, was waiting, awake.

They had parted, Nicholas de Fleury and this girl, on their wedding night. On that night, caught by chance within hearing, Gregorio had heard Nicholas receive such a welcome as, surely, no man ever received from his bride. '*Look at me. It's Simon's child, Nicholas. What shall I do with it? Kill it? Rear it? Tell Simon about it? Or let the world think it's yours?*'

Nicholas had left the room then without answering. But, ignoring advice, he had repudiated neither his bride nor her child. He had merely departed on business, leaving her as his acknowledged wife, with half his fortune still settled upon her. And he had informed her that he intended the child, when born, to be treated as his.

Gregorio did not understand, but Margot did. Nicholas had acted with the cleverness you would expect of him. He had drawn the venom from the girl's declaration by forcing it underground. And at the cost of inhuman restraint, he had denied her the satisfaction for which she must have ached.

To offer to accept another man's child as his own seemed an act worthy of the man who, to all appearances, had emerged with some nobility from the ordeal of Africa. But it had not always been so. Long ago, Nicholas had responded very differently, it was said, to men or women who crossed him. Since then, he had directed his energies towards success in business, employing a talent for strategy to force his will on men of far higher birth. There was ruthlessness there, however rarely he let it be seen.

Gregorio could not deny it, but was disarmed, Margot well knew, by the high spirits, the imagination, the courage which had always endeared Nicholas to those in his own chosen circle. Once, Margot herself had had no doubts either. Until this occurred.

Why should a girl – intelligent, capable, united in unorthodox passion with such a man and accepting his offer of marriage – why should Gelis hold Nicholas de Fleury in such hatred that, far more terrible than refusing the marriage, she had slept beforehand in the bed of his enemy, and conceived a child to bring unborn to her husband?

Why? Gelis had never said, and Margot could not ask her.

She could attempt, though, to guess. Chance having made them lovers in Africa, perhaps Nicholas or Gelis – or both – had resented the inevitable bondage of marriage. But then, by all accounts, the illicit union had continued on their return; both had seemed desirous of marriage. And yet that again was contradictory. To plan such a betrayal, Gelis could neither have loved Nicholas de Fleury nor pitied him, for all she had allowed him every liberty, over and over, and must have brought herself to respond.

But physical passion and hatred could live together. She might have been jealous of Umar, except that Umar was married. She might have resented the life of the mind which Nicholas had pursued, except that she, too, was not unread or unintelligent. Perhaps the other wives of Nicholas, his other mistresses haunted her. Or maybe it was something quite different. Perhaps, in their idyll in Africa, Gelis had truly plumbed the nature of Nicholas; had identified what other men had suspected: something that was not humane, or cheerful, or generous. She had seen perhaps that his famous stoicism was something to fear, as you would fear a wolf tormented by children. A wolf she had chosen to challenge.

Once, after she had left Gregorio to come here, Margot had asked about Katelina, the sister who had married Simon de St Pol and died in Cyprus. Gelis had turned the subject. Simon believed, Margot knew, that Nicholas was responsible for his wife's death. If Gelis believed that as well, it could account for something of this. What was transparent, however, was that Gelis had no interest in the man she had picked to father her child. He was a cipher. He had been chosen to cause Nicholas the utmost – what? Anguish? But that would presuppose affection for Gelis. Anger? Offended pride must feature in all this, of course. And outrage, because she had defiled the legitimate line of his house. His first-born would be a bastard.

Yet Nicholas had offered to make it a de Fleury, and rear it.

Margot did not believe that, although Gregorio did. That was why she had come here in the first instance – because she did not believe that a man like Nicholas would tamely accept Simon's child as his own. Nor would it matter if it were not Simon's child, but a substitute, a poor changeling brought in to deceive him. Sooner or later, Nicholas was going to retaliate, and Margot meant to be here. Not to stand between husband and wife. Not to protect this distant fair girl, oppressed and silent, whom she hardly saw and whose private torment she could only guess at. But for the child, if there was to be a child.

A solitary woman, she could offer small help, except for what comfort her presence might bring. She did not expect the girl's confidence, and did not receive it. But the weeks had been made to pass, and she had been tolerated, and thus was present, now the moment had come. The moment when Nicholas de Fleury would enter these rooms and, after nearly eight months, speak again with his wife.

She might have known that he would not honour the bidding. He came, indeed, the day after his arrival, but at first light, when the lamps still burned in the yard, and the grooms were breaking the ice in the troughs and the smell of warm bread and smoke lingered under the eaves. The gates were already open, but he dismounted and stood, in the way only Nicholas stood, while the porter trod through the crackling slush to announce him. Instead of tomorrow, he had come through the night.

Indoors, the line of light under his wife's door went out. Gelis had heard the voices and crossed to her window to look. Margot continued to stand watching from hers. There was little to see. He was alone and anonymous, his harness and cloak outwardly undistinctive, his face an obscure patch between hat-brim and scarves. Then the porter returned with the guest-house master, and their shadows moved up the path to the door, which then closed. He would be greeted hospitably, and offered rest and refreshment, for he was barely ashore and dry-shod from the sea. Presently, amid the chatter of servants and nuns you could hear, quiet and sociable, the sound of educated male voices below.

The lamp in the next room had been rekindled. The door between presently opened and Gelis van Borselen stood there, her face in shadow. She said, 'Ah. You are up. He seems to be here. Do you mind keeping your room? I shall send if I need you.'

It was an order: Unless I say so, don't speak to him. It was also something more, and worse. All that was said in one room could be heard in the next.

Margot hesitated. Then she said, 'I should like to send word to Gregorio.'

'Write a note,' Gelis said. 'I shall give it to him before he goes.' And she turned to walk back to her room.

She wore, half fastened as yet, the undergarment of one of last summer's gowns. Margot thought, as the door shut, that she looked cold in it already.

The journey, being at night, had taken longer than four hours to accomplish. Nicholas had chosen to set out twelve hours too early, knowing that Gelis would count this as one of his options, and would be prepared. The ease with which he was admitted confirmed it. It meant, of course, that she had been forced to keep vigil too.

On the way, he had occupied himself with a long, complicated piece of strategy to do with current rates of exchange for gold bullion. Between formidable ladders of numbers, the tracks of his mind kept presenting him with blocks of fragmented poetry. When it first happened, he followed the verses to the end, as his consciousness yielded them. When others took shape in their place, a painful jumble, he forced a return to his numbers.

Now and then, he fell asleep in the saddle: something that could happen in battle-lulls, but rarely elsewhere. This was hardly a battle. All he was doing, in practical terms, was settling a claim over property. He had to pursue a missing object, identify it, and take appropriate action.

He arrived at the convent. The guest-master, gazing slightly past his ear, offered him hot spiced wine, with speeches of welcome.

Refusing, Nicholas asked with equal courtesy after the health of his wife and the child.

'Ah!' the guest-master said, glancing past the other ear. 'But that she must tell you herself. A wife's prerogative. Shall I send to see if she is ready?'

'If you would,' Nicholas said, sipping water. He hated water. One day, when all this was over . . . For a long time he had been saying: One day, when all this was over. For, of course, it had to be over, one day.

Then he was upstairs, and his escort tapped on a door, and left him as someone remarked, 'Please come in.'

Please. ('*Bear it? Kill it? Rear it?*') Please was an improvement.

He went in and closed the door behind him. He locked it slowly and, turning, tossed her the key. 'Unless you want to be interrupted,' he said.

Regardless of anything, it was her face he looked at first. He had no idea what to expect. Dislike, of course. Probably something very much stronger: hatred, contempt. Possibly fear, although she would disguise that. Or worst of all, juvenile triumph.

But not that, no. She was not juvenile. She had planned it, she had carried it out, she would carry this out. She could do it in several possible ways. He saw, looking at last, that his recollection of her face was quite exact, and that she had chosen to appear firm and calm, but for a hint of impatience.

He looked down then. She wore the gown she had worn, newly landed from Scotland last June, on the day of their sudden betrothal. He remembered the close-cut ellipse of the neck, sedately matched to the beauty – the new-ripened beauty – it covered. He recognised, forcing his thoughts through their channel, the expensive fabric; the excellent seamwork. It fitted now, from bodice to hem, as it had done before.

He said, 'You must be cold,' with a calmness equal to hers.

The shutters were closed, and she had brought in extra candles and lamps. Instead of the first hours of a cold winter dawn, it might have been the eve of some extraordinary Feast of the Church. Or a doctor's tent at the edge of some battle.

It served its purpose, the light. It outlined her body, confirming what the gown had already announced: that she was not thickened with child. It showed next her firm, fair-skinned face and set mouth and pale eyes hardly defined except by their lashes and brows, unexpectedly brown. She plucked her brows, unlike her late sister, and her hairline was fashionably high, the hair light as chaff, and bound and netted as befitted a matron.

She looked like a figure of spiritual authority, rendered upon painted glass. She was five years younger than he was: twenty-four at the most. He could not read her face any longer. He doubted if she could read his.

He had left his cloak below, and his sword, although he had kept his dagger for various reasons. He laid aside his hat and gloves and sat down, as one could say was his right. In a leisurely way, he glanced about him. Then he returned his gaze to where she stood. There was no point in greetings or courtesies: it was a matter of business. He said, 'Is there news, or should I come another day? I put off several meetings.'

He had set the level: she maintained it. 'You need not have come at all,' Gelis said. 'You walked out of our last conversation. I was disappointed.'

'You want to resume it?' Nicholas asked, gently surprised.

She lifted her hand to her cheek. She said, 'I am only a woman. Perhaps you would strike me again.'

'Perhaps,' he said. 'Since it suited your purpose so well the last time. What were you saying when I left? *Whatever you want, I shall do it*? I came to give you my answer.'

She said, 'You think the offer still stands?'

'Offer? I thought,' he said, 'it was a promise. In fact, you made the same one a few hours before at an altar. So have you borne a child, Gelis, since we last spoke?'

'Let me remember,' she said. This time, she let him hear the anger. He was surprised that she expected him to react.

He said, 'You know why I have come. I am prepared to bring the child up as mine. I told Gregorio.'

'I heard,' she said.

'So there are arrangements to be made. I cannot discuss them until I know the child exists. We can make this quite brief. It would suit me.'

She stood, looking at him. He realised that of course she had considered, many times over, what his first words would be, and how he would say them. She had not expected, perhaps, how he looked. He knew he looked different. She said, 'I thought we ought to meet face to face. I wanted to tell you myself. It seems, you see, that I was mistaken. Tragically, there never was any child.'

It was not going to be brief.

He said, 'Why then did you announce it and stay here?'

'To escape you,' she said.

'I see. So why send for me?'

'I thought I told you. To see your face. To talk to you in a place where you couldn't harm me. There never was a child. I was lying. To the world, my doctor made a mistake.'

He said, 'Then you had better explain it to Simon. Preferably in a room like this with some nuns. Whatever you do, he'll slaughter your doctor. He thinks you are increasing his stock.'

'You've spoken to Simon about . . .?' She stopped herself quickly.

'As you were hoping, I'm sure. *He* didn't think you were lying. And there is Margot as well. Margot would have left if you hadn't been pregnant. So you were pregnant. Or you have to prove otherwise.'

Move; pause; move; check; move. She said, 'I could strip for you, but it's cold. Or there is a small, well-known test for strayed nuns. Infallible, too. Milk is a commodity of which Nature is astoundingly wasteful.' She waited, her hands usefully poised.

Nicholas reclined where he was. The chair-back was cushioned. He contemplated her for a long time at his leisure until she realised he was going to do nothing. Then she dropped her arms and threw his key on the table. She wore a half-smile.

'Oh, no, no,' Nicholas said. 'I'm not going to assault you; I leave all that to Crackbene. And you would have stripped if there was nothing to see. So there *was* a child, I deduce, and we can go on, but quicker.'

'Crackbene?' she said. 'What has he done? Has he done something to Simon?'

'But quicker,' he repeated with patience.

'What has happened to Simon?' she said.

He had thought better of her. She had thought it all through, surely, when planning it. He changed his position with indolence, folding his arms and lifting his chin in the air, so that his eyes almost closed.

'You want to know the consequences of your scheme? Simon was alive when I left, but I don't hold out great hopes for his future. Lucia is dead. Henry will die if I say so. Jordan is extremely uneasy, and is likely to come and put to you all the matters we have just been discussing, not excluding the test for lactating nuns. *I will not wait any longer. Did you bear a child?*'

'Yes!' she said. 'It is dead.'

The lamps flickered. Wheels rumbled out in the yard. Somewhere, someone was singing. His lids remained nearly closed, because he told them to. 'I don't believe you,' he said. 'You could not hurt me with a dead child.'

'I lost it!' she said.

'You would have provided a substitute. Without it, there was no point in scheming.'

'You are so sure,' she said. 'So sure you know everything. All right, listen. Listen. Open your eyes, damn you, and listen.

'I have had a child. Eighteen days ago. It was half-human, sexless, a freak. The nuns will tell you. They buried it.'

His eyes were open by then. He sat up, and clasped his hands gently. He said, 'Why not say so at once?'

'It was you,' Gelis said, 'who taught me to delay what will give the most pleasure.'

Her eyes were searching and bright. His thoughts flickered, random as lamplight, and then became still, before the brightness of her eyes.

Nicholas drew a breath and said, 'No!'

He rose before she could stop him. The candles streamed as he passed. He crossed the room to the inner door: the door that was shut but which showed light underneath it. He flung the door open and saw what he had guessed he would see: the invisible witness to all that had happened. Margot, who had deserted Gregorio for this.

She cried out, and he dropped his hand without touching her. Her face was drawn, the natural comeliness dimmed with fear and anxiety. He said, 'I won't hurt you. Come in. Will you come in?'

She was looking beyond him, at Gelis. He turned his head to Gelis as well, the standpost hard at his back. Then he straightened and left it. He came back to where Gelis stood. He said, 'We should each tell the truth. Let Margot come in and sit. Both of you, listen. Lucia is dead, but I didn't kill her. Henry will come to no harm. Simon is being punished, and is also bearing your punishment: I presume that is what you intended, and I make no apology. Gelis, I shall not kill the child, or renounce it. Neither will Simon claim it. If it exists, there is nothing to fear. So tell me. Is there a child?'

'Yes,' said Margot.

Gelis said, 'No. He is tricking you.'

Nicholas said, 'Margot?' The lamps burned; he felt his lips crack.

Margot said, 'Be fair. I can only tell you a little. A child. A child born alive, and still living.'

'A son or a daughter?' he said.

'No!' said Gelis again. She rose, her face livid.

Margot said, 'A son. That is all I can tell you.'

'That is all,' Gelis repeated. She stood before Margot, as if her shadow could silence her. 'That is all. Go away. Nothing more.'

'And here? He is here?' said Nicholas softly.

'No,' said Gelis. 'No, he isn't.'

'Margot?' he said.

She stood beside Gelis. She said, 'No. He isn't here.'

'I don't believe you,' he said. 'It doesn't matter. The place isn't so large. Look, it is daylight.'

He rose and passed the two women. Margot's arm was round the girl's shoulders. He laid hands on the shutters and parted them. Then he set the window ajar and rested beside it, the air on his face. Presently he said, 'The singing. What is it?'

'Hymns from the chapel,' Margot said. She seemed to wait. Then she spoke in a subdued voice. 'Nicholas? Now we have told you, will you be patient? The baby is young. It isn't supposed to be born. You can go back reassured. Tell your friends that Gelis is well. You can be certain the baby will thrive.'

'And then?' Nicholas said. He did not turn.

'I dare say you will come again,' said Gelis's voice. 'Then we can discuss what to do.'

'If you are here,' Nicholas said. He moved then, and closing the casement, fastened it slowly. 'And even if you are, the child may not be. Or may have turned into a freak again, or a mistake, or even died of some mysterious illness.' He turned.

'It will be here for you,' Margot said. Gelis said nothing.

'I intend that he will,' Nicholas said. 'And until then, he will be in a place of my choosing. Where is he now?'

'Not here,' Gelis said. She had separated from Margot.

'Where?' He was looking at Margot.

Gelis said, 'She doesn't know. Come again in a month. Come again when he looks more like Simon. Then tell me if you want him.'

Her eyes went past him to the window. Margot said, 'What is that?' and came quickly forward. Gelis hesitated and then followed her to the window. He stood aside to let them look out.

The cries were loud by then, and the sound of trampling horses, and of angry voices and blows. The voices were those of the servants, and the blows were struck by the younger grooms, and even by the fist of a nun or two. They were aimed at a troop of forty armed men which had surrounded them and was driving them briskly indoors.

His men were well trained, and obeyed orders. They used their arms in defence; they did their best not to retaliate. The yard emptied. His captain, looking up, nodded.

Gelis said, 'You broke your word. You weren't alone.'

He used a dimple, which she could interpret quicker than anyone. 'You should have had the road better watched. You broke a promise more binding than mine. But for that, I shouldn't have called them.'

'What will they do?' Margot said.

'Find the child.'

She said, 'It isn't here. Gelis sent it away. Don't distress these good holy people.'

'I shan't touch them,' he said. 'So long as they tell me where it is.'

'They don't know,' Gelis said.

'Then I am sorry for them,' said Nicholas and, walking across, resumed his seat and folded his arms.

'This has gone too far,' Margot said. She seized the key and grasping the door, unlocked it and ran from the room. Gelis made no effort to stop her; neither did he.

'So she doesn't know about Simon,' Nicholas said. 'You wouldn't care to send her back to Gregorio? This type of campaign is not for the sensitive.'

'She thinks I need protection,' said Gelis. 'What did Simon say about me?'

'All of it? I stopped him halfway, since there was nothing new in it.'

'And you fought him.'

'Over something else, yes. Hand to hand. He was very surprised. Has the child been baptised?' Below, someone screamed.

'Yes. I chose a name you would like. What will you do?' The same person sobbed.

'I thought I'd mentioned it. You can stay with the child for a month. Then you can present it in Bruges, and come with it to begin family life with me in Scotland.'

'And Simon?' she said.

He thought for a moment. 'I suppose so,' he said. 'So long as you are discreet, and he is still there and able. It might be difficult, though. Henry knows all his father's bedmates, you included. He doesn't want a brother or sister. In fact, I shouldn't let Henry too close to – what have you called this son of yours?'

She told him. With all his vaunted percipience, he had never really considered what she might do about that. He was still standing, dumb, when Margot stormed into the room pursued by his complaining captain. Margot strode over to Gelis and, grasping her by the shoulders, pushed her to stand before Nicholas. Margot said, 'Tell him. Tell him where the child is. Now. And quickly.'

The captain, arriving beside her, was breathless. He said, 'The Lady's child isn't here, my lord. It's been spirited off to some other estate. But how far away, they won't say. Sir, have I your leave to persuade them?'

Margot said, 'Gelis?' and shook her.

Gelis moved her head from side to side, smiling at Nicholas.

Know your enemy. Know what she will do, and what she will not. Nicholas turned. 'Persuade them,' he said.

'No!' said Margot, and spun Gelis round by the arm. 'Tell them what they want to know. Or I shall tell Nicholas everything. And the van Borselen family. I shall break every promise I made you.'

Gelis looked at her. The captain paused, half out of the room. Gelis sighed. Then she said, 'What a fuss over nothing! What sort of persuasion do you think they would use? And the moment it began to be painful, someone would blurt out the truth. I don't know why people always will hurry things.'

Involuntarily, Nicholas laughed. He said, 'Neither do I. But I think that, by any standards, the time has come to concede. Where is the child, Gelis?'

'Oh, well,' she said. She turned to the captain. 'Two hours away. Write it down. I don't want to be blamed if you lose the way.' And, calmly, she gave an address.

Margot released her and sat down.

'You need some food,' Nicholas said. He walked out and called down the stairs. The captain passed him, running below with the paper. Outdoor noises penetrated almost at once: shouting and the jingle of harness. From inside, below him, there continued a hubbub of voices and crying. No one came to his summons.

Nicholas swore under his breath, but without very much violence. Instead of calling again, he walked down the stairs and into the heart of the uproar. After a while, he got them to listen.

No one had been hurt, and they agreed, after a while, that young women in childbirth had peculiar ideas, and that these were of less importance than the expensive new roof they required for their hospice.

While he was there, he had food sent upstairs, and some ale. He didn't go upstairs himself, but joined the Abbess in her private parlour, and allowed himself the luxury, all the time she was talking, of one fine glass of wine.

The Abbess said, 'If you won't eat, you should sleep. We'll see the Lady comes to no harm. I shall wake you when the party comes back with the child.'

The chamber he was given was small, and contained only a bed. Gelis was a courtyard away and one floor above him, but he had left men on guard. He expected Margot would sleep. Obviously Gelis would not, nor would he. Not now.

They had to shake him awake. Eventually, he rolled off the bed, and then sat on the edge, slowly dressing. 'I'm sorry,' the captain was saying. 'I'm sorry, we got to the house but they'd gone. It seems like another troop came and took over, and rode away with the babe, none knows where. That's wicked, sir. Or do you think the mother planned it again?'

'I expect so,' he said. 'And if she's wise, she probably doesn't know the real destination herself. Well, I can't wait. We'll have to leave it. You've done well. I think you'll find they have some meat and ale here they won't grudge you, and then a barn where you can sleep for a bit. I'm going back.'

'I'll give you a man, sir?' said the captain. 'Or more, if the Lady's going with you?'

He said, 'No. I'll go alone. It's only four hours to Bruges.' He would have daylight for most if not all of it. The captain, naturally, did not persist.

His horse was already saddled when he went indoors for the last time and ascended the stairs. Margot intercepted him before he could go further. She said painfully, 'Gelis tricked you. I didn't know. She let it go so far before she gave in.' She broke off. She said, 'Sometimes I think I can't forgive her. Or you.'

'No one was hurt,' Nicholas said. He touched her, and she flinched. 'The screams were part of the play-acting too.'

'Simon was hurt,' she said. 'You say Lucia is dead, and Henry in some sort of trouble. What kind of play-acting is that? I think you should leave your wife with her child, and give up what you are doing in Scotland.'

He dropped his hand. 'Do you?' he said.

'You can't want this marriage. Open war, with a child in the middle? And it is escalating. You incite one another.'

'I expect Gregorio would agree with you,' Nicholas said. 'Would you like to come back with me, now that Gelis is well?'

'You don't want me with her?' she said.

Nicholas said, 'I was thinking of you.'

Once, long ago, Margot had been forced into marriage and fled. Once, long ago, Margot and Gregorio had been unable to marry, but now her husband was dead, and they could. Except that they didn't.

She shook her head. 'I don't want to keep secrets from Goro. I'll wait until the official birth, and come back. She has to come back then, surely. This is no life.'

He said, 'He misses you. This is one thing that should not have happened. Come with me and marry him.'

'Now?' she said. 'You think I should marry him now, after all that has been happening? No. It has been so all our lives, and it is not going to change now.'

He said nothing more. He followed her to his wife's room, and waited outside, and was almost beyond feeling when Margot came out and said, 'She is sleeping.'

Her eyes were on him. He said, 'Let her sleep.' He, too, had been felled.

Margot said, 'The child. What will you do?'

He said, 'I am leaving men here. She'll expect that. She'll probably find out how to elude them. I don't think it matters. She'll announce the birth when the timing is right.' He stopped. 'I should have liked to see the boy. Will she let me? Some time?'

Instead of replying, Margot slowly re-opened the door, as if the answer might lie somewhere inside. The bleak afternoon light showed the chair he had sat on and the guttered candles and the brazier choked with grey ash. It showed the uprights of the bed, and the pallid rectangle upon which a girl lay like a stone, like a corpse on a beach; furled in her summer-light, bare-shouldered gown, her roughened hair spilled down her back. Her hand was sunk clenched in the pillow.

Nicholas took off his lined mantle and lowered the furs, soft as snow, till they covered her. Margot started and stopped a small gesture. Outside she spoke. 'Take your cloak back. We have blankets.'

He smiled. 'I have a raincloak as well. That will do. No. Leave it. I mean it. She will hate it so.'

She looked at him. Her expression had changed. So far as he

knew, his had not. Goro was a clever man, but transparent: they made a good pair. She said, 'He has the best nurse that money can buy.' Then she ran to her room.

Riding back the way he had come, Nicholas was sensible of the difference. It was daylight. His attention, no longer compelled inwards, could play on the country about him: the bustle of birds, the sound of an axe, a fox crossing his path without haste. It was not spring as yet, but overhead the leaf-buds were thickening and the first petals were pale underfoot. He passed hamlets with pigs grunting about, and inquisitive children. There were carts on the road, and other riders, although no one he knew. Finding himself suddenly hungry, he stopped at an inn and took part in a solemn exchange on the subject of foot-rot.

Disencumbered, exposed, the spaces of his mind were touched now and then by vagrant sound; by spangles of music which occasionally coalesced into something he had heard Will Roger devise, or the girl called Katelijne Sersanders. Sometimes the verses were bawdy. He chanted under his breath, knowing he wanted something else, and then knowing what it was. He also knew where to find it: in St Donatien's, where – orderly, pious and calm – the trained voices uttered praise in the perpetual choir of divine service: hymn and psalm, collect and canticle, grail and anthem, cursed by Colard in ecstasy as he painted them into his missals. For evensong, Magnificat was what they would sing. He would be there very soon, and in time.

He was singing inside his mind when he became aware that he was neither alone nor in casual company, but that the road was lonely, the trees dark, and a group of armed men was blocking his way.

He swung his horse, looking for a way out, his sword in his hand, but it was too late, and there were too many. The attack when it came was peculiarly savage; or perhaps that was because he was so unprepared.

There was nothing much he could do, except inflict what damage he might. He used his sword against other blades and, once, slashed a face; but they killed his horse and dragged him from the saddle, cudgels rising and falling. When the sword was knocked from his grasp, he used his dagger until his arms and shoulders were numbed. He protected his head for as long as he could, but the raincloak was thin.

No one spoke. He didn't argue, or plead. They were not footpads: they had not saved his horse or cut his belt or opened his purse.

They knew who he was. They were what he had set upon Simon: bullies with clubs. Bullies with orders to frighten, to capture, but forbidden to kill.

After a while he stopped struggling, since he was patently in their power and they might prefer to save their energy, too. They saved it by knocking him efficiently on the head. By then, he had worked out whose they were.

Chapter 16

ERVING FRANCE AS he did, the vicomte de Ribérac was not a man who frequented Bruges, and when he came there, it behooved him to stay with those families such as van Borselen, Gruuthuse or Vasquez with which his son Simon and daughter Lucia were connected. Even then, it did not always suit these gentry, however eminent, to have the French King's adviser so close, and he would be installed in one of the family's country manors outside the walls, and the Duke duly informed. The vicomte was generally watched, but had many ways of evading the watchers.

Nicholas did not know the house into which, waking, he found himself being pushed and, since it was now dark and heavily raining, the landscape in which it was set was invisible. He judged, however, from the severity of his headache, that he had not been unconscious for long, and so could not be far distant from Bruges. He was pleased to think that the raincloak, though torn, had come in handy: the rain itself had revived him. Through the soreness, he felt alert, expectant, even elated. The truth was, he wanted an opponent who wasn't a woman. He wanted someone who would hit hard, and whom he could hit back.

The house was old, with worn tiles on the floor, but the door they brought him to was heavy and carved. His escort knocked and, opening it, ushered him in.

It was a bedchamber. Eating in front of the fireplace, napkin under his jowl, was Jordan de Ribérac. He attended to what was on his plate, speared something on the point of his knife and opened his mouth to receive it. His jaw movements resumed. Then he looked up.

As gross men do, he wore loose robes, buttoned tight at the wrist, with his shirt-bands not quite closed at the throat. His outdoor hat had been replaced by a deep cap of felt swathed in white pleated muslin, which tumbled over one massive shoulder and into the napkin. Both were spotted with gravy. His knife was of silver. Its matching case lay on the cloth with his wine-cup. He said, 'Untie his hands and wait outside. One of you fetch him dry clothes.'

'Monseigneur?' said the chief of his captors. De Ribérac was alone in the room.

'Untie him,' said Jordan. 'He isn't going to kill me yet. Are you, Nicholas?'

'I don't know, yet,' said Nicholas, holding his hands out. Someone did actually cut through his bonds. He added, 'You might simply have sent for me.' The men who had freed him hesitated, and then left. He stood, pensively rubbing his wrists.

'And you would have come alone?' said the vicomte. 'I don't think so. I know the warehouse in Antwerp; and the office, the apartments, the soldiery the Bank has not been told it possesses. I cannot imagine why your guard were not with you just now. On such mistakes rest an old man's feeble triumphs. And now you will undress for me.'

'To music?' Nicholas said.

'Was such the practice in Trebizond? One never ceases to learn. My son strips before me whenever he can,' said the fat man. 'To allow me to savour the contrast. Of course, I could summon my men.'

'I expect they look the same, too,' Nicholas said. 'You have heard from Simon, I gather.'

The fat man swabbed his platter with bread. 'I have heard from Simon. I have visited Diniz. I have spoken to that fool of a woman, Adorne's wife. I know what you did to my son and my daughter. I have asked you to strip.' He looked up.

'The Erring Nun Test? It wouldn't work,' Nicholas said. 'No, I'm sorry. I must be light-headed. You want to see my safe conduct.'

'Your safe conduct?' said de Ribérac. He was peeling an apple.

'A very explicit scar. Poor young Henry's noble effort at murder. I'm sure Simon sent to ask what to do.'

The knife moved round and round. 'A fabrication.'

'Before witnesses?' He found a stool and sat. There would be an attack. The vicomte liked inflicting pain, or else watching it.

'What witnesses?' Jordan said. 'Adorne's doctor, Adorne and his niece will hardly speak for you now. The man Roger is English and coercible. Your Julius may succumb to a brawl in the streets.'

It was surprising what he knew. 'And Mistress Bel?' Nicholas asked.

'Lucia's clucking hen you took roosting in Africa? See what a fine nest my daughter lies in,' said Jordan, 'through the efforts of Bel of Cuthilgurdy. She may have been soft with you once, but she will perjure what soul she has to save Henry.'

'Assuming all five to be perjured or dead, then indeed there is no case against Henry. How may I help you?' said Nicholas.

'With a little information,' said Jordan. 'What news of this child of my line? Is the new infant born?'

'Pray that it isn't,' said Nicholas. 'If it comes now, too soon, it will die. Or so the doctors are saying.'

'Too soon?'

'It isn't due until April. You know that, my lord. And child and mother are feeble.'

Jordan laid down the fruit. 'We both know it is overdue now. We both know it is Simon's. It must be born. Why are you lying? You are not fool enough to think Simon will claim it?'

Nicholas stared at him. 'But the father is Diniz!' he said. The man turned crimson. Nicholas waited for the knife, or the wine, or the apple. Or a call for the bullies.

'My dear boy!' Jordan said. By sheer will-power, it appeared, his florid skin was reduced, his eyes gleaming. 'My congratulations! So confident, and only yesterday full of terror! You speak of Diniz and Tilde, whose mediocre union will no doubt produce another mediocre child, should this one fail. I speak of your wife. What is the glorious news?'

Nicholas pursed his lips. 'She is reluctant to say.'

'But she has given birth?'

Nicholas pulled a doleful face. 'I have seen her. She is no longer pregnant. Not pregnant, that is. But whether a child has been born, she won't say.'

Jordan wiped his lips slowly, leaning back. 'But you would not have returned without forcing an answer. And if you did not, I shall, be quite sure.'

'If you find out, you must tell me . . . Do you want that apple?' Nicholas said, leaning over and taking it. 'I heard she had no child, an idiot, or a son. I couldn't tell you which was correct. What does it matter, if you don't mean to claim it?'

'Do you?' the vicomte said.

'It is her child,' Nicholas said. 'I don't mind fattening it. Life is sober enough: there is always room for a jest. Especially against the van Borselen. I shall cook and eat it next year.'

'What do you want?' Jordan de Ribérac said.

'From you? Kilmirren,' said Nicholas. 'Then Ribérac. Then an apology.'

'I am not Simon,' said Simon's father. 'Simon does not know when to apologise. I do not know what the word means. You were responsible for the death of my daughter. You attempted the murder of Simon, and no doubt will try it again. Are you prepared also to kill Simon's two sons?'

'If you want me to,' Nicholas said. 'Certainly, there is no great enthusiasm for Henry, and the new child, if it exists, is from the same stable.' He remained grave.

Jordan de Ribérac was not smiling. He said, 'Your death would solve all these problems.'

'Would it?' Nicholas said. 'My fortune descends to Gelis van Borselen and her child. The Duke of Burgundy would take great care that it never left Flanders. Apart, that is, from the portion already invested in Scotland.'

'A few houses?' said de Ribérac. 'The King would soon reclaim those.'

'My land next to Kilmirren?' Nicholas said. 'Gelis and her child would inherit that. Semple allotted it. The King won't interfere. The King needs the van Borselens, and needs Burgundy.'

'The King wants Guelders,' de Ribérac said. 'So does Burgundy. He and the Duke may fall out.'

'If Burgundy wants Guelders, he will get it,' Nicholas said. 'You know that as well as I. Scotland needs Burgundy. Or else you would have let Simon claim Gelis's child.'

'It is born,' said de Ribérac slowly.

'I believe it is,' Nicholas said. The fat man was clever.

'You believe?'

'Legitimacy is a delicate business. It has been laid aside in some hayloft to ripen.'

'Or in case you do the child harm? From your point of view, it is an embarrassment. From mine, a novelty. Give it to me.'

'In return for what?' Nicholas said.

In the silence, he could hear voices outside the door. The clothes, arriving. Someone tapped. When Jordan did not answer, they tapped again. Then Jordan directed a single obscene sentence at the door, and the voices cut off abruptly. Nicholas tossed his apple-core into the fire and stood, watching it wrinkle and seethe. '*La plus belle me devoit avoir*,' he said. 'In return for what?'

Jordan said softly, 'What would you say to legitimacy? Legitimacy for you, as well as the child. Simon accepts you as the son of his loins. You become the heir to Kilmirren. And I rear the child, your successor.'

'I was hoping you'd say that,' said Nicholas. He went and sat down, pausing to open a button or two. 'One yearns and strives and, suddenly, there it all is, and so simple. I should need a statement under oath, of course, before agreeing. I don't suppose you have a convenient lawyer?'

'I can get one,' said Jordan. 'By the time you have eaten and changed.'

'And Simon, when he hears, would agree?'

'He would have no choice,' de Ribérac said.

'In spite of Henry? Were I legitimate, a child of my marriage would dispossess Henry,' Nicholas pursued.

'Henry is worthless,' de Ribérac said. 'You have, I should think, little love for Simon's small assassin.'

'I am glad you think the five witnesses were not entirely blind,' Nicholas said. 'I am glad, Grandfather, that we are agreed. And in token of it, do you know what I should like?'

'Speak,' said de Ribérac. He, too, had seated himself, but away from the fire. His skin glistened.

'The ring on your finger,' said Nicholas. 'You remember the day we first met? I feel I should have something to remember it by.'

'Mark it, you mean?' said the fat man. He drew the band off with some trouble and gazed at it in his palm. 'It is a family ring.'

'So I see,' Nicholas said.

He waited. Slowly, the fat man held out his hand and rising, Nicholas crossed and lifted the ring on one fingertip. Below, Jordan's empty hand curled and turned white.

'Thank you,' Nicholas said. 'I was afraid you'd want my poor daughter to have it, but she has only two thumbs on each hand, and not even a human nose to put it through. But the next child might be normal.'

Jordan's hand closed on his wrist. Bearing down, he rose to his full height and stood, eye to eye. His skin, neither mottled nor red, had grown ashen. Nicholas laughed into his face. He said, 'Sign my own death warrant? Will my fortune away? Did you think for a moment I'd do it? It's time you took to your bed. You didn't even make sure that the child was a son.'

The hand bearing on his was quite painful. 'And is it?' said Jordan.

'So I am told. I think I believe it. Neither you nor I are likely to see it, I fear, for some time. But it will be reared as a de Fleury, by me.'

'If it lives,' said the fat man. 'She may not let you. She may marry again.'

'That would be difficult,' Nicholas said. 'In my lifetime, at least. Did I give the impression that I would set her aside, or even harm her? I ought to have corrected it. I ought to have mentioned it, perhaps to Gelis herself. I expect her to go where I go, once the child is proclaimed. There will be no doubt, I assure you, of the paternity of the other sons we shall have. And when I have founded my house, my home, my land, my little dynasty, I shall take a ship back to Scotland and show my wife the waste ground where Kilmirren once was.'

'Then I shall have you killed now,' said the fat man.

Nicholas lifted his free hand. It had the silver knife in it. He said, 'You could have used this. So could I. I could still make you a hostage. You would only kill me if you had lost your own sense of importance. You have never been afraid of me. You are not afraid of me now, or you would hardly have amused yourself with that offer. So why not let the race run its course? Surely you are certain of winning?'

The face opposite, the veined face with its swollen chins and broad brow and pursed lips slowly relaxed. Jordan de Ribérac dropped his grasp and, moving deliberately, crossed to the jug and poured wine. He filled a second cup. He said, 'You invoke my pride. You have some wits. Yes, I admit it. Your threats are immaterial: I have heard a thousand such in my life. But I also like battle, and can enjoy it from my chair as well as in the saddle these days.

'So, yes. I shall let you go free. You shall have a horse, and will complete your successful homecoming to Bruges, and carry my familial greetings to Diniz my grandson and his industrious spouse. Which reminds me. You have a ring of mine?'

'It is on the table,' said Nicholas. 'I doubt if you will find it suits any finger but your own.'

Since Godscalc could not, Gregorio waited, hour after hour, at the gate by which Nicholas de Fleury would re-enter Bruges. So, long after dark, he was there when de Fleury, with the rights of a burgess, passed over the bridge and was permitted to make his way into the town. Gregorio waited until he was a pace or two away from the guard, and then stepped out and took his horse by the reins. De Fleury stopped.

For a moment, looking up, Gregorio was unable to speak. Then he said, 'I have to warn you of something.'

The mask above remained a mask. Then it changed in the wavering light. The other man said, 'First my news. Margot is well. She will come back when Gelis does. Back to you.' He waited and then said, 'Not in the street. There is a tavern.'

In Bruges, they were known in every tavern. But a remote corner was found, and some ale neither wanted, and Nicholas de Fleury sat, his tattered cloak cast aside and the mud drying on his torn doublet and said, 'What?'

Gregorio said, 'The vicomte de Ribérac came.'

'So I believe,' the other man said.

'You knew?'

'I have seen him.'

His voice, his face, everything about him was wrong. Gregorio threw out his hands. 'Tell me. Tell me what happened!'

'Later. The vicomte de Ribérac came?'

'To the house. I wasn't there. Diniz was out. Godscalc was sleeping. The servants . . . He forced his way in. He had heard about Lucia and Simon. He knew you nearly killed Simon; he thought you had trapped Lucia too. He accused Diniz of – of certain practices . . . with you, with the young men who come to the house.'

'With Umar. Simon's theory. I know,' the other man said. 'Who heard him?'

'Everyone. Julius. Tobie. Tobie told him he was talking nonsense and Julius punched him. Or tried to. Then de Ribérac left. But Tilde had heard, too.'

'Heard how Lucia was supposed to have died? Heard about her husband's reputation with men?'

'To do him justice,' Gregorio said, 'I don't think the vicomte realised she was near.'

'He did,' Nicholas said.

'You have seen him? He told you?'

'In his own way. What happened?'

'She collapsed. The baby was born. A boy. Dead.'

'And Tilde herself?'

'Tobie is with her. He says she's safe now. He says the infant wouldn't have survived in any case. Nicholas?'

The other man stirred. 'You want to know about mine? My wife's? Nothing but excellent news. The birth is over. Gelis has never looked better. The child is a vigorous boy. Or so Margot tells me. It is hidden.'

'Because it came early?' Gregorio paused. 'You haven't seen it? But I thought she promised to –'

'To leave its fate in my hands? She has reconsidered, it seems. I have asked her to bring the child to Bruges in a month. I may have to leave before then. In which case she should join me in Scotland.'

'She has promised?'

'She has promised nothing. But she seems to be rearing the child.'

'Seems? Aren't you sure? Are you doing nothing to find it and –'

Nicholas de Fleury rose, knocking over the ale. He said, 'All that can be done, I am doing. I am indebted to Margot. I think we should go.'

Gregorio rose. 'Is it even baptised?' he said. 'Godscalc will –'

The other man said, 'It has been done.' The tattered cloak lay on the floor. He stepped over and left it.

'He has a name?' Gregorio said. He looked for a softening.

'Yes,' said Nicholas de Fleury. 'Gelis chose it. Her son is called Jordan.'

Within a day, there was no one in Bruges who did not know that Nicholas vander Poele, who now called himself de Fleury, was back.

He paid, first, the lying family calls, in which he described how the poor lady Lucia died, and reconciled the van Borselens, the Gruuthuse, the Duchess Margaret in Hesdin and the Dowager Duchess in Nieppe with an account of his visit to Gelis, and her good health and witty impatience. He predicted the birth would be early, which surprised very few, and further let it be known that until then his wife wanted seclusion.

Having designed to say little to Tilde, he found himself detained by feverish questions, as if the child coming to Gelis was in some way a twin of the one Tilde had lost. It needed some skill to respond. He found he had no need to talk of Lucia or Diniz: Godscalc had mended those fences. Or so it would seem.

Godscalc, Tobie and Julius accepted the tale of his visit to Gelis, as did Diniz and Catherine, and he did not mention having met the vicomte de Ribérac, who had left town again.

The house was full of commiserating women, but he was out on business most of the time.

He went to see Tommaso Portinari, and dressed for it. Tommaso's mouth did not open, but his clerk's did. When they drank, it was from the gold cups. He found out what was happening with alum, and that he needn't trouble refounding his courier service, for Metteneye and Adorne had already established one. He knew that already.

He learned that, in Tommaso's opinion, he had been foolish to recall his Alexandria agent, with the Vatachino spoiling deals everywhere and the Ottoman army roving the sea. Nicholas had personally annoyed the last Sultan. He was lucky to have le Grant keeping this one so sweet. Nicholas should speak to young Nerio of Trebizond, and Michael Alighieri the Florentine merchant. The ducal court was full of Trapezuntines with news of the Orient and pretty perfumes and manners. It would be a change from the northern wilds and their customs.

He went to the ducal court. He sent word to the Chancellor Hugonet, and the Duke himself received him in the Caudenberg Palace at Brussels. He took care to please him, deployed his excellent Greek to please others, and left privately satisfied.

He went to St Omer, and told Astorre he had to continue in the Duke's service or get out. They had words, but Astorre agreed to stay for a year.

He went to Antwerp on business to do with his ships, and took the chance to visit the office which Jordan de Ribérac had so inopportunely discovered. When he left, two men had been dismissed and one beaten: no more indiscretions, he thought, would occur.

In the second week of March, returning from another visit to Brussels, he found the printing machines had arrived. The space they were to occupy was prepared, but of course John le Grant was not present as planned: the reminder was irritating. So was Tobie's absence of interest. The manuscripts to be printed lay half compiled about his room or Godscalc's while priest and doctor attended to Tilde. Since he could not complain about that, Nicholas set to and began to collate them himself, taking clerks from the counting-house, which upset Gregorio.

When Gregorio entered his room, Nicholas assumed he, too, had come with a grievance. If he had, he didn't produce it at once. He said, 'Did you hear? Adorne is back from Scotland with Metteneye. They landed and rode home tonight with a retinue.'

'Was he limping?' said Nicholas.

'Good God, is that all you can say? I'm told he was,' Gregorio said. 'And he wants to see you tomorrow. He may have kept diplomatic silence in Scotland, but he's not going to let you off here. You'll have to go.'

'I dare say I shall. If we had a book ready, I could take him a present. But I shan't be here to offend him for long. Has Margot written?'

'Margot? No!' Gregorio said.

'Then you shall write to her. It is time, I think, for my son to be born. What would be a good date? Any preference? One might say three days from now. On the fourth day, I go to the convent. On the fifth, she receives family visitors, and a week from now she comes back to Bruges, greets her friends, and we all go to Scotland.'

Gregorio said, 'It sounds an excellent plan. I think you should write to her yourself. If she's still where you left her.'

'A garden enclosed is my sister, my spouse. She is,' Nicholas said.

'But there's no sign of the child, I should guess. That's why you want this?' Gregorio said. 'She'll have to produce it, or move it, or send word to its carers.'

'You're not going to write?' Nicholas said.

'No,' said Gregorio. 'Not as your agent, to Margot.'

'Then was there anything else?' Nicholas said.

Gregorio gazed at him. 'Only what I've said before. Let it go. Find some grounds for divorce. Send her off with the child. Pick up the life you used to have.'

'Yes, you said it before,' Nicholas said.

'Then listen to me,' Gregorio said. 'Or to Tobie. Or to Godscalc. Once you had charity.'

'Charity?' Nicholas said. 'I have decided to maintain my marriage!'

'That is not charity,' Gregorio said.

Chapter 17

THE LIMP COULD not be disguised, although Anselm Adorne set his stick aside for the hour Nicholas spent in his presence and, if he felt pain, did not show it. Nevertheless, his eyes were deep, his thin-boned face pale. And Margriet his wife was swollen with anger.

She would not leave them to talk. She made that plain even before the meeting took place in her very own house, in the Hôtel de Jerusalem.

'I will not go away! A youth who bedevilled all your years of office, until you had to beat him for it! An apprentice who stole the affections of poor Marian de Charetty, until out of love we had to agree to their wedding, even arrange it! A fellow who, now he is rich, will pick a fight with all who oppose him, and have them murdered too, if it suits him! Have him arrested!'

'Let us hear him first,' said Adorne.

'What is there to hear? He laid a trap for Kilmirren the Younger and tried to kill him! He frightened our niece half to death! He set about you when you tried to restrain him, and then when he had gone, Kilmirren's sister was found in the river! He is a murderer! If I leave him alone, he will kill you!'

'Then,' said Anselm Adorne, 'you can hand him over to the authorities, for there will be no doubt at all who is the culprit. Really, my dear. A man like Nicholas seldom kills in cold blood. He prefers to bleed his victim of power or money. He does not like the Genoese.'

'You didn't know,' Margriet said, 'that the *Fortado* crew were all rascals. You only took shares in the venture.'

'Nor was I in Famagusta when the Portuguese held out against him. But we are of Genoese blood, and his rivals. That I concede. There we are certainly opposed. But in a personal way? I think not.'

Nevertheless, Margriet van der Banck stayed with her husband, high officer though he might be, cultured though he might be, champion jouster and hard drinker though he might also be (when away from the house with his cronies), because he was her dear man, and kind father to so many fine children and had made her, in her time, hostess and companion to royalty. Her chain and necklace, carried high on her bosom, proclaimed it.

The youth, when he came, was empty-handed. Youth? Jan, her eldest, was twenty-four and this one was four years his elder and given over to Mammon, whereas Jan was learning law at Pavia and would end up serving God in the Curia, if the Bishop of St Andrews was as good as his word.

This one wore black, like the Duke did. The nice boy who used to play with her Lewisje had grown up into the self-confident merchant who had come back from Africa and driven the less well bred to mirth over the way he was chasing the van Borselen girl. Now she was his third wife and pregnant, and all the boy could think of was creating trouble in Scotland for Anselm. Causing trouble to Anselm everywhere. Wounding Anselm nearly to death.

Nicholas de Fleury was big, for an artisan. He said, 'No gift could compensate. I brought an explanation instead.'

'I do not think,' said her husband, 'that your former friend Margriet wants to hear it. She thinks I should have you arrested.'

Margriet flushed, then lifted her chin.

The young man said, 'I should not resist you. When did I ever?'

'When did you have the means?' said Anselm dryly. 'I may still commit you. If you had injured my nephew or niece, I would show you no mercy. As it is, I promise to hear your excuse, that is all.'

'It is an explanation, not an excuse,' the man said. 'I have no excuse.'

He stood with a sober face and did not look awkward, although no one had asked him to sit.

'Well?' said Anselm. She had heard him help young people who had made a mistake. He did not do so this time. She was glad.

The young man lifted his head. She, too, heard the voices. Antoon and Arnoud, the little ones. The shrill sounds faded away. The young man before Anselm said, 'My quarrel was with Simon de St Pol. I had made a pact, at some sacrifice, and he broke it. I meant to teach him a physical lesson. He is my superior in most forms of fighting: I didn't think it unfair. But I lost my temper.'

'How strange!' remarked Anselm. 'Your greatest weapon? That is how you win against Simon. You could have killed him with ease.'

'I didn't mean to kill him,' said the other.

'Or me?'

'You were lucky,' said the young man. He paused. 'I mean –'

'You mean you didn't really care at the time where you struck. Why did you want to follow Simon? To finish what you had started?'

'In a sense,' the man said. He spoke slowly. 'Not to kill him. But not to leave it like that.'

'To apologise? To get him to apologise? He was, I think, unlikely to do that.'

'Nothing so civilised,' the man Nicholas said. 'I wanted to keep fighting until he knew that I'd beaten him. And then remind him that he couldn't do anything about it.'

'He couldn't?'

'Or I shouldn't be so magnanimous about Henry.'

'Henry?' Margriet repeated, frowning.

'Henry de St Pol, Simon's son,' said her husband without turning his head. 'I don't think I told you. He lost his temper during a tourney. When Nicholas tried to help, the boy stabbed him.'

'And he couldn't be seven!' said Margriet, touched with horror.

The two men looked at one another. She became aware of a silence. Then Anselm said, 'I observe the parallel. You think I shall not prefer charges against you, in return for the advantage it gives me?'

'You have witnesses,' the young man said.

'Yes.' She knew Anselm. When he leaned back like that, he had achieved what he wanted. He said, 'And what primacy should I have? What degree of control? What, in fact, do you offer?'

'As much as I have over Simon, for what it is worth. I shall try not to displease you. On the other hand, if you push me too far, you will have to revive the case and take me to law. But I shall do my best to elude you, and you will never possess such an advantage again.'

They were still looking at one another. Then Anselm turned his head towards her. 'Well, my dear? What do you think? You have heard his suggestion. Do we accept this solatium or not?'

She said, 'Ser Anselm, are you out of your senses? He wounds you nearly to death. He asks you not to take him to law. And in return, he will *try not to displease you*, as if it were some sort of concession, and not the Christian duty of every soul on this earth!'

Her husband smiled. He had turned his eyes from her again. He said, 'You have missed the point, which indeed has been made with some delicacy. Unlike most Christian souls, this one is capable of causing you, me and our children quite an amount of displeasure. Young Kilmirren shares my misgivings, or he would hardly have left Court with Henry.'

'Simon has gone?' the other said slowly.

'To Portugal, it is said. Or perhaps France. So,' said Anselm, 'there is no need for you to go back to Scotland. And if I do not forgive you immediately, you will stay and prove troublesome here. Am I right?'

'Of course not,' the man said. 'Or, if you think so, you must arrest me at once. Or – be sure I shan't try to escape – within four days, perhaps. I should like . . . I should like to be free when my child is born.'

'What!' said Margriet. 'The baby? You have heard? It is due? Oh, Anselm!'

'It is due?' said Anselm softly.

'In a few days. I am – I was going to the convent tomorrow.' The blemished face turned towards her. 'You can believe me. You will see Gelis when she can travel. Or before, if you like.'

'Her baby!' said Margriet. 'I have a gift. Wait. I made it myself. You shall take it to her.' Rising, she sniffed through her smiles. In her thoughts she saw the little van Borselen girl, her face rosy, her hair round her shoulders, a babe in her arms. She was thinking, hurrying out, that Dr Andreas might well be wrong. That Antoon needn't be the last son: that she was only forty, and could give Anselm, surely, another.

She closed the door, and her husband sank back in his chair. 'My wound is forgotten,' he said. 'Although it is not a ruse you could employ every week. There *is* a child on the way?'

'A son,' de Fleury said. 'It is born. A mite premature, so that its birth has been post-dated a little. I should be glad if you would maintain the fiction.'

'A son!' Adorne said. In spite of himself he rose and took the young man by the shoulder. Then he found his hand and shook it. He said, 'I fear you have softened my hard heart as well. I cannot send a father to prison. I must – Let us drink to it. What excuse can we give to Margriet?'

'We are saluting your magnanimity,' Nicholas said. 'If you mean it. And what I have told you is the truth. You have a check on me, you and your family. I owe you a favour. Despite what you have done to my courier service, I owe you a favour. Concerning which, I should like to touch on the subject of horses. If I might sit down?'

When Margriet came back, they were drinking. It did not strike her as typical that, having brought nothing at all to his victim, Nicholas de Fleury should depart a free man, with a gift.

There remained Gelis.

She had not left the convent. His men, indeed, had made that impossible. It did not mean that she would comply with the directions he had given her, then or now. It was with silent amazement, therefore, that he opened and read a response.

She agreed to the birth-date. She agreed to a visit from him, and then, later, her family. The child would not, of course, be visible: its age would be patently wrong. Its premature birth would be sufficient excuse.

She would come to Bruges when he wished.

He received that letter the day after his interview with Adorne. Returning from that, he had gone to his room, where there was a pile of correspondence to deal with. Julius arrived in ten minutes: he timed him. He took quite a long time, for Julius, to assimilate Adorne's amazing restraint.

'I did give him something in return,' Nicholas said. 'You know his courier service?'

'Damned pirates!' said Julius.

'They need horses. So does Scotland. I've started a breeding programme – bought some stables and put a good man in charge. I've offered Metteneye and Adorne part-shares. They'll make money; so shall we.'

'But –' said Julius.

'And if it fails, we shan't suffer too much.'

'Nicholas?' Julius said. Smiling broadly, he affected to swing a slow punch. Good ideas always found appreciation with Julius.

It had been clear to Nicholas, long acquainted with ladies, that all Bruges would soon hear of the imminent birth of the baby. Reading the letter from Gelis, he resigned himself to telling his colleagues as well.

It appeared everyone had been anxious. His hand was wrung, his back slapped. Cooks wept. Godscalc wept. His timetable, without his agreement, was wiped clean of every appointment, and a triumphal escort arranged to take him to his wife that very day. He persuaded them, with some effort, to postpone it until the following morning, and further conveyed, with even more effort, that he preferred to make this trip without personal friends.

Everyone understood. Everyone was offended. Everyone forgave him at a bibulous supper at which he drank water flavoured with wine and parried jokes he had heard in Greek and Latin and Arabic, and usually better told. In the middle, Tilde let it be known that she wanted to see him, and when he came lifted her arms to his neck, and pulled him down to the pillow to kiss him.

In view of the paternal rigours ahead, he was allowed to retire early, and gradually the noise died down below, and everyone else went off to bed.

Not quite everyone. When Nicholas left the house, he was stopped at the gates by an anonymous figure, the rain soaking into the shawl it had clutched round its head. Tobie. Tobias Beventini, physician and pest. Tobie said, 'Where are you going?'

It was raining hard, that was true, and he was not suitably dressed. Nicholas said, 'For a walk.'

'There's nothing out there but drunks and stray dogs and a few prostitutes.' Tobie was grim.

'It's the dogs,' Nicholas said. 'I could never resist them.'

'Well I doubt, looking at you, if it's anything else,' Tobie said. 'Unless a death-wish for the rheum. When did you last have a night's sleep?'

Instead of shouting, Nicholas made his voice kindly. 'You're going to prescribe me a posset.'

'It makes a change,' Tobie said, 'from sawing out cross-bolts.'

'Yes. Well, I don't need one,' Nicholas said. 'A refreshing walk in the rain. Nature's remedy.'

'Rubbish. Per intoxicationem, three drops: five hours' sleep and no thinking.'

'I like thinking,' said Nicholas. He moved.

Tobie moved too, and repositioned himself in his path. Tobie said, 'I'm asking no questions. I'm simply saying, as a doctor, that you won't solve the little matters of Loppe, or Umar, or Simon, or Henry, or Gelis or whatever else this way.'

'By thinking,' suggested Nicholas.

'By imagining that you can do any damned thing without sleep. Like thinking. Like not thinking.'

'What about like talking things through with a friend?'

Tobie was silent. Then he said, 'I wasn't going to suggest it. I was going to remind you that you've stood injustice before. Thought it through, understood it, accepted it. Do it now, or nothing will mend.'

Nicholas said, 'I am more optimistic than you are. I think everything will mend. On my terms. Or above there will be the Angry Judges, and below will be Chaos.'

The rain fell. 'And that is straight thinking?' said Tobie. He sounded tired. He said, 'They say you've quarrelled with Gelis because she won't go to Scotland. Or they say that's why you're going to Scotland.'

'And thou shalt not sow thy field with diverse seeds, it says somewhere. Leviticus. Do you like Leviticus? Are we having an ordinary conversation now? I have not quarrelled with Gelis. The pumpkin gives birth and the fence has the trouble. Do you like quotations?'

'Is that how you do it?' said Tobie. 'Fill your mind, push it away? But what if the block comes and goes as it pleases? What if you can't stop the verse?'

'Then I come out and talk to the dogs,' Nicholas said. 'Or the drunks, or the prostitutes, or some quack with an overpriced mixture. Do you know about candied marijuana seeds? They have an amazing effect in spiced wine.'

'Five hours,' Tobie said. The harshness, Nicholas knew, was to hide the relief.

He had not meant even to appear to give in. He agreed largely because he had begun to think in Arabic and knew (O Believer, shall I direct you to a commerce that shall deliver you from a painful chastisement?) that he must cut the interview short, or soon he would speak it aloud. The well of memory. The well of his innermost being. It was one of the worst fears he had.

Indoors, the draught was duly produced and convincingly swallowed. Gregorio had said it. Keep your pain to yourself.

Next day, the ride to the convent was easy. The Bank supplied Nicholas with his liveried escort, and the gates were set wide in broad daylight. While his men remained below, the Abbess escorted him mirthfully to the upper chambers. 'She is in bed, in case she is spied upon. So anxious for your good name! And her family are coming to visit her?'

'Her family will join her tomorrow. And the boy? Is he here?'

He knew the look now; the sliding, flickering glance. The Abbess said, 'But you know better than that! The babe and his nurse are not here. But they are safe! He flourishes! I am told a beautiful child, like his father!'

'You reassure me,' said Nicholas.

Gelis was in bed, it was true, and alone. Margot's room, its door open, stood empty. No eavesdropping today.

It wasn't worth saying. Nothing much was. He saw, approaching the bed, how much time and money had been spent on the room since he saw it. The bed-frame had been changed for one of walnut, carved and painted, and the hangings were of striped voile caught back by silk and gold tassels. The towels, thick and fringed, hung by a basin and pitcher of silver, and the cushions and stools were all new, and covered with tapestry. On the table next to her bed stood a clock. When the lord of Veere came, and her cousin Wolfaert, they would find her wealthy and cherished. Even beautiful. The twilled hair lay loose upon pale embroideries; the pillows behind her were silk. Her skin was smooth; her lips soft. Round her throat she wore aquamarines, the precise icy hue of her eyes.

'Your birth-gift,' she said. 'I sent away for them. The cloak, although fine, was second-hand.'

'I thought it appropriate,' he said.

'Oh dear,' Gelis said. 'Well, shall we begin again, or somehow continue from there? We have a lot to discuss.'

'You disagree with my plans,' Nicholas said. He had worked out what she must know: about Lucia; about Simon; about Henry. About Adorne by now. His thinking today was exceptionally clear: he wished Tobie could have been present.

She said, 'You did get my letter?'

'A landmark: I was touched. You didn't mention coming to Scotland.'

'Yes, that does remind me,' she said. 'I meant to discuss that as well. I don't think you should go back to Scotland. And, of course, you can't expect me to preside over the mortification or worse of my baby's father.'

'It might tickle your fancy,' he said. 'But in fact the prospect doesn't arise. Simon has fled the country, with Henry. By fat paternal command, I imagine.'

Her forefinger moved on the coverlet. 'So he has conceded defeat. Lucia is dead. The score is settled?'

'With my accepted son and heir christened Jordan? How, incidentally, do you mean to explain that away?'

She thought. After a moment she said, 'Motherly sentiment? A loving attempt to heal your estrangement?' She cleared her throat.

'It is still going to appear very odd,' Nicholas said. 'When the score is settled, that is. I hoped you would consent to come to Scotland for that. The mortification or worse of the old man. You don't like him especially? That is, you only borrowed his name in the cause of our present skirmish?'

She said, 'Is that what it is?'

'Well, it can't be war: people get killed in war. So you'll come to Scotland?'

'Of course I won't,' Gelis said. 'I don't like Simon's father: I loathe him. But I won't help you attack him.'

'Or watch me? You won't take responsibility for your own actions? You started this,' Nicholas said.

'Then punish me,' she replied.

'All right. Come to Scotland,' he said.

'But promise to leave them alone. Jordan and Simon.'

'Simon has gone. You are saying you would rather I attacked you than Jordan?'

'If you can.'

'Oh, I can,' Nicholas said. 'As it happens, I can gratify Jordan and settle your score in one stroke. He has asked me to sell him the child.'

Once before he had seen her like that, her skin tallow-white but for a rash of stark colour. He waited comfortably, hitched on a ledge, his hands loosely clasped, his eyes unforgiving. There was no one within call.

It lasted quite a short time. Then she coughed again and said, 'What did you tell him?'

'I asked him the price. It's a good one. Jordan rears and possesses his namesake, and I become Nicholas de St Pol, legitimate heir to Kilmirren.'

'And?'

'Don't you like the idea? When I die, your son inherits everything: Kilmirren, Ribérac, the House of Niccolò. You won't see him again, but you will have our other children to console you. I hope you are looking forward to that.'

She was out of bed now, and already a few steps towards him. She said, 'You can stand there! You can stand there!'

The veils of her bedgown moved and shifted, and he kept his eyes immutably on her face. He said, 'Could you not foresee all these moves? You married into this family on the strength of your skills. You had assessed your abilities against mine, against Simon's, against Jordan's. You must at least have done that. You must surely, however much you protest, have known what would happen to Simon. Perhaps you expected it also to happen to Henry.'

'No!' she said.

'But it brought him into the game. Now your child is in, too. What is the matter? I thought the whole point was that he is expendable.'

She stood still then. 'Is he?' she said. 'Have you promised him to de Ribérac?'

'Will you give me other children?' he said. Unmoving, he watched the hem of her robe quivering. Then he lifted his eyes again to her face, but gradually this time.

She coughed again. She was only a little distance, he knew, from being ill. She said, 'Yes. If I can keep this one.'

'Oh, good,' he said; and walking across to the bed drew back the sheets tenderly and held out his hand. 'Because that's what I told M. de Ribérac. That I felt you and I might rear the boy better together, despite my illegitimate state. That, in fact, I had an odd feeling that were it otherwise, my life would not be a long one. And that, of course, we had plans for many dear offspring of quite impeccable parentage in the future.

'I am glad you agree. I hope you will come back to bed. You needn't fear that I shall climb in beside you. I dare say I shall overcome it, but at the moment I feel a certain repugnance. Will you come to Scotland?'

She stared at him, her skin glistening white.

'Or Bruges, then. You will come to Bruges, and we shall discuss Scotland. Or if neither of us can contemplate so early a reunion, we shall make other plans for our future. For our long happy future, Gelis, together.'

He threw down the sheet and walked out, carefully closing the door. The guest-master knew where his room was, and he arranged to have his men fed and, indeed, joined them briefly. They made all the usual jokes, so that he hardly had to contribute at all.

He heard by nightfall that his wife had been a little unwell and was resting. He heard the next morning that she was feeling entirely herself, and was sitting in state, prepared to receive such visitors as she must expect before evening. He was supposed to spend the day, naturally, with her. He was not sure, now, that he could. He went to see her, to find out.

He had brought garments proper for a man celebrating the birth of an heir, and was not surprised to see that she, too, was suitably lapped in rich fabrics. She looked well, and showed no sign of illness. A little paint, he thought, had been applied. She watched him cross the room, her expression agreeable. She was one of the most gifted of all his opponents, although she had failed to take his measure last night.

He said, 'I thought I should be the first to congratulate the proud mother. Did you have a difficult labour?'

She drew a short breath, and then appeared half amused, half resigned. 'Why the concern? You haven't asked me before.'

'I thought you ought to practise some answers. For example, when was he born?' He returned the smile, spreading his cap with its plumes on the bed and sinking into a seat. 'Oh, not, of course, the real date.'

'After midnight,' she said. 'An hour before sunrise. Through the night, in the dark.' Her lips were still smiling, but she spoke with her eyes fixed on his. The words came slowly and stopped.

Before he replied, he measured the carpet and priced it. Then he said, 'That was the truth.'

'Yes. Why not? I do falter in vice now and then. Nicholas . . .' She seemed to consider. 'The child is the only subject you speak of. This one, or others.'

'What else is there?' he said. He picked up his cap and revolved it. The jewel flashed, and roused light from her wedding ring.

She said, 'There are, surely, some other things we should talk about.'

'Well, no,' Nicholas said. 'I think that would be rash. I think the less talk between us the better.'

'And yet you have decided to have children by me? When you have conquered your –'

'I must apologise,' Nicholas said. 'It was not an appropriate word. But you have announced some decisions quite as arbitrary. Unless you have altered your mind? You can still repudiate the boy and the marriage. You would find it difficult, though, I should warn you.'

She said, 'You don't even know why I did it.'

'Don't I?' he said. Some of it, he had guessed. He didn't want to know more. He had no intention of putting any of it into words. It would sound odd if he did. *Your sister chose me, and I obliged. She had my child and passed it off as her husband's. You devised a singular punishment. You planned to do the same in reverse.*

He supposed that was it. There would be other reasons which were better not spoken. She knew that as well. Already, he thought, she was regretting the question. It was not to her purpose to explain, to accuse, to encumber the situation with needless emotion. With any emotion. He agreed with that, while reserving the right to frighten her when he must. It was all a question of control.

He imagined the convoluted journey she had planned for them both as if it were a battle plan, a tough and delicate model, its bridges, gulleys, pitfalls all carefully constructed and tested. She would give nothing away, risk no words that would weaken it. He understood that, as well. He said, 'Then you had better not say any more, in case I decide to divorce you after all. Meanwhile, you are still of the same mind?'

He waited. It was a risk, but a small one. Whatever end she proposed, he believed that the path towards it would be a long one; that she meant to continue as she had begun, rather than end it too soon, immolating themselves and the boy – and the boys – in some self-destructive public confession. He credited her with having entertained that idea, among others. Above the gauze, the aquamarine eyes were assessing him. He was used to that, too.

Then she said, 'I am your wife. You are prepared to call Jordan your son. If that is what you want the world to think, I agree. I will come to Bruges. For the rest, I may need a little time. So, I gather, do you. It may not be a bad thing if you were to go to Scotland without me. How long will you stay?'

'Long enough,' he said, 'to do what I have to do. I am building now by Kilmirren. A hall.' He had risen to move to the door.

'For your children?' Her voice, following him to the threshold, remained idle.

'Oh, no,' he said, looking back. 'I shouldn't think so. No. It will do until I have finished in Scotland. And before you ask, you will know when I have finished. Everyone will.'

He spoke absently, his thoughts moving into different languages which he had forgotten she knew. He had no doubt, of course, that she would discover the meaning, if he spoke the phrases aloud.

What is brought by the wind is carried away by the wind. That was one.

At night, a cotton-seed is the same as a pearl. That was the other.

She said, 'I did not want him to die!'

She was weeping. She had no right to weep.

He lasted one week before he left Bruges for Scotland. And he left before Gelis arrived.

There was some logic, he could say, on his side. His ship was to hand, and the wind – rare in March – was in his favour. If he went, he could return all the sooner. And he had given a magnificent banquet in Bruges to celebrate the birth of his heir. His wife, being frail, had not attended.

He had left his business in order. Instead of taking Diniz from Tilde, he had given him full control, for the first time, in Bruges. To Julius, dazzled, he had restored the charge of the Ca' Niccolò, Venice (but had not mentioned the other disposition he was hoping to make). To Gregorio he had proffered a choice: Flanders or Scotland.

Margot had not come back to Bruges. Margot was not even with Gelis in her convent. Margot, they now knew, was with the infant, Gelis's son whom (Gregorio had learned with reserve) Nicholas still intended to rear as his own.

It worked quite well. Gregorio said, 'I am not your spy. Nor is Margot.'

Nicholas said, 'Why snap at me? Do you think Margot cares for this arrangement? Do you think that I do? The legitimacy of the boy is the problem, and Margot is trying to protect him.'

'It seems hard on Margot,' Gregorio said. 'And, unlike you, I find lying difficult.'

'Then don't lie,' Nicholas said. 'Tell everyone the child may be Simon's.'

There was a silence. Then Gregorio said, 'You know that I can't.' Then he said bitterly, 'I'll come to Scotland.' Which was exceptionally convenient.

Nicholas threw away Tobie's pills and filled his head full of numbers. He sailed as soon as he could, and left behind an echoing empire of men who had once been his friends.

He had seen her. He had laid down his terms: so had she. The second stage (*thank God, thank God*), was now over.

And now there was Scotland, and the third, ready waiting.

Chapter 18

B Y MAY, THE Kinneil salt-pans were long free of snow, although further upriver the hills about Stirling were streaked, and the plain in which the castle rock stood was soggy and flooded in places.

Will Roger didn't mind, except that it gave his choristers coughs. Jogging between Edinburgh, Haddington, Peebles (where his little sinecure eked out his salary) and the chapel royal of Stirling, he actually began to have hopes that he would have a musical programme worth the name for the King's wedding. Standing on a box, nursing his altos, he was so intent he was unaware of his visitors until a familiar voice copied, with unfair accuracy, what he was trying to explain.

He turned. Nicholas de Fleury, of course, the dimples foully provocative. Beside him was a youngish man in a lawyer's cap and black gown, with a comic nose and a startled expression. Will Roger roared, 'The father! The father! The loins that have sired some croaking heir that doesn't know its A from its elbow! Come and kiss me!'

It wasn't entirely wise: he could feel the choir's communal stare, fascinated, faintly disapproving, wholly jealous. Conducting choirs was a pastime with heavy sexual undertones, which one ignored at one's peril. He disengaged and said, 'And who is this?'

'Your new fiddler,' said Nicholas. 'I've just come from Secretary Whitelaw. Your lodging, whenever it suits you?'

The startled expression was a fair reflection of Gregorio of Asti's state of mind, now that he had emerged from the interminable voyage of the Bank's caravel, the *San Niccolò*, which, far from sailing direct to Scotland, had delivered Nicholas de Fleury first to Southampton, then to London.

At Southampton, he had received news from Florence, Naples and Venice and interviewed merchants with business in Bristol.

In London, armed with a safe conduct from Governor William in Bruges, he had been received by the Duchess of Burgundy's mother and saw her maid of honour, Anselm Adorne's homesick daughter. The sieur de Fleury had letters for both, and in return was invited to spend an hour in their parlour. An hour that had stretched to three, there was so much news to exchange.

He also had some introductions to merchants. He talked with them all. After a while, Gregorio sent a mental apology to Julius. Whatever had brought Nicholas north, it was not a simple evasion of matrimony. Something very large indeed was afoot. Something to which, so far, he was not being admitted.

After that, the ship made two further calls, one to Newcastle and one to Berwick. So far as Gregorio could see, the Berwick call had no purpose except to let off Mick Crackbene, who disappeared for a night. It was a hybrid border town, presently Scots, with more than the usual rough trade on the wharf.

Nicholas had allowed the crew an evening on shore and, after a while, had unexpectedly followed them. Unlike Julius, Gregorio felt no wish to know about that side of his life. He himself didn't relish abstaining but he did; and he was just as young – well, two years older than Nicholas. But he wasn't married to Gelis van Borselen.

Then had come Scotland proper, and Leith, where Jannekin Bonkle had come on board, bursting with news, with the result that, instead of landing, they had left ship and transferred to another which took them up the Firth and then dropped sails to navigate the narrowed, wandering river that brought them here for a stay of one day. Here, to the King's castle and burgh of Stirling.

Gregorio had known what to expect: a collection of stone and wood buildings crowning a rock, with the thatched houses of burghers and nobles and craftsmen on the descent to the river. A natural fortress, very like Edinburgh, and very likely with all the same disadvantages of climate reported by Julius.

He had packed his heaviest cloak, as Margot would have wanted. It was a kind of lucky token, the cloak. If he took it, he would be back in Bruges before winter and he could find Margot and talk. Either Nicholas would have come to his senses or he wouldn't, in which case Gregorio would leave him. He knew quite well that Nicholas understood that as well as he did.

It was in the high winds of Stirling that the brave Bruges cloak began to lose its homely whiff of nostalgia. In the castle of Stirling, within the working offices of the kingdom, the lawyer Gregorio saw for himself how men received the returned Nicholas de Fleury: as double burgher and merchant, as investor, as a man active in business whose wellbeing – although he lacked the ducal remit of Adorne – was a matter of interest to both Scotland and Flanders.

The events of four months ago – the unseemly brawl, the wretched mishap that followed – had not been forgotten. But Nicholas de Fleury had been useful, and would be again. And, of course, his prompt action had saved the young prince in the lists. It was as well that the St Pols, father and child, had taken themselves out of the country. It meant that the Flemish banker and Scotland could settle down to some business. For one day, before anyone else got hold of him, that was what the high officers of the kingdom were doing.

And one other. A red-headed youth dressed for hunting had detached himself from his companions and stopped Nicholas on his way from the Secretary's room. The exchange was short and Gregorio was not introduced, but the huntsman, from his flush, had been pleased. When Nicholas had produced a court bow on leaving, Gregorio copied him. He had identified the badges. This was Alexander, Duke of Albany, the King's brother. The one who had stayed at Veere. The one who knew Gelis van Borselen.

He sighed. That time, although not wearing his cloak, he did think of Margot.

He followed that day most of the calls that Nicholas made. They ended in the warren of cabins where the canons, the chapel servants, and the musicians were lodged. There he was introduced to a passage stacked with musical instruments and fluted with glittering trumpets which proceeded to a room of no very great size, but so full of peat smoke and ale fumes and noise that he flinched on the threshold.

'Disgusting, isn't it?' Nicholas said and, stepping back, took down the first instrument he could see, which was a shawm. 'Which end do you blow?'

'Give it to me,' Gregorio said. It had happened once before, on the *Ciaretti*. His heart suddenly lifted.

He took it, while Nicholas reached for another. A trumpet. One of the royal trumpets, in silver. 'You begin,' he said. 'I'll sling the bells round my neck. Can you reach one of the drums with your feet?'

They didn't get very far before the doorway was crowded with figures. A tall man strode forward, swearing, and, depriving

Nicholas of the trumpet, proceeded to replace his toots with swooping notes of earsplitting brilliance. Blowing, he retired to the room. Nicholas followed, tinkling morosely, a kettledrum under his arm. Will Roger said to Gregorio, 'That's not bad, give me another,' and fell into step beside him. Then he said, 'No, they said yours was a fiddle?' and handed him one, giving the shawm to somebody else.

The somebody else was Hugo van der Goes the painter, from Bruges. Behind him were two other men he knew from the same place. They all went back into the room and sat down. You couldn't hear yourself think for Nicholas on the drum, setting the changes of rhythm. It went on for ten minutes and then Will Roger blared out a discord and threw his instrument down, collapsing on the floor. 'It's all very well for you bastards, but I've been at it since dawn. Nicol, *be quiet.*'

The kettledrum rose to a deafening rattle, and stopped. 'You think that's loud?' Nicholas said. 'You've gone rotten since I've been away. Where's the other drum?'

They hammered him heartily, taking the drum away, and he gave as good as he got. His own friends were roughest, Gregorio noticed. The rest enjoyed it as well: he had entertained them before, you would guess. But he was still an important man, and a foreigner. When, reduced to their shirts, they were all lying back laughing and panting, Will Roger presented him with a flagon of unspecified liquid.

'It should be wine; I'll get some later. Gentlemen: I give you Nicholas de Fleury, Knight of some God-forsaken Order of Cyprus, and his wife and his son. What've you called the brat? James, I wager.'

'I'm working on it,' Nicholas said. 'I'll cut you in, if you like. The first man with a ten-figure order gets to choose his own name for the child.'

'Then there's your man!' exclaimed Whistle Willie. His calloused forefinger appeared to point through the window. 'You don't mind a combine? A ten-figure order among the whole castle? Hey! *Lancelot!* Would you like to christen a vander Poele?'

A passer-by, puzzled, turned round. Nicholas, breathless, was pulling, one after another, a series of pitiful faces. 'Lancelot vander Lacu!' Whistle Willie bellowed, elaborating his point. The farce played itself strenuously out.

Gregorio listened in silence. You thought that, for a while, he had forgotten the bitch. But, of course, he had not.

*

Later, someone sent out for food, and the talk lurched about between topics of high and low interest, such as women, and horses, and arrows, and women and plate gauntlets and women. Then Whistle Willie began to sing under his breath, and someone else took him up, and soon they were chorusing away in unexpurgated versions of a number of ditties Gregorio had heard, at night, in Jehan Metteneye's house after a supper.

In the course of it, someone near the door scrambled up saying, 'My lord Duke!'

But the red-headed youth, slipping in, said, 'No, it's Sandy. Go on.'

They broke up half an hour later, royalty being an inhibiting guest, and Nicholas accompanied the King's brother of Albany into the courtyard. When he came back to collect Gregorio, they had all gone save for the man they called Whistle Willie who was sprawled in a settle, a broad smile on his earthy face. He said, 'Well, Nicol. You got what you wanted?'

The malice was friendly. Nicholas pulled another of his comfortable faces and sat down, pushing a litter of ale-mugs out of his sight. Gregorio, heavily relaxed, brought a cushion and sat on it. What Nicholas had wanted and got from this meeting was gossip.

To wit: that Hugo van der Goes and the rest of his imported craftsmen were going to be worth what he had advanced them, because the Danish dowry money seemed likely to come, and the royal wedding would take place this summer at Holyrood Abbey next door to Nicholas.

That one of the results of the royal wedding was Sandy Albany's new crop of pimples; due, it was said, to the marriage he was going to have to make with an elderly half-sister of Betha Sinclair's. *There* was a prince, Willie Roger had said earlier, and now repeated, who would be glad if Nicol de Fleury's good friend dropped dead in the next week or two.

Gregorio lifted his lids. 'Not you,' Will Roger said. 'Although I might as well tell you that you can't get through bottles like Julius. No, not you. The hairy Franciscan who's trying to bring the Pope's peace to Denmark and Sweden.'

'Called?' said Nicholas. His dimples, for once, looked involuntary.

'Called Ludovico da Bologna. He's been in Sweden for weeks. And if he settles the war, Denmark won't need to worry too much about Scotland, and Sandy won't have to go to the altar. Which reminds me. I have a note for you from the Hamiltons. They heard you were here. So, what English gossip have you got?'

'What kind do you want?' said Nicholas, taking the paper and reading it. 'There's been a rising in Yorkshire. It may not come to anything. On the other hand it might, and the York–Lancaster fight for the throne break out all over again. Which side do you support?'

'The winning one,' said Whistle Willie. 'I left England because there didn't seem to be one at the time. What are the merchants saying in London?'

'Keep in with everybody, send away your ships, and invest your money in cannon. The Queen has just had her third child, another daughter. Edward isn't as secure on the throne as he thinks he is. You'll lose your English pension.'

'Don't try it,' said Roger. 'I haven't got one. I could name a few Scotsmen who have, and so no doubt could you. You saw Mr Secretary Whitelaw, you were saying.'

'Do you think he has one? No. I've shipped him some dogs and some jousting-horses, that's all. I brought you a book.'

Will Roger frowned. He said, 'I want a really good bribe. A book?'

'It *is* a really good bribe,' Nicholas said. He stretched to his satchel and fished in it. The book he drew out was a strange shape, and cheaply boarded.

Will Roger crimsoned. He said, 'What you promised? Burgundian?'

'The whole thing, and three other pieces. Plus.'

'Plus?'

'Plus what they're going to play at Lorenzo de' Medici's wedding in Florence. Do you want it?'

'Christ, I could marry you,' said Whistle Willie. 'God-awful dimples and all. Do I want it? Do I want perfect pitch, and perpetual reeds, and a harp that doesn't mind draughts, and boys that stay boys for ever?'

'Well, you've got that one,' Nicholas said. 'You were born one. We must go. What was that about Sersanders earlier?'

'I think he wants to kill you. Don't worry. He's in Aberdeen. When he comes back, Katelijne'll protect you. She's off to Edinburgh too, with the King's fearful sister. Have you got to go? Oh yes, you have.'

He ushered them out, having answered his own question. Outside waited one of their men with a lantern. Stumbling down to their lodging, Gregorio attempted to solve one of many puzzles. He said, 'What are you bribing him for?' He added, 'Where are you going?'

Nicholas, who had come to a halt, said, 'Over that way. I might be late. Govaerts will see you back safely.'

'What . . .?' said Gregorio.

'That's what I'm bribing him for,' Nicholas said. 'He hands me notes, and doesn't tell you what's in them. Edinburgh tomorrow. I'll have you called early. Good night, Goro.'

He was back before dawn, but not much before. Gregorio, contending with other afflictions, attempted no comment.

Of the two parties leaving Stirling that morning, the first to assemble was that of the King's sister Margaret with her attendants. The second, inadvertently meeting the first, was that of Nicholas.

'You look disgusting,' said Katelijne Sersanders, calling from one side of the street to the other. 'I know why, as well. You took Master Gregorio to Whistle Willie's last night.'

'We looked disgusting when we arrived,' said Nicholas de Fleury, leaving his companions and riding slowly across. He was still dressed in black.

'No, you didn't. I saw you when we came back from hunting with Sandy. With – Sandy. I expect you celebrated the baby. How is it?'

'Celebrated,' said de Fleury. As the two parties rode on, he kept pace with her. 'I have made peace with your uncle. Have I made peace with you?'

'And my aunt?' she said. She could see poor Master Gregorio trying to place her. She turned and said, 'Anselm Adorne's niece. Sister of Anselm Sersanders.'

Master Gregorio bowed, carefully, in the saddle. De Fleury said, 'Your aunt belongs to that glorious sisterhood who revere the first-born of a marriage. For the sake of mine, she forgave me.'

'My brother doesn't like babies,' said Katelijne. 'We didn't think you'd come back.'

'So what should I do about Sersanders?' he said. He sounded interested. He was again the careless rider of Leith strand, not the bright-eyed man, soaked in blood, who had tried to drive the life out of St Pol, and had taken cold steel to her uncle.

'Apologise to him,' she said. 'He knows what it is to get battle-silly. Then agree to meet him in a fight. That will salvage his honour, for those people who suspect what happened.'

De Fleury frowned, riding beside her. He said, 'But he's good.'

'That's the idea,' she said.

'It wouldn't be enough to apologise? You would accept an apology.'

'No, I shouldn't. You'd have to do something else.'

'Katelijne?' said a gentle voice. Phemie Dunbar, come to spoil the game with tranquil good sense.

De Fleury said, as she hoped, 'Well, we have a day's ride before us. We should be able to work something out.' Then he turned and introduced Phemie to Master Gregorio, which was an excellent idea, since they should have much in common. And then, when he had presented himself to the lady Margaret, and renewed his acquaintance with the other attendants in her train, de Fleury was free to ride at her side, as the two parties blended. Dropping back, they devised between them his punishment.

She had not meant, at the outset, that it should be quite so disruptive, nor that it should gradually involve the Princess's whole party, not excluding Margaret herself. It restricted itself to the route, since the ride along the estuary was as long as anyone should wish to make in one day. But it made use of every sporting facility they could muster between them, from bow to lance to falcon, and even to one of those long-stemmed clubs which, used from horseback, could send a ball from man to man along the flats, earning points for each target.

By dinner-time they were hot and exhausted with laughter as much as with exercise. But even during the meal, which they took in the fresh air, out of baskets, de Fleury snatched up her viol and commanded her to perform, adding new rules and new contests, until she stopped eating, as he had, to compete, and the others clamoured to take part. Then the lawyer Gregorio, who had been sitting apart, came over and knelt beside de Fleury and spoke.

She knew what he was saying. He had been talking to Phemie. She watched de Fleury's profile, eyes downcast, as he listened. When he finally rose and came over, she knew what he was going to say, because they all said it: her parents, her brother, her uncle.

De Fleury said, 'They want us to stop. Have I apologised enough?'

'No,' she said.

'I didn't think so. What might we do that would convince them we've stopped?'

As it happened, she had already thought of something: a word-game. He had never heard of it before, but she taught it to him, and he invented a number of variants as they paced side by side at the end of the column. As they entered Edinburgh, he allowed her to win. It made her so angry that he reversed the last moves and beat her soundly. Shortly after, the two groups of travellers parted. Last of all, he applied to her and she absolved him.

She wondered why he had wasted a day on such trivia. She

concluded that there was no one in either party whom he regarded as interesting or useful, and that he had found some kind of repose in exertion. In the lawyer Gregorio's face she thought she recognised a trace of the same look that Phemie wore sometimes. Towards de Fleury himself she felt curiosity, and a degree of affinity, and a sensible wariness mixed with something she would not call fear.

Gregorio experienced fear. In spite of all that Julius had said, he had not been prepared for the reality: for the tall, secretive house in the Canongate which Nicholas had fitted into the enclave of ecclesiastics and merchants and from which his business was run.

He was not prepared for the scale of the banquet given for Nicholas by his landlord, who happened to be Abbot of Holyrood, and who invited to it all the men of business Gregorio had ever heard of, including Berecrofts Older and Younger in whose country-house Lucia had lain dead.

He was not prepared for an invitation to the other house the Bank owned in the High Street, nor to find that Nicholas had lent it to the convent of Haddington for the use of its Prioress and nuns. He was not even prepared (although he was content enough) to find there Mistress Phemie Dunbar, the sedate unmarried daughter of the late Earl of March, who had brought some order into the headlong, tumultuous ride from Stirling to Edinburgh instigated by Adorne's crazy scrap of a niece.

However, he had not been surprised, except initially, by the part Nicholas had played in that, or by the intensity of his activities since. It matched what he remembered of the more extraordinary undertakings of the past: the revitalising of the Charetty company through the cunning of the alum monopoly; the trading and fighting at Trebizond; the setting up of the Bank; the fitting-out and execution of the African expedition. Of Cyprus his knowledge was second-hand, but he had read the accounts, and knew when the payments had stopped for their land and their farms and the army. They said there had been a famine there recently. He had sent the reports to Nicholas, as he sent everything, but it was Nicholas who decided what to act on.

Gregorio was not alarmed, therefore, at the scale of the activity, but he was critical of its content. The major investments were good: the Banco di Niccolò had property and land, and had expended money on loans in the right quarters. There was a foreign wedding afoot, and the King and his lords required all the jewels, clothes and furnishings that implied. Julius had been right in identifying a fine profit there, and insisting that the padrone should return in person to realise it.

To a degree, the Bank had been right, too, in placing money where it would encourage business. The *San Niccolò* was already carrying timber: there was room for a cart-building workshop to supplement the familiar skills of the monasteries. Draining experts could bring fields and salt-pans and coal layers into better profit – that was why John le Grant had been sent for. There were other schemes, not yet in place. Alum, brought direct from their own special contacts, would profit the Bank and still sell cheaply to the dyers and curers. Dyeing itself could be properly taught, and good weaving. And as the country grew wealthier, the demand for luxuries would increase.

At that point, drowned in calculations, Gregorio called a halt.

'Nicholas? This is a small country, and remote. It can use some of your schemes – or could, when you first thought of them. But soap-making? Gunpowder? Paper? Cabinet-making? A workshop for embroidery looms? The demand for all those things is limited and will soon be satisfied. And almost none can be exported without meeting far greater competition in the south. You will be wasting the Bank's money.'

They were meeting in the Casa di Niccolò in the Canongate where the uses to which the Bank's money had already been put were very obvious. Travelling through the last weeks, Gregorio had visited many merchant-lairds in their castles as well as the ecclesiastics who kept house in town. He had walked with Forrester of Corstorphine to hear the new choristers in his church, and climbed the hill to Haliburton's fine keep at Dirleton where his wife Cornelia kept a painting-room for Hugo vander Goes her kinsman, already full of coloured shields for the wedding.

He had visited the Earl of Orkney in Roslin and the Church's mines at Tranent and the Hamiltons and the Berecrofts beside Linlithgow. He had seen the salt-pans beside the Lord's house at Seton, and inspected the Bank's own warehouses and lodging at Leith. He had been to Haddington, and met the Prioress Elizabeth, and heard, from behind a door, a well-played guitar which turned out to belong to Mistress Phemie Dunbar, whom he remembered he knew. He was rather thankful not to meet Adorne's niece, who was away.

Now it was the third week in May and he knew that the time had come to curb Nicholas de Fleury, for none of his other staff would. And particularly not Jannekin Bonkle, fast integrating into the traditional merchant network of Edinburgh. Jannekin thought he was commissioned by Midas, and however much gold Nicholas chose to throw into Scotland, there would always be more.

Jannekin therefore was not present, but safely engaged in the clerks' room, the miniature chancery upon which the Scottish lord Whitelaw, Secretary of a kingdom, had looked once, withholding his envy. Next to that was the secure room which held the locked chests with their wealth, and spread through the house and its yards were the other chambers and workshops Nicholas had created for the artisans he had brought or was bringing. Close to the ovens was a chamber of stone for the furnace. But access to that was not easily granted.

For the rest, the house was not unlike the two mansions the Bank used in Bruges, except for the grandeur of its great parlour, and of the bedchamber in which Gregorio now sat, preparing to argue with Nicholas.

There were other differences. In Bruges, by the end of May, the worsted bed-hangings would have given place to fine say, and the great Irish bedcover removed – the bernia which Margot had bought when Nicholas first came back to Venice and which still lay here on his Edinburgh bed, with the brazier burning low at its foot.

Gregorio said, 'Why do you stay here if you find Scotland cold? Listen to my advice. Wait for the wedding, recover your loans from the dowry, and let all but the best of these other schemes go. One single good cargo from Alexandria will give you double the profit. Kings are dangerous. If Edward of York falls, he could bring down the Medici.'

'You think James of Scotland, just turned seventeen, is going to bring down the House of Niccolò?' the other man asked. He left the brazier and sat down, a model of patience.

Gregorio said, 'I think you've punished Simon quite adequately and made life sufficiently uncomfortable for Jordan. I think you should finish competing with them and get out, before you forget that you have a Bank and a number of partners.'

'And a family,' said Nicholas de Fleury. 'Or no. You could put them down as self-supporting. Look. I understand. I agree, to a point. But banking means taking risks, and in my view this throne is secure.'

'And what circator did you get that from?' Gregorio said. 'Lord Boyd, Tom Boyd's father, has gone south on some errand and he hasn't come back. He could be plotting with England.'

'He *is* plotting with England,' the other said. 'He's promised, among other things, to have Chancellor Avandale killed when the

Scottish nobles sail in with his son and the child-bride from Denmark.'

Gregorio stared at him. It sounded true. It probably *was* true, given the kind of network Nicholas had undoubtedly established south of the border. Gregorio said, 'So that the Boyds can renew their grip of the King? If they do that . . .'

'They won't,' said the other man.

'How do you know?'

'Because I've seen to it that they won't. Have you ever met the Sheriff of Renfrew? Simon's baronial superior and neighbour?'

'No. Why?' said Gregorio. He spoke sharply because he knew now, why Nicholas had appeared so unduly patient. He was waiting for somebody – and probably the somebody whom he could hear arriving outside. Gregorio went to the window.

It was not a short view, such as you got from a window in Bruges. Behind the Canongate houses, the open land bumped its way past leekbeds and pastures and fruit trees to a narrow valley, and then rose beyond to a fine sunlit crag grazed by sheep. Immediately below, the paved back yards of this house and its neighbours were crammed with a jumble of stables and wells, bakehouses and byres, styes and henhouses and sheds.

Into this space, admitted by the vaulted passage that led from the highway, a small cavalcade was at this moment reaching a halt. It consisted of four liveried servants and a spare, middle-aged man in a brimmed hat and thick velvet overgown, now nimbly dismounting. The badge was the chevron chequy of Semple, evidence of the family's rise as seneschals and bailies to the High Stewards of Scotland. And this was Sir William Semple of Elliotstoun, acting for the ancient Sheriff, his father.

William Semple knew Nicholas. Of course he did. One of the minor injuries Nicholas had inflicted on Simon – apart from half roasting him and occasioning, one way or another, the death of his sister Lucia – had been to persuade the Sheriff to deprive Simon of his outlying leased land and to reallocate it to M. de Fleury.

Julius had described the achievement with glee. Gregorio could imagine how Simon felt. He wondered whether Simon de St Pol now regretted his willing part in the vicious scheme concocted by Gelis, however little he had understood it at the time. He thought probably not. Indeed, especially not if he guessed the resulting child to be his. His elation would counterbalance, very nearly, anything Nicholas could inflict. Which was why, perhaps, Nicholas was bent on further prosecuting his plans. Gregorio could not imagine what part the eminent Sir William Semple had been persuaded to play in them.

The answer at first seemed to be none. Sir William, seated in the chair of state with an excellent cup of wine in his hand, enquired first about the King's wedding, and the magnificent celebrations he understood M. de Fleury was advising upon. From that he moved cordially to enquire when M. de Fleury planned to view his new estate, for he hoped that he and Marian would be permitted the honour of entertaining him. And finally, he made it known that her grace the lady Mary, Countess of Arran, was presently at home at Dean Castle, and would welcome news of Gelis van Borselen and her babe.

He was a thin man, with a lean ruddy face and sparse brown hair left to curl on his shoulders. His eyes were light and sharp. Nicholas said, 'I have to see my new factor. You approve of him?'

'I helped Master Bonkle choose him. An experienced man, Oliver Semple: a second cousin of mine. A good rent-collector, a man who will get you a fair price for your hides and your fells and your cheeses, and strike a bargain for a stretch of good fishing, besides knowing what's what when you're building. He and your builder – he and Cochrane get on. Well, then. You could ride to Beltrees from Kilmarnock. There is undeveloped land further south you might look at. I do not know, of course, how deep your interest lies. But you should not fail to call on the Countess at Dean. And, of course, you will find Mistress Bel at Kilmirren. Bel of Cuthilgurdy? She is attending to the affairs of the poor lady Lucia.'

'I thought Mistress Bel was in France,' Nicholas said. Gregorio looked at him.

'She was, but she has returned. No doubt there is much to arrange. The late poor lady's house now belongs, I suppose, to her son M. de Vasquez?'

Nicholas hesitated. For a moment, Gregorio thought he wasn't going to admit it. Then he said, 'No, to me. Now his mother has gone, M. Diniz has no interest in Scotland. And it adjoins the land I already have.'

'So it does,' said Sir William Semple. 'How pleased my old friend Jordan will be.'

'So they are not the closest of friends,' Gregorio said, when their visitor had gone.

'Who?' Nicholas had rung for his page and was writing.

'William Semple and Jordan de Ribérac.'

'No. Jordan doesn't develop his land, and invests all his money abroad. Simon can't keep good managers. If I put off the Abbot, which I'm doing, we could set off for Dean Castle tomorrow.'

'Tomorrow? Why? ... Where is it?' said Gregorio, as an afterthought.

'By Kilmarnock. Sixty miles to the south-west. We could stop with the Flemings of Biggar.'

'Why?' said Gregorio. 'Or why tomorrow?'

'Because that's why Semple came here,' said Nicholas. 'I don't mind going. And I want to see to one or two things. And to look at Beltrees.'

'What are Beltrees?' asked Gregorio.

'Singular. It's the name of a towerhouse and an estate. Julius and I thought you'd be shocked, so we didn't send you the accounts.'

'This is the Kilmirren land that you filched?'

'Some of it. I've added a few hundred acres. All undeveloped and waste. And the tower was too small: I've refurbished it. It's on a hill. It'll be cold.'

Gregorio was silent. A project so large, and none of the accounts had been sent to him. He assumed he knew why. He said outright, 'How long are you staying in Scotland?'

'As long as it takes,' Nicholas said, 'to finish all I want to do. But you don't need to watch me.'

Chapter 19

THEY SET OFF at dawn, an impressive cavalcade, and arranged to break their journey at Boghall Castle, as Nicholas had suggested. Govaerts, sent ahead to solicit hospitality, would certainly be successful.

Robert, Lord Fleming, knew Nicholas. Gregorio, in turn, knew something of him. The lordship might be new, but there had been Flemings in Biggar for three hundred years, and half of them traded in Bruges. Gregorio wondered, in a resigned way, if there were pretty daughters or granddaughters.

It was a thirty-mile ride which yielded, as it transpired, a particular balm of its own. For once, Nicholas initiated little, and those around him could retreat into their thoughts and savour the landscape they rode through. Rushing streams; undulating valleys between soft, sunlit green hills; grey stone towers and thatched cots hazed with peat smoke; the bleating of sheep and of goats; herds of cattle filing to milk; the cry of a hawk, circling above in the blue air – all of it delighted Gregorio; filled him with singing pleasure, and then with an echo of contrition, for his partner in pleasure was not there.

The castle, when they reached it, was large and old, with a stone bridge crossing the moat. Riding over it, Gregorio carried with him the single piece of advice Nicholas had troubled to give him. 'The old man is aged early and shaky, but son Malcolm knows the time of day, more or less. You talk to Lord Fleming and leave Malcolm to me.'

Malcolm came out into the courtyard to meet them. His doublet, creased from the coffer, was a better one, Gregorio guessed, than he would normally wear in the country, and his hat had a feather. He was short-legged and dark and probably not quite as old as he looked: the cares of managing his father must have taken their toll.

He said, 'I had not time to warn you. Perhaps you do not object. But Anselm Sersanders has just arrived. Sir Anselm Adorne's sister's son.'

Nicholas reined in and, after a moment, dismounted. He said, 'I have no objection, unless you have. I was told he was in the north. The new Observatine Friary, and Maryculter.'

'He came south to visit his sister at Dean. You are going there?'

'Katelijne and I are good friends,' Nicholas said. 'And although you may have heard of a mischance, I hope Sersanders won't hold it against me. Besides, Gregorio here is exhausted, and I have told him too much about your good claret. We may rest here tonight? I promise there will be no unpleasantness.'

'I was sure of it,' said Malcolm Fleming, and led the way in.

Gregorio, dismounting stiffly, handed his horse over and caught Nicholas up. 'What are you doing? You half killed his uncle!'

'I know. *Tutto e fritto*,' said Nicholas de Fleury, and emitted a wail, absently, in a whisper.

The Great Hall of the Flemings was reached by a flight of stone steps and had tall windows and a fine fireplace glowing with resinous flame in the twilight. The top of the tower was in sunlight as yet: from its battlements, Gregorio imagined, one could see half lowland Scotland and the uplands of England as well, not to mention the neighbouring keeps he had glimpsed.

In the room were no nubile daughters but two young grandsons, John and David, who made their bows and were taken away, leaving only the chaplain, who rose to be introduced. Distant laughter came from a parlour. Malcolm said, 'My wife is absent at present, but come. My father sits by the fire, and Master Sersanders beside him.'

The room was long and, supper being just over, the rush-strewn floor was free of trestles and empty. Against the light of the fire it could be seen that Anselm Sersanders had risen, but that the old man was still seated. The carved back of his chair, tall and black, hid all but the turban on his head. Malcolm Fleming walked forward.

'Father. Here is Master Nicholas of the Banco di Niccolò. And Master Gregorio, both come to stay with us.'

The wind-dried face that peered round the chair was that of a mature courtier, not a man of affairs. Robert, Lord Fleming, was lavishly dressed, give or take a stain or two, and the spare bones of his face were still handsome, although his shallow-set eyes had in them a look of permanent shock, or even permanent grievance. Nevertheless, he got to his feet. 'Gentlemen, welcome,' he said.

'My lord of Fleming.' Nicholas, bowing, was always a picture. Taught by courtesans, Gregorio recalled. One need never doubt the social competence of Nicholas de Fleury. Even when, as now, Anselm Sersanders stepped sideways, not forward.

Sersanders said, 'Forgive me, my lord. I do not care to meet the man who tried to murder my uncle.'

His light-skinned face looked rather pale. It was a situation, as Gregorio had already recognised, which could explode into high farce or tragedy. Short though he was, the nephew of Anselm Adorne had much of his uncle's grace and a great deal of his athletic ability. And whatever business brought Nicholas here, it was not going to be helped by a quarrel involving skilled swordsmanship.

Gregorio opened his mouth. Nicholas laid a hand on his shoulder to silence him. Nicholas said, 'We need no lawyer in this. My lord, I have to tell you that Master Anselm is right. His uncle intervened in a family quarrel and I struck and wounded him in the heat of the moment. Happily, Sir Anselm has since seen fit to forgive me, but I have not yet had a chance to explain to his nephew. I should gladly pay any compensation he asks.'

He let his hand drop and addressed Lord Fleming directly. 'Perhaps, if Master Anselm will not speak, my lord would act as intermediary? I should be content to do as he says.'

Sersanders flushed. The veined eye of the elder Fleming rested on Nicholas. He said, 'Ane hoor with a sword is mair grief than six honest chiels with their fists. Who in the name were ye fighting?'

'Kilmirren, Faither,' said Malcolm. Like his sire, he had dropped the language of diplomacy. 'Am I not right, de Fleury? Kilmirren wasted his land, and fell into a fury when Semple let the Bank have it.'

Fleming's lips arched and straightened. He said, 'I mind. A richt crop o' weeds, the bane of his neebors, and the craws still blithe as speugs in his woods at Beltane. And they took steel tae one another?'

'He took my uncle's own sword, and lamed him with it,' Sersanders said. 'My uncle might have died. He limps still.'

'I don't wear a sword,' Nicholas said. 'I have none with me now. We were wrestling. Kilmirren fled. Sir Anselm stopped me from following. I lost my head. I shall pay whatever forfeit you wish, short of life.'

'Short of life!' said Lord Fleming. 'And that's a fine exemption ye've made for yourself. If you near louse a man frae his life, what for should ye no' tyne your own?'

'But gin it wasna meant?' Malcolm said. 'Adorne tried tae play birleyman, and got hurt for it. Here's a man admitting the wrong, and ready to pay for it. A man, forbye, of goodwill.'

Lord Fleming looked up. Across his face passed several unaccustomed expressions. Then he said, 'Aye. Aye, there's an argument. But what if the strife is renewed? What bystander's life will be forfeit the next time? Or will ye tell me that a Decreet Arbitral will suffice?'

Nicholas said, 'Will you explain it, my lord?'

The old man turned and sat with a thump. Sersanders remained to one side of the fire, his eyes fixed on Nicholas. Gregorio wondered if a Decreet Arbitral was what he thought it was, and wondered if Gelis had heard of it.

The old man said, 'Is it no' plain eneugh? It's a process for the settling o' feuds, with due regard to an action of blood that's been committed. That is to say, the baith o' ye wad mutually remit and forgive all unkindnesses and injuries done tae the other in times bypast. Master de Fleury, wad ye set your name tae that?'

'I should. But you would have to ask Anselm here for his part.'

'Master Anselm! But ye've nae quarrel wi' him, or so ye were telling me. It's Simon de St Pol of Kilmirren your tuilzie was with, and may be with again. So I ask ye again. Wad ye subscribe?'

'Simon de St Pol is abroad,' Nicholas said. 'It would be unfair, I think, to expect me to sign unless he did. But I shall agree without stint to any pact or redress you require in the other case. Perhaps Master Sersanders himself has a view.'

They faced one another, Nicholas and the boy four years younger. Sersanders looked strained; Nicholas sober. Sersanders said, 'My uncle's wellbeing is worth more than money, but it is not, perhaps, worth another life. I accept that the attack was not personal. If my uncle has not demanded public satisfaction, then neither will I. But I want M. de Fleury to confess and to apologise for that act now, before witnesses. And I wish him to meet me, with blunted weapons, at a joust of my choosing before the end of his stay. Does my lord deem this sufficient?'

Lord Fleming looked at his son, who gave a slight nod.

'Aweel,' said his lordship, scratching his head under his turban. 'Another man, Maister Sersanders, wad say ye've missed your chance of a muckle great sack of the usual money of Scotland, but I respect ye for't. Right enough, he'll apologise, and ye've leave tae broadcast it as ye wish. And as for the joust, it is ilka man's right to challenge another, and Master de Fleury will promise to afford ye the fullest contemption and satisfaction, with blunted points. Are we agreed? Sir Hugh there, where are you?'

The chaplain came forward. Lord Fleming waited, erect in his chair, while the apology was made and accepted. There was a brief, unfriendly handshake. Lord Fleming looked at the banker his guest and flung himself back, poking under his bonnet again.

'Then sit down!' he said. His turban drooped by one ear. 'Whatna foolish damned way for a visitor to chap on a man's door! Sit down, the lot o' ye, while Hugh here goes and sends for some liquor: my mou's like the well o' a glue-pig. And Malcolm! Malcolm! There's my pate-claith fell on the rushes again . . .'

After the first cup of wine, Anselm Sersanders excused himself and retired, grimly polite. Nicholas waited a while and then, obeying some suggestion of Malcolm's, drifted off with Lord Fleming's heir.

He was absent for an hour. Gregorio stayed and kept the old man company which, being a lawyer, he did not find uninteresting. Later, in the bedchamber that they shared, he addressed his fellow guest. 'I suppose you knew Sersanders would be here. Semple told you?'

Nicholas had stripped. The burn marks on his skin had almost gone, and his shadow on the low ceiling was as big as a tree. He looked more preoccupied than triumphant. He said, 'He hinted. I didn't want you to worry. God be pleased with him, Semple looks like being quite helpful.' Sometimes he fell into Arabic unawares, Gregorio noted.

Gregorio climbed into bed. It had been a very long day. They had, in the end, been given supper. He said, 'And what made you so sure that Lord Fleming wouldn't report you?'

'He's afraid of the King,' the other man said. With his bedgown around him, he had begun to set out writing materials by the candle, the brazier at his side. He added, 'Get some sleep. It's another thirty miles to Dean Castle and the other Sersanders.'

'Holy Mary.' Recovering manfully: 'But you're not the King,' Gregorio objected. 'Or not yet. Look, if you're sending a message, I'll write it.'

'No,' said Nicholas. 'Thank you. Not being the King, I can write my own letters.'

'If,' said Gregorio, his eyes already closed, 'if Simon had really been here, would you have signed their Decreet Arbitral? Taken their oath to forgive and remit?'

'If they made it a condition,' Nicholas said.

'And having sworn, you would keep it?'

'What do you think?' said Nicholas.

*

For all its recent massive extensions, the double castle of Dean, home of the Boyds by the burn of Kilmarnock, had no chamber devoted to music, and those musicians who played in the hall kept their instruments in the gallery closet, where Katelijne Sersanders soon found them. Today, engaged in a furious duet with Mistress Phemie Dunbar, Katelijne still kept an eye on the window and could see, as soon as it climbed the rise, the retinue outfitted in black which announced that difficult man Nicol de Fleury.

She said, 'Leave this to me,' and getting up made her descent as quickly as had the child Henry, alarmed by the sight of his grandfather.

Leave this to me, considering the age of the speaker, were words that might have alarmed or annoyed most grown women. Phemie Dunbar simply put her music away, rose, and went to inform her cousin Betha that the rich Fleming had come. Betha, in turn, went to apprise the lady Mary.

Katelijne, running out to the courtyard, saw that de Fleury had already reined in his horse, awaiting her. The lawyer, Gregorio, was behind him. She said, 'I told Anselm not to kill you. He didn't.'

'A Gradual Alleluia,' de Fleury remarked. He was attired today in black damask, and his hat was as big as a mushroom, its upturned brim pleated with silk. 'You aren't afraid that I might have killed him?'

'Oh no,' said Katelijne. 'I told you. He's had the very best teachers. And you wouldn't have come if you had.'

'I am regretting it already,' he said. 'I have a conditional reprieve in return for an abject apology and a promise to face your extremely competent brother in the lists. With blunted points.'

She said, 'Oh dear.'

'But I am still capable of appreciating the comforts of life, for a while. The lady Mary, I'm told, will receive us?'

'Oh, yes. Dame Betha and Phemie are here. And Hearty James, the Lady's half-uncle. And you've just missed Tony Cavalli. Do you know about Tony Cavalli, adviser to the Duke of the Tyrol? You ought to,' she said.

'If I ought to, I am sure you will tell me,' de Fleury replied. The words sounded condescending – the lawyer smiled – but she knew when he was not speaking casually. She wondered what scheme he had devised for deflecting the Lady's profound interest in his wife. He was not being protected by Hospitallers now. Whatever he did, he was going to have to answer some of her questions.

Inside, she watched his face as the chamberlain led him up the stairs and through the passages of the castle. Hung with carpets and lamps, cluttered with cushions, the hoary stronghold of the Boyds was being transformed by its mistress into an unwieldy bower of love against the return of her lord, Thomas Boyd, first Earl of Arran.

Sharing her house, studying the sallow, inarticulate girl only three years her elder, Katelijne had divined that some kinds of hunger could inhabit the unlikeliest forms. The Princess Mary, threatened with marriage abroad, had found herself instead with a young, lusty Scots husband, almost immediately snatched from her pillow. Perhaps she was even a virgin. Certainly she longed for her husband with all the fervour of Robert, her kingly forefather, who had sired, in his day, twenty-one legitimate children. Katelijne felt that for Mary, twenty-one would hardly suffice.

Confronted with this theory, Phemie, who had never married, smiled but did not reply. Betha, foster-mother of royalty, had said, 'If you wed, you will bear. That is only fair to your man. To wed in order to bear is another matter.'

'Or to wed for the joy of it?' Katelijne said.

Betha Sinclair had looked at her then. 'Very few have the chance of that. Or few of our standing,' she said. 'But joy comes with custom, often enough, if you give it a chance. You heard Cavalli. Sigismond of the Tyrol roves abroad and his wife Eleanor makes her own life at Innsbruck. But when he comes back she receives him, and he her; and although she has none but a dead child, and he has brought thirty women to bear, he and she are fond with one another.'

'You are telling me something?' said Katelijne.

'Of course. Marry whom you like and respect, but do not expect to choose whom you will marry. You owe as much to your family. And think a long time before you decide not to marry at all. It may suit Phemie, but for most women a partnership of the soul alone is not enough.'

Katelijne didn't reply. It was a litany much repeated in the last year. She knew the situation in Flanders: the Duke of Burgundy's unpredictable temper; the fears of the Flemish towns under him. She knew that, at present, her family were uncertain where best to marry her. That was partly why she and her brother were here.

They might have to depend on their links with this land in the future. It was one of the reasons why her uncle had hoped that M. de Fleury would not come back to Scotland. Katelijne wondered what was so menacing about the fair Gelis van Borselen, and whether any improvement was to be hoped for. A properly impassioned young wife would surely keep M. de Fleury at home. She even questioned Master Gregorio discreetly, as they walked up the stairs.

'After the Queen's fleet arrives? I hope he'll go back,' Gregorio said. 'I've advised it. Alexandria is safe now: he should go there. But you like it here? The air suits you better in the west?'

'I haven't breathed any of it yet: it's been busier than Haddington Priory. The Countess asked my lady her sister to lend Dame Betha and Phemie and me to help her prepare the state rooms for her husband. Then we have to ride back to Leith for the Royal Danish Arrival. Phemie and I have to sing a new laud, but we can't tell the notes from the beer stains. I'm making a flute on a lathe. The private rooms are up here. You remember Hearty James, the King's uncle?'

'Who?' said Master Gregorio.

'James Stewart of Auchterhouse, the half-royal uncle. He visited Veere. His sister married Wolfaert van Borselen.'

'Oh,' said the lawyer.

'I knew you'd be pleased. Hearty James. He got drunk with the rest at Linlithgow. You know. When they pilfered the crates from the *Ghost*. Was the compensation worth while?'

'It was adequate,' Gregorio said.

'I'm sure. Half the furnishings ended up here. Oh, look!' Katelijne said. She waited while the lawyer stood and gazed up at the roof, his cap-lappets laid back like dogs' ears. It had pleased her to discover that he recognised when she was teasing him, and didn't mind. He was a shy man, not a stiff one, she saw.

They were looking at a tall ladder, upon which stood the King's uncle, hanging a mirror. At its foot stood his half-niece and M. de Fleury, with Dame Betha and Phemie behind them. Phemie was weeping.

The lady Mary said, 'To the left. To the left. That is where you say we should have it?' A pearl had burst from her sleeve, leaving a poke of pink taffeta, and the tips of her fingers were black.

'That is where the Duchess would have it,' said M. de Fleury. 'With the little desk there, and the picture-cloth looped to the right. Gregorio, what do you think?'

Gregorio sneezed. His eyes, like those of Phemie, were watering. He said, 'Forgive me. There is a remarkable scent . . .'

'It's the mirror,' said Katelijne. 'Didn't you know? Or no, of course, all these things came on the *Ghost*. The paste reliefs on the mirror are scented. We hope my lord Thomas likes musk. And that is a book-cushion. And that is a firescreen, with inlaid wood *tinti e ombrati*, stained and shaded. Scorched, that is, in hot salt.'

'Sand,' corrected Dame Betha, who was protecting a large covered bell on a standpost.

'For fine veneers,' Katelijne conceded. 'For thick skins, there is nothing like salt. You need a globb nail.'

The royal uncle and M. de Fleury, who were the same age and equally unused to technical jargon, exchanged glances. Mistress Phemie said, through her tears, 'I have a lozen one. Can you reach it?'

'Give it me,' said Master Gregorio, and tossed the headed nail upwards, lappets flying. The royal uncle snatched, the ladder lurched, and the nail fell on top of the quilted object, which emitted a screech. The mirror shuddered.

'Steady,' said M. de Fleury. He looked at the nail thoughtfully.

The King's uncle said, 'I need to rest the mirror on something. No – Christ – don't climb beside me. Get me the nail. What did I do with the hammer?'

'In your belt,' said M. de Fleury. 'What's under the quilt?' He had picked up the nail and, walking over, was lifting the book-cushion.

'Your parrot,' said Dame Betha calmly. She raised the cotton cover, removing her hand rather suddenly as a large red-and-blue object lunged at it from within.

'*My* parrot?' said M. de Fleury.

'I am told it arrived on the *Ghost*. Perhaps you were not aware. In any case, when my lady expressed a longing to buy it, Master Crackbene thought you would have no objection.'

'I didn't know. Does it talk?' de Fleury said. The parrot looked at him evilly.

'Not a word. My lady is planning to teach it.'

'A welcome for my lord,' said the Lady of Dean Castle, blushing. 'M. de Fleury, we are receiving you with small ceremony. Will you forgive us? Once the mirror is hung . . .'

'Holy Mother,' said her uncle. 'Never mind that. I need the nail and somewhere to rest –'

'Here,' said M. de Fleury. He put on his hat, lifted the book-cushion on top and, laying the lozen nail on top of that, walked to the ladder.

'It isn't tall enough,' said the King's uncle James. 'Put a book on top. Turn over the handbasin there with the lugs. Mary, are those your red stockings? Now the nail. Now come here, and I'll let down the mirror. What –?'

The scream this time came from Dame Betha, invoking the Trinity in the vernacular. It had been preceded by a clang and a whipping of wing-feathers. The cage-door hung open. 'The wee hoor's flitted!' exclaimed Dame Betha, still in the vernacular.

All those present looked up except James of Auchterhouse, embracing the mirror, who was already higher than anyone, and Nicholas de Fleury, standing under the towering skewer of *brochettes* on his head with only his contorted mouth and chin to indicate his reaction.

'Oh!' said the lady Mary. 'Oh! Oh! He'll eat the hangings!'

Phemie choked. Katelijne, who had been attempting to keep a grave face, burst into laughter. Dame Betha, pushing her hand into the cage, extracted a handful of cereal and tossed it over the floor. Katelijne said, 'We need a net and two brooms and some gloves and three eggs. M. de Fleury? What do parrots like?'

'Other parrots,' he said. Under the weight of the mirror, the pyramid on his head had sunk heavily, bulging out and overlapping the brim of his hat: his voice sounded nasal. The King's uncle, hammer in hand, was attempting to knock the lozen into the wall. The muffled voice added, 'Sing to it. Where is it?'

'On the bed-rail. We could sing it the laud. Phemie's gone for the brooms. Oh, the windows. My lady Mary, do you want . . .'

The lady Mary had no intention of losing her parrot. She ran to both shutters and closed them. Darkness fell. The noise of hammering abruptly stopped, with a surprised oath, and the muffled voice under the hat made a remark. It could be deciphered as a desire to know whether or not he was now wholly suffocated and actually dead.

'No,' said Katelijne, feeling her way to the tinderbox. She collided with Dame Betha doing the same and fell to her knees in a patch of gravelly parrot-food. The parrot, which had been consuming it, blundered croaking into her hair, started away, and could be heard hurtling about the room like wet washing. The door opened, admitting Phemie, daylight, and an assortment of servants with implements. On a shrieked order from the Countess of Arran the door was slammed shut and darkness fell again. Amid the hubbub of voices the demands of James of Auchterhouse on the ladder remained the most penetrating. The parrot couldn't be heard, nor could Master Gregorio or M. de Fleury, who appeared to be voiceless. Katelijne lit a candle.

The parrot flew up to the ceiling, batted frantically along its leaping shadows and, shooting downwards and sideways, attached itself with two horny claws to the bosom of the King's uncle's doublet. It then proceeded methodically to wrench the buttons off with its beak.

At that point, Katelijne stopped looking in order to breathe. She could hear Phemie wheezing beside her, and even Master Gregorio, although he had picked up the broom she let drop and started forward with it. Someone threw the net, but not high enough; it came down and coped the cage and Dame Betha together. Looking up for a second, Katelijne saw the astonished, sensible face of the Earl of Orkney's widowed daughter appearing in strips through the bars like cut cheese. Then the ladder started to rock.

They rushed to steady it, but circumstances were against them. Beating at the flapping bird on his chest, Hearty James had dropped lozen and hammer and forgotten, for the moment, where he was. His slipping weight pulled at the ladder and dislodged the mirror which had been resting partly against it, and partly upon the Pisa-like tower on its human foundation. The King's uncle started to fall. The ladder slipped sideways. The mirror, heavily tilting, was saved by a series of scrambles by M. de Fleury who, scuffling below, managed to engage the help of the wall to support part of it.

The ladder crashed. The King's uncle fell, his doublet gaping, and was safely caught by many assiduous hands. M. de Fleury, teetering about, hands outspread, chin upraised, came slowly to a halt, the mirror resting perfectly balanced between the uncertain pile on his head and the wall. It could be seen that his mouth was open. Someone – Phemie? – started a round of applause. Katelijne's ribs hurt.

The parrot landed, with a thud, on the top of the mirror. The man below made a slight move, compensating. The parrot looked down. Then it sprang across and posed on the pyramid, its tail spread, its great oyster beak confronting the mirror. It pecked the glass, its eye lascivious, and pecked it again. '*Hijita de mi alma,*' it said.

The King's uncle, and those who were helping him, paid no attention. 'It spoke!' said his niece. 'What did it say?'

Master Gregorio knew. His laughter fading, he opened his mouth. The Atlas under the hat spoke before him. '*¿Salud, chiquito?*' said M. de Fleury, his voice astonishingly distinct.

The parrot pecked the glass anxiously, a thread of white encircling each pupil. It exclaimed, its voice raucous: 'My treasured ones! Kiss me, my angels! Come to me, my little mice!'

Nicholas de Fleury moved without thinking. The pyramid tilted. The parrot, disturbed, slid muttering off. The mirror, inclining backwards, began to run down the wall at a speed which human flesh could not check and M. de Fleury did not try to. He stepped away, and the mirror – glass and white paste and backing – crashed to the floor. A stench of musk rose, causing the parrot to cough. While it was doing so, Dame Betha threw her handkerchief over it, and flung it into the cage. The door shut and latched. The parrot put a claw on its swing and shoved it petulantly. '¡*Demonio!*' it remarked.

'It swears!' said the King's sister.

A handbasin, a book-cushion, a book, and a pair of red stockings arranged themselves in a pile at her feet, followed by the remains of a hat. The contrite face of Nicholas de Fleury confronted her. 'I am afraid,' he said, 'that this is not the bird that you wanted. Let me buy it back. A full refund for the bird and the mirror.'

Katelijne Sersanders prodded Master Gregorio in the back. 'It's not his fault. Tell him,' she said. 'He owes nothing. Tell him.'

She had to prod him twice. Then Gregorio said, 'No. If he wants the parrot, let him have it.' He spoke with punctilio, although his face was still glossy with laughter.

Katelijne said, 'Why? Tell me?'

'To make me happy,' said M. de Fleury. 'I always wanted a parrot. Do you need three eggs for anything?'

She was diverted at once. 'They were to juggle with. Can you juggle?'

'For you, anything,' said M. de Fleury. 'Put them back in the shells and I'll amaze you.'

Chapter 20

THE PERFORMANCE being over, there followed the business. James of Auchterhouse, paying in kind for his recent amusement, shared a flask with his good-humoured visitor and emerged from the encounter much sobered, his eyes dwelling in thought on the timid person of the Countess his niece.

The talk at table with Betha and Phemie proved to be as instructive as it was entertaining, dealing in a forthright Sinclair way with the question of the little Queen's dowry. Which, if it included the island of Orkney, was about to affect the Earl and all the Sinclairs his kinsmen. M. de Fleury knew the family Zeno whose forebear Antonio had sailed to a land west of Greenland with *their* forebear, Earl Henry of Orkney. Eighty years ago, they might have found Cathay. It was agreed that if they had only managed to set up a trading-post, it would have brought the price of silk down a treat.

The topic was raised of Sir Anselm Adorne and his daughter in England. The Countess talked about her legendary royal aunt in the Tyrol, friend and half-sister of Auchterhouse, and aunt to the King. The subject of families reminded the Countess of the happy news she had already received. She returned to it.

'A fine boy, you say. And Gelis is well, but not yet in public for – for the reason you tell me.'

'The bridal oil too close to the birth-tray. I beg your grace's forgiveness for mentioning it. I have already had a severe reprimand from our priest.'

The little Countess was not displeased. She said, her skin enlivened with interest, 'And the name? We hoped you would call the boy James. Or Thomas, perhaps. It is a saintly name, Thomas.'

'Or Nicholas?' said Katelijne. 'It is a saintly name, Nicholas.' She had been piqued, Gregorio knew, because this was one question Nicholas always avoided.

He couldn't evade answering now. He didn't try, but sat at table with his ringed hands before him and his dimples marshalled below the black velours cap now fitted over the hair his bodyservant was trained to cut flat. The unicorn horn had been worth three thousand florins. The diamond in his cap was worth two.

He said, 'Naming the boy was a difficult task, with duty and inclination leaning sometimes towards James, and sometimes towards Florence or Franck, to honour the house of van Borselen. In the end, we allowed Duke Charles to decide. He sent water from Jordan, and we baptised the child with it and after it. The boy's name is Jordan de Fleury.'

The gaze of the girl Katelijne would have made paper curl. She didn't say anything. It was the Princess who spoke with surprise. 'The name is unusual. Yet we know of the vicomte de Ribérac, who must have been baptised thus for the same reason. We shall set aside a gift for the boy and his mother. Tell his mother we wish to hear from her. Tell her that our own lord is already preparing to cross the sea to our side, and we hope she will share in our happiness.'

'I shall tell her, your grace,' said Nicholas gratefully.

Presently, while the others played cards, Gregorio sat by the fire and chatted with Mistress Phemie Dunbar about small, pleasant matters to do with letters and music, and the friends they had in common elsewhere. Only at the end did she say, 'One seldom meets a man as versatile as your M. de Fleury. You are close friends?'

It was not a question he was ready to answer. He spoke, a little ashamed of his reticence. 'He follows his bent. So far, I follow it too. How far, depends on Nicholas.'

The undistinguished features looked thoughtful. 'He does not welcome help or advice?'

Gregorio paused. He said, 'The answer, I'm afraid, is that he doesn't. He has reached where he is with nothing behind him: no great institution, no tradition, no kinsmen. Such an achievement brings self-sufficiency.'

'It brings isolation,' said Mistress Phemie. 'You know there is a convent of the Cistercian Order at Emmanuel?'

They had passed it, on their way to Berecrofts. Mystified, Gregorio nodded.

'There is a child there,' Mistress Phemie said. 'A love child, of Joneta Hamilton's. Have you heard of Joneta Hamilton?'

He had, from Julius. He had been able to guess, when his head cleared, exactly how Nicholas had been employed, that first night in Stirling. Gregorio said slowly, 'Yes. But not of the child. Is it his?'

To his surprise, pain crossed her face. 'No!' she said. She touched his hand. 'No, of course not. It is far too old, and black-haired and of quite a different mould. No. But if he does not know of it, some troublemaker may take pleasure one day in telling him, should he continue to seek the girl's company. No doubt you know men who would like to provoke him.'

'You are asking me to break the news first?' Gregorio said.

Through his alarm, he realised she was smiling. She said, 'I shouldn't presume. I have told you only so that you can protect him a little, at need. I do not want to know what is wrong. But if you do, it may guide you.'

He wondered how, hardly acquainted with Nicholas, she knew that something was wrong. He thought of the Nicholas of nearly a decade ago: the incorrigible apprentice; the young married man evincing the first gleams of brilliance; and, pervading it all, the aura of boundless goodwill. Then had come the double blow of the death of Umar and the betrayal of Gelis, after which self-sufficiency had changed – she was right – into ruthless detachment. Thinking of his long vigil that night of his wedding in Bruges, Gregorio was swept once again by the overwhelming pity he had felt for the man, emerging from his wife's room to stand motionless at the window while the first light of dawn changed into brutal, dazzling day. '*It's Simon's child, Nicholas!*' she had called. When he had told Margot of it, she had wept.

Gregorio wondered how Margot did tonight, nursing another woman's unwanted child; and whether her task was worse than his. But she had been right to go, as he had been right to come here, despite his increasing apprehension. He should have come the first time. Or perhaps he was wrong, and the uncomplicated, self-centred character of Julius had been what Nicholas had wanted and perhaps needed then. Julius would have heard, delighted, this tale of the Hamilton girl, and – carrying it crowing to Nicholas – would have enabled him to respond carelessly – genuinely perhaps – in the same vein. Whereas Gregorio could not imagine himself being able to mention it at all.

The company retired. Gregorio, procrastinating, climbed the stairs some time after his bedfellow, and entered the room they were to share with reluctance. '*¡Buenos días, caballero!*' remarked a sly voice at his shoulder. He whirled.

The parrot. He had forgotten. He had forgotten the scene with the hat. He had forgotten Nicholas de Fleury, the comedian.

He was there too, sitting crosslegged on a stool, wearing his ruined hat and a length of pink bed-curtain. He was nibbling a fig, and there were others in the palm of his hand. He and the parrot were staring at one another. The parrot, Gregorio was thankful to see, was in its cage.

'Well hurry up, I need you,' said Nicholas, still gazing at the cage.

'I'll get the ladder,' said Gregorio with a surge of relief.

'Don't think you're being funny: it may come to that. No. You've got a mirror. Hold it up to the cage and let it see itself.'

'What with? It bites!' Gregorio said. He pulled out the mirror and stood. 'Where are my gloves?'

'Never mind your execrable gloves,' the other man said, his eyes fixed on the parrot. 'You heard it. You understood what it was saying. It was talking Spanish. It was meant for me. It was talking in a style we both know, and using phrases we both remember. Go on. Whose?'

Gregorio sat down, holding the mirror. 'Ochoa de Marchena,' he said faintly.

'Ochoa de Marchena, Spanish shipmaster of the *Ghost*, which disappeared off the African coast with a cabin full of African parrots and hats, and a cargo containing three mule-loads of African gold belonging to us. Yes.'

'His parrot?' said Gregorio.

'His voice,' said Nicholas de Fleury. 'So let us re-create the cabin. So let us hear what he has been sent to say.'

The answer was nothing. The night wore on, the figs were shared, the parrot fell in love with its reflection and continued to utter endearments to its new friend but said nothing else except once, when it repeated *Holy Virgin!* in the voice of Nicholas, several minutes after mistaking his thumb for a fig.

Gregorio said, 'We were wrong.'

The parrot's friend took off toga and hat and removed an ostrich feather from behind his ear. He said, 'It's Ochoa's vocabulary. It's Valencian dialect.'

'African parrots are grey,' Gregorio said. 'Grey and red.'

There was an unexpected silence. The other man said, 'So they are.'

Gregorio looked at him. He said, 'I was wrong, wasn't I? I thought you had some deep plans for Scotland. But you do really fancy laying hands on the gold. And that business about the Tyrol, and their power-hold on the highways to Italy, and their nuisance value to Burgundy and to the Germanies and to France . . . You are going back. You're not staying in Scotland after all, are you?'

'And that's what they call logic in Padua?' The padrone's voice was different from the comedian's. The padrone said, 'I'm interested in the Bank, but I employ other people to polish its door-knob. If the situation in the Tyrol looks promising, if the Vatachino become a little too vivacious in Rome or the Levant, if the parrot comes up with a name and address – I have you, don't I, to go back and deal with it?'

Gregorio felt himself flush. He said, 'What were you doing with the King's uncle?'

'I wish I could shock you. But we were discussing the Boyds.'

Gregorio picked up the bed-hanging and threw it over the cage. The parrot swore. 'How much did you tell him?' he said. 'Hearty James doesn't care for the family, but his niece and Tom Boyd are married. He'll warn her.'

'He has,' the other man said. He settled back into bed, clasping the feather. 'She came to me later on for advice. If – for some undisclosed reason – she found herself having to pay a short trip to the Continent, would the van Borselen be prepared to receive her?'

'And you said?' Gregorio asked.

'That Henry van Borselen was old; and Wolfaert's new wife was a Bourbon; and my own wife was in delicate health. But . . .'

The feather twirled.

'But?' said Gregorio.

'But that I was sure that Anselm Adorne would be happy to have her. So what about Beltrees tomorrow? I have to leave early: I want to call at Lucia's old house, and then Semple's. You could come, or you could meet me at Beltrees. Bring the parrot, why not.'

Lucia's old house was called the Little Hall of Kilmirren. Lucia's property had once been part of Kilmirren, until Diniz had sold it to Nicholas de Fleury. The paperwork for that was complete, but the company lawyer should know, surely, what the place looked like. Also, according to Semple, someone he was rather fond of was there now. Gregorio said, 'I don't know. I ought to come with you.'

'Then come with me,' said de Fleury, and threw the feather away.

Riding north through the long, sunlit morning, Gregorio wondered what other visits his partner might have paid, secretively or otherwise, to this countryside, and what he made of it. Marsh and peat moss, lakes and patches of timber, small turf and wattle settlements with their churches and keeps, makeshift fords, dirt roads deep in mud – none of it, surely, could appeal to a man brought up in towns, used to the rich buildings, the comforts of Bruges, of Venice, of Florence.

The wild mountains of Trebizond had been set about with precious churches and monasteries, and the marble halls of the lords of Byzantium. Nicholas de Fleury, with Loppe at his side, had fought and worked in the sugarfields under the hot sun of Cyprus, but had lived in a sumptuous home, in a land still touched by Gods, where pillars, arcades, amphitheatres dazzled the eye, and painted treasures breathed in the shadows. In Africa, destitute of all but the means to survive, there was still Timbuktu.

Kilmirren lay in this green, empty land with its small towns and its rolling land contoured with cloud-shadows. The Bretons, Normans and Flemings who came here in centuries past found a country not unlike the one they had left and, settling, married into the families that they found here. So the St Pols must have come. But now, such settlers must be aware of two worlds. A man of land and power in France, Jordan de Ribérac seldom came to Kilmirren, and the lure of high living and chivalry called Simon, too, from the land and the mundane duties that went with it. Yet he would want it, for Henry. A man without land was at best a tradesman, a mountebank.

Which brought one to Nicholas de Fleury. But for Simon's denial, Nicholas, son of Sophie de Fleury his first wife, could have hoped to claim all this land in due course. He had dropped the claim. But since then, he had been given reason, if any man had, to return the injury Simon had done him.

From what Julius said, he had already inflicted on Simon – and received – as much punishment as the quarrel warranted. Lucia's death surely had not been intended, but Katelijne, who had been there, had little to say about it and Julius, who had a great deal, had not been a full witness. Nevertheless, but for the quarrel, Lucia would not have died, or the child Henry been drawn into trouble. Before others were hurt, de Fleury should bring the feud to an end. Instead, he bought land.

He could have no feeling for Kilmirren, or Scotland. At best, you could say that its language was one of his tongues; that he had merchant acquaintances; that he could make himself acceptable now and then in court circles. Set against all the rest the world offered, it was nothing.

But he also had a wife and, now, a family. Owning Kilmirren – all of it – he could do what Jordan de Ribérac had done: instal an agent, and take his comfort abroad, as a landed man with possessions and title.

Jordan would never sell. Even threats against Henry would not make him. So Nicholas de Fleury would have to acquire Kilmirren in some other way. As the son of Simon – but how could he prove it? Or as the survivor, of course, as, one by one, his family continued to die.

Gregorio caught his first sight of the castle at noon: a keep with rambling accretions, set in a large, irregular yard with high walls. Naturally it was empty: the vicomte away; Simon and his son safely dispatched overseas until Henry's misdemeanour was forgotten. The personal staff had gone with them. Gregorio wondered which lordly household had the training of Henry at such times. Anyone, probably, would be better than Simon. He reined in, finding he had come upon clusters of low, turf-roofed houses too scattered to be called a village. Twenty people and as many children had come to watch them pass, and dogs began to run at their heels. Chickens squawked and a pig stood in his way.

The de Fleury men were well trained, and rode carefully. The glance of their padrone was equable, but he did not stop. It was known they were coming: the Kilmirren steward had even offered the hospitality of the castle, in the vicomte's absence. An acceptance, however, would have alarmed him. All those who served Kilmirren would know who this man was, and what their lords thought of him. A mile away, Gregorio could still feel their gaze on the back of his neck.

Then they came to a fence and a hedge, and a kitchen garden well hoed, beyond which was the Little Hall, the two-storeyed building which had been the home of Lucia de St Pol y Vasquez.

Nicholas de Fleury dismounted. A burly man strode from the doorway – Oliver Semple, second cousin to Sir William. Gregorio had met him in Edinburgh. Semple said, 'I brought two grooms. The stables are still in good order. And good day to ye both. Ye do well?'

'Well enough,' his new employer said. 'Master Gregorio has found the ride rather long. Perhaps you and I should talk first, and he could wait for us in the parlour. Is there someone there?'

The factor said, 'How did ye guess? Ah, Sir William. Aye, Mistress Bel, her of Cuthilgurdy, rode round. If it pleases ye, there's enough in my hampers to serve the lady as well.'

'How extremely provident,' said Nicholas de Fleury. 'We shall see you later then, Goro. Tell the lady we shall not be too long.'

Bel was alone. She looked exactly the same: round as a melon in a thick gown for riding, with her pepper-grey hair bound into a stoutly ironed selection of napkins. Her skin was like unbaked dough. It had never taken the sun, even in Portugal, when he had first met her as companion to Lucia. Even when, sick and gaunt, she had arrived back with Diniz from Africa. Her face stayed the same, and her spirit, and her gravel voice saying, 'Well, Goro!'

His eyes were wet, hugging her. It had been a long time since she left Bruges for Scotland, and the news he had had of her from Julius was odd: once closer than most, she had seen almost nothing of Nicholas. And the occasions on which she had seen him were disastrous – the first, the stabbing by Henry, and the second, the drowning of Lucia. She had seemed, Julius said, to hold Nicholas responsible for everything, including the weather. Julius did not take old ladies seriously.

Now Gregorio set her down and sat down himself. There was a brazier, lit presumably by Semple's orders. Nicholas felt the cold. Bel said, as if he had spoken, 'Let Nicholas be. I ken why he sent you. I want to hear your news. Where is Margot?'

'With the child,' he said. 'You know of the child?'

He was speaking quickly. At the same time, he remembered something that ought to come first. He said, 'At least – you know the bad news, as well?'

She looked down. She said, 'No.' It was all she said.

He looked at her anxiously. 'Mistress Bel? I'm so sorry. About Tilde.'

Her chin lifted. 'Ah, Goro, I'm a stupid auld callant. Yes, I kent. Aye, I'm famished with sorrow. They're young, they'll have bairns in plenty. But the lassie would grieve.'

'We all did. It needn't have happened. It needn't have happened but for that vicious old –' He couldn't speak Jordan's name.

She said, 'I can guess. Lucia might hae given him the benefit o' the doubt, and so will I. But the good news is that Gelis is delivered?'

'Of a son she has called Jordan de Fleury.'

She was silent. Then she said, 'So tell me, and fast.'

'Nicholas hasn't seen him,' Gregorio said. 'You understand, the child came early. The news was delayed. There was a birth-feast for him later, of course, and Gelis should be back in Bruges now. Bel, speak to him. No one can.'

'About what?' she said. And as he didn't reply, 'No. All right. She is withholding the bairn. All is not well with the marriage. He is here, instead of in Bruges. Is that why he is here?'

Gregorio said, 'I don't know. No, it has something to do also with Simon. It must. But Simon isn't here; Nicholas surely can let his schemes go. He has to stop the vendetta with Simon and go back. He has to go back for his own sake. And hers.'

'And the bairn's, wouldn't ye say? She's named him Jordan de Fleury. Why?' Her eyes were directly on his.

'To cause the deepest hurt,' Gregorio said.

'The which that would do. Aye. And if ye all ken so much, Master Gregorio, whyfor are his friends not urging the man to go back themselves? What can I do, unless I hear the hale story?'

'He won't listen to me. No one else knows what has happened but Margot. And I've given my word not to tell.'

'Then Nicholas is a lucky man,' she said. 'And she's a lucky woman, your Margot, whatever you may think o' it all. The differ being that Margot deserves it.'

He looked up. She had never removed her eyes from his face. He said, '*Umar* is luckier than he is.' Then he heard footsteps on the stairs, and she dragged her eyes away as Nicholas de Fleury and Semple came in.

The factor went to pour wine. Nicholas put down the papers he was carrying and stood still, like a crossbowman judging his target. Bel of Cuthilgurdy said, 'You'll have come for your rent?'

The factor wheeled, flask in hand. Nicholas said, 'I didn't know, when I bought Lucia's land, that you had a house on it. I understood you stayed with her here.'

'Times I did. Times she wanted company. She had a furnished bedchamber, too, at the castle. You'll find a good mattress there, and some taffety skirts and a mutch cap and some preens and an Inglis brown gown in a kist, if you think that they'll suit you.'

'Diniz sold me the land,' Nicholas said.

'And his Madeira land too?' Bel said. 'With his one babe cut off, he'd be easy persuaded. He didna come with you, I see, to visit the grave of his mother and, of course, collect a few rents in the bygoing. It must have been a real trial to you both, rearranging her money.'

The factor stood, a cup in each hand. He said, 'You'll excuse me,' and laid one at her side. His employer took the other and held it out to Gregorio. He said, 'Thank you, Master Oliver. We'll join you below. Mistress Bel is upset.'

The door shut on the factor. Nicholas sat down between Bel and Gregorio. He looked at Bel. 'Whatever the complot, you could have spared Semple,' he said. 'He knows well enough where you stand. As a matter of interest, Diniz wouldn't bring Tilde to live here. And he still owns the *quinta*.'

'Whatever the complot?' Bel repeated.

'There isn't one? Then what have you and Gregorio been wasting time talking about?'

'How to send you back home,' Gregorio said.

'For Simon's sake?' He rose, smiling, and filled a cup for himself. Gregorio saw it was water, again.

Gregorio said, 'For everyone's sake. This is not how you and Bel should be talking.'

'And how are you going to send me back home?' the other man said. He was watching Bel.

'What do you see when you look at me?' she said. 'Apart from dule, dule and sorrow? Where is your babe? Where is your courage, that you turn your back and run from a failure? And what is your excuse for being here, if not the death of Simon and Jordan?'

'Why do you defend Simon and Jordan?' Nicholas said.

She looked at him. 'I have defended you in your time. Did you deserve it?'

'Most certainly not. Well, what would reassure you?' said Nicholas de Fleury. 'Gregorio, tell her. I am here in Scotland for profit. To develop some land. To set up some trade. To allow, yes, some marriage difficulties to settle themselves. But I shall be returning to Gelis. I don't mean to stay here for ever. And whatever ensues, you are secure in your house. After all, I killed Lucia to get it.'

Gregorio rammed down his cup. Bel said, 'I don't want the house.'

Gregorio said, 'Bel, the house is yours without rent for as long as you wish. Do you think he'd put you out, or exploit you?'

'She has a house at Cuthilgurdy,' Nicholas said. He cleared his throat. 'Her son stays there. If I'm right?'

Cuthilgurdy was not far from Stirling. Her livelihood, they all knew, came from there. She had once been married, they knew, but had never mentioned a family. They had never asked.

Bel said, 'You've been busy.'

'Given our last conversation,' he said, 'it seemed advisable. I have no plans for your house. If you want to leave it, that is your affair. Make your arrangements with Master Oliver.'

Her lips parted. Then she said, 'Aye. I'll do that. And now I think I will go.'

Gregorio looked from one to the other. He said, 'Nicholas?'

'No,' said Nicholas.

She left. On the threshold she glanced back at Nicholas de Fleury and Gregorio glimpsed, for a second, the look that they exchanged. His breath caught in his throat, for he recognised that he had seen it before: this silent collision of pity and pain. The woman again had been Bel. The youth – the child – had been Simon's son, Henry.

For all the rest of that journey which was to take them, in the end, to Beltrees, Gregorio was thankful for the presence of Oliver Semple, broad and weathered and slow and emphatic of speech, who rode beside his new foreign employer, and to whom Nicholas de Fleury spoke all the way, evenly, of practical things.

Until they left behind the Little Hall and Kilmirren, Gregorio did not realise how much he had been counting on Bel to reach Nicholas: to stem and dissolve the coating with which, film upon film, he was separating himself from them all. Now he saw that it had already been too late last winter. If Bel had not then shaken his purpose, she was not likely to soften him now.

Deep in thought, Gregorio rode. There was one formal call still to make: passing through Semple land, they must pay their respects to the owners. Arrived at the thick-walled fortalice of Elliotstoun, Gregorio roused and saw for the first time the long valley flashing with water and the wooded slopes beyond which they were bound. About him, the scented air sparkled with birdsong. It came to him that he was looking at beauty.

Since duty required it, he passed indoors with the rest. The goodwill of the Semples was essential but, as the afternoon waned, he saw that Nicholas was concealing impatience. They were close to Beltrees and the tower he was building. In the nature of things, he must be anxious to see it, for it was plain that his stay in Scotland was not going to be brief. He had said he was returning to Bruges. He had not said which month, or which year. Eventually he stood and made his excuses, and finally they all resumed their horses outside, and the last part of their journey began.

It was short. They rode along the south shore of the loch, the sinking sun flashing gold in the reeds and on the moorhen spinning furrows among them. Far away, fish were rising. Elliotstoun was a mile and more behind them when Oliver Semple turned his back on the water and put his horse to a flowery lane that meandered uphill between alder and thorn, winged with leaflets.

It was very quiet. Twice they smelled wood smoke and heard distant barking, and once a woman milking a cow turned her head slowly to watch them. Her face lay like a coin on sheared velvet. No one spoke. Above their heads a blackbird decided to make a declaration of joy and did so like one of Will Roger's mellower clarions. The crowded houses of Bruges seemed by comparison a

russet Necropolis. Poring over papers, exercising the legal, the
actuarial skills, Gregorio had failed to allow for enchantment.

'Wait,' said Nicholas. He spoke as if he knew what Gregorio was
thinking. He did not look round.

Wait.

The lane, ascending its last, indolent curve, began to bring them
to the crown of the long, flanking ridge they had been climbing.
For a moment, looking back in the leonine light, Gregorio saw loch
and valley changed, as the woman had been, into something of
Byzantine richness; water transmuted to satin; grass to fur, set with
escarpments of topaz and onyx, studded with beads and blisters of
gold. His heart filled, so that when his horse stumbled, he all but
left the saddle. Oliver Semple lifted his voice. 'And here we are.
But you need to go canny, my masters. These God-damned carts
fairly gut the fairway from under you.'

The lane had gone. Instead, in a welter of churned stones and
mud, a wide black highway had taken its place, driving along the
spine of the ridge from the west, torn-up bush and shorn stubs at
its edges. Tracks from it ploughed down the slope at their feet,
descending into a distant depression. And in the depression, hell
had been re-created.

Sprawled before him, raw in the sun, Gregorio saw a seething
carcass set on a smoke-blackened eminence. Vibrations of sound
shook the air. The air itself had turned rotten; the stench made
him cough. The shock made him dry-mouthed with nausea.

'I knew you would like it,' said Nicholas de Fleury.

The illusion, of course, lasted only a moment. Later, he was to
wonder at his own strange reaction, and at the conviction he had
that Nicholas had somehow brought it about. What he had seen
was only a massive building in embryo. The ribs were scaffolding;
the skeletal frieze printing the sky was formed of wheels and
pulleys, cranes and windlasses; the maggots, in cap, hose and tunic,
were workers.

The haze that wreathed it came from lime-dust and cook-fires
and furnaces, and the smell from the turf huts, the shelters, the
horse-lines and the stables that clustered below. The buzz was
human conversation, rising above the squeak of windlass, the
blows of hammer and chisel, the clack of tumbling stone. It
included laughter and the voices of women. He could see two of
them scaling the rise, a basket of washing between them, their
skirts kirtled up to the thigh. He could see a third at the door of
her hut, speaking round her raised, dimpled elbows as she knotted

the band round her hair. When she heard the horses and turned, the sun moulded itself on her body. Presently she lowered her arms and began to draw up and fasten her bodice.

The factor said, 'You can't keep them away, and it saves the chiels from stravaiging into the townships. They're nice enough lassies, although there are others just as handy and cleaner. Tam Cochrane will tell you. He's there now.'

'And we can sleep there?' said Nicholas.

'Ye'd wonder, I agree, but you can. And there's room for your men. You won't know it when there's a proper road made, and the grass grows, and we get some trees planted. Here you are.'

Gregorio didn't speak. He could already see, approaching closer, that this was not the massive stronghold of his earliest fears, from which the men-at-arms of de Fleury would descend to spoil and harry Kilmirren. For one thing, the Semples of Elliotstoun were far too shrewd to allow him to build one.

But it was not, either, the mystical palace he had begun to dread, riding up through the sunshine: the *très riche* home, born of five cultures, into which a nameless rich man might pour all his longings.

Before him, half reshaped and still building, was the residence, without walls, of a powerful man with powerful connections. The comely range of living quarters now forming round the embryo square was of a style to lodge lords and their retinues rather than a troop of light horse. The hall and chapel which adjoined it were new and far from complete, but Gregorio saw the promise of tall windows surrounded with vine-scrolls, and colonettes and capitals that reminded him of France, rather than Flanders. Next to the hall was the tower, once the only occupant of the rise and now half restored, its windows enlarged and the space between them newly banded with ornament.

Three floors of that were secure, they were told, and would lodge them that night. The master mason already had his room there, and the vaulted cellars served as tool-store and tracing-house, and supplemented the long thatched lodge in the yard, thick with powder, where the masons patiently sat, carving stone.

Cochrane, when he emerged, was also coated with powder and still, absently, held a saw in one hand. Oliver Semple, as from long practice, ducked to one side when he started to speak. They were by now dismounted, and standing scattered among the giant rouleaux of timber, the new-cut stacks of stone, the piles of lime and the mountains of sand, the baskets and barrows, the canopied workspaces where men mixed mortar or sharpened blades at a forge.

Everyone worked, and everyone looked at M. de Fleury while
working, so that the great hoist turned slower and slower and the
withy ladders became congested with climbers, and the bucket
banged on the side of the well. The faces under the caps were
friendly – dirty but friendly. Most were labourers, but one or two
were craftsmen whom Gregorio recognised. A carver, a tiler, a
cutting-mason already employed in the Casa di Niccolò in the
Canongate.

Members of a new army indebted to Nicholas.

Master Oliver, raising his voice, introduced M. de Fleury and
Master Gregorio his lawyer, and announced that it was proposed
to drink to the patron's good health at sunset. There was a satisfied
cheer, and M. de Fleury briefly addressed them. The master
mason, still gesticulating with his saw, then placed himself before
the arrivals and proceeded to lead them to the four quarters of the
yard in order to explain, with some passion, the curiosities of his
handiwork. The light faded. Gregorio followed.

None of this had anything to do with the Bank of Niccolò, or
with Venice or Bruges, or with John sweetening the Mamelukes in
Alexandria, or Astorre in Burgundy, or the trade links Nicholas
was forging with Scotland. Gregorio could not guess its significance
and, now, was reluctant to try.

He felt, in the midst of despair, a distinct cordiality towards
Thomas Cochrane, master mason. He had felt the same for Will
Roger. He then wondered if Nicholas had selected them, or the
other way round. He knew, with absolute certainty, that he would
never feel free of responsibility until he saw Nicholas drunk.
Draining his cup, he could not think, all through supper, how to
explain that to Godscalc.

The only conversations Gregorio ever succeeded in having with
Nicholas were in their sleeping-chamber at night, when the other
man was effortlessly caustic and he was exhausted. That night,
although starved for sleep, Gregorio was driven to accost him
again. 'What the hell was all that about winter herding, and stable
dung for the barley, and compulsory fencing, and pastures for ewes
with their followers? You know less than I do about farming.'

'I got it from Katelijne,' said Nicholas de Fleury. 'Who got it, in
turn, from the factor at Dean. She thinks a landowner should know
about land. I've told Oliver to keep the Semple boundaries healthy,
and leave the rough land between me and Kilmirren to look after
itself. What he does in between is his business. What do you think
of our champion Oliver? Better than Roland?'

'Jannekin?' Gregorio said. Young Bonkle knew trade inside out, but perhaps he had too many kinsmen. On the other hand, this man was a Semple.

Gregorio said, 'They both have connections. Semple has the experience, I agree. But if you're expecting to farm, why have we been making all these digressions? Perhaps the land can produce coal, or lead, or silver, or gold, to hear some; but none of it is on the ground that you've bought.'

'That's why Katelijne thought I should concentrate upon farming,' the other man said. 'And of course I shall, after the wedding. Six shillings and eightpence a sheep – isn't that staggering? And pease at thirteen shillings and fourpence a boll, and peat available for nothing at all. Don't you think I should settle down here, if I survive the duel with Sersanders?'

'Sersanders?' Gregorio said.

'You'd forgotten. The joust. Part of the wedding festivities. I've offered Paisley Abbey a window to intercede for me.'

Gregorio had actually seen the cartoon-scroll below, with a figure on it not unlike Bishop Graham. Gregorio said, 'If you stay, you will have the most beautiful small palace in Christendom. Those are tiles from the Maghgreb, commissioned surely to fit in that corner.'

'My dear,' Nicholas said. When feeding the parrot, he always seemed to drop into Spanish. 'Like God, right angles transcend creed and frontier. Tiles fit anywhere.'

'So the drums still beat,' Gregorio said. 'We had no ship there this year. But perhaps Tommaso had. Where does the news come from, with the tiles? The ibn Said? Benedetto Dei? Nicholas, tell me.'

'You ask the wrong questions,' the other man said. 'Not where does it come from, but what does it say?' The parrot poked through the bars, its eyes dilated, and tried to grip the piece of apple he was holding just out of its reach.

Gregorio watched. He had never known Nicholas to speak of this, not since those first moments in Bruges. Then he understood. Gregorio said, 'The report was true. Umar is dead.'

'So they say,' said Nicholas de Fleury. 'Even the child they thought had escaped. They will break the tiles out tomorrow. Native work has little value these days, and if Sersanders forgets his own strength, I should like to be remembered for good taste, at least.'

The parrot screamed. 'Don't torment it,' said Gregorio.

'It is only a parrot,' said Nicholas.

*

Semple's messenger reached the keep at first light, with the news just brought over from Edinburgh. The royal bride's fleet had been signalled, and M. de Fleury was required to return.

Separate word had been sent to Dean Castle. 'I hope they've mastered the laud,' said Gregorio. 'Not to mention the world's first polyphonic beer stains.'

He felt a conscience-stricken relief. Whatever awaited in Edinburgh, including Anselm Sersanders, it was in a context with which he was familiar, and involved business for which he was trained. Here, he felt like an amateur crossing a tightrope on the shoulders of an expert who wanted to fall.

Chapter 21

WITH KINGS REGULARLY dying so young, the arrangements for receiving royal brides from overseas were
generally in apple-pie order. Margaret of Denmark,
aged twelve, sailed into the harbour at Leith twenty
years to the sunny June day after Mary of Guelders, the present
King's mother, now dead. Wolfaert van Borselen and his royal
Scots wife had come in the fleet that brought Mary from Flanders.
The ships that fetched Margaret from Denmark brought with her
those triumphant Scots statesmen who, for ten weary months, had
stayed to wring her dowry out of her father. Among them was
Thomas Boyd, first Earl of Arran.

Nicholas de Fleury, a foreigner, was not among those appointed
to receive the future Queen on her landing and attend her to the
Abbey of Holyrood where, in a month, she would wed. He was not
at all interested, having long since transferred to different schemes.

His work on the wedding was done and indeed (unknown to
Gregorio) paid for. Closer than most to the superb wedding of
Duke Charles of Burgundy, and aware more than most of the
Continental connections, yearnings, expectations of the Crown of
Scotland, Nicholas had had all the time in the world to bring to
Scotland the craftsmen, the artists and the engineers who would
create for the kingdom a spectacle which would not be laughed at
in Bourges or Brussels or Florence.

His work was done; his investment was made. England had
brought down the Frescobaldi and the Riccardi by failing to honour
their loans. Scotland had paid its dues to the House of Niccolò in
another manner entirely. The wedding, in terms of cash profit, was
an event of minor importance to Nicholas. In ways not so obvious,
it fulfilled an essential part of the design.

Some of it, of course, had been executed before he left for

Beltrees: quiet meetings with the young Albany; with other officials at Court. Sometimes he took Wilhelm of Hall with him. The King had met Wilhelm, his new goldsmith.

He did not mention to Betha Sinclair how often he had been received by the Earl of Orkney her father, or how many manuscripts he had conveyed to his library. The Earl had coal and salt-pans in Dysart, and soon would have more. Soon, everyone would have more. Nicholas had introduced Hugo van der Goes to Jannekin's father, and spent time at Kinneil with Joneta's extremely shrewd parent, Lord Hamilton. He had courted, deeply and thoughtfully, all those he knew of both sexes dwelling within the rule of the Cistercian Order.

The journey to Beltrees followed these varied activities, and so did an aberration in the matter of sleep which threatened his pace for a while, until he conquered it. He knew Gregorio was alarmed, but paid no attention.

Then, after their recall to Edinburgh, three things occurred.

First, he was summoned by Sir William Knollys, Preceptor of the Knights of St John, to respond in form to the challenge by Anselm Sersanders, merchant burgher of Ghent, to a joust *à plaisance* in public, at a place and time to be mutually agreed.

He was interviewed, attended by Gregorio, in the Knights' house at Linlithgow. Sersanders was there, with the Preceptor and a priest. The priest was John of Kinloch, whom Nicholas vander Poele, now de Fleury, had once humiliated in Rhodes. Sersanders might not want to draw blood, but he had found other ways of avenging his uncle.

The proceedings were formal. It was agreed that the event would form part of the welcoming festivities for the Danes. There would be a series of tournaments. This would be included in one of them. John of Kinloch asked after M. de Fleury's injuries, so undeservedly incurred after the last entertainment. M. de Fleury reassured him. The priest then enquired after the lady van Borselen, dame de Fleury, and her husband responded as if neither of them had ever heard of a courtesan called Primaflora. Sir William finally sought to establish that he had suitable armour, and M. de Fleury replied that he had. This time, he had brought his own with him. It had seemed likely, after all, that something like this would be necessary.

It was all to be expected. All that had been unexpected was the readiness of Sersanders to be associated with the Knights of St John.

The explanation in due course emerged. Unrest in the north of

England promised to escalate into a far stronger movement against the King, Edward of York. If civil war broke out again, his Lancastrian rivals might be restored to power. And the Knights, having their headquarters in England, would have less to concern them than most, for they had always regarded Henry of Lancaster as their King.

From past experience, and from, you might add, intelligence gathered even from the sickbed just referred to, Nicholas de Fleury knew a fair amount about the Knights of St John, and those who adhered to them, and their property. So, of course, did Anselm Adorne. The very delicacy of the relationship between himself and the family Adorne gave M. de Fleury pleasure. But for the obvious disadvantages, he would have preferred it if Anselm Adorne had been here, not his nephew.

The interview with the Knights occurred five days before the State Arrival at Leith. Two days later, a hooded woman, alone, without escort, called at the Canongate residence of the seigneur de Fleury of the Banco di Niccolò.

The long, warm evenings were light; the lantern hung at the pend was hardly as bright, yet, as the last of the sunset over the castle. His porter, however, was discreet and so was Govaerts his steward, carrying the news to the padrone in his office. Govaerts said, 'I imagine this is the lady that you were expecting.'

Julius would have made a joke. Nicholas said, 'Where is Master Gregorio?'

'I believe, in the Burgh,' said Govaerts. 'The Prioress invited him, after the music. He has a lantern-boy with him.'

So, in other words, someone would know when he was coming. Nicholas said, 'Then she should come to my room. But no one else.'

Govaerts said, 'You are out, padrone? Or engaged?'

'Whatever you usually say,' Nicholas said. 'And in the manner in which you usually say it.'

After that, it would have been ironic if the lady had actually come to improve his wellbeing; but she had not. Indeed she flinched from his touch, even though the folds of her cloak must have been stifling; and he had to draw out a stool, speaking calmly, before she would sit, and then let the mantle fall back from her shoulders.

Her face was, as ever, irredeemably plain, and dogged, and youthful. She said, 'I require you to help me.'

'Whatever your grace wishes,' he said.

Later, alone in the office again, he heard Gregorio climbing the stairs. His step was a fraction uneven. Nicholas set aside his pen and sat back and deployed his dimples, all to himself, in self-parody. The truth was that if Gregorio didn't come in, he'd go and fetch him. Or something with which to replace him.

Gregorio opened the door. It had been a good evening, that was apparent. For once, he had left off the black robe of his profession, and wore a braided brown doublet with a wide-brimmed hat which was almost flamboyant. His nose, thin as a tail-fluke, was flushed. He said, 'I hear you've had company.'

'She's gone,' Nicholas said. He knew Goro's views on philandering. He added, 'So how was the music?'

Gregorio slumped in the chair with the back. 'It might just be ready in time. I don't know why you don't come. Will Roger says you're a mean bastard who won't do anything unless he gets paid for it. Listen, Dame Betha and Phemie were there. I've found out the exact terms of the Queen's dowry.'

'Tell me,' said Nicholas, with surprise.

'So you know,' Gregorio said. 'Am I as drunk as all that?'

'Mellow. No, I don't mind confirmation,' said Nicholas. 'The Queen gets Linlithgow Palace and Doune and a third of James's income. James receives in redeemable pawn the Norwegian Crown's land, rights and revenues in the islands of Orkney and Shetland, thus putting out the eye of William Sinclair, who gives up the earldom, but keeps whatever private lands his family have managed to lay hands on. And in addition, William is to receive Mary of Guelders' castle in Fife. The one beside Dysart.'

'While young Albany has to receive the Earl's daughter. That's about it,' said Gregorio. 'And have you heard about Boyd?'

'Boyd?' said Nicholas. His response this time was unfeigned.

'They've announced the first tournament. You're due to run three courses against Thomas Boyd – Arran – before the joust you asked for with Sersanders. I've protested.'

'Have you? Thank you. Why?' Nicholas said.

'Because Sersanders will be fresh and you won't. There ought to be parity. Not that there is. Boyd and Sersanders both grew up jousting, and you couldn't ride a horse until – well. That is, although you've done a lot since, it's not fair.'

'I see that,' Nicholas said. 'Well, you'd better organise a great big Dane as a first joust for Sersanders. Otherwise I'll sulk in my tent and leave the fight to my armour; I'm training six ferrets to activate it. What's it like to be drunk?'

Gregorio sat up slowly. He said, 'Was it that bad? Or that good? I have a flask . . .' He laid a fumbling hand on his pouch.

'That good,' said Nicholas. He let himself smile into Gregorio's face with its anxious, fixed stare and then, rising, crossed to the shelf where the cups were. One managed, most of the time. It was Gregorio, not Julius or Godscalc.

Gregorio said, 'I have to tell you. I was meant to tell you. She has a child, Nicholas. But it isn't yours.'

His fingers eased. The pewter slipped, but he saved it immediately. He said, 'Now there is an alarming statement, if ever I heard one.'

'Joneta Hamilton,' the other man said. 'I'm sorry.'

'That it isn't mine?' Nicholas said.

'You knew,' said Gregorio.

'Really,' said Nicholas. 'As the ultimate expert in marital and extra-marital intercourse, I can claim some proficiency. I can, even yet, identify a virgin when I am lucky enough to obtain one, and know the signs of incipient or successful motherhood as well as I know what to do about it. Or if I didn't, by God, Gelis has taught me.'

Gregorio had turned white. He said, 'I'm drunk. I'm sorry,' and uncorked and held out the wine-flask. Nicholas started to move. Before his palm struck the flask Gregorio threw it himself on to the floor where it lay, the wine spreading. Gregorio watched it and then, lifting himself, walked to the door. He turned and said, 'I didn't mean any harm. To save you from . . .'

'From this?' Nicholas said.

The door closed. He put down the cup but it fell, warped out of balance. It was as well Margot couldn't see it. On the other hand, Gregorio had come close to abusing a privilege. That wasn't why he was here.

The Canongate was draped with scarlet for the Entry of Margaret of Denmark, and the houses lining Leith Wynd hung arras and cloths from their sills. The procession, from Leith, was a long one.

Between the junction and Holyrood, the windows on both sides of the street were in demand and Berecrofts the Elder had packed his high, jutting frontages with friends and neighbours, and encouraged the wealthy foreigners on his land to do the same. Waiting, they shouted from window to window. The street was so narrow that from some upper storeys men and women could touch hands across it and the banners, when they came, would clap and slither into the windows.

In the Banco di Niccolò the upper loggia creaked with the number of neighbours and guests who packed into it, picking their

choice of meat or tartlets or dried fruit from the platters they
passed, and grasping their ale or their wine as they talked. They
wore holiday clothes, but even so they brought with them, released
by the heat, something of the odours of their calling: the smells of
hide and wood-flour and metal, of malt and pig-lard and incense.
The wives, in their tall folded headgear and necklaces, wore heavy
scent and peered round the heads of their children at the paintings,
the arras, the sconces, the chests, the tables, the enamels and the
lozenged windows now thrown wide to the street and surrounded
by flowers.

Nicholas de Fleury presided. He could have chosen to take his
merchant's seat in the swagged stands so painstakingly erected in
the yard of the Abbey. So could Berecrofts. But business came
first, and there were others who would be glad of the chance. And
it was not the King's procession today; just that of his bride and
her retinue, conducted by the Abbot of Holyrood and including
the eminent lords – Chancellor Avandale, the Bishops of Glasgow
and Orkney – who had passed the autumn, winter and spring
winkling the Northern Isles and a bride out of Denmark.

At the last moment, Gregorio left his task as joint host and
climbed the staircase to the small casement window which gave on
to Leith Wynd.

The first of the triumphal arches began at the bottom by Trinity
College, and the light southern wind smothered the sound of the
singing and trumpets, but it was clear enough from the noise that
the procession was now on its way, pausing now and then for the
enactment of some short pageant, or the recital of verse, or a song.
The main choir, including Katelijne Sersanders, had not been
wasted on the steep one-sided incline of Leith Wynd, but had been
saved for the Canongate proper, where pends and roof-tops were
crammed and a discerning audience awaited in the yard of the
Abbey. Gregorio smiled, thinking of Katelijne, and then sobered.
These young girls: what lay before them?

Katelijne, here to marry someone, no one knew who – but strong
enough, very likely, to make a success of it. Mary of Guelders,
come twenty years since from the wealthy Burgundian court to
marry James's father, but well equal to what she knew she would
find. And twenty-five years before that, the English Queen, grand-
daughter of John of Gaunt, had arrived already married to the first
King James of Scotland.

Her daughters had been less able. The best, Eleanor, had been
sent from Scotland as soon as her mother was buried and was now
Duchess of the Tyrol, and successful in all but procreation. Of the

others, Joanna, deaf and dumb, had been sent home from the French court unmarried, despite Scotland's disinclination to accept her. And aware of all of that was her niece Mary, the little Countess who had been vouchsafed a husband in Scotland and who, today, would be expected to play, for the first time perhaps, the part of a wife.

And Thomas Boyd was there. The horses came four abreast, fringed and tasselled and plumed, and between the paintpot chequer of banner and pennant and the bouncing of foxtail and feather you could see the cloth of gold of the heralds, the silver shoulders and helms of the men at arms, the host of the Danish household in its brilliant livery of gold and silver and azure with the Dannebrog Cross, and the hats tall and wide, flat and bulbous of the Scottish lords with their emblazoned cloaks, their gowns and doublets, jackets and coats in madder and russet, olive and rose.

For a long time, the Boyd banner was simply one among many, concealing the lords underneath. And then, as he passed, Gregorio saw the brown face and dark-brown hair curling thick round a stalwart neck under a hat made of beaver. A heavy chain, flashing with light, encircled a muscular chest and sturdy shoulders. The anxious precautions of Dean Castle were justified.

Then, thinking of Mary, Gregorio's gaze fell on the little girl, so much younger, who had come so far to be wed.

Margaret, Princess of Denmark, Norway, Vandalia, Holstein and all the rest, sat on a golden chair set on a litter, surrounded by the flowery gowns of her ladies. Below her tall headdress she was round-faced and small: a pansy caught among orchids. Her eyes and her smile were both fixed, and her clear tender skin was drained of colour.

Gregorio thought, Nicholas: I hope you are watching. Nicholas: I hope you are shamed into weighing your strength against what you see there, what you see in the little Countess, what you see – yes, what despite everything might lie behind what Gelis has done. And, Nicholas, what Margot has suffered because of it.

The procession passed; turned at the junction into the Canongate and, meeting the great roar of the citizens, proceeded downhill, past Nicholas de Fleury and his guests to the Abbey of Holyrood. As it passed, the boy Robin pushed through the parlour and, after much seeking, climbed to the little room where Gregorio was. He said, 'Master Goro? Are you tired?'

Gregorio turned and smiled, taking pleasure in the boy's fresh face and simplicity. Gregorio said, 'Of course not. I've got the best view in the Canongate. Come and see the end of the procession. Look: have you ever seen so many dwarves?'

'No. Come down,' said Robin. 'M. de Fleury misses you.'

He was only a child. But his gaze, clear and steady, was troubled.

Gregorio said, he didn't know why, 'I'm sorry. Yes. Of course, I will come.'

'And follow the procession. I'm going to. You should. Or you'll miss Katelijne's singing,' said Robin encouragingly.

Gregorio ruffled his hair and followed him out. Nicholas, so far as he could see, had not missed him. But the boy, you could see, thought he was God. And one could not always be sure.

Later, the Scottish envoys, having deposited their charges at the Abbey, rode uphill again and passed into Edinburgh, to report to the King at the Castle.

Later, a masque was peformed in front of the Abbey, watched by the Danish Princess from her window.

Later, in a long column of white satin, led by trumpeters and escorted by musicians, James, King of Scotland, rode downhill into the Canongate to attend a private banquet, and to be introduced to his bride. With him he brought his half-uncles, his brothers and Mary and Margaret, his sisters. Their veils blew, misting all the bold colours behind them, and a blizzard of gold from their harness passed over each house as they came. The lady Mary was white.

Later, although the food and wine had not faltered, the tribune, parlour and chambers of the Banco di Niccolò started to empty at last. By dusk, even their own clerks had gone, and Nicholas de Fleury and his lawyer were alone with Old Berecrofts and Archie, come to share a last pitcher of wine by the open windows with their drooping burden of garlands.

The Abbot's banquet was over. Returning, the lady Mary's cheeks had no longer been pale, nor her veiling so pristine and stiff. The King's ruddy face was preoccupied, and that of Albany wore a half-smile.

'Aye, aye,' said Berecrofts the elder now, from the window. 'I hear it passed off well enough. Naebody spewed, or mistook the fire for a drain, or clapped a wench to the hurt of her laces. But she's an awfu' young lass. And he isna going to wait like a monk, not with the itch he's got on him already. The Stewarts aye ripened in ae place afore they matured i' the tither. I'm told they had a table worth seeing, with Danish sea-kings in sugar afore every place. That woudna be you?'

'Well, I hope no one else is getting paid for it,' de Fleury said.

Berecrofts eyed him. 'And the wedding feast, when it comes? They had a boar's head stuffed with flax-tufts the last time. Then they set fire to the flax. Ye could hardly dae better nor that.'

'It must have been a great moment,' said de Fleury.

'Aye. But rumour says you've planned something a wee bittie different. And there's the white satin today. And the chains. I've seen gold that thickness before, but no' often. I hope you'll no' hold your breath till you're paid for it. Jamie's no' got sovereign authority yet. Ye might have to wait till the autumn.'

De Fleury drank. 'What makes you think I shall leave even then?' It was water, again. He added, 'There's enough trade for us all.'

'Aye,' said Berecrofts. 'So long as ye mind it.' He got up. 'Man, I'm auld. We'd best be off. What's this I hear about the tourney tomorrow?'

'A friendly challenge,' said Nicholas de Fleury. 'I'm well down the list. If I'm killed, Gregorio will stay on and send in the invoices. It'll be flaming boar's head for the wedding feast, though.'

Archie grinned. His father barked. They both crossed the yard and made for their house. Gregorio waited until Nicholas turned back indoors. Then he said, 'I should have realised where the shoulder-chains came from. I know they can pay for it, eventually, out of the dowry. But Nicholas, gold of that weight is going to set us seriously out of pocket in the meantime, on top of the horses, the clothes, the furnishings, the artisans and all the rest for the wedding. Aren't you getting the Bank in too deep? Even for you?'

'And their jewels. You've no idea what they've stockpiled in jewels. No. I don't think so. And the chains don't enter into it. The King didn't buy them from me. They're the price of what I've bought from him.'

'What?' said Gregorio.

'Personal entertainment,' Nicholas de Fleury said. 'Go to bed. Tomorrow night we get to share in the banquet. And before that, I have this appointment with Thomas Boyd and Sersanders. You really should have protested harder.'

'The trouble is, it's an honour,' said Gregorio. 'They decided they would propose you to do it, and I couldn't get you released. But Sersanders will have had another fight, too, by the time he meets you. And you *have* had some training. With Astorre. In Milan.'

'It was a long time ago,' said Nicholas mournfully.

*

'Of course I know. I suggested it,' said Katelijne Sersanders with what seemed to be inordinate relish. She was fifteen years of age, and could hardly know what she was talking about.

'Suggested your brother should encounter Nicholas de Fleury in the lists? I can see,' said Gregorio slowly, 'that it might appear quite exciting.' Now he came to look at her, she seemed to be smaller and thinner than ever, although elaborately turned out in a high-waisted gown with tight sleeves. Her hair fell in a long, curly tail from a caul too small for the rump of a horse.

The dress anticipated the evening: she was not summoned for duty till then, which was apparently why she was here, in the convent's town residence rented from Nicholas. Gregorio didn't mind, although he didn't mean to stay long. He added, 'I don't imagine for a moment they'll harm one another. The swords are blunt, anyway. You're going to lead your brother into the lists?'

'So I've been told. Why didn't M. de Fleury want to joust in December?' she asked. She had been stitching her embroidery and studying a piece of music at the same time: her bright squirrel-glance reached him across two sets of frames. It looked innocent.

Gregorio smiled. 'Merchants don't do very much fighting. And maybe he didn't want to face Simon de St Pol.'

'He did, later. Master Julius said he fought with Urbino's mercenaries and his own in the Abruzzi. He said you were all in the wars against the Turkish army at Trebizond. He says M. de Fleury fought in Cyprus for King Zacco and killed a Mameluke emir in single combat.'

'I wasn't there. I wasn't in Trebizond. He didn't kill him,' said Gregorio. He wished Julius had kept his mouth shut. He wondered how Julius always remembered these things, and he didn't.

The girl said, 'I know. He cut the Mameluke's hand off, and the King came up and finished him off. Then a Mameluke tried to assassinate M. de Fleury in Venice. Do you know the parrot speaks Greek?'

After all that, Gregorio nearly laughed. Then he met the cool, level stare and refrained. He said, 'How do you know?'

'I know the sound of it. When we visit you, M. de Fleury speaks to it in Spanish. Not when he thinks he is alone.'

'And it answers?' said Gregorio with false jocularity.

'It repeats what it has been taught,' said Katelijne. 'The same thing always, and a name. I heard it at Dean, and in the Canongate since. But I don't understand Greek.'

'The name is Greek?' said Gregorio.

'The name is Nikko,' said Katelijne.

*

As the tournament of December had been a rehearsal, so the first public celebration of the wedding festivities of James, King of Scotland, was a splendid precursor of the mimes, the plays and the music, the feasts and the dancing, the hunts and the shooting, and the increasingly elaborate tourneys planned for the élite of Scotland gathered for these weeks in Edinburgh, together with the foreign lords come for the wedding.

The critical foreign lords. Everyone knew that to arrange such a series of spectacles demanded wealth and experience. Not so long ago, when feats of arms dominated the event, the court armourer would not only come up with weapons and arms, but import everything else the Court needed, from golden harness to the fringe for the balconies.

Now people expected much more. Now the Italian republics and princes, damn them, imported artistic masters to devise the themes for their Weddings and Entries, and to choose and supervise the artists, the designers, the performers. When therefore lords from these lands were your guests, you must, whatever your resources, stage as brave a show as you could.

All through the autumn and winter, Nicholas de Fleury had taken on himself much of the role of master designer. Returning last month, he had reviewed what had been done, and set it on course for completion. Scattered between burgh and port, the workshops he had created were active; the spectacular machinery built; the flags, the devices, the effigies painted. The storerooms were already filled with the extra linen and silver, and the teams of tailors were cutting and sewing the last of the silk, the satin, the velvet garments into which, twice daily, the royal household would change, their clothes identical in colour and fabric.

All was in order and others were now in charge. For although the work had been his, he was a stranger-merchant and a competitor, and the men who had laboured with him were Scottish and well born and should not be offended. Added to which he had lost the taste for clambering about with a paintbrush in his hand. He had let Crackbene do some of that. In fact, some of the machines whose refurbishment Crackbene was supervising at this moment had come from the Duke of Burgundy's store, at a very sustainable price.

Nevertheless, today he had risen early and, taking a clerk, had walked uphill into the High Street, speaking to the workmen he knew, passing the time of day with the porters, stopping at a corner stage which, later, would support a doubtful fantasy to do with Scotland and Denmark. The highway was thronged with speeding servants, waterbearers, cooks. Already, before dawn, the household cows had been brought in from the Burgh Muir to be milked.

Now the rising sun shone red on shutters already open, or on windows of oiled linen and glass belonging to the homes of Thom Swift, and those of the other large merchant houses within which most of the Crown's bidden guests would be lodged. For, of course, there was little space at the Castle, where the King's rooms were already filled with his family; and the future Queen occupied the royal rooms at the Abbey.

All the lords were in town. The town houses of Fleming and Semple would be occupied, but not that of St Pol of Kilmirren, which was shuttered and closed. Nicholas glanced at it once, as he turned downhill towards the Horse Market and lists, joining with people he knew from the Castle. Simon, Henry, and Jordan were gone, and Bel had not ridden across to save anyone this time. This time, no one needed saving: far from it.

The freshness was turning to warmth. He stripped to white shirt and black pourpoint, his doublet slung on one shoulder, his cap in his hand. People called, crossing to join him. By the time he reached the massed flags of the lists he was part of a group. Entering the lists, the exchange of gossip gave place to technical problems and questions of protocol. He established discreetly that his own two courses, as he wanted, were separated: the tilting with Boyd near the start, and the sword-fight with Sersanders close to the end.

In between, Sersanders too was tilting, with a Danish nobleman. Nicholas wondered, outwardly grave, if Gregorio had contrived to match poor Anselm with a giant. He didn't think, for Katelijne's sake, that the ladies of Haddington would be helpful, even if bribed. He was reminded that Katelijne would be leading the horse of her brother, and that Betha Sinclair, when approached, had briskly offered him one of her daughters. 'For the one specific purpose,' she had added, 'of leading your horse, Master Nicol; and handing your prize, gin ye win one.'

The girls were all very young: he doubted if any could keep a large courser steady. Perhaps Dame Betha would help her.

Later, he returned to the Canongate. The day's events unrolled: no work was done, as clerks and servants rushed to the windows at every thunderous clatter of hooves. The Danish procession passed twice. At one point a cannon went off, and the sky was blackened with birds. The men he had sent to the Castle Rock came back and reported. Gregorio returned from some errand, and agreed reluctantly to share a working dinner with the padrone in the garden.

The flies kept getting into the wine but paid no attention to water. After a while, Nicholas said, 'Let me guess. Phemie doesn't like fighting?'

Gregorio lifted his gaze from his food. He said, 'Mistress Phemie Dunbar is in the Castle. I haven't seen her.'

'That's no answer. What's the trouble?' said Nicholas.

'I should say that to you,' Gregorio said.

'Why?'

Gregorio said, 'I don't know. I'm not afraid of the jousts. You won't be so stupid as to damage Sersanders or Boyd, and I don't think either would hurt you. I'd forgotten about Cyprus and – the rest of it.'

Very few people knew about Cyprus – and the rest of it. Julius. Julius and Katelijne. Nicholas said, 'So what else?'

Gregorio said, 'What about Ochoa de Marchena and the gold?'

'Explain,' said Nicholas. It used up time.

Gregorio said, 'You've bought land. You're building a castle. You talk of farming. You're in the middle of developing dozens of projects and have run up debts which may not be paid, as the projects will have to be nursed at least until the King attains his majority, if not later. You have announced, indeed, that you intend to stay some length of time, and when I objected, you said it wasn't your job to polish door-knobs. Neither it is. But you can't run a Venetian bank from a castle at Beltrees.'

He looked warm. It was a warm day. Nicholas said, 'I also said that if something needed attention, you could handle it. Are you asking me to send you home or not to send you home?'

'Neither,' said Gregorio, and then looked both angry and bothered. He said, 'I've run the Bank for you before. I can do it again. But I can't handle the gold. Maybe the whole thing is a hoax. Maybe we're imagining things. But if that was a message from Ochoa, it deserves some very fast action. And it was directed to you, not to me.'

'Why? You know Ochoa's voice,' Nicholas said. There was, as he expected, a silence. Who knew Greek? No, who would recognise the sound of Greek and be intrigued enough to listen? He went on easily, 'But in fact you are right. I did question Crackbene. The cage was consigned to me: it was on the lading-note but with no indication of the sender. He had it taken ashore when the *Ghost* was unloaded, but didn't bother to tell me when he realised he and I were both leaving. The Countess saw it, and got it.'

Gregorio said, 'You thought it was important enough to buy back.'

'I still do. But you've just described, haven't you, all the reasons why I can't do much about it?'

Gregorio looked at him. He said, 'You are saying that to withdraw now from Scotland would do more damage than the gold itself could repair, if we found it?'

Nicholas said, 'I'd put it the other way round. I really think it's worth losing the gold to stay on and develop all that I've started. If the gold exists. If the message is genuine. If the person who sent it isn't dead by now.'

'You offered Diniz half of it if he found it,' Gregorio said. He had a legal mind, had Gregorio.

Nicholas said, 'But as you said, the message was personal. Are we going to go on talking about this for ever? You don't give a damn for the gold. You are only, as always, trying to find ways to force me out of the country. I have said this already. If you want to go, go. I am not disturbing my plans in order to deliver you from temptation and your mistress from her self-imposed child-nursing. Solve that problem yourself.'

Gregorio got up and walked back to the house. Bravo, Gregorio. Bravo, Palamedes, who invented this manner of living. Nicholas got up, too, after a moment, and went off to reduce the work of three days to three hours. Or however long it was between then and his joust, his *jocundus adventus*.

Chapter 22

I
T BEGAN TWO hours before sunset, so that most of the courses were run before darkness fell, and there were only the single jousts left to take place. In case of wind, they had three hundred coloured lanterns, such as they had in Bruges and Venice in carnival-time. But, in fact, the warm, breathless weather persisted, and they were able to use the standing candelabra as well, mounted with candles so large that a single man could hardly carry a dozen.

The stands this time were two-tiered, built to face one another across the width of the lists, so that the royal party gazed at the Rock and its lesser guests sat with their backs to it. The royal pavilion was hung with cloth of gold and lined with velvet and tassels; and the knights' tents at one end were all stitched in silk with the banners crowded around them, catching the afterglow from the west. As the lamps were lit inside, you could see the shadows of combatants arming, with their pages and bodyservants about them.

The lamps had been lit first of all in the upper stand containing the musicians, where lutes and recorders and viols had been attempting to make themselves heard over the clatter, the pounding, the roars of the early encounters. The conductor was Will Roger, with the wild demeanour of a man who has embarked, at last, on a voyage which will probably kill him, superimposed on the vainglorious smirk of the same man who has managed to beg, borrow or bribe sixty trumpets and fit them out to a man in pink taffeta.

The faces of the children in the royal stand were eager and flushed: they enjoyed jousting. The children? Waiting his turn, Nicholas caught himself thinking like Adorne, like Gregorio, and was amused. James was seventeen, but a King. His bride was twelve, but would be his consort next month. Albany might be the

King's younger brother, but he had experience of the Burgundian court, the richest in Europe, and his brothers must envy him. Mar would be a force to be reckoned with, one day, and so would Bleezie Meg, today without her attendant Katelijne, who was here, of course, in her brother's pavilion.

In the gloom, he could not pick out the others, although he thought he saw Dr Andreas, and he did see the well-tailored dark robe of the Secretary. Archibald Whitelaw had studied law at Cologne. He had wondered if Gregorio knew that, but it seemed that he didn't.

It was nearly time for his first bout. To tilt against Thomas Boyd with a lance, he wore the armour he had brought with him, neither etched nor gilded but cut and jointed and pinned so that he could move almost as if he wore kidskin. Lined and polished, it clung like an animal's skin to its flesh. He had had it made not because he intended to take up a career in the lists but because there were things he wanted to do, and he preferred to survive to do them. It made it all the more ironic that he had nearly lost his life in the lists to the knife of a child, in December.

The child he had been given as his queen for the day was very young, but older than Henry. Blind with maternal solicitude, Betha had fitted her out with a cone hat with a veil, dangling oversleeves and a gown with a train. Grasping his horse-ribbon was going to be the least of it. He went to sit beside her on the bench and talked while they waited for his announcement. She had been amused by the fantastic helms in the procession – wolfheads and eagles, lyres and boars. He had told her of Marx Walther of Augsburg who wore three sausages on a spike.

His own banner, motto, badge were simple: it was not the place, although he wished it were, for something more witty. He did belong to an order of knighthood, a Cypriot one, and it was the Order of the Sword which was proclaimed, silver on blue, by the cross-hilted blade on his flag, and its motto which was inscribed on his surcoat, and round the blue and white plumes of his helm. *C'est pour loïauté maintenir*, it said. You couldn't really appreciate the joke, unless you knew both Zacco and his royal half-sister.

The fight before his began to run its three courses: Liddell against a short Dane. The Dane was skilled, but his horse was either unfamiliar or still unsteady from the voyage. And Liddell was uncommonly good: he held the lance, all twelve feet of it, as if it grew out of his wrist. They didn't even run the third course: Jamie struck the other each time full on the breastplate, and each time the lance splintered and flew.

It did no harm when it struck, with the coronel set in its tip. And these were poplar lances, made to break. You could hardly unseat a man with one of these, not unless he was an extremely bad rider, or you were especially lucky.

Cheers; applause; the Dane retiring glumly and Liddell riding forward to the stand to make his bow before the King. He was Albany's steward, and the face of Albany shone. The girl leading the horse was obviously used to it. A sister, perhaps. Nicholas turned and smiled at his little lady, and made a joke that he thought a Sinclair might understand. There was a pause.

His page had come, with his helmet and gloves. The lances stood, ready stacked, and his groom waited a little apart, holding one of his thoroughbreds. There was a spare horse, in case. He could afford it. He walked to the bay, which was fidgeting, and spoke to it.

A fanfare deadened his hearing, overwhelming all other sound. Despite its training the horse jerked its head, shivering. Then it calmed and he mounted, settling into the deep jousting-saddle. He had had it covered with blue velvet and studded with silver. One of the sets of reins also was silver-studded in a pattern of azure enamel, and his horse wore a gem on its browband. After the black of the past year, it felt like a costume of masquerade. He closed his visor. The girl looked up, her headgear stabbing his arm, her veil catching his spurs. Her lip was trembling. His page, who was prettier than she was, smiled at her too, and helped pick off the veil. It had torn a little. He touched his horse forward.

A man barred his way. In the distance, someone was speaking. The trumpets blared again, and the girl squeaked with fright: he held the horse firmly. The man in front of him said, 'Sir knight, your match has given way to another. Be so good as to wait.'

'Why?' said Nicholas. His horse, balked, tried to sidle and he held it hard. The man repeated, 'Later,' and walked away without answering. His groom came up and Nicholas dismounted with care, and allowed himself to be divested again of his gauntlets and helm. The girl gazed at him, her eyes large as eggs. He spoke to her, smiling. 'I don't know what it's all about. Perhaps Govaerts can find out.' Govaerts disappeared.

The next courses were run, and then the next, in which Anselm Sersanders took part. His little sister strode out beside him, pony-tail swinging. She had seized hold of both ribbon and reins, and when the horse attempted to shy appeared to shove it bodily forward. You could hear her talking testily and her brother responding, booming inside his helm. They presented themselves, and the lady Margaret threw down a flower, which Katelijne picked up and gave him. He had a fox's crest pinned with his sister's favour. The favour looked like, but could not be, a salt-cellar. Then she retired, and the tilting began.

The Dane he opposed was not a giant, but he was well trained and sturdy and bold. He flew from the far end as from a catapult, without diverting except to adjust his lance as he neared. They collided. He struck, and so did Sersanders. The Dane's lance splintered, but that of Sersanders, a shade less direct, skidded and glanced off the other man's armour and remained in his grasp, still unbroken. First mark to the Dane. They rode on and turned.

The Sinclair girl said, 'They're very poor-grown, the Sersanders family. If I were her, I'd wear pattens.'

'Or a tall hat,' said her knight. He glanced down at the eggs. They looked soulful. Govaerts came back, shaking his head, and resumed his place with the rest of his household. Gregorio had left the tent at the beginning. To take up his stance, Nicholas guessed, with the minstrels.

They had started the run. It was true, Sersanders was short. So was his sister. But he had the family temper, and seemed to have lost it. He swept up to the barrier this time in an explosion of rage, and the crash was such that the whole structure shuddered and the Dane rocked to one side. Then he recovered and they passed. This time Sersanders held the smashed lance, and the other had missed.

One each. With or without pattens, Katelijne Sersanders had both fists on the barrier and was jumping. The royal stands seethed. The public, massed in the dark, roared without cease. The Sinclair girl said, 'That's not a good fight. Ours will be better than that.'

'I'm glad you're feeling up to it,' Nicholas said. He didn't quite know what he was saying. It was dark. No one had come to tell him when to fight. Sersanders and the Dane had turned and were racing again.

This time the collision was so great that both stopped. Sersanders jerked backwards. The Dane, losing a stirrup, half fell and was saved by his saddle. In the fist of each was a lance broken in shards. Honours even. An extra course to decide.

'I can't look,' said the girl. Katelijne was hanging over the barrier, her long tight sleeves dangling like lobster claws.

'Excuse me,' said a man. The same man.

'Yes?' said Nicholas. He brought his mind back. It came readily.

'I fear,' said the man, 'that I must ask your indulgence. My lord of Arran has been further delayed. Rather than hold up the contests, it has been decided to proceed to the combats by sword. Your bout with the gentleman Anselm Sersanders will therefore precede your match with Thomas Boyd, Earl of Arran. Unless you object?'

'It is not for me to say,' Nicholas said. The last gallop had begun. Anselm Sersanders, whoever won, would be tired.

The collision occurred. The stand rose to its feet. Sersanders flung back his visor, a shattered lance in his hand. The Dane had missed. Nicholas said, 'You must ask Ser Anselm. I shall be fresh, and he will not.'

'I am sure he will agree,' said the man.

And, of course, he did. Pride saw to that. When they faced one another ten minutes later, Anselm Sersanders sat, secure and firm in the saddle, sword in hand. His horse was fresh but biddable under the iron hand of its maiden and his face was flushed but composed. The horse of Nicholas, unaccustomed to the smell of fright and to veils, was less manageable. But Nicholas had not galloped four times into battle, or accepted four times, as Sersanders had, the full weight of man, horse and pole against his bruised neck, and shoulder, and chest. Nicholas hadn't fought anyone yet.

Don't look bland. Don't look awed. Don't look half intoxicated.
Don't think.

It *was* a salt-cellar Sersanders was wearing. The brat. Betha Sinclair had favoured Nicholas with a handkerchief. He didn't think it was the child's. (*Don't smile.*) The trumpets blew, and he and Adorne's nephew faced one another.

Nicholas had jousted quite often before. Once as Guinevere in a wig, as he remembered. Although no, that was one tourney that didn't take place. He could handle a lance, but the sword, by now, was much more his weapon, and sport on horseback had given him an Eastern brand of skill in the saddle which Westerners complained was unorthodox. At the same time, the sword was more demanding than courtesy tilting. That is, the weapons for this kind of fight were not only rebated, they were quite different, and longer than usual.

Thirty-one blows had to be exchanged. The winner was the man adjudged to gain the most points, or the man who unhorsed his opponent. It was hard, skilful work. Nicholas always preferred to be fresh for a sword-fight. As now.

He had taken some other precautions. For this fight only, he wore an open sallet, exposing his face. It could be dangerous. But the jousting-helmet, as still worn by Sersanders, gave limited vision and, bolted to the breastplate and back, was always heavy. And Sersanders was tired.

Now the barricade had been dismantled. The trumpets blew. Sersanders and he rode to the King's stand together and bowed. The Sinclair girl, stiffened by competition, managed her veil, her sleeves and, nearly, her train. Katelijne unobtrusively helped her. Katelijne said out of the side of her mouth, 'The *Sterner* versus the *Psitticher*.'

Stars and Parrots. She knew a lot about jousting. The ladies retired. Sersanders gazed at him for a moment, his eyes unusually wide, and then lowered his visor and, turning, trotted to one end of the field. Nicholas took the other, and spurred forward the moment the trumpets blew.

Their horses looked the same. The rules said they had to be matched. There was no advantage, therefore, in ramming together and hoping to unsettle the other man so that a blow might unseat him. So they each took their time, cantering evenly, closing the gap. They had almost reached the space before the King's stand when Sersanders suddenly drove his spurs in and came hard towards Nicholas, his sword ready to strike from the flank.

Behind the visor, his eyes were unreadable, whereas Nicholas knew the glow from the stand lit his own face. He took measure, fast, with his eyes. Sersanders watched him and struck. In a dazzle of sparks, his blade met that of Nicholas, in a direct counter that nothing had signalled. Nicholas felt the other sword momentarily yield: with luck it might even have fallen. Then they were apart, and the dance could begin.

It *was* a dance. Combat was the deployment of ruses. Sersanders knew some, Nicholas others. Tellingly, the bay he was riding knew most. It was an old way of gaining ascendancy: to use a horse trained on the sports field. Not in battle, of course, but for this kind of fight, which depended on speed and lightness and agility.

Not that Sersanders was anyone's dupe. After the first moments, circling, stretching, striking, he could see well enough how Nicholas was using his weight to guide and instruct the horse, and how sensitively the horse was responding. It meant he had to change his own strategy. That, or be made to look less than professional, here, before the cream of a nation.

And that was not what Nicholas wanted. This was not merely an event in a tournament: it was an encounter of honour for Sersanders. Sersanders shamed would arouse the whole Adorne faction in Scotland. At the same time, Nicholas had his own plans. He was performing, as Sersanders was, for the King and for Albany. And he didn't intend to get hurt.

It made a good fight. He liked the feel of the sword, five feet of it, in his hand, and liked to open his shoulders, using his extra reach, his extra height. Sersanders had never fought, as Nicholas had, with mercenaries, or been trained by a mercenary leader, despite his years of careful teaching by Adorne and his father, and the perpetual practice offered by the societies.

Simon was one of the few men Nicholas knew who had done both: practised the art of chivalric warfare and also fought in the field for his own country against foreign knights and their followers. He himself had not, of course, met Simon in formal combat with weapons of chivalry. Or not yet. Or not unless you counted a few moments in Venice.

The thoughts were fragmented, and sprang from what was immediately happening – from the type of blow, of parry, of feint which recalled something else. Tzani-bey had been short. Tzani-bey had compensated in ways forbidden in chivalry. It was not permitted to injure the other man's horse, or strike a weaponless man, or change weapons. Nicholas reached the conclusion, wheeling, striking, tapping, that jousting was not really interesting. Sixteen blows. Seventeen. (*When?*)

On the other hand, Sersanders was making it interesting. Being fit, he had recovered well from the earlier fight. He had also, by now, assessed what he was facing. He had further assessed, Nicholas saw with pleasure, that the blows he faced had no malice behind them, and that he was being offered a chance, to his surprise, to engage in a bout of lively and high-quality swordsmanship.

Which did not make it easy. The swift turns, the bending, the swoops which drew roars from the crowd were not maypole dances, and each exchange of blows, single or multiple, was the result sometimes of a long sequence of movements. By now – twenty-four, twenty-five – they were both slowing a little and losing precision. Of the three metal hasps securing Sersanders's helmet in front, one had broken. Nicholas tried to keep his swordpoint from catching, and so far had succeeded. They had each, on occasion, inadvertently struck the horse-cloth of the other. His horse wore leather below, Sersanders's plate. Being accidental, the blows did not count.

Twenty-seven. Now full dark had fallen, and they trampled upon their own streaming shadows. The rectangle within which they struggled was outlined in light: lamps, candles, high-flaring torches. High on the Rock, window-light sprinkled the darkness and here and there exposed an expanse of broad wall. A flush in the air told of the stair-lamps of the Horse Market.

The news would have to come up the Wynd and into the Canongate. Then up the High Street and down through the market and here . . . *Pay attention!*

Light exploded into his face: disastrous light this time. The dazzle of Sersanders's sword, deflected up from his shoulder-plate. And the flash of his own helm, struck from below and torn backwards from his bare head.

His horse stopped. Sersanders, still in violent motion, saw what had happened and reined his horse hard, dragging his sword-arm up and back. The horse, alarmed and nervous, suddenly reared and Sersanders, unbalanced, found that one hand would not hold it.

Nicholas saw his opponent's mount rear above him, black on the stars, and the hooves begin to come down. A single roar from the stands filled his head. He saw Sersanders hurl his sword to the ground and, seizing the reins in both hands, use his weight and the rigour of the bit to try to drag the horse sideways.

He had no hope of keeping balance. The animal twisted. Its hooves clattered down, missing Nicholas. Its knees buckled. Then it fell, big as a wagon, and the crash of its steel shook the ground.

Nicholas, dismounting, hit the ground at the same time. He fled under the flailing hooves and round to where Sersanders had fallen. Sersanders lay free, on his back. As Nicholas reached him, he slowly raised one plated arm and put back his vizor. He said, 'We only got to twenty-nine points.' He sounded winded. He looked unharmed. He *was* unharmed.

Nicholas gave him a hand to sit up, and then stand. Men were running towards them. He said, 'We could both get on my horse and hit one another.'

'That nag?' said Sersanders. 'It wouldn't stand for it. I don't know what knacker sells you his horses.'

'Well, I wouldn't ever trust you with a good one. Look what you do to them,' Nicholas said. They were walking slowly across to the stand. As boys, ten years ago, they had talked to each other like that. Nicholas stopped. He said, 'You could have cut my throat. No one would have known.'

'I should,' said Sersanders. Then the marshal of the lists arrived, panting.

Nicholas stood, while procedures were swiftly discussed, and one horse was being killed, and the other led away. The two maidens, skirts clutched, arrived and clung to the group. The Sinclair girl had been weeping and Katelijne gave her a handkerchief. Anselm Sersanders and Nicholas de Fleury were invited to approach the royal stand, and informed that honours

were even, and their fair ladies would present them with what they
had won at the banquet that night. A flower fell at Sersanders's
feet, tossed by Margaret. The trumpets, defeating all speech, called
for attention, and an announcement was made. The next bout
would be the last of the evening.

'But what about ours?' said the Sinclair girl against a sonorous
recital of honours. He saw Katelijne had overheard and was struggling.

Nicholas said, 'I think we hold that in private. No, of course I
know what you mean. I suppose it's been cancelled.' He watched
Sersanders walk away with his sister. They had exchanged a sort of
salute. Whatever had happened, Sersanders had undoubtedly come
off the better. He looked up at the stand, preparing to leave the
field, and heard someone calling his name.

The voice came from the stand. As he hesitated, a page in royal
livery came running, important with the command. It sounded like
a summons to heaven. Perhaps it was.

He had to go as he was, bare-headed, his sallet under his arm.
The steps to the royal enclosure were covered with velvet, the rails
gilded and carved. He had provided the craftsman himself. And
the central chair with its emblazoned awning, from which James
the King had just risen. The regal face was unevenly flushed, and a
man in riding clothes stood, head bowed in deference behind him.

The news had come.

You made three obeisances, as in Trebizond. Then this King,
seventeen years old, said in his uneven voice, 'It has been in our
mind to send for you before this. We are pleased with what you
have arranged for our nuptials. So is the lady Margaret, our future
consort. The lady Margaret also wishes to thank you.'

Above the belt and collar of jewels, the ermine fichu, the stuffed,
golden sleeves thick with embroidery, the lady Margaret's hairless
face regarded him winsomely. He bowed and, when she held out
her hand, kissed it and spoke to her. All merchants knew the Hanse
languages. She smiled, her eyes widening.

The King said, 'She thanks you. Master de Fleury?'

Out in the field the last pair of combatants were meeting. They
had already made several strikes. No one in the royal stand was
watching them. Nicholas said, 'Yes, my lord King?'

'I owe you for more than that,' said the youth. He wore a
magnificence of ruby satin. They all did. The colour, burning
under the lamps, strove against the rows of fiery Stewart polls and
eyebrows, and lost.

The King said, 'The traitor has fled. You warned us. You were

right. We have uncovered the plots of his father. And now the man
has proclaimed his guilt. He will never come back. If he comes
back, his head will be forfeit.'

'Your grace?' Nicholas said.

'Thomas Boyd, Earl of Arran,' said the King. 'He entered the
town, saying nothing. He took to his chamber, feigning sickness.
Now we learn he has sailed. He returned to the harbour last night
and took ship. For where we do not know.'

'And took Mary with him,' said an accusing voice. Nicholas
turned. Margaret, the King's red-headed sister from Haddington.
Her lip stuck out.

The King said, 'So it appears. She, too, was said to be unwell.
Her husband has overthrown her proper judgement.'

'My lord,' said Nicholas de Fleury. 'Had we known, your friends
should have tried to detain them both.'

'No! No! It is his flight which has proclaimed his guilt! Had he
remained, who knows what lying witness he might have produced
to try and save himself! That we are spared. We had a canker at the
heart of the kingdom, and now it is gone.'

'With Mary,' said the inexorable voice.

The King turned his back on his sister. 'We have therefore
much to thank you for. In the months ahead, it will lie in our
power to show proper gratitude. In the meantime, we wish to
enhance something you already possess. You are a Knight?'

'Of the Order of the Sword, your grace,' Nicholas said.

'And is there a sword in this place?' said the King.

There was a rustle. Outside, someone was counting aloud.
Twenty-one. Twenty-two . . .

Numbers. Make friends of numbers, and they will never let you
down; never weary you; never sicken you. A sword was brought.
'Kneel,' said the King.

It was the Order of the Unicorn to which he was being admitted:
the Order of which Anselm Adorne was already a Knight. The
chain laid round his shoulders was borrowed from another, until
his own could be made. 'But you are no less a knight of this
kingdom for that,' said the King as he rose. 'And will use your title
forthwith, for it is not some mean order of Cyprus, but one known
to the world. As for your chain, Wilhelm can make it.'

'My lord King,' Nicholas said. 'I have no words. But look. I
have arranged the heavens to speak for me.'

They thought him a magician, but he had seen, in the dark, the
glimmer high on the Rock where he knew to look for it. And it was
time. It was his fortune that it was also just time.

The explosion was glorious. The great golden ball hung in the air jetting sparks and then, as every eye watched, it began to spin, throwing off garlands of light. A great sigh arose and the King's face, turned upwards was golden. He said, 'You have arranged fires of joy for our wedding. Indeed, indeed, we love you tonight.'

All the way back to his tent the skies over his head flamed and crashed and exploded in drifts of crackling colour, and men crowded round as he walked, shaking his hand and clapping the shining metal on his shoulder. His armour was a carnival of light in itself.

The third stage – the third stage was coming to its full promise at last.

In his tent were his household, their eyes shining: the pages rushing to unfasten his buckles, the serving-women clasping their hands. Friends crowded the doorway. Shedding the last of the weight, he stood in his sodden jerkin and was helped into his robe, with the silver sword embroidered at cuffs and at hem. His old Order. The insignia of the new one had been laid again on his shoulders.

'Well?' said Gregorio.

'Come,' said Nicholas. He cleared a way to the back and, sending for wine, made for them both a moment of privacy. It was a time for wine. He hadn't thought it would be, but it was. When it came, he poured it, and spoke. 'Set your conscience at rest. It was going to happen. If Arran had stayed, it would only have added to the carnage. And if his father had had his way, still more would have died. As it is . . .'

'As it is, you have a knighthood. And come this autumn, Boyd land. Boyd land next to Kilmirren.'

'And more,' Nicholas said. 'The wedding has to be paid for out of something.' The heavens rang, and colour flooded into the tent. 'That is why I am staying. I can do anything now.' The wine, after so long, was unbelievable. He said, 'Did you see the man who came in just now? The man with the gardens at Broughton?'

'He sells me herbs,' Gregorio said. 'What of him?'

'He sells me corn-marigolds,' Nicholas said. The chain blazed. The unicorn flashed blue and gold and red in the light.

'*Gule?*' Gregorio said. 'The weed? The weed that destroys healthy cornland? Why? Where . . .' He broke off.

'Here and there. The rough land between Kilmirren and Beltrees, for example. Every mile of it. He tells me it's a matted blanket of fierce orange flowers, all ready to burst into seed. Why so glum? Why fight with swords,' Nicholas explained, 'when you can do it with flowers?'

Gregorio sat looking dazed. Nicholas refilled his cup and strode out to his friends. They closed around him. Soon Sersanders would come, and offer his congratulations, and perhaps mean it. Katelijne would arrive and Betha Sinclair, who had brought up the little Countess and helped prepare the castle for her lord's coming home. But Mary Stewart and her husband were together. It was what she had wanted.

Then the banquet. Then the dancing, the speeches, the prizes, and Will Roger playing the simpleton and making music fit for Pythagoras. Then the weeks to the wedding, with all their concocted, mechanical marvels. Then the autumn, and the King's coming to power. And his.

Someone said, 'There you are.'

Crackbene's voice. Crackbene, who should be in Leith. He stood, the light flashing on his bulk and his fair, impassive face. Nicholas said, 'Come into the tent.'

Gregorio was still there. He looked up, and then stood. The unicorn sparkled but Crackbene ignored it. He said, 'I have a message for you from Bruges. They've sent others that seem to have failed. This one came on a ship. Life or death. You have to go back at once. There's Todrik's *Margaret* at Leith, ready to set sail at once for Newcastle. You can find another ship there.' He stood, his face composed and full of quiet sympathy.

He hadn't said what was wrong. It meant he had noticed the chain and was not averse to disrupting someone else's reward for his work.

Nicholas said, 'If it is my wife or the child, you will be sorry.'

'No,' Crackbene said. His pale gaze steady, he pulled out a creased packet and offered it. 'It's the old priest. Father Godscalc. They want you.'

'He's sick,' Nicholas said. He was reading. He said aloud, 'No. Worse than that.'

'Let me see,' said Gregorio.

It was in Tobie's writing, and explicit. Godscalc's life could be measured in weeks. He would survive until Nicholas came.

'I'll pack,' Gregorio said. 'Get the horses.'

He looked back. 'Nicholas?'

Crackbene hadn't moved. Nicholas said, 'Look at the date on the letter. It's taken too long. It will be over.'

The fireworks had stopped. The trumpets proclaimed the end of the contest; a voice boomed; another fanfare announced that the King's procession was about to form up and leave for the banquet. Everyone was standing outside except themselves.

Gregorio said, 'I didn't, I think, hear you speak. It doesn't matter how the letter is dated. This is Godscalc, departing life, and calling you home.'

'No,' said Nicholas. He heard himself say the word. It was not a rejection of Godscalc. It was a rejection of what going back now would mean. Whom he would see. What would happen, before he was ready for it. He thought, in a moment's odd desperation, that even Godscalc wouldn't ask him to do that. He tried to hold on to the thought.

Crackbene said, 'You won't persuade him by force.' He was speaking to Gregorio, who had made an impulsive movement. Gregorio, who was never impulsive. The tent wavered, and Nicholas wished, with a surge of bitterness, that he had managed to keep to his rule about wine just this once.

It would have been satisfying to smash everything he could see, including Crackbene and Gregorio. It would have been a release beyond measure to find himself alone.

He said, 'You go. Or Bel. Why not Bel?'

'There isn't time,' Crackbene said. 'I don't mind going. But I've worked a long night at your bidding already.'

It was like watching a hare racing over a field, watching the mind of Gregorio following that. Gregorio said, 'A long night?'

Outside, the tent-makers waited. The crowds, by the sound, had begun flowing home. The royal procession had gone to the Greyfriars whose establishment, as memory served, was the only one qualified to contain so large and prestigious a company.

Crackbene glanced at Nicholas, and away.

Gregorio said, with sudden comprehension, 'You arranged it, both of you. You arranged for Boyd to escape. You helped his wife to go with him.'

Never underestimate Crackbene. Never. Never. Never.

Gregorio said, 'Go to Bruges. Or I tell the King what you did. And why you did it.'

'Try it,' said Nicholas pleasantly. 'Crackbene would thank you. I imagine they'll hang him.'

'No,' said Crackbene. 'I think I'll be on the high seas with you and with Master Gregorio long before that. But, of course, you couldn't come back, if Master Gregorio chooses to tell them.'

Nicholas had men within reach. What of it? He couldn't silence his own shipmaster or his own partner by force. If he didn't go, Gregorio would do as he said. He knew Gregorio.

The unicorn, lightless now, had nothing to say. The crowd was silent. The King, entertaining his future bride at the Greyfriars, would be surprised at his newest knight's absence and then perhaps a little relieved, since certain accounts might not be presented at inconvenient moments.

Nicholas said, 'You will know when I call in this debt.' He spoke to both of them, but he meant it for Crackbene.

The third stage was not over. Born, it was frozen at birth because of the innocence of Godscalc, the naïveté of Gregorio, the duplicity of a Scandinavian shipmaster. And because of them all, he had to face Godscalc, and the mirror which Godscalc embodied.

Which – Do you hear me? Do you hear me? – if he had to, he would smash.

Part II

High Season:
DOUBLING

Chapter 23

DEATH WAITED, his hand on Godscalc's shoulder, and was patient. Father Godscalc, untouched by doubt, woke each thick, aching morning to a patient day which might bring him his last benison, his last opportunity for grace, his last words with the child Claes, the man Nicholas.

It had not become, he would not allow it to become a house of mourning. His spiritual battle had been fought and won in Africa; his mortal one was of minor importance. Tobie, pressed for honesty, had told him a long time ago how matters stood. It was why the book-printing had not progressed, to the annoyance of Nicholas. But he had asked Tobie to say nothing of it. If others stepped forward instead, the world would still be enriched, and Nicholas had no need of wealth. Mortal wealth.

He had many visitors. His friends of the cloth brought him comfort and filled his room with incense and prayer. The paint-stained followers of St Luke, whose guild chaplain had once been his brother, came and talked (although his brother had been dead these four years). They brought him their work, and helped Tobie hang it. It lined his chamber like fish-scales: the gold, the ultramarine, the alizarine glowing. The Hanse merchants came, bringing honey and good beer and fur for his shoulders: he liked to speak German. And a German confessor and a monk from Cologne, who happened to bring information about paper and alum. Anselm Adorne arrived with his priest, whom he knew, carrying jellies from Margriet.

Of the company, Henninc dropped by from the dyeyard every day with some novelty in his satchel: a new colour he thought Godscalc would approve, or an order in especially fine writing. And every hour, so it seemed, he had a visit from Tilde or her sister, with something to eat or to drink, or just themselves, to sit by his bed with some chat and their sewing. Tilde told him about the business; Catherine told him what Paul or Nerio had been saying and repeated their jokes. Her heart was not, he thought, engaged, but she was flattered. She deserved happiness now.

Diniz, of course, came when he could. A little tired, because the company was now a large one and the Bruges office lay on his shoulders, but he was a kind young man, and assiduous, and his loving thoughtfulness had helped reconcile Tilde to the loss of their infant.

Twice Godscalc had been startled into tears. Once, when the door opened on the brisk red hair of John le Grant, famed engineer, navigator, master gunner; one of his young men – not so young now – who had been with him in Trebizond. John, back by chance from Alexandria because forced to do so by Nicholas. But here, where otherwise he might not have been, speaking fluent Scots-German and with all the news Godscalc longed to hear from the East. At the end, when Tobie came to remind him he was tired, Godscalc said, 'I am doubly glad you are here, for although you may wish it, I do not believe Nicholas should go abroad again yet. When he comes, persuade him to stay.'

'He is coming?' John had said.

'Of course,' said Tobie.

The next time, it was Astorre. Syrus de Astariis, mercenary captain of the original small Charetty bodyguard whose services the Bank now deployed all over Europe. Astorre had taught the boy Claes how to fight, and for a while the military arts had nearly claimed Nicholas, as they might have seduced Godscalc, once, from his calling.

He would be no use in the field now – he, Godscalc, who was two years younger than this sinewy man with the sewn eye, the torn ear, the grizzled beard, who sat wide-kneed on a stool and poured out the tale of his triumphs and complaints: the wiliness of the French King – God turn him into a capon – which had landed them with the mess of Liège and was now encouraging Duke Charles to ally himself with the Duke of the Tyrol.

'See here!' Astorre said. 'Old foxy poxy Louis is up to all his tricks because he doesn't want Charles and England to join forces against him. Your brave boy Duke Charles fancies himself as a king, and would be much obliged, please, if someone would give him all the bits of land between Flanders and Burgundy so that he can piece them into a kingdom. And his grace of the Tyrol needs money – don't we all? – and is willing to sell off the Black Forest to get it, not having a daughter to trade off like Denmark. And while all this is going on the Swiss Confederates, the best fighters in Europe bar mine, are beginning to feel leaned upon. And if they ever get together, God help us.'

'I hope He will. And then what?' Godscalc said. His inner eye saw it: the siege towers, the cannon. His inner eye had always plagued him.

'Then we put up our prices,' Astorre said. 'Nicholas told us to stay on in Burgundy. I didn't want to. But he was right. Is he here yet?'

'Any day now,' Tobie said, coming in.

Then one evening Tobie came in alone. He shut the door meticulously at his back and stood and said, 'He is here.' His stillness, and the closed door, told the rest.

Godscalc was very tired nowadays. Not in pain, but aware of the labour of lifting himself into full consciousness, and the relief of sinking back into sleep. Latterly every effort to return had been a rehearsal for this hour. For these moments. *Do you want to leave me? Yes, but I dare not.*

So he looked up at Tobie, his grim, pink-faced companion and doctor, and replied to the warning, not the words. He said, 'I know what to expect. That is why I wanted to see him. Did you think it was for myself?'

And when Tobie had gone, and the door opened again, he said, without even waiting to see who it was: 'I have to apologise, my child, for the inconvenience. But the appointment was not of my choosing.'

It *was* Nicholas de Fleury, bending his head under the lintel and removing his hat. A large man, he was as quiet as an animal. Godscalc smiled, with a twist of the lips, waiting for him to move, to walk from the shadows. When he did, Godscalc searched the face he knew as well as his own.

Yes.

He said, 'Sit. You look as tired as I am.'

Nicholas said, 'They didn't tell me, before.'

'You would still have gone to Scotland,' Godscalc said. 'Don't be afraid. You won't hurt me by telling me that you didn't want to come now.'

'I ought not to have come,' Nicholas said. He had accepted Godscalc's great chair and was hunched, his head lowered as if pondering. His eyes saw Godscalc's hand on the coverlet, and he took it slowly in one of his, as if testing it.

'You can do me no harm,' Godscalc said. 'You could lie, but I'd know it. You have been a pastor to me, and so I must be to you. By letting me speak, you will suffer me to perform the last act of my ministry, to the one I love best.' He closed his hand on the fingers beneath it. 'No, Nicholas.'

The withdrawing hand stopped. Nicholas sat, his face averted, but did not move again. Godscalc could see his cheekbone, and the hint of nostril and nose, and the ends of his lashes. He saw when he opened his eyes.

Godscalc said, 'What brought us both here? A joyous adventure. Yourself, nameless, bereft, but with enough spirit to animate all this old town and its people. And enough compassion to take a woman and her fatherless family and make them part of your own upward flight.'

Nicholas did not speak. The light illumined his neck: the arch that Donatello had drawn; the forms of bone and muscle that defined the flank of his face, of his jaw. He had never had beauty. It was craft that had gone to his making, as the sculptor – and others – had seen. And the lines were still clean and uncluttered and young.

Godscalc said, 'I remember Marian de Charetty, who also died happy. I remember the courage of the years that came after, and the agony at Trebizond when you strove to do what was right. I have heard of the tragedies of Rhodes and Famagusta, and how you overcame those, and the joy and the triumphs and the merriment you created as well. Not a man of those out there would have followed you otherwise. And in Africa –'

Nicholas turned his head. He said, 'No. That is why I did not wish to come.' His eyes were dry, and grey-black as iron.

Godscalc met them. He gathered his strength and spoke calmly. ''Tis often so. The worse the loss, the more unforgiving the anger. Umar did not want to leave you, or his wife, or his children. You think he should have told you, let you try to rescue him, or at least share his fate. Don't you think he knew that? Don't you think it belittles him, to resent what he did?'

'I know that,' said Nicholas.

'With your mind only, I think. It is the first step, at least. But that is not all.'

'It is enough,' Nicholas said. He stood slowly, his hand gripping the frame of the chair. 'Father, I don't want to leave. Talk to me, but not about that.'

'Not about why you are not only angry with God, but angry with the whole human race?'

'No,' said Nicholas.

'No? Angry, then, with your wife. Mortally angry with Jordan and Simon de St Pol, despite your own asseveration; and cruel to those caught in your quarrel. And, uniquely and finally, uncaring of all those around you, your *familia*: the people who have enabled you to rise, and who love you, and who depend on you, because you have been consumed with a longing for vengeance. Why? Shall I guess?'

Nicholas said, 'I changed, that is all. I became tired of living my life as a victim.'

'And that is your answer? Is it possible,' Godscalc said, 'that you think I intend to tell anyone else what you and I are saying just now? Or that I can carry it anywhere in the morsel of time that remains? This is why I waited for you.'

The lamp hissed. A wisp of smoke rose from the brazier, brought to warm him although it was summer. Nicholas looked, too, as if all mortal warmth had been denied him. He took a step from the chair and then, turning, folded both arms along the high ridge of its back, and propped his bent brow on his thumbs. He said, 'Your guess is probably right.'

Godscalc said, 'Then let me make it. What is the greatest pain I could conceive, that would drive you to idiocy? Only that the child is not yours. But perhaps Simon's.'

'You have it,' said Nicholas. He didn't move.

Now Godscalc's eyes were damp. He continued steadily. 'He took the girl, then, by force?'

'You know it couldn't be that,' Nicholas said, and disengaged from the chair with sudden impatience. Godscalc watched him. Of course it couldn't. The consequences of rape would have been transparently simple. Victim, husband and child would be bonded together for life; and Simon de St Pol would be dead.

Godscalc lay. You would say that in this brilliant, extraordinary man Gelis van Borselen had all anyone could want on this earth; that the unruly attraction between them was about to deepen into the companionship of which they both stood in need. She had shown her mettle in Africa. Godscalc himself had experienced the constancy of her care. Yet he had been disturbed even then, sensing turmoil, anguish even, under the sardonic calm.

He had been unable to reach her, although she had wept, once, at his knee. He had stopped asking questions, fearing to drive her away: she had no parents, no siblings, no confidants. Only when she spoke to him of marriage had he begged her to search her own heart. He had been concerned for her, as well as for Nicholas.

She had listened. She had even placed her doubts, as he had hoped, before Nicholas. Then in Scotland she had planned this cruel thing, from what desperation he could not imagine. And Simon de St Pol, from his shallow resources of pique and of vanity, had lent himself to her plan. Godscalc said, 'Did Simon know what he was doing?'

Nicholas said, 'He knew she was going to marry me. I think, for him, that was amusement enough. I don't believe he envisaged a child.'

'So he doesn't know about Henry. This is not his retaliation for Henry. It is hers.'

'I take it so,' Nicholas said.

'But to reject you now? After Africa?'

'I was always afraid,' he said. 'So was she.'

That, of course, Godscalc had known; only he had never been sure of the reason. Now he said, 'Afraid of what?'

'I don't know. Of ourselves. She had other fears. She never talked of them.'

'But you didn't expect this?'

'No,' he said. 'I thought I was safe.'

I thought I was safe. The shadows moved. Sometimes the brazier seemed to steal all the air from the room. Sometimes Godscalc's lids were so heavy that he had to rest them, and wait, as now, to lift them open again. When next he spoke, he chose his words with great care. 'Sometimes a child will stoop to the unthinkable to test the depth of one's love.'

'To test it to destruction?' said Nicholas. He seemed to be whispering. Then he must have turned, for he said roughly, 'Ah, no. You know now what happened: it is done; it can't be helped; it is wearying you. Godscalc, let me call Tobie.' He was kneeling on the bed-step, and Godscalc felt both his hands around his.

He withdrew one and touched the boy's hair, and thought to draw him close, as when once before they waited together on the threshold of death; and thought that Nicholas wanted it, too. He said, 'It *can* be helped, my dear son. You must know there is only one question that matters. I don't ask what your wife feels for you. Perhaps you don't know. But despite everything, behind everything, below everything, do you love Gelis still?'

A distant door slammed. He felt the sound under his arm like a blow. Nicholas lifted his head and let Godscalc see his face, as if he no longer wanted to protect himself. Then he said, 'Someone is coming.'

Godscalc did not speak; not then, nor when the weight left his bed as Nicholas slowly knelt back, and stood, and then stepped down from the bed. Footsteps approached: the sickroom door opened quietly. Tobie stood there, his cherubic face scowling. Tobie said, 'Father, I had to.'

'I asked him to bring me,' said Gelis van Borselen.

Tending the dying, Tobias Beventini had faced many times the hard necessity of discriminating between one friend or another, of using what wisdom he had to detect when his patient was in need of peace or even when, suffering, needed his loved ones more than relief.

He did not quite know what he was doing, bringing Gelis to the room where Nicholas de Fleury and his priest were alone. Nevertheless he believed, from what he had heard, that Godscalc had a right to speak for the last time to the formidable companion of his journey from Africa; and that she had a right to his blessing.

Entering the room, he knew at once that Godscalc was spent. He also felt, more than saw, that something private was taking place, or had taken place; and that Godscalc felt it unfinished. He did not, therefore, as he might have done, either turn them all from the room, or ask Nicholas to take his last leave. He saw, in fact, that after the first shock, the eyes of Nicholas and the priest had returned to each other, and held still.

Tobie said, 'You are an obstinate old man, and you should have sent for me. Nicholas, sit down over there. Gelis, there. And be quiet, both of you, until I have finished.'

'A bully,' Godscalc remarked. He had found a special smile in the hollow face, among the thinned grey and white whiskers, for Gelis. Then he turned the smile, grown calm, grown calming, upon the man Nicholas.

Busying himself with the cup, the flask, the drops, the sponges, Tobie saw them both, Gelis and her husband, as if through the back of his head. Or if he did not, he saw them reflected in the priest's worn, smiling face.

They had been told to be quiet, and they were. Gelis was still cloaked and hooded as she had come through the countryside, once they found her. Diniz had sent men searching far and wide. The cloak was wet, and her face, when she drew back the hood, was sharpened with the speed of the journey, but ravishing still, with its light eyes and fair hair. Nicholas half rose to help her, but she shook her head and cast the cloak back herself. The hem of her gown was stiff with mud.

They both sat in shadow; he couldn't hear either breathing. The eyes of Gelis moved between the bed and the person of her husband, black on black. Nicholas, after his first gesture, had not looked at her. Tobie, moving his clean hands in and out of the light, knew that Godscalc's eyes were on his face, to test what he thought. What he thought was that he had never seen Nicholas de Fleury under such strain, and that Gelis herself had observed it.

He took his time over his business; giving Godscalc some of the space that he needed, and robbing him of the space ahead, which Godscalc did not want, and he had no right to preserve for him. Then he turned and dried his hands, and said, 'Gelis?'

She rose. The face on the pillow, once hearty, once dogged, once boisterous, said, 'Gelis, my dear. And Nicholas. Nicholas, stay.'

Gelis looked at her husband. A quick look, hard to decipher.

Nicholas said, 'I would – yes. And Tobie? Tobie would like . . .' His voice trailed into silence. Whatever he meant, it seemed that Godscalc understood it. Godscalc said, 'I see. Then, of course, Tobie must stay.'

Gelis was still looking at Nicholas. Then she turned and dropped to her knees by the bed and, after a moment, laid her cheek on the coverlet.

Godscalc lifted a hand. He was looking not at the girl, but at Nicholas. Then he smiled and laid his fingers on the girl's hair. He said, 'Shall I be the bridge?'

Tobie got up. 'Don't go,' Nicholas said.

'No. Don't go,' Godscalc said. 'If there cannot be a bridge, or not yet, then surely we two, priest and physician, have still something to offer these children. Gelis?'

She looked up. Her brow, white-skinned and polished, was seamed with short lines. She knelt back, her hand still in the crippled hand on the coverlet.

Godscalc said, 'There is not, I think, very much time. I am glad we four are here because, apart from all we owe one another, we share a secret. When I have gone, you three alone in this world will know of certainty that Nicholas has a son, and who the boy is. You know the dangers. You three, by your combined wisdom, will guide this child to manhood, from whatever distance; will think for him; and will do what is best for him, and not for you. I die trusting you to do that. Tobie?'

'Yes, Father. Of course,' Tobie said.

'Nicholas? *Whatever* it means?'

Nicholas walked to the side of the bed and knelt opposite Gelis, his wife. 'Yes, Father,' he said. He was looking at Gelis.

'And Gelis?'

'He is the son of my sister,' she said.

Godscalc waited. Tobie looked from him to Nicholas. Nicholas did not move. Gelis said, 'My child is his cousin. In all I do, I shall make no distinction between them.'

Tobie smiled and then lost the smile, looking at Godscalc. Godscalc said, 'You did not bring me your child? I should have liked to bless him. Where is he?'

She lifted her chin. 'I shall send for him,' she said. Across the bed, the grey gaze of Nicholas stayed unaltered.

'Send Nicholas. He will bring him,' said Godscalc.

Tobie stirred. Godscalc's deep eyes moved towards him, and he smiled. He said, 'I am reminded of my mortality. Let me change what I ask.

'Compared with Henry, your child, Gelis, will be fortunate. He has a young and beautiful mother who has learned from her sister's mistakes, and forgiven them. In Nicholas he has a toy-maker, a gentle protector, a man born to give children the happiness he was denied. A man who, too, has learned from the past, and is able to begin afresh, with his wife. Umar's family did not all live, but yours will. And so –' His voice faded.

Nicholas said, 'Please. Please. Tobie, help him.'

Gelis did not speak. Tobie crossed quietly, his eyes on the pillow. Godscalc said, 'I shall sleep more happily. You are not to be afraid.'

'No. We are not afraid,' Nicholas said. 'We want you to speak to us.'

'Even though, as always, it is not what you wanted to hear?' He was smiling again, a little. The sheet moved to his breathing. They waited. He said, 'Nicholas, I owe you not only my life, but my faith. Gelis, Tobias, I owe you all that followed. I shall not reward you with homilies, although my Church says I should. Tobie, trust where you have always trusted. You are right: you have not gone astray.

'Gelis – Nicholas – look at me, not at one another.' He stopped. He said, 'If you would wish me Godspeed on my way, give me a promise.'

He stopped again, to get breath. Nicholas – not Gelis – spoke. 'Whatever you want, you shall have.'

'Do you think me so cruel?' said Godscalc. 'I ask only one thing. You may think it strange. Nicholas, will you promise me not to go back to Scotland?'

None of them, including Tobie, had expected that. Gelis looked across quickly. Nicholas, his eyes on the priest's, wore a look of deep concentration. He said, 'Never?'

Godscalc said, 'No. I should not spoil a lifetime of plans. Only for now. Only, say, for two years. Would you leave them in peace for two years?'

It was a strange phrase. Dying men exacted peculiar promises. One soothed, one agreed. Tobias, wholly concerned with the shell on the pillows, only came to realise in the silence that followed that Nicholas was not going to supply a comforting answer. Then Godscalc said, 'Do you want me to tell Tobie why? No one here knows your strength of purpose as I do.'

'No. I agree,' Nicholas said.

'You won't go back?'

'Not for two years. I promise.'

The face of Gelis, looking at his, was a mask.

Godscalc closed his eyes, as though to conserve, if he could, an extra measure of energy. He said, 'I have heard more convincing avowals.' The half-smile remained on his lips.

'You want a Decreet Arbitral?' Nicholas said.

'What?' said Tobie. Godscalc opened his eyes. Tobie saw that it was self-mockery that he had heard.

Nicholas, too, seemed to be smiling. Nicholas said, 'Then let me do it in form.'

He had lifted both hands and laid them, as he knelt, upon the crucifix between Godscalc's fingers. Godscalc gathered them, and looked up. 'I promise,' Nicholas said.

The two sets of hands rested. The crucifix glowed. Tobie's eyes blurred. He did not know where Godscalc's gaze had turned, but he heard his voice, sounding strange. 'I say it again. Child: be my bridge.'

'What do you want?' Gelis said. The words had no timbre.

'I want nothing.' The once-big voice was full of pity. 'I shall exact no promise from you: I have not the right. But we all tread one path. Stay with me on this threshold a moment, and help me remember the love that we share.'

He was smiling. Gelis leaned forward. Pale brow, pale lips, pale strand of hair fallen forward, she stretched her hands to her priest and her husband. For a space, flesh on gold, gold on white, something sacramental seemed to rest in the lamplight. Then, the hands drawing apart, it dissolved.

The crucifix shone. The door opened and closed. Gelis uttered a sound of protest, or appeal. The man, the child for whom Godscalc had waited, had gone.

Godscalc lay, his gaze upon the closed door, his face full of pity. Then he turned his tender smile to the girl.

After that, few came to trouble him. Gelis shut herself in her chamber. Last of all, Gregorio knelt by the bed and received his friend's blessing before the doctor dismissed him and the German priest, waiting quietly outside, was brought in. Presently the woman came whom Tobie trusted and, leaving the sickroom in her gentle charge, he went to the parlour where the sisters, Catherine and Tilde, sprang to their feet when he entered; and Astorre opened an eye; and Gregorio turned from talking to Diniz and John.

Tobie said, 'He is sleeping. You'll see him tomorrow.'

'Shall we?' said Gregorio.

'I think so. But not very much longer. He has what he wanted,' said Tobie. 'Where is Nicholas?'

Catherine said, 'We thought that you'd know.' As Tilde had become plump and pale, Catherine had grown bright-skinned and shapely.

Tobie said, 'No. Shall I look for him? He's probably hungry.'

'I'll come,' said Gregorio. Diniz rose.

'Good God no,' Tobie said. 'I don't need to call a man to his food by committee.' He took his eyes from Gregorio's, and went out.

Tobie's association with Nicholas de Fleury went back a long way. He began his search, none the less, in a severely practical fashion, tapping at and opening the door of the chamber he used; strolling through the counting-house and its workrooms and offices; poking into this corner and that; and descending then to the yard, wandering casually from stable to storehouse. No horses had come, and none gone. He verified that Gelis was indeed in her room, and alone. He was unsurprised.

Their patron was not on the premises. He had gone out, on foot. And this time, no quack had forestalled him.

So where would a man go in Bruges on a warm midsummer night, his mind burdened with verse, or with numbers?

Once, it must have been easy. An apprentice, bruised in flesh or in spirit, would steal from his workshop like this; would tramp these cobbles, barked at by dogs but ignored by his betters. Then eventually, under some lamp, he would be hailed by his friends and swept off and consoled with cheap ale. Or he would find his way down to a basement, where a wench in her chemise would open the shutters, and then her chemise. Or if he wanted no company but his own, there were places under the bridges, or, in winter, against a warm chimney.

Where would a rich man go, bruised in flesh or in spirit? The rich had no refuge at all. Except in the past.

*

Against the later splendours of Spangnaerts Street, the Charetty
dyehouse always looked shabby, even though the offices had been
rebuilt after the fire they had had, and the house reconstructed for
Henninc, and new and better storehouses had risen in place of the
old to contain the perennial crates and baskets and sacks, the
fleeces and the yarns, the bales of cloth and the barrels of alum, the
parcels and parcels of dyes. The smell stayed the same: of wet
wool, and queer herbs, and urine.

There had always been a wall. There had always been a place in
the wall where apprentices could climb in and out to avoid the
porter, or Henninc.

Tobias Beventini of Grado, physician, was ten years older than
Nicholas, but he could still scale a wall, to the harm of his gown
and his temper. Inside the yard, all was quiet.

Once the apprentices had slept in these sheds, side by side in the
straw of the upper floors; and on Sundays filed down the ladder for
Mass, while Marian de Charetty stood at the door and neatened
their hair. Now they were used only for storage, because the
apprentices slept in the house.

The shutters were closed, and the first doors Tobie tried were all
locked. He had keys. Seized with this stupid idea, he had brought
the keys with him from Spangnaerts Street. Nicholas carried the
master. Tobie paused, and then continued to look.

It was the whine of the dog that brought him to the door furthest
away. It gave to his hand, so that the warm stench flooding out
shook his senses. It was followed by the nose of a hound. There were
always dogs, and this one knew him, and knew Nicholas. It was glad
to see him, and a little anxious. Because, of course, it wasn't alone;
otherwise the door would be locked. Nicholas wouldn't confine it,
and probably couldn't contrive to expel it. Or didn't care either way.

Tobie fondled the dog, and then went inside, closing the door.
He felt for the lamp on its hook, and its tinderbox, which gave him
a dim, unprovocative light to carry. He made no effort to call.

The ground floor held only merchandise. A ladder, inviting, led
him to the airless heat of the loft. The dog padded below, its eyes
shining. The muted light fell upon the humped shapes of sacks,
patched with labels and scrawled over with writing. He understood
what it said. Two years ago, he had taught himself in Oran, while
waiting for Nicholas to come back from the desert.

Nicholas de Fleury lay near the centre, with the dyes, the drugs,
the writing under his cheek, and his bent arm laid over them.
Tobie buried the lamp in a corner, dimming it further. Then,
sweating, he began to pick his way over.

Nicholas had been enveloped, too, by the heat. His discarded shirt, when Tobie touched it, was sodden. He himself lay on his face as if asleep; indeed, he could not have been awake and lain as still as that.

Tobie felt no professional misgivings. With Nicholas, of course, there was a history, but what he had glimpsed did not suggest fever. And however low he was brought, Nicholas fought. Conceding, tolerating, conciliating, he still pursued, with deadly accuracy, whatever objective he had set for himself. Which, of course, only he knew.

He was here because he was aware that he needed a respite. The desert had given him skills: he could identify stress, and recognise different kinds of exhaustion. Here he had sought, perhaps, the weightless peace of his boyhood. Or, more complex than that, the cradle of some early kindness linked, by the script upon which he lay, with another.

For a while, Tobie stayed. Because he was tired, he drifted now and then into sleep. As any doctor would, he came to the surface when Nicholas stirred or changed his position, however slightly. Nicholas. Claes vander Poele whom he had tended, dumb and desolate, in another place, a decade ago. He had witnessed, then, evidence of a hurt no physician could cure. And now, with the same Nicholas under his hand, a good man and a priest had proved helpless.

In time, the lamp flickered and Tobie rose to his feet. He dared not wait, and to end that shallow rest would be pointless. Climbing noiselessly down, Tobias Beventini extinguished and replaced the lantern and left, miserable because he was angry with Godscalc; and Godscalc was dying.

Chapter 24

ELD A WEEK AFTER his death, the funeral Mass of the Charetty chaplain was widely attended, the Duke himself sending a representative (Tommaso Portinari), and most of the chief burghers of Bruges and their wives crowding into St Donatien's in their black.

Apart from honouring the good man, commended by the Holy Father himself for his travails in Africa, Bruges was curious to witness the entire House of Niccolò on solemn display: Diniz de Vasquez and the two Charetty girls, one of them his wife; Tobias Beventini the doctor; the red-haired man they called John le Grant, who worked for them in the Levant. And most of all, the big fellow Claes himself, now Nicholas de Fleury, knight, who had come with Gregorio the lawyer all the way from the King's wedding in Scotland to be at the deathbed. And got there, too, the very day the old man sank into his final coma.

The lady wife of Ser Nicholas wasn't there, since she had to leave to return to her infant. And Astorre, the army captain, hadn't been able to wait. But everyone else from the yards and the house had turned up, and the business closed for three days as a mark of respect.

Good feeling, that showed, since the old man had none of his own friends or family left, barring two Germans who had found themselves in the town. One of them, Father Moriz by name, had stood up in church and seemed to be telling them about Father Godscalc's early days in Cologne. Then he had switched from German Latin to the Louvain kind, and read out a lot of things about Father Godscalc's later life in Bruges and elsewhere which were very fine, and made those who could understand them blow their noses. Later, there was a Flemish translation for the women.

The funeral feast was well done, too, for those who were invited.

And everyone leaving St Donatien's was correctly thanked by Claes – Ser Nicholas – himself at the door. They said he had had enough of Scotland and was going to stay and look after his own business now, which was only right for a young man with a wife and a baby. His first anniversary was just the other day now; but you couldn't celebrate with the old man so recently gone. And if young Nicholas married Catherine off, they'd have a wedding to go to as well.

'Ghouls,' said the engineer John le Grant as the doors to the Spangnaerts Street house closed behind the last of the guests. He didn't say it with vehemence, in case he needed the vehemence for something else. He felt drained, by death and by his first experience of Nicholas on his home ground.

He should have listened to Gregorio, with whom he had held, over the years, a long and illuminating correspondence. He knew Tobie and Godscalc and Astorre. He knew, God help him, the step-daughter Catherine. He had known the negro he used to call Loppe. He had been with Nicholas in Florence, in Trebizond, in Cyprus, in Venice, but never here, in the Hof Charetty–Niccolò, Bruges.

John le Grant, pioneer, shipmaster, gunner, had come from Alexandria to Bruges because Nicholas had demanded his services in Scotland. And now Nicholas was here, and not in Scotland. And he wasn't making toys any more, or none that John liked the look of. Living with Nicholas had always been unpredictable. Now it was like running on top of an icefield.

Astorre, who had departed, had come off best. Late in the day of Godscalc's death, Nicholas had taken Astorre to his desk and worked through the future of the army: listening; taking advice; bringing le Grant himself into the consultation, but always steering towards the plan he obviously had already made. Then Astorre, contented – even impressed – had gone off.

Then it was the turn of le Grant on his own, and he had found himself, with no levity at all, explaining once more the history of the parrot he had sent by roundship to Nicholas de Fleury.

It had been a brief conversation, for Nicholas had guessed, of course, that he was the sender, and that the bird was connected somehow with the missing shipmaster Ochoa de Marchena, who had disappeared when sailing from Africa, along with four to five hundred pounds of pure gold, owned by the Banco di Niccolò and never recovered.

And, naturally, Nicholas had also recognised the mimicked voice

they both knew, which spoke Cypriot Greek as well as sweet
French. The voice of Zacco, King of Cyprus, who had once been
very well liked.

John produced his submission. 'Whoever sent the parrot wants
you in Alexandria. And I don't know who sent it. It came to me
from an Arab trader from Tor, and he got it from a chain of other
people. I was to send you the bird, and they said you would know
it was intended for you, because of the Spanish. They meant, of
course, you would know it was linked with the gold.'

He paused. Sometimes, as now, the bastard didn't even bother
to put on an expression. He went on, 'I recognised Zacco's voice,
too. I nearly plucked and stewed the brute instead of sending it on.
Friendship with Zacco is not, at the moment, a recipe for advance-
ment.'

'It never was,' Nicholas said. 'His voice could have been accidental. The parrot belonged to his household. Or don't you
remember?'

John remembered all right. Zacco rarely spoke Greek. Zacco
called no one else Nikko. He said, 'We have to go to Alexandria
anyway. If someone wants you so much, no doubt they'll find you.'

There was a silence. Nicholas said, 'Crackbene sold it.'

'I shouldn't necessarily blame him,' said John. 'I was afraid to
write, and the bird was dumb to begin with. Did you bring it?'

'It would have been sick. I brought its repertoire. I can't make
anything of it. But why send a slow parrot instead of a fast letter?'

'Ochoa couldn't write. Or you wouldn't be sure the message was
from him. Or a parrot-cypher was safer.'

'Or it wasn't urgent.' He spoke as if the idea had just occurred to
him. Then he ended the interview.

An hour later, Gregorio was summoned and told to bring John
and Diniz to hear an outline of the company's changed plans.
Gregorio looked round and said, 'I'll get Tobie,' and was stopped
by the voice from the ice-floe. 'Why not leave him? I am sure he is
tired.'

The previous night, Godscalc's last night on earth, Tobie had
been missing for part of the evening and Nicholas for rather
longer. John, a light sleeper, had seen Tobie return. Nicholas he
had only heard. But Nicholas had gone straight to Godscalc and
had stayed, through dark, dawn and morning, until Godscalc's
sleep sank towards death.

He had supervised, then, what had to be done, before transferring
the same untrammelled competence to the company desk. He had
seen Astorre. He had talked to John himself, without excitement,

about gold. Now, calling them together, he had set himself to explain his new plans for the Bank and the Charetty company: plans which must have been worked out through that long, silent death-watch; plans which made no mention of Scotland. And Tobie, by arbitrary decision, was excluded.

Afterwards, Gregorio took John to Tobie's chamber. The doctor had had some sleep, but not quite enough: there were great purses round his pale eyes and his bald head was creased. Under the sheet he was childishly furry. Gregorio said, 'We've just had a meeting. Nicholas wouldn't send for you. I've brought you some ale.'

'I've missed you all the time you were in Scotland,' said Tobie, taking it. He waved the mug at John and drank from it as they sat down. He said, 'Has he seen Gelis yet? Since the death?'

'Yes,' said Gregorio. 'In private. She was already packed. I believe she has gone.'

'She didn't say goodbye to anybody?'

'She was fond of Godscalc,' the lawyer said.

John said nothing, for it seemed to be true. He had seen her ride out. She was red-eyed and pale. She was the same physical type as Primaflora, which was presumably why Nicholas had married her. He always seemed to get entangled with young women who didn't like him particularly, but could supply, in excess, what he wanted. Come to think of it, there was nothing much wrong with that.

Tobie said, 'About the meeting. Don't worry. I'll find him a pill for his temper.'

'What happened?' said John. 'I saw you come in last night.'

'And you told Nicholas?' said Tobie. He stopped drinking.

'No.'

Gregorio said, 'I expect you followed him, and he saw you. I was worried as well. He'll get over it. Tobie, he's not returning to Scotland. He's going to Egypt with John.'

'God's bonnet,' said Tobie. He stared at the lawyer.

'I know. He should have done it before. He should have gone to the Levant before he committed us so deeply up north. But he can return to Scotland, he says, in two years, and put all his remaining schemes back in action and collect what's due on the rest. Adorne isn't there any more; Sersanders is only an agent; there's no one else as close to the King as Nicholas was in the end.'

'And in Egypt?' Tobie said. 'He'll get the Levantine trade going to the limit at last?'

'And the missing gold,' said Gregorio. 'What do you know about parrots?'

*

It was an axiom long apparent to Gelis, that one attacked when one's opponent was weakest. She assumed that her husband obeyed it as well. She expected him to turn the death of Godscalc to his advantage, and took steps, naturally, to counter him. It was by chance that she discovered, seeking to avoid Nicholas through the night, that he had left the house early and that Tobie had followed. She knew when Tobie returned, for she was waiting at Godscalc's bedside to confront him. And Tobie was not a good actor.

She had wondered who would bring her word that Godscalc had died; and was not surprised when it was Nicholas who knocked and came in. Attack when your opponent is weakest. But if she had been sleepless all night, so had he. Or so she assumed.

On the other hand, he was a brilliant actor. He stood before her, subdued and chastened in manner, his words a model of what was considerate. His shirt was fresh, and so was the loose tunic over it. Once, she had known every garment he had. Every garment. She spoke from the window-seat where she had been sitting longer, she realised, than she knew. 'I'm glad you came back in time. Where did Tobie really find you? Some brothel?'

He smiled, but the glance that it grew from was distant. He hadn't known, she saw, that the doctor had followed him. He took a seat. 'Didn't he tell you? If you want the address, you can have it. Or did Father Godscalc exact solemn promises? What have *you* agreed to give up for Lent?'

'You were there,' she said. 'He didn't ask me to promise anything more.'

'The blackguard,' said Nicholas. 'Not that you would have kept your word anyway. I take it that you are not proposing to take Henry under your roof any more than I am. I've made some financial provision. If he kills anybody, it will pay for the defence. Otherwise I propose to have him watched, as Godscalc suggested, from a distance. I shall send you half the account.'

'Half the – He's your son.'

'He's your sister's son. I'm sure you remember.'

He had learned so quickly. Or no. He had always known how to retaliate. She changed her position a little, folding her hands. She said, 'I fear that Henry is only a pretext. You are actually proposing, in your sweet way, to induce me to foot half the bill for spying on Simon.'

'You mean that wouldn't amuse you?' he said. He settled his elbows and furled his fingers, full of interest. 'Certainly, I don't think you'd uncover any tremendous surprises. No, you're right. In fact, the situation wouldn't arise. Henry will be left where he is, and Simon and Jordan will go back to Scotland.'

'Where you will be waiting for them.'

'No, no,' Nicholas said. 'Fields and fields of corn-marigolds, but not me. You haven't been listening. Scotland is what *I* have agreed to give up for Lent. For two Lents.'

She let a silence develop. Far away, the life of the house could be heard: soft footsteps passing up and down; grieving voices. A soul dear to them all – she thought – had left the earth, and Nicholas had knelt for its blessing. She could feel those craftsman's hands resting on hers, and hear Godscalc speaking. Nicholas had been performing. It had meant nothing to him. Nothing, nothing. So, determined, alone, one worked with what did have some meaning.

She said, 'Gregorio told me what a Decreet Arbitral was, and what you thought of it. And of your interest in Boyd land in Scotland. You want it to encircle Kilmirren.'

He produced an expression, briefly, of theatrical slyness. He didn't deny it. He looked, indeed, as if he were thinking of something quite different.

She said, 'All those schemes? All that consolidated goodwill? Of course you're going back.'

'Of course you would think so,' said Nicholas de Fleury. 'But since I'm not, let's move to the next point at issue: your future. We reached an agreement.'

'I remember,' she said. Remarkably, she had kept her voice even. The next point at issue. The next item before you all, gentlemen. She was in the presence of the padrone. He had agreed that her child would be safe, and she had agreed to bear him what children he wanted. Fields and fields of corn-marigolds. Her skin contracted. She added impersonally, 'And you have overcome your repugnance.'

He pulled his fingers apart in a generous gesture. 'With great regret, I have to postpone our reunion. That is, I have to leave in a few weeks for Florence, and I may have to winter in Egypt. But I shall be back in Venice next year, and able to send for you and your son. Will Venice suit you, next spring? A happy nesting, like that of the birds?'

She must have moved. He looked up, his expression quite benign. 'I don't ask if you wish this; only if you understand it. If there is any difficulty, my attendants will find you and resolve it.'

She took her time, because she wanted to tremble. She was being given nine months. She was being given nine months because he had been telling the truth in one respect, if only one. He was keeping his promise to Godscalc. And since he had to reshape his whole future, he had released her from his immediate plans.

Also, by next year, he would think, the age of her child could no longer be judged with precision. He could introduce wife and offspring in Venice, a legitimate family. And on that basis, he would expect to beget his next child. Which was, of course, all he wanted. His reward and her punishment.

I have to postpone our reunion. She studied him. He was not a man for whom abstention was normal. Despite Tobie's vagueness, she believed that last night he had bought his own partners. He had had women in Scotland. It was a weakness, and therefore a lever. Nicholas was expert with levers. He used his knowledge of her for his own ends. He had expected to get what he wanted from Godscalc, but hadn't. And suddenly she realised why.

She sat up. The chair, which was a new one, creaked slightly. Everything in the chamber was new; all the furnishings of the wedding night had been swept away, and even the bed stood in a different place. There had been a niche, once, full of objects fashioned by children. She said blankly, 'You told him. You told Father Godscalc about Simon.'

'Well, I showed him diagrams,' Nicholas said. His tunic was lightly embroidered and his buttons were carved from blue stones. With her, he didn't bother with dimples. He added, 'He guessed.'

'Hence the oath about Scotland and Henry.'

'Sadly, yes.'

'And none about the duties of parenthood.'

'Sadly, no. Although he did try to send for the boy. If there is a boy. Is there a boy?'

'I told you. So why did you pledge your word not to go back to Scotland?'

'You tell me,' he said.

'You wanted a quid for your quo.'

'A quid for my quid.'

'You thought it would touch me, and you'd get your hands on the boy.'

'*Get my hands on?*' said Nicholas. 'My intentions towards your invisible son are entirely peaceable. Find me something to swear on, and I shall.' Again, the mockery showed. He was operating on one level. He was operating with his mind; his mind and nothing else, and that was how he must be met.

Gelis said, 'A well-head? Never mind. I've listened to you. You did make a promise. You're keeping it. I am willing to do the same. Not to show you the child, but your other requirement. You needn't wait until spring. I'll come with you to Florence.'

He began to laugh, and halted politely. His gaze brushed her hands, which had clenched. She unclenched them. He said, 'I'm sorry. You don't know about the Bank's arrangements for patrons in Florence. There is a house. That is, they'd make room for you, but I don't think you'd like it.'

His eyes were large and open and grey. He didn't expect her, this time, to believe him although – damn him – it might actually be true. He was chiefly making it clear that he did not want her. Or, amendment: he wanted her when he chose, and not before. And however caustic she proceeded to be – and she was – he had no intention of including her in his itinerary. Which made his itinerary, of course, the object of all her curiosity.

She rode out of Bruges before the rest of his meetings were over. She stayed overnight somewhere public, and she stayed the next night somewhere safe. The following day she arrived with her own private staff at the fortified hall presided over by Margot.

She saw Margot first. Next, she went to the inner room where the night-light burned, and sat down. Later, she rested her chin in her hands and started to think.

Much later, in the privacy of her own chamber, she wrote and sent off two letters. The seal on both was anonymous, and the courier who carried them highly paid. One was to her usual correspondent. The second was addressed to Sir Anselm Adorne.

In later years they would boast, in the company, about the compression of activity that enabled Nicholas de Fleury to leave when he did for Alexandria, changing and adapting all his plans. At the time, despite a swift, unexplained visit to Brussels and another to Antwerp, no one guessed what else he was doing, while the lamps burned day and night and couriers fled to the south.

He elected to take only two officers with him: John his agent, and that German priest who, appearing with his friend at Godscalc's death-bed, had stayed to deliver his eulogy and become his chosen successor as company chaplain. Father Moriz of Augsburg was not destined for Alexandria but for Venice. There – truculent, short-necked, bow-legged – Moriz would partner the patiently labouring Cristoffels at the Banco di Niccolò and cause no disruption in the high life of Julius. He would also, very likely, take control of the Bank's Venetian interests. Father Moriz possessed hidden assets.

These dispositions had been discussed and accepted by Gregorio and Diniz. While staying in Bruges (and near Margot), Gregorio would act as an intermediary between Scotland and Nicholas. Diniz was content to remain with Tilde and manage the company;

he trusted Nicholas to save him his portion of gold. The opinion of Tobie, also left behind, was not sought.

Then the safe conducts arrived, the last arrangements were complete, and the House of Niccolò's personal men-at-arms, its baggage, its household mustered to leave in their splendid black livery with the unicorn rampant. John le Grant, an individualist, wore a green doublet and a battered hat sporting an Imperial Byzantine brooch worth two sheriffdoms. The priest was robed in black, unrelieved, as it happened, by unicorns. Nicholas de Fleury bore the gold chain of his latest Order and his good-humoured expression was matched by the satisfaction on the faces of all those he was leaving behind. He could read what they were thinking.

He was returning to the concerns of the main Bank (at last). He was going to brisk up (about time) its Alexandria agency, and pursue the search for the gold from the *Ghost*. Then come the spring he would sail back to his lady in Venice and the Bank would have a patron once more. Nicholas. A family man, with a fair wife and a . . .

I want the teachers sprung of your line . . .

No. Think. Think. Keep thinking.

He said goodbye to them all. He bestowed a chaste embrace on each of his step-daughters and shook Gregorio by the hand, but could not bring himself to exchange looks with Tobie. Last of all, he leaned from his horse and spoke smiling to Diniz. When he rode off, he was smiling still.

On the tenth day of August, eleven days after Nicholas left, his lawyer Gregorio arrived breathless at the doors of Gelis van Borselen's hall in the country. The ride which had taken Gelis three days had been accomplished by Margot's lover in one. Tobie had agreed to come with him.

It had been Diniz who had provided them with the address of the ladies. Leaning from his horse as he left, Nicholas had given him leave. 'Wait a week, if you like. By then, I shall be out of the country. There are no secrets now. Gelis and I are to meet in the spring. Neither she nor I will mind if you tell Gregorio how to reach the house where you found her.'

And so, freed from his promise, Diniz had told them.

They seemed to be expected. Their jaded horses were taken away, their baggage removed, and the house-steward ushered them into a large, sunny room, its windows set wide to the late evening sun. They were brought washing-water and towels, and given wine. The steward reappeared. He was alone.

Gregorio said, 'Is it inconvenient? We shall stay of course at an inn. But we should like to speak to the ladies if possible.' He wondered why Tobie said nothing. Tobie had said almost nothing ever since Diniz had told them, at last, where to come.

The house-steward said, 'An inn? Honoured sirs, this house is yours for as long as you wish to avail yourself of it. The lady Gelis left orders.'

'Left?' Gregorio said.

'Before she went away. I am sorry: you were unaware? After she came back from Bruges, the lady Gelis packed and departed. Four weeks ago to the day.'

'We had not been told. To go where?' Tobie asked.

The man – a courteous, middle-aged man of the neighbourhood – shook his head in regret. 'To stay with friends. I do not know, I am afraid, where she was bound.'

'But Mistress Margot?' Gregorio spoke. There was already an ache in his chest.

'Went a week after that, in a different direction. Where, again, I do not know; but her message may say. She left a letter for Master Gregorio.'

He heard Tobie speak. 'How could she know we were coming?'

The man looked taken aback. 'Forgive me. I thought it was arranged. At least, I was told to wait for a month and then forward her letter to Bruges. But you are here.'

The packet came and Gregorio opened it. It was a long letter from Margot, repeating her reasons for what she was doing and asking him to understand. She said she loved him. She did not tell him where she was going. She had been upset when she wrote it, for the last words were blotted with tears. She seemed, so far as he could make out, to be saying that they would not have to wait very long.

'But she's right, you know,' Tobie said later, in the chamber they shared for one night. 'I know the word I'd like to apply to the van Borselen family. But if Nicholas comes back from Alexandria and Gelis takes the boy to Venice to meet him, Margot will be free in eight months.' He waited. 'Won't she?'

Gregorio shook his head, and Tobie waited again. Then he spoke again, trying to be patient. 'All right, Goro. I shan't wheedle your secret out of you. I'm sure Margot is safe. But look, I'm worried. Nicholas is a wrecker when he's put under duress. You know that. And he's out there with no wife and no keepers. He's cut me off and left you behind.'

'Temporarily,' Gregorio said. 'He has to run the Bank. He can't do without us completely.'

Tobie looked at him, surprised, and then hopeful. Immediately, he began to feel better. 'No,' said Tobie. 'And meanwhile, I must admit, I'm glad he's got Moriz and John. If anyone can beat him at his own convoluted games, then it's a cold-eyed bigot like Moriz and a bloodless bastard like John.'

Chapter 25

A YOUNG MASKED woman of good appearance entering the Republic of Florence with a well-accoutred retinue and lodged at an unexceptionable address attracted some attention, of course; but in July, men were less vigilant than in cooler weather, and once it was established that the lady was neither a relative of the Medici nor a prostitute, the Republic's interest waned.

So sedate and well planned, indeed, was the arrival of Gelis van Borselen that it was some time before even the ruling family realised that a relative of the Duke of Burgundy was in their midst. And even when news of her identity was finally carried to Piero de' Medici in his sickbed at Careggi, it was several days before it spread to the other vital quarters: those of the dealers and merchants and bankers such as the Vatachino, the Strozzi, and the Florentine agent of the Banco di Niccolò who did not know what to do, but who finally sent a page to her house with a box of sweetmeats and a message begging the lady to order whatever assistance or pleasure she wished.

On the same day, naturally, an urgent letter flew from the same agent to Bruges addressed to the lady's husband, his magnificence the lord Niccolò de Fleury. Gelis did nothing to stop it. Long before it arrived, Nicholas would have left Bruges for Florence. The message would pass him on the way. Or if it did not, Nicholas would hardly turn back; not with a ship already laid up in Pisa (she had checked) with space reserved between decks to take him to Egypt in September. By now, he must be only two weeks away.

Waiting, she maintained, unimpaired, the chaste serenity with which, of late months, she had conducted her life. The town might be unfamiliar to her, but the Italian merchants in Bruges had been ready to tell her about every great house, every market, every church. From Tommaso Portinari she learned where to seek her coloured leathers and silks. From Michael Alighieri, an expert on goldsmiths, she found out where Nicholas and his small band had stopped on their way to Constantinople and Trebizond, and heard the story of the *farmuk*, the spinning toy which had so enchanted the little grandson of the late great Cosimo de' Medici himself. Which had so enchanted Tilde, when Nicholas sent her one. Oh, Nicholas her husband knew whom to beguile; and when; and how. And when to stop.

In Florence, she made herself quickly at home. She installed her household in the middle-sized house discreetly found for her by a van Borselen kinsman. The permanent guest-house, so graphically conjured by her husband, proved to be wholly fictitious. The dame de Fleury, veiled and chaperoned, moved about Florence methodically pursuing her business, and showed no surprise when, at the end of the first week of her visit, the madonna Alessandra Macinghi negli Strozzi, merchant in spectacles, sent her chamberlain to call and presently followed in person.

She was sixty-three now, the matriarch of the once-powerful Florentine Strozzis, the black hair greyed, the eyes dimmed by the painful years of campaigning which, three years ago, ended when the Medici lifted the ban on her sons and allowed them to come back from exile: Filippo Strozzi, already a magnate; and Lorenzo, the discontented juvenile of Bruges, now wealthy and settled in Naples. Lorenzo's mother knew all about Nicholas.

'And so you plan to surprise your young husband. How charming. Although poor Bertuccio, your husband's agent, has been sorely alarmed. But then, one must make allowance for the raptures of first love. I am so glad,' said Monna Alessandra, 'that the young man has achieved such an unexpected and elevating marriage. I must tell you that the Republic was not impressed when he paid his first visit to Florence. There was a certain wildness of conduct.'

'He has matured,' Gelis said. 'But, of course, you have done business with him since, over the spectacles. And the Arab horses. He sent them to Scotland.'

'Ah?' said Monna Alessandra. In a leisurely way, she unhooked the spectacles that hung from one ear and, clipping them over her nose, gazed at Gelis. 'They tell me Scotland is quite important these days.'

Gelis smiled. 'They keep their neighbours occupied,' she said. 'And prevent them from interfering too much across the Narrow Sea.'

'Which suits the Duke of Burgundy and, no doubt, the van Borselen,' the old lady said. 'So it is power that interests you?'

'As it interests you,' Gelis said. She was not ruffled by elderly women. Once, when silly and young, she had thought Lorenzo Strozzi romantic.

The two circles of glass contemplated her. 'As it interests me?' repeated Monna Alessandra. 'I think not. Power for its own sake is dross. I do what I do for the survival of my family. For my sons. Yet you married late and have produced one child, so they tell me, of which you have said nothing at all.'

Gelis lowered her gaze. She said, 'As you mentioned, Ser Niccolò is . . . ardent by nature. The child came early. Perhaps, even yet, I am not wholly reconciled to it.'

There was a silence. She lifted her eyes. The old woman spoke thoughtfully. 'Ser Niccolò, I hear you say, as if a foreign knight-hood made him the equal of a van Borselen. Why proceed to marriage, madonna, when the office of lover was so clearly that for which he is best fitted? Chance-got children are no impediment, as a rule.'

The princely chambers of Bruges seldom produced this kind of astringency. It invited real answers, and for a moment, Gelis was tempted to give them. Marriage, Monna Alessandra, has its uses. To punish your lover. To teach him. To destroy him. To hold him for ever. Or even a combination of some of these things.

Gelis said, 'An orphan has less choice than you might think. My branch of the family is not wealthy and has welcomed the marriage, as you did that of your daughter. Ser Niccolò is a man of uncommon ability.'

'You compare yourself to my Caterina,' said the old lady. 'Yet in a well-arranged marriage the wife does not leave her home without the consent of her husband.'

'I am waiting for him!' Gelis said, smiling. She held down her anger.

'Oh, that is evident,' said Monna Alessandra. 'He did not invite you, and you are chagrined and, disregarding him, come. Why, I ask myself? A lovers' quarrel, now to be mended? I do not think so. A girl in love would besiege me for secrets. What did he do, my high-spirited Nicholas, when he was in Florence? What did they whisper of him when he was a young man – a young, married man – in the East?'

'You want to tell me,' said Gelis.

'I am not sure that I know. There is someone in Florence who does, if you are interested. But you are not, are you?' said Monna Alessandra languidly. 'It is power you seek. Your husband is little – was he ever much? – but the architect of this power. And when he has built to your satisfaction, you will decide, I have no doubt, what to do. Meanwhile, his death would be very unfortunate.'

The glazed circles conveyed a dry admonition, unencumbered by outrage, condemnation or threat. Gelis found herself speaking harshly. 'Rest assured. Chagrin will not induce me to hasten it. I should never kill where I love. And only simpletons kill where they hate.'

'I see,' said Monna Alessandra. Then, more briskly, 'I am glad to have the air cleared. Business does not thrive in an atmosphere of unstable relationships. It is why the proper choice of a wife is imperative. I hear Tommaso is coming here soon? Tommaso Portinari?'

'To renew his contract,' said Gelis. She took a good deal of care, now, with what she said.

'And to have the Medici select him a wife. Lorenzo is in the same situation. Both, I should hope, have lived a full life and are experienced men. Neither will choose his wife blinded with passion. In marriage as in business they may even prove more successful than you,' said Monna Alessandra. 'With your ardent but inconsiderate husband and your premature child. So I advise you again. Choose a course. If in doubt, end your marriage. If you think yourself his intellectual equal – as you may be; he is only an artisan – then bind him into a partnership, and use your sex to keep him there. You have done it already.'

They looked at one another. Gelis said, 'You surprise me.'

Monna Alessandra rose. 'You expect all elderly women to be captivated by his charm. No. He does not use those dimples with me. In return, I take him for what he is, as I take you. One has to live with one's kind, whether one likes them or not.'

'So I have found,' Gelis said.

'Yes. So I must go. You are unlikely to need me. Call on me if you do. The Bank brings me good business,' said Monna Alessandra.

In Florence that year, the month of August proved unpleasantly hot. The wealthy had long since closed their houses and retired to their delicious villas in the campagna. Those who remained tied to town collected their households each evening and rode out to their farms, away from the heat, the smells and the gnats of the river Arno.

Gelis van Borselen, awaiting her husband, found it expedient to emerge a little from her lengthening retirement, and accepted invitations to the homes of distant relatives, and to households such as that of the Acciajuoli, where her husband was known.

Because of the fragile health of Messer Piero, she was entertained in the Via Largo by the lesser members of the Medici family, who several times mentioned how exhausted they had all been by dear Lorenzo's little wedding. Three hundred barrels of *vernaccia* tapped, would one believe, and five thousand pounds of the wickedest sweetmeats – how could one lace up one's *gown*? And the gifts! Although nothing, to be sure, compared to the nuptials of Duke Charles. What had the King of Naples sent to Duke Charles?

She was quite good at that particular game, and held her own. Because of it, perhaps, she found herself included, with other young matrons, in the parties which began to mark the opening of the cooler autumn season – a pretty water-festival, or a mock battle in the Piazza Santa Croce, or a dinner party, or a dance in the Piazza Santa Trinità.

As her circle widened, other small, idle pleasures became open to her. She could have become part of the carefree bands of young men and girls of her own age who strolled through the warm streets in the evening, the men with their lutes, the girls with ribbons and posies, escorted by their liveried torchbearers, taking laughter and music and mischief from one wrought-iron gateway to another.

Once, from her window, she saw a pair she did not know linger behind: the man well made and tall, with a laughing face and brown hair. Then the merriment faded, and he took the girl suddenly in his arms so that both faces were hidden and they stood together, without movement or sound, still as sculpture. It lasted only a moment; then they walked on, their hands tightly linked, while above, she sat helplessly weeping.

But that, of course, was exceptional. The mind was the weapon, the scourge; the senses obeyed it. The mind surveyed the sweet, the seductive dish in which the sharp business sense of Florence was embedded, and compared it with the Burgundian court which, although richer, had nothing of this kind to offer. Entertainment for the wellborn in Brussels was encased in Portuguese etiquette; set about with mechanical figures. Only the common people could be freely exuberant like this – at a skating-party; round a fire; under the coloured lanterns at carnival-time. And only in childhood had she been permitted to join them.

These were the only times, and they were few, when thought strayed and pain would seat itself, mocking, in the familiar place, and her resolution for a moment would falter. For the rest, she set to completing the small, private calls she still had to make. There were not so many. Time was passing, after all. After all, it was September.

She spent an evening with a man called Prosper Schiaffino de Camulio de' Medici, who was Genoese and discontented. Leaving, she was reminded of what Monna Alessandra had said about having to live with one's kind, whether one liked them or not.

She returned the old lady's call, but talked of nothing of consequence except perhaps the grape harvest.

She rode to Porto Pisano to make the acquaintance of the Provveditore, and view the galleys – the *Santa Reparata*, the *San Antonio*, the big *Ferrandina*, the two Burgundian ships – preparing for the autumn departure. If there was to be an autumn departure. The ships for Flanders were safe. But the Levant? With the Turks the way they were? One could only prepare, and then hope. Thus the Provveditore.

She listened thoughtfully and rode back, beset by mosquitoes. The Burgundian galleys (leased to Tommaso Portinari of Bruges) would sail for Sluys in October, carrying alum. The schedule for the *Ferrandina* had not yet been announced. But space on the *Santa Reparata* was still reserved for the Banco di Niccolò, which had made handsome accommodation for its patron, his servants and their goods, about to travel to Egypt.

He was still coming. Confidence renewed, she was able to identify the messenger from Porto Pisano who reported every few days to Messer Bertuccio; just as she knew that Messer Bertuccio would receive reports from the roads to the north the moment that Nicholas came south of Milan.

Nicholas failed to come south of Milan.

September waned. The Arno brimmed because of the rain, and the sea consuls reduced river shipping and had palisades erected as usual. Piero de' Medici returned from the country, and seeing him, men talked in whispers. Messer Bertuccio called and enquired if in any way he could be of service. She saw, to her annoyance, that he was actually hoping for news. She began to realise that she had depended too much on his competence.

October arrived, and brought to Florence two visitors. One was Tommaso Portinari, come to renegotiate his company contract and be allotted a wife. The first was a stranger, whose name, announced by her house-steward, was vaguely familiar.

Nicholai Giorgio de' Acciajuoli was a tall man, grey-bearded and lean and past middle years, with all the hallmarks of his family: the grace, the cultured Florentine accent flavoured with Greek, the large, dark, cynical eye. It was only when he disposed himself, sitting, that she saw that his stick had a purpose: one of his limbs was man-made.

Smiling, he noticed her glance. 'My young friend Nicholas has not regaled you with the tale of our earliest meeting? He shattered my timber leg and was beaten for it. I am glad to see he has found himself a charming wife to curb his excesses. But I forget. Now he is a great man, and full of discretion. And has fathered a fine son, if I am not mistaken?'

'I am sure you are very seldom mistaken,' Gelis said. It was a response, not to the words, but to some challenge she had not yet quite fathomed. She added, softening it, 'But yes, we have a son. A satisfaction which I hope, with your name, that you share.'

'What a kind heart,' he said. 'But alas. Pierfrancesco, my cousin's husband, will tell you. A worthless brother or two – Bartolomeo Zorzi, what have I not done for him? – is all that I may legitimately claim, although, like your husband, I have not wasted my youth. Since you are a van Borselen and accustomed to affairs of the world, I may say without offence, I hope, that few brides can have taken a young man so exquisitely trained.'

A curious remark. He smiled. She said, 'I trust you are going to call us well matched. Or I should suspect that you think me inhospitable. May I offer some wine?'

'My dear madonna!' he said. 'In the domestic arena, the ladies of Flanders are peerless. No, I thank you. I have not come to partake of wine, and it is another form of hospitality to which I was referring. I wished to talk of the sensual arts . . . not in general, merely with reference to your husband's experience.'

'Florence,' said Gelis, 'never ceases to amaze and delight me. It is not a topic I have heard proposed in public before. It is not, I am afraid, one which I intend to debate now. I am sorry. If I cannot press you to wine, it seems that your visit has been wasted.' She rose.

He did not. He said, 'You must forgive me. This poor leg . . . Allow me the space of five minutes to gather my strength, and I shall relieve you of my presence forthwith. Meanwhile, I must reassure you. Debate was not what I had in mind. Merely some thoughts – some random thoughts on the subject of lovers and wives. You knew his first wife? Marian de Charetty? Please sit down. I am really not feeling well.'

If she had him ejected, heaven knew what he would say. She sat. She said, 'I remember the widow Charetty.'

'But of course you were young. A worthy lady, but with little to offer, save her business. But his next wife! The most dazzling courtesan in the Levant! And between – before – after the services of the princesses of Naxos! What finer grooming could a young man aspire to? A partner – two – in whom the exoticism of Byzantium, the refinements of Italy mingle in each flawless, finely judged movement!'

She moved abruptly. He said, 'No! I should not dream of embarrassing you. But I wonder what Nicholas feels when he sees the daughter of Fiorenza about to take his place, as did his wife, in that desirable clasp. Except that the son of Violante would have been worse.'

The large, heavy eyes sustained their sweet smile, challenging her to dismiss him. The thought struck her that he was drugged. Yet there was nothing vague in his speech: she felt compelled to hear all he said. He had judged her better than had Monna Alessandra. Belatedly she realised that it was Monna Alessandra who had sent him. She said, 'You seem to know my husband better than I do.'

'Forgive me, that would not be difficult,' said the man. 'Ah, your expression is meant to remind me of Africa. But carnal knowledge is half an alphabet only.'

'And you have the other half?' Gelis said. She waited, with calm, his words bleeding into her mind. Primaflora, whose arts, subtly transmitted, had become part of the vocabulary he spoke of. And also, it seemed, the princesses of Naxos. Which? And what did Nicholas – did she – owe to them in their lexicon?

Her mysterious visitor had not mentioned her sister. Since he had found out so much about Nicholas, he might even know that. Not all of it, but as much as she had known, at first.

'I have certain advantages,' the man said, 'when it comes to understanding what men are afraid of. You might find my insight can be useful.'

'How would you like me to use it?' she said.

'I knew,' he said, 'I should find your conversation agreeable. You should read more. You should read that old work by Alfonso the Wise of Castile which speaks of the shoulder of Sagittarius the Archer, the Hunter . . .

'But that is by the way. What should you do? I should like you to see that your husband does not marry again. Not, I am afraid, for his sake or yours. I am a person who takes a long view.'

'For the sake,' said Gelis warmly, 'of the next generation? Or your view extends even further?'

'Many find the idea amusing,' he said. 'It is a responsibility, to be sure, to have a child and to choose its marital partner. I may not speak of myself. But take the ladies of Trebizond. Fiorenza of Naxos has a daughter who will alter the course of your life.

Violante of Naxos has a son whose line will make sure that yours will survive. Her husband does not mind, I should say; he has his own consolation. You should know that. But you need not tell Nicholas. It will only encourage him.'

She sat, her chin in her hand, without answering. He said, 'You don't believe me.'

She stirred. 'Did you expect me to? I do wonder, however, why the length of my marriage concerns you. Why should Nicholas de Fleury and I stay together?'

'Did I say that?' the man said. 'I merely suggested that it would be better for everyone if Nicholas did not marry again. Posterity is already served.'

Gelis cast herself back in her chair. She said, 'Well, I understand now. Posterity is the problem. But why should that limit his pleasures? Men should be able to marry, if so inclined, and if the law deems them free. Why not think about gelding?'

There was a contemplative silence. Then the Greek said, 'Tell me. How did he fail? Or how have others offended?'

'It is really hard to say,' Gelis said. 'In any fashion, that is, that would be helpful. Sometimes all a man has to do is to die.'

He said, 'Or a woman, I suppose. You have been helpful, as it happens. And I would do something for you in return. This was purchased by my cousin after the funeral of the artist. I have redeemed it. I thought it should be where it belongs.'

It was a drawing on vellum. It had never been sprayed: a haze of chalk fell from the scroll as she opened it. Inside, the tones of the study were blurred, but the deftness of line had survived: the work of a maestro, though an old one. It showed a youth dropped to one knee, one hand raised, his face turned, with its open, innocent eyes smiling up at the artist. The young man was explicitly, charmingly nude.

In the corner, the artist had put his name, and a single word in Italian. She had heard it before. In the trembling hand, it looked wistful.

She became aware that her thumbnails were white; and the vellum had stretched taut between them. She calmed herself and looked up.

Nicholai Giorgio de' Acciajuoli, brother of Bartolomeo Zorzi, had risen and gone. She knew, however, how to reach him.

It was unfortunate, perhaps, that Tommaso Portinari's visit occurred the same morning.

Tommaso himself, preparing to call on Gelis van Borselen, had changed his dark managerial gown (trimmed with beaver) for a fluted doublet in damask with twisted buttons of gold, and hose whose embroidery did not conceal the interleaving of sinew and muscle between dainty ankle and thigh. An osprey feather from his hat mingled with his clinging black fringe, and his well-bred nose and high cheekbones carried the unmistakable lustre of success.

He was forty-four years of age, and his career was at last attaining its peak. He was manager for the Medici in Bruges. He was the favourite merchant and banker of Duke Charles of Burgundy, and served on his council. His pompous brother Pigello was dead; the other was manager in Milan, and Pigello's sons would perpetuate the Portinari association with the Medici. Messer Piero had promised it.

He had got to Florence before Messer Piero's health became worse and had obtained from his swollen hand the renewal of his partnership contract, securing him, for an input of four hundred pounds groat, a percentage of twenty-seven and one half on all future profits in Bruges, an increase of two and a half.

Best of all, there was no doubt that Messer Piero was going to die and his petty restrictions would perish with him – unless something wholly ridiculous happened in England. And buried with Messer Piero would be his threat to disband Tommaso's two precious Burgundian galleys.

Further, to perpetuate Tommaso's association with the Medici . . . he had been offered a wife, and had met her.

It was no hardship, therefore, to be home in Florence, at the height of the season, dressed as befitted one's station, and calling upon a member of the well-connected van Borselen family.

Tommaso stood on the threshold of Gelis van Borselen's chamber and bowed with great charm, and then, advancing, kissed her hand in court style and, stepping sideways, took the seat indicated as her house-servant withdrew and the lady Gelis sat in her turn.

She looked older. Her hair, drawn back and veiled, revealed good enough bones, but there was a self-possession one did not look for in a woman of – well, of course, she was old. Twenty-four. A first child at that age could unship a woman's figure for life, and no one would know until the buckram came off in the chamber. Birthing was best begun young. And what led up to it. Youth. Unsullied virginity. That passion to learn and to please. That kitten-like, boneless agility . . .

His hostess said, 'Are you well?' and he laughed, dabbing his temple.

'It is warm. I hurried. It is such a pleasure to see you.' He did not, these days, need to envy Nicholas.

He had several things to find out, and conducted the conversation accordingly, with annoyingly little success. She seemed to know nothing of alum, and barely to have heard of the Vatachino firm of brokers. She congratulated him on renewing his contract, and solicited his views on the Medici succession. She asked if there were plans for his wedding.

She knew about the old hag. That is, she had heard from Monna Alessandra Macinghi negli Strozzi that her son Lorenzo was seeking a bride. He had the pleasure therefore of telling her that the lord Piero de' Medici had honoured both himself and Lorenzo by directing them to take in marriage two maidens of the same parentage.

'You and Lorenzo are to marry sisters? How delightful!' said Gelis van Borselen. 'Tell me immediately.'

One did not trust the enthusiasm. One gave oneself the satisfaction, none the less, of describing one's angelic bride: the maiden Maria, daughter of Ser Piero's friend Francesco Bandini Baroncelli.

'Bandini?' said his hostess.

He did not allow his smile to diminish. Pierantonio Bandini Baroncelli was head of the Pazzi, his most serious competitors for alum in Bruges. It was the Medici way, to knit together rivals in marriage. He said, 'I am overwhelmed by the honour. Lorenzo as well. Monna Alessandra was speechless. My dear Maria will join me next year.'

'Next year?' said Gelis van Borselen.

He said, 'I have to go back to Bruges after the marriage. Almost at once. It is sad.'

'Tommaso?' said Gelis van Borselen. 'How old is your wife?'

'By next year? She will be turned fully fourteen,' said Tommaso Portinari. 'I know I may count on you to make her welcome in Flanders. Our children will grow up together.'

She gazed at him in the considering way he disliked. She said, 'You are sailing back with your ships?'

He realised she meant the Burgundian galleys. He said, 'No. They left Civitavecchia five days ago, laden with Tolfa alum.' It had been a small precaution, in case Piero had had some idea of cancelling them. Or even promising them for some crusade.

She said, 'They have sailed? They are not returning to Porto Pisano?'

He was surprised by her tone. He said, 'By now, most ships have

sailed. It is the season. I doubt if you would find any galley still
there save, perhaps, the *Ferrandina*. The King of Naples has sent
word to hold her.'

'But the *Santa Reparata* is there,' she remarked.

He was further intrigued. 'You may be right. My captain did say
that all the lesser galleys had left. But I could send, if you wish it,
to confirm. You had some goods on that ship?'

Her eyes were a thin shade of blue. Nordic blue. She said, 'A
berth. I am here to accompany my husband to Alexandria.'

'But if the ship has sailed . . .' said Tommaso.

'He will take space on another,' she said.

There wasn't another. He didn't say so. He said, 'Demoiselle . . .
Did monsieur your husband arrange to meet you in Florence?'

She looked at him. She said, 'We had no assignation. But – you
will discover – marriage thrives on delightful surprises. He does
not know I am waiting to join him.'

'You should have told him,' said Tommaso Portinari, sounding
grave. 'Alas, demoiselle, your husband is not coming to Florence.
If he meant to sail on the *Santa Reparata*, he must have changed
his plans many weeks since. The Medici have been informed not to
expect him.'

There was a little silence. 'Where is he?' she said.

'At this moment? Precisely where, I gather, even his Bank does
not know. His route was not predetermined. And, of course, winter
is now coming on. Once the snow blocks the passes, the Duchy of
the Tyrol is sealed.'

'The *Tyrol?*' she exclaimed.

'The Alpine range south of Augsburg. The mountainous country
that divides the Germanies from the Italian peoples. Your husband
has gone to do business with Duke Sigismond in person. So
reports say. I wish him every luck.'

She said, 'I was to meet him in Venice, in spring.'

'Then I am sure he will do his best to be there.' He spoke in his
dulcet court voice.

Her predicament did not displease him. The Tyrol was a
spendthrift Imperial duchy whose native resources offered low
yields for astronomic investment. Nicholas was welcome to strand
himself there and face an angry wife at the end, empty-handed.
Tommaso was fairly sure that there was no profit to be had in the
Tyrol. Nevertheless, the commercial restlessness of Nicholas annoyed him.

He looked at the wife of Nicholas with genuine pity. The man
was an artisan. There was no substitute for a formal, proper

betrothal between persons of like rank and resources, who knew what propriety was.

He said, 'I am sorry. There has been a misunderstanding, I can see. But I am on my way back to Flanders and should be happy to escort you safely to Bruges. Then you can return in the spring for your rendezvous.'

She thanked him and accepted, rather flushed. It was a genuine offer. He had calls to make. Carrying and picking up news between the agents of France and England, Genoa and Milan, he found it convenient to seem just a Medici manager about his firm's normal affairs. The company of a lady added to the illusion. A decorative lady with little interest in business.

He left soon, in excellent spirits.

He did not see her walk to a table, and pick up a drawing, and tear it across and across and across.

Chapter 26

NICHOLAS IS A wrecker.

So Tobias his physician had said, having seen it happen before: Nicholas de Fleury stopped in his tracks by some fatal collision of circumstances and responding, not as a normal man would, but with every unit of force he possessed, deployed without discrimination or scruple – unless he were halted. Tobie and Gregorio were not with him now to prevent it. Fortunately, perhaps, the world was full of others who might, although none of them – even Gelis – had guessed quite what was assembling there, in his mind.

To himself, it was perfectly clear. Since he couldn't return yet to Scotland, his projects there had to idle without him. It meant a disarrangement in his private finances which lent Ochoa's gold some slight importance. Associated with the lost gold were some minor scores which, filling time, he might clear off once he reached Alexandria. But, of course, he was not going to Alexandria at the moment. He was going to the court of Sigismond, Duke of the Tyrol.

It amused him, to keep that to himself the whole length of the journey to Ulm. There were four principal passes over the Alpine mountains to Italy. The one that proceeded past Ulm to the Brenner was not an unusual choice for August, and no one questioned his route. Of all the experienced band who accompanied him, only Father Moriz showed impatience as they rode south, clearing his throat as if he would ask a question, or desired to be given some answers. He did not, however, actually speak.

John le Grant, on the other hand, travelled with his mind fixed on his empire in Egypt, and was far from amenable when, in a private room in their warm German tavern at Ulm, Nicholas finally made his announcement.

John repeated it. 'We're going to the Tyrol, not Alexandria.'

'Yes.'

'We're expected to winter at Innsbruck.'

'Yes.'

'You're not going to Alexandria at all.'

'Yes, I am. Later. After the winter.'

'Well, good luck to you,' said John le Grant. 'For I'm going there now. That was my intent.' The chaplain shifted his feet. Le Grant glared at him.

'If you like,' Nicholas said. 'Mind you, the ships for the Levant have all sailed, but you should get one in six months or so, if you're keen.'

'You've already got places booked. On the *Santa Reparata*.'

'I cancelled them.'

'You have ships of your own.'

'They're in service. I would have told you before,' Nicholas said, 'but I had to promise to keep it a secret. Burgundian politics. Even my wife doesn't know. Poor Gelis, no meeting in the spring.'

'You haven't told her?' said Father Moriz in his deep German-Flemish.

'I couldn't reach her,' said Nicholas sadly. 'It seems that she left Bruges and set out for Florence. She hoped to come with me to Egypt.'

'Your wife is *waiting for you in Florence*?' said John.

'So I'm told. But Tommaso Portinari is due to arrive there very soon. I am sure,' Nicholas said, 'that he will see her home safely. Or you will. Perhaps you'd like to take her with you to Alexandria?'

Le Grant stared at him. Father Moriz coughed. He said, 'Myself, Master Nicholas, I hope you will not mind if I come with you to the Tyrol? It ill becomes me to say it, but from the Rammelsberg to the Schwaz, I have found nothing so gripping as the mysteries that lie under the mountains.'

'Mining?' said John le Grant.

'Ah,' said Father Moriz. 'I do not compare my talents with yours. But perhaps you have heard of my colleague – my late famous colleague – Johannsen Funcken?'

Under the red hair, the red eyebrows lowered and the fiery eyes moved and fixed. 'You bastard!' said John le Grant.

'I beg your pardon!' said Father Moriz good-humouredly.

'Not you. Him,' said the engineer. 'Also the most devious . . . Father? You knew about this?'

'No. I guessed. I knew you were a pioneer, whereas you didn't know I was a smelter. I knew that Burgundy was involved with the Tyrol and that my friend Nicholas here had certain interests, and wished to offset any reverses in Scotland. I knew that his rivals, the Vatachino, were extremely watchful. No doubt you perceived as much as well,' said Father Moriz cheerfully. 'But coming from Augsburg, I was perhaps more aware of the possibilities. It is romantic to search for lost gold, but there are wider opportunities to be gained, maybe, in an area closer to the Bank's current efforts. Am I not right?'

'I don't know what you mean,' Nicholas said. 'I just want to hunt chamois, and I hoped John would come with me.'

'Damn you!' said John. But his tone was lacking in venom and there was a renewed gleam of vitality in his eye. The priest sighed.

Nicholas was used to the signs of exasperation and the signs of relief. He knew just how far to go to get what he wanted. He didn't see why life had to be dull. In truth, he quite looked forward to some chamois-hunting.

He did not know that he was the chamois.

From then onwards, the journey was not precisely luxurious, even before they noticed that something was wrong. With the Swiss cantons hungrily eyeing them, the men of the Tyrol were perpetually nervous. The effect of the great new Burgundian pact had not necessarily percolated here, where each pinnacle had its own lord, its own castle; and the sound of the signal-horn wailed and hooted and replicated itself from crag to crag wherever strangers were seen.

As far as the ducal centre of Innsbruck, the journey was painful but passable. They met snow and mud in the high range south of Reutte, but there were elemental inns further down. They would have been more than satisfied with the noisy comfort and coarse glitter of Innsbruck, save that there was no one there to receive them. Duke Sigismond and his court had gone south. Nicholas presented his letters and dragged his retinue forth in pursuit.

They did not enjoy it. On the edge of September, bitter winds scoured the Brenner, and there was frozen mud underfoot and fields of snow on either side. Beyond, they moved downhill from winter to autumn again: from high pastures to meadows studded with pillars of hay.

Here, their way should have been clear. Instead they found themselves pursuing paths which had become steep and ill-kempt and winding, in a land without towns. The smoking hamlets that occupied higher ground shut their doors at the sound of the horns; and it seemed as if, higher yet, eyes were watching, although nothing moved but the slow-grazing cattle and the clustered flecks on the hills which were stags.

When, after a day of blustering wind and chill rain, Nicholas sent the guide ahead with Donat his huntsman to ask hospitality at the gates of a tower, Donat returned white with anger, stripped of both armour and arms, and dismissed with brusque threats of dismemberment. And yet Duke Sigismond knew he was coming. Word by now should have spread.

On the third day, they were forced to live off the land: hunting, fishing and cutting timber for fuel, without which they would have gone hungry. Dionisi his cook made a banquet. On the fourth, compelled by a broken bridge to detour, Nicholas put up a hind and successfully shot it. Then he turned, startled by a loud shout.

He saw one of his men-at-arms fall, wounded by the same kind of bow that he carried. The man who shot him sprang from the rocks, and twenty others leaped out beside him. On every side, axes flashed and spears glinted and bearded men began to rush forward, yelling. John le Grant whipped out his sword. The men-at-arms furthest off were already struggling.

It was an instinct, to fight; but the truth was that it was hopeless. The surprise had been total. The terrain gave little foothold; the path had already been blocked. The Flemings closed ranks and did what they could. Nicholas bellowed exhortations and warnings and heard Father Moriz shrieking in German as well. '*What are you doing? You are attacking the guests of Duke Sigismond!*'

John le Grant spoke between blows. 'We've been hunting on the Duke's territory. They want to take and hang us in public as poachers.' A bolt rang on his shield.

Nicholas said, 'What do you think? I'd rather stand trial than die now, even if we hang from a roof at the end of it. Father? Ederic? Donat? Do we surrender?'

'We surrender,' said Father Moriz and, lifting his crucifix, walked forward declaiming. Nicholas swore and thrusting past, managed to share the first blow that sent the priest reeling. John le Grant, uttering Aberdonian and German profanities, contrived to take most of the second. A dozen men fell on them. When they were eventually dragged to their feet and disarmed, it seemed as if surrender had in fact been accomplished: the head of the Banco di Niccolò was in the hands of a group of powerful tousle-haired men whose felt hats bore the badge of a lion.

When asked what lord they belonged to, they laughed, and threw their captives on horseback and tied them. Then they set off in line.

The bound men were all bleeding. It was late afternoon and not warm. The guide had disappeared, and they had been separated from their packs and stripped of all that was valuable on their persons. John said, 'Where are we?'

Nicholas said, 'In the Tyrol.' His head was ringing and one arm was quite dead and possibly broken.

John said, 'Nicholas?'

Nicholas said, 'It's terrible, terrible.'

'Oh, Christ,' said John le Grant, with familiar feeling. The German priest looked at them both. John le Grant said, 'He thinks he knows something we don't. Nicholas, they aren't the Duke's men. They'll take us to some brute-ignorant lord who *will* hang us.'

'Maybe,' Nicholas said. 'Upside down, I believe. They tie whatever you've poached to your feet. Remember, you shot the hind and I picked off a couple of pheasants. Do you see what I see up there?'

The others fell silent. They had hoped for a town perhaps, where a ducal officer might have been summoned. Or even for a simple encampment, for much can be made to happen under cover of night. Instead, what straddled the pass was a fortress. An old one, its walls broken and cracked, but still high enough to thwart even an optimist. Within, from the sluggish smoke rising, there was someone newly in residence.

John said, 'I'm going to do something. There won't be a chance once we're inside.'

'No,' said Nicholas. 'And if you try it, I'll kick you unconscious.'

'You've got a plan. Tell it. You know your plans never work until I've checked them,' said John le Grant. Father Moriz gazed ahead, looking solemn.

'I haven't time. Here we are,' Nicholas said.

All the while they were being pushed through the gates, and untied, and beaten across the filthy enclosure to the dungeons, Nicholas thought of the fuss Julius would have made. He missed Julius and his outbursts, on occasion. John's outbursts were, of course, not outbursts at all. Then their captors left, and the dungeon door closed and was locked, and everyone looked at him hopefully.

He said, 'All right. I've got the dice. Let's get comfortable. Then I'm putting up ten Rhenish florins as prize money.'

One of the young men-at-arms said, 'My lord, how long . . .?' and stopped when Ederic, Nicholas's manservant, looked at him.

Nicholas said, 'An hour. If it's over that, I'll double the prize money.' No one asked how he was going to measure the hour.

The wounded man was not badly hurt, but had bled a lot. Dionigi was lame. Those who were fit crawled about helping to bind up the cuts of the rest. The roof was so low that one bracket-candle lit the whole chamber. There was no food and no water, but the straw on the floor was at least fresh.

He was quite good, himself, at measuring time. John, he knew, was even better. Just short of the hour, by his reckoning, they heard footsteps approaching, and the door opened upon several men. One of them held something out. The man said in German, 'Whose is this?'

Nicholas did not reply, but waited for Father Moriz to glance at him. Father Moriz then spoke. 'It belongs to this knight. To the lord Nicholas de Fleury of Burgundy, guest of Duke Sigismond.'

The speaker in the doorway looked from Nicholas to the priest. He said, '*Diese ist der Orden van der Schottische Einhorn.*'

'That is true,' said Father Moriz.

'But you are German,' said the man in the doorway. It could be seen now that he was young, and wearing a sword under a stiff leather jacket.

'From Augsburg. That is so,' said the priest. 'Master John here also speaks excellent German, although he is Scottish. And Sir Nicholas has some of the language. We should like to meet your lord and remedy this mistake.'

Nicholas continued to look as if he had some of the language. He was pleased as well as surprised. He had expected to have to do some of that himself. He was also pleased and surprised for other reasons, in spite of the cold.

The man said, 'I have orders to take the Collar's owner upstairs. The two German-speakers will, please, accompany him.'

'And the others?' said Father Moriz. 'They require food, drink, medical help . . .'

'It will be seen to,' said the man. He set the door open, and Nicholas walked out with Father Moriz and John.

It was like another occasion. That time, they had all been in prison together – Tobie, Diniz, Astorre, as well as John. That time, he went to meet death and found something else. Death was never the worst that could happen.

The dripping stairs of this castle were nothing like those of Zacco in Cyprus. Fortified though it was, it had been built and was used as a hunting-lodge: he could hear dogs yapping and growling and had seen the good range of stables. The man in the leather jacket walked ahead, but two armed servants followed. It was a steep climb and a long walk through tortuous chambers thereafter.

Feeling had come throbbing back to his shoulder and beat in his head. The side of the priest's face was bruised, and John le Grant limped.

It seemed to Nicholas that he was exaggerating the limp. He felt alive in spite of the pain, and expectant, and wished in a sudden blind flash that he were free, as once he had been, to savour all that was happening. Then their conductor stopped and knocked on a door, and spoke to the person who opened it. It closed, then opened again. This time, the man in the jacket led the way forward and bowed. 'Your grace, the knight of the Unicorn Collar. Sir Nicholas de Fleury; his priest; and a Scotsman named John.' He bowed.

The room they had entered was of moderate size but warmed by a brazier, and the plaster walls were draped with patterned hangings and lit by wax candles in good polished sconces. The furniture, though solid, was equally good: a pair of stout coffers topped by tapestry cushions, a set of shelves on one wall bearing dishes of pewter and silver, a number of cups and a vessel of wine. There was a prie-dieu in a corner, and a basin and ewer in another, with a rack of plain towels. The master chair stood by the brazier, and the board beside it bore two heavy books and some sewing on a table-carpet of green cloth. The occupant stood by the window surveying them.

'Your grace,' Nicholas said. He heard John draw in his breath. He spoke to a woman.

She was nearer John's age than his: past her middle thirties, and already too stout for her height, although her hair still showed red under the old-fashioned double-peaked headdress. Her sleeves were fur-edged and trailed, and her high bosom was pinned with a brooch made of rubies. The stones were formed in the shape of a lion; the same as that worn by the men who had brought them.

'My grace, is it?' she said. 'It seems my nephew's making mair free than he should with his unicorns. What for was that Collar?'

Le Grant's face had turned red. Nicholas said, 'For getting your niece's husband out of the country. You may not approve.'

'Thomas Boyd?' said the woman. 'Oh, deary dear. Oh, deary deary dear.' She walked forward slowly. 'Were ye hurt just now?'

'Yes,' said Nicholas. 'Most of my party were injured.'

'Sons of Belial,' she said. 'They were to ca' canny. I told them. Jack, go and see to it.' The man in the leather jacket hesitated, then went out. The lady of the chamber who had opened the door closed it and sat just inside, her eyes lowered. She was not young, but handsome after an older fashion. Her mistress said, 'Jack Lindsay. His father came out with me and married a German. It can happen to anybody. Well, come to the fire: you look as if ye need it. I'll get my physician to see you. Does the priest not have Scots? Where are you from?'

'Aberdeen,' said John le Grant, thus addressed. He walked forward. 'Your grace.'

She said, 'You don't know who I am. He does.'

'I didn't tell them,' said Nicholas. 'This is Father Moriz, an expert in smelting. He does speak English. And John le Grant, mining engineer, navigator, gunner. He has worked in Germany as well as Constantinople. John, this is her grace the Duchess Eleanor of the Tyrol, lady wife to Duke Sigismond and father's sister to James, King of Scotland.'

There was a silence. The Duchess took the big chair and picked up her sewing. 'So you didn't tell them. Well, I have to say the Duke was forgetful as well. He's away. I wouldn't exactly know where, but of course he'll hear how ye mistook the way and got into trouble, and send to Brixen to have ye all join him. In due course. News takes time to travel.'

John le Grant said, 'This isn't Brixen? Your grace?'

'Dear me, no,' said the Duchess Eleanor. 'That's seventeen miles to the south. We'll go there directly. No, you've wandered. It's the guides. You can't get good guides nowadays. Do you like soup? My cook makes a good soup. You go off and get yourselves seen to, and we'll talk properly when you're done. You're not very old.'

Nicholas turned at the door, where the man she called Lindsay had reappeared, followed by her lady-in-waiting. Nicholas said, 'I've aged lately, your grace.' She smiled as they filed out.

She had told him just enough to let him settle everyone's doubts. First his men, cramming down ale and venison and thick, filling bread in a bare room which, though draughty, wasn't a dungeon, and had pallets already brought in for the night. By then, even the injured looked brighter.

'We were in the wrong valley. But we've had some luck from it. These are the Duchess's men, and she's here, and she's anxious to do everything she can to make up for it. We're off to Brixen, her own castle, soon, and then the Duke himself will send for us.'

The men accepted it. Niccolino always fell on his feet.

Once the ale had taken effect, he found a place where he could talk to John and the priest and the three men of his own household.

They were sober, as he was. Donat started before he could speak. 'That guide was bribed! Those places he led us to!'

'Bribed, of course. By the Duchess, one supposes,' said Father Moriz.

'Of course.' Nicholas looked across at Donat. 'Your back hurts. So does my arm. She thought it necessary. She's a capable woman controlling a twenty-year marriage to a self-indulgent, indolent profligate.'

'They say,' remarked John le Grant, 'that he has a bastard for every week of the year.'

'And they had one child, who died. He also spends money. On the mistresses. On gambling. On new castles – Sigmundsburg, Sigmundseek, Sigmundsfreud, Sigmundskron, Sigmundslust, Sigmundsfried. On birds and horses and dogs for the hunt. On the advisers he favours, and the men of culture he likes to sustain. He has already sold off all his father's land in the Confederate States, and now has mortgaged Alsace and the Black Forest.'

'To the Duke of Burgundy,' Ederic said. Ederic came from Antwerp.

'An encroachment the Swiss don't appreciate. The cantons are nervous of Burgundy and have the best fighting men in the world. The Tyrol sits between, and can't afford to pay mercenaries for anything. Sigismond thinks the Duke of Burgundy will lend him troops to protect him or – madly – attack the Swiss if he wants to. The Duchess doesn't think the Duke will. The Duchess thinks that the Tyrol needs help. Not soldiers; not at once, anyway. But investment. A way to realise its own wealth, so that no matter how much Sigismond spends, there will always be more.'

'Silver,' said John le Grant. The priest's face remained undisturbed. The remaining three looked uneasy.

'And copper. More valuable sometimes than gold.'

'And the use of your Captain Astorre and his army?' It was the priest.

'They possibly think so.'

'You sound as if you'd had a talk with the lady already. This was the meaning of your conversation upstairs?'

'She will call me back,' Nicholas said. 'When my broken head and the drink should have done her work for her.'

'She sounds an astute woman. Why has she stayed with the Duke?' This time, it was John.

The priest said, 'Ah, no. Why has the Duke stayed with her? That is the nub of it.'

The rest of the men had started to sing. Against the noise,

Nicholas talked, and the others listened, the priest and the engineer addressing one another and him, their voices considered, vehement, thoughtful. They were all flushed. Presently the man in the leather jacket came back, and walking over to Nicholas required him to follow. If you listened carefully, you could hear the thread of Scots under the German.

John le Grant spoke to Nicholas in rapid Italian. 'Maps, remember.'

The young man turned. 'There are some maps,' he said shortly in the same language. Below the Italian, too, the Scots lay submerged. If he was James Lindsay's son, then he was full cousin to David Lindsay, Earl of Crawford. Thinking, Nicholas followed him back to the Duchess's chamber. This time there was no one in attendance, and Lindsay, after introducing him, left, closing the door.

Eleanor of Scotland sat unchanged with her embroidery, a cup of wine at her hand. The embroidery had materially grown. She said, 'Pray be seated. Nowadays, I prefer to talk business in German. I am told Flemish is not unlike.'

'We can speak German, your grace,' Nicholas said.

She looked up. Her skin was uneven and ruddy, and she had the long Stewart nose of her father. Her mother had been English and royally connected. Her father, caught at eleven, had lived a prisoner for eighteen years in England. A generation later, one of her sisters had been Queen of France and another had married Wolfaert van Borselen. Few statesmen had observed the shifts and changes of power as narrowly as Eleanor of Scotland.

She said, 'I hear you have an interest in mining, and a certain amount of bullion to invest.'

'That is so,' he said. 'A considerable amount, if our surveys prove fruitful. What you have on the banks of the Inn may be as fine as the alum at Tolfa. But it requires to be expertly mined.'

'Alum?' she said. Her needle worked.

'Other minerals are heavily taxed. Crude mines may be less attractive than newly dug shafts. Good ventilation and drainage cost money. And so do my experts. Indeed, even alum has problems.'

'Then why are you here?' she said.

'To hunt,' he said. 'With your permission, this time. My men are experienced. If there is no quarry worth our joint attention, we shall tell you. If your grace will give leave.'

She said, 'I shall do better than that: I shall come with you. You will find no better terrain than this in the north, although, of course, there is fine sport to be had about Trent. We shall put off our journey to Brixen. We shall hunt. And then, if you have a proposal, you shall put it to my husband's adviser. You have heard of Antonio Cavalli?'

'Was he not in Scotland?' said Nicholas. He might have been more straightforward had he known how much she knew. He had heard, at Dean Castle, all about Antonio Cavalli. He had heard all about Eleanor of the Tyrol. And what he hadn't learned there, he had learned at court. The Scottish Court, and that of Brussels.

She was answering, undisturbed. 'Master Cavalli stayed with my niece at Kilmarnock. The lady Mary, Countess of Arran. Your wife served her once. You say the Countess has left Scotland with her husband?'

Her voice remained mild. Nicholas said, 'She was attached to him. Had he stayed, the King your nephew would have been forced to execute him. Instead they are both free.'

'If in exile,' said the Duchess.

'At least,' Nicholas said, 'exile can be revoked, unlike death.'

She said, 'For one? Or for both?'

Nicholas said, 'I doubt if the Earl of Arran would be allowed to return. His lands are too valuable.'

'You expect to acquire some?' she said. 'Or have you lost interest in Scotland? Having poached, so I am told, our good goldsmith Wilhelm of Hall?'

'I have an office there,' he said. 'And a house in the Semple district of Renfrewshire. A little land seldom comes amiss.'

She stitched. She said, 'My father is buried in Paisley. The monks still have their fustian sent from Ulm. The King my nephew would like us to send him cannon.' She looked up.

'Guns are fashionable,' Nicholas said. 'But, of course, their utility depends on the skill of the casting.'

'A badly cast gun killed my brother,' she said, and stuck the needle finally in her work. She rose. 'As you know. You have been luckier today. I am going to give you some wine. Your arm looks painful.'

They had put it into a sling. He got up as well. 'It will be stiff tomorrow, that's all. Don't trouble. I drank something below.'

She paid no attention, crossing to the board and pouring with her own hands. Her heavy robe smelt faintly of horse. He thought of other women of power in his life: the brave and delicate mother of the Persian prince Uzum Hasan; the noseless grotesque in Cyprus who had given birth to the beautiful Zacco; Bel of Cuthilgurdy, if you liked, whose influence came not through a son or a grandson but by way of a peculiar strength of her own.

Eleanor of Scotland was not a woman of Bel's kind although, coming back, she dropped into Scots as she put the cup in his hand. 'Drink it. It's a receipt I keep for sair heids. Whiles, it seems that every princeling in Europe sends his bairn to the Tyrol to be reared, and a good smack or a physic does wonders. I'm told ye've begotten a knave on your wife?'

'A son of six months.' The outer voice answered. The inner voice contradicted. A son of eight months, *eight months* by now. If it was a son. If it was anything. Four teeth in a smile. Kicking. Or crooked. Or dead and decayed in the earth.

The wine was strong, with something herbal in it. He added aloud, 'We are delighted.'

'I'm sure of it. An heir. My niece the Countess was very taken with Gelis van Borselen. I should tell ye that the wine will put ye to sleep in ten minutes, so you'd better finish it off and get gone. I'm not a great believer in conversations over the grape. Besides, I've a harder head than you'd expect. I've had practice.'

He got up. Her unsmiling face appeared made of red granite; her eyebrows were black. He realised that it was her eyebrows that he should have been looking at. The dread left his mind, and he laughed.

'Aye,' she said. 'Well, we've got one reaction that you meant. Let's see tomorrow if we can find one or two more.'

Next day, riding out at her side, he felt restored and a trifle light-headed. He did not remember going to bed, but deduced that his lapse had not only been condoned by the rest but appreciated: no one much liked being with a man who was afraid to take a drink. He wondered why, possessing such a helpful beverage, she had not tried to make better use of it. It put him in her debt. That was probably why.

He knew now where they were. The purpose of this great party – horses, hounds, huntsmen, women and men of her court and her household, with their packhorses and tents, their wagons of necessities and provisions – was to comb the mountains for game, it was true. It was also to bring before him all that the Duchess wished him to see.

That first day, she conversed in desultory German. She was a magnificent shot. Her eye to her bow, she spoke wistfully of her visits to Salzburg, that last hope of the childless. As her shaft flew, she talked nostalgically of her rambles through the salt mines of Hallstatt, merely pausing to register the accurate dispatch and fall of a pheasant, a bustard, a hare. Drawing to a halt for cheese and ale, she would get him to demonstrate the use of the short Turkish bow from the saddle, turning at the gallop to shoot into his own horse's hoof-marks.

She had learned hunting, herself, very young. The Sinclairs were excellent tutors. But, of course, she had lost her father when she was four and her mother at twelve, the year she was sent to the French court. She had been permitted to stay in France, too, although her sister the Queen had been dead for three days when she landed. What did Sir Nicholas know of the French style of hunting? They discussed it.

They stalked a herd of red deer, and made a kill. Afterwards, she gave the dogs their bread sopped in entrails, as she had given him his doctored wine. He treated her now with extreme caution.

She discovered, as he knew she would, that they had stayed at the Sterzing inn frequented by silver-miners, and had looked at the mines. They had cast an eye, before they became lost, at Gossensass. He was hopeful that she would steer him to Bruneck and wondered if, after Brixen, she would take him where he really wanted to go. He thought now that she would.

Whenever she mentioned workings, John began to ride very close, and so did the priest. Nicholas had made no real assessment of Father Moriz, other than that he was experienced, self-reliant, and rather too loquacious. It seemed enough for the present.

In any case, after the wine and a heavy day's hunting, few of them felt as brisk as the Duchess, whose special draught had brought not only sleep but a curious detachment which lasted for the whole of that day. She spoke of Hallstatt, and the thin, clear air inside his head connected it instantly, as it should, with the salt mines of Taghaza. His thoughts did not go beyond that, because his personal embargo was absolute; but so far as it went, he experienced no distress. It was as if all substance had been withdrawn from his mind, leaving nothing but ether. It was not disagreeable.

The sensation continued all day, and was still present when they reached the temporary lodge within which it was proposed they should sleep, and the Duchess commanded an expedition to provide fresh fish for supper. The stream they found was rushing and cold, and the trout so plentiful that the party stayed until sunset burned on the peaks, and transformed the roaring spate into flame. Nicholas said, 'A mill could work here.' John looked at him.

'It could,' said the Duchess. She had stopped. 'They are most useful on bigger rivers, near towns. You have seen them.'

'Floating mills,' Nicholas said. Then he said, 'No, that's nonsense. The stream is too small.'

To his vague confusion, she took him up. 'Are you interested in water? Come with me. And your two colleagues. No' — to her chamberlain — 'we shall not be long. We are walking the other way up to the lodge.' And, turning, she led the way uphill, and away from the river. Her officers stood watching, and then returned to their business. The senior lady-in-waiting stood longest before turning back.

Now the slope they were mounting was wholly dark. The sun had left the river below and was slipping higher and higher in the opposite wall of the valley, the distant mountains still dazzling behind. The route the Duchess had chosen was steep and rough and full of boulders: when Nicholas offered his arm, she took it. It was, he found, only a courtesy: she was as sure-footed on the hill, despite her shortness and bulk, as she had been firm in the saddle. John le Grant and the priest, protectively climbing behind, must have already guessed that the safeguard was unnecessary.

In turn she, too, must have satisfied herself about their adequacy on hills. She said, 'In the Tyrol, you have already discovered, huntsmen require to be mountaineers. Now it is easier to talk, away from the noise of the water. You are afraid of water? Of the water back there?'

It was dark now below, where the river had dashed and swirled a moment ago, the flames surging. He did not want to speak.

The Duchess said, 'Think of water. There is no harm in it. Cold, fresh, rushing water, sweet and blessed and plentiful.'

Cold, fresh water swirling about him. Not starlit ice, but a bridge hanging with fire. And from before and behind, death approaching, because he had bidden it. Approaching not for a yellow-haired woman — not yet. But for himself. He knew, before it happened, that whatever possessed him was again about to give voice. When it did, the verse was unknown.

> *Ta femme sera de la sorte*
> *Dans les parois de ta maison*
> *Comme est une vigne qui porte*
> *Force bons fruicts en la saison.*

A wash of pain followed, and he fell.

He did not drag her with him, because she freed her arm a moment before, almost as if she were expecting it. At the time he was only aware of the shock of meeting the ground; and of the exclamations of John and Father Moriz behind. The Duchess spoke. 'Leave him. He is not, I think, hurt.'

'No,' said Nicholas. He began to collect himself, and his

thoughts. He had taken the fall on his right side, his good side, and his right hand felt odd. Otherwise there was nothing wrong. He had been dreaming, of what he could not quite remember. Of water. He said, 'My hand.'

The Duchess said, 'It's a real treat, now and then, to be proved right. Gentlemen, are you fit?' Her eyes gleamed in the dusk. Nicholas got to his feet.

John le Grant, coming forward, said, 'Your grace, we didn't fall. Are you all right?'

Nicholas grunted. The Duchess said, 'No, *you* didn't fall. You felt nothing. Neither did I. The alchemist who walked here with me some months ago didn't fall either, but he stopped at the same place. The water he found – the excavation is covered – will serve the lodge when it is channelled.'

Father Moriz said, 'Naturally, the work left the surface uneven. But no harm has been done.'

John le Grant brushed that aside. 'How did your expert find water?'

'With a plumb line,' said the Duchess. 'I brought one. Or simply by the sensation he feels in one hand.' She spoke to Nicholas.

He said, 'If I had another cup of wine, I could do it again?' He could not see her expression.

She said, 'The wine had little to do with it, except for clearing your mind. Natural forces need space.'

He said, 'I think you are reading too much into a fall. You are saying that you think I divined the presence of water? And that you *expected I would*?'

'Yes,' she said. 'Oh, be angry. No man likes a stranger walking inside his head. But if you know about me, then I know more about you. Your friends tattle. There is a physician who says that you dream.'

'Everyone does,' Nicholas said.

'To be sure.' Her voice was bland. 'Aye, well. I won't ask what you were dreaming down there, but something about that river struck deep. Enough, I hoped, to bring alive this gift if you had it. You have.'

'I fell,' repeated Nicholas. His shoulder hurt. He wanted to shiver with cold.

She continued patiently. 'And it is important. To you, and to me. For if you can divine the presence of water, you can divine other things.'

'No,' said the priest. It had the weight of a command.

'It comes from God,' said the Duchess Eleanor. 'Do you doubt it?'

'I have seen it done,' said John le Grant. 'But why Nicholas?'

'Either of you might have had the same power. Many do. I suspect,' said the Duchess Eleanor, 'that it might have been more convenient for the House of Niccolò to discover such a gift in one of its clerks, rather than the man at its head. But you have him. And he is valuable. So let's go up and get warm and talk this over.'

Nicholas said, 'You said you have a plumb line?'

He saw the flash of her teeth as she smiled. Below and above, servants were waiting with torches. She said, 'A canny man, your Nicholas de Fleury. Aye. There you are.'

The object she produced from her cloak was a toy: a ball of hazelwood on the end of a long hempen string. With a little work, it would have made a good *farmuk*. Nicholas took the string between finger and thumb and let the thing dangle at arm's length, the ball at its end swaying gently. It gleamed faintly in the dim torchlight, its shadow lost in the blackness of theirs. He watched, keeping still.

The ball was increasing its swing. The cord rocked in his grasp: he tightened his grip of it. The swing became stronger and wilder. Now it described not a line but an oval, a circle. The ball cast itself outwards, dragging, leaping, and began to gyrate in a large ragged ring with a power that made his arm crack and began to flay the skin from his finger. It made a moaning sound, circling: *Oh mill! Oh mill! Oh mill! Oh mill! Oh mill!*

It throbbed and growled: **What hast thou ground?**

Nicholas hurled the thing from him.

'Yes,' she said. 'Well, you're as well to know. Come. We'll be catching our deaths.'

Chapter 27

'I FORBID IT,' said Father Moriz. 'Whatever my secular training, I have your souls in my charge. The Duke defied the Church; now the Duchess dabbles in wickedness. You will refuse, or I leave.'

The German gnome had turned into a firebrand. Fortunately, Nicholas thought, they had been given some time alone, he and John and the priest, before the Duchess commanded their company. The lodge being small, they were crowded into a room the size of a garderobe, but at least they weren't outside under canvas. He felt as if he had either just been very ill, or was about to be. He said, 'All right, I agree. I don't do that again.' He sucked his forefinger, which kept bleeding.

'Well, we know why,' said John. 'You were scared bloodless, admit it. Of a bob on a string? All right: I've never seen it done that way before, but divining-rods aren't new. The Queen of Sheba walked in on her webbed feet and gave the secret to Solomon.'

'I suppose it's a precedent,' Nicholas said.

John calmed. He said, 'Well, you suffered a shock. But, Father, the finding of water can't be a sin? Moses did it.'

'The Lord God is speaking through Nicholas?' the priest said. 'Or just through Eleanor of Scotland's webbed boots?'

Nicholas said, 'I don't think you can fault her private life or her faith. The Tyrol needs silver. It argues courage to seek it in this way.'

'She let you take the risk,' said Father Moriz. 'What happened to the diviner she spoke of?'

'He died,' Nicholas said. 'She didn't hide anything. She arranged for you, a priest, to attend. We are not being compelled to do this.'

'But we'll lose our chance at the mines,' said le Grant. 'Moriz, if we used a rod and found another Tolfa in Italy, would the Holy Father condemn us?'

Father Moriz put his hands on his knees. He said, 'The Pope is in Rome. Nicholas is here, and in danger. If the Pope endorses the divining practice, then I might change my mind. On the other hand, I might not.'

'Moriz!' said John. 'Such uncanonical pride! What would the Cardinal say?'

'Nothing,' said Nicholas. 'He's dead, after an acrimonious dispute with the Duke over silver mines. Do you suppose Nicholas of Cusa used rods?'

'I thought you didn't want this,' said the priest. His face, coarse as a tuber, was attentive and his eyebrows stood out like brushes. He said, 'I saw what happened.'

John said nothing. Nicholas said, 'I may not want it, but I shan't stand in your way. It is for you and John to argue it out.'

'But you must have some view,' the priest said.

Nicholas said, 'It is a mystery. The end product is potentially good. If I felt physically threatened, perhaps I simply wasn't prepared. It was also a . . . vivid experience in other ways. One would have to learn to control it.'

'You could pray,' said the priest.

John said, 'You could pray with him. The rod could be blessed. Surely this is a life-giving mystery, not an evil one. Confined to the wilds of the mountains it threatens no one; no one but our employers will know of it. You have faith. You have studied the God-given stores that lie under the ground. You must believe this miraculous key to their whereabouts will do nothing but good?'

There was no need, really, for Nicholas to speak any more. Between then and their audience with the Duchess Eleanor, John did all the persuading for him.

Hence, when in due course they took their places before her, the Duchess Eleanor was pleased to learn that the discreet use of the divining-rod, closely supervised by Mother Church, had been added to the services the Bank was about to propose. They discussed these in detail, and also their journey to her castle of Brixen, and the explorations they would make in the south. What that entailed was left unspoken.

The discussion reverted last of all to the Duke, and the strategy to be followed (the word was not used) when the lord of the Tyrol finally summoned them. 'It may not be,' said the Duchess, 'for a week or two. He is in a district he especially favours, and the hunting is good. Also, he has business to transact with some broker. You may know him. A man called Martin, representing the Vatachino company of merchants.'

She was sewing again. The silence was quite brief. Nicholas said, 'Our paths cross, from time to time. In fact, the Vatachino interests coincide sometimes with ours.'

'So Master Cavalli was saying. He is with the Duke,' said the Duke's lady. 'He knows my mind. He will see that nothing is settled unwisely.'

She laid down her needle, licked her finger and, reaching for a new length of yarn, picked up the needle and forcibly fed it. When she held the thread taut, the needle hung like a very thin poacher. She looked up and smiled.

'So,' she said, 'you must be glad that you have something unique to offer as well. A cup of wine, now, to help the three of you sleep on it?'

The wine proved to be ordinary and Nicholas, who had refused it, felt cheated. Back in their room, John le Grant manufactured outrage by the bale.

'I thought she said she didn't know where the Duke was? *The hunting is good.* I'll wager it is. I wager she knows every mistress and every bastard; we'll probably find half of them guests at Brixen. But the bitch! Not telling us . . .'

They had been over it five times already. '. . . Not telling us about the Vatachino,' Nicholas supplied. 'Well, there's a lot we didn't tell her. And she says they won't have concluded a deal. And I believe her.'

'Yes! Because now she knows our terms, she'll use that to push down –'

'John?' said Father Moriz from his pallet. 'Could we have some rest, do you think? It has been a long day.'

It had. A day Nicholas would rather not have had. No. One did not run away, however devastating the revelation had been. John had been partly right. It was loss of personal control that he feared; and the happenings today, part illusion, part reality, had combined two manifestations of it. He had not wanted to go on.

Well, now he was compelled to. And although he had tried to deny they existed, he had early started to realise that he would have to confront the episodes in his life he did not understand, and try to deal with them.

He did not envisage switching from numbers to prayers, but need not say so. Like John, he wanted Father Moriz to stay. It occurred to him that Father Moriz had a very good idea to what degree his various skills and doctrines were held in esteem. It further occurred to him that Father Moriz was bent on changing those proportions, and very likely had had no intention of leaving at all. This German was a man of conviction. One did not have to make allowances for Father Moriz.

John, half undressed, was still up and still talking. Nicholas slammed over and struck out the light. There was an astonished roar.

He wished he had taken the wine.

The castle of Brixen, when they reached it, was as crowded as every other home of the Duke's at which, by that time, they had stayed. By that time it was evident on what Sigismond of the Tyrol was exhausting his inheritance. The palace-fortresses were the work of a nervous man, never sure of his countrymen, and of a vain man, cousin to the Emperor of the West, who liked to carry from castle to castle a scholarly entourage, a continuous stream of eminent guests, a herd of countless liveried servants.

John, attempting to assess his expenditure, had based his guess on the size and quality of the Duchess's hunting-party, on the magnificence of its hounds and its horses, its birds and its weapons and the priceless harness of its mounts.

Now they were familiar with painted chapels dressed with silver and gold, with libraries of singular books, with chests and shelves which carried, still, the remains of the ancient treasures the House of Habsburg had acquired or been given: the silk dalmatics, the sabres, the crowns with their jewels and enamels, the crystal goblets and altar-frontals, the caskets and relics.

In Brixen, significant and well escorted as they were, the company of the Banco di Niccolò merged into a community of many hundreds, of which the Duchess, lately their apparently sole companion, was the hub. In their daily excursions abroad, there were others now to guide them. And once they were in the hills, there was no longer any pretence that their business was hunting.

They visited mines, and the mountain slopes beside mines. In the Tyrol, the word for a miner and for a mountaineer was the same. And Nicholas used both the pendulum and the hazel rod he had been given and found silver twice in a week. The first time, it was a bag of coins concealed underground. The second time, it was genuine. An hour with pickaxes showed what they had discovered.

Each time, wet and exhausted, they came back to the warmth and bustle of the town and the castle and, retiring, wrote out their reports, once in code for themselves and once in edited form for the Duchess. These were carried to her by Lindsay. All the rest of their entertainment lay in the hands of noblemen who were her household officials, who introduced them to the sweating halls, packed with people and dogs, where the castle's lesser guests and resident household supped; and conveyed them to the quarters where the other guests of great estate, with their retinues, received them in rooms equally packed.

There was a great deal of noise: so much that even the clamour of the Cathedral bells hardly penetrated the walls of the castle. It was at Brixen also that they discovered the Duchess's pipers. She employed three, as well as a number of trumpets. Nicholas slept very little and, when he did, kept senselessly dreaming of Kerasous, once in the empire of Trebizond. He couldn't imagine a reason, unless it had to do with alum or Amazons, both of which Kerasous and the Tyrol had in common. At the end of the first week, the mistress of the Duchess's ladies took him in hand, appearing at his side in the hall when a gambling dispute between Teutonic princelings was reaching its height, and both the singers and the dogs had become inaudible.

In the quiet of her chamber, he thanked her. Her name was Gertrude. A graceful woman, no longer young, she had been in attendance all through his first expedition with Eleanor of Scotland. Here, she was in charge of the cohort of young, well-born maidens who formed the Duchess's retinue. Most of them had been educated at Sonnenberg, the convent whose laxity had so enraged the late Cardinal Bishop of Brixen. It reminded Nicholas, briefly, of Haddington, which reminded him in turn of other things. The woman said, 'I know you prefer water, but the wine is weak, and has nothing in it that will harm you. Sit down. Close your eyes, if you wish.'

'That would be ungracious,' Nicholas said.

She said, 'I brought you here for your own sake, not mine.' She was thin as a gazelle, with a long face and deep eyes below her elaborate headdress. The jewelled bands on her sleeves were very fine. She poured a goblet for herself and sat opposite, the cup in her hands. She said, 'Her grace means you well, and has told you the risks. But it is greedy, the pendulum.'

'Greedy?'

'Of life. Of energy. It is German, I think.' She smiled.

He said, 'Why do you say that?' Presumably she had been told to do this. He could not guess, yet, what she wanted.

'Because the civilised world regards us as boors. We think it a banquet to lay a plain cloth and put on it a dish of poached and boiled eggs, a plate of minnows, a bowl of turnips and a platter of peas in the pod.'

'You are quoting?'

'From the Burgundian envoys recently entertained by the Duke. They were offered bread on the point of a knife, and wine from two brimming silver-gilt cups, the squire holding the lid of each cup under Duke Sigismond's chin as he drank. The Duke wore a robe he had already appeared in at Arras.'

He summoned his energy. 'They must eat heartily, who inhabit fierce lands. They hunt in France and Scotland and Italy, but face only the beasts.'

'Other travellers have been less generous,' the lady said. 'Our nauseating food, our bitter wine, our coarse customs, our unsafe roads and disputatious, turbulent unlettered peoples – that is how the German States are regarded by those from softer countries. Cardinal Bessarion is godfather to the Emperor's only son, but was thankful to leave. Prosper de Camulio – do you know him? – thought us barbarians. And Pope Pius! How he hated Vienna, and his time as the Emperor's secretary.' She paused. 'Aeneas Piccolomini, he was. He came twice to the Tyrol. Duke Sigismond took him stag-hunting.'

Nicholas kept his voice mild. 'They knew one another, I heard, when the Duke was a boy at the Emperor's court.'

'He formed the Duke's tastes in many ways, Piccolomini. He taught him which books to esteem. He was not in Holy Orders as a young man, of course.'

'He had elevated standards,' Nicholas said. 'As I remember, he was critical of the common people of Scotland as well – poor and rude, with their cabins covered with turf. Although the women were white and beautiful and very prone to love, he remarked.' He waited.

'One of them gave him a child. He was less impressed by the Duchess's father, who was murdered the following year. He considered the King small, fat and hot-tempered, and content with less state than one of the meaner burghers of Nuremberg. I have heard the Duchess quote that.' She was silent. Then she went on.

'When Duke Sigismond was sixteen, he asked Piccolomini to write a love poem he could send to his mistress, and he did. She succumbed, I am sure: his verses were paeans to desire. "He who has never truly felt the flames of love is but a stone, or a beast," he wrote to someone else. "Into the very marrow-bones of the Gods has crept this fiery particle." He was a good teacher, Aeneas Piccolomini.'

'You are explaining a marriage,' Nicholas said.

She smiled faintly. 'Oh, the Duke of Burgundy arranged the marriage, not Piccolomini. Rude though it is, the Tyrol lies on the highway to Rome. It is the way the barbarians came. It has to remain in Imperial hands. So the Duke of the Tyrol was married to Eleanor, Princess of Scotland, a country too distant (whatever its aspirations) to endanger the imperial succession. And the Duke of Burgundy won an ally north of England. Indeed, the Duke married his niece to King James, the Duchess's brother.'

Nicholas stirred. 'You are saying that the third King James is showing an inclination to aspire?'

'I am sure he would not be so ill advised,' his hostess said.

'No. And you are also saying that the marriage between the Duke and the Duchess Eleanor must endure, because any other alliance would be dangerous?'

'Fortunately,' said the woman called Gertrude, 'my lady has studied him, and he is comfortable with her. She is level-headed and can achieve much when he is absent, although she cannot cross him – few can – when he is here. She knows the courts of France and of Brussels, and has effected what changes she can without many resources. She has made him into a collector of books, and encouraged him to regard himself as a student of advanced thought. She has made friends of some powerful women and men, and she is not unhappy.'

'And the succession?'

'I do not think,' said Gertrude dryly, 'that the Emperor is altogether disappointed that they have not produced an heir. It may even be another reason why the marriage is encouraged to continue. And meantime, as I said, she studies his needs.'

He had wondered, looking at the red-faced little Duchess and her troop of winsome attendants; thinking of the half-grown young he had already seen in the castle. The Duke of Burgundy could afford to beget powerful bastards who would form a circle of reliable leaders but never usurp the place of the heir. Sigismond's love-children were seeded like grass, brought up amiably and amiably cared for, but born of no line that might threaten the Imperial throne.

The woman was watching him. She spoke gently again. 'I respect the Duchess,' she said. 'She has been impressed by you. She asked me to find out if there was anything you might want. The castle has some resources. But I think you need rest.'

Nicholas smiled, although he had not been unaware of the charms of the Duchess's maidens. He said, 'I know my place as a guest. I am glad to be here. You are kind.'

He looked at her directly, and she smiled in her turn. She said, 'That, too, in my time. But there are several younger and prettier to choose from. Or it might simply suit you to sleep. There is an inner room here.' Her voice was soothing and had become very soft.

His lids closed. He thought at first the lamp had gone out. The room was cold and quite dark, and he was overcome with a lethargy so immense that it was beyond him to open his eyes or to move. 'I'm sorry,' he said.

'No. Stay where you are. I will lock the door. Now.' She stopped speaking. There were movements: the warmth of a brazier pulled close, the weight of a blanket, something soft into which his head sank. She said, 'Sleep where you are. You can have a bed later.' She spoke hastily, as if she knew what was wrong, and disapproved.

When he woke later, it was to the same shadowy chamber lit by the flickering red of the brazier and a single lamp, shining on the waist-length hair and pale bedgown of a woman sitting quietly watching him. Gertrude, whose bedroom it was.

She said, 'You must be warm.'

Under the rug, he was still fully clothed. She rose and stooped to draw the cover away. He smelled a scent deeply placed. She was about Marian's age. The age Marian would have been. He said, 'I am not sure what happened.' She was bringing him wine.

'You found silver,' she said. 'They will ask you to look for other things. It is not just the climbing which tires you. The other man died.'

'She told me,' he said. His throat was dry, and he drank.

'But not why. He was not looking only for metal. He could find anything. Anything. He could find, and he could cure. Sick people came, and he sent them away well.'

He put down the wine. He said, 'Don't tell Father Moriz.'

She stood by the small tongues of flame, her own cup in her hand. Her fingers, like her face, were long-boned and fine, and the damask of her gown was half opaque. Oh God, a tub of water. Steam, and long hair, and untouched fires, ready for rousing. That was not a dream.

The woman beside him spoke with insistence. 'I have told you the truth. It killed him, for he took the ills on himself, instead of making himself only the instrument. He told me. If Duke Sigismond finds you have this gift, he will not let you go.'

Steam, and a bath, and a conflagration. 'The Duchess will tell him,' he said.

'No. Nor will her household.'

He said suddenly, 'He could find *anything*?'

He had startled, even frightened her. She, too, put down her wine. She said, 'He found a man who had died in the snow.'

'How?'

'He knew him. He thought of his face.'

'But if he didn't know him? If he didn't know what he looked like?'

She said slowly, 'Then he could not find him. Unless he had something – a shoe, a glove. What is it? What is it? I am to help you. She said I was to help you!'

'No one can help me,' he said. It was not quite true. Marian, Katelina . . . Their paths had crossed, and if he had given, he had taken as well. But no one had opened this door to him. *He could find anything.*

His cup, which had been empty, was full. His hands, which had held his cup, had gathered something else. Her gown lay on the floor.

He woke at first light, in a bed, in what he perceived to be the inner room. He was alone, but remembered not being alone. No one else was there, either in this chamber or the next. He dressed, and left.

Very soon now, Nicholas supposed, he would receive his summons from Duke Sigismond, and would be able to move, finally, into the arena he had chosen so carefully to compensate for the one he had lost. He had still, of course, to face the Vatachino, his enemies; but he had few misgivings, and felt confident that – of the two years of his separation from Scotland – this segment at least would be well spent. What happened over the rest of the time would depend on how well he had read the mind of his wife of a year and four months.

He set himself to wait, and also to be careful. He had received a grave warning. He had received a passing gift, which he acknowledged for the courtesy that it was. And there had been bestowed on him – unearthed for him – a talent of singular price.

He could find anything.

Winter advanced upon autumn. It was known, now, that Nicholas de Fleury was locked in the Tyrol. The news had reached Julius at Venice, and had stolen from there to Alexandria, from where it spread to a man called David de Salmeton.

Julius, who never lacked confidence, was not afraid of what the

Vatachino might get up to in Egypt. In six months, John le Grant would be there, and Nicholas with him. If in the meantime Nicholas chose to negotiate loans and hunt chamois in preference to joining his wife, the Bank could afford it. And Julius could look forward, himself, to another year at the helm of the business.

His henchman Cristoffels made no complaint, although he missed the German priest he had been promised. De Fleury had sent him a personal note about that, as sometimes he did. Occasionally, Cristoffels fulfilled special commissions without reference to Julius. One such had concerned the Genoese Prosper de Camulio. Another had taken him to Murano, to a family called Buonaccorsi with whom Nicholas had apparently struck up a friendship. The making of spectacles in Murano still brought the Bank extraordinary profits.

At the same time, and purely for his own interest, Cristoffels kept an eye on the island of Cyprus, where the King's marriage-bed was still empty. The resulting reports he filed and kept for himself. The padrone had not asked to be told about Cyprus.

Intelligence about Nicholas de Fleury reached Scotland in stages, relayed across the country from Govaerts in Edinburgh to Oliver Semple and Cochrane at Beltrees, where the embellished tower was proceeding to completion, and the horizon was blackened with pyre-smoke from heaps of dead marigolds. The castles of Kilmirren and Dean were, of course, empty.

As soon as she heard, Katelijne Sersanders turned up in the Canongate office and extradited the parrot to Haddington. The Berecrofts boy helped. Being busy at sea, the shipmaster Crackbene wasn't consulted.

James, Lord Hamilton, received the news thoughtfully, and conveyed it to Joneta, his natural daughter. Then he sent a hind to his son-in-law Davie whose uncle Jack had gone abroad and married a German.

When told, Whistle Willie said nothing, but kicked a specially made drum with the side of his slipper. The King, with his jewel coffers full and his Palace finished and furnished, was more philosophical. When, instead of de Fleury, another distinguished foreigner arrived, James of Scotland made him all the more welcome.

Gregorio, in Bruges, was not philosophical.

He had compelled Nicholas to come back for Godscalc. His other reason, unconcealed, had been to halt his foolhardy over-extension in Scotland. In this he had succeeded. The haemorrhage of silver in Scotland had ceased, but others had stepped in to reap all the benefits. And Nicholas had repaid Gregorio as he had repaid the interference of Tobie: by cutting him out of his confidence.

Nicholas had said nothing, leaving Bruges, about going to the Tyrol. He had encouraged Gregorio to look for Gelis and Margot while already aware, it would seem, that Gelis planned to waylay him at Florence, and that Margot would not be there. Margot had written to him twice, but had not come to see him, nor told him where to come. Presumably she was with the child. If there was a child.

And, of course, Nicholas had not gone to Florence. He was not going to Alexandria this year. And if he had changed his mind about that, did he intend, on leaving the Tyrol, to meet his wife and child in Venice as planned? And if so, what next? Put them both on a galley and take them through Turk-infested seas to hunt for his gold?

No. Margot was not going to be free in eight months. Nicholas had allowed Godscalc to debar him from Scotland, but in the wake of that one decent promise had, as usual, cheated them all.

So Gregorio was not moved to sympathise when Gelis van Borselen returned from her wasted journey to Florence, nor when she paid her one visit to Spangnaerts Street. She did not bring Margot, and professed not to know where she was.

He knew (and had told Margot) that the child born to Gelis had been fathered by Simon. He hadn't told anyone else. Gelis never attempted to speak of it, knowing his views as she must. Perhaps she recognised, from what Margot told her, that he would preserve the child's name so long as Nicholas did.

But that was all. He himself would never forgive Gelis for what she had done. For what she had made Nicholas do. For what had happened to Nicholas.

Chapter 28

IN THE WAR Gelis was waging, the contempt of Gregorio played a part, but only a small one. She called at Spangnaerts Street, certainly, to check on her credentials: meeting the searching blue eye of Tobie; the warm regard, born of Africa, of Lucia's son Diniz and hence of young Tilde his wife. She did not stay there – she had taken up residence in her former house outside Bruges – but it was November, and couriers always passed between Nicholas and his officers, wherever he was. Gregorio would not tell her the news, but the clerks would.

In fact, there was little. He was still in the mountains, and had received some messages, but those he sent had more to do with Bruges and Venice and Scotland than with any plans of his own. She had got more information out of Tommaso.

Then Tilde's sister Catherine had joined them with her handsome friend Nerio who, it appeared, was familiar with Florence. Gelis thought him inquisitive, but did not seek to avoid his questions about the Medici and Monna Alessandra and the Acciajuoli family. He knew – as did some of the others – the one-legged acquaintance of Nicholas, but had never met Donatello. She did not mention the drawing. All in all, she supposed she had proved that she had not passed her time in libidinous living.

She left her husband's house soon, and found no reason to make frequent visits thereafter. She was not likely to be lonely. Bruges would always find time for a wealthy van Borselen. Chaperoned by her maid and her manservant, she accepted the invitations that came her way from the upper merchants and nobility of the town, and her cousin Wolfaert van Borselen's new wife was happy to entertain on her behalf.

It was there that she first detected a certain unease which evidenced itself in the burgh as an undercurrent of dubious excitement.

Eventually, Wolfaert told her the reason. Mary of Scotland was coming to Bruges. His niece, the Countess of Arran, whom Gelis had served. After months of exile in Denmark, in Germany, the Princess was coming, together with her refugee husband, the Earl, Thomas Boyd.

'Here?' Gelis said. 'They want shelter? Isn't that dangerous?'

Wolfaert had shifted his bulk. 'Extremely awkward, at least. The Earl has been condemned to death for attempting to harm the Scots King, and all his lands forfeited. My father is Admiral to the Duke. The Duke is married to the English King's sister. To invite my unhappy niece to this house would have implied some sort of Burgundian endorsement. No. She and her husband are going to stay with Adorne.'

'Poor man,' she said.

'Anselm? Save your pity. Anselm Adorne will find a way of safeguarding his family. Meantime, I have told you all this for a reason.'

She could guess. 'You don't want me to serve the Princess again.'

'It would not be politic. Again, Adorne has come to the rescue. He is bringing his own sister's daughter Katelijne, who has been in royal service in Scotland. That should be enough, together with his wife and the two nuns, his daughters.'

'The Countess might ask for me,' Gelis said. 'Perhaps she even met Nicholas in Scotland.'

'I believe she did. It is fortunate,' said her cousin, 'that your husband is to be absent this winter. If he has plans to develop in Scotland, a friendship with Thomas Boyd and his wife is the last way to advance them.'

Wolfaert, a stolid man, was nevertheless always worth listening to.

Paul, his bastard, was even better. He did not remember, of course, his father's good-sister Eleanor who had come to Veere for the Guelders betrothal. But after she disappeared to the Tyrol, Aunt Eleanor had exchanged news with her van Borselen relatives.

He had a list of books he was supposed to be reading. She had sent a gift when his father remarried. He had been fascinated by this man she had hired who could find people.

'Who?' Gelis had said.

'I don't know his name. Aunt Eleanor employed him to help them find mines. But he can find people, too. Strangers, even. All he needs is some small thing they owned.'

She had contracted to stay for a week. Wolfaert was surprised but not, she thought, sorry when she elected to return home forthwith. The ride took most of the day. Arriving, she brushed her expostulating steward aside and went at once to her room, where lay the parcel she had received just before leaving. A parcel and letter from Nicholas.

The letter told her what she already knew: that he now proposed to make his Alexandrine expedition next year. He was in the Tyrol at present, but would travel south in the spring; when his plans were clear, he would send her particulars. He hoped she had enjoyed her sojourn in Florence, and that she had returned to find her son well. He enclosed a gift for the first anniversary of his birth, whenever that might occur.

She had read the letter, and found its casual tone disconcerting. She had not unwrapped the parcel. She opened it now.

She had seen Nicholas at work. She knew better than most his solitary preoccupations, given some scraps of wood and wire, and an objective. Now she saw another example.

Made for the child named after his most formidable enemy: a little soft toy whose mechanism had been sunk deeper than baby fingers could delve, whose feathers frilled, whose wings fluttered and whose beak, primed by its spring, opened to emit, sweet and shrill, a nursery song from her own Zeeland childhood.

He must have heard her sing it, long ago. Long ago, when he was getting her sister with child.

She might, but for Paul, have taken it as a piece of flamboyance. Instead, sick with anger, she carried the thing into the kitchen and cast it into the oven and watched it burn, erratically brilliant, its beak emitting thin screams and flakes and fragments of song.

The cook stood aside; the cook-boys watched fascinated. Her steward, unexpectedly entering the room, stopped abruptly and was overtaken by a fair man of exquisite appearance, following more quickly than was customary on his heels. 'My very dear and virtuous lady!' said Simon de St Pol of Kilmirren. 'At last!'

Today the west windows were shuttered and the lamps lit in the spacious room where she and Margot used to sit in the summer. Simon's hair, as he found a seat, glittered like ducats.

No one who met Simon de St Pol ever forgot him: the blue eyes and fine, almondine features, the straight back, the tapering hands. Beneath the fur-weighted skirts, the superb thigh-hose and boots, his body – as she had cause to know – was uniformly fair also, although not without scars.

Scars were all he had in common with the only other man with whom she was intimate, and even these differed. Simon's had been earned in knightly combat and war. Those of Nicholas were the weals of the servant and the hacks of hand-to-hand combat. Simon had asked her, once, to demonstrate where and how the skin of Nicholas had been marked. The kernel of intercourse, with Simon, was always sunk in a fruit called comparison.

She had responded, although not necessarily truthfully. It irritated her that, recalling such details with ease, the face of Nicholas often seemed to evade her except as a sculpture of some ancient Celt: the spaced roundels of eyes; the bladed nose; the lax lips; the dimples – those baleful footprints – that straddled them. All that was living about it seemed to erase itself for long spells from her memory, whereas for example she could at any moment have drawn the shape of his hands, which were large, and did not taper.

Simon was sitting at ease. He always sat consciously well (so did Nicholas). He said, 'Why didn't you come to Scotland? I was hoping your husband would bring you, but I realise he may have some misgivings. So you have settled for a future in matrimony?'

'You mean, why have I not ended the marriage?' said Gelis.

'Not exactly,' Simon said. 'I mean that you are rich, and are living in a manner that suits you. The day of your marriage! Nicholas, oblivious, solemnly releasing me from every commitment! When did he find out? You might have warned me.'

'It slipped out,' she said. 'Did it matter?'

His expression deepened into one of rebuke. 'Not to me. But if you marry a savage, you have certain responsibilities. He murdered Lucia my sister.'

'I heard –' said Gelis.

'You heard she drowned in an accident. She drowned because he thought she was me. I shouldn't blame you. What should a well-bred woman know of primitive impulses?'

She stared at him. He brought his gaze down from the ceiling and spoke warmly. 'But you aren't afraid? He made no threats? What did he say? I wish I had been there when you told him.'

'Do you?' Gelis said. 'Oh yes, I see. At least he would have killed the right person.'

'Acid as ever,' he said. His voice was comfortable. 'Well, at least you have come to no harm. And now, let me see this wonderful child.'

She had never thought he would come. She had weighed it – *put yourself in the other man's place* – and concluded that she was safe: that Jordan, if no one else, would stop Simon proclaiming this connection, or claiming whatever child she produced. The trading power of the van Borselens would protect her. And the damaging power of Nicholas, capable of informing the world that this was the child of his wife and his father. She said, 'I'm afraid the child isn't here.'

Her voice must have been strained. Simon said, 'Oh come! What do you think? I don't want to steal the brat: Henry would kill him in a moment. I just want to see what he looks like.' His smile deepened. 'A father's natural pride. What have you called him?'

She was composed enough now. 'Jordan,' she said. 'I named him myself. And I'm afraid he really is not here. He will live with his nurse until he is older.'

'Jordan!' he said. He had white, unbroken teeth; unusual in a champion jouster. 'You do dislike Nicholas, don't you? Forced to pass off the child as his own, or admit he can't satisfy his own wife. Forced to rear a son of mine whose very looks –' His voice quickened. 'Is that why the child is not here? Nicholas hates it so much?'

'He has never seen it,' said Gelis. 'That is why it is in the country. There is no need to concern yourself. He doesn't know where it is.'

'He knows where you are,' Simon said. 'I'd spend some of that money, if I were you, on good bodyguards. You can't hide a young lad for ever.'

'No. But at the moment, as you'll understand, the place ought to be secret. I have protection. He has his own way of punishing people, but he has not tried to harm me so far. And *my* sister, of course, is dead already.'

'You're an amazing woman,' he said. The lines left his brow and he shifted the hand at his chin so that one finger lay along the line of his lips. He spoke through it. 'Of course, he wants you.'

'He is in the Tyrol,' she said. Her breathing calmed. She rang the bell at her side and ordered spiced wine of the kind that he liked. He was smiling. It had all happened so quickly that she was still wearing her riding boots and short gown. Servants came and went.

'What is he doing in the Tyrol?' Simon said.

She shrugged. 'Promising Captain Astorre and his army to Sigismond. Unless the Duke gave him different orders. He went to Brussels before he went south.'

'Really?' said Simon. He recovered. 'I'm told the Burgundian commissioners are the most hated men in Alsace. The cantons are becoming alarmed. Was Nicholas the right man to send?' His expression now was amused.

'It's a rough country. It should suit him,' she said. 'And, of course, there is the silver. He has taken John le Grant with him, and another man. If Sigismond becomes rich, he can seize back all his Swiss land.'

'I heard a rumour,' Simon said. He had begun sipping his wine.

Gelis smiled. 'Bruges is full of rumours. You know, because of Nicholas, that the Adornes have to lodge Thomas Boyd, the Scots traitor?'

'Because of Nicholas?'

'He helped Boyd escape. And the Princess Mary, his wife. So Adorne's wife insists. She is a little resentful,' said Gelis. 'A change of ruler in England may help. Are you sorry for Anselm Adorne? He is Genoese and invests in Genoese projects. Perhaps in the Vatachino, for example.'

He said, 'Is that what Nicholas thinks? He could be right. Adorne put money into the Vatachino's African venture. He could be the broker behind them. The only names I hear, and I hear them too often, are de Salmeton and Martin.'

'There is a third man,' Gelis said. 'The Bank have been competing for contracts against a man called Egidius. From what I know of Nicholas, he probably has him identified by now; and Adorne's interest as well. Nicholas has very good spies.'

'I shouldn't mind knowing what he finds out,' Simon said.

She put down her wine. 'I doubt if he would tell you,' she said. 'Of course . . .'

'It would help me,' he said. 'It would help Jordan. The Vatachino are wrecking our Portuguese trade.' He had carried his wine to his lap and settled it there. The light glimmered over the long, undulating line of his limbs, down to the lazy, crossed heels. He looked up. His lashes were gold. He said, 'I know we are rivals in trade, but the Bank would hardly suffer – and if it did, would you really mind?'

'Where would I reach you?' she said.

His fingers moved on the cup, and then began slowly to stroke it. He said, 'I am going to Scotland, since Nicholas obligingly has left it. You might change your mind and come back. He has two reasonable houses at least, if the women have left.'

'The women?' She was meant to ask.

He gave the wine-cup two admonitory taps. 'Oh, Gelis, you know what you married! All sorts, all ages, in public, in private. Not so many men, since the negro. But Adorne's niece was a child. Even the Cuthilgurdy woman sickened of that, I was told.' His voice was deprecating, but not loud. He shifted a little.

Gelis said, 'Adorne's niece? Katelijne Sersanders?' Wolfaert had
mentioned her. She must have been fourteen when she went to
Scotland. Just sixteen, by now. She found her eyes were on St
Pol's hand, smoothing round and round the sunken, silver ellipse
of the cup.

'In his sickroom, naked,' said Simon. His fingers stirred, but her
eyes had stopped following. *Not so many men, since the negro.* One
forgot that Simon treated candour, too, as a mistress.

One forgot, too, how noiselessly he could move if he cared. She
became aware of his scent, very close. Her hand was gently taken
and his wine-cup folded into it; in a soft movement the goblet was
laid against her own cheek and held there. It was heavily warm,
and an inch from her lips. She felt him stretch, and knew he could
reach the door, and the key.

She wanted – She knew what she wanted, but it was not this. A
long passage of arms lay before her, and she could not have
Nicholas driven to end it by Simon. She pulled herself free, the
wine spilling. He exclaimed. The door flew open. A child's voice
said, 'It isn't here!' A child entered.

'Henry!' said Simon and, releasing her, straightened. His eyes
were black. He said, 'I told you to wait.'

'I wanted to see him,' said Henry. 'I wanted to tell him not to
grow up and bother me, because he's only a bastard. Are you the
mother?' He was speaking to Gelis.

Her sister's son. Now nearly nine years of age, the blue-eyed,
golden-haired baby of her dead sister Katelina van Borselen, wife
of Simon and mistress of Nicholas as, in reverse, she had been.
Only the straight brows and the set of the mouth brought his
mother to mind. It was Simon who brought him up now. But she
had sworn an oath to Godscalc. So had Nicholas. She searched the
boy's face, and saw nothing of Nicholas there but one dimple and a
certain stubbornness, perhaps, in the jaw.

Are you the mother? It was his father's child he had been searching
for and would have killed had he found it, very likely. He had tried
to kill Nicholas. She looked at the white, angry face and wondered
what madman had made him believe that a half-brother had power
to supplant him. Then she thought of the fat vicomte whose name
she had used as a weapon. She sat where she was, the wine staining
her breast, and said, 'I am Gelis van Borselen, dame de Fleury. I
am your aunt.'

Simon swore. Transfixed as she was, she almost smiled.

The boy said, 'That's what I thought. He got you under him and
you grew him a baby. Are you growing another?' He was looking

her up and down. He added conversationally, 'I do that too. With the cup. They like the wine in little drops.'

The words, in a child's mouth, made her spin round upon Simon. He said, 'He eavesdrops. He was brought up by sluts. A St Pol does as he is told. You were told to stay at the inn.' He had the boy by the arm. The boy looked at him with hatred.

Gelis said, 'Henry? There is no half-brother here you need be jealous of. There never will be another. I will promise. Simon, will you promise too?'

'What are you talking about?' Simon said.

Gelis said, 'That Henry will be your heir, and no one will ever supersede him. That is all he wants to know.'

'Well, he ought to know that already,' said Simon. He had become rather flushed. He addressed the child, glaring: 'Do you want to go to Scotland? Just tell me.' The child was silent. 'Because if you don't, you're behaving in just the right way. You've insulted your aunt. Apologise.'

'I'm sorry,' Henry remarked.

'You heard what she said. You'll leave her baby alone.'

'If you say so, my lord father,' said Henry.

'Get out,' said Simon.

The child looked at Gelis, and left.

Gelis found she was shaking. She stopped herself. She said, 'Dear me. Perhaps your father was right, after all.'

'About what?' Simon said. He was breathing fast, his eyes still on the door.

'In offering to recognise Nicholas as his grandson. Your son.'

'What?' Simon said. He said it quite slowly.

She raised her brows. 'You didn't know? Your father offered to purchase my child. In return, he would recognise Nicholas as your son. Nicholas would inherit Kilmirren and Ribérac, and young Jordan would follow, not Henry. Unhappily, Nicholas wouldn't agree.'

'That's impossible,' Simon said, and half laughed. She waited. He said, 'My father *proposed* . . .'

'Ask him,' she said.

'And Nicholas *turned down the offer*?'

'He tends to take the long view,' Gelis said. 'I suspect that, once your father had got what he wanted, Nicholas would not have lived very long. And, of course, he hasn't seen the child, as I said. He has persuaded himself he has a use for an heir. Certainly he has money to leave. Are you not pleased about that?'

He was untangling his thoughts, pacing fretfully. 'I should be, if you were parting. But you're not. You may have other children.'

'Was that what Henry interrupted? A precaution?' she said. 'Then you heard me give him a promise. He will have no rivals born of me and his father. I think you should leave.'

Simon looked up. He came across to her and held both her hands. He said, 'Forget Henry. Promises to children mean nothing. Gelis: Katelina tried to please, but you cannot doubt which of you is more gifted. You are wasted on Nicholas. Come to Scotland, to me.'

She thought. 'Perhaps,' she said. 'When I have been to Alexandria.'

Gelis van Borselen was aware, since she had not been invited to Alexandria, that to arrive there would take some ingenuity, and that there was therefore a great deal to do. But before she embarked on her preparations, there was one visit she felt compelled to make time for.

Margriet van der Banck, arranging the Hôtel Jerusalem for royalty, was pleased to see her, but unable to speak more than two consecutive words without breaking off to admonish, encourage, direct or sometimes chastise the flock of helpers who – hammering, sweeping, painting; climbing stairs with stools and chests and hangings; or staggering towards the kitchens with boxes of platters and pans – were turning the residence of Anselm Adorne into a place fit for the Scottish traitor Thomas Boyd, Earl of Arran, and his wife, the King's sister.

The distraction of Dame Margriet was in fact a convenience: it prevented any but sporadic references to the little baby, and Dame Margriet's gift to the little baby, and the absence of the little baby's father. In any case, Dame Margriet did not dwell on the baby's father, who – Gelis remembered – had been ungrateful enough to wound Anselm in some scuffle in Scotland. Anselm was back now, of course, from his second trip – so successful! The young King so charming, so generous! – and was preparing for the difficult meetings he was to arrange for the spring and the summer: meetings which would decide once and for all the trading arrangements between Scotland and Flanders. Who else could do it but Anselm?

Anselm Adorne himself, discovered in his office guiltily attempting to work in the face of the tempest of renovation below, cleared a seat for her and said, 'I have no doubt that you have come, like the rest of Bruges, to see the parrot. It is on the floor above, with my niece Katelijne. How are you, Gelis?'

'Chastened,' she said. 'I thought, after the way Nicholas treated you, that you ought to know that he was going abroad. He is, but not until next spring. I am sorry.'

He touched her hand. 'Nicholas and I are not enemies. Oh, I know what happened in Scotland. He did what he did in desperation, not out of cold blood. I won't deny' – he smiled – 'that he is a stimulating opponent. He had a scheme for a stud farm which would have ruined Metteneye and myself if I hadn't guessed what his object was. But I should never wish him ill, Gelis. He is a rare individual. Cherish him.'

'Do you need to tell me? I married him,' she said; and gave him a smile. 'I must go. You are busy. It cannot be welcome, this visit. You have leave of the Duke to entertain the Princess and her husband?'

'What do you suppose?' said her host. 'So long as the visit is private, and the Duke is not involved. The problem will arise, I imagine, when it is a question of baptising the infant. Ah! You did not know that the lady Mary is about to bear her first child?'

'No,' Gelis said. Wolfaert had said nothing of that – fearing, perhaps, that she might be moved out of pity to offer her services. That, then, was why the homeless pair had been forced to end their hapless wandering; to seek a place for the birth worthy of the Princess's rank, and where the child would receive public acknowledgement. She said, 'Does King James know of this? Will he not regard you as shielding a traitor?'

'I have consulted King James,' said Adorne mildly. 'His first reaction was just as you say. But he is fond of his sister, and she will not leave Thomas Boyd. And few others in Flanders could take her. One would not wish such a dilemma, for example, upon Wolfaert.'

She felt herself flush. She said, 'Wolfaert did not send them to you.'

Adorne looked contrite. 'My dear! Did you think that I imagined he would? No. They came because no one else could suitably give them asylum. Or because they had a little advice.' He tilted his head. 'Have you never wondered – were you never told who contrived their disappearance from Scotland?'

There was amusement in his voice, and some irony, and a hint of weariness. She lost all the air in her lungs, and recovered it slowly. '*Nicholas?*'

He laughed. 'It is, I imagine, a fairly safe wager. And to think I forgave him my injury! Indeed, I received his magnanimous assurance that he owed me a favour. Do you suppose that this is it?'

'I don't know,' said Gelis. 'But, speaking even as his wife and a partisan, let me say that I hope you will balance the score. Ser Anselm, I must go. Should I see the parrot?'

'Yes! Yes, of course,' Adorne said. 'And Katelijne. You will remember her as a child – and, to be sure, she is still small for her age, and troubled by weakness – but I have to admit, although she is my own niece, that there are elements in her that Margriet and I find quite extraordinary.'

'She has no husband arranged?' Gelis said.

Adorne smiled. 'Talk to her, and then tell me what I should do. Perhaps she should wait for your son.'

The parrot had red and blue feathers and was in a cage, talking Greek. That was the first jolt. The second followed immediately.

Beside the cage was a stack of striped linen edged with old-fashioned reticella embroidery. Crosslegged on the floor next to that sat the girl Katelijne, paintbrush in hand, giving her undivided attention to an immense carved receptacle with a hood. Her eyes, in the kindest phrase, were over-focused, and her tongue adhered to her upper lip like a bat.

Gelis moved. The tableau dissolved. The girl jumped to her feet, hauling down her gown which had been tucked round her hips. Her eyes adjusted. She said, 'Oh, it's a woman, thank goodness. I thought it was my uncle. How do you like it? Their cradle.'

She did not say whose cradle it was: the arms of Boyd and the royal arms of Scotland made explanation unnecessary. It certainly, thought Gelis, was not for herself. Small and slight as a leaf, with loose brown hair and hazel eyes in a pale, earnest face, Katelijne Sersanders looked no more than fourteen years old – even less. The age Gelis had been when she found out what her sister and Nicholas were doing.

Gelis said, 'I'm sorry. Your uncle sent me upstairs, I think, to get me out of the way. It was a bad time to call. I'm –'

'Oh, I know who *you* are,' said the girl cheerfully. 'Gelis van Borselen, dame de Fleury. You *are* lucky. Aren't you lucky, married to that idiot of a man? Isn't it *awful*?'

'You mean Nicholas?' said Gelis equably.

The girl gave a peal of laughter. 'No, the cradle. I hope you had a nice one. He couldn't wait to get home and see the baby. Is it nice being married? Do sit down.' She cleared a book from a stool, swept her paints to a tray, scampered her fingers down the edges of all the piled linen and deposited it in three different stacks on a shelf, was sworn at by the parrot, rolled up some sewing and brought over the brazier, swore in unison with the parrot, picked up and slapped away some music, and sat down with a thump on the predella. 'Is it nice?' she repeated. She had a smile that darted about, quick as a fish.

'Being married to an idiot?' Gelis said. She felt breathless. The parrot was cackling.

'We all thought he was wonderful,' said Katelijne. 'You nearly didn't get him back. Those poor golfers! The marijuana seeds in the wine! Staggering about with the mirror for Hearty James! The dog-races . . . and I can't imagine where he learned to cheat like that at cards. Was it your jew's trump? I hope you didn't mind that he gave it to me. It was a wager.'

'It wasn't mine,' said Gelis. 'Did he play it?'

The girl laughed. 'He liked the drums better. But you mustn't think he caused mischief all the time. He learned. He built. He found out about farming. And the music – well, he probably told you.'

'You tell me,' said Gelis. The parrot made a remark.

'It needs Whistle Willie,' said the girl. 'I can't describe it. Not just his voice. But some people carry about music buried like that, Willie says. Sometimes no one ever knows that it's there.'

'Whistle Willie?'

'Will Roger. You've heard of him.' Katelijne was looking at her. The girl said, 'Perhaps you haven't had much time together. I'm sorry. Can I tell you anything more? He did miss you.' She was eight years her junior and spoke as an equal. But this child had never shared a bed with Nicholas, nor thought of it. The girl said, 'I do apologise for the parrot's being so drunk. My cousins have been giving it wine, and it shows off.'

Gelis said, 'Like my husband, it seems. I was glad when he came back from Scotland. We were all concerned over the quarrel he had with St Pol. Sometimes Nicholas loses his temper.'

The mouth gave itself a judicial screw. 'He can be very *silly*,' the girl said. 'You must lose patience, too. The fight with M. de St Pol was quite unnecessary, and then he lost his head. My uncle was hurt. He didn't plan that, but he made pretty sure that M. de St Pol was going to have an uncomfortable time in other ways. Did he tell you? About buying up Kilmirren land, and smothering his ground with corn-marigolds? Then later they found the Kilmirren hides stank, and the cows all gave diuretic milk?' The girl's face had turned pink. She said, 'I'm sorry. It shouldn't be funny.'

'It sounds fairly typical,' said Gelis dryly. 'What would he have done had he been well?'

'Oh,' said Katelijne. She paused. 'You know what happened? At Henry's age, children are stupid. Your husband pretended thugs were responsible. M. de St Pol should be grateful, in spite of everything.'

'Was he really hurt?' Gelis said. 'Nicholas?'

The direct eyes studied her again. 'It was a knife wound close to the heart. You can't blame the child,' the girl said. 'But Dr Andreas was concerned for a day or two. The shock to the body; the shock to the mind. But you know Dr Andreas.'

Gelis remembered Andreas of Vesalia. She said, 'The shock to the mind?'

'I don't know what it means,' Katelijne said. She seemed to hesitate. She said, 'He thinks your husband has dreams.' The parrot gabbled.

Gelis manufactured a smile. 'Most people do.'

The girl was looking down. She said, 'You don't know Dr Andreas predicts the future? He studied at Louvain: he claims to recognise others who have the same arts, or are possessed of similar powers. He thinks your husband is one.'

Gelis said, 'I have never known any man as earthily human as Nicholas.' She spoke as to a child. The parrot squawked and spoke too.

'I don't understand either,' said Katelijne. 'But he went straight to the river. He found the body. He knew it was dead. And other things, Dr Andreas says. Was there a library, once, he was afraid of?'

Silence. Some little time later, Gelis realised she had not replied. She said, 'I don't remember. My dear Katelijne, I think both you and Dr Andreas attribute more to my husband than you should. He is in the Tyrol, engaged in some very unromantic commercial activities.'

'Divining for silver?' said the girl.

Gelis said, 'Prospecting for silver, I'm sure. The divining, I am told, is in the hands of some charlatan or other who claims to be equipped to find anything.'

She stopped smiling, for the girl was looking at her strangely again. The girl said, 'There was a diviner, but Cavalli said that he died. They were seeking another.'

Gelis said, 'Katelijne! Are you well?'

'Yes, of course,' said the girl. The smile flashed. 'Dame Margriet will tell you it's time for my rest. I'm so glad you came. Will you wait? There's some music Willie sent, and these notes, when you next see M. de Fleury . . .'

The door had opened and Anselm Adorne stood there smiling. 'Katelijne, my dear. We must let Dame Gelis go.'

She went. The last thing she saw was the ferocious face of the child, brush in hand, eyes focused on the terrible cradle.

One week later Gregorio of Asti, called from the counting-house, entered his chamber and found there Margot, his lost love and mistress. She looked older than he remembered, and fearful, and speechless.

He gathered her into his arms, and she wept.

She would not tell him why she had returned; only that she was free at last, and could stay. She could not tell him anything of the child, because she had sworn.

He stroked her hair, and felt only distress.

Chapter 29

WHEREAS IN BRUGES and Venice and Scotland the last weeks of the decade were blustery and busy and wet, the Tyrol advanced towards the new year in the deep isolation of snow.

Chamois-hunting, by tradition, ended in the last days of December, before too many people were killed. Sigismond, as ruler of the Tyrol, had no qualms about breaking tradition if he felt restless, or particularly successful, or if he wanted to place people at odds, or achieve ascendancy over them. Chamois-hunting in the peaks of the Tyrol was for men.

The Duchess Eleanor, who was an excellent shot, always stayed at home, when they happened to be living together. The cart with the girls then left discreetly. After the zest of a kill, a man would throw to the ground anyone he could find, and after, the wine and the collops were glorious. There were enough girls for them all. Naturally, the Duke took his own satisfaction first. He liked his companions to watch. He spun it out sometimes, to tease them. He had stopped once, and had a man caned.

The man whom Eleanor had brought had been with Duke Sigismond three days when the big hunt was planned. He spoke German and shot well and did what was expected of him, after the kill and before it. His prowess at everything was a degree below that of the Duke, as you would expect of someone touting for business. Unlike the red-haired fellow Martin last week, who had wanted to show what he could do. He had gone away with a bolt through the arm. Nothing too painful: his business propositions had been good. Sigismond had accepted them.

Alum and silver. This man de Fleury was after the same: he knew that from Eleanor. The fellow was percipient. He had let Gertude get him to bed. He had held, assiduously, to other matters of proper conduct. He might forget himself quite spectacularly when he learned that the deal was already done, and he had lost to the red-haired (wounded) Martin, agent of the Vatachino. It was a pity to ruin good sport by telling him all that too soon. It was winter. There was plenty of time to deal with the chevalier Nicholas de Fleury.

John le Grant said, 'He's playing with you.'

'I know,' said Nicholas.

'The fact that he punctured Martin in mistake for something with antlers doesn't mean that the Duke didn't conclude a deal with him. You may be gambling your life over nothing.'

'Prayer will save me,' said Nicholas. He had never yet managed to make Father Moriz utter an oath.

In any case, the matter was academic. They were already dressed and ready to go: Nicholas and Father Moriz and John indistinguishable from the other men in the party in their hooded hats and thick quilted tunics dragged down with their knives and spearheads and crampons, their horns and axes and satchels and the wooden rings which would ease a long walk on snow. Moriz, who had hunted chamois before, was armed with a throw-spear, as were the Duke and black-haired Cavalli, his current favourite adviser, who had been absent until now. None of the Duchess's men had come with the Duke: not even Jack Lindsay. None of the Duchess's men had spoken to them since the two households joined.

John le Grant, an expert in matters of trajectory, had brought his crossbow, and persuaded Nicholas to do the same. Among the dozen other hunters, the spear was by far the most popular. Its chief attribute was silence: necessary whatever the sport. But of course a crossbow, well fitted and covered, could also be silent. Even on flat ground, chamois-hunting would have been dangerous. In the mountains, and the way Nicholas was, it was unwise for other reasons as well.

If final proof of that had been needed, his companions would have received it the previous day, in the course of an ordinary hunt up the side of a valley, when the hounds had put up a boar.

The sale of cities and the mortgage of provinces had paid for the splendour of Sigismond of the Tyrol's kennels and stables. Other princes kept dogs by the thousand, uniform in size and performance, and trained in sensitive packs. Sigismond's hounds were bred for their voices.

John had heard of hound music before, but had never experienced it. If a man had enough wealth (or enough credit), he might scour the world for apt dogs of every shape: healthy fleet dogs with one thing in common – the disparity in the sound that they made. From these, he would choose and blend his perfect pack. Then, on the day of the hunt, the lord would dispatch them to their task and, taking his place of advantage, would sit in the saddle and listen, and watch.

The prey fell to music. Notes on the staves, the hounds bayed, each voice proclaiming its name and its place, signalling the course of the chase and ending in the soaring climax, the paean of the kill.

Yesterday, Sigismond had conducted such a hunt.

It had begun late in the day. They had shot in the morning, and had been confined ever since by falling snow. By the time the sky cleared, the sun was low in the west and the mountain-shadows were filling the valleys. Then word came that the kennel-master had traced a young boar close at hand. Sigismond hailed the pack and set off.

There being an order of rank to be observed, the three minor guests of the Duke of the Tyrol had ridden among the last of the party, and were still traversing the slopes when the dogs were released. Distantly, the horns produced their bronchial stutters; the barks and yelps died away; the horns spoke again. Then, remotely, a texture of sound made itself felt.

It was not, at first, at all like the voices of hounds. Muted by space and by the swiftness with which it was travelling, it seemed to lie low and mutter, like a storm building at sea. Then it resembled more the sound a water-wall makes when it meets resistance: the snap of splintering wood, the hollow thud of breached canvas, the clangour of bells, the shrill chime of stressed rigging. Then it swelled. Then it lifted its voice, and its voice was an organ.

Nicholas stopped.

The sun still dwelled on the peaks, but there were stars in the sky. Intent on scaling the hill, le Grant did not at first notice: it was the priest who called him back. The few riders behind them began to pass. John said, 'What is it?'

'Nothing,' said Father Moriz. 'It's going to be dark very soon: perhaps we should wait for the torches. See, someone is climbing to bring them.' The sun had left his shoulders already; his face blazed like a nugget inside his good fur-lined cowl. Beyond the side of the hill, the ground rolled and dipped to the valley where points of light, paraphrased between mounds, showed where clusters of riders had gathered. A horn, flattened by distance, began to create valances of imperious sound. The organ stopped.

'A kill,' John le Grant said. The hunt-servant ran up, and he leaned down and took one of the torches. It revealed the priest's bulbous face, its eyebrows wary. They both looked at Nicholas.

Nicholas said, 'Well, let's get on.' His skin was damp. It reminded le Grant of Trebizond. It reminded him, even, of something he did not want to remember.

Le Grant said, 'Are you having marsh-fever? In the Alps?'

'If I want to. Would it be a record?' said Nicholas.

His voice sounded almost right: like that of a sober man under some slight medication. Father Moriz arrested his reins. Ever since Brixen, the priest's tongue had been sharp. He said, 'What were you afraid of? It is only a hog.'

'I don't know,' Nicholas said. Then he said, 'Yes, I do. Something that happened in Scotland. It's over. Let's go.' And he pressed his horse forward again.

The others followed. The last of the light had now gone, and ahead the sky was deepening to night. The snow was grey and the riders scattered over it black. As the three of them rode, the curve of the hill began to obliterate the lights ahead, one by one. The horns had ceased, and all the hound music had died.

Without warning, Nicholas spoke. 'I am going to lose it.'

'What?' said the priest. He drew alongside. Ahead, all the lights were now masked, and only John's torch guttered and flared, his enquiring face stark in the light.

'*Hersia ad tenebras*. The Tenebrae Hearse,' Nicholas said. 'There's a good three-part setting; I've sung it. The tapers extinguish one by one, or they should. Will you give me your torch?'

His voice was normal again. John hesitated, and then held it out. As he did so, the hound music seemed to float upwards again. With an exclamation, Nicholas snatched the brand and, raising his arm, hurled the torch into the night. Darkness fell. All noise stopped, save for a thin, disembodied, musical scream that faded into flakes and fragments and tatters of sound.

'I have lost it,' Nicholas said.

There was a space. Then he said, 'I'm sorry. Your only light. Let me go ahead. We should pick up the flares as soon as we've rounded this shoulder.' Which, of course, they did.

Nicholas himself, at this time, was concentrating on leading as normal a life as he could in abnormal circumstances.

He knew by now that he had certain powers, and had found ways of extending them. He could not only detect the presence of water, of silver, of copper; he could guess the depth at which they lay, and their extent. From what tests he had been able to make, these predictions were accurate.

He did not feel it necessary to reveal all that he knew but even so, after the first cynicism had subsided, he found that his gift, whatever it was, had so altered people's perceptions as to blur the purpose for which he was there, and even distort the talks he held with the Duchess's advisers on behalf of his Bank, which should have been succinct and business-like, but instead were suffused with misgivings. He made what progress he could.

When the initial prospecting ceased and he was invited to travel with the Duchess's court to Duke Sigismond, he felt intense relief. A pretty, petulant man of forty-two with his long, fair fringe, tip-tilted nose and kittenish eyes, Sigismond of the Tyrol was more intent on proving himself and his guests in the hunting-field than embarking on difficult questions of business.

It suited Nicholas. At first, haunted by his new-found ability, he had speculated on his chance of becoming the most accurate bloodhound in Sigismond's pack. He was thankful to find that the dogs were still better than he was. They scented what was living and moving. His senses provided him with the emanations, shifting and muddled, of every place where their objective habitually trod. He could lead them very well to where it had been the previous week.

Those, of course, had been the ordinary hounds, not the others. Sound, it seemed, was another influence to beware of. It was as well to know. The Duchess, in her wry way, had said that.

He had, then, to learn to shut out that side of his perception. It meant reinstating the blockage by numbers. The mental effort was strenuous but it was still better than the exhaustion of Brixen.

When he had completed his business, that would end. His gift would remain: a weapon he had never dreamed of possessing, which would very likely win him the game, even if he lost the occasional throw. Whatever it meant to lose the occasional throw.

He wished he didn't need the metallurgical skills of Father Moriz. He was glad, as he had never expected to be glad, that Godscalc was dead. He was finally pleased to be climbing with Sigismond on this hunt which, he was well aware, had not been arranged for his pleasure. To succeed here, he required nothing but human skills and a little flamboyance, and the prize at the end was worth reaching for. He trained all his thoughts upon that.

There were fifteen in the Duke's party, but many servants climbed

with them, and yet more were deployed in the passes to net those
beasts which might escape, and to aid, in their various ways, the
ducal hunters.

They left their mounts at the foot of the range, and the first part
of the climb was across a long slope deep in snow. The wickerwork
prints of their snowshoes, round as butter-stamps, followed the
single trails of the professional huntsmen, climbing to the first
ridge. The mountains soared above them, dazzling white against a
pellucid blue sky.

The chamois was an antelope. Nicholas had seen its skull
displayed often enough, Roman and fragile, with its twin back-
swept horns and the cavities of its black, mourning eyes. The
chamois was an exclamation, a lilt, an animal with the elevation of
a bird, light as smoke, whose hooves hardly printed the snow as it
traversed the peaks and soared between gullies and ledges. To kill
a chamois, a man required agility, and endurance, and strength. It
was the ultimate test exacted by princes, and often the ultimate
doom.

Sigismond of the Tyrol led the way, and kept Nicholas de
Fleury at his side. At the proper time, the snowshoes were untied,
and soon after the thick leather boots were fitted with crampons
and the axes were out, clawing their vertical path. Father Moriz,
his lips moving, exercised his spear-hilt and settled his toes into
their succession of crevices, with words of advice to one side for
John, and to the other for Nicholas, when he thought the latter
could hear him. Then the group of men which contained de Fleury
moved upwards and out of his reach.

The numbers had gone. In the intoxication of the air, the searing
light from the snow, the magnificence of the panorama forming
below, Nicholas climbed without weight, without cares. If
Sigismond wished, Sigismond could kill him: he was close; he had
the weapons, the skill. On his other side climbed the Venetian who
was at present the Duke's most favoured servant: Antonio Cavalli,
the busy envoy and expert on horses who had visited Dean Castle
in Scotland that spring. Around them were other intimates of the
Duke: nobles, churchmen, and men of learning who had discovered
that to keep his interest they must not only quote Pliny, but hunt.

The climbing strained every sinew. Here the snow was soft;
there it was impacted like stone; in another place the rock, stripped
by gales, was striated with ice. And climb they must, for the
chamois were not here but high in the peaks. After two hours of it,
some of the party had flagged and turned back. After another hour,
Sigismond, smiling, responded to a signal from above and led the

way to a fault, shielded from wind, where his huntsmen had nursed a small fire and were unpacking meats and fat flagons from baskets.

Sigismond said, his gapped teeth harrowing a long, bristling bone, 'The Duke of Milan hunts with leopards. The lady my Duchess tells me they tried it in Scotland, but the people complained.'

'I heard it was the leopards which complained,' Nicholas said. 'Like elephants, they are not fond of the cold. Should you wish to experiment, I can supply you with muzzles. James of Cyprus has them fashioned in gold, although he fails to use them enough.' Smiling, he touched his arm, acting a wince.

'How did you cheat *him?*' said Sigismond.

Nicholas set down his ale. 'One learns from one's betters,' he said. 'My lord, you have a complaint?'

'I, your host?' Sigismond said. 'Princes are resigned to being exploited. You proposed to the lady my wife to excavate, for a certain sum, a field by the Inn which would yield me a fortune in alum.'

'That is so,' Nicholas said. The Duke's household, close about him, chewed without looking up.

Between words, the Duke's teeth grated spasmodically on the bone. 'My advisers tell me that such alum cannot be sold. The rights to sell in the Tyrol are already possessed by Bartolomeo Zorzi, appointed by the Holy Father to vend Tolfa alum.'

'Your grace distresses me,' Nicholas said.

'Do I? Then consider the silver mines,' the Duke said. Combing free the last of the meat, he threw back his arm and sent the whitened bone into the void. His unwiped lips glistened. A servant knelt hastily with a cup, but did not trouble to hold the lid under his chin.

'The silver mines?' Nicholas repeated.

'You bring letters of friendship from Burgundy, but Burgundy prefers me impoverished. Were I to mine silver, I could win back all the land I have pawned to him. The mines you will claim to discover are worthless.'

'Of course,' said Nicholas, 'I bow to your judgement. You are abandoning, then, all hope of restoring your fortunes with silver?'

'On the contrary,' said the Duke. 'I see no redress in the matter of alum. But there are those, less self-interested, who can promise me all the money I need through the simple right to sink and operate mines. You have heard, no doubt, of the Vatachino. Their agent Martin sat only last week where you sit. He owes nothing to any prince, and less than nothing to Burgundy. I have granted him the contract.' He stood. 'I have shocked you.'

'No,' Nicholas said, standing also. He wished the Duke had been four inches taller. 'I would have done the same, in his place and yours. So does your grace mean to continue?'

'The hunt? Why not? Let us go,' Sigismond said.

John le Grant caught up with Nicholas shortly. 'What was that? Why tell you that now?'

'To see what I would do. Father Moriz?'

'Yes, my son,' said the priest. He did not sound particularly fatherly.

Nicholas said, 'Take care. Take care, both of you. It won't last long, but this is where you have to keep on your toes.'

John le Grant groaned.

He was right. Having established a position of conflict, the Duke amused himself over the next stage of the climb by practising refinements. These were relatively small in scale. Of two pitches, the worse would always fall to the Fleming; if a man ahead slipped, it was the fingers of de Fleury upon which his heel would begin to descend. Once there was a brief avalanche which caused John, too, to cling to his hold, and even the priest was not exempt from minor mishaps.

Even so, they were no more than dangerous gestures. The climb itself was demanding enough. For a man from a flat country, Nicholas congratulated himself on acquitting himself reasonably well: for that, he had the mountains of Trebizond and Troodos to thank, and his recent hardening in the heights about Bozen. The others were much the same.

Sigismond, he had to acknowledge, was a natural mountaineer, and so were the young aristocrats and hunt-servants about him. Broad of shoulder, powerful of thigh and ankle and knee, the young men were the ones who gave him most trouble. They vied for the attention of Sigismond. There was a certain bonhomie in the group, but nothing like, for example, the rough, libertarian exchanges between huntsman and King that were common in Scotland; and the jokes were guarded rather than free-running and bawdy. They were all afraid of their master. Nicholas supposed he ought to start being afraid of their master as well.

The weapons came out shortly after, when word came at last that they were close to their victims, their prey.

The wind had risen, scuffing snow into their faces: for some time now they had been climbing in silence. The herd they sought was one which had challenged the Duke for many weeks, because the chamois had picked a terrain from which the exits could hardly be netted: for the few that escaped the wrong way and were caught, there were dozens which were able to fly to safety. They had, then, to be killed on the spot.

Sigismond waited now till the party had gathered, smothered in the jetted steam of their breath, their beards freezing, their clothing soaked with exertion. At his signal they armed; the crossbows were uncased, the bolts ready; the spearpoints fitted into their sockets. Father Moriz hefted his weapon. His legs were snow-caked to the thigh, his face hacked out of veined marble, but his hands were quite steady. John's features had the blue-white drawn look of the thin-skinned, but he, too, handled his crossbow with precision, glancing at Nicholas now and then. Below, the mountain range filled all the space to the horizon; a porcelain pattern of white and blue shadows against which puffs of snow spouted and vanished like gunsmoke. The pale sun dimmed and glinted like a tavern sign wrung by the wind.

The Duke signed to Nicholas and pointed to a spot just behind him, and Nicholas took his crossbow and moved quietly to occupy it. He knew the young Count at his back, one of the worst offenders on the way up. The next man was the swarthy Cavalli, and behind him was one of the four Kämmerer – chamberlains – another young man of rank. The master huntsman, in whose footsteps they would follow, waited in silence ahead. The Duke took his place at the head of the file, and the others fell in: John and Father Moriz, Nicholas saw, had been relegated to the end. Then the huntsman turned, and they set off to follow him. The wind, rising still, continued to pick up snow and throw it into their faces. Their spears tugged and nodded.

They had been told what to expect: an exposed twenty-foot traverse and then a sloping channel, guarded by rock, which spiralled up to the plateau at the summit. There the animals lay. Beyond the plateau was empty space: on one side a sheer drop to the ground; on the other a gorge, a chasm between this mountain-top and its neighbour whose sides were unclimbable. It formed, however, the bridge of air by which the chamois made their escape if disturbed. Soaring over the gap, they were instantly safe in a petrified forest of needle-peaks which no human being could climb.

This time, they would never reach it. The end of the steep, irregular terrace led to the plateau itself. Halfway up, the archers would halt to span and bolt crossbows. At the top, bursting forth, the hunters would form a ring, their backs to the chasm. Then the chamois could do only three things: attempt the passage, by now entirely netted and blocked; leap to death over the outer, sheer wall of the mountain, or run in panic to jump to freedom in the usual way – towards the gap, and the bolts and the spears.

They were pretty animals, but the world was full of animals. This was not to do with animals, as it happened, but a prince's reputation among his peers. It had also to do with chastising a vassal of the Duke of Burgundy, to whom Sigismond had reluctantly sold so many excellent possessions, and who had not, so far, provided the hearty support Sigismond would have liked.

Nicholas expected, and was on guard against, a painful accident with someone's arrow or spear once the hunt had begun on the plateau. The tearing kick behind the knee came while they were still on the ledge, and was far more dangerous – perhaps even worse than had been intended, for it is difficult to knock a man half off his feet when your own footing, even in crampons, is also precarious. It came, he thought, from the Count.

At the time, he did not think too much at all, finding himself tumbling towards an unimaginable drop with all the wrong kind of momentum. His crossbow shot into space and his belt-hook bit into his doublet. No one spoke – that would have disturbed the chamois – but at least the man ahead stopped. Someone flung out an arm, and someone else grasped one of the leathers crossing his shoulders. It was enough to change his direction: he wheeled round and cannoned into the man standing in front, who half fell. He fell himself, but safely, along the length of the ledge, and found himself lying on his back with a spear at his throat. Above him, looking down, was the huntsman. Beside him, getting slowly to his feet, was the Duke. The huntsman's face, turned to the Duke, wore a query.

There was little doubt what it was. Nicholas lay still. The point of the blade, razor sharp, had already entered his skin: something ticklish ran from it sideways. Everyone else had drawn back.

Far above, carried down by the wind, came the noise of an animal farting. The Duke's eyes moved. The huntsman stood. Then the Duke jerked his head and, turning, resumed his silent way while the huntsman, repossessing the spear, moved his lips briefly and followed, leaving Nicholas to get to his feet.

A hand helped him: that of the grinning young chamberlain. The Count, his eyebrows lifted, had passed and gone on. Nicholas could see le Grant trying to force his way close, and shook his head at him. The snow was littered with good yew shafts from his quiver, flickering in the wind. He bent to collect them and nearly fell a second time from the weakness of his knee. It was then that he remembered that his crossbow had gone. In any case, it was a two-footed bow and he probably couldn't have spanned it, or not immediately anyhow. Father Moriz might lend him his spear. A well-thrown spear could kill at forty yards, whereas a steel bow would do three hundred or more. He had been careful not to bring a steel bow.

Nicholas collected himself and, limping stolidly, began to make his way upwards again. He had nearly killed the Duke. The Duke had nearly had him killed. Honours even.

Just below the plateau they gathered in silence again, and the huntsman crept forward. There was no doubt now that the beasts were up there: Nicholas could smell them, and their snuffles and grunts penetrated the whistle and moan of the wind. Whistle Willie, you should be here. His eyes were bloodshot and his cheekbones ached with the wind, but it had covered their movements. Until now the sound had been steady, like the distant roar of a horse-race, or a battle. Now the roar was catching its breath: it was gusting. Bad for spears. Crossbows should manage. Nicholas waited.

Someone tapped him on the shoulder. He turned. The chamberlain, offering him his own crossbow, fully spanned with a fork-headed bolt in the groove. The man, smiling, indicated the spear he already carried. Nicholas held out his gloved hand, cracking his lips in a smile. He had hardly taken the bow when he heard a shout from ahead. The chief huntsman, calling, had leaped to his feet and was leading the way to the plateau. The rest floundered after, plunging up to the summit to meet the full buffeting force of the wind. They spread out, gasping, while their eyes streamed and froze and their weapons drummed and tossed in their grasp.

The animals, perhaps thirty in all, were grouped at the far end of a wide, uneven space, lumpy with snow where some low undulations and crannies offered them shelter. Some were resting, knees and haunches sunk in the haze of uplifted snow. Others, already upright on straying legs, were springing aside like blown leaves; the twin spurs of their horns appeared at once whimsical and perplexed. The Duke aimed, tightened his fingers, and the first quarrel flew to its kill.

Chapter 30

BUT FOR THE WIND, it turned out more or less as the hunt-master had predicted. Faced with the advancing body of men, the sudden stampede of animals checked and the group ran jumping from place to place, high as puppets, while the snow stank and steamed from their panic. Some of the young pranced round the brink and crazily leaped, or equally crazily attempted to scrabble over the edge, as if descent on that side had been possible. These were lost. The older beasts, however, ran sideways and tried an outflanking movement.

They were allowed to succeed. Those which reached the incoming ledge were taken by the men waiting with nets. Those which made for the chasm were picked off as they came. By that time, the plateau was strewn with dark carcasses, and the snow was red and yellow and brown. The remnants of the herd clustered trembling together, their breath white, their eyes wide.

There was a pause. The crescent now broken, men moved about, gasping; tugging out and refitting spears, bending, feet braced, to strain the crossbow cord up to its limit. A longbow could manage ten arrows in the time it took to prepare a crossbow for one. But a crossbow for hunting was deadlier.

Nicholas was collecting spears, Moriz beside him. Someone – the chamberlain – was calling to him. The chamberlain said, 'Are you doing nothing, M. de Fleury? You have not even shot your first bolt!' Some flakes of snow, descending, spotted the blue and red of his face.

He had shouted. They had all been shouting, from excitement and to be heard in the wind. The Duke turned. Moriz said shortly, 'He can't span.'

It wasn't quite true. His leg was just less than agony now: he could have managed. Nicholas said, 'I was waiting for just the right moment.'

'Then it has come,' said the Duke. 'You see my men at each side, moving forward. They have stones. When we are ready, they will use them to induce the herd to rush forward. As they pass, we shall kill them. You will take your position over there, and you will shoot.' A sprinkling of flakes, thicker now, drove between them.

'My lord!' said the master-huntsman.

'My lord?' Nicholas said, cupping his ear. 'My lord was speaking?' He left Moriz and made his obedient way to the Duke, hurrying as much as was possible.

He reached the Duke. The Duke said shortly, 'Shoot this time. Over there.'

'At the chamois?' said Nicholas, lifting the crossbow. He sounded surprised. Nevertheless he took aim, steadied, and made to press the release.

'*No!*' said the Duke and his chamberlain in unison. The chamberlain, who had begun to hasten over, suddenly stopped. The Duke raised a hand and delivered a blow that almost broke his guest's wrist. Sigismond said, 'Do you know what you are doing?' The man Cavalli had appeared at his side.

Nicholas lowered the bow and stared at his wrist, and the Duke. He still looked surprised. Snow fell. 'I wondered,' he said. 'That is, why you wanted me to fire from the front. It would just have driven them backwards over the –'

'My lord!' repeated the huntsman, arriving. 'We must leave. There has never been seen such a harvest as we have already. Let us collect them and go.' Already the mounds in the snow were grey and white.

'And lose the rest? No!' said the Duke. 'Make the signal. And you' – to Nicholas – 'stand over there.'

The face of Nicholas cleared. 'Beside the chamberlain?'

The Duke glanced at him. 'I will speak to you later,' he said, and lifted his hand, giving an order. The huntsmen, armed, formed two uneven lines. At the sight of the signal, a confusion of shouting broke out in the distance, accompanied by muffled thuds. The feet of the small band of chamois plucked at the snow, and their heads turned like vanes on a steeple. Then the boldest put its nose down and rushed forward, and the others came too. They leaped as they came, soaring over the moraine of their dead. As they came, the huntsmen shot, all except Nicholas. And the Duke, who was a brave man, one saw, did not move from his side. Nor did Cavalli.

Three chamois escaped, floating over the gorge to the pinnacles on its far side. One left blood in its tracks. On the plateau, men were running now, dragging together the kill, roping and lifting it.

There was no way to take it down except over the shoulders, and everyone save the Duke was expected to bear what he could. The bows and spearpoints were bagged, the quivers closed. It was hard now to see from one end of the plateau to the other, and below, the marbled landscape faded and vanished. 'Faulty alum,' said Nicholas hoarsely; but no one understood the joke except himself, and he didn't repeat it. He kept meeting John's furious eye: the chamberlain avoided him, but Antonio Cavalli kept close and helped him take one of the beasts on his back.

Cavalli said, 'How is the knee? It will be difficult, going down.'

Nicholas looked round, so far as he could. 'Well enough. At least I shall be going down at my own speed, not someone else's. I have to thank you for that.'

'You wore a stout strap,' said Cavalli. Their faces were too stiff to smile.

Last, Father Moriz came up and spoke to him. It took the form of a diatribe so vehement that the snow fell off the priest's eyebrows. Nicholas moved off with the others, still listening. He hoped all the time that Father Moriz was going to swear, but he didn't. In the course of it, John inserted himself beside them by adroit management of a well-directed haunch and two hooves. He said, 'What happened? They pushed you.'

'They pushed him, and then gave him a steel bow,' said Father Moriz. 'He didn't use it. In this cold, it would have snapped when the bolt was released.'

'It might have hurt someone,' explained Nicholas.

'I know what a steel bow does when it splinters,' John le Grant said. 'It might have gone through your skull. It might just as well have killed the man standing next to you.' His voice suddenly faded.

'That's why I was standing next to him,' Nicholas said. 'Luckily, I think he guessed that I knew. What have you got on your back? I've got an ox on my back and you're carrying an overgrown rabbit. I wish I hadn't come. I'm going to spend the rest of my life like a horseshoe.'

He went on talking, because he felt like it.

It was not a descent for weaklings, but neither was it beyond a band of strong and experienced men. The guides led, prodding the snow with their spear-butts and shearing the rounded ledges to reveal their true dimensions. In some ways it was easier because the soft snow provided a grip. In others it was terrible because the wind thrust the snow into their noses and eyes, and twice obliterated everything in a dense white haze in which particles seemed to rise and fall from every direction at once. Then they halted and crouched until it was over.

Along with them in the searing pure air they carried a miasma of blood and perspiration and dung. They also carried, wrapped about them, the beneficent warmth of strong pelt and powerful bodies still hot from the kill. To rest was not entirely a hardship except, in the case of Nicholas, when he came to stand up with the weight on his back. The second time, Father Moriz gave him his spear and a hand under the elbow.

Since it occurred to no one, least of all Nicholas, to be concerned for an animal, there was a subterranean cheerfulness under the strain. When, halfway down, the snowfall stopped and they were able to halt at a platform to make a fire, and release their burdens and eat, men began to smile suddenly and call to one another. Nicholas stretched his legs beside Father Moriz and John. The Duke had turned his back on him, so no one risked greeting him – yet. Nicholas didn't mind.

He felt happy. He had only recently realised that he felt happy. For a considerable time – for a day – he had been released from everything but physical danger. His difficult gift had not been required, nor had the interminable exercises by which he kept himself sane. He had thought of nothing but each moment as it came.

It would end soon. But, his feet lacerated, his knee on fire, his face cracked and every muscle screaming in protest, he was content.

They were met an hour after that by men battling up from below, who took the beasts from them and led them down cleared ways to the bottom, where the great sledges had been brought, each pulled by eight plumed and iron-shod horses, and covered with velvet fringed awnings with the Duke's crest in gold. The carts for the chamois came after.

There were braziers fitted inside each sledge, and a place for spiced wine and fresh meat and cushions. They moved off as the last of the light left the sky. Then the torches were lit and, under the canopies, faces glowed red round the braziers. The runners hissed over the snow; the moon rose; they ate and drank and laughed, and became sleepy; and woke, and drank and laughed and argued again. At some point the Duke, in the leading sledge, broke into hearty song, and the roar of a bawdy hunting chorus surged down the chain, and was followed by others. When the lights of the castle appeared, the cheer that rose was not at all sober. The sledges entered the gates and stopped, and men staggered out, Nicholas stumbling among them. Two or three fell. The others waited, respectfully swaying, for their Duke to emerge.

Duke Sigismond of the Tyrol left his sledge on a chair carried by two liveried men who, with twenty others, had run from the building to serve them. The Duke's hat, fallen awry, showed his fair hair puffed over his face, which was rosy and swollen and lay to one side, on his shoulder. Experiencing a jolt, he opened one large shallow eye and uttered a thick but not unamiable obscenity. A short, bulky shadow at the top of the stairs suddenly moved and walked briskly indoors.

The Duchess. Her expression, Nicholas saw, had not been one of disgust, or impatience. What she had felt was relief.

One day her husband, who shared his favours with so many others, would fail to come back, or would come back to her dying or crippled. She hunted: she knew what the risks were. Hazily, Nicholas wondered if the absences helped: if the times they were living apart were easier than the times like these, when she was aware of every folly and danger. He wondered if she would leave the Tyrol if Sigismond died; or stay, as her sister had stayed to become permanent Dowager Duchess of Brittany. He thought she would stay. She would be better in the Tyrol, he thought.

The darkness was back: the weight lay again on his temples. 'You should have stuck to water,' Father Moriz remarked.

'There wasn't any,' Nicholas said.

Father Moriz had him under the arm, and was supporting John le Grant on his other side. For a gnome, he was strong. He said, 'Nicholas, I can understand a few tongues, but not that one. Never mind. I can recognise an excuse in any language. Come along. You will need some wits about you, I think, in the morning.'

The Duke's wits being in the same state as his own, it was afternoon the next day before the summons came: the illustrious and powerful prince lord Sigismond, Duke of Austria and Styria and Count of the Tyrol, requested the presence of Nicholas de Fleury, Knight of the Order of the Scottish Unicorn, resident of Venice and Burgundy.

'Ouch,' said John le Grant. 'Neither of them the happiest of attributes just at the moment. Are we coming too?'

'No. You both drank too much,' Nicholas said. He didn't want them with him. If he was right, the Duke didn't either. In the event, he went to the Duke's chamber alone.

Sigismond looked unchanged, except perhaps for a little extra fleshiness under the eyes. In the short time he had known him,

Nicholas had seen him make some extraordinary recoveries. Sitting now in his chair of state with his brimmed beaver hat banded with pearls, his quilted coat shawled with fur, his rings, his chains, his belt, his pendant and brooches, this was Sigismond, Duke of the Tyrol, in his princely persona. Nicholas – who had gone to some pains as well – did the right thing and knelt, and was allowed to rise. There was no one else in the room except Antonio Cavalli.

The Duke said, 'Your knee pains you?'

'Yes, your grace,' Nicholas said.

The Duke paused. 'You deserved it. You could have killed me. You would not have lived very long after that.'

'No, my lord,' Nicholas said. 'I regret it. Unfortunately, my alternative was immediate death.'

There was another pause. Cavalli looked down. The Duke said, 'There is another matter.'

Nicholas bowed. He had not been asked to sit. Cavalli was sitting. He was wearing a neat doublet and a round cap and he was dark as the men from between Trent and Venice were dark. He had a relative in the German fondaco in Venice. Nicholas said, 'Yes, my lord Duke?'

'The bow,' Sigismond said. 'The steel bow.'

'I was given it, your grace,' Nicholas said. 'To use it would have been suicide. I knew it was not by your will.'

Once, the Duke must have been a ravishing child. When he asked the future Pope, for example, to write him those love letters. Now the two lines deepened at the root of the tip-tilted nose and the pink arched lips drooped. 'I have mentioned,' said the Duke heavily, 'the man who calls himself Martin, of the company called Vatachino?'

Spring came. Summer flowered. His headache disappeared. Nicholas said, 'You mentioned, my lord, that you had decided to allot him the right to mine silver. It is not for me to censure a rival.'

'In that case, you must be unique,' said the Duke tartly. 'Are you too high-minded, also, to present any case of your own? You appear to be a remarkably poor envoy.'

'Certainly,' Nicholas said, 'I am a representative of my lord of Burgundy in so far as I bring his goodwill and letters. In the matters of alum and silver, I represent only myself and my Bank, and am as free as Herr Martin to bring wealth to the Tyrol from both.' He paused respectfully. 'The mountainside did not seem the appropriate place for debate.'

The Duke's hand tapped on his knee. He said, 'Wine, man!'

without turning his head. Cavalli got up. The Duke said, 'How, free? You have a business in Bruges. Whoever finances me will offend Charles of Burgundy. I should instantly redeem my pawned land. I should be strong enough to make war on the Switzers, who in turn will blame him. You didn't think of that?' Cavalli brought him a great cup of wine which he seized and drank off. Then he tossed the cup on the floor, where it cracked a tile. 'You didn't think of that?' he repeated. 'Or you plan to make so much profit from me that you don't care?' Cavalli picked up the cup and retreated with it. He cast a glance at Nicholas as he passed.

Nicholas said, 'My lord, none could have put the problem better. May I speak?'

'That is what you are here for,' said the Duke. He was still angry.

Nicholas shifted, but only a little, on his damaged leg. He said, 'In my opinion, my lord, Burgundy will never permit you to redeem the land you have lost, no matter what money you raise. On the other hand, she would appreciate a rich neighbour, able to recruit its own armies against the Switzers, provided only that the cantons did not turn their anger, in turn, against Burgundy.'

'You are repeating my point. They will, if I license a Fleming.' He had another cup in his hand. He said, 'You tire me. Sit down.'

'I am sorry, your grace.'

Nicholas sat, without looking at Cavalli. Cavalli said, 'Perhaps Ser Niccolò would take some wine?'

He clearly knew the Duke well. A wave of one hand indicated permission. Nicholas said, 'Water, for preference. But thank you.'

'We don't keep water,' said the Duke. 'You don't answer.'

'I feared to tire your grace,' Nicholas said. 'There are ways to prevent the cantons from blaming Burgundy, and even ways of preventing Burgundy from blaming me. Just as there are ways of selling alum without depriving Bartolomeo Zorzi of his papal profit. And if such ways met with your grace's approval, I can offer you, at the end of it all, a contract markedly better than any the Vatachino put forward.'

'You don't know what that was,' the Duke said.

'I know Martin,' said Nicholas. He took the wine Cavalli had brought him and looked at it regretfully. He said, 'But, of course, you said the contract was sealed.'

Cavalli looked at the Duke, who was frowning. There was a beading of wine on his fur. 'Recent events have unsealed it,' said the Duke.

*

'You're drunk,' said John le Grant enviously.

'I'm not,' Nicholas said. 'You'll be telling me the Duke is drunk, next.'

'So?' said Father Moriz. They had been pacing the floor, waiting for him. They looked nervous. It surprised him that they thought anything could go wrong.

'So we've got it,' Nicholas said. He sat down, and did his best to enunciate clearly. 'He gets his loan: six thousand pounds in French money and two thousand in Scots. We have a licence to mine the Inn alum for three years, and the new silver seams as soon as we can get a man through to Lyons. I knew Sessetti and Nori when they were with the Medici at Geneva. The Duke wants us to send him Astorre. I have to see the Duchess in private, but Innsbruck will manufacture the cannon: Father Moriz will set up the smelting and then go on to Venice.'

'And you?' the priest said. He sat down, looking breathless. 'Wait. What about the deal with the Vatachino?'

'Cancelled,' Nicholas said. 'Smacks for ungentlemanly conduct. Martin bribed a couple of men to be nasty, and they were a little too nasty for the Duke's political comfort. And personal comfort: he might have been killed. So no contract. And only three chamberlains.'

'So you're staying,' said the priest.

'John and I will set it up and stay over the summer. No Alexandria. I'll send somebody later.'

'Will you?'

'Egypt can wait,' Nicholas said. 'So can the gold. This is bigger.' He realised too late that neither Moriz nor John had put the question. A third man had come into the room.

Father Ludovico de Severi da Bologna, Patriarch of Antioch, wore the unorthodox habit, heavily stained, of his original calling as a wandering Observatine friar of the Franciscan Order. His girdle had, perhaps, been used as a lead-line for pig-lard and his battered crucifix was the size and weight of an axe-head. There was no sign of his hat. Where Father Moriz was short of body and leg, Father Ludovico was of medium height and stoutly boned, from his nose to his considerable rib-cage. Apart from the ruddy skin of his face and his tonsure, all his surfaces appeared covered by an explosion of curling black hair.

Nicholas knew him. The history of the past decade had been punctuated by thundering collisions between himself and the Patriarch in various parts of the world. Father Ludovico had been last heard of in Sweden, trying to bring the Pope's peace to the

Scandinavian wars. John knew him from Cyprus. John had known, Nicholas realised, that da Bologna was here. He had just kept quiet because he was sulking.

Nicholas said, 'The wine wasn't as wonderful as all that, and I only got to try six of the women. Father Ludovico, go away.'

'I've just come. I see Satan has got you again. You are helping him in Christ's work?' said the Patriarch, casting an eye on his fellow priest.

'He managed the drink himself,' said Father Moriz. Nicholas was entertained.

'And so tell me about the cannon,' said the Patriarch, sitting down.

There was the kind of silence that often occurred in his presence. Then Nicholas said, 'You're not getting it. It's for the King of Scotland. Anyway, we've done you a much greater service. We've shown Duke Sigismond how to get rich. If you want money, come back in six months.'

'The Turks may be in Vienna in six months,' the Patriarch said. His voice rolled.

'Well, they may go away again. Bessarion had a low opinion of Vienna.'

'Money, how?' the Patriarch asked with apparent interest. 'Ah! The silver mines! And, perhaps, the alum? You are exploiting the Tyrol alum in defiance of the papal monopoly?'

'No,' said Nicholas eventually. 'That is, papal markets won't really suffer. We're sending ours north, beyond Flanders. Scotland takes alum from anywhere.'

'I see. And the silver?'

'Oh,' said Nicholas airily. 'The silver has nothing to do with us. We stumbled across it. But the French are sending to mine it. They've a lot of experience. Lyons.'

There was the kind of silence that happened sometimes when he spoke, as well.

The Patriarch was smiling. His eyebrows, unlike those of the younger priest, arched like shredded black wool. He said, 'And the cannon?'

'I told you. For the King of Scotland,' Nicholas said. 'It took a lot of trouble to arrange all of that. I shouldn't like anything to disturb it, or there wouldn't be any money for anything. You *are* here for money?'

'The Pontiff,' said Father Ludovico, 'is much concerned for the soul of Duke Sigismond, since his return to Mother Church. The spiritual health of all the Germanies concerns him. Partly. Chiefly, I came to see you.'

He had been afraid of it. All the happy wine in his system disappeared. He said, 'In this weather? Why?'

The Patriarch of the Latins in Antioch sat down and stretched his feet to the stove. His boots were patched and his hose were heavily felted. He said, 'The Lord visited me with an inspiration. We like to keep an eye on you. I wondered if you'd heard the latest from Scotland. Is there anything to eat here? I had a hen from that woman Gertrude, but that was this morning.'

He had been here since morning. Nicholas could see Moriz and John exchange looks: eventually Moriz got up. 'I'll see to it,' he said, and went out.

'An expert on metals, so I'm told,' said Father Ludovico. 'No doubt he prays over them. It must teach him a lot. You were better off with Godscalc. Pity, that.'

'What about Scotland?' said John, which was helpful of him.

'Oh, gossip. You may have heard it already. Couriers getting through?' the Patriarch said.

'They're not as persistent as you are,' Nicholas said. 'What news?'

'Well, the King's married – but you knew that: you helped him celebrate. Then his sister went off with her husband – but you knew that too. I'm sure you knew that. Then Anselm Adorne went, and was created a knight – Were you created a knight? Will God never cease to surprise us? Then Sir Anselm went back –'

'Back?' said Nicholas.

'To Scotland. That would be after you left. The death of poor Godscalc. You gave up material things in order to be at his side. The Lord will honour you for it. And it will please you to know that your friend Anselm Adorne reaped the benefit.'

John had stopped looking at him. 'In what way?' Nicholas said. But he guessed.

'The land,' the Patriarch said. 'The land the poor silly girl forfeited when she absconded. All the estates belonging to Arran her husband. The King partitioned it out. This servant, that friend – even some musician, I hear, received plenty. But Sir Anselm – now there's royal generosity – was given a barony. He is Heere van Cortachy now. A good bit of well-paying land in the north-east, so they tell me. And since Adorne is to lodge the Princess Mary in Bruges – did you know that? – the King has been properly lavish with bits of Boyd land to help the new Baron there with his expenses. That is,' the Patriarch said, 'although the King wouldn't mind Thomas Boyd's head on a hat-stand, he wouldn't let sister Mary come to want.'

'So the Princess and her husband are staying in Bruges?' Nicholas said. The door had opened and Father Moriz came in, a servant following. A hearty smell of meat joined the thick air from the stove.

'By now. At the Hôtel Jerusalem, with the good Vrouwe Margriet as his hostess. The new Baron himself, of course, is not there, and so will escape any ignominy. Is that ale? Take it away.'

This time, Nicholas refused to respond. The Patriarch, intent on the board, had already unfastened his knife-case.

Father Moriz took a seat not far off. 'The new baron? You speak of Anselm Adorne?'

'Now my lord of Cortachy,' elucidated the Patriarch, filling his mouth. 'Back from Scotland with more on his mind than trade meetings. He's planning to travel this spring. Quite a programme. Rome, of course. Genoa. Egypt. He should be in Alexandria by the summer, and Cyprus and Rhodes, they say, just after that. A holy pilgrimage, naturally. A visit to friends. The Levant is stuffed full of Adornos. A son's going too, and a niece. They say he's leaving next month, with the Duke of Burgundy's blessing.'

It was like one of his own traps. So neat, so comprehensive, so final. Anselm Adorne, waiting only for his departure, had scooped the honours in Scotland and was now proceeding to forestall him in the Levant. And so the snare could be closed.

'No,' said Nicholas.

Father Ludovico concentrated on his food: his mouth was as full as a nesting-box. Behind the mess was a smile.

John said, 'Nicholas –'

'No,' said Nicholas for a second time.

Father Moriz said, 'I think, Nicholas, that you will have to listen. And, very likely, have to go.'

He did not need to listen. He knew why the Franciscan was here. Ever since the first missions of the Observatine monks to the East, Ludovico da Bologna had travelled the world, from Persia to Tartary, from Rome to Egypt, from Poland to Germany at the bidding of Popes. At the bidding of Bessarion, Cardinal-Protector of his Order. He had lived in Jerusalem for years, and had failed, as Nicholas had, to reach Ethiopia.

Because Nicholas travelled too, they frequently met. And wherever they met, it seemed to Nicholas, his private and business activities were immediately commandeered for the Patriarch's purpose, which was to cajole and threaten Christians and Muslims alike to halt the advance of the Ottoman Turk.

For that, he preferred Nicholas to be in the Levant, not

submerged in a vast operation for Duke Sigismond. The threat to spoil this winter's work was real enough. The other threat, it was clear, was that posed by the discerning, the increasingly competitive Anselm Adorne.

Shrewdly, the Patriarch was proposing a scheme which was not in itself unattractive. Nicholas had always meant, at some point, to visit Egypt. David de Salmeton was there. The gold was worth looking for. The agency needed attention. He had eighteen months still to run of his penitential exile from Scotland. And on the most private level he did not think, at the moment, that he could contemplate another meeting with Gelis.

Nevertheless, the fact remained that he did not want to go to Alexandria soon, or stay long; and he resented being manipulated. So his first impulse had been to refuse. He had refused.

But he knew all the time that he would go, because he could not stomach what else he had heard. He didn't like what had happened in Scotland. He objected to the fact that, having been pleased enough to see the Bank in the Tyrol, the Duke of Burgundy had now apparently given Adorne the key to the Levant. He could not allow all his plans to be endangered by an adversary as smooth, as adroit, he now knew, as Anselm Adorne.

The Duchess Eleanor gave a farewell feast for her three visitors in the early spring, when the ways had cleared and all the preliminary work for the mining was done. She held it at her preferred castle of Meran, for the tumultuous double courts had again separated, with their horses and dogs, their hordes of servants and permanent and semi-permanent guests; the chaplains, the entourage of honour, the Court Master, the stewards, the Marshal, the chamberlains (lacking one). The men she and Sigismond liked to keep about them: the lawyers who were also humanists; the highly qualified churchmen who collected books and advised, and wrote poetry in their spare time. They had an astronomer. They had had the Patriarch of Antioch for a short time and had been thankful, as always, when he left.

Her father had been a great poet, writing in English and Scots before and after he was freed to rule his country. Her sister the Queen of France had composed verse. She and Sigismond collected books and commissioned translations: there was always a room full of scribes somewhere, some of them men of renown. Sigismond had good Latin but little French: she had had a French romance put into German for him, and had helped with it herself. German was very like Scots.

Books kept her company when he went off to his castle on the lake to put the romances into practice. There was a fiction that she didn't know what went on in Sigmundsburg, even while she was sending doctors to women in childbirth, and bringing their young to fill places at court. But she had friends: Albrecht of Bavaria, who sent her books, and Mechtilde of the Palatinate. And books and manuscripts were always coming from Augsburg. She had got one from Rome to give to the Abbot at Neustift. She had used books, long ago, to placate the Archbishop. Their advisers borrowed them. Their advisers stayed with them, she sometimes thought, because of them. And they were a pleasure, sometimes, in themselves, if not always. She was not as intellectual as Mechtilde, who had founded a university.

She had found that the young merchant Nicholas had an interest in medical and mechanical treatises and was reasonably familiar with the classics, but had read few romances. He was comfortable to chat to and play cards with, and he could sing. She called him Nicol, which indicated a measure of guest-friendship but not more. He and the priest and the engineer had been accepted by their equals well enough once it was plain they spoke German, and were not the Welsch, the French-speaking Burgundians no one could tolerate. None of them presumed.

She thought, and so did Cavalli and Lindsay, that Sigismond had dealt with the mining contracts extremely well, and he was happy, in any case, to leave the detail to others. He would want to know, however, exactly how and when the loan money would come.

She knew how he would spend it. On buildings. On roads, if he listened to what everyone said and was wise. On war, if he didn't and wasn't. If the loan hadn't come in this fashion, he would have raised it from some other source, with far more potential for harm. This way, they might be able to afford all that Sigismond was going to spend anyway.

Now the planning was done, the equipment here, the lodgings for the workmen arranged. A mine was a temporary village, needing cabins, water, ovens, a church. It had interested her to visit the three men in the office they used in the castle. The last time, she had found de Fleury alone at the table, his fingers slowly smoothing a map. The placid occupation was contradicted by an air of extraordinary tension. Then she saw the jewel strung from his hand. He was divining.

She had once seen the other man do it: the man who had died. She knew it was possible. In the Tyrol, their maps were too poor.

The other man had been poring over a drawing of Florence. He wanted to see, he had said, in what street his mistress was sleeping that night. She remembered how worn he had looked. Now, she hesitated.

De Fleury must have heard her, and turned. His face against the light was not at first distinct, and she smiled, stepping towards him.

She said, 'Weel, Nicol! What sinistrous trick have we here? You've become crafty now at your trade?'

His hand moved, half palming the stone. She waited for him to stand. When he did, he had uncovered the bob and laid it on the map. His back was still to the light. He said, 'Duchess.'

She looked at him, and then made up her mind and walked forward to study the map. It was large, but not professionally done. She thought, from the ink on his fingers, that he had probably drawn it himself. It showed the streets of a large town and some of their houses. On another sheet, laid aside, she saw the plans of three dwellings. She recognised two. One, unmistakable because of its church, was the Hôtel Jerusalem, Bruges. The other was her own late sister's house, that of Wolfaert van Borselen in Veere. She realised that the town on the map must be Bruges.

She said, her voice kindly, 'I interrupted. Ye were seeking your wife. Did you find her?'

He spoke, his voice slower than usual. 'No, your grace. I didn't expect to find her. She stays outside Bruges.'

'Then who? My family, would it be?' She let him hear the reserve.

'No! No, your grace,' he said immediately. 'Another lady. I found her. I had been . . . concerned for her safety.'

'And is she safe?' the Duchess asked. She moved, inducing him to turn round. She saw it was as she suspected. She said, 'Am I allowed to know her name?'

'Of course,' said de Fleury. 'Her name is Margot. She is the close friend of Gregorio, my manager. She went missing.'

'But now she is back?' the Duchess said. 'You can tell that?'

'It seems so,' he said. 'They are both there, in the house that we use.'

'Then they are at ease, and you too. But don't fall sick for their sake,' said the Duchess. 'Spare your gift. Or you'll find me ill pleased that I taught you.'

'Never that,' de Fleury said. 'You showed me a way. If it does me harm, then most likely I deserve it.'

Their eyes joined. 'Aye,' she said. 'I jaloused that already.' When she turned at the door, he had already crushed the maps from his desk and discarded them.

It was their last meeting in private. Soon he was gone, with his entourage and companions. They would cross the ridge and descend the sunny slopes of the mountains where the apple blossom sparkled in ice and the southern warmth beckoned.

She did not envy Nicholas de Fleury, although she would not forget him. Indeed, in her way, she incorporated him in her planning much as he, in his turn, had used her. She did not know that she had been the fourth stage of a plan which – because of a death – had undergone a masterly reconstitution.

Nicholas de Fleury had been debarred from the chase of his choice. No one had said he couldn't fire from the coverts. Or return, once this diversion was over, to see what he had killed.

Chapter 31

ALEXANDRIA, THE JEWEL on the northernmost sea-strand of Egypt, was one of the romantic places of the world to which Nicholas, on his wedding day, had promised himself to bring Gelis, his wife. It suited him to enter it, without her, three months after leaving the Tyrol. He had John le Grant at his side and a few writings attributable to a parrot.

He did not leave his main arena without thought. He had listened to Moriz. He made sure, before going too far, that Anselm Adorne was genuinely committed to the same journey. (Priests were not immune to slips of the tongue.) But the warning proved to be true. The Baron Cortachy was not only armed with safe conducts and ducal letters of credence, he had made a will preparatory to leaving. It confirmed, as nothing else could, his rising importance in Scotland and Flanders.

The Baron had bequeathed his best sapphire to the Bishop of St Andrews, for love of Maarten his son. A stained glass window with the Adorne coat of arms was promised to the Charterhouse monks outside Perth. To mark his funeral, that of a prince among merchants, ells of linen in grey, black and white were stipulated for the church and his lying-in-state; and a file of twenty-four men, robed in black, from the weigh-houses. The bells of three spires were to toll, and a thousand poor men to receive alms. Bruges would remember its eminent citizen, Anselm Adorne.

Shriven, ducally sponsored, Adorne had planned to set out in February, and hoped to celebrate Easter in Rome. Seven companions had been invited to ride with him: a chamberlain in holy orders, two merchant kinsfolk, a niece, a monk, a ducal chaplain and an eminent burgess of Bruges. A son was to join at Pavia.

So Nicholas de Fleury was told. He did not know, because the message did not reach him till later, that when Anselm Adorne finally left, the number of his company had increased by two.

Proceeding in turn, Nicholas de Fleury travelled south from the Tyrol with his metallurgical padre and John. They called, on the way, at some of the mines. They stopped at Bozen, which had a market favoured by Venetian traders. They arrived in Venice in March. Julius sent the Bank's grand oared boat to Mestre to meet them, and Nicholas saw Father Moriz assessing the silken canopy and the gilding and the carving and the preposterous liveries. Nicholas spoke to the oarsmen, who looked frightened, and then took his place and was silent.

He felt odd. It should have been terrible, this first return to the city he had left two years ago, rich and comforted and full of childish desires. But as the islands beyond Mestre slipped past – Murano, San Michele – and the familiar skyline appeared, with its golden domes and towers and palaces; as the boat skimmed through the winding canal and into the great thoroughfare of water that led to the Rialto and the Bank, he was touched by something like the warmth of the old days, returning to Bruges.

Bruges was no longer home. He had lost Bruges, with everything else. On the other hand, this was a place he had made. He understood, for a moment, the disappointment that lay behind Cristoffels's stiffness and Gregorio's past disapproval: disappointment that, having created this astonishing bank which he was entering now, this great mansion full of activity of which he should be the head, he had left it to others to run.

It was being well enough done. Funded as it was, it could hardly help but succeed. It was hardly his fault that he had spent, in his life, less than the makings of one year in Venice. He hadn't chosen to go to Cyprus. He had had to leave for Africa, or the Bank would have failed. He had never ceased to communicate, except when circumstances made it impossible. The fact was, however, that he had guided it in the main from a distance, and of the people coming to shake his hand now – Padrone! Padrone! – he knew only half.

He understood, but that didn't mean that he would change the course he had laid down because of it. It was his life he was living, not theirs.

Nevertheless, he arrived, and made himself known, and proceeded to launch a dense programme of work that was to last through the rest of March and the most of the following month. He sat with the clerks, and spent nights with the letter-books and ledgers, Moriz at his shoulder with Cristoffels and Julius. Summoned, the agents came in from their branches: Florence, Genoa, Milan, Naples, Rome; and he took the patron's chair behind the big table, his officials beside him, and heard their reports, and asked his questions, and gave his orders.

He was arming the company, as he must, against Adorne. And there was time. Adorne was still on his way. The agents were home, primed and briefed, long before the Baron Cortachy and his train reached their cities. And as Adorne began to pass through, the reports arrived of what he was doing.

He was meeting merchants, that was clear. Many, of course, were related to him. It was also, however, something of a triumphal progress. Anselm Adorne was being greeted, entertained, even fawned upon by the rulers of each republic or duchy he passed through, and was being royally treated.

An early report, hurriedly scribbled, said that he was being represented in some regions as an envoy of the monarch of Scotland. A second message contradicted the first. He carried Burgundian credentials of ambassadorial weight. The chaplain in his party was de Francqueville, one of the Duke of Burgundy's personal confessors. The report from Milan, sent in the third week in March in a rainstorm, mentioned that the Duke and the Baron had hunted together with leopards. The lady Gelis van Borselen, dame de Fleury, had accompanied the party.

That packet came as Nicholas was leaving for a meeting appointed by the Great Council. He read the letter as the *barchetta* swerved and splashed on its way to St Mark's and the mallets of the smiths and the shipwrights and the caulkers thundered far off in the sheds of the Arsenal. He wondered, with part of his mind, how well off they might be for timber. John le Grant said, 'What is it?'

Nicholas folded the paper away. 'My wife is with Anselm Adorne.'

John le Grant opened his eyes. With the milder weather, the cold sores had gone, and the redness from around the white eyelashes. Oddly, the vigour of the engineer's manner had also diminished. It was as if he had determined to distance himself from something he feared or distrusted. Now he said only, 'Your wife is coming here?'

'Time will tell. At the moment, they're all on their way to pick up Jan at Pavia.'

Adorne's oldest son had just completed a jurist's course at Pavia. From Pavia to Venice was three days by fast boat. It had always been possible that Gelis would circumvent the postponement and try to join him on terms of her own. She would be angry, too, about Florence. There was, of course, no word of a child.

John said, 'If she comes, will you take her with us?'

'I should think she'd find that very unpleasant,' Nicholas said. 'Not to mention dangerous. No. She could wait with Julius, if she likes, until we get back.'

It had a feasible ring. Talk of danger was well founded at any rate: the noise from the Arsenal was as significant as it had been six years before, when he had sailed from Venice to Africa, leaving a city going to war.

That time, it had been summer. This time, Easter was late so that the place was filling with pilgrims as well as mercenaries: rich and needy from every nation preparing to go to the Holy Land; finding and hiring a dragoman; buying their mats and jars and chamberpots and feather beds and mattresses and basins; their wax lights and tinder, their salt meat and hen-coops, their locking boxes for money; their trinkets of rings and crosses to take and have blessed. And, in between, visiting shrines and relics; investigating the islands; being conducted through the Arsenal; viewing the Doge; and admiring the elephant trained to dance behind bars.

Soon the poles with their red crosses on white would go up in front of St Mark's, and they would rush to book their places on the great galleys going to Jaffa: twenty ducats on leaving and twenty ducats on arrival for the privilege of lying a month toe to toe with diseased and vomiting strangers in a hold dimly lit by four hatchways, and crossing a sea menaced with war.

The meeting he was going to had to do with that war: with Sultan Mehmet's threat to end the Venetian Empire with eighty thousand men and a war fleet of eighteen years' building. The Doge and Council had stopped asking Nicholas de Fleury to join them in person. He had paid them much of the gold they had asked for, and had lent them the *San Niccolò* and the *Ghost* to join the ships going to Crete: it was up to the Signoria to crew them. He had sent leave, through Julius, for any of their own men who wished to join the Captain-General. The Captain-General was not of the highest competence but Paul Erizzo was, the Venetian commander on the spot.

The Doge had accepted his gold and his ships. Subsequently, he had not only freed Nicholas de Fleury from war service, but allotted him additional privileges by virtue of his forthcoming mission to Egypt. The Doge, too, had been harangued by Ludovico da Bologna.

That, then, was disposed of. And God knew Nicholas didn't

have to hunt for reasons for not taking Gelis. It irritated him, none the less, to have to prepare for a confrontation. He hadn't planned to leave until Easter was over, and all the ceremonies that launched the sailing season just after: the Corpus Christi processions, pairing pilgrims with senators; the Marriage of the Sea on Ascension Day, when five thousand ships accompanied the Bucentaur of the Doge to the neck of the Lido, where the Doge cast a ring in the sea and then invoked the Lord's blessing in the church of St Nicholas, saint beloved of mariners; saint whose power, they claimed, could endow the childless with sons.

He had counted on having weeks more in hand before he joined the *Ciaretti*.

He spent a few short-tempered days. The news, when it came, was brought by a courier from Genoa. Adorne was there with his son and the others. They were proceeding to Rome, and the lady Gelis van Borselen was still with them. The doctor had stopped at Pavia.

'The doctor? What doctor?' had said Julius impatiently. This dispatch had been brought to the padrone in his chamber, and after reading it through, Nicholas had called the others to hear.

'Guess,' said Nicholas. 'Who is the expectant nephew of Giammatteo Ferrari, the wealthiest professor of medicine in Pavia? Who has managed to achieve a free trip to see his frail uncle, and perhaps even view his frail uncle's printing presses?'

'Tobias Beventini?' said John le Grant. He eyed Nicholas.

'Tobie?' said Julius. 'I thought he disliked his uncle.'

'He doesn't dislike his uncle's library,' Nicholas said. 'And the old man's own children are dead.' He glanced at Father Moriz. 'You met our Tobie. He nursed Father Godscalc.'

'Oh, I know him,' said his metallurgical priest. 'We spoke a few times in Bruges.'

'Did you?' said Nicholas. He was aware of saying it sourly, for it explained a number of things. The rest of his mind was on the other problem.

John le Grant was thinking on the same lines, it seemed. He said, 'You say your lady's still with Adorne?'

'They're spending Easter in Rome. After that, instead of sailing from there, they propose to come north and take ship from Genoa. Adorne has a programme of calls he means to make on the way to the Holy Land. Corsica, Sardinia, Tunis – the voyage could take seven or eight weeks.'

'What will she do?' le Grant said.

'Stay with her party,' said Father Moriz unexpectedly. 'For if she comes here, no doubt she knows you will attempt to obstruct her.'

'That's what I thought,' Nicholas said. It surprised him that anyone else had worked it out. He could, of course, send persuasive friends to try to separate her from Adorne and bring her back home. He could go himself. But even if he contrived to get her away, it was hard to know how to keep her from going to Egypt, unless pinned down in irons. And that was not – not yet – part of the game. Anyway, as soon as she was alone, she'd take ship somehow. He had resigned himself to that.

He decided to leave Venice before April was finished. He had some business to do in Florence. If he got to Alexandria in June, he could keep ahead of her all the way if he wished. He could vanish.

He made his final calls. He had not avoided the homes of those Venetian merchants who had married the sisters from Naxos, but he had not, as it happened, spent any time with the princesses alone. One of them was the mother of Catherine, the girl married on paper to Zacco. The future Queen of Cyprus was sixteen and Zacco, of course, was his own age exactly. Nicholas happened not to encounter the girl, but received a box of Greek sweetmeats and a sugary farewell from the exquisite Fiorenza her mother.

Although her kiss was deep, his response – once automatic, overwhelming – was reliably absent. He wondered if, at twenty-nine, this was usual. First the years of natural joy; then the rule of passion closely confined by society; and finally conjunction to order, as with Sigismond's whores. If he had to, he could become the lover of Fiorenza or Violante once more, but he was no longer driven by appetite. It seemed likely he never would be again.

Which was convenient. Nicholas left Venice satisfied, no matter how he left the Venetians.

The elderly galley *Ciaretti*, highly taxed (as privately owned galleys properly were) and loaded by Livornese boatmen (as was the rule) moved out of her own Porto Pisano at the end of May, bound for Alexandria. With her she carried her patron, Nicholas de Fleury, Knight of the Unicorn, and for sailing-master she had John le Grant, fulfilling again the role he had occupied at his first meeting with Nicholas. Or half the role. Then, he had also been sailing-instructor.

Nine years before, his first ship, she had carried Nicholas and his company to all that awaited him in Trebizond. Now she was expendable. He had lent his better ships, for one reason or another, to the Signoria. They were well insured. He disliked both of them.

Behind in Venice, the Bank under Moriz, Julius and Cefo was

primed to subside into its usual routine, but with more than its normal vigour.

Behind in Florence remained a number of satisfied merchants, a busy agent, and various amused or astonished representatives of the families Medici and Strozzi. A week before their departure, Alessandra, purveyor of spectacles and mother of Lorenzo Strozzi, had let Nicholas take her hand, lying back in her chair attended by the sisters Antonia, the future wife of her son Lorenzo, and Maria, bride but not yet bedded wife of Tommaso Portinari of Bruges.

Alessandra had said, 'Marietta would never have done.'

The sisters looked down. 'No,' Nicholas had agreed. Everyone knew whom Lorenzo's first choice had been, and why it had been firmly scotched.

'I have to tell you,' Alessandra had continued, 'that I fear that you, too, have been irresponsible in your selection.'

'You disapproved of my wife,' Nicholas had said. 'But a van Borselen is not to be sneezed at.'

The matriarch of the Strozzi family had almost smiled. 'I am unlikely to disagree. I assumed, for that reason, that you would wish to keep her, although her precipitate arrival last autumn seemed childish. It is clear, having spoken to her, that she is so far from childish that she poses a problem.'

He had released her gnarled hand and sat back, displaying amusement. 'I am used to capable women, madonna.' The girls peeped at one another, and away.

She said, 'Oh yes, you see me, a widow, managing my possessions. You saw your first wife, also a widow, do likewise. I daresay the same applies even to courtesans.' Her spectacles slanted. Her mantled head, lifted, brought the cords of her neck into view. 'A married woman who runs after power, signor de Fleury, may end as a rival to her husband, instead of a partner. You should have asked the good Duchess Isabelle to pick you a bride. Sweet maids like Antonia and Maria ask nothing more than the arms of a good husband about them, and to experience the joy that many handsome children will bring.

'There is no happiness like it,' had continued Monna Alessandra, bestowing a fond if absent smile on each of the sisters. 'Those who pretend otherwise are misguided, and must depend on a good man's love to correct them.'

It had been an extraordinary conversation, too good to keep to himself. He couldn't tell anyone. What she was saying was, *Get her to bed.*

*

The last message to reach him from Venice began so ominously that John le Grant enquired what it was. Nicholas read the gist of it aloud.

Instead of proceeding to take the slow-moving great ship from Genoa, half of the Baron Cortachy's party had elected to travel instead by one of the faster pilgrim galleys from Venice. They had arrived in Venice. They had even called at the Bank. They wanted spectator seats on a boat for the Ascension Day ceremony.

'Gelis?' had said John le Grant at that point.

'Wait. No,' Nicholas had said. 'The monk, the Duke of Burgundy's chaplain and Daniel Colebrant. Only three went to Venice. The rest stayed with Adorne.'

'Taking the leisurely trip via Tunis,' le Grant said. 'So you'll be in Egypt before your lady, right enough. But she'll be expecting you. Are you going to let on that you knew she was coming?'

'Oh, she knows that,' Nicholas said. 'She knows I'd be tracking Adorne. I was bound to be told she was with him.'

John said, 'So what has she done with the boy? Left him with Margot in Bruges?'

'The Patriarch didn't say so,' Nicholas said. If Margot was in Bruges, then certainly she came there alone. He added, 'It'll be all right. There are nurses.' As always, John left the subject as soon as its interest had faded. He never had to check John.

They made only one call of note before finally leaving the Italian mainland. Lorenzo Strozzi, thirty-seven years old and a little plump and a little naked of hair, was waiting in person at Naples to embrace Claes his young playmate from Bruges, and sweep them to his sumptuous mansion.

Plied with comfits and Candian wine, they congratulated Lorenzo on the beauty of Antonia his betrothed and conveyed the salutations of his lady mother Alessandra, and found themselves launched with remarkable speed on an agenda of solid business exchanges to do with spectacles, the Catalan market, and several agencies which they shared.

As befitted the company advisor to King Ferrante of Naples, Lorenzo knew all the gossip of Naples and a good deal of the gossip of Rome as it referred to the affairs of Bruges and the Tyrol, and Venice, and Scotland. About the gossip of Cyprus he was even more forthcoming.

'It's true. Zacco doesn't feel committed to his little Venetian Queen: they're only married by proxy. Rome has had overtures from him. So have we. We had a message from Zacco last week. If he repudiated Catherine and married our King's lady daughter, what would Naples do for him in return?'

'A lot, I imagine,' Nicholas said. 'It might come cheaper for Zacco than Venice. Why don't you put together a nice dowry with a lot of ships and soldiers and trading concessions wrapped in it, and see what he says?'

'Is that your considered opinion?' The Charetty army had once fought for King Ferrante of Naples. Naples respected the Banco di Niccolò, not least because of its political acumen.

'Unless the girl has two heads. You'd get a good bargain. And a jumping-off place in the Levant, with some luck. We spoke of alum.'

'Yes.' When they talked about money, Lorenzo's eyes always shone. He said, 'You're going to send an offer to Persia? To Uzum Hasan?'

'And put a proposition to the Sultan in Cairo. The possibilities,' Nicholas said, 'are infinite.'

'And I take it you think that it's safe?' Lorenzo said. 'Your going to Egypt?'

'Since I helped kill the Mameluke commander in Cyprus? I think it's quite safe,' Nicholas said. 'It's a new Sultan now. They didn't close down our agency even when Khushcadam still ruled, and John has been accepted for years. They need our trade.'

'Everyone does,' said Lorenzo Strozzi, a touch smugly.

'What was all that about?' said John le Grant later, in his new, neutral tone of enquiry.

'Just to see if he would rise to something,' Nicholas said. 'Isn't he *rich*?'

The rest of the voyage was less tiresome than Nicholas had expected. On board ship, there was always something to do, especially when, as now, she was heavily armed, with bowmen and gunners to exercise. The *Ciaretti* was his ship, intimately known to him from several glorious voyages: he could do anything that he wanted, day or night.

Between Naples and Alexandria they fired no guns in anger and lost only one man: a page wasted with sickness. That was a tribute to excellent provisioning, because the ship made few calls, steering clear of the Venetian islands. In normal times a trading galley like this, well supplied with fresh water and food, could be kept virtually free of disease. The pilgrim galleys were different. With their foul crowded holds and mixed races, the passenger galleys were breeding-beds for bloody fluxes and fevers, their wakes pierced by sinking bodies shackled with stones and packed with rank ballast sand in their shrouds.

That would be why Anselm Adorne was hiring his own roomy vessel from Genoa, instead of choosing the galley from Venice. Or such, at least, would be one of his reasons. Adorne would learn, too, soon enough, which of his companions succumbed when at sea. Gelis would not be one of them.

Once, Nicholas had taken a sea-chart below and spent time with it, until his shipmaster took it away. The attempt to divine that way had failed, although he had imagined a faint stir on the map about Tunis – but that might be because he expected it. There was no sensation at all from Alexandria. He desisted then, thinking it more satisfying to employ his ordinary powers of reasoning, and to project what he knew of his wife's. She had several options, depending on why she was doing this. His mind, roving through all his neatly developing conflicts, kept returning to base; reviewing the fulcrum, the axle, the crab of the whole complex structure.

He would spend his second wedding anniversary in Alexandria. Wherever she was, Gelis, too, might recall what the date marked. Godscalc had died two days before the last one. Two years was not a very long time. Even a decade was not too long, if you were enjoying yourself.

The African coast then was not very far off. Nicholas watched for it, mostly from somewhere high in the rigging. Working the ship, he went barefoot in shirt and drawers, which no one had liked much at first: a patron should look like a patron, and not only when going ashore. He had fifty seamen and a hundred rowers, three to a bench. None of them was a slave. He had bowmen, helmsmen, trumpets. Ships' officers and crew changed all the time, and he knew none of these well, but had established an easy enough way with them all. He joked now, up in the mast-basket, looking over the sea.

The Egyptian coast, being alluvial, was always hard to pick out. Further east, you could tell the mouth of the Nile by the brown stain and the fresh-tasting water. But Alexandria, according to John, was nothing like the dramatic amphitheatre of Trebizond: just a long rim of limestone and sand and two spits. If you were fifteen hundred years old, you would have seen the palace of Cleopatra on one of them, and the great beacon had once stood on the other, four hundred feet high, with its flaming, glittering eye scanning forty miles of the ocean. Eunostos, Port of Safe Return, they had called it.

Now there was just a bonfire stuck on its base to guide mariners into the harbour, with a clutter of mosques and towers and a battery of bombards below it. Cleopatra's palace had gone, although there was an obelisk (said John) which would tell him where the Emir's palace now was. And he would see minarets and a couple of watch-hills and, visible from a long way, a tall red pillar where the Temple of Serapis and the Citadel of Rhakotis had been.

But Alexander, if he still rested in the city he was never to see, encased in gold in his coffin of glass, lay fathoms under some mosque, and there were tumbledown ruins and pillars where the Mouseion and its library had been. Al-Iskandariyya, eighteen hundred years old, for a thousand years a capital city and chief source of learning, was now shrunk to this, a trading port of the Mameluke Sultans of Cairo. And the remains of St Mark, the pride of present-day Venice, had been smuggled out pickled in a barrel of pork.

Sic transit. Everything changed. The sun was piercingly hot, but he was ready for that; for all of that. Below, he saw John le Grant neutrally watching him.

Thirty miles from Alexandria the Emir's ship came, as was the custom, to board them; to take details of their names and their cargo and send these by pigeon to the governor, who would fly the news by the same means to Cairo. This wasn't the Tyrol. By the time the *Ciaretti* reached Alexandria their reception, one way or the other, would be assured.

He was fairly sure of a welcome. Six years before, it would have been different. Then he and his army had been fighting for the island of Cyprus, hated for a hundred years here since one of its kings had taken Alexandria with an army of mercenaries – Scots, Venetians, Genoese – and left its people massacred in the ruins which had never been rebuilt. Six years ago he wouldn't have been welcome because he served Cyprus, and because he and Zacco the King had just managed to kill Tzani-bey, the Mameluke commander in Cyprus, and all his army.

Zacco had bought forgiveness from Cairo, and his merchants traded with Egypt again, even though one Muslim at least had tried to kill him for what he had done. In Venice, Nicholas too had been a target that year. But Nicholas no longer drew fees from Cyprus; and there was a new, astute Sultan in Cairo, and an Emir in Alexandria whom John le Grant had cultivated with success. The *Ciaretti*'s guns were there, but they were covered in peace and submission. It was left to the Mameluke vessel to fire a salute.

Truth to say, through the flame and crash of it, no one spoke. They were traders; they were not a Venetian galley, and the banners they flew were well known by now in the Middle Sea. But mistakes were sometimes made by Muslims wishing to gratify larger neighbours. Then the smoke cleared and instead of the glitter of scimitars you could see the coloured clothes, the tall hats, the white turbans at the rails of the opposite ship. Her oars steadied her, and she prepared to lower a boat. A flourish of trumpets spoke from the *Ciaretti* and the other replied. The *Ciaretti*'s sails began to come down, and John le Grant raced below, reassured, for his hat with the brooch and his coat.

When he emerged, the Emir's officials were already climbing aboard and Nicholas was preparing to welcome them. The sun sparkled on gold. John saw with relief that the newcomers were mostly familiar. Self-important, disagreeable, greedy, but people he knew. No palace revolution, then, in his absence. It meant that the Emir's policy, too, was unchanged. It didn't mean more than that.

He introduced each man to Nicholas, and Nicholas made his responses in Arabic. They had argued about that. It was not expected; in some quarters it was even held to lower one's standing. Le Grant used it himself, but then he wasn't head of the company, and he kept his Scots accent throughout, in case anyone thought he was making concessions. But Nicholas didn't. He spoke the beautiful measured Arabic of the schools, seldom heard even among Mamelukes, and they looked at him with attention, filing aboard and down the steps to the great cabin.

The party seemed to be complete. Nicholas had turned and John was ready to follow him when a dry voice spoke in Tuscan from the gangway. 'Well, Niccolò!'

Nicholas wheeled. John le Grant stared at the man in European dress who had spoken; at his baggy boots and short coat and brimmed hat with the under-ties fluttering. The frowning eyes in the sun-pinkened face were not looking at him. John exclaimed. '*Tobie!*'

The doctor's gaze flicked to him and held.

'He thought you were in Pavia,' said Nicholas. 'He thinks we are surrounded by demons who can be in two places at once. Are you all here? The eminent Baron Cortachy and the rest?'

'No,' said Tobie. He stepped forward slowly. 'No, they all rode north to sail from Genoa. We found a boat and came earlier.'

'We?' said Nicholas. He looked perfectly normal, except that he was still speaking Arabic.

Tobie looked at him. He said, 'Gelis is still with Adorne. You know she joined us?'

'Yes,' said Nicholas. 'And you stayed at Pavia.'

'Yes. Well, I heard my uncle was dying. He isn't. I caught up with the rest. I saw she wasn't up to the journey to Genoa, and found a ship that would bring us direct. She's much better now.'

Nicholas looked at him in silence. He gave the impression that he wasn't sufficiently interested even to guess.

'Who came with you? Who is with you?' said John.

'Adorne's niece,' Tobie said. 'The girl. Katelijne Sersanders.'

Chapter 32

LATER, THE GIRL said to Tobie, 'Was he pleased to see you?'
They were in Alexandria, in the House of Niccolò's rooms on the first floor of the larger Venetian fondaco. Handsomely built by the Mamelukes, it took the form of a rectangular building enclosing two immense courtyards, placed in a garden surrounded by extremely strong walls. It was one of a dozen such khans in the city, each providing its nationals – Genoese and Venetians, Catalonians and Tartars, Persians and Florentines and Cypriots – with lodging, office, warehouse and trading-counter at once.

Nicholas was not there, being still incarcerated with the customs officials, securing his passes, displaying his cargo, submitting to the interminable weighing and argument that would determine his tax liability. Even with John and the Venetian Consul to help, it would drag on for hours.

Katelijne Sersanders sat at a table, where she had been grinding something in a small mortar. She had plaited her hair and tied it out of the way on the top of her head. She was wearing a thin cotton robe with a girdle, and there was a smear on one cheek. She looked up.

Tobie said, 'No. He wasn't pleased to see me.' He sat down. The table was littered with saucers, boxes and jars, a piece of unfinished palm mat and several books. He said, 'What are you doing?'

'Improving on yesterday's mix. It's a secret: I told you. I should have gone on board to meet M. de Fleury, not you. It was too much like the time he came out of the Sahara. When you were waiting for him at Oran.'

He said, 'They wouldn't have let a lady on board. But you're right. Too soon after Oran; too soon after Godscalc. Godscalc was part of Africa too.'

He had stopped wondering at himself for talking to this girl about Nicholas. He had been with her now for four months: ever since he had left Bruges in February in the knightly cortège of her uncle, bound for the Holy Land.

His reasons for joining Adorne had been complex. The girl was ill, and he liked her. He would be able to visit that old devil Giammatteo in Pavia. And he had become haunted by the feeling that Nicholas in the hands of Father Moriz and John le Grant was still not good enough: that they would both let him get his own way. For nine years, Nicholas had needed someone to stop him, but only one man had, for a while. And the one man was dead.

Tobie had seen Katelijne Sersanders before, as a child. Meeting her again in the Hôtel Jerusalem he had been disturbed, as a doctor, to see how slight and pale she had become; how the quicksilver energy had drained away, leaving her prone to sudden fatigue and seized with perpetual headaches. She had smiled from brilliant eyes all the same, and had spoken with all the readiness he remembered.

'Dr Andreas is very forbearing, and doesn't seem to find it an insult that my family should rely so much on St Catherine and not on his potions. But he says the climate in Alexandria is good, and the sea air should help, and the martyrdom of St Catherine on top of all that should spell perfect health. Only he can't come with me.'

She had been speaking in February when persons of eminence were beginning to gather for the birth of the Countess of Arran's first baby in March. Of course Katelijne was tired: she and Adorne's wife between them had borne all the travail of the Scottish Princess's arrival with her handsome, smouldering husband. And later the husband's father, Lord Boyd, had favoured them with his presence as well. Poor Margriet, lady of Cortachy. Poor Katelijne.

It was fortunate, then, that the physician Andreas of Vesalia had arrived with the rest of the party from Scotland, come to stay for the birth and the christening. There were two of these who were strangers to Tobie but who brought Gregorio to life when they called on him: a woman called Betha and another called Phemie of the Sinclair family. Tobie left them together, and continued his own easy befriending of Margot which arose from philanthropy rather than choice, much though he admired her. Since she had come back to Gregorio, the strain between them had been obvious. As Gregorio wouldn't talk of the cause, Tobie had to assume that Margot's loyalty to Gelis and her invisible child was somehow responsible. He sympathised with Gregorio.

Then Bel of Cuthilgurdy arrived, and Tobie felt immediately

better. She had a new grandchild, and fell into comfortable chat with Tilde and with Margot without asking questions, and carried off the Sinclair women to cheer up Anselm Adorne who, in a resigned way, was making his will.

That was when it appeared that Andreas had to stay to look after the Princess, and there might be a place in the excursion for a footloose physician.

By then, the number of reasons for leaving had increased by at least one. The ceremony of the birth would be followed with terrible inevitability by the ceremony of baptism. Margaret, Duchess of Burgundy, was going to be godmother. Eleanor, Duchess of the Tyrol, was to travel north to see her royal niece's first child. The Hof Charetty–Niccolò was already awash with bales of satin and silk as Tilde and Catherine prepared to dress themselves and the company and Diniz.

Tobie made it known, with regret, that he proposed to leave Bruges with Anselm Adorne and his niece Katelijne as their physician. He found, with annoyance, that the company was to include John of Kinloch, a priest he had cause to dislike. He later learned, with mixed feelings, that Gelis van Borselen was going as well. But it was too late, then, to change his mind.

The situation had made Tobie deeply uneasy. All he had originally known of the grown woman Gelis had been learned from Godscalc, and he had formed a mental picture of a beautiful, independent, valiant girl who had been with Nicholas in Africa for half at least of the three years he had spent there, the watershed of his life. Nicholas had gone to find gold, but he had been prepared to pay the price that was necessary, and had suffered with Godscalc, and nearly died. His reward had been the great friendship with the black scholar Umar, who had once been a slave and had become his teacher. His reward and his punishment, for Umar, after sending him home, had been lost in the tribal rebellion that followed. And with him, it seemed, had been lost the healing power of all Nicholas had learned from books, and learned from the desert.

Returned, Gelis and Nicholas had married, but had not stayed together. Until now, Tobie had conformed to the general conclusion: the idiot had got her with child far too soon. On this journey, he had revised his opinion. Then, thrown into the company of Katelijne, he had found as she convalesced that she had formed one or two opinions herself. And because she was wholly uninvolved, wholly without envy, wholly tolerant, and extraordinarily perceptive, he responded by telling her what he knew.

Not all of it. The secret of Henry he kept, even when she described, with pity, the blow that had nearly ended his real father's life. He did speak of Umar, and Africa.

For a long time after that, she had been silent. Then she had said, 'How many people are given the chance of that kind of love? A black slave; a judge. He withdrew M. de Fleury from a pointless life; gave him silence, gave him teachers, gave him wisdom, and then died. People mourn in queer ways; then they stop.'

'If they are allowed to,' said Tobie.

The hazel eyes had looked up from the pillow. Katelijne said, 'The lady of Fleury is jealous of Umar?'

'Maybe,' Tobie said. 'Umar had a loving young family ... babies ... It was partly what drew Nicholas home, Godscalc thought. For the first time, Nicholas wanted that for himself.'

The girl had seemed to think. She said, 'The lady Gelis never speaks of your Umar, even when asked about Timbuktu. She would, if she hated him.'

'Does she hate Nicholas, then?' Tobie had said.

'Oh, no!' Katelijne said. There was a long silence. Then she said, 'You are saying, why hasn't he seen his own son?'

'I don't think it's for lack of trying,' Tobie said. 'If he stopped short of force, I think it was only in case he goaded her into doing something extreme. I don't know why she should deny him, but young mothers are sometimes irrational for a while. She may not have wanted a child. A bad birth-experience may have led her to blame him. There may be something wrong and she is ashamed of it, or even trying to spare Nicholas from the knowledge.'

'Or she may be jealous,' had said Katelijne.

He frowned. 'Of Nicholas? In case he steals the love of the child?'

'Perhaps. Or,' she said, 'of the child. In case it steals the love of Nicholas.'

They looked at one another. She said, 'They are very alike, M de Fleury and his wife. Trade, calculations, puzzles, mechanical devices, the manipulation of money.' She paused. 'She refers to him lovingly, always.'

'Lovingly,' Tobie repeated. She didn't speak. Tobie said, more lightly, 'Isn't everyone interested in money?' He watched her face.

'Are you?' she said.

He had been disconcerted by her before. This time he just said, 'You should meet my uncle. I rest my case until then.'

Curiously, neither he nor the girl ever talked about reaching Alexandria ahead of Gelis van Borselen. Only, at Rome, Katelijne –

Kathi, she had asked him to call her – took this turn for the worse. By the time they had sailed she was practically recovered.

Nicholas arrived very late at the fondaco, long after the groans and braying of asses and camels and the clamour of many voices, shouting in Italian and Latin and Arabic, indicated that the cargo had been released, dues paid, taxes implemented, and was being installed in the warehouses. He ran up the stairs and came into the rooms, cap in hand, his hair like astrakhan from the heat.

He shone. Occasionally in the past Tobie had noticed this property in Nicholas: that, however tiresome the moment, a chance happening, like a spark, would set some fire running, and he would radiate a burning and transient happiness.

Nothing in the abrupt, cold reception on board the *Ciaretti* had prepared Tobie for that. He thought the successful landing was perhaps the cause; or sudden hopes for the future; or the assimilation of the truth that Gelis was not here. He even thought it might have something to do with the girl, until he saw the quality of the gaze Nicholas directed towards her. It was not admiring or fond, but neither was it the look a man allots to a pet marmoset he is training. It was the sort of greeting he had seen Nicholas give to an exceptionally bright clerk of his own company; and the girl's smile, responding, was as frank.

Nicholas said, 'And have you a Scots title as well?' It wasn't especially cutting.

'Are they infectious?' she said. 'Perhaps you're right. I feel a unicorn growing in, now you mention it.' She had put her feet into shoes and replaited her hair and changed, as everyone did, into something clean for the Consul's table at supper. They never went on the street after sundown: the Mamelukes locked the front gates.

Nicholas said, 'I thought you were ill. What was wrong?'

'Too much energy,' said Tobie, surprised into sounding protective. 'She used it up. She doesn't want to use it up again.' Nicholas was wandering round the low-ceilinged room, looking out to the gardens on one side; looking down on the other through the ruddy sun-dazzle at the courtyard with its vaulted storehouses and shops, its handsome tiers of lodgings completing the square.

From the next room you could see the back gardens, but not the wall at the bottom which divided them from the road and the sea. Nicholas looked, and then came back to study the courtyard. Tobie could see Kathi itching to get up and join him.

Nicholas said, 'There's an ostrich tied to a tree.'

Tobie said, 'No!'

'Well, yes. It's been there all year,' said John le Grant, coming in. 'There's another outside.'

'I meant,' elucidated Tobie, 'no, you are not going to race them.' He gazed warningly at Nicholas. 'I found her practising.'

'Then you shouldn't have told her the story. So what have you been doing all these weeks?' He sat down.

John said, 'Nicholas. I've got Achille below.'

Below was the counting-house. Achille was the under-agent who had been managing their affairs. Nicholas said, 'Achille can sulk in his tent for an hour: I want some wine and some gossip. We are allowed wine?'

'At an exorbitant tax rate,' John said. 'You don't drink it.'

Nicholas looked taken aback. Tobie studied him with some interest. Nicholas said, 'How good of you to remind me. I do want to know one thing right away, while you're fetching it. Will you find out where the Vatachino are lodging?'

'I can tell you,' said Kathi. 'David de Salmeton's in Cairo. But before he left he took rooms in the Catalan fondaco next door. There are two sub-agents still there.'

'Next door?' Nicholas said. 'Which way?' John, his hand on the door, had turned back.

'That way. You can see it from the other side of the room. Past the garden wall and over the lane. The second-floor loggia.'

Nicholas got up and looked. He said, 'How do you know?'

Kathi shot across the room and returned with a bag which she presented, open, before him. It was full of bright fabrics and papers of needles and thread. 'I went to the silk-sheds with the Catalonian Consul's wife,' she said, closing it and sitting down. 'Damask and samite. Fairly good but not uniform. And then she came over here, because our baths are better than hers and she has a complaint. Dr Tobias told her what powders to use, and I went with her to the drugs market – Dr Tobias is teaching me how to mix drugs – and in return she took me to St Nicholas – that's the Florentine church – instead of St Marie's – that's the Genoese – and I met the mistress of the Consul for Pisa who likes botanical drawings – have you seen the plants they have in the gardens? – and wanted to talk about David de Salmeton. In fact, she showed me a curl of his hair.'

'Lovelocks!' said John le Grant. John le Grant had cast an Aberdonian eye on the handsome David in Cyprus.

'Well . . .' said Kathi, looking at Nicholas. Her eyes were glinting in a way Tobie knew all too well.

Nicholas said, 'I'm speechless. I think I'd feel safer with Achille. You have shocked Dr Tobias.'

'I just wanted you to know,' she said, 'that I have independent sources of information and don't mind sharing them. Otherwise you'd suspect an Adorne conspiracy. That is, I'm going to watch you and my uncle competing, and that's comical enough without taking sides. When are you going to the Emir?'

'Tomorrow,' Nicholas said. A servant pushed open the door, bearing a tray, and, passing through the room, went to place it on the shaded verandah. John le Grant was behind him.

'I haven't met him,' said Kathi. She waited until the servant had gone. 'Are you going to give him the falcon?'

'The falcon,' Nicholas repeated. He had been on his way to the balcony. He turned, his hand on the door. Tobie sat, leaning back, watching them both until he saw John watching him with astonishment. He wiped the smile off his face.

Kathi said, 'Yes. Or was that for the Sultan, and the essence of violet for the Emir? Anyway, they'll be pleased about the copper bars and the Rheims linen – I thought you weren't supposed to bring copper? – although I don't know if you'll get fifty florins a bale for that amount of wool cloth. But you might.'

She stopped, her round face ineffably smug. Nicholas shut the door and came back into the room. 'You know my cargo,' he said.

She smiled. 'I thought I'd better warn you. Everyone usually does. Achille probably didn't bother to tell you, because grain is so short. You know we don't have any bread? It's the time of year. And there's a lot of camel-meat, but not much of any other, unless you've brought some with you?'

Nicholas sat down very carefully. 'You mean I have some secrets left?' Then he added, '*Grain?*'

She waited, smiling. Very slowly, Nicholas closed his eyes and tilted his head back against the wall. 'Pigeons,' he said. He opened his eyes again and gazed at Tobie. 'You rat, you're allowing all this to happen.'

'I know,' said Tobie. He felt warm. 'I've had it since February.'

Nicholas shifted his gaze to the girl. He said, 'Let me get this quite straight. My ship approaches the harbour. It is boarded by the Emir's officials, and news of its owner and cargo is sent to the Emir by pigeon. You *intercept the pigeon?*'

'And send it on afterwards,' said Kathi virtuously. 'You can tell which they are by the mark.'

'Katelijne, you'll have your hair made into bowstrings,' said Nicholas, 'and John and Achille and I will be expelled from the bellies of bombards. You know you must stop it at once?'

'I have,' she said. She looked unperturbed.

Nicholas said, 'What about the ship that came in after ours. Tobie!'

Tobie looked blank. The girl said, 'No, I've stopped. I didn't do that one.'

Tobie said languidly, 'You mean you didn't bother to go up and read off the note. The pigeon's probably still on the roof. The Emir's probably combing the city for it.'

'How do you get to the roof?' Nicholas said. And during the ensuing scramble, 'Tobie! I thought that girl was supposed to be ill? What are you here for?'

'To stop her doing things like this,' Tobie said. 'Now you can take over.'

There were banks of plants on the roof, and some melons, and trees in tubs, their blossom scenting the eternal Alexandria breeze as it tempered the heat. The sun, sinking over the blood-coloured sea, sent long shadows over the flat surface and, below, the courtyards were also filling with dusk, with only the tops of the palms showing bronze. The murmur of voices rose up, with some laughter, and a clatter of dishes. With the working day done, the men and women and children who lived in the fondaco were emerging into the balmy air and mellow light to take their ease; strolling in the gardens, entertaining guests from other fondaci, greeting the newly arrived officers of the *Ciaretti* and waiting, no doubt, to be introduced to the banker who owned her.

From here, you could see the harbour quite clearly, and the galley's tall masts, some half a mile out. The port was crowded with flotillas, although not with Venetian galleys, impressed this year for war. There were only two of these, but four from Genoa, and a swaying raft of fishing vessels and pinnaces. All of them were Christian vessels, and so confined to the easterly, dangerous harbour, closely under the eye of the cannon and easy to guard and restrain. The sails and rudder of every ship in the harbour had been impounded from the moment it arrived.

Kathi's voice said, 'Oh, no!' Tobie turned.

He knew, of course, what she had been doing. He knew the discreet corner where she laid out her lure: the fragments of biscuit and powder and fruit that she thought might tempt the appetite of a passing pigeon. She waited until she heard the trumpets, as a rule, and then came up here, shaking her tin in the way the Emir's pigeon-keepers shook theirs.

She stood in the same corner now, but instead of reaching her palm to the birds she was kneeling in the midst of the mess, gathering something into her hands. Tobie said, 'A patient? What's wrong?'

'It's dead,' she said.

'An ordinary pigeon?'

'No,' Nicholas said. He had been kneeling beside her. 'Give it me. No. One of the Emir's. There is the mark, and here is the message.'

Tobie said, 'What do we do? What has killed it?' It was stiff, its wings a trifle open, its eyes shut. Nicholas was turning it over, examining it.

Nicholas said, 'It's still warm. There's nothing broken or cut. There's not a feather displaced.'

'Poor thing,' said Kathi. 'Then it was sick. It could have died anywhere.'

'All the same,' Nicholas said, 'you don't want it found here. The street, perhaps?'

'The cats would get it,' said Kathi.

'Well, let them. They'll get a good price for the message.'

'Or we could cook and eat it,' said Tobie, his appetite suddenly roused. 'Camel's meat palls, I can tell you.'

'*You* can cook and eat it,' Nicholas said. 'I'd want to know what it died of. Katelijne, what did you feed it with?'

'It wasn't that,' she said.

'I know it wasn't, but what?'

'I saved some grain,' she said. 'Just a little. I did want to be sure.'

'Yes. Well, you did capture my bird, which is what you were after. So this one got more of the same? Just grain?'

'I can tell you,' said Tobie. He knew what she had been pounding. He reeled it off.

'And that's all?'

'More or less. I did eke it out,' Kathi said. 'Maybe it's your fault. Would candied fruit kill them?'

Nicholas stood very still. Against the flaming sea and the sky he looked like a menhir. He said, his voice gentle, 'My candied fruit?'

Kathi looked at him. By contrast, the low sun made her look ruddy. She said, 'It was wrong of me. I saw the box: your servant was throwing it out. I asked for some of the pieces.'

'No. It wasn't wrong. Why was he throwing it out?' Nicholas said.

'I thought you had told him. He said it was because it had been opened and ants had got into the spaces.'

'It had been opened and some of the sweetmeats were missing?' Nicholas said.

'You didn't know,' said the girl.

'No. Katelijne, will you go downstairs and get Tobie to wash your hands for you, very carefully? I'll clear up here. Then when I come down, I want you to show me which boy gave you the box. Don't be worried: I shan't be angry with him. I only want to find out when it was opened.'

Tobie said, 'Where did it come from?'

'I don't know,' said Nicholas. But there was nothing left, now, of the aura of contentment, of relief, which had come with him to the fondaco.

'The boy died,' Tobie said.

'The box was untouched when we sailed. It was broached before we reached Alexandria. The cabin-boy had access to it, and died.'

Kathi was not present. The public part of the evening was over. Freshly dressed, they had presented themselves below, the guests of the Consul, the newest arrivals at the fondaco. What delicacies the galley could provide had been presented; the news from home had been told, the evening had ended in laughter and music. Katelijne had retired. And now Nicholas had to satisfy both John and Tobie.

John said, 'He died of sickness. You still can't be sure.'

The page had been interviewed. Frightened to tears, he had been patently innocent. The box had been opened at sea – he had seen it in the padrone's chest in his cabin, and some of the sweets had been missing. Now, told to be careful, he had found and brought to the table the battered carton and some of its contents.

It lay before the three of them now. Nicholas said, 'Tobie? I suppose you are here for some purpose. Can you test it?'

'Yes,' said Tobie. 'So can you. Eat it.'

'Thank you,' Nicholas said. 'Is there no other way?'

'No,' said Tobie. 'Or yes. Feed it to someone or something.'

'Nicholas?' said John le Grant.

'Good night,' Nicholas said.

Alone, he laid the sweetmeats before him. Alone, as John's voice had suggested, he took the little string in his hand and held it steadily poised, his thoughts on the trifles before him. The candied fruits given by Fiorenza, mother of Catherine, Queen of Cyprus. Fiorenza, wife of Marco Corner, sugar-grower in Cyprus, farmer of silver mines on the frontier between the Tyrol and Venice. He asked, as he had learned to ask, 'Will this food do me harm?'

And the jewel, stirring, swayed, began to circle, began to race, began to hurtle in a circle so wide, so fierce, so frightening that it tore the skin from his finger.

He rose, with difficulty. Recalling the way, he climbed the steps to the roof and stood, far from the swept grain, the interred pigeon. The wind blew from the north, and the sky was powdered with poisonous stars.

Next day, Nicholas de Fleury, knight, presented himself at the gate of the Emir's palace, and was admitted to his audience. Because he was a merchant, he and his retinue were escorted between a double file of Mameluke horsemen, impassive in their long robes and scarlet furred headgear, the golden orbs of their maces matched this time with the full armoury of sword, bow and quiver. The horse-cloths were of damascened satin. Drummers in silk coats preceded them.

He was not permitted a horse, but the mule he was given was exceptionally fine, and he used his own silver harness lined with red velvet and studded with immodest jewels. He wore, too, a merchant's robe of full-length brocade, not this time in black, but of cloth of silver and crimson, and his cap, although plain in shape as a pillbox, was adorned after the fashion of the Emir's own wives with pearls and Indian rubies, cunningly set. Across his shoulders he wore the chain of his Order, with the unicorn gleaming white in the Alexandria sun.

Pilgrims were harshly treated in Alexandria. Pilgrims paid tax after tax, impost after impost; were kept incarcerated on arrival; were forbidden to leave without permits; were harried, made to walk everywhere, charged impossible prices for the simplest of services; even forced to adopt heathen robes, for otherwise the unruly, the uneducated among Alexandria's natives would stone them. They stoned them, none the less.

But merchants – even though Christians, even though blameworthy, too, for the terrible massacre perpetrated by Peter of Lusignan and his crew – merchants were the lifeblood of Egypt, and treated honourably. The Emir, instructed from Cairo, welcomed Western merchants to Alexandria, taxed them circumspectly, and allowed them wine and such other luxuries of the flesh as they might require. And if it so happened, one day, that the actions of Venice or Genoa or Catalonia did not agree with the Sultan's expectations, he could always hold their merchants as hostage.

The fountain in front of the palace was working, although blown in the wind like the tattered palms that stood on either side. It still

pleased Nicholas how green Alexandria was. He had stepped ashore
expecting sand. He walked forward, composed rather than braced.

The steps of the palace were of marble and the floors inside
made of mosaic. The pillars and wall-linings were marble as well.
It reminded one of Trebizond, if anything. There was no stucco,
no honeycomb arches anywhere. The hall of audience was well
kept also, and the Emir in his white five-horned turban seemed
affable. Nicholas began the long walk to the dais. John le Grant
followed him. Nicholas had been offered, and had refused an
interpreter.

It was still a shock, a little, to see so many robed figures about
him, and to accept that none of the faces was black. Nicholas
approached, said what he should, and delivered his letters of
credence and his gift, which was not essence of violet but a cloth-
of-gold robe twice as costly as the one he was wearing. This man
was not the Sultan but he was important: an Emir of many
thousands of lances; the military governor of the second city of
Egypt, which provided a great deal of the Sultanate's wealth. The
men around him were Mamelukes, officers of the administration
and the army; and civilians who were Muslim merchant princes
themselves, inhabitants of the great marble mansions that still
stood, here and there.

They were here to assess him. The meeting was purely formal:
the talks he had asked for would begin in private, and later. He did
not have to think very much, kneeling, bowing, taking his seat for
the prescribed glass of sherbet. He knew the etiquette. He knew
even what they were thinking. He had lived and thought as they
did for a long time. And he wished them to know it. It was why,
from the beginning, he had used his Arabic.

He knew already, as he sat, that their curiosity had been roused,
and that they would, by now, know something about him. He
answered what questions they put; mentioned names; quoted once,
briefly, from Abu al-Faraj. John, silent beside him, would follow
some of it, and would know he was speaking of Timbuktu. He
didn't know what John made of that, and didn't much care.
He praised Alexandria, and said it would please him to pass his life
there.

The Emir liked that. Further meetings were touched upon.
Nicholas and John rose, retreated and left. A box of quails followed
them, and a wicker basket full of grapes and melons and passion-
fruit, and a small barrel of figs, carried by Mameluke servants.

At the gates of the fondaco, the Mamelukes saluted and left, the
captain with something pressed into his hand. John looked at the

baskets. 'Katelijne will be pleased. She can take some of it with her.'

Nicholas walked through the arch, unbuttoning his robe as he went. 'Where is she going?'

'Tobie's taking her to her uncle's fondaco. He says he didn't bring her here to be interrogated about what her uncle has done so far on the journey, and it wouldn't be ethical to expect him to report on Adorne either.'

Nicholas turned. 'I haven't asked him to. Or her. Yet.'

'Well, don't. And he doesn't want the girl mixed up with poisoned sweets either. Where did those come from?'

'A disappointed admirer. Poor Tobie. Is he courting her?' Nicholas said. 'What fondaco is he putting her into?'

'The Genoese. Of course he isn't courting her. He's her physician. He likes her. He doesn't want her overexcited. Oh, Christ.'

'What?' said Nicholas, completing the unbuttoning. A page, appearing, took off the garment. The silver weave was almost too stiff to fold. Underneath he wore a white shirt and black hose. He pulled off his hat and handed it over. The ostrich, bored with its tree, slung its neck towards him and hissed. He said, 'No. You've got too many feathers.' Across the courtyard and beyond the next range of buildings a kite floated in the blue sky.

John le Grant said, 'It's hers. Tobie and I saw it last night after we left you. She had this amazing idea.'

'Which you told her not to go on with. I see now why Tobie wants to remove her. What idea?'

They had walked through the second courtyard and were emerging into the garden, which was shady with fruiting, mysterious trees. There were small birds in the palms, clinging to the long berried sprays, and orange butterflies flirted. A young woman in Venetian dress stood with a child, feeding a gazelle with morsels of bread. She turned and smiled at them. The courts they had crossed had been empty of all but skipping servants and the animals of the little menagerie. The men were mostly indoors or in the warehouses or at other fondaci.

The windlass squeaked, bringing water up from the depleted wells. All Alexandria was built upon cisterns, replenished by rain, filled to overflowing when the aqueducts brought the miraculous flood of the Nile, as it would in September. It was why the city was green.

The wind blew from the sea, and distorted the jets of a fountain. 'There she is,' John le Grant said.

Chapter 33

NICHOLAS LOOKED. It was Katelijne, with a kite. She wore a thin muslin dress, slightly torn, and no hat. She had also taken off her shoes. Her arms and legs, which were bare, were unacceptably brown and touchingly thin. Her tongue was out, and she was gazing at her kite, which was in the shape of a frog. She hadn't seen them.

'What is she trying to do?' Nicholas said. From where she stood on the grass, the wind had blown the kite out of the garden and over the lane that adjoined it: soon it was going to break against the walls of the neighbouring fondaco. He supposed she was learning. You didn't have to be in Alexandria for more than a day to discover that all children flew kites. The cool northern breeze, always present, was the gift of Aeolus to kites.

John said, 'She's trying to lift a map from the main Vatachino offices.'

'*What!*' said Nicholas. He started to laugh.

'She discussed it all last night. The wind holds the kite to the shadowy side of the building; the balcony doors are all open for air; you slide the kite down until you reach the loggia you want, direct the kite over the balcony wall and let it travel on into the doorway.'

'Where someone seizes it.'

'No. She was going to wait until she saw them go out. The map's on a stand; you can see it. And the kite is covered with gum.'

'Mixed by Tobie,' said Nicholas. He had broken into a run, still hiccoughing slightly. Katelijne, without looking round, repossessed her tongue but continued to concentrate her attention on the control of the kite.

John, hurrying after, said, 'He didn't think she really would do it.'

Nicholas arrived. He said, 'Magnificent. Down. To the left.

There's a gust coming. Steady. Up. Let me help you.' He stretched up, his fingers high on the cord. He said, 'Let us magadise. Is that the balcony?'

The frog was ridiculous. The frog looked, in a bad light, like Sigismond, Duke of the Tyrol. It clung, leaped and clung like a leaf down the wall of the opposite building, then suddenly curled itself under and sped like a bird for a doorway. There was a shout from inside. Katelijne tugged. The kite reappeared with a sock on it. Katelijne said, 'Oh, bother.' A woman ran out on the balcony and pulled off the sock. Katelijne said, 'It's one floor down and two along to the left.' The kite, fanning uncertainly, rose a little, revealing its surface to be pocked with small objects. One of them was a sponge. John started to weep.

Nicholas said, 'How many along?' He had his other hand on the cord.

Kathi said, 'Not that one.'

It was too late. Silkily gliding, the kite disappeared over a balcony, slithered across its tiled floor and presented itself in some inner sanctum. There was another scream, followed by a howl from a baby. 'Oh,' said Nicholas. A different woman came out holding a baby, a spoon and the kite. The three travelled rapidly forward; then the woman let go the spoon and the kite soared upwards once again, the spoon embedded in it. Heads, male and female, began to appear on other balconies and voices could be heard, distantly ejaculating in Spanish. The Vatachino balcony was still empty. Nicholas aimed at it, and Katelijne jumped about at his feet. 'Up! Out! Over a bit! Higher! That's it!'

The frog steadied itself on the balcony. An Orthodox priest, emerged from the next doorway, stood in his tall hat and black robe, gazing at it. The kite flipped over the balcony and hopped into the Vatachino's empty room, fluttering about the frame upon which the vellum was resting. The priest, resting his hands on the dividing railing, peered inside after it. Nicholas put a slow, steady strain on the kite.

It popped out like an owl from a tree. Pasted across its wide cheeks was the paper. It sped past the priest, who leaped back, and soaring and dancing consented to be driven high into the sky and steered backwards and into the garden. The balconies of the Catalonian fondaco were rimmed with animated faces, pointed fingers, and audible emanations of annoyance and laughter. Nicholas stood, the kite flying on a short cord above him, and bowed; Katelijne curtseyed. John le Grant sat on the grass chortling. Then Nicholas reeled down the kite and pulled off the rectangle that was stuck to it. Strings of soft glue plastered his hands. He let the kite out on its cord and then stuck peg and cord in the grass, leaving the kite trapped to float in the middle air. All the time he did it, he was looking at the map.

It wasn't titled, but it was clear enough what it was, even when disfigured with smears. It was a map of Alexandria, the town they were living in. There were the two harbours, Muslim and Christian, with Pharos between them. There were the two intersecting main streets: the one that led inland to the Pepper Gate and the one that crossed it and led to Rosetta and Cairo. There were a lot of other streets roughly filled in, and some mosques and some churches, and a bit of the area outside the walls: Pompey's Pillar and Lake Mareotis, the reedy stretch full of waterfowl that was once joined by canal to the Nile.

There was nothing on it about Alexandria's defences, or about fondacis and markets. It was not the map of a spy or a trader. It was a simple record of streets. None was named, but three had symbols drawn in against them. Each was a letter of the Greek alphabet.

John said, 'You've spoiled their map. They'll never find their way out the door after this. Was that what all this was for?'

'Yes,' said Katelijne. 'Though we didn't know it.' She sat back, looking at Nicholas. 'The parrot. You wrote down what it said?'

The laughter left Nicholas suddenly. He said, 'Yes. What reminds you of that?'

The girl said, 'It spoke Greek. What did you make of it?'

John le Grant stared at them both. Nicholas said, after a moment, 'Some was nonsense. The rest was a fragment of service from the Greek Orthodox ritual.'

She looked at him. Then she said, 'Trebizond and Cyprus?' and smiled. 'I didn't get that. I got something else.'

Nicholas said, 'I thought you didn't know Greek.'

'There is this Jew,' she said.

'I thought he was teaching you Hebrew,' said John le Grant.

'That's in the mornings. He teaches Greek in the afternoons. He has fifteen languages. How many do you have?' she said to Nicholas.

'Not enough for this,' Nicholas said. 'Talk quickly.' Distant noise continued to emerge from the next fondaco. People were beginning to come towards them over the grass.

'He says,' said Katelijne, 'that when the Greeks planned Alexandria, they named all the streets with a letter. Being Greeks, they laid out the whole place in rectangles. So, by naming the letters and the points of compass, you could describe any location you wished.'

Nicholas said, 'The parrot said nothing of that.'

'Not to you,' Katelijne said. 'It had to be drunk.'

John had begun smirking again. Nicholas said, 'And?'

She said, 'It sounded like gibberish. It wasn't. It was street names and compass points based on the original highways. You know. Four thousand palaces, four thousand baths, one thousand two hundred greengrocers and forty thousand Jews. My Jew knows the old Greek names of the streets.'

Nicholas looked down at the map. 'And the Vatachino knew three of them. How?'

'I can't imagine,' she said. 'But David de Salmeton is away, and you're here. You can prove out the message. I can pretend I'm an idiot and hand the map back as if it were all a mistake. Unless, of course, there's going to be a riot.'

He became aware, lifting his eyes, that the noise from the fondaco had greatly increased. Instead of dispersing, the inhabitants of the balconies had crowded even thicker. Their gaze was all trained in one way.

The balcony of the Vatachino company was still empty. The neighbouring balcony was wholly occupied by a kite in the shape of a frog. Nicholas wheeled. The stake with its reeled cord had gone. John said, 'It pulled loose five minutes ago. I didn't want to interrupt you.' His freckled face gleamed. Nicholas looked up, and so did the girl.

The kite was not alone on the balcony. In fact it was being held by four or five people, all talking with great animation. Glued to the kite, they now saw, was the priest of the Orthodox church, still wearing his hat. He was talking as well. To one side of him, carefully snipping, a barber was detaching his beard. He completed the task as they gazed. The priest stood, his face naked, his manner as perplexed as that of a newly halved twin. The frog, disengaged, sprang to its full unfettered height and set out in the direction of India, wearing eighteen inches of beard and a spoon.

John had started to cry again.

'We shouldn't laugh,' Katelijne said. 'But it is rather funny. It's Alexandrian. It's like the jokes they used to play in the Mouseion. You know, rewriting the whole of the *Odyssey* without using the letter S. You couldn't do that.'

'I could if I had a lisp,' Nicholas said. They had begun to walk quickly over the garden in the direction of the nearest door to the courtyard. 'I suppose they called it the *Iliad*. I could do you a good line in Ls.' John was running behind, his hands held palm outwards like chicken-wings.

Katelijne started also to hurry. She said, 'Mind the fountain, it'd make the glue run. The Mouseion produced some nice verses as well. *Who sculptured Love and set him by the pool, Thinking with liquid such a flame to cool.* And take Callimachus.'

'I'm trying to,' said Nicholas. 'Why are you holding up your hair?'

'I can't let go,' she said. 'Berenice was lucky. Were those your best hose? How do we open the door to the yard?' She held the map in one hand by a corner.

'I'll do it,' said John and, advancing, used an experienced elbow. The courtyard inside was filled, but no one stared at them. It was feeding-time for the animals. The Venetian Consul's wife, wearing a fine beaded headdress and a gown with puffed shoulders, saw them and came over smiling to Nicholas. 'What has happened! You have been throwing off ceremony, having successfully finished your audience! Then I see you are better suited than any of us to assist. There. That is for the hog.'

'The hog,' Nicholas said. It was not a query. Behind him, someone was choking.

The lady said, 'You must have seen it. We keep it to annoy the wretched pagans. It is perfectly tame. Over there. Pour it into its trough.' She smiled and walked away, leaving him standing looking after her. Attached to his hand was a bucket of pigswill. Katelijne said, 'Oh! Oh! Oh!'

John was pale with emotion. He said, 'Oh God, oh God, I can't stand it, I have to go somewhere and –'

'You can't,' Nicholas said. 'Can you?' He began to walk away. 'On the other hand, I have this bucket of pigswill. No, on this hand, as it happens. Here's a door. We take the pail to our rooms; you help me get it off, and I'll help you put on your gloves. Katelijne, go away. Have a bath. We'll come for you.'

Katelijne continued to nudge him. It wasn't Katelijne. It was the hog, trying to get at the bucket. Katelijne was behind, kneeling on the fondaco's tiled floor silently rocking herself, with one hand on top of her head and her forearm over her eyes.

John said, 'That's it.'

'The pig won't like it,' said Nicholas.

The Jew said, 'It is a poor map, but it will serve. You are looking for the great Alexander's treasure?' Below the obligatory yellow turban his face was broad rather than long, with a short black beard and brown eyes from which all trace of irony had been banished. He gazed mildly at the three of them, and the girl. The girl shouldn't be here. They couldn't find a reason to exclude her.

'Next time, perhaps,' Nicholas said. 'Is that what everybody does?' The man was a scholar, said Tobie, and had come recommended by the Consul. Tobie had interviewed and appointed him. He had been teaching Katelijne for three weeks. Kathi, as Tobie called her.

Tobie was there now with John and the girl and himself, his small round nostrils inflated, his cap already dragged off his bald head. In a moment, he would start sneezing. The map on the table was not the original, but a copy hurriedly drawn up by John. The Jew said, 'It saddens me to cause disappointment. You have, then, some other purpose?'

Nicholas said, 'A friend has posed us a puzzle. It depends on the street names. These are the names we have been given.'

The Jew took the paper. He said, 'What do you know of the city? The whorehouses? The markets? The houses where you can buy smuggled aphrodisiacs and jewels?' He spoke in accented Tuscan, the language they had begun with.

Nicholas said, 'Tell me, is it true? Sixteen hundred years ago, out there on Pharos, seventy rabbis in seventy huts translated the Hebrew scriptures into Greek? Do you think no one read them?'

The Jew looked up. He said, 'Your Greek is Trapezuntine.'

Nicholas said, still in Greek, 'So I know, at least, the legends of the cities Byzantium ruled. There is the Canopic Way, leading to the Gate of the Sun and to Cairo. There is the Street of the Soma, crossing it. There were green silk awnings spread over both, and colonnades and mansions of white marble so dazzling, they said, that the men and women of Alexandria wore only black. There was the tomb of Alexander, there the Mouseion, with its observatories, studios, library; there the shrine to Hephaestion. I want no lecture,' said Nicholas. 'I want to know what I do not know, the names of the streets.'

The Jew said, 'You do not want your companions to know.'

'No,' said Nicholas. Then he added, 'Lack of knowledge will not harm them.'

There was a silence. Then the Jew said, 'I believe you.'

Katelijne said, 'Truly, we admire the city. You must forgive us if we are ignorant.'

'Ser Niccolò has explained,' said the Jew. He had returned to Tuscan. 'I understand. Only I am not sure if I can help. These are letters referring to obscure streets, whose whereabouts are not precisely known. I shall do what I can.' He frowned, his pen working over the map. 'There. Possibly there. And possibly there. Does that meet your expectations?'

They all gazed at the map. The streets he had marked were those the Vatachino had already identified. 'It might do,' said Nicholas. 'Is that all?'

'I do not know the three others,' said the Jew. 'I deeply regret. Of course, I shall exact no fee for such trifles.'

Nicholas walked out with him all the same, to engage him in friendly talk and persuade him to accept what was fitting, and was given in turn a painstaking receipt which he slipped into his purse. Returning, he found Katelijne gone, and John and Tobie glaring at each other. John said, 'He's told her what it's about.'

Tobie's handkerchief punished his nose. He withdrew it. He said, 'You said yourself. Without her, you wouldn't have known what to look for. Of course I told her.'

'About Ochoa and the parrot,' Nicholas said.

'And the gold,' John said grimly.

'Then it's just as well,' Nicholas said, 'that the Jew's information was rubbish. If the streets are where he says they are, the directions mean nothing. Or the parrot was lying. Take your pick.'

They both gazed at him. He laid out the map and explained it. Tobie went away, finally, sneezing.

John said, 'Well?'

Nicholas said, 'You mean you still remember your Greek? All that time digging holes in Constantinople?'

'And in Trebizond,' John le Grant said. 'She's Adorne's niece. I follow the reasoning. I wish you didn't have to keep it from Tobie, that's all. Anyway. What did you really find out?'

Nicholas took a paper out of his purse and, laying it beside the maligned map, opened the inkpot and took up his pen. He said, 'Read them out, and I'll mark them. Then read out the compass directions.'

John read, and he wrote. At the end, Nicholas laid down his pen. On the map was a cross. John said, 'What can possibly be there? It's to the east of the Soma. It's a small street, but still near the centre. It could be rubble, occasional mansions, ramshackle cabins. How can we know what to look for?'

'You have forgotten the rest of the message,' Nicholas said. 'I know what to look for. I shall tell you tomorrow when I have found it.'

*

One did not leave on such an errand dressed as a merchant, armed with a new permit, accompanied by servants and Mamelukes. That was for later, when the formal meetings took place. Nicholas slipped out of the fondaco on sandalled feet at sunrise next morning, as soon as the gates were unlocked, and emerged into a road already busy with the pent-up surge of countrymen bringing food into the city, and fishermen slippery with scales from the strand.

The camels, held up through the night, slouched their way through the slotted doorways in the double walls and the rising sun gleamed on the turbans of the guards on the same walls, and on the hill, and flashed upon this dome or that minaret. Above the clanking of bells, the shuffling, the sound of voices, the hoof-beat of a Mameluke's horse, the braying of asses, came the first sonorous note of the morning invocation of the muezzin.

He had his prayer rug within his robe, and spread it and knelt, as everyone did, prostrating, fulfilling the ritual. No one looked at him twice: a man in a worn robe and cap, with his head and lower face wrapped in white cloth. He would have to begin to grow his beard very soon. The lightness of his eyes usually passed: they were common enough among Berbers. He broke off his prayers to curse, in fluent Arabic, as someone stepped on his hand. He needed to know this city, and this was the best way to do it.

He did not, therefore, go straight to the street with the cross. He acquainted himself with the poor quarters as well as the rich: the tall, fragile houses of driftwood and rags with their tattered awnings, set among vivid trees; the naked children; the women whose eyes glittered through almond holes cut in their headcloths, who walked erect beneath crowns of white napkins, green herbs, and red amphorae of oil or of water.

He stopped and bought a loaf of flat-bread at an oven and watched a dice game, chewing peacefully until, throwing a coin, he got himself an invitation to join, and squatted in the dust for a while, the dust being the board. The dice were cowrie shells. It was a game he was good at, but he lost more than he won, and joined in the jokes, and capped them, using the Arabic of the Maghgreb for safety. There clung about the place, faintly, a memory of last evening's hashish. After a while, his nose twitching, he threw a coin to a boy stirring *ful madames* in a great pot still stuck with night-ashes, and bought them all bowls of bean porridge so thick he could eat it with his fingers, and did. It was three years since he had tasted it. He talked through it, half forgetting what he wanted to know, but not forgetting completely.

He learned that a man had to be careful, or the Mamelukes

would be there in a trice, two or three on their horses, whipping you back to your work, for how could the Mamelukes live in luxury unless common men slaved? They said the streets of Cairo were never safe: that women were raped in their beds, and men too; that bands of Mamelukes would stop anyone, strangers or Cairenes, demanding bribes, or wrenching the turbans from the heads of good men for the few dinars they kept in the folds. And what were they but foreigners themselves, the mongrels? Greeks, Circassians, Kurds, hardly able to understand what a man said? Was there no end to the rapacity of the Sultans and emirs? There was a man who died leaving a hundred and fifty parcels of bands and belts and robes of honour. There was the Vizier Abdallah b. Zanbur who, on his arrest, left behind him six thousand belts and six thousand Circassian kaluta-hats: had he six thousand bodies and heads? This Sultan Qayt Bey could not control them, even though he was once head of the army. The Mamelukes had elected him. He had been a slave to a Sultan himself. He had fetched fifty dinars.

'We will be rich,' Nicholas said, 'when the Turk is rich. When the Ottoman fleet takes Negroponte, Modon, Crete, Corfu, Venice itself; when the Turkish army takes Vienna, all Muslims will be rich.'

They looked at him then, even though they had won all his money. 'Art thou a fool?' said the oldest. 'Dost thou imagine the Mamelukes, their mouths greasy with the dripping of flesh-meat, will wish the Sultan Mehmet to come with his Janissaries and take their golden spurs and their sable coats from them? No. They will oppose one another, sword to sword, and it is we, the carriers of water, the workers in the bath-ovens, the fishermen who will suffer.'

'Verily, thou speakest wisdom,' Nicholas said. 'But what is it to us? The drowning man is not troubled by rain.'

He was sorry to leave.

After that, he found himself half seeking familiar sights. He spent little time in the bazaars, where the Market Inspector patrolled, the scales borne before him, his sharp eyes watching the brass, the silver, the costly scents changing hands and the foreign merchants and their wives moving about in thin slippers, attended by their Mameluke guards. He lingered more in the commoner markets where the mats, the trays, the baskets were laden with other riches he had forgotten: not just the pomegranates, the figs, the pickled lemons small and fine as apricots, but the lean wild dates and the beans, the lettuce and watercress, the heaps of

sorghum and cucumbers, the furzy millet, and the frying cheese
smelling of Tuareg. Passing, he abstracted a handful of roasted
melon seeds, just to taste them on his tongue.

He left, after a while. This was not what he was here for. Not for
this: not for the smell and sound of the camels, and the forgotten
habit of running a rider's eye over shoulder and haunch. Not for
the impulse to click his teeth, and mount, and go. And be free to
go.

His mind, taking charge at that point, put a stop to the mood
and sent him on, briskly, about his proper business.

Fortunately, the city changed its character nearer the centre,
where the streets were wider and straighter and there were traces
still of the double columns that once lined the way, and the
mansions of the wealthy Alexandrians stood in their chipped marble
grandeur, a pole of lanterns before every door, the fine carpets and
pieces of damask billowing from their balconies.

In Alexandria, everything fluttered and flapped near the sea. It
was only when you followed the street of the Soma up the slow
incline to the crossroads and then turned aside, into the Canopic
Way, that the blessed north wind was shut out, and the smells of
musk and dung and cooking-oil clothed you like flannel. The
Mouseion and the temples had all been built on rising ground,
within the embrace of the wind.

Soon, he was quite close to the street on the map. He had
memorised all the roads; even in the wilderness of the suburbs he
had been able to trace them, here and there, and give them the
letters indicated by the Jew. He had made a point of visiting
the prison of St Catherine of Alexandria, a sunken cell surrounded
by railings with a Mameluke outside, noisily fleecing a group of
threadbare pilgrims from Germany. There had been a chapel near
by, with its door shut, surrounded by rustling trees.

Katelijne had been here, with Tobie. Protected by a merchant
fondaco, they would have paid less than the pilgrims and been
better treated. It was a matter of Christian belief that here, in the
third century after Christ, Catherine, daughter of a Cypriot
governor and over-versed, perhaps, in the liberal arts, had been
imprisoned for her faith and then exposed to a contraption involving four wooden wheels and some blades.

Emerging scatheless from these, she had succumbed to the sword,
but, beheaded, had vanished from sight, being translated by angels
elsewhere. He knew the legend. It touched him that, having travelled
so far, Katelijne should have found, it seemed, the health and
contentment that she'd sought. He walked on, and emptied his mind.

He had told John he knew what he was looking for. He scented it first in the air. He heard it next above the rumours of noise from the streets all about, in the silence of a narrow street containing little but rubble and houses reconstructed from rubble. The sound of four voices, lifted in exultation. He stopped.

The church was old, and so sunken that he climbed down a bank to its doors. The marble it was made of was pitted, but the gardens behind it were green, as was the burial ground. A Christian cemetery, although not a Latin one. Nevertheless, a Frank dying in Alexandria could be buried here, if his friends paid enough and if he didn't mind Mamelukes shouldering his coffin. Tolerance was here also, at a price. Nicholas walked down and touched the carved doors.

They gave before him. Inside was a young monk, bearded, robed and hatted in black. Nicholas spoke to him in Greek. 'I am a Christian merchant, who would beg an interview with the head of your convent.' He lifted aside his headcloth as he spoke, but made no move to thrust past.

The young man said, 'You are welcome, my lord. If my lord would wait, the closing hymn is being sung.'

'I shall be glad to wait,' Nicholas said.

The garden within the cloisters was small, with some flowers and a fountain, and a few graceful birds he thought must be tame, because they came towards him as he sat. He remembered that in Timbuktu there had always been pets: monkeys, parrots, a songbird or two. In Timbuktu the markets had been full, like these, of innocent, cheerful, hard-working people leading a strenuous life, but not an unhappy one.

In Timbuktu there had been the intellectual and physical well-being that comes from a flourishing trade, and the communal spirit that arises also from the perils deriving from man and from nature: the vagaries of the river; a sudden falling-out among tribes. But in Timbuktu one did not live and breathe commerce. One took what sufficed; and then walked the length of a street or a square and there would be a mosque, a school, a scholar's home or a *kutubi*, a bookseller, where one would leave one's slippers and enter, leaving commerce behind. Or that was what had been in Timbuktu.

A man came into the garden; a man who walked with authority, black veil flying, a crucifix chain swinging beneath his grizzled beard. The singing had stopped.

Nicholas turned towards the newcomer, and spoke. 'My lord Abbot? I am Nicholas de Fleury of Bruges. I am told you have a message for me.'

The Abbot looked at him. He said, 'This is the Church of St Sabas the Sanctified. You are not Greek?' He was elderly but not old, and looked stern. The young monk stood deferentially beside him.

Nicholas said quickly, 'I am told you have in your church the pillar St Catherine was chained to. I have a young friend who is sick. I would pray.'

The Abbot said, 'You should have said so. Come in.'

The basilica was not large, and seemed dark even though, stepping down, Nicholas saw the sky through a high row of windows. Then he saw how the low-hanging lamps glowed on frescoed walls and glinted on the little, dark ikons which fronted the short line of chapels, and shone on the carved side of the pulpit, and lay red and warm on the thick granite pillars. The fragment of St Catherine's marble, incised with the cross, was not very large, and a painting by St Luke was too blackened to convey very much.

His companion made a sign, and there was a discreet movement as the two remaining choristers left. The Abbot looked directly at Nicholas. He said, 'You speak Greek. You wear the robes of an infidel.'

'I have lived in infidel countries,' Nicholas said. 'I have lived and traded by the Joliba, at the behest of Cardinal Bessarion, in whose care resides the family of the Despot Thomas, former prince of the Morea, at Rome. I have also heard your rites in Nicosia, and in Trebizond. I am, by upbringing, a Frank. My name is Nicholas de Fleury, Knight of the Sword to James, King of Cyprus. I hold his badge in my hand. *C'est pour loïauté maintenir* is its motto.'

The Abbot took his hand and held it under the lamps, studying the fingers as much as the badge. He said, 'And to whom do you keep loyalty, my lord Nikolaos?'

'To those who are loyal to me,' Nicholas said. 'And those who, like the Blessed Saint Ekaterina, have suffered in prison. A bird brought me a sign. The sender will have rewards both material and spiritual, provided I leave here without hindrance.'

The Abbot smiled. 'What evil do you fear? We are monks; we are poor. We have our treasure already in heaven. You could kill us all with your fists: our nature is mild; we should not resist you. It has been enjoined on me only to see that the object entrusted to me is delivered.'

'Have I given proof enough?' Nicholas said.

'I am satisfied,' said the Abbot. 'Come with me.'

The object he spoke of was a leather scrip, of the stout, plain kind carried by pilgrims, already much worn. Inside was a wooden writing-tablet already prepared. Nothing was scored on the wood or incised on the wax, which was smooth and white and unblemished. There was no writing implement with it.

'This is all?' Nicholas said.

'It is all. We are told,' said the Abbot, 'that nobility on earth may be earned by the sword, but nobility of the soul must be sought in stony ways and through hard endeavour. I have to tell you to rejoice that you have been chosen.'

'I do,' said Nicholas thoughtfully. He put the worn bag away, and drew out another, which was heavy with gold. The Abbot looked at it. The Abbot said, 'You are generous. By honouring our church, you honour yourself. I will summon the brother best fitted to receive your donation.'

It was one of the singers, cowled and soft-footed, who came to the sound of the bell and, on the Abbot's instruction, stood before Nicholas and took possession of the bag with its coins. His eyes remained dropped; his words of thanks were pious and humble. His crucifix glittered, unduly exposed, for instead of a beard there rose above it a half-naked chin, from which a ragged black fringe still depended.

'As I have said,' the Abbot remarked, 'our nature is mild. We do not resist. We have found that the Lord takes care of His own, and we praise Him.'

Demurely the monk held the gold. A muscle twitched in his cheek.

'Amen,' Nicholas said. 'I am ashamed. Does the Lord give receipts?'

Chapter 34

FINDING NICHOLAS GONE, John le Grant cursed, got hold of Achille, and set to work reassembling and apportioning his cargo. Tobie looked in on him once to mention that he and the girl were moving to the Genoese fondaco immediately. It annoyed John profoundly. He had counted on Tobie's support in handling Nicholas de Fleury.

He retreated thankfully to his chamber at noon and found Nicholas walking about, a rib of meat between his bared teeth, sorting out garments and flinging them over his shoulder. There was a powerful smell of hot candle grease.

Told to put on his second-best coat, John said, 'Be damned to that, I'm hungry. What happened?'

He caught, just, the shank Nicholas threw at him. It looked as if it had come off a market-stall. 'Tell you later,' Nicholas said. 'Hurry up. Meetings, meetings. We're late for the Emir.'

In fact they were not, and the ensuing conference at the palace covered all the pre-arranged ground and ended with some worthwhile concessions. It was the unscheduled conversation that followed that made John uneasy. Rejoining their cumbersome retinue, he was unable to remonstrate, being hauled in turn to the Persian and Syrian fondaci and the houses of two wealthy Egyptian merchants. He noticed that Nicholas, all of a sudden, seemed to have discovered his bearings.

The business talks were reasonably successful, being with people John le Grant knew and regularly negotiated with. Nicholas acted as the padrone, evincing ignorance when it would serve, and using his weight when that would serve too. They worked well as a team. The topics were cotton and corn; the glass and sugar handled by their Damascus sub-agent; the raw silk that Turcoman merchants could send them. They discussed and apportioned their interest in the spice fleet, which would arrive in September.

It came twice a year. Too big for the Red Sea and its shallows, Chinese junks and heavy Indian ships which had left Calcutta in February would unload their jewels, their silks, their spices, their perfumes and their parrots at Jeddah. From there, taxed and packaged, the sacks would travel by fleets of small vessels to Tor, and thence by camel-train to Cairo and the north. No foreign traders, of course, were permitted in Cairo, the capital. Foreign traders dealt in Alexandria, or nowhere.

Every meeting, having dealt with the spice, went on to wring its hands over the war which had half emptied the harbour. Across the sea two weeks ago, a Turkish fleet big enough to cover six miles of sea had sailed to Euboea, the prized island possession of Venice, and deposited soldiers there. Three days later the Ottoman Sultan himself had led an army to the opposite shore and was now confronting the capital, Negroponte.

Negroponte was the chief naval base of the Venetian fleet in the Levant. Without it, merchantmen would have to beat their way to Modon and Corone; local rulers would riot; the Turks, owning the harbour, could use it to attack whom they pleased. What happened to Negroponte would affect every man's business, every man's country. Alexandria was full of rumours, and each day a new scare would run through the city – the Sultan had brought his heavy artillery, the straits to the island were bridged, and even greater armies were pouring across. Nicholas, listening, made soothing remarks about Venetian strength, but said little else. John was glad when the last meeting ended.

On their way home, they passed the Tartar fondaco. Even at the fading of day, the slave market was busy and full, the sellers proclaiming, the handlers with their short sticks expertly tumbling, exposing, clinically presenting their wares at fifteen ducats apiece. The slaves were from the Black Sea and beyond, and of all shades from ochre to tawny.

John ignored them. Nicholas said, 'Krim Tartars. We'll call there tomorrow. They sell them with exactly the same routine in Lagos. I suppose they have an intercontinental market phrasebook.'

When he spoke like that, it was as well to ignore it. 'Why call tomorrow?' said John. 'We don't need to work every day. Adorne isn't going to arrive any moment.'

'I don't know,' Nicholas said. 'Remember Gertrude's tales about Basle? She says men throw coins into the steam baths and order their mistress's maids to up-end and fetch them. The maids love it, according to Gertrude. If they don't mind, maybe nobody does.'

'Maybe they don't. Are ye deaf?' le Grant said.

'About tomorrow? Yes, I've planned meetings,' Nicholas said. 'And I know Adorne can't come for a while. But I do want to arrange him a welcome. And I do want to be elsewhere when he receives it. You as well. Should we call on Tobie and see if there is any news?'

'You want to be elsewhere when Gelis arrives?' le Grant said.

'I didn't invite her,' said Nicholas.

The Genoese fondaco had a chained leopard in the patio and a Consul, Signor Pietro de Persis, who would visibly have preferred to unchain it on discovering that his visitors were bankers from Venice. He did, in time, send someone upstairs to enquire if the Signorina Caterina and Messer Tobias would receive them: eventually they found themselves in a suite even larger than the rooms Venice provided. Nicholas said, 'He doesn't like us. We could feed candied fruit to his leopard.'

'I have a better suggestion,' said Tobie. 'Feed it to the harbour drummers and trumpeters. No one's had a proper night's sleep for a month.'

'Since the Turkish fleet went to war,' Nicholas said. Unbuttoning and then dropping his gown, he was exploring the room. In its furnishing it was remarkably like the one the girl had occupied in the Venetian fondaco, largely because the same objects were strewn all about it. 'Well, Dioscorides?' he said. He sat down and picked up some drawings.

The girl, too, looked much the same, although marginally neater than when flying the kite. 'Well, Teiresias?' she said.

The silence was almost non-existent. 'You *have* been learning. Who from?' Nicholas said. He laid down the drawings and looked about him. John sat down, attracting a quick glance from Tobie.

'I had a good teacher in Ghent,' Katelijne said. 'I wondered why you needed the Jew. I thought the map would have been sufficient. Anyway, what did you find?'

Nicholas did not answer. John le Grant, drawing breath, saw that Tobie was frowning. Tobie had heard of Teiresias of the rod, blessed with prophetic insight. Tobie said, 'I thought the Jew couldn't help.'

'No,' said Katelijne. She was looking at Nicholas.

Nicholas said, 'How did you know?'

'The van Borselen,' said Katelijne. 'The Duchess Eleanor writes to them.'

Tobie said, 'What does she know?'

The girl's eyes were on Nicholas. His gaze was on his hands. He had picked up some palm leaves and was plaiting them. He said, 'She knows that pigs sometimes find truffles, but not when there are no truffles to find.'

John was silent. He had already guessed that. If Nicholas had consulted the Jew, it was because he had already tried and failed to find gold by his own methods. Tobie said, 'I think you will have to tell me what you mean. John?'

'He is a diviner,' John said.

Tobie stood. Nicholas, without looking up, indolently continued with what he was doing. He said, 'I have given myself a special bonus. The Duchess is pleased with her silver mines.'

'She should be,' the girl said. She added, 'You know divining is supposed to be harmful?'

'Not at all,' Nicholas said. He spread his hands and lifted what he had done. It was the beginning of a basket, such as Katelijne had been trying to make. He said, 'I thought the knack would come back. Harmful? Only to those who don't know how to manage it. It recognised the candied-fruit poison.' He looked up.

'And who it came from?' It was Tobie.

'Not that.'

'But it didn't find gold?'

'No.'

'And the Jew couldn't help?'

'No,' said Nicholas.

'But you would have come to Alexandria anyway, to compete with my uncle. Where is he?' said Katelijne. 'Go on, tell us.'

'Kathi, no,' the doctor said. 'It isn't a competition. We know. We heard his ship was going to Malta, then Sicily. He should be here in ten days. The way things are, they won't sail further east.'

'I hope not,' said Nicholas. 'There is a considerable wailing and gnashing of teeth in the city. Poor Paul Erizzo.'

John looked at him. Up till then, he had never mentioned the name. Paul Erizzo, Bailie of Negroponte, had been Venetian Consul in Cyprus when he and Nicholas and Tobie had been there. Now, long past his tour of duty, he had stayed to lead the defence of Negroponte against Sultan Mehmet.

Tobie said, 'The news is better today. The Sultan has called on Negroponte to surrender, and Erizzo has told him to go away and eat pork. He's going to try to hold out. They've had some reinforcements from Crete, and Venice has fifty galleys gathering there. If a Venetian fleet got to Euboea in time, they could break the pontoon bridge to the island, strand the Turkish vanguard and prevent the rest of Mehmet's army arriving. You may be proud of the *Ghost* and the *San Niccolò* yet.'

'I hadn't heard that,' Nicholas said. 'Trust the Genoese to hear all the gossip. And your uncle is coming?'

'And everyone with him,' said Katelijne. 'Can't you divine people at all? If you can manage silver, can't you pick out your Gelis? Don't you have a chart? If I get a chart, will you teach me?'

'No, he won't,' Tobie said. He moderated his voice. He said, 'Whatever Nicholas does is his business. This is not something for you.'

'Then it shouldn't be for M. de Fleury,' she said.

'You convince him,' said Tobie. 'Anyway we've proved it already. A Genoese in a fast boat from Tunis can tell us more about your uncle's ship than a conjurer. Nicholas, it's taken on African passengers. When they arrive, they'll have someone with them.'

A leaf fell. Nicholas picked it up. Tobie swore suddenly. He said, 'Not . . . No.'

Nicholas looked up. 'So, who?' he said.

Tobie had changed colour. John saw the girl considering him, her hands very still. Tobie said curtly, 'But he might bring news. It's Benedetto Dei, the Florentine merchant. He's been in the interior. And someone who sounds like one of the ibn Said brothers. It can't be good news, Nicholas.'

No one spoke. Nicholas resumed plaiting slowly. John le Grant wondered if the girl had any idea what had happened to Nicholas in Africa. He himself knew, because Godscalc had told him. Tobie, who had brought Nicholas home, certainly knew. John cleared his throat, and Tobie looked at him. John said, 'I think you had better stay until the ship comes, hadn't you, Nicholas? I can go to Damietta on my own. I've done it often before. Then you can join me.'

Nicholas continued with what he was doing, but a prosaic dimple formed and vanished in one cheek. It signified, without speech, that he knew exactly what John was trying to prevent him from doing.

Katelijne said, 'Didn't you mean to stay till the ship came?' She looked perplexed.

Nicholas said, 'Well, what do you think? Only business is business, and we thought for a while we should have to sort something out at Damietta. But John can go and I'll stay.' He laid down his knife and, placing the piece of weaving on the floor, began to gather the cuttings. 'So what about you, Katelijne? What will you do when the good Baron Cortachy comes? Show him Alexandria? Are you going with him to the Holy Land?' He was looking at Tobie.

Tobie, unusually, got in an answer before she did. 'No, she isn't,' he said. 'That is, she'll spend some time with them all in Alexandria, and travel as far as the Garden of Balm, if you know where that is. Her uncle wants her to bathe in the pool. Then she'll come back here and stay at the fondaco until her uncle has finished his pilgrimage. Am I right?'

She was amused. She said, 'Did we give any secrets away?'

Tobie went pink and then laughed. He said, 'Never trust the opposition.'

She said, 'But he isn't the opposition, he's your friend, isn't he?'

Tobie and Nicholas looked at each other. Then Nicholas gave a laugh. 'Katelijne,' he said, 'Tobie's only friends are the patients he's treating. The trouble is, he tries to treat so many at the same time. We must go: they'll be locking the gates. I've used up all your leaves.'

She looked at the piece of work. There was nothing amateur about it. To John's eye, it was indistinguishable from true native weaving. Katelijne said, 'Can you make hats?'

'Yes,' said Nicholas. 'Buy some straw and I'll show you tomorrow.' He looked at Tobie, but Tobie was looking down.

That time, John said nothing until they were in their own Venetian fondaco, and alone. Then he said, 'You will stay? I'll go on to Cairo.'

'Yes. It was as well not to mention it. Yes, I'll stay. It doesn't mean, my dear ingenious John, that I mean to alter my programme.'

'She's a nice girl,' said John le Grant.

'Certainly she is. She knows about her uncle and myself. Tobie will protect her.'

'Poor Tobie,' said John.

'Not at all. Tobie will enjoy it. So when should you leave? In a week? Then we'd better get the other meetings in place. Let's look at the papers. Bring up Achille.'

The sun was going down. All the others, work done, were in the gardens or on the roof of the fondaco, sipping their wine in the milky breeze, watching the sky changing over the sea, and the masts, tipped with lights, rocking together in the calm of the harbour. He could hear the sparrows bustling in the palms, and the drilling voice of some bird, repeating the same few notes over and over. Nicholas was sitting, the lamplight on his papers.

John came back and sat down. He said, 'You haven't told me. What did you discover this morning?'

Nicholas said, '*Tête-Dieu,*' and flung down his pen.

'Don't you think I've been fairly patient?' John said. 'I'm asking you whether you've found a clue to the gold. I thought that was one of the reasons why we were here.'

Nicholas said, 'We're also here to get this agency up from its knees, plaster the cracks the Vatachino have made in it, fortify the bits that Sir Anselm Adorne undoubtedly has got his eye on, and make some very long-term arrangements indeed looking East. That's enough, I should have thought, for the moment.'

'All right,' John said. 'I know our concern is the trade, not the gold. But what you know, I've got to know. Or where will the Bank be, supposing next time you do eat the pigeon?'

There was a silence. 'You have a point,' Nicholas said. 'The other way of looking at it is the opposite. It might be safer if you didn't know.'

'To hell with that,' said John mildly. 'I'm not moving from here until you tell me.'

Nicholas looked at him. Then, slowly, he pulled one of his faces and sat back.

John said, 'Aye. Wheels within wheels within wheels. You don't need to tell me. You get lost in the gears and forget what you were making. There are business secrets, and they're different from personal secrets. This is a business secret, and I'm in the same business. So is Tobie.'

Nicholas had relaxed. Still leaning back, he said, 'Well, he's in the Hippocratic business as well. Let's leave Tobie until he has decided whose secrets he's keeping. I don't mind your knowing.'

'Oh, thank you,' said John.

'I hadn't made up my mind what to do about it, that was all. So. I did find the place on the map. It was a church: the Greek Church of St Sabas. The object they gave me had been left, as the parrot was, by someone unknown, with instructions and money enclosed. It came in this.' Nicholas stretched and flung on the table the well-used pilgrim's satchel, its cross still faintly embossed.

John drew it towards him and opened it. There was nothing inside. He looked his question.

'I burned it,' said Nicholas. 'It was a writing tablet, an old one, with the wax filled in, but blank. Have you seen a message sent that way before?'

John shook his head.

'You would have enjoyed the Medici ciphers,' Nicholas said.

'This wasn't a trick worth the name. You melt off the wax and the message is cut on the wood underneath. In this case, just the name of a place. Guess what it was?' His eyes in the lamplight were grey as water, with hollows beneath. He had wanted to get rid of the paperwork, it was suddenly clear, because he had wanted to work with the rod.

John said, 'You were in a Greek church, not a Latin or Coptic one. And this is a Christian purse, indicating maybe another church, or a shrine or a monastery.' He paused. 'There is a Greek church at Tor. That's where the parrot was brought from.' In the silence, he visualised the Red Sea and small, clamorous Tor, with its brackish wells and its palms and its harbour; the place where the camel caravans gathered to bring the Indian merchandise north. Cairo was eight days north of Tor. He said, 'There's a monastery there.' A flourishing monastery, he remembered, with a plantation of two thousand date palms. They would have a place to hide gold.

'Not Tor,' Nicholas said. His voice expressed more than the words.

John took a long breath. Then he said, 'Sinai.' If it sounded grim, it was the way he felt.

'Yes,' Nicholas said. 'Not Tor but its mother-house, set in the heart of twenty-four thousand square miles of wilderness, and reached by many days of excruciating travel, most of it vertical. Like Moses, we have been called to Mount Sinai.'

There was a pause, filled with breathing. 'You can't take Gelis there,' John said.

'I don't propose taking Gelis anywhere,' Nicholas answered.

John left, supposedly for Damietta, in ten days. He had several important errands in Cairo, one of which was to locate the whereabouts of David de Salmeton, whose rooms in Alexandria they had so recently and stickily raided. Left to himself, Nicholas settled down and, concentrating on the agency, began to fill twenty hours with work every day. At the end of a week of it, he fulfilled a long-standing engagement and called at the fondaco of Cyprus.

The agent had once worked in the Treasurer's office: Nicholas knew him. Gradually, impoverished by Cairene tributes and failed harvests and general turmoil, James, King of Cyprus – Zacco – had lost the power to pay the army Nicholas had provided him with, and one by one had withdrawn his substantial privileges. There had been other reasons for the schism as well.

Since his return from Africa, the reports from the Bank's agents in Alexandria and Damascus had indicated a change. Nothing direct – no messages, for example, from the King himself or Marietta, his cropnosed mother – but a hint here and there that matters were open to adjustment. Nicholas had instructed John to ignore them. He did not want to pick up the life or the friendships of seven years ago. He was pleasant, therefore, to this man and his clerks, but did not tell them what they were striving to learn – whether, as a man of independent wealth, he sided now with Venice or Cairo.

Zacco was married, by proxy, to the daughter of Marco Corner of Venice and, until she had children, Venice itself was her heir. She had no children, because Zacco had not yet met her. Zacco had not yet met her because, very patently, he couldn't stand the idea of becoming a Venetian colony. Something which Lorenzo Strozzi of Naples, for example, had understood very well.

If Venice took over Cyprus, she would establish her warehouses there, and the Mameluke Sultan of Cairo would lose both his direct trade and his tribute. If Negroponte fell, the Ottoman Sultan of Constantinople would possibly move into Cyprus before anyone, causing his fellow Muslims in Cairo equal pain. Nicholas said, 'What's the news from Negroponte?'

He knew already it was hopeful. Paul Erizzo had discovered a traitor, and employed the knowledge to mislead his enemy. As a result, fifteen thousand Turks had been killed. 'All the same,' the agent said. 'Constantinople fell to those guns. The walls of the capital cannot survive such a pounding. Signor Paul has sent to beg the ships of Venice, the ships of the Religion, to make haste from Crete.'

One of the ships which would come to the Captain's aid was the *Ghost*, once the *Doria*: the same vessel Paul Erizzo had used long ago to help capture Nicholas and take him to Cyprus. Venice had wished to acquire credit with Zacco, and had hoped Nicholas would do what he had done, which was to clear Zacco's foes from the island. Zacco had been grateful, up to a point.

As for Erizzo, Nicholas had formed a respect for him and his pretty daughter. Nicholas held all Venetians in respect; especially Fiorenza, wife of Marco Corner, sugar-planter, who had presented him with some choice candied fruit. The agent had produced a similar box, just a moment ago, but Nicholas had felt he must regretfully refuse. He made to take his leave, having learned as much as he could, and having conveyed what he wanted.

The agent said, 'But my lord will come again, and spend longer? There are many friends who wish to be remembered to you. Perhaps they might tempt you to visit Cyprus yourself?'

'It seems unlikely. I am not staying in Alexandria,' Nicholas said. 'Although I admit I have a great curiosity about one thing.'

'Yes? Yes?' said the Consul. They were standing. He was a short man of Cypriot blood: what they called a White Venetian.

Nicholas said, 'I had always dreamed that one day I might possess a parrot as beautiful as the one belonging to the King's illustrious lady mother. Is the bird still alive?'

The Consul's lips parted. 'Madame Marietta's parrot?'

'A red-and-blue parrot. It stood by her chair.'

'I know it,' said the man. He looked simply surprised. He said, 'A magnificent bird, I agree. Indeed, I agree. But it is no longer there.'

'It died?' said Nicholas sorrowfully.

The agent smiled. 'I fear it has gone through a gate as difficult to unlock as that of death. It was presented by the lady Marietta to a convent.'

'A convent?'

'Well, a lodging. A house serving some property of the Franciscan monks between Nicosia and Famagusta.'

'Not Psimoloso?' said Nicholas. 'I should have guessed. I should not, of course, dream of depriving the good friars of their pet. Think no more of it. And now I must go.'

The Consul accompanied him to the door. He said, looking outside, 'You have a good guard? Is that all your guard? You have no attendants of your own?'

He had three servants, which was enough, along with the Mamelukes. The Consul said, 'But you should have more. The Emir knows. He should have provided you with more men. It is in his own interest.'

'More men against what?' Nicholas said.

The Consul looked up with what appeared to be genuine alarm. 'You did not get my special message last week? About the sister of Tzani-bey al-Ablak?'

'About Tzani-bey's *sister*?' Nicholas said.

'She who paid an assassin to attempt the life of our King. The man failed. But it is said that she holds you, too, responsible for the death of her brother in Cyprus. Here perhaps you may think yourself safe. But be careful. And if you leave the city, guard yourself every moment,' said the Consul. His face was full of sincere anxiety. 'I cannot understand it, monseigneur. I left you a message. M. Pierre said he would give you it himself. You must know him. M. Pierre de Persis, the Genoese Consul.'

'Yes, I know him,' Nicholas said.

His hand ached. He visited the baths every morning to drive the stiffness away from his shoulders and neck. It didn't matter. He had found the ship. It was coming. Very soon, Anselm Adorne would be here.

Chapter 35

RUNNING BEFORE A summer storm, the ship containing Anselm Adorne, Baron Cortachy, and his companions reached Alexandria on the afternoon of Tuesday the seventeenth of July. At the entrance to the foreigners' harbour, she was thrown into a passage choked with classical marble from the great tumbled lantern. The vessel struck the stone twice, the shock nearly springing her planks and throwing all the exhausted passengers to the deck. Recovering, she made her way into the haven at last, and took her place half a mile from the shore. The customs boat conducted its usual search.

It also brought orders. Until the following morning, no one must land or receive friends or consuls on board. No explanation was given.

However disappointed and weary they felt, the newcomers did receive some sort of welcome. Regardless of nation, seamen already inside the haven poled their way over and, swarming aboard, lent busy hands to the labour of dropping anchor, furling the sails and dismantling the ship, as enjoined by the law.

The skiffs lay about her for a long time. Finally, the customs boat left, the violent activity ceased, and the big Genoese ship was left to float, battered, in the late sun, with the sound of faint music and reviving laughter to tell that crew and passengers and helpers were at last able to toast their arrival in Eunostos, in the Port of Safe Return.

Nicholas de Fleury stood on the fondaco roof, watching them. He was alone.

Earlier, warned by tambour and trumpet, all the staff of the consulate and its merchants had crowded the space where he stood, agonising over the incomer's struggles; cheering when she at last made her way safely in. She was too far off, of course, to distinguish passengers. Men and women were like *ghabr*, like dust; like the minute script they tied to the wing-feathers of pigeons. Wherever Gelis was standing, or Dei, they could not distinguish him either.

Lingering there, he had been startled, like the rest, when a voice shrill with alarm had raised itself far below in the courtyard, repeating a phrase over and over in a thick Venetian vernacular. Nicholas had been among the first to leave the roof, bounding downstairs, the others pouring behind until all the men and women of the fondaco were crowded together below. There the Consul, holding the man by the shoulders, was speaking. Then the man, weeping, repeated what he had said.

Nicholas had stayed with Achille and the rest for a while, then had found it oppressive. When he came up the second time, he had the roof to himself, and the view of the harbour. The sounds that floated over the water were not very different. After a while, the small boats began to leave the big Genoese one by one, rowing across to their various ships, and Gelis's vessel swung to its anchor. It was two hours to sundown, and outside the harbour the storm-waves crashed gold on the spit. He was not thinking about Gelis, or Dei. A few hours ago, he had been thinking about nothing else.

Tobie's voice spoke at his elbow. 'I came when I heard. Negroponte has fallen.' He paused and then said, his voice shaking, 'The bastards.'

'Who, the Turks?' Nicholas said.

'No, the Genoese. The bastards are celebrating.' Tobie paused. He said, 'What have you heard? Your Consul will know more than ours.'

Nicholas said, 'It was taken at noon five days ago, fighting street by street. They have butchered every male over eight. Erizzo gave himself up on condition he kept his head: they have sawn him in two at the waist, and beheaded his daughter. It was worse than it might have been because Mehmet thought he was losing: the Venetian Captain-General brought seventy ships up the strait. But instead of breaking the bridges, he took fright, it seems, and sailed back to Crete. So Mehmet gave his troops all that they wanted.'

Tobie moved, but Nicholas didn't look at him. 'So we've still got the *Ghost* and the *San Niccolò*, those two happy ships. Even the Duke of Burgundy's two galleys would have been safe: Tommaso might risk them next time.' He broke off and said, 'Oh, damn them.'

Beside him Tobie swore, too. The harbour, so peaceful a moment before, had erupted into a cacophony of noise; of blaring, hooting and warbling, of the clang of bells and the thudding of drums, punctuated by the erratic thunder of cannon. The Turkish ships of the western harbour had just heard the news, and those from their fondaco were rushing to join them. As they watched, boats laced with turbans began to skim towards the Christian galleys. The tumult gusted into the city as if roused by bellows.

'Hound music,' Nicholas said, and made as if to break away suddenly.

Tobie gripped him. 'No. Listen. It's happening too in the streets. Leave it to the Mamelukes. The Mamelukes are probably as sick over the victory as we are.'

'They can't police the harbour,' Nicholas said. 'I hope to God the Genoese keep their heads.' The harbour now was full of small boats, and the sound of screeching and banging and jeering as they circled.

Tobie said, 'The *Ciaretti* have a good crew. And Adorne's ship will be full of Muslims for Mecca. He's an experienced man. He'll look after her.' He didn't specify whether he meant the girl or the ship, and Nicholas didn't ask. They watched.

The Genoese kept their heads, and all the merchantmen, pinned helplessly there in the harbour. They stayed below, and offered no provocation. By sundown, the amusement had palled and the harbour was beginning to empty, although the streets within the city were still full of deafening noise. The wind had freshened. Nicholas said, 'You've missed the curfew. Come down and have something to eat. Will Katelijne worry that you didn't come back? How did she take this?'

'She's a Sersanders,' Tobie said. 'She's heard war discussed, and seen the results of it. She was afraid for her uncle. The Genoese here didn't even care about that.'

Nicholas said, 'Don't you remember the Cypriots when the Genoese left Famagusta?' They had reached his room. There was no one there. The fondaco echoed with muffled sound; the outpourings of misery and bereavement. There was nothing they could do. He found some cold meat and two flasks; one of wine for Tobie, one of water for himself.

'Still?' said Tobie. 'Why water, Nicholas?'

Nicholas arranged things and sat. He had been standing for a long time. He said, 'You ought to go to the Tyrol. You either become an abstainer or crapulous.'

'And this?' Tobie said. He had found the bob on its cord and pulled it out.

'That's to help me find water,' said Nicholas. 'Tobie, I don't want to fall out again.'

'But you don't mind having company,' Tobie said. He was shrewd enough. He went on, 'All right. What would you like done tomorrow? De Persis says all the merchants will be allowed to come on shore, although perhaps later than usual. Adorne has already sent over his letters. Credentials from the Senate of Genoa. That gets him officially into the fondaco.' He stopped.

'Really? The Senate of Genoa?' Nicholas said. 'And he called himself a Burgundian envoy in Milan? I thought this was a family pilgrimage? The route has been a bit odd, and I'm not sure what shrines he visited in Tunis or Sousa or Monastir, but doesn't he intend to go to the Holy Land?'

'I'm not going to tell you,' said Tobie. 'But you know he's to be here for some weeks, and you know how pilgrims would be treated. At least he can live decently in the meantime.'

'Claiming to be a merchant. Yes, it's natural,' Nicholas said. 'Modified dues, guards of Mamelukes, use of the fondaco. He may even have to pretend to do business, poor man.'

There was a short silence. Tobie said, 'Have you done something?'

'I don't remember,' Nicholas said. 'You were asking me about tomorrow.' He hadn't intended to torment Tobie. It didn't matter. What was going to happen would happen, with or without Tobie or Anselm Adorne.

Tobie said, 'I was asking you, as I remember, about your wife. Do you want to come back with me for when Gelis arrives? Or come later? Or would you like me to bring her alone?'

It was the aggravation he meant it to be, in that it thrust before Nicholas a decision he had not so far made. He therefore said all the more briskly, 'I would like to see Dei first. Or whoever has come from Africa. Would you let me arrange that, and then send you word about Gelis?'

Tobie said, 'I suppose so. Although if I know Gelis, she will do what she wants.'

'Which will be?' Nicholas said.

Tobie said, 'To join you at the first possible moment, and stay with you. To which she is entitled.'

Nicholas said, 'Yes, of course. Look, I've stopped you eating. There's the wine. If I can find a servant, I can have John's bed made up in a moment.' He paused. 'Or do you think Katelijne might be anxious? The streets are quieter. The Consul might be able to bribe someone to let you go back.' The sounds of weeping were fainter, but they were still there.

Tobie said, 'You're right. Perhaps that would be best.'

It took Nicholas by surprise: Tobie seldom changed his mind, or not at least without argument. Seeing him off in due course, he found himself puzzled as well as relieved. He had wanted company, but not of a kind that would ask questions, or quarrel. He tried to think what company he wanted and his mind, of course, gave him the answer. The useless answer, for neither could come.

Not until the following afternoon did the Emir of Alexandria consider it safe to allow into the city the captain and passengers of the ship which had arrived, so inopportunely, at the moment of the Ottoman victory. Later still, formalities over, the noble and puissant lord Anselm Adorne, Baron Cortachy, walked into the city of Alexandria at last, and was conducted to his spacious rooms in the Genoese fondaco where his niece Katelijne ran glowing into his arms, and Dr Tobias, her physician, smiled breathlessly.

It had been Kathi's idea to watch from the roof. It had been Kathi who first saw coming, escorted solemnly by the Genoese Consul, the small party of five weatherbeaten, richly dressed men attended by a large retinue of servants and Mamelukes.

There were no women among them. There was no one, either, resembling a Florentine or a Maghgribian trader. 'Benedetto Dei and the other man aren't there,' Tobie had exclaimed.

'Gelis van Borselen isn't there,' had said Kathi, much more sharply. Then she said, 'Dei would go to the Florentine fondaco. I don't know where the other would lodge, but I'm sure M. de Fleury does. Where do you think his wife is?'

'At the Venetian fondaco,' said Tobie sourly. His heart sank at the notion of the news from Africa and Gelis arriving together. Gazing below, he observed that Adorne, now much nearer, had lost none of his grace of appearance or manner, although deeply tanned and more spare than he had been. He walked, conversing lightly, with his gaze lifted to the fondaco, as if hoping to catch a glimpse of his niece. Tobie said, 'We ought to go down.'

Kathi in turn was smiling fondly down on her uncle's broad hat. She said, 'He looks well, doesn't he? He so loves managing things. He'll know where she is.' She turned and ran, Tobie following.

Below, embrace and exclamations over, Anselm Adorne turned from his niece to shake hands with the doctor. 'You have looked after her so well. I want to hear all about your journey from Rome, and what you've been doing in Alexandria.'

Kites, thought Tobie. Pigeons. Visits to churches? He coughed and opened his mouth. 'We want to hear about you,' said Katelijne, taking her uncle by the arm and sitting down with him. 'And Dr

Tobias would like to have a word, if it's convenient, with the lady of Fleury. You know why?'

Anselm Adorne looked at the doctor. He said wryly, 'I suppose, having seen the *Ciaretti* in the harbour, that I do know why. I'm sorry, that being the case, to disappoint you, and Nicholas. The lady Gelis isn't with me.'

The tone of voice was perfectly level, and Tobie's pulse settled. He said, 'She is still on board? Or – I hope she hasn't suffered some mishap?'

Adorne smiled. 'So far as I know she is well. In fact, I thought to find her already here. You didn't know that she left us? After you sailed, she decided she would rather travel the quick way, by pilgrim galley from Venice. Our other three friends had already departed to do the same thing. She left to join them.'

'And did?' the doctor said.

'So far as I know. And if she did, did so safely: the galley arrived at Jaffa without harm. We heard as much on our way. But from Jaffa to here is no great distance. I thought she would have arrived.' He frowned. 'You make me anxious. Nothing can have gone wrong?'

Tobie realised he had been staring at nothing. He said swiftly, 'No. I am sure there is a simple explanation. The galley arrived, and three important men and a lady would hardly avoid notice, I'm sure. In any case, I know where to ask. I'll go now and find out. You'll want to speak to Kathi, and rest.'

He smiled, shook hands again, and held Kathi's eyes for a moment in warning. They had had an oblique talk, that day, about the ethics of their odd situation. She was loyal to her uncle, and he had to steer a path between his duty to her and to Nicholas. She knew quite a lot about Nicholas now, but he didn't think she would chatter. She seemed young; a stranger might think her no more than childishly pert. They had not seen her, as he had, weak and sick and still displaying the same bright curiosity; the interest in others which had nothing self-centred about it.

On his way out of the fondaco, prompted by civility and by a curiosity perhaps less well intentioned, Tobie stopped to shake hands with the rest of Adorne's party with whom, after all, he had travelled from Bruges for three months. He greeted them all: Jan, the lank, fair son, bored with weeks at sea with his father; the young friend Lambert van de Walle, who had imagination and might make a good merchant one day; the older merchant Pieter Reyphin who was of distinguished Ghent blood, like the Sersanders, and was shrewder than he looked. And the priest, John of

Kinloch, who had always loathed Nicholas and had been as aggressive and as contemptuous on the journey as he dared, out of Adorne's hearing.

They all asked after Katelijne. He saw that she was their mascot, and they would never really forgive him, because he had whisked her away.

He left and, grimly anxious, went about the business that mattered. He knew where to find Benedetto Dei. He knew, too, who might have word of any pilgrims travelling west from a Venetian galley at Jaffa. He made both calls, and, emerging soberly from the second, stood for a moment, pushed by the crowds, and studied the vast scarlet sky.

It was near the hour for the curfew. He knew that this time he would have to spend the night at the Venetian fondaco. He entered the gates and stayed a while in the garden. The sun went down, and he was shaken with sneezes.

Because they came ashore after noon, it was some time before Benedetto Dei and Abderrahman ibn Said reached their respective lodgings and the messages that awaited them both. Dei, with the aplomb one would expect from an agent of Tommaso Portinari, decided that Nicholas de Fleury could wait, and went to bed. Ibn Said went immediately to the Venetian fondaco.

He had gone when Tobie made his way there.

Achille, showing Tobie into the room, said, 'But as you see, the padrone is not here. Come tomorrow.'

Tobie said, 'The gate's shut. I can't come tomorrow. Of course Ser Niccolò's here. Where is he? What's the trouble?'

'None,' said Achille. 'He is sleeping.'

'You said – Get out of my way,' said Tobie rudely. The man jumped. Tobie didn't even need to push him aside. In the rooms, which were empty, everything seemed as usual except for one thing. Tobie said, 'If you really wanted to protect him, you shouldn't let anyone in. The place reeks of drink. Where is he?'

'I don't know,' said the man.

Tobie wondered how Nicholas had frightened him. He said, softening his own manner a little, 'Look. No one will blame you. Everyone is under strain today. Did Ser Niccolò have a visitor?'

The under-agent clasped his hands. 'A Muslim gentleman called. I brought sherbet.'

'But not after the Muslim visitor went. What was his name?' Tobie said. 'Was it ibn Said?'

'Very like,' said Achille. 'A merchant from Timbuktu, or his brother. He talked, and went away. It was daylight then. Later, the page came from lighting the candles and told me.'

'Told you what?' The candles were lit.

'That Ser Niccolò would not let him come in. I waited. Then I came myself. I lit the rooms. But he had gone.'

The man was pale. Tobie said, 'If you went round the fondaco tonight, you'd find a good few men drowning their sorrows. Go to bed. I'll spend the night here. He'll come back, or I'll find him.'

He must have sounded reassuring, because the man went.

Standing in the silent rooms, Tobie considered a paradox. Of all the men he had known, Nicholas de Fleury had the gift of entering the minds and thoughts of others. Now Nicholas de Fleury was the object of analysis, and it was for his doctor to guess whether this night he required rescue or privacy. For there was little doubt about the news he had received. The tragedy lay in the news still to come.

In the end, Tobie set out to find him. The gates were locked. Nicholas de Fleury must be within the confines of the fondaco. He began with the roof, and worked down.

Nicholas heard him come over the grass. He heard because he was lying on it, his shoulders and head supported by the trunk of a tree. He supposed that, if he had asked him, Tobie would have explained that wine after abstinence doesn't necessarily result in oblivion. He stayed because he felt too delicate to move, but without much hope that Tobie would pass him. He felt Tobie kneel, and opened his eyes. Tobie said, 'Umar is dead.'

Nicholas said, 'Oh, yes. But we knew that already.'

'Now you can accept it,' said Tobie.

'Now I know the details, yes. It is a great step forward,' said Nicholas. His stomach knotted and he told it to unknot.

Tobie said, 'I'm sorry. It was bad, then. I'm sorry. Do you want to tell me?'

The words became lost, in some fashion. Some time later, Tobie repeated them. He appeared now to be sitting beside him. Nicholas said, 'I'm sorry. Something I drank.' The wind had risen again but it was very warm, and the trees tossed against the twinkling windows of the fondaco. The spray from the fountain, blowing across, was quite pleasant. He made an effort and thought about Tobie. Then he remembered. He said, 'So did you see Gelis? You didn't bring her, I hope. She might go home and never try to come back again.' He thought the idea vaguely funny and smiled.

Time passed. The words hung about, and when he next came to himself they were still there. He said irritably, 'Well? What about Gelis?'

Tobie was on his other side this time. Tobie said, 'Hold my arm. I'm going to lift you up and take you to bed.'

'I don't think so,' said Nicholas. 'You're not as pretty as Zacco.' He stayed where he was. 'What about Gelis?'

'She's all right,' said Tobie. 'Look, get up. You can't stay here all night, and I want some sleep if you don't.'

She's all right. Would anyone, placed as Tobie was, use that off-hand phrase to speak about Gelis? Nicholas said, 'Why are you lying?'

Tobie was silent. Then he said, 'Come upstairs.'

'No.' All at once, it was easy to be sober. Nicholas said, 'Tell me. Now.' He reared up like a dyeframe triangle: spine braced, palms between rigid knees.

Tobie knelt back on his heels. He said, 'She isn't here. She changed her mind and took the galley from Venice.'

Nicholas remembered. He released his hands and placed them on either side on the grass. He said, 'The party who wanted places on the Ascension Day boats?' He was surprised, but relieved. The galley had arrived safely at Jaffa: the Consul had said so. He said, 'So where did she go?'

Saying it, he recalled the contradictory impression he had received from Tobie's first words. He said, a little more sharply, 'Shouldn't she be here by now?'

Tobie said, 'Come upstairs.'

Nicholas looked at him.

When Tobie did not speak, Nicholas said, 'You have told me. Now tell me the rest.' Every physical complaint had gone. Everthing had gone, except hearing.

Tobie said, 'The galley arrived safely at Jaffa, but had been forced to stay at sea because of the war. Her food and water were tainted, and illness broke out, and spread. Forty-nine pilgrims died on the way. Among them were the three who had been with Adorne: the Duke of Burgundy's chaplain, the monk from Furnes, the merchant Colebrant from Bruges, and a fourth who joined them late, whose name was not recorded, but whose wedding ring was brought ashore with all the rest of the luggage.'

He paused, and then said, 'It bore your name and hers. It was all there was. Those who perished were all buried at sea.'

The fountain wakened him, or the unyielding stone under his cheek. The cold was so great he was shaking. He said, 'They rescued an earl and a bishop.'

Someone beside him said, 'There were survivors. One day, you will hear the whole story. Not now.'

Nicholas said, 'I must go.'

The voice said, 'There is nowhere to go. Come upstairs. Come with me. Nicholas?'

His name was Claes, Nikki, Nicol. His name was not Nicholas. What was his name?

Who sculptured Love and set him by the pool, Thinking with liquid such a flame to cool.

Someone was shaking him. He said, in explanation, 'My mother is dead.'

And the other man, in anguish almost as great as his own, seemed to say, 'I know. Is that not the root of it all? I know, Nicholas. I know.'

Wine after long abstinence has a curious effect. Waking and sleeping through the long night, Nicholas de Fleury was aware that Tobie was somewhere in the same room, but could not always think why. Towards morning he remembered very well. Soon after that Tobie himself fell asleep, his chin masked with fair bristle, circles under his reddened lids. Nicholas rose and, presenting himself early at the baths, was clean, shaved and dressed by the time Tobie awoke. He had also spoken to Achille, and had a tray brought with food enough for both. He did not try to eat himself, but laid the tray beside Tobie's pallet. He said, 'I have to thank you.'

Tobie pulled himself up. After a while he said, 'What do you remember?'

'All of it, I think,' Nicholas said. 'Gelis died on the galley from Venice. Some things will have to be done. I don't know how the child is being cared for. The news will have to be sent to her family.'

'I can do that,' Tobie said. 'I shall tell Adorne, as well. And the child, presumably, is already in the best hands. Gelis expected to be gone a long time.'

'But not quite so long,' Nicholas said. 'Would you do one more thing for me? Would you prevent Adorne or his niece coming to speak to me?'

'They will understand,' Tobie said.

Nicholas experienced a fleeting amusement. He said, 'I doubt it.'

Tobie left later, having satisfied himself, Nicholas assumed, that despair was not about to drive him into doing something irrational.

He had not asked what Nicholas intended to do, understanding perhaps that as yet he had little idea. His own main concern, from the outset, had been to appear as normal as possible and to get rid of Tobie.

It seemed that Tobie had somehow diverted Achille as well, for no one came near him except a page who scuttled out with the tray, and some time later appeared with another one. Nicholas let him leave it. The interruption made him realise that the pain came from his hands, cramped round the arms of his chair. Then it was dark, and the daily hubbub lessened below, and gradually the intrusions – everything – stopped.

And everything *had* stopped. Wheels within wheels within wheels. John had said that. So withdraw the innermost wheel, and silence falls. Nothing happens, because nothing makes it happen. The panorama is frozen. The mechanical figures cease to climb. The outlying animations – in Scotland . . . in Flanders . . . in the Tyrol, Venice, Cyprus, Egypt, Persia – all slacken as well, and sink below, weighted with sand from the ballast. Joining the wheel already broken, which he had never fully acknowledged till now.

There is no cradle under my roof . . .

I want the teachers of your line to help instruct the poor fools sprung of mine . . . All now truly gone, from today.

From yesterday. Time was passing. So what was he going to do? His mind reached that point, always, and jibbed, and went back. Back, and back. And then forward again. *Was it quick for him? How was it for her?* Slow this time, and seeping: seawater, fresh water; the pendulum swinging. If the mould was broken, how could you ever put anything together again?

Some time during the night he lit a candle and, sitting, dazzled, took out his maps and his jewel. His hands beat slowly and heavily, as his heart did, and he thought that was bad. Although he knew it was pointless, he cast over Jaffa and all the coast that lay between there and Alexandria, but of course there was nothing. He waited, and then thought to ask the jewel what he should do.

Divining tools cannot make choices. Remembering, he set himself, with an exhausted kind of persistence, to ask specific questions. Should I go here? Or here? Or here? It amused him, distantly, to leave his future to fate when suddenly he had no care for the future. The sparrows were chirping and the morning wind was stirring through the window before he remembered the question he had not thought to ask.

It meant another map, one he had just acquired. He got it out, moving stiffly, and glanced outside at the lightening sky. Soon the gates would be unlocked. Soon anyone could leave if they wished. He lifted the cord, thinking of several things instead of concentrating on one.

It was odd therefore that the jewel should begin to move for the first time in the positive direction; that the cord should rasp on his finger as it sped, and that it should rise, as it so seldom did, to its full spinning height.

He knew then that he didn't want to go back to empty rooms in Bruges, or Venice, or Scotland. He didn't want, and might never want, to confront familiar faces or to take prosaic decisions, as if life had merely suffered an interruption, and could continue, somehow, in another way.

It came to him that he had felt this way before. He thought it curious: a childish flaw he believed he should have outgrown. But at least he didn't fancy he could work his release by flinging himself mindlessly into battle for any man. It reminded him of Erizzo, who would not, either, have been vouchsafed a tomb; a casket bearing a legend; a coffin marked by some dying white cyclamen and a fillet of grass. His mind, bruised with thinking, slid back and clung yet again to the question the jewel could not answer. Perhaps because that was why, in the end, he did not want to go back to Bruges.

He made his decision. He put out the guttering candle, changed his creased clothes and, returning, summoned Achille while he began to write letters. One of these he sent by hand to Tobie. Before noon, Tobie had arrived and was announced. He was not alone. Anselm Adorne, Baron Cortachy, had come also, with Katelijne his niece.

It was an example, there was no doubt, of Tobie's authority, not his lack of it. He had not promised, in so many words, not to bring them. Both Adorne and the girl had been primed: he wore a look that was grave as well as friendly; she gazed at Nicholas with simple compassion but not with surprise. He knew how he looked. He had seen it reflected in the eyes of his servants, of Achille. Adorne, plainly dressed without any outward manifestation of his new honours, took his hand and said, 'We have a reason for coming, otherwise we should not have intruded. Nicholas, we are so sorry. We pray for you, and for her.'

It looked almost genuine. He was a handsome man, fine-featured even when tired, and he sounded sincere. Katelijne also came forward and, seating herself, shoved back the veil she had worn for the streets. She said, 'I'm sorry. Dr Tobias brought us.' She paused and added, 'You always said he had too many patients.'

It meant something. He suspected vaguely what it was. He said to Adorne – to the Baron Cortachy – 'It was good of you to come. I trust your pilgrimage has fulfilled so far all you expected of it.' His mind was far from clear. He did not want it clear.

Adorne said, 'Our journey is of no matter. It is yours that concerns us. Nicholas, we hear you are leaving Alexandria?'

Tobie, without speaking, had carefully removed his straw hat and was mopping the shining bits of his scalp. His eyes, when he looked up, were round, blue and threatening.

Nicholas said, 'Yes. I'm going to join John le Grant. My agent.' He had sent for a merchant's pass for Damietta. From Damietta, if you had money, you could disappear anywhere. You could disappear before that, if you had the right dress and spoke native Arabic and had the friendship of Abderrahman ibn Said, who happened to be going to Cairo.

Adorne said, 'That was what I understood. It is what I plan to do too, but not for several weeks. Nicholas ... I have a great favour to ask you. Would you take my niece and Dr Tobias with you? To Damietta?'

'Now?' Nicholas said.

Adorne smiled. For the sake of his niece, perhaps, there was only a hint of anxiety in his face. He said, 'Of course, if she waited for me, she would have my interpreter. But Dr Tobias thinks she should seek treatment now. You have heard of Matariya, the place of the Garden of Balm and the Well of the Virgin? It is reached by sail up the Nile from Damietta. It means hiring a boat, and although Dr Tobias speaks well, his Arabic is not as fluent as yours. Would you help them?'

'Or perhaps John might, if you can't,' Tobie said. His tone, like his gaze, was intimidating.

Tobie had guessed, of course, that John hadn't stayed in Damietta. He had probably guessed that Nicholas planned to meet him in Cairo. He certainly suspected the discomfort and worse that Nicholas had prepared here for Adorne.

True to his code, Tobie had kept all this from Adorne but he was here, wordlessly staring, to intimate that there was a price for his silence. Katelijne was to leave Alexandria with Tobie before the unpleasantness began. And Nicholas was to accompany them.

Nicholas attempted, from the profligate store of his masks, to select one that was deprecating. He said, 'You surely can manage without my help, or John's.'

He had addressed the remark to Adorne. But Katelijne, as he ought to know, was never greatly interested in pretence. She said,

'We were only being polite. You'd be better for a little while with Dr Tobias, and I'm willing to share him with you. I had a cousin who drank for six years when his father died.'

Adorne said, 'Katelijne!' Below his tan, he had flushed a little. Then he laughed.

Nicholas said, 'That's quite an analogy.' His head swam and he sat down.

'Not from sorrow: he found his father had two previous wives and a lot of legitimate sons. It was the shock. It will wear off.'

'Kathi is an expert,' said Tobie. 'But it is true. We are travelling in the same direction; we would welcome your help. And perhaps you would welcome our company.' He was glaring again.

Nicholas said, 'In that case, what can I do but offer it gladly? Will Tobie make the arrangements?'

Adorne rose. 'He will stay with you now. You have relieved my mind enormously. I hope perhaps in return you will draw some comfort from the arrangement. Although, God knows, the loss of a wife and a lover is something that no man can suffer lightly. I will not attempt to tell you what we feel for we, too, have lost our companions. Friend, I confide my niece to your care.'

Nicholas stood. He said something. Adorne left, and the girl, who looked over her shoulder, a tooth sunk in her lip. The door closed. Tobie said, 'Sit down. Don't bother saying it. I'm going off to pack, then I'll come back to help you. In the meantime, take this. You'll get a few hours of sleep, and then we'll all get some good out of you. And I'll look after that.'

He had picked up the jewel. Nicholas roused himself. He remarked, 'A nut, a ring, a pebble – anything on a string would do just as well.'

'Then get one,' Tobie said. 'But don't get attached to it. It's the mystique that does all the harm.' His gaze dropped to the maps and the candle grease on them, but he said nothing further. He put some pills on the table and left.

Nicholas lifted a pill and examined it inconsequentially. He might take it. He had come to Egypt for a brief season, expecting to rouse some new game and lay a few snares for the old. He had time to fill in.

But although he was leaving Alexandria, this time it wasn't the end of a stage, a phase completed, a milestone satisfactorily passed.

You couldn't reach or pass milestones when the travellers had failed; when the journey had come to a halt.

Part III

Close Season:
THE EMPTY FIELD

Chapter 36

THE WAY TO THE Garden of Balm is by water, sailing blown by the wind between sweet-smelling shores rich with cane sugar and vineyards, date palms and orchards, floating not in a bath but a cradle, to the music the Nile makes.

Many months later, Nicholas came to recognise the drugs Tobie had given him. At the time, he was hazily aware of the long day and night ride to Damietta; the absence of any effort on Tobie's part to find the departed John le Grant; and the relative ease with which Tobie produced sufficient ungrammatical Arabic to obtain a boat capable of sailing upriver.

The fiction that Nicholas intended to stay at Damietta seemed to have dissolved. The fact that he was on his way to Cairo appeared to be taken for granted. Since no one could now transmit the information to Adorne, he supposed it didn't matter. The Garden of Balm being located at Matariya just short of Cairo, itself six days away, he assumed that he would part company there with the rest.

The days of the journey flowed past and were lost in much the same way that time, numbers, calculation sank from consciousness after his son – his son Henry – had tried to knife him to death. The presence of the girl Katelijne perhaps enhanced the illusion.

It all seemed remarkably simple. Tobie, the girl and their servants were dressed in the coarse robes of pilgrims; Nicholas, in a last flash of commonsense, as their dragoman, in the Arab clothes he had worn in Alexandria. He had not shaved since they left. He was not hungry, but the girl had brought baskets of delicacies: figs and melons, grapes and dates, and Tobie bartered for rice and plump quails, eggs and fish on the way. It was like the Joliba, except that Bel was not there.

The consonances were perpetually soothing. The honey-smell of bubbling sugar swam over the water so that he thought they were passing Episkopi, and he was charmed to notice sea-lizards stir by the shore, disturbed by the boatmen's small tapping drums. On the Gambia, they rapped the wood of their boats with their oars. Gelis had done it for hours until she was exhausted. He wondered, drowsily, if there would be any orgies. Katelijne said, 'What are you smiling about?'

He smiled back but did not, then, reply. On the shore were camels, buffalo, water-wheels. Because the water was low, the boat kept in mid-stream: once they were stuck on a shoal, and he wakened to find they were all being compelled to slide overboard and wade through the water. Katelijne was supporting his arm. He said, 'What are you holding over your head?'

'You've wakened!' she said. She had become very brown, except over her chin where the veil went.

He said, 'Well, it seems to be daylight. It's an 'ud.'

'I told you he'd know it,' said Tobie. 'The prince of enchantment. She wants to teach herself, but she didn't want to disturb you.'

Then he looked about him: at the boat, at the river, at Tobie, and said, 'What has happened?'

'Nothing,' said Tobie. 'What you needed to happen. There is Matariya. You can't go to Cairo without calling there. So you might as well come.'

It wasn't quite true that he had no other means of getting to Cairo, but he was well enough pleased to remain. Tobie, he realised, had withdrawn whatever treatment he had been receiving. As the hours passed, Nicholas de Fleury came to himself.

He had thought, once, to find truth in the desert, in that world of infinite space, of stark and painful simplicity that leads the mind and soul inwards.

He had failed in that, and had found the failure terrible. Now, brought here by others, he was a convalescent in a different place. The scented gardens of Matariya – the airy pavilions, the profusion of sweet spring water sparkling in the hot sun, brimming in the wide, shady hall with its painted arcades where flowers and swimmers floated together – these healed not through the mind, but through the senses. Truth had been withheld, but he had been deemed worthy of comfort.

The gardens belonged to the Sultan. Its custodians were well accustomed to the pilgrims who came to drink at the white marble basin from the well-spring touched into being by the Holy Family, fleeing from Herod. The distressed of all races came to the baths for relief. And in the innermost garden, the garden most jealously guarded, grew the vine-like balsam plants which the Queen of Sheba, it was said, had brought and given to Solomon. Their oils, envied by kings from their anointing to their entombment, were prepared in the Sultan's own palace at Cairo and became gifts of diplomacy, or were sold in their ivory phials to the rich. Here, the breaking blossom soaked the air with its scent; and hair, skin, clothes were perfumed for nothing; for love.

Katelijne bathed every day. He did not see her, nor wanted to. It was far from the Timbuktu-Koy's palace, and the innocence of Umar's wife Zuhra and the courage – or he had then thought it courage – of Gelis. Pictures entered his mind, now and then, of these moments which he had long driven out. They did not disturb him, or not in a way he was yet aware of. They fed a softer puzzlement that was now taking its place beside the anger and the misery. The haunting sense of bewilderment would, he supposed, never leave.

To his surprise, he did not have much time to think. Tobie came with him when he swam, and challenged him to fierce races which upset the other bathers and did nothing to reduce the endearing slight pot of Tobie's stomach. Then, girdled into damp robes, they would rejoin Kathi in their pavilion, with its open terrace full of fluttering birds. She was taming a crested bird with barred wings called an upapa. She was also making friends, in a determined way, with the water-wheel oxen. She was always doing something.

They spoke Arabic a lot, because he was supposed to be their interpreter, and they both wanted to learn. Sometimes, when Tobie and the girl were together, he would hear them going over their lessons. It amused him to have Tobie, in this at least, as his pupil. It was he who suggested that the girl might also like to extend her Greek. It helped restore his own fluency. He was not sure if he was going to need it. Whatever plan he had conceived now seemed to have lost much of its point. If there was gold in Sinai, John could fetch it.

For the rest, the daylight hours passed, all of them filled; all of them marked by the tread of the oxen and the creak and splash of the wheels, turning, turning, up-ending the cycle of water-jars to fill the veins, the canals that watered the balm-garden. Just as distantly on the Nile the river was beginning to rise, a foot every day as the sweet, life-giving water, sent by God, moved into Egypt on its sacred, annual journey. The blessings of water, which could give, and take away.

Nicholas had never played the 'ud, the little lute she'd saved from the water, but he had seen it done, and he knew how the five courses should be tuned. He sat adjusting them before Tobie's astonished gaze, announcing each one as it was done. By the time he got to the third, Tobie said, 'How do you know that's a D?'

'He carries keys in his head,' the girl said. 'Didn't you know?' And to him, 'Don't you wish Whistle Willie were here?'

'No,' said Nicholas. 'I don't want him interfering: I want to set a Koranic chant in antiphony with a Gregorian one, and add in some tritones. Who would martyr us first?'

'There are two wheels in the garden,' said Kathi. 'What's that?'

'That's a salamiyya. I bought it from a man at the baths. You blow into it.'

'You surprise me,' said Kathi. 'Now tell me you don't have a drum.' She turned to Tobie. 'He had to leave Scotland because of the way he beat drums. Did you have them in Africa?'

The first direct question. Until later, he didn't notice it. He said, 'I've seen them used for sending messages. I could make one if you could saw me a log. We shouldn't be popular. It can speak for forty miles from a river.'

'You could send a message to John,' said Tobie blandly.

Nicholas said, 'I could send one to you, if I thought you'd understand it. What's all that?' Within half a day, the girl had become surrounded by litter.

'Flea paste,' she said. 'Dr Tobias found the ingredients. And that's a sketch of the ostrich. Did you know there was an ostrich?'

'No?' said Nicholas, with one eye on Tobie.

Tobie said, 'I said all I have to say in Alexandria.'

'Anyway, what was it like when you rode one in Bruges? What did you do with the water-wheels? There was a story –'

Tobie said, 'Stop it. I hear you. You're feeling well. But stop it. Go on drawing.'

'I could draw you,' the girl said to Nicholas. She had lifted some paper.

Without thinking, he rose to his feet. 'No, thank you.'

She tilted her head to one side. 'I don't blame you. It wouldn't be very good. Have you been drawn before?'

He thought of Colard Mansion and relaxed, smiling. 'A few times. When they think they can get away without paying.' Here and there, when he came to think of it, a sketch or two must still exist: a chart, a map of Claes vander Poele.

A map. The simple sketches of Colard would never hurt him. Then he remembered a workshop in Florence and felt the blow of full understanding, rather than instinct. The after-blow was much worse.

He sat down and said, politely, 'I'm sorry. Of course I don't mind. I'm sure it would be splendid.' But she had put the paper away and, in doing so, had discovered the dice.

It happened sometimes like that: he was not going to forget for very long. But the swimming relaxed him, and he slept for a few hours every night, even though he might lie awake for the rest. He assumed Tobie knew it, but he didn't intrude. In arranging all this, Tobie had done all the prescribing he meant to do.

The girl was fond of Tobie, which was good. Her conversation with himself, wholly haphazard, did not avoid the delicate subjects, but didn't probe them. Mostly, it returned to their joint experience of Scotland. She seemed to take it for granted that, with Bruges and Venice too painful, he might consider settling there. 'After all,' as she pointed out finally, 'presumably my uncle didn't manage to obliterate everything you were doing, although he is very clever. There must be a house or two left?'

'I doubt it,' he said. They were devising a surprise, without the knowledge of Tobie, for the drunken knights in the next pavilion. As the Nile filled it brought more boat-loads of pilgrims, some of them noisy.

'Such as Beltrees? Near Kilmirren,' she persisted. 'You know you'll have to do something about the boy Henry. He thinks he's a reprieved murderer. And you like Bel. She would help. You'd find a lot of differences healed.'

'They'd be sorry for me?' he conjectured.

'Oh, yes. It wouldn't last long, so you'd have to make the most of it. Mind you,' she said, 'you must be wondering what to do about your own boy. Look at the mess Simon made, bringing up a child single-handed. You would probably ruin yours too. You've forgotten to fit that into that.'

He had. He took it back and repaired the omission rather silently. The child. If there was a child. It was, indeed, the question he had not resolved. It would be seventeen, eighteen months old, if it existed. He had realised some time ago that Margot would feel free, when she heard of Gelis's death, to tell him the truth. He thought she would write to Alexandria, or Gregorio for her.

Meanwhile, of a certainty, Margot would find the child and take it into her keeping. Sustained by all Gelis had owned, it would want for nothing until he could reach it. And if it did not exist, she would surely write and tell him that, too.

The question was whether he could bear to go back in advance of that letter. To go back to find nothing, possibly, but fresh cause for bitterness. And if he didn't go back ... If he stayed and made some effort to nurture his business it would be October, November before he would hear. Then, if he wanted, he could return on the last of the spice ships. He wouldn't hold the *Ciaretti* so long. If the child was alive, it would have passed another three parentless months. But many boys did.

He reached that point – the usual point – and realised the girl had continued to work quietly in silence. He stopped then, and looked at her. 'More generous than a rooster, more loving than a camel. I haven't thanked you.'

'What?' She knew just enough Arabic. She looked round, at first distracted, then rather pleased.

He dropped back into French. 'You and your Dr Tobias. I probably shan't do what you think I should do, but it won't be for want of help and companionship. And after all this, Kathi, what about you?'

She conveyed a shrug by inclining her head. She was smiling. 'Home, and marriage.'

'You want marriage?' he said.

She looked surprised, and then laughed. 'I don't want a convent. Yes, of course. I'm fortunate. We can afford a good dowry: my family know all the men of my age who would suit. We are all linked together already.'

Heel naturlijk. She spoke with her usual candour. There was wisdom behind it. She was, he saw, one of the few in whom the intellectual passions far outweighed any other; who, health allowing, would accept what her family proffered and become – on her own vivid terms – a fulfilled wife and mother. He envied her, for a moment, what he had never possessed. Then he said, 'Christ, Thundering Poison is coming. Hurry, hurry. Hide it.'

In Cairo, John le Grant, who had his own means of receiving news from Damietta, heard with some disquiet that Nicholas, instead of travelling alone, had left Alexandria with Tobie and Adorne's own niece, Katelijne Sersanders, passing as their interpreter. He next heard, even more inexplicably, that the party had stopped at the Garden of Balm, and that Nicholas was still there. He learned the reason that evening, when entertaining some Maghgribian friends who had called to take the air in the small belvedere of the house he always leased, well north of the Citadel, between the University and the Turkish and Syrian and Turcoman khans.

His guests brought with them a stranger, but one whose name he had cause to know: Abderrahman ibn Said, a trader who did business between Timbuktu and Tlemcen. When the others left, ibn Said remained behind. Then he spoke in Italian.

By now, everyone knew that the Medici were trading with the Sahara, and that the ibn Said brothers were part of the chain. This man knew both Nicholas and his wife, whom he called the madonna Gelissa. He had shared Adorne's ship to Alexandria, and he had spoken to Nicholas, who had entrusted him with His Excellency's address.

John said, 'I am sure he can rely on your discretion. Western traders, as you know, are not permitted in Cairo.'

'But you pass for a man from Tunisia: this is known, of course. One would not dream of betraying it, and Your Excellency's beard is growing already. No,' said Abderrahman ibn Said, stroking his own very fine whiskers, 'your noble padrone confided in me because, then, it was agreed we should travel together. But alas, it was not to be so. You have heard the sad news of Negroponte?'

It had reached Cairo by pigeon two weeks ago. John le Grant nodded.

'Such a disaster for Venice. Florence weeps for her. Alexandria, you may imagine, was in a clamour. And then I had to impart to Ser Niccolò my information about his very dear friend Umar ibn Muhammed al-Kaburi. So piteous.'

He was not an unfeeling man, ibn Said, and the terms he used, talking of the massacres at Timbuktu, were discreetly muted. But what he was relating was the manner of Loppe's death. Loppe whom John le Grant, too, had known in Cyprus and Trebizond. All the perpetrators, of course, had been crazy for gold, and it was known that rich men often swallowed their jewels, or forced their children to eat them. They had found the last of Umar's babies, in the end.

He stopped speaking, Silence enveloped them. Then John said, 'Forgive me,' and rose and crossed to a table where the flagon of fenugreek stood. There he hesitated.

The turbanned head turned. Ibn Said said, 'When Florentines visit, I keep Florentine habits. If you have wine, I shall share it. I have more to tell you.'

And so he heard about Gelis.

He saw the man out himself and came back alone and sat at his darkened windows, looking down on the crowded souks of the city; the jostling turbans, white, blue and yellow; the hoods, the headcloths, the veils, the caps of children, random as fish-scales;

the baskets, bundles, trays carried head-high like capitals in a river
of text. The swifter passage of a mounted Mameluke, mace on
shoulder, whip hand held high. The call as the Criers of the Nile
began to approach, borne on horseback from distant souks: *People
of Misr! People of Misr! Praise Allah! Rejoice! The river has risen
six marks since last night!* The flood was close: you could sense the
excitement, the expectancy in the air. He smelled hot meat, and
ginger, and hashish. But his thoughts ran elsewhere.

It was all too clear now what had happened to Nicholas. The
only mercy was that Tobie had been there. And bringing the girl
had enabled them all to leave Alexandria.

He could not imagine what Nicholas would want to do. He was
supposed to be joining John to travel to Sinai. But that was a
journey to try a fit man, never mind one who was sick, or suicidal.
He had arranged with ibn Said to visit the Garden of Balm as a
Muslim. It was all he could do: see Nicholas, speak to him, and
above all speak to Tobie. And Nicholas would have to be got out
before Anselm Adorne came to find him. For any sympathy he had
felt for Nicholas would have given way to something different by
now.

He went to Matariya next day on a ramshackle donkey, grimly
suffering the punishing ride across the immense, bustling city to
pass into the quiet green land of gardens and orchards that lay to
its north, fringed with the great homes of the rich. Close to
Matariya one could glimpse the walls and belvederes and flowering
trees of still greater palaces, one of them the Qayt Bey's own. The
Garden was his, and sometimes the pilgrims were dismissed and
sent to stay in the village, so that the Sultan's men could set up
their fine silken awnings and spread carpets and cushions, and load
plates of silver and gold for some banquet.

Arriving today at the Garden and showing his credentials, which
represented him as one of those whom pilgrims hired to seek
lodgings and permits, John thought for a moment that some such
eviction was indeed occurring. Within the gates, a violent fracas
seemed to be taking place. At the centre of it was a short figure
with a slipping veil and a vocabulary which seemed to be a mixture
of Latin and Arabic. The man looming beside her, garbed in a
frayed robe with a striped cloth round his head, and translating in
voluble Arabic, was Nicholas. His eyes, though unusually sunken,
were ox-like with innocence. In the shadows behind them stood
Tobie. John shuffled purposefully over and asked him for money.

Tobie drew in his breath. Belligerently, John repeated the
demand, while Tobie's expression wavered between relief and

apprehension. John said, in the same atrocious Italian, 'Is that Katelijne Sersanders?'

'Yes,' said Tobie. He gave an inappropriate scowl. 'They've just offended the entire German nation, but I think they can talk their way out of it. Come indoors. She's not supposed to see you.'

'Adorne is here then?' said John. He bent his head, scuffing at Tobie's heels.

'Not yet. I suppose she might tell him. But honestly,' Tobie said, 'I don't think it matters.' Inside, he pulled the covering over the doorway and led the way through to the terrace where he turned. He said, 'You won't know what has happened.'

'I do,' said John. 'That's why I'm here.' He waited.

'And you're wondering what you've just seen?' Tobie said. 'It's nothing to be afraid of. It's the first stage after shock: a longing for any kind of distraction. She's been magnificent. And he's almost ready to think. Think rationally this time, I mean.'

'To the extent of planning?' John said. 'Does he want to go home? Or would the other thing have some advantage? Would he be fit for it?'

'Fit for what? Business in Cairo?' Tobie said. Then he said, 'Don't be a fool. I'm not going to tell Adorne.'

The voices continued, combatively, outside. John sat down. He said, 'We got word of the gold. He's been directed to St Catherine's, Mount Sinai.'

'You're jesting,' said Tobie. He sat down as well, staring at him. He looked as a doctor would, embarked on a long, testing case. After a moment he said, 'No, you're not. Yes, he could do it. I don't think he could concentrate on very much else.' His voice changed. 'How did you hear about Gelis van Borselen?'

'Ibn Said. A trader who came on Adorne's ship. He told me about Loppe as well. So I knew what to expect.'

'I didn't,' said Tobie. 'Will you tell me?'

At the end, he walked out to the terrace. He said, 'I can't advise. He'll have to make this choice himself.'

John waited. Then he said, 'You'll have to stay with the girl?'

'Until her uncle comes. After that, I don't know.'

'She looks well,' John said.

Nicholas, bowing himself out of the quarrel, followed the girl solemnly into the pavilion and then, catching her eye, recapitulated the previous two minutes in mime. She had embarked on a spasm of laughter when she caught sight of Tobie and tried to look apologetic. There was someone with Tobie.

Nicholas said, 'John?'

To Nicholas de Fleury, it was like a continuation of the mime.
He spoke: Kathi vanished; Tobie changed expression and John le
Grant said, unprompted, 'I know about everything: ibn Said told
me.'

'Oh,' said Nicholas. He looked about.

John said, 'I'm not staying. But you'll have to move. Adorne will
come soon.'

'Ha! Gand! Mauvais Gand!' said Nicholas automatically. His
chin itched, and he scratched it.

John said, 'The house in Cairo is there. You can use it if you
want to be quiet. The agency's finished anyway. That clever
bastard David de Salmeton got in before me. He guessed
Negroponte would fall, and persuaded the Sultan to pin his faith
on the Vatachino and the Pope and the Genoese. If I could find
him I'd kill him.'

He looked as if he meant it. He had tinted his skin. Nicholas
wondered where he got the dyes. It was quite a feat for a red-
headed man to pass himself off as an Arab. Cairo would be hot.
There was nothing he wanted in Cairo. Nicholas said, a little
plaintively, 'I was going to swim.' He looked at Tobie.

There was a silence. John said, 'Adorne will be here. It wouldn't
be fair to Katelijne.' After a moment he said, 'I have things to do.
Think about it. I'll have to leave in an hour.'

He walked out of the room, and Tobie followed him. Kathi had
disappeared. Nicholas felt as if he had been given extreme unction
and left to commune with his soul. Inspecting the contents rather
of his mind, he was forced to the opinion that he couldn't stay at
Matariya. The Baron Cortachy, no doubt hourly approaching,
would arrive in understandable fury and would immediately
denounce Nicholas, in turn, as no dragoman. So he had to move
on.

When they all reappeared, as they did, he had already assembled
the few possessions he had and was ready to leave for Cairo with
John. John's response, learning this, was a deeply Aberdonian
grunt. Tobie cleared his throat, then said nothing. Kathi regarded
him. 'How? Why?'

Nicholas said, 'Skipping like a dove or a passing cloudlet. Why?
Self-preservation. I told the Emir of Alexandria that your uncle
was a rich pilgrim masquerading as a *burjasi*. A merchant.'

'You did?' she said.

'And that, despite the Genoese credentials, the lord Anselm
Adorne was really the sire de Cortachy, knight and baron of

Scotland, that perfidious country whose soldiers helped to destroy Alexandria.'

She said, 'That was a long time ago.'

'Not to Alexandria. I also mentioned how the Genoese fondaco had penetrated the customs house next to it and retrieved half their taxable merchandise. They'll get into terrible trouble. I'm sorry,' he said. 'Nothing personal. I imagine your uncle and his party will be here fairly soon. Tobie had nothing to do with it.'

'Thank you,' said Tobie with anger.

'And I thank you for your ointments, charms, and miraculous potions. What will you do?'

'Wait for her uncle. Blame you,' Tobie said.

'That's right,' said Nicholas. 'And Kathi?'

'Wait for my uncle. Blame him and you,' she said. Below the judicial lip, her chin had compressed like a biscuit.

Nicholas said, 'What is it they say? Blessings are in the hands of the one who has power.'

He did not expect them to recognise the quotation. It was John who said, 'Power is God's, Glory is God's, Dominion is God's. Who do you think you are? Are you coming?'

Confounded, Nicholas looked at him, and then at the others. Tobie scowled. The girl looked downcast, but threw him a grimace. He smiled apologetically in return and, lifting his packages, obediently followed John out of the Garden.

Cairo, Mother of the World – city of intrigue, city of turmoil, city of spies – was seldom deceived by the foreigners who slipped within her walls. Many vanished. Those who were allowed to remain were the unofficial diplomats, the tactful men of affairs whose presence promised some advantage to the Sultan and his advisers. The only fee such people had to pay was that of absolute discretion. Whatever disguise they might choose, the general run of Mamelukes and Cairenes must never penetrate it. And concomitant with that, the foreigners were aware that their every word, their every movement was watched.

These were the terms on which John le Grant made his regular visits. Given patience, the system provided for certain approaches, certain meetings, certain opportunities for discussion at the highest of levels, and occasionally with the Sultan himself. When these did not occur, it was an immediate sign of dislocation, even of danger. He had warned Nicholas. They were out of favour. And he could do little about it until he found out more about David de Salmeton, who had ousted them.

High on its spur of the Maqattam Hills, the Citadel of the Sultan looked down on the domes and minarets of the city, and on the broad Nile beyond with its islands moored like palm-masted ships. The report of the Informers came first to a house in the north of Cairo owned by the great Mameluke official, the Muhtasib, and went from there to the even greater Grand Emir, the Dawadar Yachbak, who asked that the matter be pursued.

It was noted that the merchant's agent who came regularly from Alexandria had recently visited the Garden of Balm, bringing back with him a friend who passed for an interpreter. It was reported that this was probably true, in that the man spoke native Arabic, sometimes with a Maghgribian accent, sometimes of the kind taught in the schools; sometimes with an inflection such as they had in Bursa and Constantinople. The man was not therefore a trader, as suspected, but was more likely an Ottoman spy. He was followed.

This did not greatly concern the native Cairenes, long accustomed to a floating population from al-Maghgreb and al-Andalus, from Syria and the other Arab-speaking countries of the East. His name, Nicomack (father of Aristotalis), was common enough, and he used the patronymic ibn Abdallah, given to converts.

In the course of a handful of days, he hardly became a familiar figure in a city with a population several times that of Paris, but he made acquaintances. Students in the Mida Alley pastry-shop found him amiable when he stepped in to watch the contortionist, and prepared, if amused, to barter his jam-filled fatir for their stipend of bread. The dice-players round this or that fountain welcomed him with his few dirhams and his stories, which were good enough for the Guild; and the dyers at Batiniyya were flattered by his interest, and pleased by his readiness to argue or to pay for a bowl of liquorice-root, or something savoury from a pedlar. When he found his way, as he did once or twice, to a house of pleasure, the flute-players appreciated his enthusiasm for their art, and the girls, who were often the discarded concubines of a man of importance, were heard to express the same sentiments.

It was noticed that he did not respond to the invitations extended to him in the street when some Mameluke's mistress, veiled and robed on her mule, would have her eunuch bend and speak to him as he sat arguing in the very path of the travelling shower from the water-camels. Thus he was cautious. On the other hand a Moorish merchant, hearing him versifying to music, invited him upstairs to his harem to recite a qit'ahs and sing, and he accepted. Later the merchant reported the women greatly moved although, of course, they remained behind the wrought screen. He had sung Berber songs, followed by others of some refinement.

Sometimes, on such occasions, he seemed to enjoy wandering about those alleys whose gates were not closed after dark, or sometimes, like the rest, he had to make himself scarce when a group of Mamelukes, finding themselves idle after the evening prayers, left the barracks bent on mischief. Then it was not wise for any man's wife or daughter to be found in the streets, and even boys were not safe. Whatever happened, it seemed that Nicomack ibn Abdallah had a patron or friend, for he always left in good time, and seemed sure of shelter.

His patron and friend took a different view, and made it plain at the outset. 'This isn't Alexandria. I'm here on suffrance; you're not supposed to be here at all.'

'I know,' Nicholas said.

'They'll spot you as a stranger.'

'They have already,' Nicholas said.

'If I can't track down David de Salmeton with money, how can you do it in bath-houses and bazaars?'

'It's a challenge,' Nicholas said. 'You seem to think he's taken our place with the Sultan. Don't you want to know how?'

'Aye,' said his agent. 'But I don't think you're going to find out pitching about like a duck with its head off. I thought we were going to Sinai.'

'Then why not go?' Nicholas said. 'Since Cairo seems so alarming.' Then he drew breath and said, 'Look. You're a Venetian agent: the Sultan won't touch you. He still needs Venice. Genoa and the Knights of St John can't hold off the whole Ottoman Empire, and Adorne can hardly deliver a Papal Crusade. They can't even prise two ships out of Tommaso.'

John said, 'Of course the Sultan won't kill, but his Mamelukes could get out of hand. Mistakes happen. Or David de Salmeton would be happy to oblige, with or without the help of Adorne. You've got to be careful. Don't you see that?'

Later, he wondered how he could have been so naïve. At the time, there was a pause, then Nicholas laughed. He said, 'I suppose I do. Or they could always blame Tzani-bey's sister.'

'Tzani-bey's *what*?' John le Grant said.

'His sister. She hired a man to kill Zacco in Cyprus six years ago. Now she's threatening me. Or so rumour is trying to make out.'

'But you don't believe it?'

'After all this time? She wasn't even responsible for –' He broke off, his manner vague. 'No, I don't believe it. But it's an excuse, I suppose, if they need one.'

He sounded undisturbed, which was as maddening as it was cause for concern. John le Grant spent his time thinking up ways to control Nicholas.

He met perhaps his greatest failure the following day, their eighth in Cairo together. He was himself tired and out of patience by the time he confronted Nicholas, who returned late as usual to their chamber, his high-buttoned galabiyya lightly scented with cinnamon and spiced food and hashish. He blinked in the lamplight, but not as if drugged.

Le Grant said, 'Adorne is in Cairo. He came yesterday.'

'Oh,' said Nicholas. He unfastened and let fall the robe, and sank into the window-cushions. Instead of hose, he wore linen trousers, once white, and his shirt was wringing with sweat. He added, 'With the whole group?'

'Tobie and the girl are still at the Garden. But Adorne's five are all here, straight from Alexandria in the foulest of tempers. Your Baron Cortachy has already been to see the Katib al Sirr, the Clerk of the Secrets.'

'It seems a curious pilgrimage,' Nicholas said.

John said, 'The Katib al Sirr issues permits for Jerusalem. That's the excuse. But of course he is setting up something else. This, surely, is the partner the Vatachino have been waiting for. And Adorne must know you are here. The niece will have told him.'

'If they stopped at Matariya. Aren't you thirsty? I could empty a goatskin.'

John rose and crossed to the table. 'What do you want?'

'Pure alcohol, if you have it. No. I'm on *qirfa*. Or salep would do. Did you know that salep is made from fox testicles? Or perhaps it's the plant that they brew it from. *Vincite fortes*. Have you heard Filelfo referred to as *triorchos*? Are you surprised?'

'No,' said John le Grant grimly. He gave him his drink. It was only cinnamon. Nicholas did not always stick to harmless decoctions, John knew. The irresponsibility of it all continued to irk him.

Nicholas said, 'What do you want to do about Adorne?'

John took his own drink and sat down. The wind-scoop on the roof breathed down a little air, and the cooling-jars tempered the heat by the window. It was still very hot. He said, 'They're lodging with Cami Bey, one of the four official interpreters. That's usual. But the Chief Dragoman visits them too. He knows Adorne's family. He helped one of the Doges of Genoa – one of the Adorno Doges – over the export of alum from Chios.'

He waited. The island of Chios, source of much of Genoa's wealth, had been the world distribution centre for the precious rock-powder alum until the mainland mines fell to the Turk. Alum had always been one of the Bank's special interests.

'So?' said Nicholas. He had closed his eyes. He *had* taken something, then.

'So go to sleep,' John said shortly. 'I'll deal with it. You wouldn't like to go home, would you? It would make running this business a lot easier.'

Too late, the word 'home' struck him as poignant. He felt remorse and resentment together. Resentment won. He said, 'I thought you would have known all that already. What do you talk about, squatting under trees in the Meidan with dogs sniffing about?'

A dimple made a shallow appearance, and went. 'The availability of girls. Whether the Arab term *madina jamaiyya* is a correct interpretation of Plato's *politeia* and if not, what is. The cheapest place to buy lupins.' He opened both eyes and shifted his shoulders, without removing his weight from the lattice. He then closed his eyes again, but went on speaking. 'All right. We do not, we really do not think that Anselm Adorne is solely a pilgrim. His sponsors may be Scotland and Burgundy, but he has serious investments in the Genoese colonies. So he is here to promote Genoa, now that Venice has lost Negroponte. To all his plans, I am his principal obstacle. And the river is rising. The spice ships will be coming next month.'

'The emirs know I am here,' John said.

'Then you must assume that Adorne will be told, and hence David de Salmeton. If I haven't been wholly energetic in hunting the Vatachino,' Nicholas said, 'it is because it seemed very likely that David de Salmeton would discover me first. Now he'll find both of us. Perhaps we should both leave?'

'Give up Cairo?' said John. 'Alexandria? The whole Levant project?'

'Why not?' Nicholas said. 'There's always Sinai. Let's go and find gold in Sinai.'

'You don't mean it,' said John. He was so vexed that it took a moment to perceive that Nicholas had closed his eyes once again and seemed to have fallen asleep.

It meant, at least, that he wouldn't disappear into the souks during the night. John spent an hour at his desk with his ledgers, had himself brought something to eat, confirmed that Nicholas was still asleep on the cushions and, turning out all the lamps, went to bed.

Rising at six hours next morning, he found himself alone. The servants were obedient and helpful, as always. A man he knew had come with a message. His generous guest, the interpreter Nicomack ibn Abdallah, had received it and departed, leaving a note. They presented the note.

Nicholas had written it in clear, but in Flemish. It summarised the news brought by John's spy, detailing Anselm Adorne's movements the previous day. Adorne, it seemed, had seen several emirs and a number of resident merchants and dealers, some of them Moorish, some of them Christian. He and his party had spent the afternoon barefoot visiting holy places – St Sergius, St Barbara – in the dress of Copts. He had laid plans to cross the river and climb Pharaoh's granaries the following day. He had hired camels and sent to buy provisions for that, and for what seemed to be a much longer journey.

He had been seen in the house of the Patriarch of the Greek Orthodox Church of Alexandria to whom, it was said, he had confided a great sum of money in return for the services of Lorenzo, a Cretan, a monk who was familiar with deserts, and would guide the Baron to his own monastery.

There was no need, really, to read all the rest. John knew the name. Brother Lorenzo from Crete, whose help Adorne had won at such cost, was no ordinary monk. Brother Lorenzo from Crete was manager, treasurer and steward of the church and convent of St Catherine's, Mount Sinai. Adorne, apprised by Tobie, by Kathi, by the devil, was aiming to reach the Sinai gold before they did.

Nicholas did not even append an opinion. He merely wrote that he had departed, as he hoped John would wish, to visit the Baron Cortachy and discuss matters of mutual interest. It was obvious, in the interests of the business (he added), that John should not follow.

It was obvious. It was obvious that only part of the futile vagaries of the last week had been due to inattention – to sheer incapacity, wrought, perhaps, by despair. The rest had been deliberate. Whatever was dangerous in Cairo, Nicholas had been willing to draw on himself. *Pitching about like a duck with its head off*, was the way he himself had described it. It had been partly that, too.

Outside, the rising sun tinted the domes and the towers. John blew out the candle. The city, awake, was already busying itself: the water-camels by the thousand filtering their way tinkling through every alley; the echo of braying as the riding-beasts were forced to their stance; the distant calls: *A hatchery of chicks is ready and will be emptied this day!* And the faster hoof-beats of the Criers approaching under their banners. *Rejoice, people of Misr! The river has risen seven marks during the night!*

Chapter 37

HERE WAS A Seraph in the courtyard of the Second Dragoman's house. Its meek, pimpled head drifted past second-floor casements attached to a long neck, a trunk and four legs. At first, the pilgrims had taken it for a toy on a cord.

Anselm Adorne, Baron Cortachy, did not wish to be reminded of Alexandria, home of such toys. In Alexandria, extirpated from the civilised comfort of the Genoese fondaco, they had been refused a safe conduct to travel out of the city, and kept under guard until prepared to disemburse the gigantic sum the Emir now saw fit to charge them. Meanwhile fresh officials continually pestered them, demanding dues, imposts, fees for some imaginary service, all of which they were forced to pay. Leaving finally, they had covered the sandy miles to the river by night, supposedly for fear of Bedouin bandits, arriving exhausted and half dead of thirst at noon.

The journey to Cairo could hardly be spoken of – the switch of boats; the commandeering of their wine by drunken Mamelukes; the wading up to the shoulders in water over lacerating ground when the crew suggested the vessel could not otherwise progress between current and shallows – none of them would forget that, or what (or who) caused it.

When, therefore, Anselm Adorne learned that he had a visitor and saw, by opening his lattice, who it was, he refrained from waking Jan, who slept late like all students, or young Lambert who was as bad; or – even worse – the other two. Instead, completing his attire, he descended alone and quietly to the parlour he and his party had been given.

Nicholas de Fleury stood up, releasing the cloth from his face. His beard, though strong, was of only three weeks' growth, and had been darkened. Pale against tinted skin, his eyes were large and curious as those of the Seraph. He wore a white buttoned robe of thick cotton.

Anselm Adorne said, 'Ah. Nicomack ibn Abdallah, I believe. What may I offer? Have you eaten?' The servant waited.

'I wish nothing, my lord,' said the other man. He spoke Italian with an Arabic accent. Adorne signed to the servant, who left. Then he sat, folding his own blue galabiyya over the skirts of his doublet. De Fleury, he saw, wore native clothing apparently to the skin. Adorne said, 'I suppose you have come to apologise?'

Nicholas said, 'You expected me?' He was still standing. It was very early. Behind the lattice, they were watering and sweeping the yard. The Seraph lowered its neck.

Adorne brought his eyes back. 'I saw you from above. You would have been foolish not to come to Cairo, since I had so naïvely dispatched you to Matariya. I hope you are not going to apologise, for I have no intention this time of forgiving you. Four of my party have never harmed you and the fifth was a sick girl.'

'Tobie removed her,' said the other man.

'You are right to give him the credit,' Adorne said. 'Now I have something to tell you. When you were a boy and transgressed, you were punished. I am not your magistrate now, but I do have some power. In particular, I have the power to have you arraigned for attempting to kill me in Scotland. I am proposing to use it.'

The other man's face didn't change. It had shown no alteration from the beginning. He said, 'You have the right.'

Adorne felt himself frown. He said, 'Do you understand what I am saying? When we both return to Bruges, I shall lay formal complaint against you both there and in Scotland. I do not need to tell you what will follow, unless something occurs which forces me to change my mind.' Exasperation suddenly seized him. He said, 'What delusions are you labouring under, Nicholas? You have proved yourself capable, able to generate wealth, able to take part in the world's affairs. Is that not enough? I have enjoyed our duel, so far as it went, but need you press it further?'

The anger was against himself, as much as anyone. Obedient, patiently standing, the image he saw insistently before him was that of Claes vander Poele, the submissive, sweet-natured youth he had known.

Nicholas de Fleury said, 'So far as it went?'

Adorne sighed. He said, 'Sit. Of course you are gifted. Of course you have used those quick wits to master every opportunity that appears. But every man has his limits. You must recognise yours. You came to Scotland. You befriended the King's sister Mary.

You persuaded her to flee with her husband to me, so that her land would fall vacant, and I should lose face. But what happens?'

'Tell me,' said the other. It sounded flat.

'Do I need to? My credence with the King was always bound to be greater than yours. In your absence, the land fell to me. With a change in the English wars, the Lancastrians challenged York, and the Duke of Burgundy thought it politic to favour both sides, and was not displeased that I should shelter Thomas Boyd. And the King of Scotland, anxious for his sister, rewarded me for protecting her. While I,' Adorne said, 'thought it wise – and was given leave – to absent myself from my house for as long as Boyd and the Princess were staying there. A situation which, in the long run, has not turned out to your advantage. But I am not to blame.'

'I see that. It is my fault that you are following me,' the other said.

'It is your lack of foresight,' Adorne said without rancour. 'Coupled with some ill luck. The death of your priest brought you from Scotland too soon. You were not to know, leaving Alexandria, that an Indian spice ship had reached Damietta and twenty thousand camels entered the city the day after you left it. We received harsh treatment, and for that you will pay. But there were some compensations,' Adorne said, 'before we were arrested.'

'Then are we not even?' said the other. If it sounded less than peaceable, the difference could hardly be named.

'No, we are not,' Adorne said. 'You must learn. Or you will never know your proper place in society. So think of what I have said. Reconsider your plans. You have a good business in Bruges and in Venice; your associations in the Levant are recent and slight, as are your attempts to found a business in Scotland. I suggest you go back to Bruges. I even have something to tell you. It concerns Gelis, your wife.'

He had spoken briskly, because he was angry: he was dealing with a man, as he saw it, only four years older than his own son. When de Fleury said nothing, he looked at him and saw a face grown as blank as a shield.

Adorne said, still more crossly, 'I am not taking some sort of revenge upon you. There is no positive news, but a fact of some relevance. While we were in Rome, a Scots orator expressed a wish to come with me to the Holy Land. He was delayed by business, so my ship sailed from Genoa without him. I have since learned that, disappointed, he then attempted the journey from Venice.'

He stopped. Nicholas de Fleury said, 'Please go on.'

Adorne said, 'It now seems that he travelled on the same galley as de Francqueville and the rest, and died with them. If so, this unfortunate man may have been the fourth member of the party, not Gelis. But there is no absolute proof. And there remains the mystery of her wedding ring. If she were not on board, how did it come there?'

Marian de Charetty, on her wedding day, had looked into those prodigious grey eyes. Adorne himself had faced them often enough, stick in hand, full of exasperation that he still hoped was good-humoured. Nicholas de Fleury lowered his gaze. He said, half to himself, 'To mislead me.'

Exasperation overcame Adorne once again. He said, frowning, 'By getting another to carry it?' It made no sense. The girl was hardly to know that her friends were going to die.

Nicholas said, 'No, of course. I spoke without thinking.' His face conveyed, briefly, a polite mixture of bafflement and apology. Behind that could be glimpsed something of much greater intensity, matched in degree to his present extreme pallor.

Adorne rose. He said more kindly, 'It is not certain. But word will come. I suggest you go back to Damietta and take ship for Venice. If they have no news, go to Bruges. Surely your wife is what matters.' A voice called outside, and he frowned. The voice came nearer. The door crashed open.

'Father?' said Jan, his student son. Then his gaze passed to de Fleury who, drawing a breath, had looked up.

'*You!*' said Jan Adorne. 'You, you false-hearted animal!'

And another voice, even more inopportune, followed behind. His secretary, priest and chamberlain, John Gosyn of Kinloch, entering, exclaimed: 'Claes vander Poele, as I live! You have apprehended him. I shall call the Dragoman. We shall see what the penalty is for a Western merchant using an assumed name and Muslim costume in Cairo!'

'No,' Adorne said. De Fleury got up, his eyes intent on the priest. He would know, of course from the doctor that John Gosyn was the John de Kinloch he had crossed in the past. Adorne continued adroitly. 'No, Father John. This young man's punishment already awaits him in Bruges. We are Christians. It is not for us to throw him to the heathen. For my sake, the Chief Dragoman will put him on a boat for Damietta, where there is a house of the Knights of the Order. They will send him to Genoa. My relatives will take care of the rest.'

Once, a schoolboy in Bruges, Jan Adorne had applauded the impudent marriage of an apprentice. Now he said, 'Father, he would only escape. He is a barbarian. Let barbarians deal with him.'

'He is a Christian,' said John de Kinloch reflectively. 'And might well try to escape. But what could he reap from such a foolishness, other than painful martyrdom or lifelong obscurity?'

'You hear,' said Anselm Adorne to his prisoner. 'Shall I call on the rest of my party for their opinion? I would consign you to Genoa, my son would let the Mamelukes have you, and Father John, if I understand him correctly, feels indifferent, since any escape will bring its own punishment. And indeed, you would be naked of gold or resources, for John le Grant and his house would be watched.'

For a moment he thought that his pace had been a little too leisurely, and that Reyphin and Lambert would appear. Past experience of Nicholas de Fleury would suggest a ready recovery, followed by action. But that was not always the case. Anselm Adorne ended, and Jan immediately began to say something, but de Fleury paid as little attention as if Adorne and he had been alone in the room.

De Fleury said, 'True to the hand, the tongue, the loins. The choice is mine, you are saying. *Ainsi soit-il.*'

He moved on the words, while indeed he was speaking. Jan, throwing himself in his way, found himself left stumbling behind as the lattice was wrenched open and de Fleury ranged the balcony and then encompassed the steps to the courtyard. By the time they reached the gates, the crowded alley beyond showed no trace of him.

Returning, Jan was pale with anger. 'He laughed!'

'He was looking up at the Seraph. It was too tall to be ridden,' said Adorne pacifically. 'Alas, when I have informed the Dragoman, I fear he will not laugh long.'

John of Kinloch made the sign of the cross. 'We should pray for him.'

Adorne saw his son had calmed. Picking his way round the room, the lad stopped and turned. 'What will happen to him? Claes?'

Adorne sat. He said, 'He is not an agent, like John le Grant, following the expected forms of behaviour. He is a rich and powerful young man who has chosen to mingle disguised in the marketplace and whose company, it would seem, already lies under the Sultan's displeasure. He has done what is forbidden, and may lie in prison for life. He may be tortured to find what more he has done. If they think him a spy, he will be put to death afterwards.'

'How?' said his son. Then without waiting he said, 'But he has killed people. He tried to kill you.'

'So he deserves to be punished,' Adorne said.

Had they looked, they would have found Nicholas close at hand, although not in the street. The mosque was small, and its madrasa no more than a tree in the yard under which the teacher sat, his boys intoning around him. Inside the mosque, his sandals laid sole to sole neatly before him, Nicholas occupied a corner, impalpable as a shadow. For the moment, he was as safe there as anywhere. And he could not have gone further. No man should be asked to die twice.

Ma fat mat: what is sped is dead, said the Arab. But what had sped was not dead. He believed the insubstantial thing he had heard, for there were so many reasons for believing it. And most of all because someone had made sure the message should reach him. Someone who – perhaps? – had been most alarmed to discover that the game had unwittingly stopped.

It was quiet. Men came and went noiselessly on the carpets. The buzz of prayer was thin and homely, and quite unlike the thrilling resonances from the Jingerebir. His thoughts began to assemble again, doubtfully, as if afraid of abuse. He did not at once remember the dangerous talent he had found in the Tyrol: the gift he had already employed on this journey before arresting its tortuous, finely judged progress. When he did, he drew a short breath. Then he closed his eyes, and concentrated his thoughts on one thing.

Presently he rose, having performed, deep in thought, the rite he knew so well, and went out through the school. On the way he capped a delighted child with his headscarf, and bought another, chaffing the vendor, from among those that hung for sale on the wall. Then he set off towards the Khan el Kalili bazaar.

He remembered where he had been sitting, the day the eunuch had leaned, scented, beside him and whispered an outrageous invitation from his mistress. He remembered where he had been trading verses and music when the other, more courteous approach had been made; and the house he had been taken to.

It was not hard to find it again: a merchant's home, rising two timber-built storeys above the shop-arches below, with its windows projecting over the alley. Fear of Adorne was not in his mind, nor even concealment. He stood looking up at the worked wooden mashrabiyya, behind which anyone might be watching. So hidden, the merchant's concubines had witnessed his entertainment that day. He had felt invaded by their desires, their agitation as he sang. It had disturbed him. He had not asked himself why.

No one stirred, or came out. But no one barred his way when he climbed the steps and, passing an unguarded door, entered the same room as before. Inside, someone was sitting alone, a fan languidly stirring. Nicholas stopped. The person spoke without turning. 'Dear me, Nicholas. You are becoming predictable. She said you would come.'

The voice was that of a man. Recognising it, Nicholas felt little surprise. Equally, he was half prepared for the rush of bare feet which immediately followed; but although his knife was in his hand, he had little chance to wield it before he was knocked down.

He was aware, between the second-last blow and the last, that the fan was waving thoughtfully over him, and the same voice had made a remark. 'She said you would do that, as well.'

The speaker's face, the beautiful face, was that of David de Salmeton.

When Nicholas did not return, John le Grant hired a number of burly men who had occasionally served him before, and presented himself at the Second Dragoman's house. The Baron Cortachy, descending immediately, eyed the escort and said, 'Your companions are welcome, but might prefer to wait in the courtyard. If you have come to enquire after your friend, all I can say is that he came, and left very soon after. Pray search if you wish. He is not here.'

John le Grant, whose nature was admirably practical, took the invitation at its face value and searched. He ended in Anselm Adorne's parlour. Adorne and four others were there. Le Grant said, 'Where did he go?'

'To prison, I trust,' said a young man.

Adorne's son. John had never seen him before, but nothing was surer, from the fair looks to the French inflection of his schooling in Paris. Le Grant said, 'Do I gather that you denounced him to the authorities?'

'As he denounced us.' That came from the chaplain, a spare little man with crossed teeth. They were all speaking, as strangers did, in mongrel Latin. This man's accent was Scots. John stared at him. He said, 'Cyprus. John de Kinloch of the Order. I heard you were here.'

Anselm Adorne cut in abruptly. 'Father John is my chaplain and chamberlain. Believe him, if not me. Nicholas de Fleury has injured us; injured me, personally. I offered him justice in Bruges, and he fled. Where he is, we do not know.'

John le Grant gazed at them all, and finally at the priest. He said, 'So it's a proud day for God's Church, and for Scotland. You know what the Mamelukes do to men they take to be spies?'

'The choice was his,' said Adorne. His voice was deliberate. 'In his place, I should have agreed to return quietly to Bruges; especially as his wife might be there.'

'You told him that?' John le Grant said. Then he added, consciously moderating, 'You have proof?'

Adorne looked at him. 'Evidence of a possible error, that is all. I should have fabricated a better story, I assure you, had I wished to. I shall tell you what I told him. Strangely, he seemed to find it more conclusive than I did.'

John le Grant listened. As Adorne couldn't do, he understood. *To mislead me*, Nicholas had said. If he believed that of Gelis, he would have grounds for thinking she was alive. If a man could divine anything, he could divine his bride's ring. And if Nicholas thought her so wayward, perhaps he did not want a reunion with her in Bruges – the tempting exit from the Levant that the Baron Cortachy so much desired. Yet surely, all these weeks, the attachment between man and girl had been patent. With the loss of Gelis, it had been as if Nicholas himself had mislaid his purpose in life.

Adorne was still talking. Suddenly, it seemed to John that he had heard enough. He got up. He said, 'I think I want other company. The dung-cake makers would do. Whether Gelis is living or not, Nicholas believes that she is. You told him that, and then set the Mamelukes after him.' He looked round them all. 'The Vatachino and you. Do you think you have only Nicholas to contend with? I advise you to watch out during the rest of your travels – and when you go back to Bruges – and to Scotland. Today you have started a war. And I have to tell you that the devices of war are my business.'

He left, without being halted. Once at home, he gave certain detailed instructions to his staff and, leaving circumspectly, made his way to the house of a boatbuilder who was entirely willing, for a consideration, to lease him a room a safe distance from the river at Bulaq. From there, he sent a messenger north bearing a message, written in Flemish, for Tobie. Tobie received it.

At the same time, Anselm Adorne, Baron Cortachy, far from dwelling on the splenetic threats of young Niccolò's red-headed friend, had become deeply embroiled in the frustrating and troublesome arrangements for his imminent departure from Cairo. It was with some alarm, therefore, that he found himself called to receive, unannounced, the minute, repressive figure of Katelijne Sersanders his niece. She looked well, which allayed some of his fears. Nevertheless, he hastened towards her. At her expression, he stopped.

She said, 'Didn't you expect me? If you threatened M. de Fleury, Dr Tobias was bound to change sides.'

'Change sides?' said her uncle, smiling. 'You make it sound like a battle. I doubt if Nicholas de Fleury is in any danger, but if Dr Tobias wants to join him, he is welcome. I have no quarrel with him. I look at you, and you are blooming.'

'I'm glad you think so,' said his niece Katelijne. 'So you have no objection if I come with you to Mount Sinai, to St Catherine's monastery? I felt she spoke to me in Alexandria. I felt the Blessed Saint wanted me there.'

'My dear!' said Anselm Adorne. 'Hardened sinner that you are, your devotion needs no further proof. Indeed, I am sure you misheard. Catherine of Alexandria would be the last to exact a month in the wilderness from any young maiden. Heat; thirst; the dangerous traverse of mountains; the presence of merciless Bedouin? Believe me, such is not in her mind. Of course, you will stay for the Abundance. We leave immediately it is over. You too will leave – I shall find you an escort – to return to the fresh air of Alexandria until I can come back to take you to Bruges.'

His mind on camels, he touched her hair, smiling. His wife Margriet could have warned him. He was familiar with motherly wives and the skittish ways of other men's mistresses. For the rest of womankind, he drew on his knowledge of poetry. It was not a very safe guide.

It might have interested Nicholas, had he been sufficiently detached, to discover that French was the language in which he responded to the white extremes of physical pain. His tormentors, noting the emerging lapses from Arabic, professed to detect in such wilful incoherence yet another ruse to conceal the prisoner's true identity as an Ottoman spy. After the third interrogation, the muffled figure of the Chief Dragoman himself descended the steps and condescended to turn over the wily French-speaker with the toe of his slipper. The act released a discernible odour: he had come, indolently dressed, from his wives' deep and various carpets.

'Know that God hateth impudence,' was all he said. The trap-door closed, and presently his minions returned with their orders. 'For this, more salt. After that, thou wilt speak thine own tongue, or pay a forfeit. A forfeit for every word. A little beating, of the kind thou knowest well: nothing that scars. Dost thou hear?'

Nicholas answered. Whatever he said, it must have been Arabic, for they did no more than empty the salt-bag and leave, plunging him once more into darkness. The salt was forced into his mouth, not applied to his skin. His skin was unbroken. When he had finished retching – a profitless exercise – he lay on the dried filth of the floor and waited for the haze of agony to disperse.

Servants being accustomed to blows, he had in recent years gained an undeserved reputation for stoicism. It did not mean that he was impervious to pain. It meant that he was not affronted by it, and could even agree, sometimes, that it was merited. More important than that, he had learned that bodily pain was less to be feared than the other kind. His lack of tolerance now could be traced to the fact that his present condition combined both.

David de Salmeton and Gelis. Two years ago, they had been in Scotland together; they had sailed to Flanders in the same ship. He hadn't believed – still did not believe – Simon de St Pol's suggestion that de Salmeton and she had been closer than that. But, adroit and subtle officer of the Vatachino, de Salmeton had shown himself an exceptional adversary ever since their first meeting in Cyprus. His company had lost face in Africa, and had been intent on mastery ever since – in Scotland, in the Tyrol, in the Levant. They had ousted John here in Cairo. They had not, so far, offered physical violence at first hand, although he himself had not always been so particular. Annihilation in the business field had been their preferred and most evident aim.

Until now. Until Adorne had been injured; forced to harbour the Boyds; exposed to ignominy and expense in Alexandria. Then David de Salmeton had set the trap and, knowing he would not fail to come, had delivered him not to the Sultan or the great emirs to whom official complaint might be made, but to some underling, whom even the Chief Dragoman could disown.

The cellar in which Nicholas lay was not one of the well-equipped prisons which occupied the basement of any official large house. It was empty, communicating by trap-door to the upper floor, and by locked doors to other cellars or passages on either side from which no sound emerged. When they had learned all they wanted to know, they could bury him here, and deny all knowledge of him. And if he were found, there would be no mark on his skin.

So de Salmeton and Adorne must have planned. And Gelis had helped them.

The veiled woman whose eunuch had conveyed that lewd invitation – that had been Gelis, testing, taunting. She had been there, on his first visit to the merchant's house belonging to David de Salmeton. For his second, she had constituted herself the bait in the trap – she who had sent her wedding ring on a pilgrim galley to Jaffa so that her real whereabouts would remain undivined.

He wondered by what means she had sailed from Venice, and where she had landed. With de Salmeton's help, it would not be difficult to find a berth and travel swiftly, reaching Jaffa, Damietta, Cairo ahead of them all. She knew, or David de Salmeton must know of the gold. From Katelijne to Adorne to de Salmeton. It had been a simple chain.

Knowing his gift of divining, she had used it against him, as she had sent Margot home; as she had stopped him – stopped the hound music, the child's music with fire. And now she had made her own kill.

He had thought her dead. *How was it for her?* Cool and careful and sly, it had been for her: a chain of elegant links smoothly fitted together and leading him here, as he had dispatched her to Florence. They played games, and she had won by choosing a short game in the end, against all he expected. While Umar, who might have forgiven her, was horribly dead.

He found himself hoarse, as happened at times when the pain remained at its height for too long. No one could hear him, but he set himself to prove, as he must, that he could exert his will and be silent. After a while, the glare receded and he made one anchor, then two; then wove between them a chain, a net, a mail-coat of numbers.

When Tobie presented himself at his door, John le Grant, Aberdonian, engineer, maker of mines, stood with his white eyelashes wet and gripped his shoulders. When, some time later, Katelijne Sersanders was announced, the engineer told his servant to say that he was out.

'No,' rescinded Tobias. Made aware of firm opposition, he amplified.'She's not just Adorne's niece, she's intelligent. See her. She may have something to tell you.'

After the kite episode, privately, he had known as much. But Adorne was her uncle, and he, John, had declared open war on the man. Also, she was a child. He said, 'Is it fair?'

'Let her be the judge of that,' Tobie answered. If he had fallen in love, it was not obvious.

Entering, small as a robin, Katelijne Sersanders made her mind known at once. 'Do you know where M. de Fleury is? Do you know?'

'No,' said Tobie. 'Ask your uncle.'

She tore off her cloak and sat down. She said, 'I was right. Someone's got him. So, who?'

John le Grant said, 'Your uncle denounced him. Try the Mamelukes.'

She said, 'We should have heard. And you would know if he was hiding. I think something is wrong.'

'Your uncle doesn't have him?' said Tobie.

The girl looked at him with something kinder than contempt. 'He offered him justice in Bruges. He isn't vindictive. But, escaping, M. de Fleury may have fled into trouble. That is all I came to say.'

'Trouble with the Mamelukes?' John le Grant said.

The large hazel eyes made him ashamed. She said, 'I thought you were concerned about David de Salmeton.'

It was Tobie who said, 'John, sit down. Kathi – come, sit, we are sorry. You say Sir Anselm has done nothing so far as you know, but Nicholas has disappeared, and you suspect the Vatachino and David? Is your uncle anxious about him?'

'About *M. de Fleury*?' she said.

'No. Obviously not. But you are?'

She sighed. 'Shall I go home? He's a man. He has friends. He's in trouble. *And I don't want my uncle blamed.*'

'Ah,' said John le Grant.

'Tell me, Kathi,' said Tobie.

She held out something white. A small packet, sealed with waxed string, upon which an address had been written in an inept and straggling hand. She said, 'I promised to have it delivered.'

'Yes?' said Tobie.

She said, 'From the Pisan Consul's wife. A lock of her hair.'

Tobie sat up. The girl said, 'It is one step, that is all. If M. de Fleury has been trapped by a rival, you will have to find him. If he is being secretly held by the Mamelukes, that is more difficult. They won't give him up to you, to a Frank. You would need help. Cairenes who are not Mamelukes. Do you know any? Does he?'

'None we could trust,' said John bluntly. It was true. Here, the Bank did business in limbo with the Sultan and his Mameluke emirs – when it did business at all. The Muslim traders did not like it. Even his boatbuilder would admit all he knew, were he asked.

'Wait,' said Tobie. 'Nicholas may. John, you told me the open risks he was taking. Didn't he mix with the doctors and the students?'

The girl said, 'From the University? You mean from al-Azhar?' Her eyes had opened: pools bottomed with gravel; the irises specked with sharp colour.

Tobie said, 'Yes.'

The word struck John with its baldness. He looked at the girl. She had flushed. She said, 'So.'

There was a silence, which seemingly impelled her at length to jump to her feet. She said, 'I mustn't keep you. I suppose you are leaving? My uncle means to set out for Sinai immediately after the Ceremony. Do you think it will be soon? The river rose thirteen more qirats last night.'

John's eyes met those of Tobie. John said, 'Are you bidden?'

Her teeth gleamed. 'To Sultan Qayt Bey's flotilla? Oh, no. We are pilgrims, taking our humble place in small skiffs and not required at the Nilometer, the banquet or even the Act of the Breach. But all of consequence in Cairo will be there.'

Her clear eyes studied John, and returned to search Tobie's face. Tobie said, 'Kathi —'

She was at the door. She moved as quicksilver moves. 'No. He is my uncle,' she said.

The nature of the fourth interrogation was such that Nicholas knew there would not be a fifth. For one thing, the Chief Dragoman had attended uncovered. And the questions, which had always been cursory, were now vacuous. They had always known who he was. It would have been convenient, no more, had he confessed to being an Ottoman spy, permitting them promptly to put him to death, publicly impaled by the al-Wazir Gate. Since he had not, they would dispose of him in secret, and John would not suffer.

There was no redress, for he had come to Cairo disguised and without sanction. No diplomatic crisis would follow his non-reappearance in Venice or Flanders. His would be one more unexplained disappearance of the many which occurred in the souks and alleys of Cairo; his body left stripped, his flesh masticated by curs.

He was being prepared for a second terminus, a mandatory departure; something he had never been disposed to arrange for himself but might be content to accept. (Gladly? Meekly? Infested by fatigue and stupidity, Bel would say. Bel . . .) Which he might or might not be content to accept, living as he did in a welter of pain, the focal point of hatred such as he had never imagined.

He had been incalculably wrong: all his senses, all his instincts proved worthless. (*An arrow shot across the wilderness within the wilderness must fall.*) Of course there was no child: he had lived in a fog of illusion. He lay as the Dragoman spoke and so distant had he become in his banishment from all that was warm and human and natural that he neither heard nor understood what was said. Soon the man left. Halfway up the ladder he stopped, and added something in anger, and laughed.

Presently, the others left too, repeating the laughter. Nicholas did not register its meaning or cause. Since he now spoke neither Arabic nor French, they had not carried out their threat, and his fingerbones – all his bones – were unbroken. With the part of his mind that was Arab he appreciated the humour. He could have moved, crawled, gripped with a few broken bones. He lay in the stifling darkness, uttering sounds until death or sleep overcame him.

He sneezed and, being still alive, opened his eyes. The trap-door was open, and the torch that hung below it was lit. The draught was not what had disturbed him: a fan, glinting with jewels, stroked his lip. 'My dear man, how you stink!' said David de Salmeton, disposed with the grace of a vine on the staircase.

Once, it had seemed a sin to doubt beauty; to think that anything less than goodness could dwell in a face and form such as this, or within Simon's golden perfection. The childish belief clung all the longer in that it was allied to a morbid awareness, a misdoubting of envy. One should love beauty for its own sake, he believed. In time, he had learned to understand the impulse, and control it. It was one of the many worthless lessons he had learned.

He looked up, beyond the mouth of the trap-door, but Gelis did not seem to be there.

His rival said, 'It is unseemly to gloat, but I wished you to meet your successor. We had planned to integrate the Vatachino with your Bank in twelve months, but you have run it down a little too quickly: we did not wish to take over a destitute house. Your flair – you had some flair – deserted you in your Scottish transactions.' The charming voice made a pause. David de Salmeton had come, as a vain and clever man would, to make his victim aware of his fate; to hear him protest or plead.

Your Scottish transactions. For a threadbare, ludicrous moment, Nicholas reviewed his Scottish transactions; summoned to mind the fierce and complex activity which had filled his every waking moment in Scotland and then, bridging the chasm of Godscalc's death, in the Tyrol and Venice, in Florence, Naples, Alexandria, until the cable had snapped and all he had set in motion was stilled. Stilled now, in all its destruction, for ever.

He returned to de Salmeton's words, and felt a pang of amusement. He did not show it. He had deliberately left no private instructions: for Scotland, for anything of the long, complicated design upon which he had been launched. When he died, the victory of his enemies would be half, perhaps three-quarters assured. His Bank would probably fall, to the triumph of the

Vatachino and Anselm Adorne, and Simon de St Pol of Kilmirren
and his fat father Jordan. And, of course, Gelis. *I wished you to
meet your successor.*

He had said nothing aloud. From malice, then, the man broached
the same subject. 'By the way, the lady your wife sends her
regards, and wished me to assure you that she is in health, and all
her friends and kinsfolk relieved of their premature mourning. She
has gone to Mount Sinai. Something about a parrot, I gather?' He
smiled, his eyes attentive.

It was, of course, the first independent confirmation that Gelis
lived. Nicholas believed it. The oblique reference to Margot was
sufficient proof. He had convinced himself of it already although,
he must now admit, his judgement was faulty. De Salmeton spoke
again, bland as barbed fur. 'What, Nicholas? So poor a spirit? The
stable-boy sulks, but surely the knight dies with a quip on his
tongue?'

Allah and the Hallows requite thee.

'Forgive me,' Nicholas said. 'They didn't warn me your presence
was lethal. The lady my wife, then, was too busy to call? I should
have had her admitted.'

De Salmeton stirred, as if the tone of the remark had surprised
him. Then he said, 'Time passes when one is occupied, and
pleasure makes one forgetful. We parted late, and she asked me to
be her ambassador, as you see. I shall report our modest success.'
Despite its grace, the set of his body was wholly masculine. It was
what had attracted Zacco, wayward Zacco. A woman, a starving,
warm-blooded woman would find it hard to resist.

'Do,' said Nicholas. 'You are staying, then, for the dénouement?
The Dragoman may make a small charge. Or perhaps, on leaving,
the lady paid you your wages?'

His mind, moving on, left his words behind. His lack of attention,
being genuine, was not particularly intended to goad, but succeeded, causing his visitor to caress the plumes of his fan, and then
to extend them in a slow, exotic gesture. Nicholas didn't notice
them until it was too late.

There was nothing much he could do. The cellar was small. He
did move, with all the grace of a frog, lurching sideways to adhere
to the furthermost wall. De Salmeton merely increased the range
of his arm. The feather-tips floated down upon Nicholas, drifted
along the distorted length of his limbs and, settling curled at his
feet, began to caress the flaps and bubbles of membrane upon
which, once, he had walked.

The initial screaming was quite automatic; no more to be

diminished or halted than any other act of uncontrolled Nature. De Salmeton seemed not to expect it, and dropped the fan. Nicholas, mutating to pitches lower and hoarser, was aware of nothing outside his immediate task except perhaps a shade of deathly contempt. He felt the other man watching; after a while de Salmeton said something and, lifting the fan, began to walk up the steps, having apparently found the entertainment too raw. Before he left, locking the trap-door behind him, he turned and looked lingeringly down, as if to imprint some choice scene on his mind.

A picture to describe to Gelis, no doubt. Nicholas wondered what torment she felt, to need comfort like that.

The pain, in time, returned to its habitual level, its progress marked by occasional sounds. His lips were paper, his tongue parched, but although desolate with hunger, he could not have swallowed. He drifted out of consciousness and returned.

De Salmeton had forgotten to put out the torch. It revealed the accumulated filth on the floor: his nose no longer distinguished the fetor. It also showed that, on two opposite walls, the doors had been unlocked and stood open.

He lay and looked at them from under his lids. One doorframe emitted dank air, and provided a glimpse of a passage. Beyond the other, receding into darkness, was what appeared to be a chain of other cells, each communicating with the next. All were open.

The rooms looked like his own, although he could not swear he saw steps. Still, there might be trap-doors in their ceilings with locks and frames weak enough to be forced. When he had first arrived, he had repeatedly tried and failed to break open this one. Now he lay for a long time, breathing irregularly. The truth was, he was unwilling to think. He found he resented this tampering with his options. He had conceded. Gelis ought to be satisfied.

In any case, there were other entirely practical obstacles to do with his feet. There was also the fact that he did not know which way to travel. Someone had opened the doors. If he waited, they would come for him. With a handcart, perhaps.

No one came. He woke from a long dream, uttering a name, and found the torch had gone out. He lay a while longer, entertaining some sort of internal dispute, after which he felt impelled to gather his limbs with distaste and drag himself clumsily forward. He made for the door to the cellars which, of course, he could no longer see. Matins of Darkness.

He drew himself across the threshold and lay, his head on his arms, listening to a distant chirping of rats, who were presumably communicating with each other in archaic Egyptian, not French.

They squeaked over a range of three notes, the middle being a quarter tone up from B. He could not seem to find any numbers. He was a *sifr*. A zero. An empty space in a long, faint row of figures. He sank into a suspension of consciousness and became less than nothing.

He dreamed he met Osiris, God of the Afterworld, to whom he explained, against his better judgement, that he was not ambitious of the honour of martyrdom, and was therefore going home. Osiris called him an unthrifty, changeable hoor. They were both speaking Scots.

Look on the face of Love; that you may be properly a man.

Do not, at least, run away.

Chapter 38

IT WAS THE fifteenth day of August, the day of the Feast of the Assumption, and the Nile, rising, stood at last at the Great Mark that meant harvest, and life.

Cairo, Metropolis of the Universe, lies between deserts, and the Ceremony of the Abundance of the Nile, the Wafa el-Nil, was the crown of its year, for it marked the moment when the mighty river, travelling for hundreds of days from its unknown source in the Earthly Paradise, delivered the mysterious summer inundation whose rich black mud, spreading into the fields, would nourish corn and cotton and sugarcane, bean and date palm, watermelon and cresses, and feed the children of Egypt that year.

The mud and the water which – dashing along aqueducts, rushing into cisterns and wells and springing through sluices and channels – turned the baked land into lakes and moated parterres and nielloes of dancing, glittering silver, of fresh sweet water come, like a miracle, in the parched height of summer.

When, on the fifteenth of August, the Watchers on the island of Roda saw the water had risen to fifteen cubits and sixteen qirats on the Nilometer, the thirty-two feet or *qefa* of tradition, they rode shouting and clashing their cymbals through the city and up to the Citadel, upon which the Sultan Qayt Bey caused it to be announced that the Ceremony of the Abundance of the Nile would take place that day. Retiring, he donned his ceremonial many-horned turban (known as the Syrian Water-Wheel), and prepared to ride out to his parade ground on his white horse with the golden saddle and stirrups, and his harness with the great pearls, and three rubies the size of fowls' eggs upon his back saddle-bow. (Allah be praised.)

The word came to the people. As the Heralds and Criers rode about town, the workshops closed, the stewards of rich merchants hung out precious cloths, and the women put their children into fine tunics and slippers. The cooks burned their fingers packing their ovens and filling the vats full of oil for the pastries; while all those who sold in the markets made sure that their best goods were prepared to set out for the evening, when the children of Cairo (Allah be thanked, it is the Wafa el-Nil) would be hungry.

Meanwhile the emirs of ten and five thousand, the Heads of Alleys, the Masters of the Sword and the Pen began to gather up at the Citadel, where the young men were already practising their drill, and the senior Mamelukes were racing back from their privileged lodgings, their blackamoors scampering alongside with their weapons. The great emirs paced in more slowly: the Grand Emir Yachbak; the Second Emir of twenty thousand lances; the Emir Akhor, the Comptroller; the Agents of the Exchequer; the official Bearer of the Sultan's Slippers; the Katib al Sirr, the Clerk of the Secrets. The Emir Madjlis, the Master of Ceremonies was everywhere. The tall fringed caps looked like a flock of red lanterns; the turbans like puffs of smoke, or piled curds, or sugar-cones shawled in black; the shot and watered silks glimmered and the swords flashed to make the eye water, while the kettledrums prattled and barked and the trumpets assaulted the ear. (Allah alone is omnipotent, who has sent us this joy.)

It had all been prepared. Only the precise date could not be told beforehand, or the extent of the flood. The best might still be to come: a height of eighteen cubits, nineteen perhaps, if the fire-signals from upriver were to be believed. More than twenty, if it came, was not a blessing. But Allah disposed.

The sun rose. In the city, the guests of the second degree began to assemble: heads of guilds, nobles and sons of Mamelukes, Men of the Turban. Then merchants from the superb Islamic khans: the Persians, Syrians, Turks. Then such folk as the Maghgribis, the Alexandrians, the converted Christians, the Jews and Copts from Old Cairo, those Franks who were being discreetly shown favour. The pilgrims. The lower classes.

Those who could not afford boats lined the alleys, climbed to roof-tops and packed into upper rooms that shook and trembled over the alleys. The privileged guests made their way to the river where the Sultan's ceremonial barges covered the water. Under the awnings, their gilding seemed mellow as honey. The guests began to climb in. They included an emir of mechanical interests and a Syrian dealer in alum. Between them, in snow-white headcloth and elegant galabiyya, walked David de Salmeton, with the Portinari merchant Abderrahman ibn Said at his elbow.

They were seen. Across the carpet of boats, from an ancient

felucca with an awning of canvas, Jan Adorne tugged the sleeve of his father's coarse robe. 'Look at that! Why not us?'

His cousin Katelijne said, 'You *know* why. He's an agent of the Vatachino but your father is here to represent Genoa. *Genoa*.' Her voice, muffled by veiling, was impatient. Jan had never admired her: she made him feel dilatory; she reinforced, by her presence, his father's impression that he was lazy. He hadn't been allowed home in five years. It wasn't his fault if she was made to wind up like a spring. Like a kite. She had got into trouble over *that*.

Lambert chimed in. Lambert said, 'Don't be silly, Jan. The Sultan has to keep in with the Venetians.' He smiled foolishly at Katelijne. Lambert was Jan's second cousin and an ally, except where girls and beards were concerned. They had a running series of bets over both.

Jan said, 'He got rid of Claes soon enough, when Father complained. And their red-headed Scotsman isn't doing much business. Doesn't the House of Niccolò count as Venetian? Maybe it doesn't.'

John de Kinloch and Meester Reyphin both smiled, but his father said angrily, 'Be quiet, all of you.' When the Chief Dragoman called over in greeting, he hardly answered. Preparing for the afternoon's journey had made the Baron Cortachy thin and bad-tempered, and his beard, now it had attained some dimension, had white threads in the fairness. Certainly, there had been a lot to arrange, and the emirs and the Dragoman had kept changing the rules until at last, with an oath, his father had actually thrown away the bundle of dog-eared notes he had inherited from Great-uncle and Grandfather as if they had become so much rubbish. Of course, things had changed. And Grandfather and his brother had been on a different mission. One less complicated. Nothing could be more complicated than this one. Jan Adorne groaned, and saw Lambert grin. Lambert knew what he was groaning about.

The processional route from the Citadel to the river being three miles in length (no one in his senses in Cairo built next to the river) the sun was quite high by the time the Royal Saddlecloth emerged by the water, followed by the musicians and pages in yellow silk; the Mameluke Guard; the Standard-bearer; the singers; and finally the Mace and Poniard and Parasol of State, under which appeared Qayt Bey's immense snowy beard glowing saffron. The elephants had recently died, but a good proportion of his hunting cats were represented, followed by the glittering cavalcade of the Mamelukes. The noise was annihilating, and reached its

zenith as the Sultan, dismounting, took his place in the floating
chamber, pillared in gold, carpeted in jewelled silks which, unfolding its cloth-of-gold sail, proceeded to undertake the brief sail
to the designated place of the Ceremony. Twelve hundred boats
followed.

The Syrian dealer in alum said, 'Is the heat too much? We shall
be there very soon. I fear my words have not entertained you.'

'On the contrary,' said the trader Abderrahman ibn Said. 'In
Timbuktu the flood reaches the cutting in January; it would have
arrived in Mopti the previous autumn but, being larger, spreads
widely and slowly. We rejoice for the Joliba, as you do for the
Nile.' He spoke, since his companion was silent. Messer David de
Salmeton was of course an astute man, but did not have the finesse
of Messer Tommaso. At present, he was gazing elsewhere. Ibn
Said saw that he was looking at two following boats. One held a
group of Christian pilgrims dressed as Copts. The other seemed of
no consequence, containing artisans flying the guild flag of the
boatbuilders, together with a number of excited young women
whose chatter and shrill ululations pierced through their veils.
Then he saw a face that he knew, and another.

Alexandria. The two men were well hooded and robed, but he
placed them at once. He said, in a quiet voice, 'You see them,
Messer David? Ser Niccolò's agent, le Grant; and beside him the
doctor, Tobias.'

'I see them,' said de Salmeton. He spoke slowly.

A thought struck the Maghgribian, and he turned back to the
boat with the Copts. Of course. He knew this party too. They were
protégés of the Chief Dragoman in the next vessel. He began,
'Why, that is –'

The other, interrupting, finished his thought.'Sir Anselm Adorne
and his friends, enjoying their fill of Cairene curiosities. Their last
opportunity, I believe. They leave for Mount Sinai tonight. Do
you envy them?'

Ibn Said gave a delicate shudder. 'I say he is a brave man.
Moreover, not one I should like for an enemy.'

'You are thinking of what he was made to endure in Alexandria?'
de Salmeton said. 'Don't you think M. de Fleury deserved whatever
reprimand he has received?'

'It depends,' said Abderrahman ibn Said, looking once more,
with curiosity, at the boat which flew the guild flag. 'He is not
there. They have expelled him from Cairo, perhaps. They have
warned his friends to have nothing to do with him.'

'Perhaps,' said David de Salmeton. 'Perhaps his friends also long to go to Mount Sinai, and are content to leave him behind. Perhaps he wearies them.'

He had never experienced blindness, but he had worked on night campaigns many times and, provided he could concentrate his attention, could measure time as if by the hour-glass. By the end of one such invisible span he had progressed through two cellars. It did not sound much, but it included a disastrous ascent of the steps by which David de Salmeton had left, and a final determined attempt to force the trap-door.

For a moment it had given way, and he had caught his breath as light appeared. Then, tearing itself from his grasp, the hatch had been flung back by strong hands from above, and against the square of terrifying light had loomed an unknown head and shoulders, and a pair of powerful hands, and a stick. The first blow struck him aside; then the man, jumping down, beat him to the bottom of the steps and, grunting, left him. He himself had, by that time, made a great many offers and tried, weakly, a great many memorable tricks, none of which had any effect. From the floor, he saw the fan of light shrink as the trap was shut and locked once again, and he was in darkness. All he had gained was the knowledge that upstairs, in the real world, it was daylight.

After a bit, he had reached an agreement with himself to abandon that room, and see what he could discover elsewhere. The answer so far was nothing; not even a ladder. Nevertheless he intended to proceed to the end, for the lack of draught denoted an end. Then he would return, and try the passage. Lastly, he would attempt to dismantle the steps. It would have been quicker to walk, but the only time he had tried that, he had fainted.

He began, like a child receiving a rusk, to contemplate anger.

Only the great emirs, the imams and the Mamelukes disembarked with the Sultan on the island of Roda (where, the Rumi pretended, Pharaoh's daughter had found some child of their faith in the rushes). Two miles long, riding the Nile like a galley close to the shore of Old Cairo, Roda had once housed the Mameluke army. Its southern half still erupted, here and there, with the remains of the towers that had once surrounded its barracks, but most of the brick had been cleared for the summer palace and garden to which, duty over, the Sultan would repair for his feast. His first task, however, was to lead the way to the Nilometer.

Since the time of the Pharaohs, a measure had stood, a subterranean column sunk in the southernmost tip of this island. Its base, a millstone, was set at great depth, lower still than the bed of the river. Enclosing both pillar and base was a spacious rectangular building too magnificent to be considered a well, lined with steps and pierced by three tunnels which led to the river, each at a different height. In the centre of this, its weight on the stone, stood the ancient pillar of measure itself.

The pillar and its encasement were presently six hundred years old. Those who had engraved its deep marks had done so only five hundred years after the Romans, two centuries after Constantinople had ruled. Then, as now, the Nile was the bringer of life.

Because the measure stood largely underground, the golden cap of its cupola seemed no more than mushroom-high among the almond blossom and palms of the island; its drum, inlaid with precious materials, having the form of an elegant pleasure-house. Having prayed, the Sultan stepped through the bronze doors and took his place on the concourse within. There the deep pool brimming about the pale, octagonal pillar, the water-light rippling over the surfaces of glass and ceramic, the sun glowing through the ring of carved windows presented indeed the aspect of a summer kiosk. The gentle flux, always moving, kissed the ancient pillar and rare scents beguiled the senses: musk and rose, violet and hyacinth. Light from above and below illuminated the heavy cross-beam with its invocations, and chased the other inscriptions in stone that banded the pit: *Hast thou not seen how that God has sent down out of Heaven water, and in the morning, the earth becomes green?*

This the Sultan saw. But soon enough, when planting and harvest were over, the waters would recede, and the Watchers, unlocking the door, would step into a foul and echoing chamber, its depleted pit streaming with slime; the upper exquisite arches of its conduits exposed and empty of life. So, when life returned, one rejoiced.

The Sultan emerged, and the Criers announced that the Abundance of the Nile was confirmed. The people cheered, and the feasting began.

'You can't be feeling sick,' said Jan Adorne, relieving his cousin Katelijne none the less of her uneaten melon. 'The water's hardly moving. You could walk from here to the shore on the boats.' A man, proving the point, came clambering over with two handfuls of smoking kofta on skewers.

'Leave her alone. It's the heat,' said Anselm Adorne. 'Look, the Mamelukes are beginning to move. They'll be setting off soon.

Katelijne, do you want to see the next part? We could go home, if
you like. Perhaps you should rest a little before we set out.'

Jan looked at Lambert. 'We couldn't,' he said. 'How could we,
until it's all over? She'll be all right.'

'I'll be all right,' Katelijne echoed. Because she wasn't eating,
she kept her veil down. She sounded grim rather than sick. Jan was
annoyed, personally. After the Sultan came out of the Nilometer
he had seen David de Salmeton escorted across to the island, and
some of the chief Muslim merchants; even the Greek Patriarch of
Alexandria, a party of Copts, and the Greeks from Abu Sarga and
the church of St Barbara, the favourite saint of the Duchess
Margaret's mother. They were all sitting in the flowery shade
beside the Nilometer, enjoying the Sultan's choice table.

They were so close he could see the Vatachino agent gazing at
him between every supercilious bite. Or perhaps he was gazing at
de Fleury's men, who sat passively in their boat among the artisans
and their wives, holding something they had bought from the
pickle-vendors. Once his father had made to call to them, but had
apparently changed his mind. Katelijne ignored them.

On the island, people were stirring at last. The emirs with yellow
sashes were those favoured, he had been told, on the sports field.
They played horse games with six hundred people. He saw the
Greeks get to their feet, and a surge of the pale blue turbans of the
Copts. He recognised, at a distance, Brother Lorenzo, who was to
guide them to Sinai. He saw, with despair, that the Sultan was
going to pray again. The men surrounding the ruler were the
imams from the theological college on whom the Sultan's luck
depended. He was always improving their buildings. Jan said, 'If
you don't want that mutton?' to Katelijne.

The Ceremony of the Abundance was one which greatly moved al-
Ashraf Qayt Bey, for all the many times he had attended it in his
sixty-odd years, although only two of them as Sultan. His predeces-
sor, that model of vanity Khushcadam, had much preferred the
second ceremony, the flamboyant Act, which he was now embarking to perform. It was, as usual, difficult to clear space for his
barque, even though the Mamelukes did their best. He saw, but
tried not to let it disturb him, that alcohol had been circulating
once more, and the soldiers just out of his sight were becoming
rowdy and careless in the use of their whips.

He stepped aboard, his emirs and judges about him, and the
glare of gold from the sail struck through the gathered silk roof of
the cabin. Behind, the vast wooden carpet of boats changed pattern

and raised their sails to steer close to the wind: quills of silk, quills of exquisite linen, quills of commonplace sacking. Music made itself heard. His barque, borne by the stream, proceeded half the length of the island before leaning gracefully to the turn which would carry it to his own Cairene shore and the Khalig. The crowds on the bank, garbed for holiday, looked like a ribbon of flowers; the trills of the women flocked over the river like swallows. He smiled, and turned to where the silk handkerchief lay.

A communication was taking place between one of his *ulama* and a boy in the water. It ended. He saw the boy depart at great speed, dipping, scrambling to the shore, half by boat, half by swimming. On the way he flung an arm over the boatbuilders' vessel, and seemed to call with some urgency.

The *alim* was a professor he revered. He scorned to question him. Just before they touched the Khalig bank, the Sultan glanced behind and noted that the boatbuilders' vessel had lost two of its passengers; and that the Frankish merchant he had recently favoured was nowhere to be seen. His professor of law, on the other hand, was firmly seated, a priestly hand on the shoulder of one of his flock. On the shoulder of the Chief Dragoman, who had been attempting to rise.

Then the barque touched the bank and was secured, and amid a din that made his ears ring the prince Qayt Bey stepped ashore to the earthen mound that plugged the throat of the Khalig and called for prayer, and then for trumpets, and finally threw aloft the silk kerchief that signified the Act of the Breach; that signalled to the wielders of the scores of raised mattocks that the dam between the great canal and the Nile should be levelled, and the glorious Abundance permitted to surge into the cisterns, the gardens, the viaducts of this his city of Cairo.

Jan Adorne said, 'You're crying! What are you crying for? I think it's exciting!'

John le Grant said, 'He's following. God damn him, he's following. You go. I'll stay and stop him.'

'There isn't time,' Tobie said.

The dam being earth, the trench that breached it, attacked by hundreds of mattocks, widened, deepened, and finally broke its way to the river. The onslaught of water, tossing high as a tree, horrified the Sultan's white horse, and they had to calm it before he put his foot in the stirrup and prepared to ride back to the

Citadel. Around him, the faces of his people shone like newly plucked dates.

Some stayed to scream in the spray and plunge their hands in the volleying water. Some began to race the flow as it travelled, swift as translucent lava, furred with dust. Some ran to watch where the wheels, dragged into motion, had begun to heave the water up to the viaduct and the viaduct itself began to weep threads of moisture. Some ran to the thundering mouths, hazed with mist, where this branch or that tumbled into the underground cisterns, roaring so that the earth above shook.

The rest of the people, singing, laughing, blowing whistles and drubbing their tambourines, poured through the souks to the taverns and markets whose stall-keepers, practised of old, had run ahead to spread out their wares.

Tobie and John le Grant ran among them. It was a slow run, involving the exercise of persuasion and force upon an impacted mass of animals, wheelbarrows and insouciant persons travelling in unpredictable directions and disinclined to give way.

The distance to the house they had been told of was not great, but the souks of the quarter were maze-like. Both men were scarlet and sodden with sweat when their method of progress began to meet with the disapproval of a group comprising the owners and clients of a pastry-shop in the Mida Alley. Standing before the two Franks, they issued an ultimatum which John unwisely rebuffed. The pastry-shop owner called aloud. Every able-bodied man in the vicinity came to his assistance. The last anyone saw of the two Franks, they were being driven forward with quail-sticks, the bells rattling and ringing with each blow; the assailants' laughter rising raucous above them. The two men uselessly stumbled and fought. Their cries rose from distant streets, and then faded.

Listening, David de Salmeton laughed. He didn't underestimate this remarkable Flemish banker – that, indeed, was why he had kept the engineer and the doctor in sight. But de Fleury's house was well guarded. No one could enter or leave without being seen. And soon it would matter no more. This was a game the Vatachino had won.

Nicholas, who did not like losing games, would not at that point have agreed. He had, after all, passed several methodical hours putting his various theories to the test in those areas open to his unreliable physical resources. He had learned, from the sound of footsteps above, that all the premises over this chain of cells appeared to be occupied, but that voices did not seem to carry either way. He had found that there was no exit beyond the last room, whose door was studded with metal and locked. The commotion of rats was loudest there, and a smell that made him draw back.

His hands and knees by now were painfully raw; they had stripped him of all but a breech-clout, and he would have to use that, too, if he wanted to stand. Later, rearranging his schedule, he settled patiently to dismantling what he could of the steps, and made himself a primitive mounting block, which he used to test other ceilings. He found one more trap-door and, kneeling, pushed against it with a plank. When nothing happened, he clenched his teeth and got to his feet, using his shoulders to wield his stock with more force until the agony made his senses swim. Just before he lost his balance, he gave the trap a great double blow that echoed through the whole chain of cells and could not fail to be heard above.

What happened next he must have missed, lying at the foot of his jumble of wood. When he opened his eyes he was conscious of light and sniggering voices, and looking up saw the trap-door open and packed with dark grinning heads. When he moved, someone called out in Arabic and, lifting an arm, tossed down a streamer of fire which landed, crackling, upon the timber beside him.

He roused himself. As he attempted to crush it, a burst of light announced that another was imminent. Then it hung in suspension, the voice of the thrower raised in noisy dispute. Abruptly, the second flame was withdrawn. The voices rose in a crescendo. Without warning, the trap-door thudded down once again, and the bolt was driven home.

He was not meant, then, to burn. He saved, sluggishly, one flickering brand and somehow extinguished the rest. Cherished, his single torch showed him again the cellars from which he had come and, at the opposite end, the opening of the passage he had still to explore. He created a second brand as reserve and left it burning. Then he took the first and edged his way to the passage. The rats kept out of the way; hosts of green light in the dark, but now he saw the slither-marks, too, of his other companions. There had been more than he thought.

There were no trap-doors or doors in the passage. After a while it turned sharply right, and became narrow. Like the cells, it had been paved. It ended at the point of junction with a much wider corridor, set at right angles to his, and equally dark. Barring the way was a grilled iron door, set with mortar and heavily locked.

He believed, for a while, that he could break the door, but found he was wrong. Thrusting his torch through the bars, he saw that the other passage, too, was made of featureless brick, with no sign of doors to left or to right. The complex appeared to run the full length of the building, which he imagined to be some sort of warehouse, a secondary building used by the Dragoman for private dealings, or summary justice.

He stayed at the grille for a while, banging it with a loose brick; making play with the brand and his voice to attract outside attention but without wasting much energy. If he had been close to anywhere public, they wouldn't have opened even these few, useless doors. He wondered if David de Salmeton was reclining somewhere, sipping wine, smiling and listening. He felt sure that, before the end, David de Salmeton would come. He wished it had been Gelis instead, and that she had not escaped him to Sinai. It was what had kept his mind awake, assembling all he wished to say, once, to Gelis.

The flame was low. If he wanted to save it, he would have to return, depressingly, for fresh wood. He had already rejected the idea, once rather tempting, of setting fire to the heap under the trap-door to see what would happen. What would happen, he suspected, was that the watchers above would immediately quench it and he was not in any form to prevent them. Or to do anything involving rapid movement, much less acrobatics.

He decided, all in all, to stay where he was, although it was unlikely that the ubiquitous John or Tobie would manage to find him. He gave it little thought: his interest in them, in all his former circle was slight. Adorne was going to Sinai, to Gelis; but he didn't think John or Tobie would make for the gold without trying to find him. Of course, they might conclude that he had gone there without them. He had been known to do such things before.

He dwelled, for an uncharacteristic moment, on the various things he had done since he became conscious that he could usually outguess other people. If those were his sins, then he had committed them. He wasn't going to apologise now.

The torch was nearly out. Upstairs, it might still be day: the trap-door had emitted, that last time, a flash of transient sunlight, and he had even heard sounds: the cloudy roar of some sort of festivity. Reminded, he stopped his desultory banging and listened.

Silence, as always. The small stirrings of animals. The beat of his heart. And something else. Beyond the grille, to his left, a rumour of sound he was unable to place, a noble resonance in which, straining, he seemed to identify a tessitura of bowstrings, the sonority of an organ, the hollow reverberation of drums. He listened, the hairs pricking on his arms. Then, overlaying the single thundering chord, still sustained, a soft roll on the timpani that seemed close and becoming closer . . . that filled the channel outside with sound . . . and then abruptly translated itself into a heaving, tangible presence.

A tide of rats erupted into his sight. They emerged from his left and poured past his grille in a frenzy, crowding back upon back, arching along either wall, spurting eventually through the iron apertures at his side to blunder past his shoulder and neck, racing into the dark of the passage behind him.

Rats. Rats fleeing from the sound he had heard; the sound which now held the muted thunder of a storm building at sea; the sound a water-wall makes when it first meets resistance: the snap of splintering wood; the hollow thud of breached canvas; the clangour of bells. The sound of the element for which these cells, these passages, these corridors had been designed.

He had not been locked into a prison. He had been trapped in the cisterns of Cairo. And what he heard was hound music.

Chapter 39

To DAVID DE SALMETON, hastening through the crowds in his embroidered headcloth and exquisite galabiyya, every moment drew him nearer to the consummation of his magnificent plan. With the disappearance of the only two men he need fear, he could devote his attention to outpacing the water; to traversing those few souks and alleys which would take him back to the warehouse below which some malevolent person – the sister, was it, of the late emir Tzani-bey al-Ablak? – was wreaking her vengeance on this meddling Flemish merchant.

He anticipated only the most minor delays. The crowd was nothing; mostly women and children bent on merry-making and easily made to give way. He found a group of pedlars more obstinate, strolling before him arm linked to arm, their laden platters roofing their caps. Accosted, these were at first deaf, and then astonished, and finally anxious to make him a customer. It cost him some moments.

It was stupidity that confronted him next with a basket, pulleyed down from an upper mashrabiyya to be packed from a portable cook-shop. The oven stood smoking beside it; none could pass and the cooks paid no heed to the crowd dammed up behind them. Accosted, they invited him to jump over the oven, stirring up the flames with some glee for that purpose. A distended dog, stepping out of the basket, began relieving itself over the stew and then, taking more time for technique, over him. Losing patience he forced his way on, kicking over the basket. He turned a corner and broke into a run.

The sound of water was audible now. It came from under his feet and from behind walls and echoed gurgling from the green of small parks and the courtyards of mosques; in the deepest wells it groaned like a mandrake. It would be approaching the warehouse.

He would be too late to see the shock of its entry. He would be in plenty of time to witness the rest. He wanted to be sure, that was all.

He was in the final stretch when he was brought to a halt by the camel and the crowds penned behind it. It was a large, indolent camel accompanied, it would seem, by a boy with a scoop in his hand. He pushed his way to the front, thinking that one man could pass. People laughed, and someone crowed like a cock. They didn't know, the fools, who he was. He walked into the road.

At first, he didn't believe what he saw, for he left matters of provender to his cooks; had never heard the dawn calls, and had never troubled to visit a hatchery, where six hundred eggs would give birth in a day; from which six hundred chickens in due course would emerge to be led through the souks to the poultry market.

Lacking a mother, the chicks adopted the boy whose broom swept their yard, and when the same boy swept them out of the yard, they followed him as they would a mother – and this despite the truth that many were no longer chickens. Hence the precaution – the camel – to tend the fruit of such accouchements as the journey might hasten. Its panniers were full of warm eggs.

David de Salmeton had made no study of poultry. He observed, beyond the ship of the desert, a broad river of prickling movement from which floated a vocal floss of thin cheeping. He saw ahead a carved cedarwood doorway, but before he could pass, it was silted with chickens. A mosque presented itself, its doors prudently closed; a chirping drinking-trough offered no foothold; a stucco-grilled window was already crowded with daffodil feathers.

They were only chickens. He stepped out, his resolve made, and saw the man ahead lift his broom in defence, and the boy run to the camel's pannier.

He could arrive late, or pelted with eggs. He dropped back. After all, de Fleury would wait.

Nicholas met the water face to face at the grille, and held on long enough not to be hurled against brick by the first, towering crash of its fall. When he did lose his grip and drop under, he became part of a swirl that surged and sucked him back through the passage, bumping him as a branch might be bumped in a mill-sluice. He did not lose his senses, although he found himself coughing and choking, unable to keep his head out of water. He was swept back to the centre, and caught the remains of the ladder, and clung. The water poured and, as the level rose, he grasped higher and higher.

His legs tossed, the pain from his feet reverberating in his loins. Creatures struggled and fluttered about him, furred and feathered and naked. The wings of a bat splashed and beat at his neck. Snakes were fluid, beautiful swimmers. He had seen an asp, in the last of the light, passing him loop by loop like a poem. Something struck him: a block from the steps, swirling and banging his shoulder. His shoulder was numb. A blow to the head, and he might lose his senses.

What senses had he to lose?

Et tes fils autour de ta table . . .

What sons had he to lose?

'Lord?' someone said. The water washed over his face. 'Lord? My master Nicomack ibn Abdallah?' The voice came from far away. From the end of the passage. From the grille.

He said in Arabic, 'Yes? I am here.'

Someone exclaimed. Above the noise of the water, quietening now, he seemed to hear several voices. There came a chime, and another. The sound of a tool on the grille. His hand slipped and, choking and retching, he gathered his strength and pulled himself higher, twining himself on the remains of the steps as David de Salmeton had done. There were three more steps above him: he had tested. Soon, the water would fill them. It didn't matter. Someone had come.

Then, grating above him, the bolt of the trap-door began to withdraw.

He hissed a warning, and heard an answer, and dropped.

The Mamelukes lifted the trap-door just in case, they remarked, the water was high and the Frank emerged to trouble the lord, which their master the Chief Dragoman would deplore. They used the derogatory term with an air of innocence: as a Frank himself, David de Salmeton knew he was there on sufferance. Nevertheless, he craned forward, holding the lantern, the perspiration dripping after his run.

His first thought was how cool it appeared, the dark water lurching below with its glottal voice, its streams of light-gilded foam; the pleasant silvery sound of the fall in the distance. The level, steadily rising, was already well above the height of even the tallest of men.

Then, his eyes opening to the dark, he saw how the glittering surface was marred with litter, and suddenly began to fear that he was too late, and that he would see nothing of the other man until the cistern was shut off and drained, and his body was left with the rats. Then he noticed something pale move, and laughed and said, 'Come. Come to the ladder and tell me how you have decided to give your Bank and your gold to my friends.'

'Then I may as well stay,' said de Fleury. It was a visible effort to float: his head and shoulders rose and fell with the incoming flux and his face, leaving and entering the light, appeared plangent black upon white like a mask. Zacco should see him now.

David de Salmeton said, 'You find life isn't worth living? How sad!'

There was a pause. The water, ceasing to surge, was merely flickering. The other man said, 'I object to the company.'

'You would like to kill me? You had the chance. But I am only one person. You would have had to kill Martin, and Egidius, and our owner. And you don't even know who that is. Shall I tell you?'

Below, the wooden blocks, hitting the walls, were spinning and dancing. Behind him, the Mamelukes shifted, but David felt no anxiety. Long before this spent man could swim, he would have stopped him. And, indeed, de Fleury was making no effort, except the consummate one of keeping afloat. The other man said, 'Have I met him?'

'Oh, yes,' said David de Salmeton.

'Then,' said the other man, 'I imagine it is Anselm Adorne. Tell him I shall await him, wherever I go. And all the rest of you.'

'And Gelis?' de Salmeton said. 'Or is that too ungallant, even for you? At least she should take joy in her widowhood. I shall see to that myself. So. Have you changed your mind, my dear Nicholas? Your fortune in exchange for your freedom?'

'Not even if you meant it,' said the other man. His voice fell attenuated on the air. As the water had risen, so the echo had gone.

'No. I would hardly ask for what I already have. So this is farewell. You can't be surprised. It was, forgive me, an unequal contest. I am told, however, that drowning is not an unpleasant end, compared with torture. I have to make you my excuse over that. I gave the Dragoman no such orders. However. Will it ease the pain if I set you a task?'

'I shall hear you out,' de Fleury said. As he tired, he was coughing continuously.

De Salmeton expressed courteous amusement. He said, 'You mentioned Sir Anselm. He had something to give you. I have it. Indeed, it belongs to you: you and your wife. Can you guess what it is? All the way from Jaffa to Cairo?'

And he held up the wedding ring of Gelis van Borselen.

The reaction repaid all his pains. Now de Fleury tried for the first time to move. Now, using the last of his powers, he attempted to throw himself over the water; seize the steps; snatch the ring.

It was laughably out of his reach. Nevertheless, at the first movement, de Salmeton pulled back his arm. '*So dive for it,*' he remarked; and tossed the ring low and far into the water.

He looked to smile into the glittering eyes but the man had thrown his head back, striving to follow the trajectory; to distinguish the ring as it dropped with an invisible gulp in the darkness. Then there came the sob of drawn breath, and the crash and spatter of water as the other man dived.

'My lord?' said the Mameluke behind him. 'Shall we unblock the rest of the conduit?'

'No,' said David de Salmeton. 'Let it brim. What is a little water? The Chief Dragoman will not mind. Then, when we are sure, we can open the lock and let the level drop back.'

He stayed some moments longer to watch. He had, however, thrown the ring deliberately outside the circle of light, and no matter how far he held out the lantern, he could see nothing now but the swaying, chuckling water, completing its rise to the roof. Whether or not he dredged up what he wanted so badly, Nicholas de Fleury would not survive to enjoy it, that was sure.

He lay in a beautiful mosque. The dome above him was profusely inlaid; damascened with turquoise and gold-leaf and ivory, within which the sacred name unfolded over and over: *In the name of God, the Merciful, the Compassionate.* From the fretted roundel of windows the amber light of late afternoon suffused the structures of lattice about him, sheening the walls and columns of marble, lighting the deep-carved bands of Cufic inscription: *We send down rain as a blessing from heaven, whereby we cause gardens to fruit, and grain to issue to harvest.*

He smiled; moved. He thought of rain, puddling the yard; hissing into the dyevats. Rain alternating with snow, causing Astorre to curse as he dragged his army over the mountains. Rain in depressing, slow slurs which sent the masons obdurately indoors, even though one last course of bricks would see his furnace secure, his plan for Scotland one stage further. Rain in soft, melting torrents dissolving a city; forming a tent for his love . . .

Hast thou not seen how that God has sent water . . . ?

His eyes, half open, dwelled on the inscriptions. God had sent water. He was in the presence of water as he lay. At his hand, beyond a wooden tapestry woven by angels, he saw a white octagonal pillar with curious marks. Leaning a little, he saw that it rose from a rectangular pool, whose surface shimmered and moved in a way that made him uneasy. He recoiled at first, and then came slowly and fully into his senses, to find himself wrapped in shawls and laid upon deep, soft-piled carpets; watched by five men sitting quietly on cushions.

The two nearest him smiled. One said, '*Allah-u akbar*. We felt we must explore with you further the Platonic interpretation of *madina jamaiyya.*'

Voices calling; hands attacking a grille. Other hands bearing him upwards; carrying him choking from water to air, from air to water; from water to oblivion. Students. He said, on a breath, 'God is great.'

A new voice said, 'They saved you. They saved us from getting killed, from making fools of ourselves. We all owe them our lives.'

Tobie. Tobie sitting with John, crosslegged, quietly, as the central pool dimpled and simmered.

Nicholas pulled himself up on one elbow. Below the shawls he was dressed, Cairene-style, in white lawn. His bones, too, were of lawn, and where his stomach and head once had been, there was nothing but air. He had swallowed the Nile and, patently, relinquished it; and along with it, all the taut needle-mesh of his torture. His feet and head ached, that was all. He said, still half astray, 'Where am I? How did you do it?'

They all turned. The fifth man said, 'You are in the Nilometer, Nicholas: in the private ground of the Sultan. Men are waiting to speak to you. I have said I will bring you when you are ready.'

The language was the classical Arabic of the schools. He knew the voice. He knew the face, unwithered by age, of the imam of the Sankore Mosque. In Timbuktu, he had passed his last night under the roof of this man.

Nicholas said, 'Katib Musa,' and, moving somehow, placed himself under his hands. The hands stroked, concealing his tears.

The voice above him was calm. 'Nicholas, did you not remember? Timbuktu is the daughter of Cairo. You had only to ask.' And after a moment, 'The others have gone. Take your time. We have had a great sorrow, you and I.'

On such a night of festivities, the Sultan Qayt Bey did not propose to reappear outside the Citadel. Instead, he sent his Grand Emir back to the island of Roda to occupy the pavilion where the Feast of the Abundance had just taken place, and where the professors of al-Azhar, the doctors of law, the religious leaders of his people had advised that a meeting of importance might best be secretly held.

Seated upon the dais in the innermost room of the kiosk, the Dawadar Yachbak felt no resentment: his wives were insufferable on such occasions; his concubines overexcited. The claims of the Frankish merchants the Vatachino had been expertly debated and, on the best of advice, had been found to excel those of the banking firm with Venetian affiliations. It was known that Franks, needy of God, sometimes went to great lengths to deride or damage a rival, and the truth could not always be distinguished.

When it appeared that a mistake had been made, he himself had enquired why the Frank from Timbuktu had not gone immediately to al-Azhar the Resplendent, the oldest, the greatest University in the world, and asked them to support his credentials. Three at least of its judges had fled to al-Azhar from Timbuktu and knew the Frank well: his care for that city; his respect for its law and religion; his eminence in the world of trade; his wealth. Especially his wealth.

The story ran that he had lost his principal wife, and hence his zest for life. Such things happened. A further report seemed to say that the wife was alive, and at Sinai, to which the man was currently hastening. Hence the urgency of this meeting, the Italian doctor had said – the doctor who had come to the University with this news, and whose knowledge of esoteric medical writings, he had been told, was not to be despised.

He recognised the doctor at once, as the three Franks were now presented before him: short and pallid and hairless. He knew also the man they called John, the Alexandria agent whose black-tinted beard had been glimpsed, now and then, in its true shade of inedible orange.

The man Niccolò, the former Nicomack ibn Abdallah, was crippled, he knew, and therefore permitted to take three steps and make his courtesy from the cushion placed in front of the dais. His companions took their places beside him and the Qadi called Katib Musa stepped to join the secretaries and lesser *ulama* who sat on either side of the Executive Secretary himself.

There were no interpreters present: not the Chief Dragoman, nor even the Second. None was required, since the merchant spoke impeccable Arabic. The Dawadar Yachbak said, 'Allah is great. It pains me that one of my race hath so injured you. When he is found, the servant of the sister of the late emir Tzani-bey shall pay the full penalty.'

'God is great,' the merchant Niccolò said. 'And displeasing to God is man's vengeance. I would pardon him.'

'Thou art merciful,' said the Emir Dawadar. He approved of

what he saw. Thus were Mameluke leaders selected. Discounting weakness, one looked instead for the spirit which kept the back straight, the eyes level, the language and etiquette properly observed and deployed. He said, 'It is nevertheless a rash man who comes unrecommended. I am told thou holdest no mandate from the beys of Spain or of France or of Burgundy, and bring no charge from the Splendour of the Sect of the Cross, the exalted ruler of Venice?'

Seated, his hands light on crossed knees, the merchant Niccolò bent his head. 'I am humble. Yet is not my empty wallet worth more than that of some ambassador dispatched before Negroponte, whose remit has fallen to ashes, and who speaks with the tongue of dead men? I have a Bank. I offer its resources and wisdom against the Ottoman Turk. Its resources, as thou knowest, are founded on gold. Its wisdom consists in belonging to no prince, but knowing the hearts and intentions of many.'

'Thou? A merchant?' Yachbak mentioned. He leaned back.

The other remained, his hands lax, his broad shoulders still. 'Where will the spices go, that travel from Tor this coming month, and what will they bring in return? Who will handle the silks of Uzum Hasan? Who will provide the copper cauldrons for sugar; the round ships full of wood for fine artefacts? Who can supply gold, from which dinars (or ducats) are minted? Who can sometimes say, to this country or that, "Thy desires are indeed great but these are thy debts, and where is the remedy?"'

There was a silence. 'One spoke of timber,' said the Grand Emir at length.

Two hours later, at the seventh hour after midday, the Emir Dawadar used his judgement to call the interview to a halt. The scribes wrote on, scratching the paper in their desperation. So much. So much had been discussed, hinted, touched upon.

Cyprus. How had this man guessed so much of Cyprus? This time Qayt Bey had hesitated to increase the tribute again: this man had shown how it should be done.

He knew the bey Ferrante of Naples, and was already engaged in the fine cross-negotiation concerning the marriage of his daughter. He could not know – could he? – that a son of Ferrante's was here, in the Citadel, freely serving as a Christian Mameluke?

This man, this merchant Niccolò, exchanged messages with Uzum Hasan, the greatest opponent in Asia of the Ottoman Turk. He knew the inner workings of the Knights of Rhodes, and the subtle strife over alum. He knew where timber was to be had, while of course observing the laws which forbade – pronouncements of infidels and idolators! – the release of ship-timber to Egypt. The man had leased two ships to Venice for Negroponte, and when the merchant Niccolò spoke, the bey of Venice often listened. This Frank owned an army. And he – pleasing to Allah – was a man who had wished to save Sankore, and all in the city, and whom the Qadi Musa esteemed not as a son, for such would have been foolish, but as a man of singular strength, for whom a master had yet to be found.

Towards the end, when the tray of cold carob drinks had arrived, the Dawadar had drawn attention to the importance of the matters raised, and lamented the lack of opportunity to continue their discussion next day. He had been informed, of course, of the lord Niccolò's plans. He held them in reverence. Nevertheless, despite the apparent delay, he would swear that the lord Niccolò's journey to Sinai would prove even more swift since, given time, it was in his own power to provide mounts, provisions, guides, protection and permits, as a result of which the flight of a bird would seem slow.

He did not say, for it was not his place to mention it, that a rival party of Franks had already set out for Mount Sinai, and were presently lodged at Birkat al-Hadjd, for what length of time he had not yet quite decided. He merely assumed that speed had a value, and was unsurprised when the merchant agreed to his suggestion. He had been certain, in any case, of the other two.

Soon after, being of good breeding, he left the pavilion, his companions following, and without exacting a ritual withdrawal by his guests. They stood none the less, including the merchant Niccolò, to whom the Qadi spoke a few words, receiving and giving the Muslim kiss on the shoulder before turning away. Glancing back from the door, the Grand Emir saw that the sledge had been brought, which would take the man to where he would sleep until he left Cairo. For a few hours at least, his safety depended on being thought to be dead.

The sledge, hung with awnings and deep in tasselled silk cushions, was heavily scented. Dropped there, experiencing every after-effect of shock, pain and exhaustion, Nicholas alternately shivered and showed a disastrous inclination to laugh. Tobie said, 'For God's sake, give him some air. I'll stay. You go back to the house. De Salmeton's got to think we don't know where he is, and don't much care. He'll assume we're both after the gold.'

'He'll assume you're after it,' Nicholas said. 'You look like an alchemist.' He breathed quickly a few times and came out with another whole sentence. 'We did it.'

'*We* did it,' said John. 'You'd have been floating about that precious cistern wrapped up in asps if Tobie hadn't battered his way round all the pastry-shops and the riwaqs turning out students. Or come to that, Katelijne did it. It was her suggestion.'

Tobie said, 'Aren't you going? You can talk about all that tomorrow.'

'Katelijne?' said Nicholas.

'Suggested the University. Well, kind of. You know her. She wouldn't let down her uncle. But Tobie had told her about Timbuktu, and she must have seen the connection. So did you, of course, you bastard, but you weren't proposing to use it. Well I hope,' said John, who was apparently drunk on carob juice, 'that you've learned your stupid lesson.'

Nicholas lay breathing. Tobie got rid of John, who could be heard accosting high officials on the subject of boats. The noise over the river was ear-splitting. Tobie returning, said, 'This is the place. It's just a pleasure-pavilion for the number three wife. Or something similar.'

Nicholas laughed, and regretted it, and was got indoors and amazingly, upstairs, where it was cooler. He said, from the mattress, 'Does Katelijne know?'

'Know what?' said Tobie, exploring shelves. 'Water. Sherbet. I asked for some – yes. Here it is. Know we found you? No, she'll have left Cairo by now. They all left immediately after the Abundance. Should I send and tell her?' He turned.

Nicholas said, 'Adorne may be head of the Vatachino.'

'Oh,' said Tobie. Then he said, 'You were tortured. He wouldn't do that.'

'No. That was a mistake,' Nicholas said. There was another silence.

Tobie said, 'I don't think she'd tell him.'

'It depends,' Nicholas said. 'In any case, I'm not sure it matters. When they drain the cistern, they'll know.'

'I wish you'd killed him,' Tobie said.

'Adorne?'

'Christ, no. At least – no. I meant David de Salmeton,' said Tobie. 'Look, it's cooler outside. I'll pull you out to the balcony. Anyway, everyone ought to see it once. Egypt *en fête*. Cairo celebrating its bloody Abundance.'

After a while, when Tobie had got tired of fussing and had gone off to find something to eat, Nicholas hauled himself up from his couch and, piling cushions, made himself a nest from which, between the folded-back screens of the mashrabiyya, he could survey Cairo over the water.

He rested his chin on his arms. He hadn't yet slept, but the shrieking nerves of his feet had calmed down; and the pain and sickness were beginning to cede to a promising languor. His mind, deadened by the effort of the latter few hours, had begun to stir idly again.

Behind him, the desert sky had turned red: it was within a half-hour of sundown. Across the narrow skein of river that separated Roda from the city he gazed on a scene hardly changed down the centuries: the people of Egypt thanking their God for the Nile.

The profile of the Maqattam hills – robbed, they said, to clothe Pharaoh's granaries – must still be as always it had been; and the sky above it as always tinged rose and lilac and a clear, high, turquoise blue. A muslin moon had appeared beside the towers and domes of the Citadel, now prickled with light, and the viaduct arches descended, as they always had, from there to the river, as if scrawled in thin chalk.

Behind them and about them were the domes and towers of Cairo; fig and pomegranate, tulip and iris; a Persian garden in mosaic and gilding. Sprays of jewelled glass bloomed, taper by taper, among the great houses, throwing rainbows up into the stucco, blushing upon marble, striking sparks from a fountain, or the silver and bronze of a door. In the last of the sun, carved in stucco, in sycamore, the outlines of chevrons, of stars, of the Name of God in all its forms flowed across the city as if blotted upon it.

Thus Cairo as he had seen it, alone, in the days of his wandering. Tonight the river and city were one. Tonight, the shore gardens and fields were outlined in silver tinged with the red of the sunset. Date palms rose from arabesques of sparkling water; thickets of herbs stood between silver grids; mosques lay in roseate pools and water moved like an arrow from lake to widening lake, flashing, searing the eye.

Because of the dazzle, he did not at first notice the boats. He heard them first: a shiver of bells, then the rise and slur of the flute, the finger-drum's hiccough, the eerie drawl of a fiddle. His eye and ear attuning, he presently saw the vessels themselves, glinting with the jewels of their passengers; the wings of their sails set with lights and with bells. He watched them until, the light fading, they changed into streams of glowing dragonflies mounting the brimming veins of the city; fanning the air with slight music. Fires of joy rose silent over the Citadel and burst like pollen in the last of the sun.

The flood of the Joliba, the Nile. Rejoicing, placating, the Bucentaur in Venice with its five thousand escorting vessels attending the Doge and his solemn Espousal. *God be praised, the ocean has opened again.* Those who dived got to keep what they found, and were assured of good fortune.

God be praised; God is great.

Kiss any arm you cannot break, and pray that someone else breaks it.

Tobie's step. Nicholas unclosed his fist, releasing what hung at his throat, although Tobie must surely have noticed: had even possibly knotted it there. Its shape was imprinted in blood on his palm: they must have had to break it out after he surfaced.

This ring. This circle of hatred.

This milestone which signalled: The hunt is resumed.

Part IV

THE WHIPPING-IN

Chapter 40

THE ESSENCE OF the problem, if you were to ask Jan Adorne, had little to do with the dangerous journey itself: with the heat, the sandstorms, the cold, the trackless wilderness of barren grit, the precipitous mountains, the circling Bedouin, the treacherous guides, the stinking food and dried wells, the wild beasts and the vermin, the horror of picked corpses of men and of camels. He was prepared for all that. He had been prepared for Alexandria, for Cairo.

That was the trouble. Here he was, a man on the greatest adventure of his life; and his father was with him.

He loved his father, of course. But other people made their way on their own, or with friends their own age, not with little girls and old men. He might not have minded had they gone straight from the Nile to the Holy Land, where you were herded about by the Muslims, and no one had any initiative. But outside the Holy Land, his father – it was now clear – was always going to take command. And even more so on this expedition.

Not many pilgrims came this way, and a lot of them died. The Sinai peninsula was a wilderness. It was where Moses did all his wandering, and heard the voice of the Lord coming out of the Bush that burned but was not consumed, and received the Tablets of the Law from the top of Mount Sinai. Naturally, Christian hermits had been drawn to the site; had come to live by the score in huts and caves until, in the fifth century after Christ, the Emperor Justinian of the Eastern Christian Church had had a fortified monastery built at the Bush. And after the body of St Catherine had been carried by angels from Alexandria into the mountains, the monks had found it and taken it into their church.

The monastery was still there, alone in the wilderness; a vestigial fortified city, containing the smallest and richest independent church in the world, protected by all those to whom it was useful: the Western Church of Rome, the Eastern Church, Greek descendant of Byzantium, and the authority of Mohammed, as expressed through the imams of the Sultan of Cairo. It had a mosque inside, as well as St Catherine.

Jan Adorne did not know why his father proposed going there. It was not for the sake of Katelijne – he had not offered to take her, originally. Of course he himself was devout. There were Crusaders and Knights of St John in his ancestry; the family had always been concerned with the Levant; their private church reproduced the Holy Sepulchre. He came to gain merit, and from piety.

He came also, Jan took for granted, to settle some matters of trade and to exchange information, not necessarily on his own behalf, with other lords and informants. The Duke of Milan and the Duke of Burgundy had each, in the past, sponsored the tour of a noble pilgrim whose duty was not simply to report on the marvels of travel. It was possible that his own grandfather and great-uncle had combined patriotism with pilgrimage. It was remotely possible that James, Lord Hamilton had made his tour of the sainted shrines for the same purpose, and that Father was performing the identical office for the present Scots King. A waste of time, in Jan Adorne's view. He had a low opinion, at the moment, of Scotland.

All right, the Adornes were great men: Doges, ducal Receivers; their homes used by princes. Everyone knew Anselm Adorne was pernickety: *para tutum* was the family motto. He had been a kind enough father, and generous. He was used to organising. He was not accustomed to being crossed. When, as became clear, stout Reyphin, however jolly a drinking companion, couldn't hold his wine or his water or keep his head in an emergency, his father had gritted his teeth and given him the clerking to do.

When, as he might have expected, he grew thoroughly sick of long-faced Kinloch and his complaints and his sermons, he had set him to compile a Flemish-Arabic dictionary to supplement the one they already had (which had included, before his father had vandalised it, the words 'Woman, will you sleep with me?' in thirteen dialects). When Lambert and Jan himself became too noisy, his father became at first sardonic and then, as his temper worsened, issued penalties.

But when his father wanted to do something, he did it. When he wanted to see someone in Cairo he disappeared, bare feet, Coptic blue robes and all, and only turned up when the Dragoman needed paying. When they had to abandon all the diversions of the

Abundance to trail out to the first staging-post of their journey, Jan and the rest were left among the Arab tents at Birkat al-Hadjd while his father wandered off before dawn on some errand. In the event, he didn't return until noon, which would have let them swim at the Garden of Balm if they'd known. He said someone had delayed him, and was angry when some officials arrived who delayed them still further. The only person to leave happy was Kathi, who had received a message she wouldn't show anyone.

And that was the last thing. Cousin Kathi, the ailing, the *female*, had pleaded to come, and his father had let her.

Lambert was ecstatic. Jan was not. They had to drop their swearing-competitions, and the secret refills from the wine-skins, and the wagers Brother Lorenzo thought sinful. Not that Kathi minded wagers; but she was a girl, and couldn't keep secrets.

Normally, it was fifteen days to Mount Sinai. His father said he wanted to do it in nine. He said they could count on twenty-five miles a day at the rate that a laden camel could go, which was two and a quarter miles every hour. There were only four places where they might find some water. They set out crouched in panniers, two to a camel, and from the start, began their travels in darkness, eating cold food because fires might warn robbers. They had six camels and a guard and three drivers and Brother Lorenzo. Jan kept his wax tablet at his belt, so that he could say he was making notes all the way. Their first full day, they set out by moonlight and didn't dismount at all until evening. He grew tired of Lambert always calling to Kathi, who was perfectly well.

The Sinai peninsula lay between Egypt and the Holy Land, its upper edge along the shores of the Middle Sea. Moses and the Holy Family had crossed it in different directions. It hung like a breech-clout between the gulfs of Suez and Aqaba, which forked at the top of the Red Sea. After rounding Suez, they travelled down the side of the Red Sea, and were shown where the Children of Israel had crossed. He had wanted to stay there. The water was deep blue and pleasantly ruffled, and full of coral and curious fish and extraordinary vessels. Also, they were on a beaten highway of sorts and were making good time.

Father, however, would have none of it. Three days out, they had joined, for better security, a large caravan belonging to the Emir of Tor, and Father was in a ferment of anxiety, claiming that they kept forgetting to behave like Greek monks (their disguise), and that the Governor was growing suspicious. The wretched Scots priest kept grumbling as well.

The Emir's concubines had come along with him. They travelled in exquisite panniers, fitted with cushions and curtains and awnings. He and Lambert and Kathi had gone to admire them, which may have caused the misunderstanding which led to their eventual parting. Under the veils, some of the girls were quite pretty. The worst offender was Kathi, who was dressed like a boy and got her face scratched.

In the end, they sneaked away before dawn on the sixth day, just before the junction where their road led them inland. Continuing south, the Emir's party could no longer trouble them. On the other hand they were now alone, but for the ever-composed Brother Lorenzo, their single guard, and their camel-drovers. Here, among the limestone rubble, the low hills whose hollows were filled with wind-designed russet sand, were no tracks. And ahead, about to close in on them, were the mountains through which they must weave, changing direction whenever they required to avoid danger: danger from Bedouin troupes, Bedouin ambushes; danger from the pebbled heights, the scorching wind, the dearth of water. He had not really been frivolous. He had been afraid, and anxious to push it aside while he could. But he was not going to admit that.

That night, on their own in the desert, his father gave him a lecture. It had to do, as usual, with the spiritual objects of pilgrimage, with Jan's place as heir to the family tradition, and with the example of pious devotion which a young man of his high education would be expected to display.

Jan listened, saying nothing. It was all right for an old man like his father to speak of a symbolic tryst in the heavenly kingdom. His father had one foot in it already, and would probably get there this journey, if he didn't stop his eternal agitation. Jan Adorne loved the Baron his father, but at the end of all this, there awaited him (if he was lucky) some portentous dull job in the Curia. Time enough for solemnity then.

At the end, as usual, he was sent off to write up his notes, despite his objection that brigands would be drawn to the sight of his candle. Then, he saw, Kathi was being marched aside for a session on her own.

She knew she deserved it. She was stiff. She had been frightened, of course, as Jan was, but she had also been dazed by the novelty all about her: by the sight of the Red Sea at sunrise, laid like turquoise silk on white clay; by the hills that had edged the sea plain – stacked brown slabs, dun-coloured tabernacles inlaid with ivory; baroque cliffs banded with shadowy patterns and rock faces fringed, fluted, garlanded, or carved like a rood screen with lotus leaves and lions' paws. All done by the wind which, swirling last night, had filled all she had with hot sand, and flayed her skin till she covered her face. She did not mind anything. She would rather be here than anywhere else in the world.

Her tent was not far away: even when travelling in company, they slept in a circle round about their possessions, or their camel-drivers would steal what they had. And every day, whether they were in company or not, came the demands from the drovers which Brother Lorenzo dealt with so calmly. Demands for extra wheat for the flour they mixed to a paste on a sheepskin and cooked into cakes on turd fires; for cheese and raisins to buy the goodwill of (putative) robbers. Demands, of course, for more money, without which they would suddenly be reminded of an urgent appointment in Damietta.

And from today onwards, naturally, they would pretend – until Brother Lorenzo reminded them – to forget the way to St Catherine's. Brother Lorenzo, with his firmness and his fine local Arabic, had saved them more than once when her uncle's patience had given way.

Kathi worried about her uncle Anselm, as she supposed he was concerned about her. As their journey since Bruges had unfolded, marked by turbulent travel and indifferent food and the increasing strain of his responsibilities, she had watched him begin to lose the even temper and the suppleness of the jousting-saddle which had always been his. It made her angry, sometimes, that he had been forced to leave home. Or at least, had been put in such a position that he felt it advisable.

Sitting facing him now, she spoke, ashamed, in the dim light. 'You are right. I am sorry. I don't deserve that you brought me.'

He said, 'I brought you because you wanted to come.' He paused, and then said, 'You have been in such high spirits. I should not chide you.' Then he laughed and said, 'Who taught you the song? Dr Tobias?'

She didn't know he had heard. She had learned it in Scotland, and was teaching Lambert in secret.

> *Bon regime* sanitatis
> Pro vobis, *neuf en mariage:*
> *Ne de vouloirs* effrenatis
> *Abusez* nimis *en mesnage;*
> Sagaciter *menez l'ouvrage,*
> *Ainsi fait* homo sapiens,
> Testibus *les phisiciens.*

The next verse was worse. She could only make her peace by

answering what he really was saying. She said, 'I was going to tell you.'

'Ah,' he said. He seemed to hold himself a little less stiffly. He said, 'I should not make it more difficult for you. You have, I think, done your best in a conflict – in a conflict of interests in which you should not have been placed. We speak, I think, of Nicholas de Fleury. I do not want to hear what you should not say.'

'He wouldn't mind,' Kathi said. 'It was Dr Tobias who wrote to me. M. de Fleury has come to no harm, and will have left Cairo by now.'

His eyes were downbent; the light played upon his cracked lips. She wondered how long it was since he had sung, or touched the strings of a lute. He said, 'I knew you wanted to come. Which of us did you think needed protection?' He looked up. 'No. I can guess. You didn't tell me till now. So he, too, is on his way to St Catherine's.'

It was not put as a question. She said, 'You guessed?'

'I was told.' He did not say by whom. He said, 'I am trying not to harm him, Katelijne. It is difficult. I have a great stake in Scotland. Your brother is at Court. England is still in a turmoil; the Knights of St John are suffering; my house is suffering. And there are interests you know nothing of, in the Black Sea and elsewhere. I am anxious about what is going to happen in St Catherine's monastery. He is not going there principally for the gold.'

'You *know about the gold*?' she said.

He looked up. 'Ah. Yes, I know. Does it seem to deny all I have just said to Jan? My life is God's before it is Mammon's.'

She did not answer. Instead, she said, 'You have set poor Jan a wearisome task. Will he thank you?'

She saw him stiffen again. 'Perhaps not,' he said. 'Perhaps he is made for secular life. Perhaps the new husbandman spoils the first shoot of the vine, and it blossoms but does not come to fruit. I should be sad.'

She said, 'Are you sad, then, at my news?'

The face he showed her was startled. 'Of Nicholas? No!' He placed his hand in reassurance over hers. 'Where would we be without such a competitor? Such a bold, extravagant, unpredictable spirit? No, I am relieved. You have lifted one burden from my shoulders. Although one should send to St Catherine's, don't you think, to warn them what is coming? A warning such as the Scythians sent to the Persians: a bird; a mouse; a frog –'

'An arrow,' finished Katelijne; who seldom recognised when silence was golden.

It did not occur to either of them that Nicholas de Fleury might already be there.

It need not be a jewel. A nut, a ring, a pebble will seek out the person you want, provided you are willing to spend what is asked of you.

The day after the celebration of the Abundance, Nicholas left for Mount Sinai. It was, of course, against Tobie's advice. The previous night, Tobie had come back to their rooms on the island and forbidden him to make the attempt.

'What does the gold matter? You can't ride; you can't walk. Sail to Alexandria. De Salmeton can't harm you there. We'll come with you. The Sultan will alter the pass. Surely all that matters is Gelis.' He had paused. 'You do believe she's alive?'

Coming in, he had turned up the lamps and set one deliberately at the other man's pillow. He sat down beside it. Nicholas continued to gaze at the ceiling. 'Yes, I believe it,' he said. He eased his shoulders distastefully.

Tobie grunted. 'John thinks so as well. He has another funny idea. He thinks she arranged her own apparent death.'

Nicholas looked down his nose. It presumably saved him from moving his head. 'She didn't mean to. She didn't want me to divine where she was. Now she doesn't mind.' He depressed one cheek and returned his gaze to the ceiling leaving the bearded dimple, as it were, in Tobie's possession. Tobie analysed it and spoke, with some disbelief. 'Gelis is at Mount Sinai?'

'Yes.'

'And she wants you there?'

'En défaut de mieux.'

'What else is she hoping for?' Tobie said with impatience. 'Nicholas? Whatever you are trying to say, you are not saying it.'

'It doesn't matter,' said Nicholas. 'Put the light out. At least you see I must go. I don't want you or John. You can make for Alexandria.'

'I shall certainly put it to John,' Tobie said. 'I feel bound to come with you, myself. That child Katelijne is going to need help.'

Nicholas lifted his head. Tobie said, 'Didn't you know? She's with Adorne, dressed as a boy. I've told her you're safe: she'd be worried.'

Nicholas swore.

Tobie said, 'Your brain worked better than that at nineteen.

You've told me half. Do you want me to guess at the rest?' He saw, as he was speaking, that in fact that was what he must do. It dismayed him.

He remembered then, as he occasionally did, that he was the elder, and experienced in medicine. He said, his tone changing, 'Tell me, then. Who gave you the ring?'

'David de Salmeton,' Nicholas said.

Tobie heaved a deep sigh and, rising, walked to the window. He spoke without looking round. 'Gelis sent it, or gave it, to David de Salmeton?'

He turned. Nicholas didn't speak. Tobie said, 'It wouldn't surprise me, or many others, if you confessed to an estrangement. You were quick to get her with child. But you've persuaded yourself that de Salmeton did what he did with her sanction? That she wishes you dead? Why should she?'

'I don't know. You must be right,' Nicholas said. 'I ought, though, to see her at Sinai. Before Adorne and his niece can arrive.'

Slowly, Tobie began to see light. He said, 'It's the gold. You think Adorne and she are in league? You think she has discovered something – perhaps she called at St Sabas? She knew your Captain Ochoa, who lost the gold from the *Ghost*. But, Nicholas, you made her rich yourself. She can't be serious. She is playing a game.'

'Games are for children,' Nicholas said.

'So she isn't playing a game,' said Tobie slowly. He looked at Nicholas, and saw what he should have seen all along. He said, 'She is punishing you because of her sister . . . She is withholding your son in reprisal for Henry, the child you got on Katelina van Borselen? She married you to torment you? Is it possible?'

'It is, for children,' Nicholas said. 'Sometimes they grow up. No one need worry. It is my affair; my particular skill if you like. I could learn to enjoy it.'

Tobie stared at him. He said, 'And when you thought she was dead . . .'

'I was sorry,' Nicholas said. 'I had such good plans. But now I can reactivate them all again. Or, of course, make a definitive strike.'

The journey to Sinai was bad, despite the Mameluke escort which browbeat the keepers of water-wheels and uplifted whatever it pleased of kid or lamb, and set about light-fingered Arabs with maces. So long as they were close to Suez and the Sultan's influence the advantages were distinct; but the leaderless, warring tribes of the Bedouin were another matter, and once they had passed the Tor junction, the Mamelukes were afraid. Some of the soldiers were renegade Christians from Catalonia and Sicily; some from the Balkans. Tobie and John addressed them with careful politeness in several languages.

Nicholas did not speak at all unless directly compelled. Under these conditions it was possible, at the start, to contemplate a ride of forty miles every day: on one occasion they covered fifty. In that frying wind, sleepless and beaten by sand, with nothing but thick, foul water to drink, it made the first part of the journey as punishing as the mountains no doubt would be, and what lay beyond. How he bore it was his affair.

Halfway through, he began walking a little. By the fourth day he was able to dismount with the rest when, labouring over a plateau, they reached the edge of an escarpment too steep for a burdened animal to climb down. There was a track of sorts, winding down; and he did not have a chamois, this time, on his shoulders. He stood, before attempting the descent, and looked at the great panorama of mountains before him. The Mameluke captain was speaking to Tobie. 'I remember the first time I stood here. I gave thanks to Allah. I do it again. Do you see them? That is Mount Sinai, and the mount of St Catherine is behind it. Don't be deceived. They are not near: the clear air just makes you think so. Can your lord manage? Shall we carry him?'

'He can manage,' said Tobie. Sometimes – just sometimes – Tobie managed to say the right thing.

The cliff took five hours to descend, in heat which was all but unbearable. At the bottom, sluggish with exhaustion, they prepared to make camp, putting up tents and foraging for fuel for the cooking-fires. Nicholas did his share but hardly ate when the time came, preferring to withdraw to his tent. Tobie followed him after a while.

He had perhaps been lying down, but was now seated in the Moorish way that was habitual to him, facing inwards. The tension that surrounded him was like the air of a storm, muttering danger. Tobie said sharply, 'Don't use it again. Stop it. She is there. You know she is there.'

The ring swayed and then stilled: Nicholas gathered it up with its cord and turned. All their faces had been altered in their fatigue. He said, 'It's a way of passing the time. She is there. And something to do with the gold. The ring isn't perfectly sure. I'm not certain the ring is quite trustworthy.'

Tobie came in and knelt, without touching the ring. Confiscating it wouldn't help matters: he had been told as much one time before. He said, 'What will you do? Why not end it; divorce her? The child is what matters.'

'Well, yes,' Nicholas said. 'Except that there you have the salient point. Just as the marriage was a pretence, the child seems to have been a figment as well. That is, it may not have been born. Or if born, it may not have survived, and another put in its place. It seems, in any case, increasingly likely that a child of Gelis doesn't exist.'

Tobie said, 'I'll find out whether it exists or not. In ten minutes. You needn't be there.'

Nicholas gave a laugh. He said, 'Oh, I should like to be there. You don't really know Gelis, do you? Or me?'

Tobie looked at him thoughtfully. Then he grunted, and got up and left.

There was no one he could discuss it with, without betraying the truth about Henry. He was not sorry. The chief virtue of John was his toughness, and the fact that with him you couldn't sit and look at your navel. It was what made him so valuable to Nicholas.

The journey continued. As the heat thickened towards evening, they deserted their stifling tents and sought shade between rocks, within fissures, in the shallow caves which lay, bubbles in cheese, along the smooth slopes. Then there came the chill of the night.

They toiled among ranges of hills whorled and streaked in different colours. Mountains shone as if greased; wrinkled peaks reared red and purple on the horizon, then walls of rock closed about them again. They came, once, upon vast tumbled boulders, their sides carved with dates and names carefully spelled out in Latin. Pilgrims had passed this way. They had other evidence: the sun-dried corpses of four men and their camels. There was not enough grit to make them a grave.

There was one moment of ease, when they were led to an oasis, bowered in date palms, where pretty girls brought their goats to the springs and a whole village ran out to greet them. They stayed an hour, for food and water, and hastened on.

It seemed worse, after that. Even Tobie fell silent on the sixth day, the longest and worst, when winding passes took them as much away from their destination as towards it, and their guides did not speak. The camels swayed, their tread spaced and deliberate, soft as a man in his slippers. The dazzle of sun from the harness made him sneeze, and his lips cracked and bled.

Then someone shouted, and he wiped his eyes and saw the defile was ending at last. Ahead, the sky had suddenly opened, blue and clear, and he could see an apron of stone, another plateau from which a track appeared to lead to lower ground. It was not until he reached the edge of the escarpment that he saw how high they had come.

He looked down upon a vast, irregular plain whose floor was not ashen, but scattered with flowering bushes. Surrounding the plain were red mountains, reduced by the immense scale to shapes that were ruminant, submissive in line; lobed and rounded by wind and by snow; travelled over and over again by their own shadows, altering subtly through the millennia.

The air was fresh as clear water, and carried the odours of honeys, of resins, of balm. He could see below the yellow of terebinth, and the fronds of the tamarisk bush which bleeds the sweet dew of manna. Sky, mountains and plain lay soundless before him: light, colour and scent all wrapped in absolute silence. The mountains leaned, humble under their heaven. Tobie sank to his knees.

The Mamelukes had wandered apart, chewing, talking; their laughter hiding a note of awe, of relief. John was standing beside him, his unseeing gaze far ahead. Nicholas, who ought to be beside them, was not to be seen.

Tobie said, 'I might as well not have been born.'

John stirred, and looked down.

Tobie said, 'There is the healing before us. And I am not a priest.'

'Get your priorities right,' said John le Grant. 'A priest can't do much with a corpse. You keep him alive; I'll find a religious to sort him. There must be someone.'

He waited, good-naturedly. After a while, the terebinth made Tobie sneeze; he blew his nose and got up. The next day, they arrived.

To the eye of a bird, or an angel, the building would appear a charming toy set in the wilderness and furnished with a dainty and luxuriant garden; a miniature enceinte: a sturdy replica of four mighty walls, buttressed, battlemented, of the kind to shelter a doughty Order of Knights, the household of a powerful Pope, the bustling court of an Emperor. Those who lacked wings were forced to seek it in the recesses of a long, rocky gulley where it had been set by its builder against the lower slopes of the mountain they called Gebel Musa.

To the bloodshot eye of Tobie, entering the gulley as the day ripened to sunset, the hoped-for shelter ahead was obscured by flashes of fire; by the glare of the broken ground up which the cavalcade climbed, led by its shadows; by the ineffable light from the mountain which fell, bathing their skins and their clothing like the lamps of Cairo at dusk in a fury of daffodil, madder and chalk. Gebel Musa, rising to God on his right, with the lamps of God glowing within like the flame on an altar.

Then they saw the cypresses high in the valley, not childish at all, but standing like spears against the seams of waterless rock, half obscuring something that blazed just behind. Nearer still, the trees parted. They saw that the ruddy glare struck from towering masses of wall, sixty feet tall, thick as a man, formidable as the faith they defended. It was only the mountain which made them look small.

It was then that Nicholas, a passenger all through the journey, rode up to his captain and issued his first and last order.

It was his right: he was the man the Mamelukes were protecting. Impressed and startled by his Arabic and his absolute assumption of command, they would have obeyed him anyway, Tobie saw. John, his hair tangerine in the light, looked suddenly wary. The Arabic was not too hard to decipher.

In essence, the lord Nicholas de Fleury wished the Mamelukes to remain where they were, while he and his friends approached and entered the monastery. They might, in the meantime, disengage the lord's baggage. Presently, they would be told what to do. Then, rested and provided with fresh supplies, they could depart when it pleased them. The conclusion had to do with formal thanks for the company's protection and the handing over of a small canvas bag, at which the captain's face became very bright. Nicholas moved about, shaking hands.

He was turning off his protection. It was the first Tobie had heard of it. He looked at John and, moving up, began, in turn, to take his leave of the soldiers. By the time he and John had finished their duty, Nicholas had begun to walk to the monastery. He was not using his stick. Tobie set off to follow, with John. Neither spoke. Soon they could hear nothing behind them: all sound extinguished by space and by silence.

Nicholas walked. Behind him, Tobie could feel his own heart thudding heavily. It was densely warm, but at his back a feather of air touched his neck. A bee passed. Cicadas buzzed, and somewhere a camel-bell stirred. From a stand of dark trees on their right came the sound of trickling water and a rumour of perfume: the tang of fruit, the nectar of blossom, the root- and leaf-smell of herbs. From the walls blazing above them descended a teasing mélange of spiced bread and warm grapes and incense, mingled with a forgivable odour of normal humanity. Nicholas turned right, into a courtyard. It was as if he knew where to go, or was being summoned.

The great main door, with its surround of ancient stonework, was sealed and barred. A postern stood to its left, also closed. There was a wall-walk above. Someone must have seen their arrival. Nicholas stood.

Hens clucked. An inner door snapped. Far within, pigeon-script on the ear, two men argued and another repeated the same liturgical phrase over and over. Someone was hammering. The postern banged open suddenly and a priest came out in a determined way; not a Greek, but a man in the hat and robes, scuffed and stained, of a Patriarch of the Latin persuasion.

'I thought,' said Ludovico de Severi da Bologna, 'that you weren't coming. Now I see you walked all the way from the Tyrol. Where's your escort? Bring them, bring them. Master John. Dr Tobias. And wait.'

'Why?' said Nicholas, returning his stare with one quite as inimical.

'Because I don't like the look of you,' said the Patriarch of Antioch. Tobie, his stomach clenching, remembered him. His beard was as rough as a bearskin, and even his fingers sprouted hair.

Nicholas said, 'Then you will have to leave me outside, for this is how I am. Is my wife here?'

'The Bedouin would strip you by midnight,' said the Patriarch thoughtfully.

'I don't think so,' said Nicholas. 'I have a company of Mamelukes waiting down there. How many monks do you have?'

'Is that a threat?' said the priest.

'Not necessarily,' Nicholas said. 'I can wait until she comes out. I thought she wanted to see me.'

Tobie moved forward. He said, 'He has two guarantors, if you will accept them. Perhaps she will see me? If she is here?'

Neither Nicholas nor the Patriarch gave him a glance. The Patriarch said, 'He knows that she's here. He communicates with the devil. The monks wouldn't like that.'

'But you haven't told them,' said Nicholas. 'So you have a guarantee of my good behaviour. Don't you find it hot?'

'No,' said the Patriarch. 'You will, by the time you've got your men here and the baggage indoors. I'll see you after Vespers.' His beard shifted. He turned and began to go in.

'And my wife?' Nicholas said. He spoke very softly. Immediately after, a singing echo made itself heard from inside the monastery, revealing itself as a cascade of small muffled chimes, light as dance music played on a dulcimer.

The Patriarch glanced over his shoulder. 'Tomorrow,' he said.

'And where?'

The call to Vespers had stopped. The Patriarch cast up his eyes. 'How should I know? Where you will not be disturbed, I imagine.' His voice was jocular. The door banged behind him.

'Nicholas –' Tobie began.

Nicholas stirred. 'It would be helpful,' he said, 'unexpected, but certainly helpful if, from now on, you would speak only when there seemed something worth saying?'

He would have replied, but for John. John said, 'Look at him. No.'

Tobie pulled his arm free in annoyance. He wished, for a moment, he were back in the desert.

In the monastery of St Catherine, built five centuries after Christ, there were three objects worthy of veneration: the church, with the remains of the saint; the chapel outside its choir, which contained the roots of the Bush; and the Library, in which reposed the most ancient ikons and manuscripts outside those held by the Holy Father himself.

There was the well, beside which Moses met the daughter of Jethro. And there were also many small chapels, designed and painted by hands long forgotten. There was a mosque, hastily fashioned a few centuries before out of a guest-house, which ensured the spiritual comfort of the monastery's Arab servants, and also the continued protection of the Sultan of Cairo. There was a Frankish church, a simple rectangle of wattle and mud which equally ensured that any adherents of Rome could preach and worship in a place which, because of its singular situation, had passed unscathed and unknowing through both the division of the East and West churches and the destruction of most of their images.

As well as that, of course, there existed the cells of the monks, once four hundred, now forty; built small and meagre as swallows' nests, one upon the other about a rigmarole of crooked balconies, half-secured ledges, cock-eyed awnings, bottomless courtyards and ribbons of steps within the eternal constancy of the walls. St Catherine's represented the architectural accretions of nine centuries; their artefacts laid reposefully one on top of the other, mysterious in their lapses, in their ignorance, in their disconnected records and memories as any of the ancient relics of pagan Egypt. And to the guest-house, near to the Franciscan chapel, were the Venetian banker and his two partners led.

They had travelled at racing-camel-pace for seven days, rarely stopping for more than three hours' sleep at a time. They had been under constant threat of attack from warring Bedouin, and in danger of losing the way. Despite all the power of the Sultan, they had been starved and parched, frozen and burned by that flaming sword, the sun's heat. At the end of the unloading, their baggage piled in the guest-room they were to share, the three most recent pilgrims to the monastery of St Catherine washed themselves, exchanging their lice-ridden shirts for fresh ones, and were ready when the Patriarch called to take and present them to their host, the Abbot who ruled the independent bishopric of Sinai.

He blessed them, and wished them repose, ordering a tray of fruit and some bread to be sent to their chamber. They were asleep before it arrived.

Later, Tobie woke and stumbled out, his eyes swollen, to find the latrines. A lamp hung among vines showed him the steps. The air, innocent of wind, was fresh and scented, but with the warmth of the evening still lingering: the night was not more than half spent, he imagined. Comforted by the silence, he looked about.

Within the black mass of the walls, the monastery had withdrawn into the secrecies of private vigil. Lamps flickered, masked by the leaves of a tree, or glimmered through trellises, or touched the white shell of a dome. There was a light, far below, under the north-eastern wall that came, he thought, from the roof of the church. When he held his breath, he thought he could hear the murmur of chanting, or the whisper of someone in prayer. Far away outside the walls, he heard a thin, grisly wail that he knew for the call of a jackal. He stopped again, coming back, but could hear nothing, the lamps hanging in silence. He supposed they were extinguished at dawn.

He left the chamber door open, so that he could take a moment to locate his mattress in the dim light. John was sleeping. Nicholas was not there at all.

John, when he shook him, was at first angry. 'You know what he's like. He wakes, and can't get back to sleep.'

By then, Tobie had lit their own lamp. 'So he dressed? Robe, cloak, boots? Satchel?'

'*Satchel?*'

'And stave,' said Tobie, suddenly breathless. He sat down. 'I thought at first he had some crazy idea about the gold. Then that he meant to find and break in on Gelis. Maybe –' He broke off.

John said, 'I don't see it. He knew he was meeting Gelis tomorrow.'

'Did he? That was what Ludovico da Bologna said. Do you trust Ludovico da Bologna?'

'No. Nor would Nicholas. But he doesn't tell absolute lies. He said tomorrow.'

Tobie said, 'But today is tomorrow. The new day starts at sunset. It's tomorrow.'

John gazed at him. He said, 'So what else did he say? A place? *Where you will not be disturbed.*'

'In a monastery?' Tobie was thinking aloud. 'She'll be dressed as a man, it goes without saying; but hardly with a room of her own. Perhaps sharing one with the Patriarch, discreetly divided? Da Bologna could move out and let them meet there.'

'But he didn't say so,' said John. Then he said, 'He looked up. Tobie, da Bologna looked *up*. And Nicholas has taken a stave.'

They found Ludovico da Bologna in the Latin chapel, reading to himself by candlelight from a sheaf of cut, unbound vellum. Pinned to the coloured mats on the walls were papers of perhaps lesser authority: amateur poems to St Catherine, left by her visiting pilgrims. The door opened so violently that mats and poems fluttered and flapped.

The Patriarch said, 'Shut the door, man. There's wax everywhere.' He turned round, keeping his place in the papers.

'Where is she?' said Tobie.

'Where you think. Unlikely, isn't it?' said Ludovico da Bologna. 'But if she was fool enough to climb, and he to follow, it's their business, not yours.'

'In the dark?' John said.

'It'll be dawn before you could get there. Pilgrims climb in the dark. They sometimes stick. They sometimes lose heart halfway up and come back. They rarely fall off. Whatever was going to happen,' said the Patriarch of Antioch, 'will already have happened. Why not stay here, and I'll put up a nice prayer?'

Chapter 41

ONCE UP IN the wind it was bitterly cold, and the chipped stars and faded moonlight chilled the spirit. She had been cold long before she set out.

She had climbed Gebel Musa twice already, in daylight. She knew the slow way, the path that camels and asses could take. She knew the direct, punishing way, the Sikket Sayidna Musa, the path of Moses which led through the steep ravine at the back of the monastery to the foot of the mountain, and then by graded inclines to the well – the water of Moses – where, in sunlight, the sweet water was desperately welcome. It gave strength for the next ascent, to the narrow plateau upon which had been built a stone chapel.

In the dark, now, she could hardly see it. But she had a good memory, and a sense of direction and of levels, and so far she had hardly stumbled. She rested a little, to keep her strength, then crossed the other ravine to the first of the gates. The tall stone archway at which, once, pilgrims were stopped to make their confession. There was no one there now.

After that, she was glad that she was light-footed and strong, for the stiff climb began. From this point there were steps, over three thousand of them, mounting steeply to the night sky between the towering, slabby walls of the mountain, chill on either side in the darkness. There was no resting place, then, until the second arch, which led to the broad grassy slope on which were set the triple chapels of St Marina the Virgin, Elisha, and Elijah. The last place one could stop was a ledge just before the summit, where she remained for a moment, listening.

There was no sound, before or behind. She was alone. She climbed the last hundred steps to the uneven spread of the pinnacle.

In daylight, one made this final step burned by the sun, drenched with sweat, aching and breathless from the climb, from fear of the height, from wonder at what one could see of the world laid below. The Mount inhabited by God and frequented by angels, where trumpets rang, and the Lord spoke unto Moses.

The Mount of the Law, to which men looked for justice.

It was not flat. There were boulders and recesses and an ancient chapel ritually used by the monks but now locked for security against the insults of rambling parties, as Ludovico da Bologna had warned. He had brought her to Sinai, because it suited him. It suited Anselm Adorne, it suited de Salmeton to know what was happening. They all had an interest in Nicholas de Fleury.

She had watched him walk into the monastery. With more patience than any lookout of old, beset by armies, she had crouched by the wall-walk and gazed, hour after hour, when she came back from her climbing. Long before the monastery servants, she saw the approaching dark smudge of the Mamelukes, sparkling with steel. She knew, when he stopped them out of sight, that he did not want St Catherine's to guess how few they were, in case they refused him. Then she saw him walking up to the door.

She recognised the men with him, whom she had expected. The journey had changed them. His own face at first was unclear, although she watched him intently. When he arrived under her gaze and stood still, she saw, stripped in the light, at last, what the Patriarch saw. And her mind also spoke that single word of misgiving.

Wait.

Wait, before I open this door. This is not the man I expected. This is not the danger I expected. This is something unknown.

Now, the wind shrieked in the darkness, and around her was space, and the presence, unseen, of age-old rock and precipice. If Mount Sinai touched heaven, heaven was desolation. Desolation and anger were what she had brought. In both, she was expert. Gelis van Borselen, dame de Fleury, wrapped her cloak about her, and sat down, and waited.

The sound, when it came, was infinitesimal but she knew that what she had heard, far below her, was a small fall of rock. Presently she saw, in the blackness, a minute comma of fire swaying, bobbing: a brand in the distance. A comma; a sentence. He was coming.

She had a talisman. Nothing tangible: a series of words, a few scenes. Because of them, she had never lost her resolve, and would not lose it now. As the sounds of movement came closer, she stood.

One man's footsteps, irregular because of the irregular rock, and interspersed with the click and thud of a stave. The brighter light of a brand; a burning brand, certainly consumed and therefore several times refreshed, and held by the same person: there was no guide, no servant here. And then, immense in the darkness, moving up the final few steps, streaming with fire and with shadow, her opponent. She heard his breathing.

At the top he came to rest, as if waiting. He had paused before; she had heard the delays. He was not in a hurry. She thought of stepping forward; forcing him into premature speech, but she knew him too well. Unless it suited him, he wouldn't respond. And when he did respond, every word would have its place in the game. The resumed game. The different game.

All this time he was looking at her; one sexless, anonymous figure facing another across the limited space. When at length he moved, he merely walked forward two paces and stopped again. Then he lifted the torch, the sleeve falling back from the vertical line of his forearm. It was like the signal for the launch of a race, or for the start of a series of contests. The light sped across her face and his own, identifying them to each other. The face was the face of the man she had seen below; stony in its concentration. Then he drew back his arm, and hurled first the brand, then his stick into the darkness.

They dropped, the stick first, the other lumbering wrapped in its flame. Finally they both tilted and fell, jerked about in the wind like spent arrows. Fire-dust lingered in snatches, then went out, leaving absolute darkness, and cold.

He said, 'C'est alors la fin? J'espère que oui.'

I take it this is the end? I hope so.

She used the same elegant language they both spoke. 'The end of what, mon époux? Of our match, after only two years? Of life? Hardly.'

The word was licked from her tongue by the wind. She could hear his uninflected voice through the bluster of sound. 'Comme il te plaît. I am armed; so are you.'

The knife lay out of sight under her girdle. She said, 'I protect myself. What other end do you mean?'

'The end of deception,' he said. He waited. 'You have brought your wrongs here, and me to hear them.'

'And then you will use your dagger?' she said.

Until then, they had been standing. Now she saw, as the sky emptied behind him, that he had found a rock, and had lowered himself upon it. It was not far away, but not threatening. He said, 'You wouldn't have come if you thought that.'

'I considered it,' she said. She felt able, now, to move to a ledge and sit down herself. Her limbs trembled. She said, 'But I have the child.'

'So you say,' he said. 'Did Simon ask you to go back to Scotland?'

She had realised, in the last few moments, that it was possible that she was going to die. She had seen the change, as the Patriarch had, but had not understood it. She clenched her teeth to still them. Then she said evenly, 'He usually does. As you see, I refuse.'

'You should have gone,' he said; and sounded amused. Then he said, 'It's cold. Let's get it over with. Why the drowning in Cairo? Revenge for Lucia, of course. But why not the long game? Because you can't pretend there's a child any longer?'

'Drowning?' she said. Faintly, she could distinguish his features. The mask was not one she knew. He was holding something in his hand.

He said, still amused, 'You know nothing of it. It was arranged by Tzani-bey's sister. But you recognise this?'

She was too wise to move. 'Tell me.'

'Your wedding ring. From David de Salmeton.'

'Well, of course,' she said. 'I wanted you to know I was alive. I didn't know you were going to give in. That is really what you mean? You can't keep up? You want to end it?'

'I am going to end it,' he said. 'But first, I want to know why you did it. I want to hear you admit there is no child. That is all.'

She could see his face. She could see the rocks growing distinct all about him. She could see the gold in his hand. He suddenly stood.

So did she. She said, 'Then listen. My object is to remind you of pain, as often as possible, and for as long as possible. Barring accidents, therefore, I am not likely to shorten my programme. If Alessandra Strozzi writes to you, you will know that I have said so already. You may believe it.'

'I do,' he said. 'I know you hate me. I thought you would want me to learn why.'

'I think,' she said, 'that I shall tell you at another time, in another place. At the end of my choosing.'

'And the child?'

She smiled. Always, the child. She said, 'You doubt the existence of Jordan de Fleury, eighteen months old and walking? I brought you a lock of his hair. Give me the ring, and you may have it.' She took the little pack from her sleeve and held it, unopened.

The sky was opal; the gable crosses of the little church outlined against it. She could see Nicholas some small distance away, standing with rock-like stillness as if in prayer, or awaiting a mystical experience, except that his hands were not joined, but placed hard over his arms.

'*Univiva, unicuba et virginia,*' he said. 'My unsullied bride: no.'

The sky brightened. He did not move. He had guessed.

'Then let the wind take it,' she remarked; and slipping her fingers into the little pack, eased it open and held it aloft. The gesture was not unlike his own. The slip emptied, in a whiff of gold fluff.

His darkened eyes followed the sparkle, while his hand idly fingered the ring. He said, 'And that is all the proof you have to offer, here on the mountain of law?' The roof of the chapel behind him was rosy. Behind and below, like the seething, chopped tides of the sea, combers of violet and red were emerging.

She said, from a sudden fear which manifested itself as crude anger, 'Should I have brought you his head?'

'Whose head would you have brought, I wonder?' Nicholas said; and bounced the ring in his palm. He closed his fist over it. 'False to false. It would have been the right coinage.'

She said nothing. He was looking at her. He said, 'If you know I can divine, you know that I couldn't fail to recognise a deception.'

'It was the boy's hair,' she said. 'You have never seen him.'

'It was not from any child born of you,' Nicholas said. His voice, suspended in the great spaces about them, was quite calm. 'So it means the child doesn't exist. We have uncovered one truth, at least.'

The wind blew, and stirred her cut hair. She had to decide, now, quickly, whether she believed in his powers; and then how to play this hand he had dealt her. She said, 'He does exist. I didn't want you to trace him. I hoped you couldn't divine.'

'And yet you burned what I sent him?' he said. He added, 'It argues, certainly, that he existed last year. Or a substitute you didn't want found.' He paused. 'Or again, if there was no child, there was no need for a toy.'

The song, faltering in the flames. How had he known? But of course, he had Simon followed. She said again, 'He does exist.'

'Yes,' said Nicholas. He turned aside a little. She couldn't tell whether it was in agreement, or caused by some other thought. He said, 'You need him to appear to exist, to control me. Otherwise I should hardly be here, for example. But as you see, I am beginning to demand more proof than that. And if you really do have a son, you will require to produce him at some time in any case, to bear my name and inherit my fortune. So why not now?'

'To save him from you. You tried to kill Simon,' she said.

The sun swam above the horizon. He stood, outlined in burning red, and looked down on her.

'But he is not Simon's son,' Nicholas said.

She looked at him.

He sighed: perhaps in impatience; perhaps from something else. His voice when he spoke was still colourless. 'I have some experience of women,' he said. 'I know about Simon: how he managed fatherhood in his youth but never again, despite all those years of assiduous profligacy. The birth of Henry restored all his confidence, but no successors have come. It is unbearable to him. He lies.'

'He has admitted it to you?' she said.

'No.' He turned. 'It is not difficult to prove, if one takes trouble. He is sterile.'

'He was my lover,' she said. With an effort, she, too, kept her voice tranquil.

'I know that,' he said. 'But the child you bore is my son, not Simon's. You hoped at first that I'd harm it. When it was born, perhaps you found some pity for it. You have jewels enough.'

'Jewels?' she said.

'I –' he said, and stopped; she didn't know why. Then he resumed, in the same voice as before. 'If that is so, then let me reassure you. I know that he is my child.'

The sun, vast and red, had no heat in it. She didn't refute it. There was no reason, now. She said musingly, 'You knew all the time? Or suspected, and then testing, testing, became gradually certain. How typical, Nicholas. No one can tell, then, what you would have done to a true child of Simon's. Drowned it, perhaps? Set the dogs on it?'

He said, 'I could have forgiven you had it been Simon's.'

The air they breathed was dyed red. Her throat closed. It made a sound, opening.

'And now . . .?' she said. 'You came, you said, to make an end. But without me, you won't find the boy. Not for years. By the time you find him, he will be someone else's, like Henry.'

'I might risk that,' he said. But he had paused, for a moment, before speaking.

She spoke quickly, then. 'What would you give, Nicholas, to share his childhood? Isn't that what you are bargaining for, now that you know he is yours? And the stakes, surely, are higher. What would you give now to see him?'

He didn't move. 'I am sure you are going to tell me the price.'

'Nothing impossible. The gold that you and Anselm Adorne think is here. You will, of course, have to find it before him; and remove it somehow from the monastery and transmit it to wherever I am.'

'You are leaving?'

'I thought the Patriarch would have told you. He and I are leaving this morning. Unless you take another decision.'

She watched him. Her life depended on what she had said, and how she had said it. On what he believed. On where they were.

He said, 'I gave you half of all I have. I see that even that is not enough.'

Then he said, 'I see you have bought time and, you hope, your life.'

She said, 'I had a knife, too.'

'Ah yes,' he said. '*I should never kill where I love. And only simpletons kill where they hate.* So I am to find Ochoa's gold and give it to you? How should I find you?'

'By the ring,' she said. 'But you would have to return it to me.'

He stood, his head bronzed, his face with the still, Celtic look she could not always remember. After a while he said, 'Then give me your hand.'

Now it had come. Good or bad, the outcome was fixed. She stood while he crossed the short distance between them, and took her hand, and fitted the ring on her finger. The metal was cold. Then he said, 'There was a ritual, the last time I did this.'

The embrace was all she expected: insult, threat, preliminary to what he had decided to do. His hands took hold of her back and her arm, forcing her close. She had started to pluck out her dagger but at this stage, it could be no more than a token. His grasp prevented a strike: she could do no more than maintain the point against the folds of his clothing. If she had wanted to kill him, she would have had to do it much earlier, in the dark.

His eyes were open. She held them; conveying all she felt of resistance without attempting to struggle against his continuing, altering touch. His remembered touch. By shape, by texture, by context she recognised one by one small familiarities to do with his hands, with his cheek, with his lips. In place of the intellectual game she was playing, a physical template suddenly locked sighingly into another; as if, lulled by instinct, this nerve or that muscle had begun to soften and sink. They stood, enclosed within an invisible mould, private to them, and sealed tight. The sky flamed and far below them, acre upon acre, the mountains flickered, welling into the light. They were on the Mount of the Lord; and the edge was one step away.

Nicholas said, 'Walk over with me.'

The air was gold. A bird soared below, also ethereal; golden. His breath had checked, like that of a swimmer about to glide under water. (Below the sea of Zeeland, that summer, the act of love over and over, hungry as sharks under water.)

She said, 'Go alone. I have a child.'

He freed her.

She stood cold on the brink, looking down upon the flaming reservoir of the wilderness; looking out upon space; upon silence; on nothing.

He began to move slowly, in which direction she could not tell. Then she heard the sound of his footsteps receding. Pebbles tumbled below. He had no stave, but it was day. She had managed without one. *Canst thou bind the Unicorn with his band in the furrow?* Ludovico da Bologna had joked. She knew that she could. And she had.

    In time, her shuddering ceased, and she made her own way down from Gebel Musa. By sunset, when Anselm Adorne arrived, she had long left the monastery.

Chapter 42

THIS TIME, Jan Adorne gave the orders; beating the camel-drivers; shouting down Brother Lorenzo; berating the monks when they began to emerge from the door. His father was sick.

Tobias Beventini, who had his own reasons for feeling sick, ran down from staircase to staircase and met the party struggling through the third iron door: the priest; a middle-aged man bowed with weariness and two young men supporting an older one who was trying to walk. A child exclaimed, '*Dr Tobias!*'

She made a believable boy, booted and slight, with half the length of her hair gone. The doctor in him wanted to respond to the note in her voice, but instead he clapped her shoulder and said, 'Well, well. Can I help?' And turning to the travel-stained monk who seemed to have been their guide: 'I know the Baron. Let me give him a hand.'

There was only one other guest-dormitory, adjacent to theirs and, like theirs, mud-floored and empty. He bundled up his own mattress and carried it next door for Adorne as a temporary measure. With a certain ruthlessness, he took John's as well. John was elsewhere, having expressed a violent antipathy to Anselm Adorne and all his friends except young Katelijne. Nicholas, of course, was also absent, but his mattress still showed all the blood. Tobie, swearing under his breath, got his medicine box and some basins and towels and started getting things into order next door.

'It's the flux,' said Katelijne. 'He had water with worms in it. We all had, but he used up his strength quicker than we did. And the last mountain, we all had to climb down but he couldn't, and the camel stumbled and everything came over its head and Jan and Father John saved his life. He doesn't know what he's saying. We should have camped, but we came on instead. We haven't stopped since just after midnight. Friar Lorenzo wants to help, but he's exhausted as well. Can you give Jan something?'

'What?' said Tobie. As the boxes and baskets arrived, she was stacking them in a far corner, unpacking some quickly, handing others to the boy Lambert and the merchant Pieter Reyphin, telling them what to do. John of Kinloch was praying.

Jan was outside, shouting at Friar Lorenzo. The sound reverberated through the silence of the evening and his father's face, sunk in the pillow, turned uneasily. Katelijne said, 'He nearly killed one of the guides in a temper. He needs to break down and cry.'

Tobie rose to his feet, a full cup in his hand. He said, 'I'll see to it. Do you think you can give this to your uncle? Then I think you should go next door while I look at him. It's my room, but it's empty.'

She was kneeling already, her hand lifting her uncle's head. She said, 'Is M. de Fleury with you? Is he all right?'

Tobie said, 'They're both here. John and Nicholas. I'll be back in a moment.'

Outside, he sent the monks away, to Jan's fury, and there was no witness to what he did next. But it solved the problem of Jan Adorne. He thought, sourly, that Jan Adorne was lucky.

John came back after Compline. Nicholas, as usual, did not come back at all. Tobie explained the situation in a murmur.

John turned and looked at the blankets screening the end of the room. 'She's in here?'

'She's had enough. They're all sleeping. I'm going to spend the night by Adorne. We'll see better what to do in the morning.'

He was treated to one of John's pregnant silences. Then John said, 'Did you tell them? That Gelis had been here?'

'No,' said Tobie. 'I didn't even tell them that Ludovico da Bologna had been here, although they'll probably find that out from the monks.'

'And Nicholas?' John le Grant said.

'I don't know where he is. Neither do you,' Tobie said.

She woke, remembering that she had come to the shrine of St Catherine. During the last third of the journey, when adventure had given way to something distressing and frightening and difficult, she had found herself forgetting the reason for it, although Father John and Brother Lorenzo said their offices, and her uncle read every night from the Gospels, as long as he could.

Today she opened her eyes upon an ikon set on a sunlit white wall, and to silence. By her bed was fresh water and a dish with bread and some grapes. When she put on her robe and opened the door, she looked upon green leaves and roof-tops and heard, here and there, the murmur of voices, and a beat too far off to be music. She looked up. Beyond the walls, all around her were immense mountains, made small by the infinite space of the sky.

She turned along to the neighbouring dormitory and scratched at the door. Her uncle's voice spoke from inside. He was alone, lying hollow-cheeked and calm on his pillows. 'I am better,' he said. 'They are in the Latin church. You and I will go there tomorrow.' She kissed him, crying from simple happiness.

Because she was young, they let her wander. Jan had given her the boy's name of Stephen, which had something to do with Ekaterina. She couldn't pretend to be Greek, but she had enough of the tongue to speak, shyly, to the monks she met, and was ashamed when, taking her for a boy, they made her a friend.

The Rule of St Basil enjoined poverty. They had no suppers of duck and red wine, no flattering habits of luxurious fabrics, no music, no dancing, no opportunities to entertain the great of the land, or exchange with well-bred avidity the gossip of court. Their robes were patched and any shade, coarse as sacking. They ate once a day, alone in their cells after evening prayers. Eschewing meat, their fare consisted of rice and peas, soup from their own lentils, with the fruit from their orchards, and water from their two deep, sweet wells. They pressed their grapes and their olives and sold them, keeping only the oil for their lamps, and a little wine for half a glass on a feast day. The grain for their bread came, once a year, across the desert from Cairo.

They worked, priest and monk, from the Abbot himself down to the least of them. They had servants – the Bedouin who prayed in the mosque – but they themselves ordered everything. She stopped by the well Moses used and helped to fetch two buckets of water: one was holed, and she carried it to someone's bench to be mended. She sat under a tattered awning cleaning lamps, and went down to the tables where they were sieving grit out of grain, and further down to the bakehouse, where they were loading loaf-pats on to racks and rolling dough into batons. A corn-mill grumbled, and someone was washing bread-stamps. When they were used, the Burning Bush would decorate every crust.

The oven was the biggest she'd ever seen, and they timed the batches by chanting. She mumbled Hail Marys through a generous dole of figs and soft bread, and produced a solo for biscuits. She peeped into chapels and found a scriptorium, full of ferocious smells, where two monks were painting and one was mixing colours. She stayed a long time, with her tongue out.

She went to look at her uncle, and found him tucked on a wooden bench outside his room, with a glass of milk and a platter empty but for some egg crumbs. He was asleep. Inside, Dr Tobias was also asleep, stretched on a mattress with his mouth open.

She went out to the gardens, and found John there, supervising a correction to one of the water-wheels. Caterina delle Ruote, patroness of wheelwrights and mechanics. There were vegetable beds and orchards and pasture, each section rooted in earth brought by camel-trains, and watered from channels led from wells, and from cisterns filled by precipitous snow-streams. The fruit trees were in parturition of small, rotund apples and pears, plums and pomegranates, each tree demure in a circle of water. There were almonds, and olives, and a small, fine fruit she had seen pickled in Alexandria.

One of the brethren plucked one for her to eat. 'You may never again taste it fresh, they have such a brief season. The Arab does not like to say, Never. He says, Tomorrow, when the apricots are here.' He smiled, watching her pleasure. His Arabic was as fluent as Brother Lorenzo's. Without Friar Lorenzo to deal with the Bedouin, they would never have reached here from Cairo.

She walked on, attended by flies. There were bees. She found a keeper lifting combs, his netted beard a-glitter with wings. There were donkeys and one or two cows. She fed the chickens.

She watched a man repairing a wall.

She addressed a caged songbird in Greek.

She explored the northern wall-walk from one shaky end to the other.

When the rings finished chiming for Nones, she extended her interest to empty mud cabins.

And found him.

He was writing. She had gone to the Library first, being sure of success for some reason, but had only found a place of crowded disorder and dust, which made her long to rearrange it.

Now she saw that he had been there, for there was a manuscript laid on the matting beside him; and he had a board on his knees with some paper on it. The ink and penbox before him were his own.

She said, 'Jan's going to need some of that. Paper for his terrible book.' She smiled and disposed herself crosslegged on the dirt, the way M. de Fleury was sitting. He always looked right, as the Arabs did, although his feet weren't bare as hers were. Hers were filthy.

He considered her. She reciprocated. She assumed he knew how he looked, and didn't need to be told. The beard, dark at the tip and yellow next to his skin, drew his face into unaccustomed lines continued by the loose open fall of his upper robe. Underneath were scars and contusions and lice bites. She said, consumed with discovery, 'It's the robes and beards. We all look Byzantine. Look at you. Jesus Pantocrator.'

He looked down in a speculative way, then lifted and joined his third finger and thumb. There was a graze on his forefinger. He said, 'I'll admit it, provided you'll have a look at Bacchos and Sergios on horseback. Sergios especially. What book is he writing?' It came close, in a cursory manner, to the banter of the black knight in Scotland.

She said carefully, 'Jan? Uncle Anselm offered this trip on condition Jan writes an account of it all for King James. King James of Scotland. In Latin.'

'That helps,' said M. de Fleury. 'Will it be actionable? Among those who can read it?'

'You aren't in it,' she said. She drew a light breath. 'It's just a travel book, but it's a strain, and Jan isn't himself. And my uncle's been very ill. And M. le Grant blames him for whatever happened in Cairo. I don't think he should.'

'You don't?' he said.

She shook her head, then stopped abruptly. The loss of her hair was still strange. She said, 'He may take steps against you in Bruges. He didn't harm you in Cairo. Although, I'm sorry, I see someone did.' She didn't ask what had happened. It would only risk reviving the grievance.

He said, 'If he did, you did much to repair it. No one has a quarrel with you.'

She said, 'But my uncle, and Jan, and the others?'

He still had his pen in his fingers and an air that wasn't even impatience. He said, 'My friends are very set in their prejudices but, you know, the confrontation won't last very long. The man who first discovers the gold will leave promptly.'

She felt herself flush.

He said, 'You wouldn't be here if you had found it. You may tell your uncle that I haven't found it either. Was there anything else?'

She said, 'You wouldn't be here but for my kite, and the parrot.'

His eyes were grey, his manner dry as ashes. 'Of course. But the gold is mine, as it happens.' After a moment he said, 'You are tired. Ask Dr Tobias to give you something.'

She said, 'Ask him to give you something. And my uncle. How can you come here, and think about gold?'

'There is a good precedent,' he said. Where the Golden Calf had been worshipped, there was an oratory down in the valley. The paper under his hand was a diagram, not a manuscript. And the paperweight lying upon it was a pebble, knotted into a cord.

She said, 'There are twenty chapels with altar gold in them, and possible hiding places by the hundred. You will lose your mind, and not trace it. Talk to the Abbot. Talk to Brother Lorenzo. He comes from Crete. Tomorrow we're going to pray in the church, and see the holy tomb and touch the relics. Then we climb Mount Sinai at night after Mass, and after dawn, we're going on to the top of St Catherine's. Will you come with us?'

'Why?' he said.

She unfolded her dirty feet and stood. She said, 'Because you are a stupid man and so is my uncle, and I don't want to see you smite one another from now till the Day of Resurrection. I can't cure you. The Lord might.'

He gazed at her, or through her. 'Then why not leave it to the two of us?' he suggested. 'Or theologically, is it a quorum?'

The Arabs arrived as he spoke, thundering up on their horses outside, thirty feet under the delivery gable, to get their dole of bread loaves lowered by windlass. It was why they left the Christians unmolested. She looked, hoping to see him startled, but he remained where he was.

He said, 'The monks are generous. They send fruit and gums to the Sultan. The Emir of Tor is partial to Sinai water and grapes, and remits to Sinai a modicum of the Tor customs. The King of France has offered an annuity of two thousand ducats. A magnate of Crete has made a princely donation of twice that amount. The demon gold has its uses.'

'I know what you are saying,' she said. 'But still, it is for the Convent. And some think that the purity and prayers of the Convent may balance the sins of the world. So, if you find the gold, what will you use it for?'

'Trade,' he said. 'As your uncle would do. It is our métier. And you might say that, without it, there would be no world to save.'

When she turned to leave, he made no effort to keep her.

In fact, he remained where he was, rolling up the plans before the monks filtered back from their service. When Tobie came to see to the dressings, he was already standing bent under the ceiling, apparently prepared to make his way back to the guest-quarters.

'We've put the girl in your room,' objected Tobie.

'Then get her out,' Nicholas said.

'Adorne and the rest are next door. They'll have you flung out for witchcraft.' He sounded furious.

'They will anyway. Katelijne has seen it,' said Nicholas. He had the scroll under his arm.

'She found you?'

'She was looking chiefly, I think, for the gold. I'm not sure it's here.'

'What?' said Tobie. Since the desert, his face seemed to wear permanent lines.

'The only place left is the church. Do you think he could have hidden it in the church? The saint's bones? The Bush? A God-fearing pirate like Ochoa?'

'If he didn't, he went to some lengths to get us here.'

'Oh, a lot of people did,' Nicholas said.

Tobie was silent. Then he said, 'Is that what you're looking for? Gold?'

'Yes,' said Nicholas. 'I know what you are asking. I saw Gelis. She has gone with da Bologna. I'm not following her. She didn't, I think, have anything directly to do with what happened in Cairo. She doesn't want me dead – or not yet. Sometime I shall tell you what happened, or part of it. But first, I want to settle this matter of gold. If it isn't here, we can leave.'

'And go home?' Tobie said.

'This isn't home?' Nicholas said.

It had been a stupid question.

The Abbot, leading the procession into the basilica, was alert to the enmity of the two sets of Franks walking behind his Council of Fathers. He had been warned of it by Lorenzo; and, of course, the two chief protagonists had each come, if briefly, to see him. The Flemish-Genoese nobleman on holy pilgrimage for whom Brother Lorenzo had formed a respect; and the Flemish banker with Venetian affiliations who had arrived with the Sultan's recommendation.

He knew, as it happened, what they both wanted. Westerner fell out with Westerner; Bedouin with Bedouin: it was the nature of man. A bishop as well as an abbot, he ruled his communities of Sinai, Pharan and Tor with considerable intellectual vigour, and had so far resisted the pressure to alter the habit of centuries and divide Greek from Frank. Both had faults. The proverbial vulgarity of the Franks; the subtlety and guile – *Graecae blanditiae ac fraudes* – of the Greeks. He knew some Latin. The Flemish banker spoke Greek.

Justinian's doors, twelve feet tall, folded open before him. *This gate of the Lord, into which the righteous shall enter*. Carved out of cypress nine hundred years since, they were deeply scored with the names and arms of Crusaders. He hoped his guests, walking behind him, would notice. A special Sinaitic company of the Crusaders had protected the monastery. The effect of the basilica and its history was one of the stronger spiritual weapons in his armoury. The mountain was the other.

The church being built on the site of the Sacred Bush, at the lowest level of the convent, newcomers were always awed by the height of the roof-timbers, and by the double column of red granite pillars whose arches separated the nave from the aisles. The first impression, though, was of the blinding dazzle of light upon gold. The Abbot was proud – sinfully vain – of the multiplicity of his lamps, fed by their own olives, grown in God's sunlight. The convent was continually blessed by gifts of fine lamps.

He led the way down the nave, noting the February ikon askew, and the exquisite smell of the Sultan's new incense. The Franks behind him were wealthy. One of them had brought a girl. He was worldly enough to know when it happened; his monks were naïve and noticed little, and he used his own discretion, provided proper conduct was observed. He did not propose to emulate the brotherhood which had protested that its well, unless specially tended, had the misfortune to turn men into women.

The Franciscan, Ludovico da Bologna, had brought a woman as well, and had taken her away. But he had confessed, and explained, and left an offering.

The Abbot, reaching the end of the nave, passed beyond the low marble balustrade into the chancel and turned. His vestments rustled. He supposed they had only seen him before in patched black, or in his floured bakehouse apron. Soaring behind him in the vault of the apse was one of the glories of Christendom: the mosaic of the Transfiguration, old as the church. He saw the light from above it fall on the upturned faces before him. The singing began, and he took up his candle.

Saint Ekaterina would forgive him if he pondered now and then, through the ritual. They prayed. He led them from altar to altar over white marble and blue, while they marvelled at the holy legends set like damask under their feet, and the holy pictures thick with gold all about them. In the Burning Bush chapel, where it was forbidden to enter with shoes, he saw that the Venetian Fleming had made use of his indulgence, and walked on woollen hose. His manner was reverent. The attitude of both parties had been grave and tense, rather than elevated. The girl who called herself Stephen knelt by the marble under which the Roots still reposed, and stared at the Venetian's feet.

The hose were not, of course, in contravention. Wool was permitted. The man had said, smiling, that he had left his soles on Mount Sinai and did not propose to go back to get them. The Abbot knew that was true. The woman had come down the mountain, but the man had stepped aside to the chapel of St Marina halfway. (St Marina, the holy virgin who had passed her life as a monk. How odd. Had he known?) At any rate, the man had been brought down in the end by the Franciscan Patriarch and his friends.

The Latin Patriarch. It was nearly time to open the Coffin. The Abbot had known Ludovico da Bologna for a long time; as had Lorenzo. The Latin Patriarch was a friend of the great Cardinal Bessarion. The Patriarch had been, in his time, a protégé of Pope Eugenius and his successor Calixtus, who had favoured Ferrante of Naples and who had led the Aragonese to the Council of Florence, that failed attempt to join the Eastern Church to that of the West. (Typically, the Coptic delegate from St Antony's had arrived late.)

Ludovico da Bologna had lived for a considerable time in Jerusalem. He had spent years on missions in the East, and had taken Ethiopians and Byzantines and Persians to Rome. He had tried to travel to Ethiopia, and had encouraged this man Nikolaus to attempt it as well. While repelled by the Patriarch's habits, the Abbot could not wholly decry what he was doing.

It was time to open the Coffin. He made a sign for the hymn, 'Let us praise the divine Ekaterina,' to be followed in due course by the Kontakion and the Megalynarion. The merchant Nikolaus at least, one supposed, would understand them.

The final resting place of the ever-memorable Ekaterina, once Dorothea, was under an arch to the right of the altar. Standing at man's height from the ground, the marble coffin was small, the insatiable hunger for holy relics having diminished the sacred frame through the centuries. Nevertheless, as always, the Abbot felt an echo of the terror, the compassion that had seized him when, a young man, he had stood thus, and watched the magnificent cloth lifted aside and the great key inserted and turned by the Sacrist. And men of the world though they might be, the pilgrims standing there now with their tapers on each side of the tomb were also reduced to a deep, waiting silence. The girl-boy, though brave, was painfully white. The key clicked and the Sacrist drew back the lid.

The nobleman, Adorne, Baron Cortachy, began to move forward.

The Abbot, leading his monks to the coffin, saw the movement from the side of his eye, and the hand of the Sacrist restraining the gentleman. Only when the brethren had made their reverences would the pilgrims be allowed to approach and salute the Saint, and touch to the relics the precious articles they had brought to be blessed, while dropping their offerings into the casket. For those who had brought no rings, no medals, the convent supplied snippets of silk, soaked in the precious oil of the sanctuary lamps, and touched to the bones. The oil itself, with all its healing properties, could also be carried away. Pilgrims came to Saint Ekaterina through much suffering, and were not sent away empty-handed . . . *for she preached Christ in the stadium, and trampled upon the serpent, and spat upon the knowledge of the philosophers*, sang his monks triumphantly, waiting behind him. The Abbot bent over the Coffin.

All was as it should be. The beautiful diadem ringed the fragile skull, lacking the jawbone. The left hand lay, white as milk, its long fingers adorned with fine rings. The curved ribs and the disarticulated leg bones lay under silk, rendered the colour of honey from the fragrant oils they once exuded. Around, in cups and caskets and boxes, were the precious gifts left for the Saint. No man, even the humblest, ever left less than a ducat.

The Abbot kissed the holy fingers, and stepped aside as his monks followed suit. Then, as was fitting, he summoned the chief of each party of pilgrims, the man Adorne and the merchant Nikolaus, to stand one to each side of the Coffin and, setting their candles aside, to stoop and pay their respects.

They stood looking instead at each other. The dazzling riches below lit their faces, causing the Abbot to admire the tableau: the brilliant carved tomb; the two fine men, one older, one young, their features made spiritual by the light, and by the fatigue of their long and difficult journey. Then the younger one, his face luminous, spoke two words in Latin. 'You may have it.'

'So I thank you. Where have you hidden the rest?'

It was unseemly. The Abbot spoke sharply in Greek. 'Do you worship? Or do you return to your quarters?'

'We worship,' said the younger one quickly; and, bending, kissed the Saint and moved on. The other, hesitating, did the same; and then paused to empty his satchel and present its contents, deftly, one by one to the relics. It was done with reverence; indeed, his expression throughout was one of concentration mingled with something like anguish. His son's gaze, fixed on him, was anxious; and the stripling looked ready to faint.

The Abbot did not speak, and remained at his post as they made their reverences in due course and moved on. He stood with the Council of Fathers while each of the remaining guests stepped up and bent, and did his duty. His eyes, from the first moment, had remained on the article the Fleming had noticed and to which, he was certain, his remarks appertained. An ostrich egg. An ostrich egg cleaned and mounted, in the manner of those which hung from the ceiling. An ostrich egg filled with gold grains.

That, at least, was what appeared to be the object of contention. There was another egg, from the same donor, as the Abbot happened to know. But that held nothing at all but a small inlaid box with some flakes of soap in it.

Comely virgin-martyr, intoned the brethren, watching avidly. *By thy godly wisdom didst thou vanquish the enemy.*

The last pilgrim stooped and fumbled, the last ducat or two shivered its way down with the rest.

Decked in grace and virtue, O Ekaterina, thou camest with joy to thine Immortal Bridegroom; O maid of God.

'My lord Abbot?' said the Sacrist.

'They have gone? Lock the Coffin,' said the Abbot. 'But give me the key.'

'He raised his voice,' Jan Adorne said. 'My father. In the Abbot's quarters. I'm supposed to be training for the Church.'

'I'm sure it will be all right,' Kathi said. The Abbot's small set of rooms was nowhere near the guest-quarters. 'The Abbot will make allowances. M. de Fleury looked very calm, and Friar Lorenzo is with them.' Meester Reyphin was wrapping up all his blessed rings and Lambert was biting the places where his nails ought to be. Dr Tobias and M. le Grant, who had also come out of their chamber, stood together by the gallery rails talking in low voices. Everyone smelled of incense.

Jan said, 'But what did he see in the Coffin? What were they talking about?'

They were supposed to be in the Refectory for a celebration after the ceremony, and carving their names. The ceremony that was supposed to make her feel better. She felt sick, and wondered if they were still expected to climb the mountain. The two mountains. Jan said, 'Don't you know what is happening?'

Addressed, Dr Tobias turned round. She saw that he and M. le Grant had reached some decision. The doctor said, 'It's to do with gold, Jan. There was some of our Company's African gold in the Coffin. The three mule-loads of gold that were stolen. We came here, and so did your father, to look for it.'

Kathi closed her eyes. Now the poem would never get done. Jan said slowly, 'My father is here on holy pilgrimage.'

'We know,' said Dr Tobias. He gave her a worried glance. 'We know his prime object. The other matter is minor. In fact, the gold may not be here at all. There is a lot of it to hide. The person who took it may have passed through, and simply left some as an offering. Nicholas – M. de Fleury said your father could have it. That is, he won't claim it himself.'

'What has it to do with my father?' said Jan.

Kathi said, 'We'll know, won't we, when they come out? Come on. You've got two stanzas yet, and the painting. I'll come and help you.'

Within the Abbot's quarters, the dispute had reached a very similar point, and the echoes of Anselm Adorne's voice rang round the low walls, striking the interleaved ikons like mallets. His eyes looked fevered.

The Abbot said, 'God is here. You have no need to cry to Him. I will hear the truth, and He will advise.'

Brother Lorenzo translated, using Latin for decorum, rather than the Italian dialect of their journey from Cairo. Brother Lorenzo said, 'My lord Abbot understands that the gold in the Coffin, unique in character, was previously stolen. It happens. A thief repents. M. de Fleury has no wish to remove it. Are you saying it has some value for you?'

'I am saying,' said Anselm Adorne, 'that within these walls, were I to search, I should find all the rest of the gold. Or were I to ask M. de Fleury, he could take me straight to where it has been placed to await him. Unless, that is, it has already found its way to the Sultan? With the apples and plums, and the phials of sweet oil and the raisins?'

Brother Lorenzo drew in his breath. He saw, by a small change of attitude, that the Greek-speaking Frank had emerged into a state of semi-awareness. Interpreting for the Abbot, he was accordingly forced to be accurate. He knew he did not need to convey a warning.

The Abbot said, with distaste, 'What rubbish is this?'

'Mamelukes brought him here,' said Adorne. 'By some miracle, before he left Cairo, M. de Fleury contrived to reverse every misfortune and obtain the dizziest privileges of the Sultanate. I ask myself what guerdon he promised.' He paused. He said, 'This place was built as a fortress. It is a valuable fortress still, to whoever maintains it. And it already possesses a mosque.'

The Abbot was silent. When he spoke, it was in a slow, measured voice, soft but deep; and it continued in its solemn cadences for a long time. When he ceased, Lorenzo saw de Fleury's eyes fixed upon him.

He returned the look. Then he turned to the Frankish Baron, and began to translate.

'You must know that you have caused great offence. The lord Abbot would ask you to leave immediately, save that he would deny no one that grace that comes from scaling the Mount of the Lord, and he recognises that there is error lodged in your heart and your tongue which the Lord can seek out better than he.

'My lord wishes, however, to say this. As Bishop of Sinai, he informs you that there is no gold within these walls or these gardens, or anywhere within his rule, and if you wish to parade your disbelief by crawling, kneeling or visiting caverns, you are welcome to do so. My lord will not even withdraw from you the indulgences, the privileges, even the chivalric honour which the Blessed Saint Ekaterina has bestowed on you this day, for fear you accuse him of some trick, or some prejudice against the whole race of Franks. Tell him what you wish to do, and then leave his house.'

Adorne jumped to his feet and stood over de Fleury. He said, 'I cannot tolerate you, or what you represent, any longer. You bring your sordid ambition to a holy place and infect what you touch. You have no faith, no beliefs. You are rich; you want more. You came for the gold, and nothing else. What have you done, from the moment you came, but search for it, like a jackal seeking a corpse?'

He had dropped into Tuscan. The Abbot's face, frowning, moved from one man's face to the other but Brother Lorenzo understood.

The younger Frank did not try to interrupt. At the end he said, in the same language, 'You can't believe the monastery capable of such wrongdoing. The Abbot is speaking the truth. The gold is not here. But even if it were, what has it to do with you? You are on pilgrimage here, and so is your son, for your souls' sake.'

His voice, which had been hard, withdrew its intensity towards the end as if he had restrained himself, or had been subdued by the balm of some opiate. Brother Lorenzo, seeking his superior's eye, spoke in Greek. 'My lord Abbot. The Baron is ill. Leave him to me.'

'And the other?' the Abbot said. He glanced at de Fleury, recalling himself.

De Fleury suddenly spoke, of his own accord, also in Greek; rising to stand before his rival the Baron. He said, 'Brother Lorenzo is right; my compatriot is unwell. We should neither of us have set tongue to the words you have heard, and I can only thank you on my knees for your lenience. My lord of Cortachy plans to leave, I am sure, as soon as his pilgrimage is completed. I, too, will disembarrass you of my presence. I have placed before Brother Lorenzo that which I beg you will accept, for the good of the Convent and the Blessed Ekaterina and all whom you serve.'

'I have seen it,' said the Abbot. It lay, covered with a cloth, in a niche in the wall. He did not glance at it. The man Adorne, unable to follow the Greek, said something under his breath.

De Fleury turned to him and said in Italian, 'I was only making your apologies, and mine. We are free to go.'

The Baron Cortachy, erect and pale, began to say the correct words at last, in formal Latin, and Lorenzo translated them. The Abbot bowed stiffly and Adorne knelt and kissed his foot, his drawn face hidden. The younger man turned back and waited. The Baron Cortachy rose, bowing, and left.

The Abbot said, 'Let him go. I wish you to show me what you have brought.' Brother Lorenzo crossed over and uncovered and brought back the object in the niche.

It was a great chalice made by a master, the match of the one that Charles of France had given them sixty years earlier; its knop similarly inset with enamels. Its worth could not be gauged, not without expert valuation, which it would have.

The Abbot laid it on the stiff liturgical shelf of his lap, gold on gold, and moved his fingers, wondering, round the prayer-engraved rim. 'We thank you,' he said. 'And we are prepared to hear that you have set your heart on redeeming some of the lesser gifts left to St Catherine. I have had both objects brought.'

Again, Brother Lorenzo walked across and came back, bearing with an air of slight distraction the two ostrich eggs which had lain in the Coffin. Presenting the first, full of gold, he saw the other man shake his head, smiling and, smiling himself, laid it gently aside. Then he presented the other.

'I would take it,' said Nicholas de Fleury. 'But not without your consent. And I should pay for it.'

The Abbot smiled. 'The price is one ducat,' he said; and continued to smile, in a benign way, as the box, small as a button, was lifted out of the egg and placed in the other man's palm.

Nicholas de Fleury said, but as a statement rather than as a question, 'It is forbidden to tell me the donor.'

'It is forbidden,' said the Abbot in a friendly voice. 'Nor can I distinguish what it contains. Your perception may be greater than mine.'

Detached from the blown egg and the mouldering sarcophagus, the little box lay confidingly, you would say, on the man's broad, hardened palm. He touched the clasp and laid back the shell of the lid, revealing the phial to be empty but for a minute heap of transparent slivers. He smiled, without lifting his eyes.

'The box is of gold,' said Brother Lorenzo.

He had nowhere to go. Katelijne Sersanders, fierce in her concern, saw her uncle, unfamiliar in his distress, thread his way through the maze of alleys and arches, along the vaulted corridors, up the haphazard staircases of the community of anchorites, termites of Justinian's monastery. Long before he arrived, she had pushed everyone out of his room and into the next.

She saw him pause on the threshold, seeing it empty, but he was too tired, she thought, to wonder why, and too grieved to wish it otherwise. Stepping softly behind, she saw he had crossed to the crucifix on the wall and knelt before it. Then he covered his eyes.

She drew the curtain over the door and backed away.

'What?' said his son. 'God in heaven, what are you crying for *now*?'

'Hunger,' she said. 'And if you're not going to the Refectory, I am. Dr Tobias?'

He had been watching as well. 'Yes. The Refectory, immediately,' said Tobie.

When they came back, Anselm Adorne was lying still on his mattress. It was dark, and they would be required to rise not very long after midnight to hear Mass and to prepare for the climb. They would be away until nightfall next day, and had still to arrange for the food they would have to take with them.

Dr Tobias and M. le Grant had shown no enthusiasm for the expedition. M. de Fleury having once again vanished, no one knew of his intentions, but Dr Tobias thought that he, too, would remain. The meal had been uneasy, but in the presence of the monks and the Abbot, nothing untoward had been said.

Having several untoward things she wished to say, Katelijne Sersanders took a lantern and made her way, with discretion, to that small gallery high under the wall where she had once before found M. de Fleury.

He was not there. She walked from level to level, brushed by low devotional murmurs; touched by moths; accosted by whispers of prostitute fragrances. Above the walls, above the patchwork of roofs hung the sky, with St Catherine's star and the dark, silent ring of the mountains.

Below the star, there was a light in St Catherine's church of the
Franks. It was the usual lamp, hung before the iconostasis beam
with its four painted figures, but she sensed somewhere a shadow,
and when she opened the door, the palm-leaf mats masked another
sound, she thought, by their stirring. Then Nicholas de Fleury
said, 'Come in. I have found a remarkable poem.'

She had hoped to discover, through him, an understanding of her
uncle's condition. But if he had knelt it was to commune, not to
weep; if he had sought solitude, it was not from personal agony. His
voice was abstracted and sweet, as if music was not far away, but his
mind had not yet had time to turn to it. She said, 'What happened?'

'A misunderstanding,' he said. 'Your uncle was convinced that
the gold must be here, and the Abbot invited him to look for it. It
isn't, of course.'

She said, 'You believed it was here.' She hesitated and then said,
'I thought it was yours.'

He had put on a kindly face. The dimples, the trenches in his
face, in his beard even looked natural. He said, 'It is, but people
forget. Your uncle had some idea that it was meant for the
Mamelukes, as part of a plot to invite them in strength to St
Catherine's. The Abbot explained that there were no stocks of gold
and no plot, and when your uncle seemed unconvinced, invited
him to search the monastery for the gold, if he liked.'

'He was shamed,' Katelijne said.

'I am sorry,' he said. He made it formal.

She said, 'So am I. I had better go. We are climbing tomorrow.'

He seemed less interested, now, in deception. He said, 'As you
must guess, I have done my duty by Mount Sinai already. Take
your uncle. Be careful. But it will help you and him.'

'Did it help you?' she said. She identified his expression. It was
well intentioned, and absent.

He said, 'I got what I deserved. And later, a prize I didn't
deserve. Sore feet, too.'

She said, 'It was your wife?' And when he looked at her, 'They
said the Patriarch of Antioch had been here, with a young man.
Someone who worked for a while on the irrigation wheel.'

'Did she?' he said. 'Yes, it was Gelis. She has gone. We have
arranged to meet again, in proper gender.'

'You thought she was dead,' Kathi said. 'She wanted you to
meet on Mount Sinai.'

'She has a touch for drama,' he said. 'Land of salt, land of
manna, land of fauns and of satyrs. Place of temptation – oh, that.
To humble thee and to prove thee, I bring thee here.'

She waited until he looked round. He said complainingly, 'You are a very quiet child.' Then he touched the poem. 'Jan's?'

Jan's. The coat of arms, nicely painted, identified it. He had worked on it all through the desert. His father had told him to. Every pilgrim party was supposed to compose one. And studying it was the man Whistle Willie invited to lyrical battle.

> *Salve virgo Katherina*
> *Salve quidem castissima*
> *Stirpe regia regina*
> *Fuisti nobilissima . . .*

He didn't read it aloud. He said eventually, 'The last two verses scan.'

'Good night,' she said. Against her intentions she smiled, implying that she perceived and accepted the compliment, and was immediately filled with remorse. She crept into her chamber, and arranged herself behind her improvised screen, and considered with furious despair the prospect of a night and a day climbing mountains with Anselm Adorne and his son.

She fell asleep.

Coming back in the quiet of the night, Nicholas de Fleury found the lamp lit in his part of the guest-quarters, and his two business partners awaiting him. John le Grant said, 'All right. Now you're purified, sit down and tell us.'

'About the gold,' Nicholas said. He had hoped to have a moment with Tobie. But after all, it didn't matter. Nothing mattered too much.

'That's why we're supposed to be here. But the St Sabas message was wrong, or out of date, or maybe the parrot was drunk. The gold isn't here, only a puckle left in the tomb. Who did that? Ochoa?'

All the way to Sinai, the notion of a hard-swearing Catalonian sea captain immured in a monastery had confounded Nicholas. Now he laughed. 'No. Ochoa hasn't been here. Just the token dust in the egg, to lure us onwards.'

He spoke with confidence. It was true that the gold wasn't here: he would have believed the Abbot, even if his pendulum hadn't told him. His pendulum had told him, over and over, about a presence of power in the tomb. And of course, had been right.

John said, 'Lure us here? Why?'

'Or lure us beyond here?' said Tobie. 'Is that it?'

Sometime, he would have to talk to Tobie about Gelis, who had been the bait which had brought Nicholas to Mount Sinai. Gelis, and his discontent over Adorne. He knew, from John, that before Gelis walked out of the monastery she had been confronted by Tobie and treated to a barrage of questions which she had refused, with apparent indifference, to answer. He also knew that it was Gelis who had sent Ludovico da Bologna to look for him when he had failed to return from the mountain. She didn't want the game to end before time.

Now he said to the others, 'A lot of people are trying to push us about for various reasons: business, personal; because of the gold. The gold is what we came for: we haven't got it; and Tobie's feeling, last time we spoke, was that we ought to abandon it and go home. Meaning west. What do you think?'

Tobie's face had altered. He said, 'Home. As soon as may be. Diniz won't mind. The Bank can stand it.'

'Seconded,' said John le Grant. 'It's getting too dangerous. If Adorne thinks he can plod on and find it, then I wish him good luck. We can aye pester him with some litigation, even if we've no chance of winning. He might even drop charges against you for half killing him.'

'There is that,' said Nicholas. Tobie looked at him. Nicholas said, 'All right: we agree. Alexandria? The spice ships will be in: the Sultan's goodwill should go quite some way to compensating for the gold. We'll need camels and an escort to take us there: a few weeks of business, then back on the first ship to Venice. We could be there by November. Achille will have news of Scotland and the Tyrol.'

'Scotland?' said Tobie.

'I can go there next year,' Nicholas said.

They extinguished the lamp very soon. John fell asleep. Some time after midnight, mingled with the psalms of the night office, came the subdued sounds of stirring next door, as Adorne's party prepared to visit their church before leaving. Nicholas, listening, became aware of movement much closer than that. Tobie, too, was quietly dressing.

For the sake of young Kathi, of course. Perhaps even to watch over Adorne, not yet restored to full health. In war, Tobie served like this, riding, walking, his box at his side; treating those he despised and those he hated, impartial with everyone. A good physician daily faced the great mysteries; it was not surprising that Tobie, too, might want to scale Mount Sinai, and stand on the peak of St Catherine.

John slept on and Nicholas lay, all his mind concentrated, like a spear, on one thought. After a while, when it was quiet, he rose and went to where the little box waited.

Chapter 43

KATELIJNE CAME TO the end of her strength on the second
mountain, the Mount of St Catherine, which was over
eight thousand feet high, and took five hours to ascend
and three to come down. Guided by Brother Lorenzo,
they had already climbed Mount Sinai before dawn, and prayed
with Father John in the chapel. From there they had descended
the west side to reach the convent of the Forty Martyrs, which was
ruined, but maintained its precious gardens, and where two monks
in a hut brought them water and fruit.

There was no path up St Catherine, and although from the top
they said they could see the Gulf of Aqaba and the Gulf of Suez,
the Red Sea southwards to Tor, and the whole peninsula for as far
as it would take six days to travel, Katelijne stuck halfway up, and
Dr Tobias stayed with her.

When they came back at dusk, most of them were hardly able to
walk, and the girl was in a camel-litter. Guiding her through the
postern vault, Tobie heard the squabble inside the monastery at once.

Reduced by space, even voices upraised in anger remained slight,
although it was evident that the sound came from above, where the
monks' galleried cells clung to the north wall. John was not in their
room. Tobie got the girl settled quickly, and ran.

It was over by then: the cell empty, and only John standing
outside, in a fury which he turned on Tobie at once.

'So where were you? You knew he was doing this?'

The bloodied fingers, the deepening eyes: yes, he had known
that Nicholas was divining. Tobie said, 'They found him at it? Or
someone told them?'

'Both,' said John. 'For my money.' His fist was split.

'Kathi knew,' Tobie said. 'But she wouldn't tell. Perhaps Gelis
guessed, and told Adorne. What happened?'

'The worst,' said John. 'Three silly monks, convinced they'd seen the devil conjuring spirits. If Brother Lorenzo had been here, it would never have happened. Anyway, they burst into exorcising prayers and wails, and when Nicholas got up, tried to snatch his pendulum and set fire to his maps. I don't think he was in his proper senses: he'd been concentrating too long. At any rate, he fought back, and the fire caught their robes, and I got there in time to save them and sit on him.'

'Heavily,' suggested Tobie, who at times had some admiration for John.

'My fist caught his jaw,' admitted the engineer. 'They've locked him up somewhere and gone off to report to the Abbot. Was it exciting on the two mountains?'

'Five broken pilgrims,' said Tobie. 'And the girl in collapse, if you call that exciting.'

The anger left John. He said, 'It was far too heavy a day. You were mad to allow her.'

'It wasn't physical,' Tobie said. 'Much the same kind of nervous overspill that sometimes afflicts Nicholas, I suspect. She knows more than most about what's going on, but not quite enough to make sense of it. What was he divining?'

John looked surprised. 'The rest of the gold, surely, damn him. Then he'd have reversed all our plans. He could never really bear to let Adorne find it.'

'I suppose so,' said Tobie. 'Well, he's lost his chance. They'll fling us out now. Or put a stake through his heart. Or set fire to him.' He waited for John's heaviest grunt. They both knew it was serious.

They got off with expulsion; or a departure as soon as an escort could be collected. It was hardly pleasant, even with the Abbot exercising his authority to calm the more timid monks and Brother Lorenzo adding helpful allusions to the Rod of Moses. A man who could discover water could not be wholly the Devil's.

The ordering of mounts and guides and provisions began. Nicholas, returned to interim confinement in their chamber, looked spent and bemused rather than fiendish. The charred maps had been taken, but the pendulum had been returned by the Abbot, with a private exhortation, to Tobie. He kept it hidden until he and Nicholas were alone. Then he produced it.

Nicholas looked at it.

Tobie said, 'I am so very sorry. It's empty. Take your time.' With any other man, he would have touched him.

Nicholas said, 'You know what was in it.'

Tobie put the box in his hands. 'Yes.' On a long campaign, there were always children. Mothers died. He had suckled a babe from his finger; seated a child in the crook of his arm and pressed out the fringe of its toes so that he could use the small shears from his box. The clippings fell, half-moons and slivers, fine as muslin.

A whimsical kind of memento, until you remembered what divining made use of. This child had been at least a year old. Tobie said, 'You knew as soon as you saw it? How did you know?'

'Before I saw it,' Nicholas said. He had opened the box. As Tobie had said, it was empty. It was the first thing the Abbot had done; shake its contents into the fire.

Nicholas said, 'I was given a wisp of hair, supposed to be his. I felt nothing: it wasn't. I could feel this through granite and marble.'

'Gelis brought you the hair?' said Tobie. He spoke gently.

Nicholas said, 'When I didn't accept it as proof, she offered to show me the child, at a price.'

'The gold?' said Tobie. 'She wanted the gold?'

'She wanted to watch me compelled to find it. That was all. She wouldn't know, you see, that someone had left this.'

It was like being in camp, moving among wounded, speaking carefully. Tobie said, 'Someone? The Patriarch? But, Nicholas . . . what makes you sure Gelis didn't help him? She could have had the box made. She must have provided what was in it. She could have made certain that someone would empty it before you could touch it. One of them must have told the monks what you were doing. They didn't find you divining by accident.'

'But,' said Nicholas, 'you see, it doesn't matter. The power stays, even though it is empty. I know where to start.' His voice strengthened for the first time. 'I don't know where the gold is. I don't need to know. I can find the child.'

Tobie said, 'If you do, you will need me. Not for the child. For yourself. Do you understand?' It was the least he could do. He should be forbidding this.

He saw Nicholas realise it. Nicholas said, 'I know. It will stop.'

'It may take longer than you think,' said Tobie dryly. 'You said you knew where to start?'

'I know where he is,' Nicholas said. 'Here, in the Middle Sea, on an island. I have to sail from Gaza.'

Gaza would take six to eight days to reach. It was on the Middle Sea. Alexandria and Gaza lay at opposite ends of the Sinai coastline. Tobie said, 'It takes you further from home. You don't know which island?'

He remembered as he spoke that the maps Nicholas had used for his divining were burned. There would be others at Gaza. They had an agent at Gaza. He began to say, 'Could it be Crete?' and then stopped, looking at the other man's bent head. The box lay in his hands. Tobie rose quietly and left, without troubling him with anything more.

That day the problem resolved itself because of the illness of Kathi.

It had worried Tobie, her collapse. Her uncle, himself over-tired, had been at first inclined to belittle it. He had been distraught, on his return, to find the calm of the monastery further destroyed, and the culprit – the practitioner of the unnatural art – to be Nicholas. Then came the discovery that his niece Katelijne had known of it.

In the end, Tobie turned Adorne from her room. 'He uses the gift to detect minerals. It isn't unknown. If you possessed such an ability, wouldn't you use it to find gold?'

And – 'No! On my soul, a thousand times no!' Adorne had said and, rejecting Tobie in turn, had brought Brother Lorenzo to view his young nephew Stephen (at a distance), and to confirm his belief that the Holy Land, with all its miracles, would surely effect a complete cure.

At the bedside, Brother Lorenzo murmured politenesses. Outside, he turned. 'Forgive me, but this I must say. You have no doctor. The Holy Land is Mameluke country, and travel there can be harsh and distressing, as you have already found. Would you not prefer to choose some quiet place where Stephen might wait out the rest of your journey? A return perhaps to my own island of Crete? To St Catherine's community there?'

It was a sensible offer and Adorne, prevaricating, longed to accept it. The monk set out to persuade him. 'I could take him and see him well cared for. He would find some interest in our ikon workshops, our trade.'

It was impossible. 'I am afraid not,' said Adorne, with regret.

The monk bit his lip and seemed to gather himself. 'Also, the ladies of my family would make him welcome.'

The tone of voice was enough. With mixed relief and despair, Adorne answered at length. 'I see you have guessed. I am ashamed.'

Later, stiffly conveying the news to the doctor, Adorne found Tobie unamazed.

'Monks are wiser than you would think. I thought the Abbot suspected the sex of our Stephen.' He studied Adorne. 'D'you think less of the Father for letting it pass? Katelijne was the only one with a real reason for being here.'

'Do you think so?' said Adorne. 'You felt nothing, gained nothing from the mountain? I know, of course, your friend did not. As for the Abbot, I think he would have let her stay longer. It was this despicable matter of necromancy which forced him to cleanse his conscience in other respects.'

'And, perhaps, the little argument you yourself had over the Sultan,' Tobie said sharply. 'I suspect we all came for mixed reasons, but some of them weren't bad. Are you sending Kathi to Crete?'

'If Brother Lorenzo can arrange it,' Adorne said. 'We hope to leave her in good hands in Gaza, and the brethren themselves will take her from there to the island. I think he is right: she needs quiet. I know you were worried about her and I was wrong to be angry. I am sorry.'

'And you want to know where I am going,' said Tobie.

Adorne said, 'I am not interested in the gold.'

'Neither are we,' said Tobie gravely. 'It appears that we, too, are going to Gaza, the three of us. We could set out on our own, or along with you all, depending on how you feel about the contaminating presence of Nicholas. The friar might have views.'

Adorne was silent. Then he said, 'And after that?'

'I don't know,' Tobie said. 'By ship somewhere. We haven't decided.'

Perhaps the man was concerned for his niece; perhaps not. He wondered if Adorne ever thought of the strain imposed on a very young girl, set to travel with men, and pretending to be one of their kind. It could be done: you saw that, too, on campaign. Buckets, cloths, unremitting struggle and vigilance on top of the genderless joys of rough travel: plucking Pharaoh's lice, big as almonds, from her clothes; vermin out of her hair. Gelis, too. He despised Gelis, but never doubted her courage.

Then he looked at Adorne, and thought that yes, he knew what he had asked of Katelijne, or she had begged him to allow. Below the civilised charm was the magistrate, the champion jouster of many hard fights. The man of conscience, but also the man of long sight and great ambition, despite all his protestations to Nicholas. Anselm Adorne, Baron Cortachy, was an antagonist whose steel was still only half felt.

Adorne said, 'I cannot be pleased, after what I know of Nicholas, and the impressionability of my niece. But I have to say that, if you will be there, I should be grateful if you would help us escort Kathi as far as Gaza.'

Gold, thought Tobie, had a lot to answer for.

He found himself thinking again of camp life, and his time as an army physician. Between battles, you could discuss what you were doing – even with someone like Captain Astorre who might not understand, but who knew the cases, and recognised the importance of handling them properly.

The present situation felt much the same, but Tobie was alone. That is, he had John's impersonal, professional help, but John wasn't entangled in the miseries of his patron's idyllic third marriage, or the problem of the ephemeral child. And without revealing the truth about Henry, it was hard to explain.

He carried to John, as a substitute, a business proposition. A caravan was gathering which could convey Adorne's party and themselves as far as Gaza. From there, they could as well take ship west to Alexandria as suffer the tedious journey by land. They would be in time for the spice market, and the galleys sailing for home.

They were sitting, for privacy, in the empty Refectory. John said, 'You're getting better. It sounded quite plausible. As I see it, he's been divining again for the gold, and he thinks it's in Gaza?'

Driven to it, Tobie invented. 'He didn't intend to do anything. But he got a response somehow from Gaza, and once he gets there, there might be another sign. If the gold is there to pick up, he'll do it.'

John said, 'We agreed to go back.'

'We *are* going back,' Tobie said. 'Do you want to carve your name?'

John looked up. The four arches, the end wall, every available space was covered with signatures. *Anselmus Adournes* and *Jo. Adournes, 1470* had been engraved for posterity on the second archway nearest the door, *Lambert Vander Walle* had found a space on the third, and *Pieter Reyphin van Vlaendren* had spread himself along the outside frame of the window. Adorne, of course, was now a Knight of St Catherine, and able to add wheels and swords to his collection of badges. John doubted if Nicholas was. He said, 'Beside all that? Do you fancy it? I've left my mark, if anyone cares, on the water-wheel.'

'I've left mine on the mountain,' said Tobie. 'Two long skid-marks in the shape of a cross.'

He fell silent. Nicholas de Fleury had said much the same, lightly. *I've left my soles on Mount Sinai.*

It was brutally true: he had walked down the mountain in blood. He had climbed it only hours after the racking seven-day race to steal a march on Adorne, and little more than a week after the cisterns in Cairo. And he had climbed it to meet the person whom – surely – he had once loved, and who had very possibly ordained both the suffering and the attempt on his life.

That night, neither Tobie nor John had tried to follow him up Mount Sinai. *Whatever was going to happen will already have happened*, the Patriarch of Antioch had said; and they had left him in prayer. Waiting, John had fallen asleep and then Tobie himself. It had been the Patriarch of Antioch who had risen from his knees when, just before Terce, Gelis van Borselen had walked down from the mountain and come to show him that she was back, and had neither caused harm, nor taken any.

She would have expected to hear, of course, that Nicholas had already returned. Perhaps she had already been told at the door that this was not the case. By the time that, disregarding all propriety, she flung open the door of their chamber, rousing John and Tobie from sleep, Ludovico da Bologna was already outside the monastery, harrying servants and saddling camels and a mule.

Standing cloaked and wild-faced in the doorway, the rosy buildings, the sunlit mountains blazing behind her, her man's hair stuck to her brow, her man's dress dishevelled and stained, Gelis van Borselen showed her race, and none of her femininity. She said, 'Where is he?'

Tobie sat up, and John stirred. The mattress beside them was empty. Tobie said, 'He went to meet you. He hasn't come back. What has happened?'

She said, 'Do you care?' and walked out. He scrambled after, half dressed, flinging on clothes. He caught her arm and she turned. She said, 'We met on the mountain, and he came down before me. He hasn't arrived. Go back to sleep: Father Ludovico will find him.'

Then, cursing, Tobie had pulled on the rest of his clothes and his boots, and with John had raced outside, where the Patriarch was already moving off. Gelis had made no effort to come. Looking back, Tobie saw she was standing outside the door, deep in shade, and surrounded, as in an ikon, by the archaic roundels and crosses cut in the wall against which her head rested. As he watched, she sank to the ground, her eyes on him.

She was still there when they came back with the litter. They had set off at speed. When the path at last became too precipitous, it was the Patriarch who had flung himself from his mount and, lifting his skirts, sprang aloft with great strides of his powerful legs, matted with hair thick as fir needles on the swell of his calves and his thighs. It was Ludovico da Bologna, too, who reached the three chapels first and sent the roar down the mountain that brought the servants hurrying up.

Sickened, Tobie and John had stumbled after, and caught the stretcher as it came down with Nicholas lying in it, unconscious. He had left the summit knowing, surely, that he could never walk down, and had found his way aside so that Gelis would pass. His feet were raw flesh, and his body less firm than the manna which hardens at night, and liquefies into dew in the sunshine.

A speck against the monastery door, Gelis rose to her feet as their cavalcade picked its way down from the slopes. The Patriarch gave a halloo to signify rescue, success. She waited until they arrived, and the servants had unshackled the litter and lowered it. Then she walked over. Tobie said, 'He will be all right.'

For a moment, as the pallet lay on the ground, Gelis van Borselen knelt, one hand on its edge, and studied her husband. The page's hair, tumbling over her cheekbones, revealed only the straight nose, the sweep of brown lashes, the mouth pulled small, with an effort that could be felt. Her fingers were white, but she did not uncramp them, or touch him.

She said something, very low. Then, as if too tired to move, she released her grip and, rising slowly, turned back and walked into the monastery.

Tobie stared after her. John said, 'Well, you're the doctor. You don't expect wives to soil their hands on sick husbands, do you? What did she say? It wasn't thank you for bringing him back, by any chance?'

'I don't know,' Tobie had said. But he did.

Wearily, sardonically, inexplicably, she had said, *Walk over with me.*

John had not climbed the mountain again. Tobie had. So had Adorne, with some pains, and for no reason but to offer homage to God at the portals of Heaven. About his faith, at least, Anselm Adorne was not cynical. Unlike Nicholas, who, whatever penalty he had paid, had used the place as a circus. Exasperated, Tobie had caught himself saying as much. He said, 'You don't have much reverence, do you?'

That had been after the descent from St Marina, when Nicholas had begun to revive and Gelis, impervious, had left. 'How do you know what happened?' Nicholas had said. 'Intercessory prayers; a solemn renewal of the nuptial pledge. The oil of pardon, the oil of prayer. For every woman who makes herself a man shall enter into the Kingdom of Heaven. We believe, we confess, we give glory.'

'Don't,' said Tobie.

'Eve,' continued Nicholas, 'should display a body like unto his, but of marvellous diversity. I do endorse that. By sexual intercourse the world had its beginning, and by continence, it will receive its end. There is something to be said for that, too.'

Tobie said, 'I'm not asking what happened. I told you.'

'I don't mind,' Nicholas said. 'Everybody comes down with something. Seven years of indulgences and seven quarantines, several times over. I get a bonus for St Marina.'

It came from fever and weakness, but it was time it was stopped. Tobie said, 'You make it sound paltry. If there is anything paltry on that mountain-top, Nicholas, by God you and she took it with you.'

'I expect we did,' Nicholas had said. 'And we brought it down again with us in sackfuls. And a couple of old tablets we found. Honour thy father and mother. They were cracked.'

'They are not cracked for Jan Adorne,' had said Tobie in sudden anger. 'He has not always enjoyed this journey, or his father's tongue, but he has taken care for him. He slept in a leaking skiff one whole night on the Nile, to give his father some rest. Does he write like a man full of spleen? *Tant que je vivrai –*'

'*Tant que je vive*,' Nicholas had contradicted. He had moved restlessly, the bitterness gone.

It had puzzled Tobie. 'Have you read it? Jan's tribute in his book to his father? "*Ipse ego dum vivam et post dura fata sepultus, Serviet officio spiritus ipse tuo.*" *Tant que je vivrai*, I'd have said, was the better –'

He broke off the argument, for Nicholas had simply continued to speak. Although the first words were the same, it was not a translation of Jan Adorne's work and it was not, of a certainty, the sentiments of a son to a father:

'*Tant que je vive, mon cueur ne changera ... Mon chois est fait, aultre ne se fera ...*'

Nicholas stopped.

'Where did that come from?' said Tobie. 'That isn't Jan's.'

'No. I don't know,' had said Nicholas. 'It came into my head. Setting aside our fathers and uncles, could we get on with my feet?'

It had been the end of that exchange. Whatever had transpired on the mountain, Tobie was told no more of it then. Nor did he ever find out, in that place hallowed of God, whether Adorne's reading was true and Nicholas had neither sought spiritual healing nor been able to find it. But whether or not they had left their mark on the mountain, it seemed to Tobie that none of them was likely to leave unmarked himself.

Chapter 44

KATELIJNE SERSANDERS never afterwards recalled much of her journey to Gaza, which occupied more than a week of her life.

She had come to Sinai. She had come through a land of drought and of the shadow of death; a land that no man passed through, and where no person dwelt. She understood the words of Jerome: 'To me the city is a prison, the wilderness is paradise.' She understood, but did not agree.

She remembered taking painful farewell of the Abbot and of the monks who had befriended her, and whom she felt she had deceived. She clung to Brother Lorenzo, who was coming with them. So, she learned, weeping, was Dr Tobias, who had rescued her once before from this limbo of weakness and confusion. John le Grant, whom she also knew and trusted, had come with him.

And, mysteriously, Nicholas de Fleury. The man with keys in his head, the horseman and swimmer of Leith, the singer, the owner of parrots and impresario of tournaments, of secret torments, of strange and terrible death in the snow. The man who could cause a princess to disappear, and laugh like a girl over a frog, and weep – so she had been told – at the feet of a wise man of another race, another religion. And weep and laugh for other causes as well, including near-death at the hand of a child. A man in whom she took a great interest.

She was ill, but not too ill to be gripped once again, as she was carried away, by the wonder of Sinai: by the stillness, the peace, the limitless silence. The awning swayed, and her eyes were drawn to the sky which hung, pellucid blue, from horizon to horizon; to the stacked, melting shapes of the mountains framing the tilting plain of Raha; the broad valley that led to the towering range of St Catherine; and then, as she lifted herself a little, to the sloping gulley of Wadi al Deir, the valley of the monastery she had left, whose walls were the incandescent face of Sinai and its opposite sisters, and where reposed – a dark pocket of green, a slip of red – the monastery of the Blessed St Catherine, to whom one brought one's griefs and from which one departed with nothing so facile as perfect health or perfect contentment, for a scream in such space was a whisper. From which one departed perhaps with an infinitesimal portion of wisdom, and some understanding.

She thought, from something Dr Tobias had said, that the desert north of Timbuktu must have provided something like that. She thought of her uncle and M. de Fleury. You could complain, if you were talking to God, that it was hard to win to such peace and then find it ruined by anger and bitterness. God, who had probably been to Pavia, would simply retort that had they all collided anywhere else they would have not only quarrelled but killed one another. She lay discussing the matter with God.

For many hours; for a day and the better part of the next, the stillness remained with them; the majesty, the silence, the space; and the tamarisk sweetened the air. Then they were among the steep defiles, the dusty mountains, and drawing their weapons at the sight of a file of small horses racing towards them, or giving soft answers to the snarling men from a Bedouin encampment, or wakening by night, tent and clothes sodden with dew, to hear the jackal packs howl, and wonder if the guides had abandoned them.

She slept, and woke, and slept, and tossed in her fever of unrest over Jan and Lambert and poor Meester Pieter and Father John, whom she ought not to dislike. She thought her uncle sat and spoke, and then saw it was Dr Tobias sitting beside her, opening her shirt with practical fingers; clearing the parasites; scouring the bites with fresh lemon; combing her hair; feeding her with bread dipped in warm milk. And that the man he was chatting to was M. de Fleury, sitting on her other side tearing salt meat and producing a solemn and studied rendering of the conversation of the three monks who cleaned the latrines while reciting their daily offices which caused even Brother Lorenzo to choke.

She laughed too, and sometimes cried. No one seemed to mind.

The sea at Gaza was blue, the date palms green, and the magical pass Nicholas carried brought him the finest rooms in the khan and the assiduous attention of the Emir and all his Mamelukes. He accepted it all as quite natural. Just at that time, he was like a man drunk on *kif*. For the sake of the girl, he made some effort to ensure that Adorne and his party of pilgrims were well housed and treated, although it was difficult. For two days, Tobie commuted between the two sets of lodgings. It was the second week in September, and Nicholas knew how to find what he wanted. Everything else would have to wait.

For a seigneur such as Nicholas de Fleury, advice in Gaza was there for the asking. Fishing vessels of many kinds plied between ports. Galleys and roundships abounded elsewhere, and passages could be bought for any destination my lord had in mind. There were maps, yes, of course. If my lord possessed a little silver, some coins, there were drawings to be found of all the islands, the coast, the land of the Grand Turks himself. My lord had only to ask.

The local agent, a Syrian, called the first morning, bringing packets from Damascus, and from Achille in Alexandria. All of them contained coded letters from Gregorio and Julius, duplicated to every factor on the African coast.

Nicholas handed them to John and to Tobie to read, gave the agent a number of fairly obvious instructions, and returned to what he was doing. John, as the Alexandria manager, read them through, made some notes, and then locked himself in a storeroom with Tobie. The place smelled of carobs. Tobie sneezed. John said, 'You've seen all the dispatches. I'm going to Alexandria. Now. If Nicholas doesn't follow, I'll have to leave there and go back to Venice.'

Tobie said, 'You should probably go.'

He looked profoundly uneasy. Amidst his own annoyance, John felt sympathy for him. He had never envied the other man the half-intimacy which had always existed between the doctor and Nicholas. He had seen how one could find oneself drawn into the complexities that lay beneath the composure. He said, 'I've heard the fairytale of the gold. Can't you tell me anything?'

Tobie said, 'Not much. Nicholas has something he has to do on one of the islands. After that, he'll probably come.' He scratched his nose and turned over a paper. 'These results are all right. The Bank isn't in trouble.'

'It isn't. But Nicholas specifically planned a short absence. He'll have been away for four months. And we were cut off in the Tyrol last winter.'

'Well,' said Tobie. 'He had the opportunity to exploit the Tyrol. Then Adorne threatened to usurp us in Cairo. And there was the chance of the gold.'

John said, 'I'm not disputing the reasons. Meeting his wife at Sinai was another. But look at all this. Scotland ought to have proper attention: that estate is built, and needs to be run. If he'd installed me as he promised, they'd have engineers by now, trained in simple irrigation and drainage at least. What's that expensive goldsmith up to? And how are they getting on in the Tyrol, with Moriz stuck in Venice because Nicholas isn't there? And what's worse, if they are managing to dig silver, what are they spending it on? If the Tyrol blows up in the Duke of Burgundy's face because of Nicholas, what will happen to Diniz in Bruges?' He paused and said, 'That bloody parrot,' in a voice he realised was fretful.

Tobie looked at him. He said, 'He would only come back here as soon as he could. Best get it over with.'

His guess was right, then. John said, 'Zacco. It has been Zacco behind it, all along?'

'I think,' said Tobie, 'that Zacco is the least of it. But yes, I think Nicholas has always known he was being coaxed, from point to point, towards Cyprus.' He broke off and said, 'He may not go, even yet. Not unless it coincides with his other reasons for being here. After what happened, would you go back to Cyprus?'

'I don't know,' said John le Grant. 'But whatever he's doing, you'd better go with him and sober him up. There is still a real world out here, even though he's forgotten it.'

No, he didn't envy Tobie.

By then, Katelijne Sersanders was beginning to feel herself once again. Sitting on her balcony, the sea sparkling below, she was surprised when Dr Tobias, on the second day, mentioned that John le Grant was departing to Alexandria alone. He also intimated that her uncle and Brother Lorenzo were anxious to speak to her.

They were admitted. Her uncle looked disturbed and unhappy; the Cretan was calm. She gathered – from Brother Lorenzo rather than from her uncle – that the scheme to send her to Crete was defunct. Since the disaster at Negroponte, the monks of St Catherine could neither send a vessel for her nor receive her. On the other hand, there was a convent of Clares in Nicosia on the island of Cyprus. Cyprus, birthplace of St Catherine.

Katelijne thought of Cyprus and St Catherine. Her mind travelled beyond St Catherine to Venus, who seemed preferable to what she knew of the Minotaur. Cyprus was on her uncle's itinerary for November. He could call for her when he had been to the Holy Land. It transpired that an important caravan was just about to leave for the Holy Land, and it was desirable that the Baron Cortachy should travel with it. And Jan, and Lambert, and the other two. And Brother Lorenzo.

Kathi said, 'So who would take me to Cyprus?'

'Why, Dr Tobias,' said her uncle quickly. 'Otherwise I should never have suggested it. Dr Tobias is also going to Cyprus. Until we come, he will look after you.'

Kathi gazed at him and he flushed. It was Brother Lorenzo who said in his collected, soft Tuscan, 'It seems that M. de Fleury has found occasion to travel to Cyprus and has commandeered a ship. Your uncle is concerned, but I have told him that he has a niece of good sense, who will take no harm. The Signor de Fleury has been asked not to trouble you, and Dr Tobias will remain with you until you are settled. What do you say?'

She agreed, in a subdued voice, and remained looking subdued until they left her.

When Nicholas de Fleury called to see her, as he did shortly after everyone else had departed, she treated him to the same forlorn gaze. She said, 'They've made you take me, I'm sorry. Because you can't leave me here.'

M. de Fleury said, 'No trouble at all, if you want it. You'd have to marry, and the going price is six hundred camels. But your Arabic's reasonable, and your uncle, I dare say, could afford them. On the other hand ...' The encounter ended with the kind of escalating nonsense she had got used to in the Garden of Balm.

Then he had thought his wife dead, and the levity at Matariya had all been inconsequential; a way to escape from what was too much to bear. Now, it seemed almost real. As if, despite the fatigue, the strange dimension he sometimes escaped to, he had been touched with hope, with something not far from elation. Or perhaps, as before, he was simply using the gift he had, which children also have, to push trouble away.

She saw Dr Tobias was anxious, and remembered the flat way in which M. le Grant had made his farewells. But then she had also seen how some men and women liked to claim him. She did not know why he was going to Cyprus except that it was for something, she saw, more important than gold. She only hoped, for his sake, that he found it.

The ship, when Nicholas and his party finally boarded her, was nothing out of the way: a rather battered small trader with some primitive cabins in the poop. The voyage was, however, usually short: only two or three days, and the girl was much better. Indeed, it was more comfortable than Nicholas had expected, there were so few other passengers.

His mind was not really clear. He was happy in a strange, detached way to do with the sea and the sunlight and the white sails curving above, and an island ahead which was still three-quarters unreal; an enchanted isle conjured up by the pendulum glinting, glinting over the maps through the night. This time, he wanted to be so very sure.

Below the happiness, of course, was the black well he had never thought to dip into again. Tobie had drunk from it already: he saw it all in his face, and then saw the girl watching them both, trying to fathom unaccountable moods.

In Ghent, in Bruges, a family of position would discuss the island of Cyprus, fortress and garden, torn between siblings: Carlotta its Queen, and James – Zacco – her illegitimate half-brother. Six years ago, Zacco had prevailed, wresting the crown from Carlotta, expelling the Genoese from Famagusta with the aid (yes, the Sersanders would know) of Nicholas vander Poele and his army; with the help of Astorre, and of John, and of Tobie. Of Diniz. Of Umar.

He had been well rewarded, for a time. He had been given or promised land, villas, estates, appointments. Given also, something even approaching deep friendship.

It had fallen apart, and he had left. When he lost his possessions, after that, it was no more than befell most of Zacco's beneficiaries. The island was becoming impoverished; the Mameluke Sultan at Cairo was greedier than before. In Cairo just now, Nicholas had encouraged him to be greedier still. In Naples, he had promoted a bold, a different marriage alliance that might seem, on the surface, only to the King's greater benefit. Nicholas was not the mortal enemy of Zacco, although some might think he had cause to be. There were, however, some scores to settle, which in a leisurely way he was doing. He had passed too much of his life playing the victim.

Anyone who knew about Cyprus would know some of that and, of course, recent events. How Venice, afraid to find the Turks entrenched on the island, had married Marco Corner's daughter to Zacco the young lion, helpless and raging to find himself torn between masters. However much Nicholas had made life difficult lately for Zacco, he did not expect Zacco to retaliate. Not unless he lost control more than usual. And that, too, Nicholas could deal with nowadays.

The rest of the matter of Cyprus only Tobie knew, of his present companions. He did not speak of it, and neither did Nicholas. Even when the island appeared, violet, green, scented, feathered with palm trees, no one remarked when their course took them to Famagusta. Most ships used the great harbour. The chapel of St

Catherine was nearby, and the lodge of the Knights Hospitaller, and the Convent of St Francis. It was right that present good should be allowed to drive out past tragedy.

Nicholas looked for the girl and found her in the bows, learning how to drop a bob line. She had, at least, changed into one of the gowns he had contrived for her in Gaza. It had the same failings as the doublet he wore: she looked like a Chinaman going to Mecca. She looked cheerful.

His thoughts drifted again, and he put himself out of the way and watched the island coming closer. The landing didn't concern him: he had no goods to declare; no employment to seek. He knew where to find suitable lodgings; the pendulum would tell him, to an inch, where to go next. And then, quickly, he would leave.

Afterwards, sane, he wondered how he could ever have been so naïve.

Tobie, who was frightened, had tried to prepare the girl a little, since Nicholas seemed to be on another planet. He couldn't believe, yet, that he was on a ship sailing into this harbour with Nicholas, who had never felt moved to talk about what had happened six years ago at Famagusta, or what had happened at the fort of St Hilarion, where his brilliant attack on an enemy had turned to desperate tragedy. As his attacks so often did.

Of course, there had been lighter moments. Tobie had described some of them to the girl. The Arthurian joust, for example, with himself as the Loathly Damsel and John le Grant as the Lion, and Nicholas in two yellow plaits got up as Guinevere. And then he had come to a halt, remembering how it had ended, with the death of Lucia's husband. Lucia, whose own death Katelijne had seen.

He had talked, a little, of the siege of Famagusta, and the last starving days of the city, but had not explained that Nicholas had shared in that agony, or that this was where the mother of Henry had died. Kathi did not even know that Katelina and Nicholas had been lovers.

He had hinted at the youth and beauty of Zacco, but had said nothing else. He knew that she sensed something imminent of more importance to Nicholas than the acquisition of gold. She had no way of knowing that he had come for his son. He didn't realise that, thinking of Zacco, she would draw other conclusions or that she, too, was grieved, and not only at the prospect of two months in a convent of the Clares.

She had been silent on the voyage; watching M. de Fleury;

sympathising with whatever dilemma was producing all the hurried anecdotes of Dr Tobias. She knew, in the part of her mind that her tutors admired, that Cyprus was a vast, fertile island in the eastern part of the Middle Sea; and that Venus had been born there a long time before St Catherine, and that Cleopatra, who had lived in Alexandria without meeting St Catherine, had been presented with Cyprus by her lover Mark Antony.

She saw Dr Tobias was afraid, and that there was therefore no point in mentioning that she personally was panic-stricken. And that someone had to do something about M. de Fleury.

She stood grasping the rail as the vessel bucked its way into the harbour at Famagusta, seeing nothing but a large crowded port smelling of fish, tar, weed, wood smoke and hot cooking-oil. It did not seem to her odd that the trader, instead of waiting for guidance, dropped its sails and rowed in a busy way past all the other vessels swinging at anchor until it reached a spot immediately under the city's sea-gate, where it lodged.

On the quay before the sea-gate was a carpet, upon which stood a man in elaborate half-armour, flanked by two files of soldiers. One of them held the Lusignan banner, the crimson lion and the Cross of Jerusalem, which also flowed from the walls of the city and from the building she took to be the Citadel. A skiff put off, to the sound of trumpets. A skiff painted in red and gold.

She saw M. de Fleury look round. The master of their little vessel was suddenly nowhere to be seen. The skiff arrived, and M. de Fleury walked down the steps and crossed to the ladder. Then he came back to Dr Tobias.

'The Royal Bailie is waiting to welcome us. We are to go to the Archbishop's Palace. Leave the boxes. Servants will bring them.'

'We were expected?' said Dr Tobias.

'We were brought,' said M. de Fleury.

Of course, he was right. From the moment they stepped foot on Cyprus, it was obvious that everything had been planned: the day and night in Famagusta, with its luxurious lodging and deferential ceremony. Then the journey of over thirty miles to the King's capital, performed with every attention to the rigours of the late summer heat, the requirements for rest, shade, delicious refreshments.

Veteran of seven months of travelling, of the angularities of the journey to Rome; of the discords of Alexandria and Cairo; of the miseries of the wilderness, Katelijne blamed her recent weakness for the loathing which Famagusta instilled.

She was used to ceremony. She was not vain: the glorious silks of Damascus, swiftly sewn into robes, veils, chemises, were grand enough for her standing; as they provided suitable coats and doublets for the two men, who were treated like princes.

Her sense of terror came from the two men: from the doctor, who walked through his part stony-faced; talking, bowing; conversing. And from M. de Fleury, who behaved at the beginning like the man in black at Leith strand, amused, urbane, wholly detached from reality. Because, to begin with, he was dealing with strangers.

Then, later, he was not. Entering the Palace, he stopped when a monk, gliding forward, clasped his hands. At the banquet, which their deprived interiors could barely enjoy, a nursing brother of the Order of St John had stepped forward and holding his arms, had embraced him. When he was entertained at the Citadel the following day, a woman had broken from the small crowd at the door and, kneeling, had kissed his feet. She had had a child at her side.

He had knelt and raised her, and spoken to her for a little, before the procession moved on. Beside her, Katelijne could hear Dr Tobias swearing in various languages he thought she didn't know. When they caught up with M. de Fleury, he smiled at her as he usually did, but only glanced for a moment at Dr Tobias.

Later, setting out for Nicosia, she heard Dr Tobias say, 'Don't go, Nicholas. Unless you know it is there.'

And M. de Fleury said, 'Do you think, by any chance, that I haven't already refused?'

'And?' said Dr Tobias.

'Look out of the window,' he had answered. But she knew already what he meant. Since they landed, they had been guarded. And watched. And surrounded.

She had tried to question Dr Tobias. He had been soothing. 'You know monarchs. They like their own way. And the convent of the Clares is in Nicosia. They were very good – they are very good. Of course, we want to see you settled and happy, and ready for your uncle to come in November.'

Then they entered Nicosia and instead of being taken to the Clares, she found herself in the women's quarters of a magnificent villa, with maidservants and a page to look after her. Tired from the journey, she had still gazed upon it with some respect as the cavalcade came to a rest at its gates.

Neither of the men looked overwhelmed, or at least, not with gratitude. Dr Tobias indeed had exclaimed something aloud, although not in French. '*The bastard!*'

'Well, he is,' had said M. de Fleury. And observing her face, had

added, 'We lived here once before. The King wishes us to stay as
his guests. We are to attend him at the Palace tomorrow.'

'Katelijne as well?' the doctor had said.

'Yes,' said M. de Fleury. And again, had turned aside from any
possible questioning.

They were sent robes. This, she discovered, was usual. One had
to become accustomed to the mingling of the Byzantine with the
French with the Venetian. The one for M. de Fleury fitted exactly.
They cut a cubit off hers and had it hemmed before she was up,
wakened by an acrimonious exchange in French the import of
which she did not then understand. Then the official escort arrived
and, embedded in prancing horses and plumes, they went to the
Palace.

The building was grander than the royal apartments at Holyrood
but not as grand as the Princenhof in Bruges, or what she had
heard of the Sultan's apartments in Cairo. There was a lot of
marble, because of the hot weather. Otherwise, its style was vaguely
French, with some Milanese painted furniture. The Palace was less
gripping than the man who lived in it.

Most of the men about him wore Western court dress: doublets
and jackets in light silks because of the heat; small hats; fine jewels.
Many were dark-skinned, perhaps Spanish or Sicilian; and a fair
number – the marshal, the admiral, the chamberlain, she later
learned – made their bows as if they knew M. de Fleury and the
doctor very well. The King's mother, Marietta of Patras, wasn't
present. That is, you would notice someone lacking a nose.

The man on the throne was all Dr Tobias had told her except
that he was not young: she guessed him to be near the end of his
twenties, like M. de Fleury. He was tall, too; and held himself as
freely, beneath the rich clothes. His hair was loose and waving and
brown, and his face was lean and amused. He stood as the announce-
ments were made, and she dropped into a well-practised salute,
and Dr Tobias and M. de Fleury advanced and bowed. Then M.
de Fleury walked forwards and knelt.

That was in order. Now he would have presented his credentials,
except that he had none, not having sought this encounter. Nor
would an envoy have lifted his chin after kneeling and dared to
look the monarch straight in the eyes.

James stood, holding the gaze. Then he laughed and, stepping
down, crossed the space between them, touching M. de Fleury
lightly on the shoulder as he passed to stand, in a waft of jasmine,
before Katelijne herself. She dropped into a still lower curtsey and
he stepped back saying, half smiling, half impatient, 'No, no. Let

me see.' And studying her, continued over his shoulder, 'She is very small, mon compère, but very well. Well enough. How old?'

He was addressing her. 'Nearly seventeen, roi monseigneur,' she said.

'Sixteen. The age of young Diniz when he stayed with you. The age of my wife. You know I am married?'

He had turned back to M. de Fleury. M. de Fleury said, 'I had heard, my lord King.'

'Something told me,' said Zacco of Cyprus, 'that you had heard. Would you not be better standing? Have you nothing to give me?'

M. de Fleury stood. He said, 'My lord, I had not expected this honour.'

'But you do not object?" said King James. His face and that of his guest were as bland as the occasion demanded. Physically, it was different. They stood facing one another, Katelijne fancied, like two heraldic animals at once opposed and supporting; violence only an inch away.

M. de Fleury said, 'There are compensations.'

Beside her, Dr Tobias drew in his breath. James of Cyprus said, 'I hope so. You knelt. But I would give you the kiss of a friend.' And laying a long-fingered hand on the other's shoulder, he leaned forward and kissed him on the cheek. 'There,' he said, stepping back slowly. 'You see. You had something to give me, after all.'

Dr Tobias stirred. M. de Fleury said, 'Monseigneur, I am glad. I only hope that the King thinks it sufficient.'

They were not speaking loudly, but the very silence in the room added to the weight, it seemed, of every breath that they took. For a moment nothing was said. Then the King smiled. 'I had forgotten your style. Other men, who love you less, might be offended. Today, of course, you are surrounded by lovers. Come. Meet them all. Take wine. Listen to my musicians. Later, refreshed, you and I will open our hearts, and it will seem as if the years between had never existed. Yes, my Nikko?'

She was already tired, and the hours that followed were a labour, although in normal times she would have fallen ravening upon the feast spread before her of opposing personalities, of conflict, of emotion. Some sense of it came to her, and an appreciation, too, of the etiquette, part Byzantine, part Savoyard, which regulated the conduct of both sexes, and ensured that she was placed in the keeping of women of birth who spoke Italianate French and saw to her comfort.

She had forgotten the reference to music. The strains at first hardly reached her over the chatter; then she realised what she was hearing and sought Dr Tobias who turned aside, looking distracted, but was unable to help. 'Ask Nicholas. There were no musicians that I remember in our time. The Cathedral plainsong, of course.'

The chamberlain, a Sicilian, was more forthcoming. 'The taste for French music? It dates from the days of my lord's grandsire: much of it was composed here. Lately, my lord has thought to renew it.'

'He has found good singers,' said Katelijne. She saw that, at last, Tobie had thought to look for M. de Fleury. She wondered why James of Cyprus, uninterested in music six years ago, had elected to introduce it tonight. But of course, he was in touch with the Venetian court. He was married to Catherine Corner, even though he had never met her. And M. de Fleury, she remembered, knew Fiorenza of Naxos, Catherine's mother.

The strings wove their pattern; the voices twined; conversation gave way to some attention as courtiers took their ease on stools and cushions to listen, sipping wine, talking in murmurs. Dr Tobias, returning from somewhere, found a cushioned surface beside her and sat down. The ballads were gallant rather than explicit, but they varied little in theme:

> *Je prens d'Amour noriture*
> *Nete et pure*
> *Et doucement norissant;*
> *Pour quoi doi bien estre amant*
> *Jusqu'a tant*
> *Qu'en mon cors la vie dure.*

> I take my nourishment from love
> Sublime and pure;
> So lover must I stay so long
> As life endure.

Katelijne said, 'Did you find him?' She concealed the impatience she felt. She could always find M. de Fleury if she tried. Of course, it took time and energy.

'Nicholas?' said Dr Tobias. 'No. I'll take you home soon.'

'Why?' she said. 'Did he ask you? Where is he?'

'I don't know,' said Dr Tobias. 'He and the King have both gone.'

Chapter 45

THE GRAND VILLA they took him to was one he knew: it was Venetian. For a moment, arriving there with his heavy escort in the dark, Nicholas imagined he was going to see the husbands of the two princesses of Naxos, and thought it might be quite amusing, with Zacco at his side. Then he realised that another member of the Corner family would be occupying it now.

The King, cloaked beside him, said, 'You forgive me, Nikko, for stealing you from your little girl and my music?' His tone was playfully insulting. He had his Sicilian chamberlain and a Florentine agent with him.

'Not yet, my lord,' Nicholas said. The heavy wooden gates opened on gardens: it was an ancient palace. A fountain played, giving him a moment's unease. They were, of course, expected. His visit had been planned from the beginning, like his other arrivals in Cyprus; and by the same people, or some of them.

He had been restrained every step of the way and further hampered by the presence of the girl: on the initiative of Brother Lorenzo, he assumed; that powerful monk of St Catherine's who would know Ludovico da Bologna so very well. The bones of the scheme had been apparent to anyone of intelligence long before, and Nicholas could have no complaint: for various reasons he had allowed it to happen. So long as it led him where he wanted to go.

A well-dressed man emerged from the light of the villa and bowed, his steward behind him. The King called, 'Ah, mon père.' And to Nicholas: 'You know Andrea Corner, Marco's brother? To him, more than anyone, I owe my present nuptial bliss. Come.' And he dismounted by the lanterns in a billow of silk, his smile angelic. Just before leaving, Nicholas guessed, he had started to drink. Perhaps because Nicholas had done the same.

It was unlikely that Andrea Corner would notice. He made the
King a full and practised salute and turning to Nicholas, greeted
him in the flattering style of an equal. He was, of course, a rich
man; or had become so since crossing to the King's side from that
of his sister. He had chosen to speak French, Nicholas observed,
although Zacco knew Latin and could make himself understood, if
he felt like it, in the argot of the Venetian Arsenal. When he liked,
his tongue could rake like his leopards.

Now, of course, he was older. They both were. They were each
watching and weighing the other, to see what experience might
have added, or dimmed. Zacco took the stairs with the muscular
drive of an animal and stood at the top to be admired, his lip
curling. Nicholas suddenly smiled in return. So let battle com-
mence.

The great salon on the first floor was not large, but a dozen
could sit there in comfort, and seven were already there, standing
as the King entered. One of them was the Patriarch of Antioch.
Next to him, surely, was the new Venetian Bailie, the brother of
Paul Erizzo, the dead hero of Negroponte. And next to him, rising
from cushions, was a group of robed men whose leader, stepping
forward, Nicholas knew from an encounter in Florence, a decade
ago. Hadji Mehmet, senior ambassador of the lord Uzum Hasan,
ruler of Persia.

A delegation to the King of Cyprus from the third greatest
Muslim prince in the world. No. Correction. A delegation, not yet
official, not yet recorded, to assess the consequences of the Turkish
conquest of Negroponte, and to discuss an alliance against the
Sultan of Turkey between the powers whose interests were
represented here. A league of defence. A league of offence was not
out of the question.

He wondered, as the introductions were made, who represented
the Sultan at Cairo. He wondered who represented the Knights of
St John and the other Italian states. He wondered what in detail
they wanted of him: his ships, his army, his debtors, his wealth. He
understood absolutely what Ludovico da Bologna had done to
bring him here and why. And he thought, with a lift of the heart
that turned him dizzy, that this time he would get what he wanted.
They could not afford to deny him.

He shook hands with the others but embraced Hadji Mehmet,
dredging up the kind of Arabic he had forgotten and seeing his
pleasure reflected in the other man's face. Ten years ago, after the
fall of Constantinople, Ludovico da Bologna had come to the West
trailing a delegation like this, begging for troops and for money.

Since then, Nicholas – and John in his absence – had cultivated the agents of Uzum Hasan, and had exchanged artisans and letters. It was one of the reasons why Venice was lenient with Nicholas. It occurred to Nicholas that he himself might be held to represent the Sultan of Cairo.

Then the King had made his way to the single chair and seated himself, and the business began.

It lasted three hours and packed into that period, allowing for the requirements of diplomacy, as much as a group of able men might manage in the way of presentation of facts, of argument and counter-argument, of ideas, and of conclusions. As issues became revealed, so did personalities.

Zacco, to whom they nominally deferred, declared his position in an odd combination of boredom and vehemence. He reminded them of the danger that Cyprus might be taken, for example, by the duchy of Milan, and planted with Genoese. He reminded them that he, the King, had sent men and ships to the coast of Turkey. If he weakened himself any further, the Turk might conquer his island – a far deadlier master than Cairo. The Sultan would deny Venice trade and ruin him by imposing impossible dues. As it was, unless the Sultan of Cairo reduced his demand – five thousand, eight thousand, at one time sixteen thousand ducats a year – he, the King, could not even afford to repair his forts, never mind pay for troops and cannon.

Having said what he came to say, he seemed in no mind to repeat it; but if the argument ran in another direction, he showed impatience and, towards the end, even some violence. His chamberlain, murmuring, sometimes restrained him. The Florentine agent Squarcialupi reported a rumour from Italy: the Pope planned to summon Italian princes to Rome to pledge money and troops against the Ottoman army. The outcome of such a meeting must, of course, affect all those in the path of these dogs.

The proposed Italian league, Nicholas noticed, was not new to Ludovico da Bologna, or to the envoys of Uzum Hasan. Any non-Christian alliance, naturally, would have to be sanctioned by the Pope. Long practised in foreign petitioning, the Latin Patriarch and the Turcoman lord were the most rewarding, perhaps, to hear and to watch. In many ways, it was the Patriarch, below the impossible barrage of outbursts, rebukes, contradictions and disclaimers, who was leading the meeting. And Andrea Corner was his ally, not only for Venice, but for the Knights of St John, the fighting Order which battled the Turks from their island of Rhodes.

There was a castle of theirs in the south of Cyprus. 'What does the Grand Commander of Kolossi have to say?' Nicholas said. He doubted if there was one. They had promoted the last one, John Langstrother, to head the Order in England and Scotland, where the man came into favour every time the Lancastrian King was in power and out of favour every time it was York.

Like Anselm Adorne. And like Adorne, the Order favoured the Genoese. And was disliked by the Sultan of Cairo. And was tolerated, you might say, by Venice ... He knew his face was perfectly bland.

Andrea Corner said, 'What can I say of this great nursing Order, this bulwark against the Ottoman Turk? Except that, being of many nations, its voice is divided. You know, Ser Niccolò, of the prejudices of the man who has served in Kolossi, in Scotland, and in Bruges as John of Kinloch. You know, more seriously, of Anselm Adorne, Baron Cortachy, who has tried to imprint the Genoese point of view upon the Sultan of Cairo; whose itinerary is to embrace, we are told, this island of Cyprus, and that of Rhodes; and who will no doubt pause at Chios and Lesbos before travelling home by who knows what route. He plans to go to Naples.'

'On pilgrimage?' Nicholas said.

'Adherents of the Knights of St John have every right, we suppose, to consider themselves to be pilgrims,' Corner said. 'But in this instance, the clarion call for aid may be confused if men hold back, thinking they must be supporting either Venice or Genoa. There is no doubt which can summon most aid against the Turk. The Order has the men and the will to support them most ably. Properly guided, they will fling their might, as King James has already done, to support the emirs of the Anatolian coast against Turkish attack: they will guard the seas against onslaughts on Crete or on Cyprus.'

'I trust then,' said Nicholas, 'that the lord Hadji Mehmet and his companions intend to speak to the Knights at Rhodes and to the magnates of the West before such a confusion of interests occurs?'

'We leave for Rhodes in two days,' said Mehmet. 'We shall be in Venice in a matter of weeks.' In public he used his native language and an interpreter although, as Nicholas knew, he spoke both French and Greek. He added, 'If the Knights cannot help us, however, we may be unable to follow the good advice of Ser Andrea. We may be obliged to wait for the Baron Cortachy and sue for help from the Genoese of the Order.'

Zacco said, 'What do you mean? The Knights will help you.'

Corner cleared his throat. 'Monseigneur, you have heard what the lord Uzum Hasan requires. Ships, cannon, hackbuts, metal-workers, gunnery officers – the Order can provide little of that.'

'They have money!' said Zacco.

'Well,' said Ludovico da Bologna. Suddenly, below his ceremonial clothes, Nicholas felt his skin tighten. He kept his breath even.

'Or if not, Venice has?' Zacco had decided to sneer.

Andrea Corner said, 'Venice has artillery, or her merchants, like Ser Niccolò here, could provide it. But all her present weapons and money are already committed to war. Venice has been fighting unaided for Christendom for too long already. Only Rhodes has some access to gold, were she permitted to employ it.'

It was so neat, so lethal, so exquisite that there was never any doubt but that he would rise to it. 'To how much gold?' Nicholas said.

'Over four hundred pounds. If they are permitted to keep it.'

'You surprise me,' said Nicholas. 'It must amount to something like three mule-loads. The ownership is uncertain?'

'I shouldn't say so,' said Ludovico da Bologna. 'Morally, it belongs to the Knights. Without it, they could never afford to buy what they need from Venice to arm Uzum. Weapons. The use of an army. Ships. Silver and timber.'

'Timber?' said Nicholas.

'Egypt needs it. They used to get it from the Karamanid Emirate on the Anatolian coast. There are some concessions on the Venetian border which have been in dispute with the Tyrol. The same with the silver. But of course,' said Andrea Corner, 'there would be no question of legal processes now. And Cairo would be strengthened in their resolve to help Venice and Cyprus. What does Ser Niccolò feel?'

Laughter welled, but he knew better than show it. Beneath all the formality, he was being told that the thieves of his African gold were the Order of the Knights of St John, captors of the *Ghost*, and, no doubt, of Ochoa de Marchena. From there, step by step, it all followed. And now, with supreme and brilliant insolence, he was being offered compensation. Don't fuss, and we shall use it to pay you for your excellent services.

If he agreed, he would have no gold to offer to Gelis.

He could find the child without gold.

He said, 'I am not sure that I am interested. It would depend on what men and supplies I should be required to provide, and on what precise terms.'

Ludovico da Bologna said, 'Particular, aren't you? So are we. We'd expect you to go with Hadji Mehmet to Rhodes for their views. Then we'd all know after the Papal meeting at Rome what the Italian states are doing. By the time Mehmet here comes to Venice you should have worked out your figures and we'll all know the answers.'

'I should be the sole dealer?' said Nicholas.

'If you want to be,' Corner said.

'And if I decide to refuse?'

'Someone else gets the business,' said the Patriarch. 'And you get nothing at all, or, if you prefer, a lot of expensive litigation. You don't need to decide now, tomorrow will do. The Order is sending a galley.'

'I hope you will come,' said Hadji Mehmet in Arabic. 'Come to Rhodes. Then meet us in Venice. You will not regret it.'

He was smiling. Nicholas said, 'Never ask an innkeeper the way.'

'Of course. But it will benefit yourself as well.'

'Perhaps. I hope I shall be able to accept by tomorrow,' Nicholas said, just loud enough to be heard by the Patriarch, who was not unconversant with that language.

The door had opened and servants were bringing trays of pastries and Candian wine. He seemed to remember that Corner was paid in sugar and wine: it was not the thick, sweet Commanderie wine of the Knights, whatever his new fondness for the Order. He wondered if the meeting were formally over, and decided that it probably was. He said to the Patriarch, 'Are there still some Greek bishops in Cyprus?'

After barely one bite, the Patriarch seemed clothed in sugary hair. 'Four,' he said. 'And the Church of St Sabas, over at Karoni in Paphos. And the Karpass, up in the north-east. The Bishop of Famagusta has his home in the Karpass. Beside the monastery.'

'The monastery?' Nicholas said. Someone had refilled his cup, but exhilaration still won over tiredness. Zacco was lying back, staring at him.

'The one you're thinking of. The monastery of the monks of St Catherine's of Sinai. A couple of cabins in the Karpass, since your day.'

'Brother Lorenzo must go there occasionally,' Nicholas said. 'Who else do you know? Father Moriz?'

'Everyone knows Father Moriz. I'm going to take the Turcomans home. Can you hold off getting drunk till I call on you?'

'Nikko?' said the King's voice.

'I don't know,' Nicholas said. 'Call on me and try. How do you get on with my wife?'

'Ah,' said Ludovico da Bologna. 'You'd need to be sober to hear that.'

'Caro,' said the King; and this time he was standing beside him, his cloak over one shoulder. 'We are riding back.'

The King, at least, had decided that the meeting was over. Everyone stood. Farewells were said. Outside, the fountain played and the horses, their escort, were waiting. The Florentine agent had stayed behind and only the chamberlain Rizzo di Marino rode silently at the King's other side. The King said, 'If you loved me, you would kill him.'

It was not clear whom he meant, or even to whom he was speaking. Then the Sicilian said, 'You know it is impossible.'

The King turned to Nicholas. 'When Charlotte died, I stripped him of everything. Everything.'

'I am sorry,' Nicholas said. Now he knew. Careless father, perpetual lover, Zacco adored his natural children. Charlotte, aged six, had been promised to Sor de Naves, his Constable, as a bribe, and had died at twelve, the previous year, on the verge of her marriage. She had been the eldest of his illegitimate children and, of course, he had none yet by Catherine Corner, to whom he had not yet been introduced.

Nicholas said, 'You blame Andrea Corner?'

'Oh yes. He poisoned her. I stripped him of all his possessions. But I had to give them back,' Zacco said. 'I owe him too much money. You don't wear the Order I gave you?'

'I couldn't take it to Sinai,' said Nicholas.

'And you are married to a van Borselen? My grandfather married a Charlotte de Bourbon. We are related,' said Zacco and laughed. 'Are you not glad that I – ?'

'No,' said Nicholas. They had come to the gates of the palace.

'She was barren,' said Zacco. 'Your wife. And dead, of course, now. We are here. Come in.'

'Forgive me, roi seigneur,' Nicholas said.

His arm was gripped. 'No. That I will not,' said Zacco. 'Unless you are afraid?'

'No, roi seigneur,' Nicholas said.

'Because you are cleaning Andrea Corner's boots with your tongue? You know that he sends every month to know why I am not receiving my bride?'

'He is afraid you will marry King Ferrante's daughter,' Nicholas said.

'Monseigneur,' said Rizzo di Marino, and laid a hand on his reins.

The King continued studying Nicholas. 'You know a lot, don't you? Or you think that you do. I was told that you called at Naples on your way to Alexandria and were kind enough to discuss my marriage with Lorenzo Strozzi.'

'I wanted you to go ahead with it,' Nicholas said. 'And place yourself in bad odour with Venice. Did you think I wished you a trouble-free life?'

'She was a prostitute!' Zacco said.

The name of Primaflora had not been mentioned, and he didn't propose to mention it now. He said, 'My lord, I have to go.'

'No. I want to talk. Bring him,' said Zacco. Di Marino tightened his grip, then released the King's reins. The escort moved close.

Nicholas said, 'My lord, I have a journey to make, and it is late.'

'An excuse. What journey?' said Zacco. 'It is night.'

He had been going to lie. Instead, he said, 'I have to ride to Famagusta on an errand. It is so that I can decide on my answer tomorrow.'

The lustrous eyes studied his without changing. Whoever knew that particular secret, it was not Zacco. Nicholas found he was very glad. Then Zacco said, 'It is more than thirty miles. On that horse?'

It was a hired one; well enough. He had begun to explain, but was stopped. The King said, 'You will take one of mine. Or something else. I remember you once had a racing-camel.'

'It will be barren,' Nicholas said. For a moment the King looked at him; then dismounting, he threw back the reins and walked off, without looking behind, over the courtyard. The chamberlain glanced at him, and then followed. The escort waited, then scattered. Nicholas watched for a moment, then moved. Before he had turned to the road, a groom was at his side, calling.

With him was the horse which Zacco had been riding, still saddled, with the red Lusignan lion on its horse-cloth. 'My lord says,' said the groom, 'that this will be sufficient to gain you entry to Famagusta, should the gates be shut when you arrive.'

He looked at it; then, dismounting slowly, took the velvet reins and laid his hand on the horse's white neck. The groom said, 'What of your own, my lord? I am to ride it home for you, or stable it.'

He didn't want questions. He said, 'Stable it. I shall send for it tomorrow,' and gave the man a piece of silver once he was mounted. There were lanterns hung among the lemon trees. Outside Nicosia the grape harvest had begun: it would be the fig festival soon. Riding from Nicosia in the past, the road to the south was the one he had been used to: the road that lifted over the hill and wound down to the sea and to Kouklia, and his estate; and the shrine of Paphian Venus.

It was warm. The sky, sprigged with stars, had none of the clear, open quality of Sinai, even at night. Two hours before dawn, the star of St Catherine, of Venus, would hang to the east and south of the monastery. It was the same sky: it would shine upon Cyprus as well. The Bride of Christ, the pagan goddess, born both in one isle.

He it is who appointed for you the stars, that you may be guided by them in darkness on land and on sea.

A hatchery of chicks is ready and will be emptied tomorrow.

He was not tired, but clear and empty, like the air over Sinai.

At first, when Nicholas didn't return, Tobie tried to get the girl to retire and then, failing, settled down with her to wait for an hour. After that, she seemed to agree that it would be better to sleep, taking her reassurance probably from his manifest state of annoyance. She was actually asleep, he thought, when the hammering came to the door and the porter led in Ludovico da Bologna, under the delusion that he was about to discuss something with Nicholas.

The idea that Nicholas was not in the house was not one he readily entertained. Striding here and there, flinging doors open, he wakened not only the household but Katelijne, who sat up and gazed at him in astonishment. 'So where is he?' demanded the Patriarch.

'With King Zacco, I should imagine,' she returned crossly; moving Tobie to a mixture of admiration and alarm. The Patriarch grunted and withdrew.

In the chamber, 'Is he?' he said.

'How should I know?' said Tobie. 'I haven't seen him since we were all at the Palace. What are you doing here?'

'Sometime,' said Ludovico da Bologna, 'I'll tell you, when you've managed to get that man under control.'

'I'm only his doctor,' said Tobie. 'If you're talking about spiritual health, maybe you should begin with his wife. She's here, is she? On Cyprus?'

'God save us, of course not,' said the Patriarch of Antioch tartly, and banged the door shut.

It opened again almost immediately and Katelijne came in, wearing a sheet. 'Who was that?'

'Haven't you got a bedgown yet? It's all right, he's a priest. Ludovico da Bologna, the –'

She sat down. 'The man who came to the monastery. We heard. He brought the lady Gelis to see M. de Fleury and then took her away. Will he go to the Palace and make trouble?'

'I think,' said Tobie, 'that even the Latin Patriarch of Antioch would hesitate before doing that.'

'But he wouldn't say why he was here. Would he go to the King's mother?'

'You were listening,' said Tobie accusingly. He regulated his thoughts. 'The King's mother isn't here.'

'Yes, she is. She sent her ladies to look after me at the Palace. I didn't know that Henry's mother died in Famagusta. The lady Gelis's sister.'

He had no trouble concentrating now. He said, 'She was caught in Famagusta while the siege was on, and was injured by the King's cannon.'

'By M. de Fleury's cannon,' she said. 'Or so they said. He and M. le Grant directed the siege.'

Cropnose. What was the King's mother playing at? Tobie said, 'They ended it as well, at some danger to themselves. Nicholas was captured, and spent the last days nursing the starving. Nursing Gelis's sister until she died.'

'And Diniz. Diniz had been caught in Famagusta as well?' the girl said. She had been told the whole story, he could tell.

Tobie got up and said, 'Well, if we are not going to sleep, we might as well make ourselves cool.' The water was fresh, and he mixed it with fruit juice and brought two goblets over. He sat down beside her. 'The King's mother has a great deal to do with her son's life. She knows Nicholas, and her ladies were probably sent to tell you what they did. Do you understand?'

'I suppose,' said Kathi, 'that that is a compliment. So Diniz didn't think M. de Fleury was responsible for his aunt's death?'

'Ask him when you get home,' Tobie said. 'He will tell you he made some mistakes when he was here. He fought Nicholas, and wounded him, too. As badly as Nicholas wounded your uncle. That was a misunderstanding as well.'

'But Diniz and he are friends now,' Katelijne said.

Tobie said nothing. He could see no grounds for friendship between Nicholas and her uncle. Nor could he point out that between

Diniz and Nicholas there was a kinship of marriage, and perhaps even of blood.

The girl said, 'Where is she buried?' When he looked startled she repeated impatiently. 'Katelina van Borselen. Was she brought home and buried at Veere? Or at Kilmirren with her husband's family?' She had a picture, perhaps, of Henry visiting his mother's grave.

Tobie said, 'She died during the siege, so her funeral Mass was in Famagusta. She left a letter asking to remain there.'

'Where?' said the girl. She was frowning.

'You were there,' Tobie said. 'The Cathedral next to the Archbishop's Palace.' He had stepped into it briefly himself. He had known where to look, but there were no coffins visible now in the aisles. He remembered the building during the siege. It was immense: golden and Gothic like Rheims: built for the coronation of Lusignan monarchs. The Cathedral of St Nicholas.

He waited for her to name it, but she didn't. If she had noticed, Nicholas had only entered the central door for a moment and stood, looking in. Tobie wondered what else the old bitch had got her women to tell her. About St Hilarion, for instance. Naphtha and poison. And the truth about Tzani-bey al-Ablak.

He sat with her for a bit, sipping his drink; half expecting the door to open and Nicholas to come in, perhaps with the Patriarch with him, bickering expertly. After some time, it became apparent that she had been told nothing more, and that she now understood that she would learn no more from him. Her lids had started to droop.

It was a surprise therefore when she opened them and said, 'Why does nobody stay with him?'

His own head had started to nod. He lifted it. 'Who?'

'M. de Fleury. You went off to be a camp doctor. Master Julius stays for a time, Master Gregorio stays for a time. The same with M. le Grant, Master Crackbene.'

Tobie sat up. 'We must get some sleep. You ought to look at other companies. They switch their people about, to learn skills and use their experience. It isn't a bad thing to let people go now and then, and get them back with more to offer.'

'Tommaso Portinari's been in Bruges since he was twelve,' said Katelijne Sersanders. 'The Medici family all live in one district in Florence. Can't you keep up, or doesn't he want you, or don't you want him? I heard the Patriarch.'

Tobie tried to remember what the Patriarch had been saying. Something about failing to get Nicholas under control. One could see the problem: it was nearly dawn now. On the other hand, he didn't see why he should be blamed. He said, 'I don't think, Kathi, he'd take kindly to ephors. It probably works best as it is. We all take a share, and he doesn't get tired of us, and vice versa.'

She didn't reply. He said, 'You don't agree?'

'No,' she said. 'But there isn't much point in saying so. I'm sure it's what he thinks he wants, and maybe you think he wants. But this way, who will ever get to know him?'

'I don't know if I want to,' said Tobie. He didn't know what made him say it, except that he was tired.

'I know you don't. None of you do,' said Katelijne. 'Because you're all afraid, in the end, of what you'd find.'

Chapter 46

I T WAS STILL DARK when Nicholas entered the land-gate of Famagusta.

He had stopped twice in the course of the long ride. A woman milking a goat by candlelight had given him some dates and a bowl of the milk, still warm; and he had picked up a handful of dried carob pods, wrinkled and sweet.

At the deep gate the sight of the King's horse, its head hanging, had roused astonishment and alarm, but then one of the guards had recognised Nicholas despite the beard and the grimed tabby silks, and eagerly claimed him in talk. He parted as soon as he reasonably could, and made his way, pace upon pace, yard upon yard, through the narrow dirt-packed streets of the silent town. In the square, he stopped before the incense-breathing mass of the Cathedral, and looked up to where the night-burning lamps lit the carving within the three great porches, and defined the triangular gables above, created for the island of Venus more than a century before by French hands. By a craftsman versed, like ibn Hayy, in geometry and astronomy; and *formulating with passion various astronomical equations.* Oh, with passion.

It was between Matins and Prime: had there been any sound, he would not have entered. As it was, he tied the horse to a ring, and made his way slowly inside and knelt. The tiled floor was clean. The roof soared dark over his head; the altar was far away, crowded with paintings and statues.

He had knelt here before, in physical pain which he had forgotten; in agony of another kind which he could never forget. Gelis had no need to remind him, over and over, of what had become of her sister. Katelina van Borselen of the long brown hair, the dark eyebrows, the round, small breasts . . . who had commanded him to her bed. *Gelis says that you're the most passionate lover in Bruges, according to all the girls she's been able to ask.* Then, unknown to him, had become pregnant with his son, and had married Simon to conceal it. Arigho. New corn, the first fruits of the harvest. And who had ended here, attempting to punish him, and herself, as now Gelis was . . . As he supposed Gelis was doing.

Except that in the end Katelina had forgiven him and, he thought, herself: the pain blotted out by the act which had caused it. Palpitating moths, and a waterfall, and Aphrodite. A sunlit vale in Rhodes where he had found her in terror, and had brought her joy, peace, release. Even though she was by then Simon's, and he had been forced to pledge himself to someone else.

He could never tell Gelis that, although sometimes he made himself remember, before the memory was overwhelmed by what happened afterwards, when he found Katelina here, dying, in a starving city under a siege directed by himself.

Gelis knew about that. He could never tell her the rest. He could never say, Your sister was a sweet lover, and urgent as you are, and wilful as you are, but never, never with the glorious madness that you bring, that you brought . . .

He was in a church. *Hunc praeclarum*, this celestial chalice. His hands, and Godscalc's, and those of his wife, making a promise. He had made no promises to Katelina, nor she to him. *She has won the Truth; she is in Paradise*, they had said. He prayed, kneeling, that it was true. Then his thoughts turned to the corn, the second fruits of the harvest.

The child was not here, within the precincts of the Cathedral. He had known that from the moment he passed them, arriving in Famagusta, just as he had also known that Gelis was not on the island. The summons he felt was not from this place: the beat in his heart and hand that had begun today like a pulse and was now like the *dumm*, the deep sound that came from the drumhead when it was struck in the centre. The phial from St Catherine's tomb hung concealed from its cord round his neck but he did not need it here.

In some crypt, somewhere within the embrace of the Cathedral, Katelina van Borselen lay now. Tomorrow he would ask to be taken there. Tonight he knelt, thinking of her and her sister. Then he rose and walked out, to answer the summons.

The Cathedral servant, following him to the door, took his coin. The Archbishop's men would look after the horse. Fabrice was the King's man, after all. Above his head the rose window was dark, that had thrown a coverlet of jewelled light over the rows of cheap coffins. He hoped to find what he was here to find before sunrise. *What would you give now to see him?*

He knew Gelis, he thought. She had made a promise, upon a condition she knew couldn't be met. The treasure was out of his reach; but the search for it would fetch him here, to Famagusta, the place where' her sister had died. That had been her objective. But Ludovico da Bologna had also been involved: a priest who had helped her for his own ends, but who would surely see, also for his own ends, that Nicholas received the reward he was due, whether Gelis knew of it or not.

So his reasoning said. The pendulum made reasoning unnecessary, but still, he felt safer consulting with both. He was being induced to seek a place of past anguish, where a child of eighteen months could be reared unremarked until needed.

So, not the tomb, nor the Cathedral. Not the house, now nothing but rubble, where Katelina sank to her death: he had seen that on his way to Nicosia.

Not – as it turned out – the church of St Anna, where dead children were left.

Not the hospice of the Knights of the Order, where he had tended the dying, with brethren who did not agonise, then, over which Republic they came from.

That left the monastery of the Franciscans, where he had been cared for, after Tzani-bey al-Ablak had died.

The *dumm* took him there. There was never any doubt that it was right, although he stopped on the way and unlaced the little gold box, and let it drop from his fingers. And arrested it, flinching, as the skin was flayed from his flesh. Of course, Ludovico da Bologna was a Franciscan.

It was nearly dawn. The bell, when he pulled it, jangled slowly and the eyes of the porter were filled with sleep. When he said who he was they stretched open, and so did the door.

My lord was expected. My lord: the young man whom they had nursed with loving anxiety six years before. The Abbot, brought from his devotions, welcomed him and would have offered him refreshment. Nicholas did not know him but saw faces, peeping behind, that were familiar but no longer gaunt. He asked to join in their prayers and, kneeling before their well-kept altar, was sensible of the warmth of their approval and friendship. At the end, as light began to imprint each painted window, he asked if he might be allowed to see to the business he had come for.

Again, they patently knew what he meant. He followed them to their guest-quarters, recognising every corner, every passage, and returning their gentle enquiries, although the blood beat through his heart like a river-drum, and trilled through his head like the *zaghruda* of fear, or rejoicing. At a simple door, they stopped, smiling. They produced keys and turned back the lock. Then, with an air of teasing benignity, they retreated and left him alone. A bird burst into song, and the cloister garden exhaled august scents.

For a moment, such was the pressure, he could not see. Then he raised a hand and lifted the latch. The dim light of dawn showed him the cell.

A small, simple room with a crucifix.

A cot, empty.

A screened hearth, with two fragrant logs burning: the only source of light inside the room. He stepped forward, closing the door.

The red, uncertain glimmer trembled over the floor. A piece of sacking lay heaped by the hearth, from within which struck a glint of soft colour.

He approached it slowly. A round, fair shape became apparent, and a tumble of gold, at rest in the glow of the firelight.

His eyes dazzled. He stood, afraid for a moment. Then he passed forward quietly and, kneeling, laid his palm on the mound of warm sacking. Under his hand nothing moved. Then he felt, probing, frightened, the dead, resisting outline of metal.

It made a whimper, falling apart; but the blocks, the pipes, the bags of bullion that made up the heap were incapable of protest or fear, and in no need of comfort, being lifeless.

The light swam in his eyes; the pounding leaped from the gold at his throat to the other that lay at his feet and shook him between them. There was nothing else in the room.

Like had locked into like. He had found his lost gold, not his son.

An hour later, as the sun rose and the litany of Prime floated through the warm air, the Patriarch of Antioch made one of his unexpected but not unwelcome descents upon the Convent of the Franciscans at Famagusta and, shaking the dust from his terrible habit, commanded a flask of good water and a few platters of whatever the Convent possessed that would relieve a traveller's hunger. Then he sent someone to look for the sieur de Fleury.

He rather expected there would be no delay. When the door thundered back on the wall he looked up from his pigeon and said, 'I tell you to wait, and instead you're off, *cito, cito, cito*, like an underpaid courier. I hear you've been given a present.'

'Do you want it?' said Nicholas de Fleury. His voice said all that was necessary.

'Regard it as a pourboire,' said Ludovico da Bologna. 'Will you have some water? The child isn't on Cyprus.'

'Your little piece of frippery thought he was,' said Nicholas. He pulled out the phial and let it swing from his neck. He ignored the water.

'Only God is a lasting friend,' remarked the Patriarch. 'Or is it really the fault of the phial? It seems to have thought that you wanted the gold.'

'You left the gold there?' said the other.

The Patriarch stretched his hand for the honey. 'No. Your wife, I assume. I don't know how she managed to get some. Oh well, maybe I can guess.' He lifted his bread. 'She certainly knows how to rile you.' He watched the other man's fists begin to slacken, and took a large bite.

'Well, look at it this way,' said de Fleury. 'It saves me having to help Uzum Hasan, once I've got my army together and managed to lay hands on the rest of the bullion. No gold, no child, didn't she say?'

'I got a better bargain than that,' said the Patriarch. 'I seem to have finished the pigeons.'

'I am sure you will leave me the feathers,' the other said. He sat down. His sword, when he came in, had been rammed not quite home in its sheath. 'What bargain?'

'That was what I was going to tell you. Do what we discussed. Let the fools have the rest of your gold: it'll come back to you tenfold as their merchant. You'll coin money, ha! Sit round the table with all these scared princes and show them how you can help them throw back the Turks. There's no one better qualified. You might have trained for this moment – Trebizond, Cyprus, truck with blackamoors, Muslims with rings in their noses. They're the rulers, but chance has made you the man they require. So throw your weight about now. Convince them an alliance will work. Help me bring them to Venice this winter, ready to plan and ready to fight, and you'll get your reward.'

'Twenty-five per cent in the hundred,' said de Fleury. His face was like a hand-coloured woodcut.

'Oh, that,' said the Patriarch. 'Certainly that. You'll notice that I'm not appealing to your better nature, not being sure that you have more than one. But if you still want a look at the boy, then you'll get it. You do your work, and the mother will bring him to Venice at the time of the conference. Can you wait three months for that, or have you a bladder that can't hold its anger?'

'Like the widow's cruse,' de Fleury said, 'I seem to have constant cause for replenishment. The answer is no. She will cheat, or you will.'

'She won't,' said Ludovic da Bologna. 'I'm a priest. She fears God, even if you don't. She'll do it.'

'Good,' said de Fleury. 'But you would break any vow for God's sake.'

'You noticed,' said the Patriarch. 'That's true. I have sold myself, and God has bought me. But I'll keep my word. It's been a useful lever, your matrimonial tiff, but I don't flatter myself I can use it for ever. You'll make up, or get tired of the battle, or maybe even decide to get rid of one another. It can happen.'

He let the silence develop. De Fleury said, 'You were prepared even for that?' Now the room had warmed, moisture showed at his temples.

The Patriarch said, 'It was risky. I thought I guessed right. If you came down from that mountain at all, you had three months more of fighting left in you both. A lot more perhaps. And she fears God, I told you. How old are you?'

You could see he wanted to think. Instead, he said, 'Why?'

'Because you'll find yourself taking some decisions if you go through with this; and Venice will be the place you'll have to do it, I'll guess. You'll be thirty soon?'

'In December.' He was still full of fury, but tired. The Patriarch, who had ridden thirty-four miles himself, felt little sympathy.

'And your birth sign is Sagittarius. Centaur, bowman and hunter. So is the girl's.' The Patriarch took the rejected flask, poured some water and pushed a cup across to the other, who took it without thinking. He drank.

The Patriarch prompted. 'The Sersanders child will be seventeen on St Catherine's Day. Time for her to marry.'

'She expects to,' said de Fleury. 'And her uncle will bring you the news if I rape her. What decisions do you think I might be old enough to take when I get to Venice?'

'Are things happening too fast for you?' said the Patriarch. 'If all goes well, if all the powers agree and an alliance is made against the Grand Turk, you could spend the rest of your life in the East. On the other hand if your mind is set on family matters, you've laid the groundwork for a very nice little empire in the West: trading and fighting for or against Flanders, Burgundy, France; not to mention the Magnificent Lords of High Germany and the Tyrol. And once the English have stopped killing each other, the Kings of Scotland and England will come to your door.'

'Do I have to choose?' de Fleury said.

'East or West? At twenty, no. Range the world. At thirty you choose, or stay rootless. There's an Arab name for the state. And before you think of saying it –'

'I know,' said de Fleury. 'You're rootless for God. Have you seen my son?'

The Patriarch considered. A fly had dropped into the honey. He let it drown. He said, 'I think he exists.'

There was a silence. 'And that is all?' the other man said.

'My mistake,' said the Patriarch, astonished. 'Of course I have seen him. He sits on my knee. I have taught him to pray for you daily. I thought you were old enough to expect the truth.' He waited. He said, 'If I thought he did not exist, I should have told you. In any case, one way or the other, Venice will solve that for you. Do what I ask, and you will see him in Venice. Or you will know the truth, once and for all: that I promise. What is your answer?'

He agreed, looking strange. The Patriarch thought it might have been achieved more quickly, but didn't complain. M. de Fleury would, of course, require to return immediately to Nicosia and report to those with whom he would now be working. 'You had better,' remarked the Patriarch, 'acquire a fresh horse.' He did not offer to ride back immediately himself. Some things were best left to Nature.

A horse to take him to Nicosia was easily come by, although not of the quality of the one which had brought him; and the journey took five hours instead of just over three for that reason, and also because he was stopped after the first twenty miles by a squadron of the King's guards, sent to arrest him for stealing the King's horse and saddle.

It was a return, after a little too long, to the conduct Nicholas associated with Zacco, the young lion of Cyprus. He resented it enough to resist, and broke one man's leg and nearly killed another before they got him subdued; and that largely because, as ever, Zacco had forbidden his soldiers to wound him. As ever, it was the soldiers who suffered and, as ever, the soldiers adored him.

At the Palace, Nicholas was locked in a room which possessed, at least, the luxury of a feather bed. He lay down to think, and awoke to lamplight and Jorgin, the King's servant, accompanied by pages bringing a tub of hot water and fresh garments.

Jorgin, six years older, did not smile and Nicholas made no approaches. The arrest had been nothing, an impotent gesture; Zacco needed him as he needed the Venetians, and probably hated him quite as thoroughly. Overlaid by the new, the old wounds throbbed as he lay in the bath-water, constituting a history, that was all. He had already reviewed, many times over, his conversation with Ludovico da Bologna, and had identified how he had been taken, step by step, to his final – his interim decision, and led away, equally, from the thing that had happened so quietly, so cruelly, in front of the fire. Not consoled, or conciliated. Just led away.

He thought that Beelzebub probably looked like Ludovico da Bologna, but that equally the Patriarch owned that penetrating, unsentimental form of insight which permitted him, if allowed, to nick the Achilles' tendon of the soul, and twist the remains to his purpose.

He was also an adequate horseman for his age, having, it seemed, ridden last night at least as far as Nicholas had. Otherwise Zacco would not have been able to snap, as he did now when Nicholas, clean, was brought to his chamber: 'I was told you had gone to take ship from Famagusta.'

Thank you, Beelzebub. The lamps were low, but the room smelled of yesterday's scents. It was a seduction scene Zacco had abandoned half planned, although the bedchamber in its own right was enchanting. Its loggia hung above gardens, and Zacco, watching him from its balustrade, had stripped to shirt and hose under a loose-girdled bedgown. The silk was Caspian, the embroidery Venetian, the jewels no doubt obtained through Squarcialupi or Benedetto Dei from the Orient.

The King said, 'You raise your eyes a great deal for a merchant, not to mention your steel. Where did that come from?'

He held the little box by its cord. They must have taken it from his room while he slept. He remembered wrenching it from his neck when they locked him in, and then throwing it on the floor, along with his soiled, ceremonial cloak.

Nicholas said, 'From the monks at St Catherine's, roi seigneur. I am sorry about the horse. I had a visit to make, that was all. I have decided that my company can agree to take part in the plan the Venetians have suggested.'

'The plan I have suggested,' said Zacco. His colour had risen. He flung the box, and Nicholas caught it. 'You should take better care of it. You are going to Rhodes, I am told; to Rome; to Venice. Afterwards your home, of course, will be here.'

'I have no property here,' Nicholas said. 'Nor do I want any.'

'You are wrong,' Zacco said. 'There is a list on the table of what you own.'

It lay under the lamp: his eye had fallen on it already. The vineyards were all good, and there were two sugar estates. Zacco said, 'Of course, Venice will not like it, but they can deny you little now. And if nothing else attracts you, there are the three pretty ladies from Naxos who are certain to visit. My father's wife, the lady Fiorenza, for example.'

'I thought you called the lord Andrea your father?' Nicholas said.

'I forget which is which,' Zacco said. He unhitched from the balustrade and sat. 'There is wine on this table.'

'So long,' Nicholas said, 'as you don't ask me to taste Fiorenza's sweetmeats. I don't want this property.'

Zacco said, 'Be careful.' It was a warning. He had whitened.

'I don't need to be careful,' Nicholas said. He had not touched the wine, or approached.

'You think I need you?' Zacco said. 'You?'

'You need the Venetians.'

'And you are afraid of them? You think they would get rid of you?' He paused. 'Sweetmeats?'

'A figure of speech,' Nicholas said. 'Monseigneur, I must go. I have to report, and to speak to my people.'

'I threw them out,' said Zacco carelessly. 'When I thought you had gone, I found I needed the villa. The girl is at the Clares'.' His eye fell, in turn, on the document under the lamp, and his lip suddenly twitched.

All the wayward charm was still there. It was hard not to smile back, until one remembered how dangerous he could be. Nicholas said, 'The Venetians will no doubt take in Dr Tobias, and me too.'

'You have a talisman against poison?' said Zacco. 'I could find a use for you.' He stood. 'You will stay. Refuse me, and I will never forget it.' He picked up and held out the sheet. When it was not taken, very slowly he opened his fingers and let it drop to the floor.

'My lord,' Nicholas said. The box cut into his palm. 'My lord, that is why I am refusing.'

He had thought, after he left the room, that they would try something else: that the King's mother would have him sent for, but she did not. He did not even go back to his bedchamber, but recovered his horse from a stable where no one spoke to him. Then he went and found Tobie at the house of Andrea Corner.

Corner embraced him on either cheek, gripping his shoulders and finding out several bruises. Tobie heard him out when they were alone in the guest-chamber. He told him all the salient facts, except for Famagusta. At the end, as was to be expected, Tobie was having trouble keeping his temper. He dragged his hat off and aimed it into a corner. 'Right. You know where the gold is, and you're giving it up in return for certain rights. You have committed the company?'

'On my own personal whim? Yes,' said Nicholas. 'To my services. Until the turn of the year.'

'When the plans and figures come to be discussed in detail in Venice. Do you mean to do all that on your own as well?'

'Julius and Moriz will be there,' Nicholas said. 'Cristoffels. You, if you want.'

'Yes, I want. Poor Diniz. He ought to know what has happened to his half of the gold. And John. Don't you think John might want to have a say in the way the company is going? Even where you are going?'

'I have no objection,' Nicholas said.

'You would leave me to arrange it? You don't want me in Rhodes.'

'No. But what about the girl?' Nicholas said. He was aware of a certain vagueness.

'You're thinking like a sponge. The girl doesn't need me: she has to wait for her uncle. Adorne. Remember the good Baron Cortachy? Forestalling you wherever he can, along with the rest of the Vatachino. Do you think they're going to let you become the accredited middleman for all this without some very nasty opposition indeed?'

After a while, Tobie added, 'Nicholas?' and stopped marching about and sat down opposite.

Nicholas realised he hadn't answered.

Tobie said, 'Listen to me. You thought you could track down the child, but now you say that you couldn't: Gelis knows how to outwit the pendulum. Or I think that's what you said. So how do you know you won't commit yourself to all this, only for her to mislead you in Venice as well?'

'Because Ludovico da Bologna made her promise,' Nicholas said. He perceived that he shouldn't have said anything.

'You didn't say you'd met Ludovico da Bologna,' Tobie remarked. 'Where? Nicholas, where have you been?'

He would find out. When Tobie wanted to, he always found out.

'Famagusta,' Nicholas said. 'She left a little of the gold there, and the box led me to it. Made of the same gold, I suppose. I thought it was going to be the child, but it wasn't. I gave some to the Franciscans, and brought some for Diniz.'

He paused and added, 'The Patriarch thinks that Ochoa's probably sailing the seas under strict supervision as a master in the Hospitallers' galleys. Licensed piracy. But he did try to tell us, through the parrot.'

He saw, this time, that it was Tobie who had been stricken dumb. He found he wanted to continue. 'The Patriarch was using us both. Gelis and myself. He knew that gold alone wouldn't take me to Cyprus, but that I might follow a clue to Mount Sinai; especially if I found Anselm Adorne was competing. And he persuaded Gelis to go there and wait for me. I don't suppose she needed much persuasion. She wished me to go to Cyprus as well, and left the box – you were right – just as he left some gold to prove it existed.'

He paused. He said, 'I was bound to try and find her, you see, after what happened in Cairo. And she was bound to try and force me to Famagusta. From the Patriarch's point of view, he had time to put off before Uzum's Envoys were due to reach Cyprus. He may have hoped the Mount of the Lord would achieve miracles, in which case he was wrong. At any rate, he says he has stopped intervening. He expects Gelis and myself either to halt of our own accord or kill one another.'

He waited again. Tobie's extraordinary, incoherent distress brought him a positive resurgence of calm. Nicholas said, 'So do bring everyone to Venice. It's going to be something worth watching.'

In a few days he had departed, with the Persian delegation, for Rhodes. Tobie sailed from the same port for Alexandria; and found the Florentine agent, Mariotto Squarcialupi, travelling with him.

The Patriarch of Antioch, a practical man, paid a pastoral call on the convent of the Poor Clares, Nicosia, and held a friendly conversation with Katelijne Sersanders, whom he had previously encountered in bed, when seeking the fellow de Fleury.

De Fleury had not had time to call on her, it appeared, before departing from Cyprus. Dr Tobias had told her some of the news. She was perfectly content at the Clares', and had been taken to St Catherine's tomb, the Lusignan chapel, and the place where St Catherine's father King Costa had lived before unwisely accepting the appointment as viceroy of Egypt in Alexandria.

The Patriarch formed an unusually good opinion of Katelijne Sersanders and put it to her, before he left, that she ought seriously to consider her namesake's example and become a bride of the

Church. She said she would give it some thought. The Patriarch returned, well pleased, to the Dominicans and composed a letter to Gelis van Borselen who was then, he had cause to believe, on her way to a discreet lodging in Genoa.

Tobias Beventini arrived in Alexandria and held a fraught conversation with John le Grant in the midst of the spice market, as a result of which a number of letter packets marked *cito, cito, cito* left for various ports. Two berths were booked on a fast galley going to Venice.

Anselm Adorne, Baron Cortachy passed through Beersheba and Hebron and entered Jerusalem on the eleventh day of September. Having visited the Mount of Olives, Bethlehem, Jericho, Nazareth, Galilee and seven other places, he arrived in Damascus on the sixteenth of October, where he was met by the Vatachino agent called Martin, and accepted a courtesy invitation from the sub-agent of the House of Niccolò, carrying out instructions from his colleagues further west. John de Kinloch, impatient to reach Rhodes (where he was to remain) had been brusque, but nothing upsetting occurred.

Lambert van de Walle acquired a rash, and Pieter Reyphin contrived to buy a barrel of wine. Jan Adorne continued his diary. Towards the end of October, the party took ship from Beirut for Cyprus. The man Martin went with them.

Leaving Achille in charge, John le Grant and Tobias Beventini set sail for Venice. In Venice, Julius held back the invitations to two receptions and questioned Father Moriz, not for the first time, about what exactly Nicholas had been doing in the Tyrol. He learned, to his surprise, that Gregorio had been sent for from Bruges.

Discussions opened with the ambassadors of the lord Uzum Hasan on the island of Rhodes, attended by Nicholas de Fleury and, subsequently, by Ludovico da Bologna, Latin Patriarch of Antioch. The Grand Master of the Knights Hospitaller of St John was not unsympathetic to the proposals brought to the table, but there was some dissidence among the Knights from the Genoese sector.

A message arrived at the Burgundian camp at St Omer causing Captain Astorre, that thoroughly professional soldier, some disquiet. He applied for permission to visit his patron in Venice and was refused. Concealing (he thought) his relief, he dispatched his apologies to Master Gregorio in Bruges. Master Gregorio left for Venice accompanied by some large wallets of papers and Margot his mistress.

A packet made its way up to Leith and was delivered to Michael Crackbene when he put in from his current voyage. It contained information, but no summons to Venice. Govaerts, the Bank's Scottish agent, continued to receive the usual dispatches and deal, as best he could, with the demands and enquiries proceeding from Beltrees, from the noblemen Semple and Hamilton, from the Berecrofts family through all its generations, and from the King. Simon de St Pol and Mistress Bel of Cuthilgurdy each made appearances from time to time in the Kilmirren district, but neither communicated with him. Meeting Whistle Willie these days, he spread his hands and shrugged. It had been found that he had no ear for music, and flutes made him dribble.

The party of Anselm Adorne, Baron Cortachy, arrived on the island of Cyprus and was treated to a grand reception by the monarch King James, who with solemn pomp invested the baron with the Order of the Sword, a Cypriot order of knighthood and a fitting successor to the honour the Baron (*Equites Hierosolymitani*) had just received in Jerusalem.

His niece Katelijne, a recent ornament to the Convent of the Clares, attended the ceremony and congratulated her uncle, who was visibly moved to see her well and composed. One of the young men in the party, no doubt her cousin, flung his arms around her and kissed her. In due course they took their leave of the King and set sail for Rhodes, where they arrived too late to meet the delegates from the lord Uzum Hasan of the White Sheep Tribe of the Turcomans, who had had occasion to visit the Hospitallers and had left the previous day.

In the Castle of Angers, René of Anjou summoned his newest page Henry and, when the lad arrived, sent him to find his grandfather, the vicomte Jordan de Ribérac, to whom he delivered a letter. The seal was familiar, and the superscription showed that it had come via Marseilles from Egypt. Jordan de Ribérac, scanning it, said, 'I fear, monseigneur, that I shall have to ask your permission to leave. A matter of business in Venice.'

'Can I come?' said Henry.

To his surprise, his grandfather seemed to consider it. Then the old man said, 'No.' The fat old man. Chamberpot Jordan.

In Bruges, the Princess Mary said, 'And your niece Katelijne is better? You have heard? Is she coming home? Does she know the lord James my son is here in her cradle?'

'I'm sure she does,' said Margriet, dame de Cortachy, taking the baby to give the wet-nurse some rest. When she gave it her finger to suck, it stopped screaming. Her fingertip was shrivelled and pink, and had grown too tender for sewing. The Duchess had told her she was wearing herself out, but it was the least she could do, with Anselm still being away and Lord Boyd so impatient of noise, even from his own grandchild. She eased her finger out of its mouth, and it screamed.

On the island of Rhodes, a feast was given for Anselm Adorne and his son by the Grand Master of the Knights Hospitaller of St John of Jerusalem and his nephew the Prior of Capua. Sharing the honour of a place at high table was Tobias Lomellini, the Genoese Treasurer of the Order.

In praising the Order for its generosity, the sire de Cortachy referred to recent Ottoman threats against Rhodes and urged the Order – speaking of course in his own voice, and not that of the Pontiff or Burgundy – not to abandon its historic distrust of the Republic of Venice.

It was then the thirteenth of November. Two days after the Baron's departure, the Council of the Order met and resolved to inform James, King of Cyprus, that the Order would not oppose any pact he wished to make with the Sultan of Cairo, and with the Grand Karaman and the seigneur of Candelore, the Muslim neighbours of Uzum Hasan. Subject to the outcome of the forthcoming meeting in Venice, certain funds were being held by the Order against the arming of such putative allies.

Anselm Adorne sailed towards Brindisi, with the intention of making his way, via Naples and Rome, back to Bruges.

Katelijne Sersanders became seventeen years old to outward appearances, and inwardly approximately three times that age. She gave up attempting to rewrite Jan's Royal Book in any language.

The agents of the Vatachino communicated with one another: Martin in Syria to David de Salmeton in Cairo; David de Salmeton to Egidius; Egidius to the address which was only that of a company of couriers. It was agreed to stand back and leave the developing situation to Anselm Adorne.

Nicholas passed the first day of his new decade in Rome, among those delegates who had answered the call of Pope Paul and Cardinal Bessarion for an anti-Turk pact among the Italian princes. Seven days later the meeting took place, and such assurances were received that the Pontiff ordered salvoes of joy to be fired wherever Christians were gathered.

Discussing it later with his Rome agent, along with Lorenzo Strozzi and a pleasantly drunk Cardinal's Secretary, Nicolas said, 'Will it stick?'

'Our bit will,' said Lorenzo, speaking for Naples. 'We need all the help we can get. But Milan won't sign in the end. And I don't know about Florence. You know the Medici: they don't want to lose trade.'

'It won't stick anyway,' said the Secretary. 'Not when all the Western powers turn their backs, having something worse to worry about. You don't know what I know.'

'Let me guess,' Nicholas said. 'The Lancastrian King is back on the throne of England.'

'That's old,' said Lorenzo. 'The King of France helped put him there.'

'Ah,' said the Secretary.

They looked at him.

He said, 'But you don't know on what conditions. The King of France wants England's help in his wars. And England has promised it. And so France has declared war on Burgundy.'

There fell the silence of genuine shock. Then Nicholas cleared his throat. 'So what happened to Edward of York?'

'My lord?' said his agent. 'That I can tell you. He fled to Holland. And was given shelter by the governor of Holland, the lord Louis de Gruuthuse of Bruges.'

'*What!*' said Nicholas. He put his hand over his cup. He said, 'The Duke of Burgundy's lieutenant-general is sheltering the deposed English King?' His hand was trembling with suppressed laughter.

His agent said, 'Yes, my lord. In a private capacity, as you would guess. The Duke is not officially aware that the King is within his domain.'

'While the Hôtel Jerusalem, in the same town, is harbouring Thomas Boyd and his royal wife from Scotland, early and fervent supporters of the Lancastrian King. How very difficult,' Nicholas said, 'for the poor wife and relatives of the peripatetic Baron Cortachy and his heir.'

Lorenzo gave a chuckle, then sobered. With marriage, he had become a shade portly. 'It's funny, but look. There'll be no money coming now from the West. If the Turks are going to be stopped, we have to do it between us.'

'That's all right,' Nicholas said. 'I'm doing nothing on Tuesday.'

He stayed until Twelfth Night was well over, amassing facts and making his adjusted calculations. In a period of intense activity and little sleep, he lay awake all through one night bothered by an illogical fancy that drew his thoughts towards Florence. The next day he was called to the Curia, and the opportunity to change his programme was lost.

When he did stop in Florence, going north, he felt nothing more than traces of emotion to do with Godscalc, and perhaps the child he had befriended, who had died. He called on old Alessandra to give her news of her son, and found her frail and short-tempered, as if she could see the last page of her account, and did not like what she read. At the end, she said, 'You did not take my advice.'

They had been talking about spectacles and about silk. He cast his mind back.

'Oh, business!' she said. 'You have grown like all the rest: you think business consists of nothing but percentages, contracts, delivery dates. I thought at one time you had some understanding of people. Charity.'

Then he took her meaning, although he was still surprised. He said, 'I was grateful for your letters. One's wife is less easy to command, perhaps, than one's sons.'

'I should not blame you,' she said, 'if you had fallen out of charity with that one. I should get rid of her. As for my sons, since you make the comparison, I did no more than order their lives until they were capable of doing so for themselves. If you have all you came for, I am tired.'

Anselm Adorne arrived in Rome on the eleventh of January. The Cardinals of Rouen and St Mark were amiable, as was that popular churchman, the Chancellor of Burgundy's brother. The Pontiff agreed, hardly solicited, to give a second audience to the counsellor of his dearest son, the redoubtable Charles, Duke of Burgundy.

In point of fact, the Pope had some cause to be interested in those countries the Baron had visited, as had Cardinal Bessarion. The Cardinal's sympathies were Venetian, and the Pontiff's – surprisingly, fortunately – were not. In the end, the Baron came away with the prize that he had hoped for, or one of them. A post in the Pontiff's own household for Jan Adorne, graduate of Paris and Pavia, his son.

To Jan, of course, it set the stamp, at last, on his future, and made the whole slogging business worth while. Their lodgings rang with his jubilation. His cousin Kathi said, 'When?'

'When I've seen you all safely back in Bruges. I'm to come back immediately. If we hurry, we could be home by February. I could be back here by May. I shan't have time, of course, to write out the Book.'

'You wouldn't,' said Kathi, 'take a small wager?'

'Why?' he said.

The girl said, 'Well, do you think you can go back to Bruges yet?

With the Princess of Scotland giving birth in your house beside the traitor Boyds, father and son, and Edward of York rampaging about incognito in Oostcamp as guest of one of the Duke of Burgundy's governors?'

She looked earnest rather than smug; but Jan was still vexed. She had been like this, virtually pickled in vinegar, since they picked her up from Cyprus in November. He wondered if Nicholas de Fleury could possibly have arranged it all. Claes. He had been in Rome when the big conference was being held. He'd gone north quite recently. They said he was making for Florence and Venice.

In a way it was no surprise therefore when his father came to mention that, unfortunately, they would not be able to go straight home to Bruges. Instead, he thought Jan would find it amusing, as a treat, to spend a little more time in Italy. Florence. Bologna. Ferrara. Even Venice. Venice in the days before Lent was surely something they might allow themselves, after all their privations.

But Jan knew it wasn't the allurement of Martedi Grasso that was drawing his father. It was the diabolical plotting of Claes.

A galley of the Knights Hospitaller of St John, putting off from Rhodes just after Twelfth Night, began a rough journey west, bearing with it a contingent of Knights and the same experienced, much-exercised Turcoman delegation from the prince Uzum Hasan which had already visited both Cyprus and Rhodes. Their destination this time was Venice.

The lawyer Gregorio, after a difficult crossing of the Alps, finally made his way to the Ca' Niccolò in Venice along with Margot his mistress. They received a welcome from Julius, together with a faint impression that he thought they had come to see what he was spending on parties. Cristoffels and Father Moriz showed genuine pleasure, and took them off very soon to find the doctor and John and exchange gossip. Later: 'And so where is Nicholas?' Gregorio said.

'Coming,' said Tobie. The word, or its echoes, sobered the lawyer. He looked at Tobie and John, and saw a warning. Later, the three of them met.

Shutting the door: 'It's Gelis, I assume,' said Gregorio. 'We know she travelled part of the way south with Adorne, and for a while she was thought to be dead.'

'She came to Egypt,' said John le Grant. He cleared his throat. 'There was trouble in Cairo, and she found her way to Mount Sinai. We don't know where she went after that. But she's supposed to be coming to Venice when Nicholas does. You don't know where she is?'

'She moves about,' Gregorio said. 'She's been in Genoa. She writes to her family. Every now and then she disappears, or perhaps she just wants some privacy.'

'And the child?' Tobie said.

'I don't know,' Gregorio said. 'No one, not even Margot, knows where it is now, or if it's alive. And I have no information about it. Margot made a promise to Gelis, and nothing that I know of would make her break it.'

He left presently, being tired from the journey, and Tobie sat for a while in silence with John.

It seemed, although no one had spoken, that something had been said. John said, 'I think you should do it. You know what Gelis made him go through. Margot would listen.' After a while he said, 'She was married once, wasn't she?'

'He is dead,' Tobie said. 'She never lived with him.'

'But Margot has been free ever since? Do you know why she hasn't married Gregorio?'

'Yes,' said Tobie. 'She consulted me.'

John's freckled face with its white chin was intent. 'It's a medical matter?'

'It's private to them,' Tobie said. 'But it has a bearing. There is deformity in Margot's family. Some are born normal; some are brutes. Every generation suffers from it, and they all know, as she does, how to nurse the afflicted. That is between you and me.'

John said, 'Does Nicholas know?'

'No,' said Tobie.

After a while Tobie said, 'I shall go and see her. But if she agrees, we should have to tell Gregorio.'

Then it was February, and they were all there, in Venice. Few of them would recognise all the threads which had brought them there. Most of them were aware, now, of the kind of calendar of which they were part, although they might not have counted the stages. The sixth, which had started in Cairo, had brought the game, lure by lure, to one field.

In the north, soon, another hunt, another season would open. It was time that this one was called home.

Part V

THE PRISE

Chapter 47

NICHOLAS DE FLEURY arrived last in Venice, with no more ceremony than, say, a ducal chancellor performing his annual audits. The boat went to the mainland to collect him, since he had given the precise time of his arrival: communications had never ceased flowing between himself and the Bank. He had with him the small household he had collected to look after his personal needs, and he had asked for no one to meet him but a clerk with a box of the most recent papers.

He read them through sitting under the hood on the misty voyage to the collection of islands that called itself Venice. His small staff, mostly Catalonian, stood huddled in the open air, talking in low voices as the Grand Canal opened before them. He proposed keeping them with him.

By the time he stepped ashore at the Ca' Niccolò, he had added the news of the last few days to what he already understood of events in the ten months since he was last in Venice, and the five since he had departed from Cyprus.

That much was essential. What was also essential was a sense, impossible to obtain at a distance, of shifts of balance less quantifiable. He gave his mind to it now, accomplishing, swiftly, his practised patron's arrival into his Bank.

The six he wanted were there: Gregorio and Julius, Tobie and John, Cristoffels and Father Moriz. Margot had come with Gregorio, but was off on some woman's business. Diniz had been left to manage Bruges, but had given his willing consent to the investment of the gold that should have been his. One supposed that investment was the word.

And Astorre, of course, had been forbidden to leave the Duke's camp, which was perfectly sensible. He would have sent him back himself, had he come.

He had summoned no one from Scotland but had had notified
Antonio Cavalli in the Tyrol who had set out at once, he was told.
Naturally. Cavalli was a Venetian: the Palazzo Cavalli was not all
that far from the Banco di Niccolò. Or he might lodge at the
Fondaco dei Tedeschi. That was close to where the Scots usually
stayed.

Nicholas knew, from those who were watching Adorne, that the
Baron was travelling north with his son and his niece. Why the girl
was coming he could not imagine, unless van de Walle and
Reyphin, both continuing home, had been considered inadequate
chaperones.

Adorne could not, of course, hurry home without getting mixed
up in politics. And Duke Charles would not now be much
interested in his reports, although the merchants of Bruges certainly
would. As for King James – the other King James – he would have
to whistle, one supposed, for his Book.

Well, men whistled. Nicholas called his six executives together
and informed them of his reading of what the Bank would be asked
for and what they could provide as part of a strategic plan against
the Grand Turk. He heard their comments. He asked Julius to
give his interpretation of the Signoria's thinking; and then added
his own estimate of what the Turcoman and Karaman rulers, the
Knights of Rhodes, the Mameluke Sultan and the King of Cyprus
(*bien plaintive de tous biens*) could offer, and the degrees in which
they could be helped. He then set all that against the Bank's other
business and resources and passed round some fresh calculations.
He did not talk of the war in the West. Their minds on the East,
no one queried it.

Gregorio said, 'You anticipate difficulty with the Knights of
Rhodes. With Genoese interests.'

'Anselm Adorne is on his way,' Nicholas said. 'The Knights
went so far as to exclude him from their discussions on Rhodes,
but I suspect he guesses they are coming to Venice: even that this
time he might catch Uzum's envoys. I fancy he also realises that if
we help Uzum Hasan overrun these particular Ottoman lands,
Venice will end up with all the former Genoese alum and perhaps
even the mastic. As well as all the usual trade in silk and jewels and
scents and rhubarb roots and beautiful women.'

'You mean that we shall,' said Julius.

'If we choose to favour Persia, yes,' Nicholas said.

'And the Genoese?' Gregorio persisted.

'They have a base on the Black Sea called Caffa,' Nicholas said.
'Ludovico da Bologna has just gone there. He may get back in time

to explain, with diagrams, how Caffa deserves to be protected. It won't help Adorne or the Vatachino, but it will placate the Genoese among the Knights and even in Genoa. So when are the Persian envoys due to arrive?'

'We think in eight days,' Julius said. 'The Knights sent them in a squadron of galleys from Rhodes. The word is that they should come by next Thursday, take a day or so to recover, receive some attention, and then meet ourselves and the Senate on the Monday before Lent begins. So we have to know what we're doing before then.'

'It shouldn't be impossible,' Nicholas said. 'I grant you we have a lot of ground to cover. And as we cover it, it might be as well to start some quiet talks with some of the Senators. Julius, Cefo? You know which ones, and when I should see them. It would be nice to meet the Knights and the Persians with something already understood. Gregorio?'

'It would be sensible,' Gregorio said.

'I thought you were sleeping,' said Nicholas. 'Perhaps it has gone on rather long. There's a lot to do. The same time tomorrow?'

'And that's what happens when you climb to the top of Mount Sinai,' Julius said. 'You come down with a lot of commandments.'

'I know. He didn't notice the balloons,' Tobie said.

Julius made a grimace of good-humoured acknowledgement and flung himself down. 'Well, it *is* Carnival-time.'

Tobie said, 'Oh, come on. There are two weeks of it left. I'm sure you'll manage some of your banquets and balls.' He stooped and picked up Julius's hand, with all the rings on it. Having examined it, he let it drop back.

'Mind you, I don't understand the Serenissima's serenity. By all accounts they were cutting their throats after Negroponte – bringing the Captain-General home in chains hardly helped. All their credit and glory departed; nothing left in the East but Crete and a few bits of islands, and the Duke of Milan about to march over here, and deprive them of Crema and Brescia. What are they having a Carnival for?'

'Because Moses de Reedy is going to take care of it all,' Julius said. 'Or he will, if all goes well at the conference. What do you mean, what are they having a Carnival for? It's Carnival-time.'

'Then I'd better go and put my funny face on,' observed Tobie with acidity; and went to find his fellow conspirators.

John was with Gregorio, who appeared sunk in doubt. 'I don't think you should tell Nicholas what we've done. He hasn't asked, anyway.'

'Don't you look at his face? He doesn't need to ask, he divines,' Tobie said. 'He knows Gelis isn't here. She doesn't have to come until after the meeting. The morning after. That was the pact with the Patriarch.'

'So she won't do anything until after the conference is held,' Gregorio said. 'So don't tell him.'

'I don't see why not,' said John le Grant. 'The way he is now, he'd hardly register a small thing like a family.'

'The way he is now,' Tobie said, 'he'd fly apart like a spring-loaded shield. Wait for ten days. Wait till after we've seen Hadji Mehmet and the Knights and the Senate and it's all resolved, one way or another.'

Five days after that, in a downpour, Anselm Adorne, Baron Cortachy, made a consciously impressive arrival by hired boat from Chioggia and put up with friends at the Ca' Giustinian on the Grand Canal, since the rooms of the Knights of St John were already spoken for. With him was his promising son Jan, shortly to join the papal household, and his niece Katelijne Sersanders.

Two days after that, on a Wednesday, his niece took a hired maid and a page, and had herself poled across the Canal to the large, square building, fronted with mooring posts, which everyone referred to as the Ca' Niccolò.

She wore a cloak and gown from Rome and a mask she had bought in Ferrara after she had begun to suspect what Venice was going to be like. She knew already that the buildings would be more refined and highly decorated than in Bruges, and that its network of waterways was infinitely more splendid and dense, and that the Carnival would be more aristocratic than the ones she was used to.

It had occurred to her that her uncle's patron James, King of Scotland, would probably rather have an account of the Carnival than a blow-by-blow description of the Tomb of Lazarus, but she had been wise enough not to suggest it. She sat with her gaze fixed away from her gondolier, whose lissom body was unclothed from the waist downwards except by coloured hose, and whose eyes, beneath his feathered cap, kept sliding sideways in the manner depicted, for different reasons, in ikons.

Up till now, similarities to Egypt rather than Bruges had kept coming to mind: the pattern of moving light on the underside of bridges and the wind-patterns of sand; the ranges of structures inlaid and banded with white and gnarled with protuberances like the mountains of Sinai. Water, swollen and flooding, coursed through the canals like an animal; like the water released at the Abundance. Even the pillared magnificence of the Doge's Palace, glimpsed from afar, had the look of a woven reed village, its cabins on stilts.

But she was in Venice, not Sinai. She stepped ashore with her suite and, treading over a mat of coiled streamers, entered the marble halls of the Banco di Niccolò.

She had to wait. A page brought her a posy of flowers, and another brought her a concoction of fruit juice and offered to look after her attendants. A third finally took her up a grand staircase from which she glimpsed rooms filled with tables and clerks. They all looked frayed. M. de Fleury, when she was shown into his room, displayed all the unforced composure of a spinning top which has picked its own speed. He seemed pleased: her visit had coincided, perhaps, with a statutory restorative break. '*Salve virgo Katherina*,' he said, offering her a seat.

The beard had gone, allowing him the use of one or both dimples. The incandescence of the journey to Cyprus had also gone. They had not met since the evening in the royal Palace at Nicosia: *Je prens d'Amour noriture*, followed by his departure. Whatever he had wanted other than gold, he had not got, or kept it. She said, 'About Jan,' since he had, as it were, introduced the subject.

He poured two goblets of wine and kept one. Nicosia had changed that, too, she had noticed. 'No. First, about you,' he said. 'I was sorry not to visit you at the Clares. Was it tedious?'

'They were very garrulous,' Kathi said. 'They talked about other guests they had had, and showed me something of Cyprus. The Monastery of Cats. Kouklia. Famagusta. They are extremely well endowed by the King's mother. About Jan. He's fond of his father. He can be silly.'

He sat down, the cup in his hand. 'Oh dear,' he said. The remark might have applied to part or to all of her speech. He added, 'I thought Jan had been offered a post in the Apostolic Threshold. *Seriously* silly?'

'Not enough to kill anyone,' Katelijne said. 'But extremely eager to return any recent blows to the family pride. I suppose, too, that this is a time when the lords of the night watch are off duty.'

'"During Carnival, all jokes are acceptable,"' he quoted mildly, and drank, thinking. Then he smiled and looked up. 'Thank you. The warning is noted. So what about the *Relazione*, the Great Book? Is it finished?'

She took a gulp of her wine. It was strong. She said, 'I've seen the last words: Conclusio Peroptima et Salubris, Amen. I think that's all he's written, apart from the beginning. But he's headed it up with his father's name and all his titles and most of the four orders of chivalry.'

'Four?'

'He got another one in Jerusalem, and one in Cyprus. The Sword. The same as you have.'

'That *is* serious,' said M. de Fleury. 'No wonder Jan thinks it a crime to interfere with such eminence. All the same, I don't think you should be involved. You'd be safer in Bruges.'

'I doubt it,' she said. 'Anyway, I'm fond of him, too.'

'No one in the world could doubt that,' said M. de Fleury.

He changed his tone. 'It has hardly, all the same, constituted a health cure, this trip. Unless the Blessed Virgin St Catherine has managed to make up for the imbecilities of the rest of us? Have you brought something back from Alexandria? From Cyprus? From Sinai?'

She looked at him. 'In health? They say I am better, but perhaps Dr Tobias could have cured me at home.'

He said, 'Yes, in health. I am sorry. Spiritual wellbeing is not my affair.'

'No,' she said. 'In any case, it's all too recent to tell. I should put it aside. Put it green in the straw, and leave it to ripen. In six months we shall all know what we've brought back.' She stood. 'I must go. My uncle is presenting his letters to the Doge this morning.'

He rose as well. 'We shall see one another in public, I am sure. We are not savages. And all your other friends here will want to meet you.'

At the door she said, 'There is one other thing. Simon de St Pol is in Venice.'

For a moment he was absolutely still. Then he said, 'You are sure?'

'My uncle called at the Ca' Frizier, the Scots lodging. He knows the family. He said M. de St Pol was there.'

M. de Fleury stirred and then smiled, opening the door and gazing peaceably beyond it. 'Then let us hope he doesn't meet Jan Adorne.'

She said nothing. He turned. Then the two dimples deepened and deepened. He said, 'Col Dieu, he has.'

On Thursday the twenty-first of February, the squadron of galleys of the Knights Hospitaller of St John of Jerusalem dropped anchor in the basin at Venice and the embassy of noble Knights stepped ashore, among whom were Tobias Lomellini of Genoa and the chaplain, Father John Gosyn of Kinloch. With them was a Persian delegation of over one hundred gentlemen, led by the lord Hadji Mehmet.

The Signoria, warned of their coming, sent a suitable party to welcome them and to conduct them to their lodging. From there they brought back, after due expressions of gratitude, the Persian ruler's gifts to the Doge, which included ten barrels of caviare, five bundles of carpets and twelve parcels of silk. On Friday, once rested, the lords of Persia and their conductors were received in ceremonial audience by the Doge, and a number of less formal meetings were arranged, to culminate in a presentation before the full Council on Monday.

Returned to their lodging, the Knights and the delegation expressed their readiness to receive the Duke of Burgundy's Envoy that afternoon and, when the Baron Cortachy arrived, engaged him for three hours in unheated discussion.

The Genoese Knights of Rhodes, not averse to Western food and good wine, accepted the Baron's invitation to dine at his palazzo. The remaining Knights and their turbanned charges found it more convenient to remain where they were and entertain the merchant Nicholas de Fleury in the manner already arranged between them on Rhodes.

The meeting lasted into the night. It was understood in the course of it that the deployment of certain resources of gold was still under discussion within M. de Fleury's company, who were prepared to open informal talks between then and Monday's meeting with the Signoria. It was difficult at times to follow the argument, such was the racket of trumpets, singing and uninhibited shouting outside. It was explained that at present Venice was in Carnival.

Jan Adorne, excluded from the deliberations of his father, took the advice of his new and urbane friend, the chevalier Simon of Scotland, and had himself fitted with an exquisite costume ready for Martedi Grasso, the crescendo of unimaginable excitement which on Tuesday would finish the Carnival. The hose and shoes were of silk, and the hood and mask made entirely of cock's feathers. Between now and then, he wore his best taffeta doublets with a black mask and cloak, as Simon recommended. Simon said he was going as Dionysus.

As the son of the Baron Cortachy, Jan Adorne was not of course in want of a guide or companion, but he was impressed, despite himself, by St Pol's familiarity with the city, and with certain houses in it.

Jan was an orthodox young man, and had behaved himself in Paris and Pavia as orthodox students did; but on this journey he had been forced to observe unnatural standards of conduct. The all-important post in his grasp, he had permitted himself at last to gaze at the wealth in the windows of Florentine goldsmiths; to smile at the pretty girls smiling at him from garlanded Ferrara balconies. And now here he was, masked, in a city tumbling into the unlicensed frenzy of Carnival, its roofs merry with flags, its exquisite buildings garlanded, its squares and lanes blowing with silken awnings and tassels, hung with cloth of gold, with damask, with carpets, and crowded with handsome people, and music, and laughter.

Whatever Simon did, Jan could do. He chose his own mistress, for example. That is, stumbling out of the heat and heavy scents of one of the houses Simon took him to, Jan became aware, as he swayed, of an exquisite masked girl on a bridge. The mist, rising like smoke, made it seem that she floated; a slender wreathed body suspended in air, one narrow, gloved hand holding back a fold of her cloak. Her face, cowled in black, was formed of white porcelain: a pure oval mask whose sleek, still eyes studied him above the rigid flare of the delicate nostrils, the parted, ceramic lips. Her headdress was a crown of silk roses.

He thought she was waiting for someone. But when she had his attention she moved, her white-gloved fingers pressed to her throat, her steps moving softly down the far side of the bridge and away. He heard a breath of laughter, and when he reached the crown of the bridge, found lingering there a scent he did not know. Far ahead, in the mist, a cloak floated. She had been waiting for him.

Behind, Simon called his name, and the girl with him giggled. She was a handsome whore, the best in the house, and Simon had not let him share her. That was his right: he was the teacher, and there were other things he and Jan were going to do together. But that night, Jan had something in prospect other than a harlot of the second rank, however exclusive the establishment. The cloak fluttered ahead, and he followed.

Julius said, 'You know Jan Adorne? I thought I saw him last night coming out of the Coccina brothel. Masked, but the same bony shoulders. Wasn't he supposed to be reserved for the Church?'

'So were you,' Nicholas said. 'So what were you doing in the district?'

'Attending the Martinengo banquet. Where you were supposed to be. Nicholas, it's the Corner reception tonight for Hadji Mehmet and the Persians. Half the Great Council are going, and the wretched Corner girl will receive. I refer to Catherine, the nominal Queen of the très haut et très illustre grand roi de Jerusalem, de Chypre et d'Arménie, your particular friend Zacco. It's ordinary dress, with a mask and a cloak. Or at least, the best dress you've got. We're all going.'

'You mean you don't want to discuss any more numbers,' said Nicholas.

'No, I don't,' Julius said. 'If we're not ready for Monday, we never shall be. All we have to do is decide what we're going to offer. One last meeting.'

'All right,' Nicholas said. 'I'll come to the palazzo tonight if you'll all present yourselves in my room tomorrow morning. One last meeting. And if you want to complain, complain to Tobie. I was going to do all this myself until he showed me how selfish that was.'

The reception given by Marco Corner and his wife Fiorenza, princess of Naxos, was – other than that of the Doge – the finest of all the entertainments offered in Venice during the span of the Carnival. The central figure was, of course, Catherine, Queen of Cyprus, their fourth child, released from her Paduan convent and done up in satin and pearls with a train. She was opulent, fair, and embossed under the paint with heavy spots. Their son George and the girl's seven sisters attended her.

The food and wine were both lavish, and a stage had been erected in the courtyard upon which a play was performed, followed by music. The dancing continued for most of the night.

Nicholas went, and remained. Julius threw himself into every extravagance, while minding his manners. Tobie and John tended to sit side by side, displaying identical sinuous smiles above slackened shoulders. Gregorio, whom the days were making increasingly haggard, muttered something suddenly and went off during the mime. Anselm Adorne came and sat beside Nicholas. He slid the mask from his face. 'Our Ambassadors appear to be enjoying themselves. You and I are not in accord, but there is no reason why we should ignore each another. I have to thank you for caring for Katelijne.'

'The Clares did that,' Nicholas said. His mask leered; his eyes remained cold.

Adorne spoke to the eyes. 'I have no apology to make, I am

afraid, over your divining. It is condemned by God, and a blasphemy. I do find it difficult, however, to pursue you into the courts about the other matter. Partly because of Dr Tobias, and partly because, being opposed to you in business, I should appear to be belatedly vindictive. I refer to my injury, and also to the wretchedness and expense to which you exposed us in Alexandria.'

'I see,' said Nicholas.

'That is all you have to say?' said Anselm Adorne.

'To you, yes. I might say a little more to David de Salmeton,' Nicholas said. 'At the moment, it is not particularly wise to say anything. As you say, we are on opposite sides, and the lord Hadji Mehmet has been watching us since you sat down.'

Adorne rose. He had flushed. He said, 'Thank you for pointing it out. You will forgive Katelijne for not having thanked you herself. She is here, but I thought it best to keep her with me and with Jan.'

'I am sure you are wise,' Nicholas said. 'Those who know only spiritual pleasures must make, in the end, the best guardians.'

Later, Fiorenza of Naxos danced with him. 'You have been avoiding your hostess!'

The long file weaved round the salon. She held her gown with one hand and the fingertips of the other rested in his. She moved them into his palm. Her mask was made like a bird, with wings and feathers and jewels, and her sleeves were so thickly embroidered that they bruised his arm when they swung. At the moment, everything bruised him.

He said, 'I thought you might not wish to speak to me, now that King James has become so undecided. The Despot's daughter is charming, I hear, and quite slim, and Cardinal Bessarion is, of course, rearing her. But in the long run, the daughter of King Ferrante might be more useful.'

She dropped his hand, her face turning up. Then, glancing over her shoulder, she took it again and resumed her swaying progress, wheeling, curtseying. Coming back to him again she said, 'Your sense of humour is unique. I hear King James offered you some of the best estates on the island. Marco was delighted. You will be our neighbour again.'

'Here, perhaps. Not, I fear, in Cyprus. I refused them,' he said. She had, of course, known.

'Niccolino!' She breathed it.

'Well, Zacco *is* going to marry,' said Nicholas. 'That is, I suppose he is going to consummate something, some time. And

Marco doesn't really want me making more money than he does. I think you should be quite pleased if I stay out of Cyprus and co-operate somewhere else for a change. I really do co-operate quite well, when I feel like it. Is that the end of the dance?'

She appeared to think it was. He decided he would give himself another hour, provided he could find Cavalli, or Cavalli could find him. Antonio Cavalli, most favoured envoy, servant and adviser of Duke Sigismond of the Tyrol, had become a frequent visitor at the Casa. The occasion was business, of course: part of it to do with the mining the Bank was financing, and part with Duke Sigismond's most recent explosions of energy, none of them likely to gladden his neighbour of Burgundy.

'What do you think will happen?' Nicholas had said.

'In Burgundy? Oh,' had said Antonio Cavalli, 'I believe the Duke will frighten off France and then set himself, God bless and preserve him, to work for his crown. He aims to end his life as a King or an Emperor, and he may well succeed. Nor do I see how my lord Sigismond could hold out against him. You may be able to mine your silver in peace, if you have patience.'

Such conversations were useful, and so were the other exchanges one might have on occasions otherwise useless, such as tonight. Nicholas saw Cavalli presently, and indeed they left together, since Julius had kindly left him the elaborate boat with curtains and tassels which the Bank used for its social occasions. Cavalli was glad to be offered a seat.

Now the mist was quite thick. Other boats slipped like shadows among the dim lights, and the sound of music and laughter was pierced by the cries of boatmen like distant birdcalls from every canal. The air was dank, even melancholy after the warmth of the salon, and when they slid between the poles outside the Palazzo Cavalli. Nicholas experienced some reluctance to see his passenger leave. He was not invited in. An elderly friend of the Duchess Eleanor resided with them and kept early hours, said Cavalli, excusing himself.

It was understandable. Company had only seemed inviting, for a moment, because now that the calculations were done, there were spaces left in his mind; mooring poles where anything could slip in and find itself lodged. Nicholas waved a smiling good night and had himself taken back to the Bank.

Tomorrow, the decision. The next day, the ducal Palace. The day after, the height of the Carnival, and the verdict, and the meeting with Gelis. If she kept her promise. If she feared God or Ludovico da Bologna, as she did not fear him.

If, after the discussion tomorrow, he could keep his part of the bargain.

Next morning, six men sat with Nicholas round the board in his chamber, and Father Moriz, who occasionally used his cloth to chasten a patron, opened the talk with a prayer. Under the bat-like eyebrows his eyes rested on Gregorio and transmitted calm. Gregorio felt a dim sense of gratitude. He didn't, as yet, know much of Father Moriz: it was John and Nicholas with whom the metallurgical priest had spent the winter in the Tyrol, and Julius and Cefo with whom he had since worked in Venice. He was only now coming to receive Tobie's confidence, and of course he had hardly met Margot before she went off. Father Moriz knew nothing of Margot, except that she and Gregorio had been together for a very long time. Until recently.

Then Nicholas took over the meeting.

It was not, to begin with, controversial. It ran, point by point, over what Venice and the half-formed Christian–Muslim alliance were going to ask them to do, and how far they should do it. Having presented the case, Nicholas himself intervened less than usual and where points of difference arose, showed an unusual tendency to leave the outcome to be settled by vote. Each time it happened, Tobie looked cross.

Occasionally, and without recourse to Nicholas, Gregorio felt required to remind the other five of the likely views of Astorre or of Diniz. He tried not to do it too often. It encouraged Julius, and later Cristoffels to observe that, in devoting so much to the East, the Bank risked neglecting the West where, after all, the core of the business still lay. It was a valid opinion.

The use of their highly trained mercenary company was a case they proceeded to argue. Before the Duke of Burgundy's war, this force was intended for Uzum Hasan, if not Cyprus. Now (it was gradually accepted) it made more sense to leave the troop where it was, between Burgundy, France and the Switzers. They would also need to retain arms and gunners, leaving fewer of both for the Levant.

Father Moriz said, 'It will have occurred to you that we are now tendering substantially less help than was talked of in Rhodes, and to that extent we are deriving less use from our gold. We dismissed the idea of claiming it back, but perhaps we should talk of it. We should be forced to, for example, if Venice rejects our proposals and appoints the Vatachino as their suppliers.'

'We should never get it back,' said Gregorio. He made it sound conclusive.

'I think we could,' Julius said. 'You're thinking of Flemish law. And if we could, why do we need to help Uzum at all? Why not put all the Bank's resources at the service of Burgundy? They've got Astorre and a lot more already.'

'Preserve me from two lawyers,' Nicholas said. 'We've been into all that. We'd never get the gold out of Rhodes, or not without paying its worth in litigation.'

'And it looks magnanimous,' Tobie said. 'Our contribution to Christendom.' Gregorio looked at him, then away.

Cefo said, 'What, then, if we leave the gold with the Order, accept some limited contracts, but put all the rest into the Western wars? It might make sense. If the Turks can't be stopped, then they'll overrun Cyprus and Cairo, and the African trade may compensate. You've heard the Portuguese have sailed much further down the coast since you went?'

'If they overrun Cairo, they will overrun North Africa,' Nicholas said. 'I'd rather help Uzum.'

'I shouldn't,' said Father Moriz. 'I'm with Cristoffels and Julius. I think we let them keep the gold, and look West.'

'Leaving them to trade with the Vatachino, and pay them out of our gold?' said Gregorio.

As he hoped, they thought about that. Then Julius said, 'No. We go to litigation. As I said, I think we'd win. It's our bullion. And anyway, it would freeze the gold meantime. Venice and Uzum would have to pay the Vatachino themselves for whatever they buy. Which they can't.'

'That's very clever,' said Cristoffels. Although frequently depressed by Julius, he recognised, as they all did, that he had flair.

'In fact, that's the answer,' said Father Moriz. 'Offer what help you can; prepare to be outbid by the Vatachino; and claim back the gold.'

'I don't agree,' Gregorio said.

'Nor do I,' said John le Grant.

It was the only time they had ever had an outright disagreement. At the end, when no one had moved his position, Tobie said, 'Nicholas? Something needs saying.'

At last. Gregorio gave a sigh compounded of relief and annoyance, and gazed at Tobie, who was glaring at Nicholas. Two obstinate men. But it was time for Nicholas to admit to his personal stake in this decision. If he wanted to see his son, he must throw his weight – and his gold – behind this Turcomani–Venetian alliance. It might not matter, if they were lucky. They might not be lucky.

Nicholas said, 'Nothing needs saying that hasn't already been said. Decisions of this order don't hang on my whim. We vote, as is fair.'

Gregorio said, 'No!'

Julius said, with irritation, 'What do you mean, no?'

'He means,' said Nicholas, 'that he thinks he knows more about my business than I do. So let me remind him that even I can see genuine advantages in both propositions. The Persian alliance was my own preference. But losing that might mean recovering the gold. And people will sometimes do a great deal for gold.'

He had spoken blandly enough. Julius smiled, but Gregorio understood very well what Nicholas meant. For the sake of the gold, or its promise, Gelis might break her pact with the Patriarch. And there were advantages in being seen to support Burgundy – advantages which had not been so apparent at the time of the negotiations in Cyprus and Rhodes. Those were two of the reasons why Nicholas was willing to let this debate take its course. Another was personal – he did not wish to reveal his predicament. And lastly, Gregorio thought he saw in him an unreliable confidence – as if, with Gelis approaching, he had imagined some increase in those strange powers which would bring him what he wanted. It was unlikely to be so.

Julius said, 'Then let's settle it. Three of us are willing to give up the gold for the use of the Persian–Venetian alliance, and three prefer to support Duke Charles of Burgundy, submitting the ownership of the gold to the due and slow processes of law. Nicholas has the casting vote.'

Cefo said, 'What about Diniz and Captain Astorre?'

Julius said, 'Well, there's no doubt, is there, about them? They'll choose Burgundy every time. Nicholas, isn't that so?'

Of course it was so. It meant that the Patriarch's scheme was about to be abandoned. Gregorio made a last effort. He said, 'Nicholas, Tobie is right. No one should be asked to decide without knowing the facts. That gold was meant for the war against Turkey. You are committed – we are morally committed – to giving it up for that purpose.'

'Not until tomorrow,' Nicholas said. 'And you have all the relevant facts in your hands. So let us go round the table again. And those who can, speak for Astorre and Diniz.'

They voted. The issue was crucial: the vote would never have been necessary if the King of France had not gone to war. It would not have taken place had Nicholas allowed three of them to explain what hung on it. As it was, it produced a foregone result. The House of Niccolò, concerned at the change in Burgundian affairs, must take formal steps, with reluctance, to reclaim its gold, and must modify the help it could offer to Persia.

The notes were written up and agreed. The meeting dispersed. Tobie remained behind.

'Remorse?' said Nicholas. Now everyone had gone, his face had lost its mobility. The word, far from being bitter, seemed almost meaningless.

Tobie sat down, and waited until Nicholas did. He said, 'It means you can't deliver what the Patriarch asked, and so won't see the child. But perhaps Burgundy and the Tyrol and Scotland now seem to be bigger game, and you don't really mind. Or perhaps you think you can manage on your own, and you may be right at that. Where are the maps?'

Nicholas rubbed his face slowly, as if pressing thoughts from his skin, either to summon them or to repel them. No words came. His right fingers were scarred. Without waiting, Tobie got up and opened chests until he found what he wanted, and spilled the scrolls on the floor, working his way down to the bottom. He said, 'You don't have one for Florence.'

Nicholas rose also, slowly. You could see his mind assembling facts. He said, 'You think she is in Florence?'

'She?' said Tobie. He fought against all his instincts, which told him to be merciful. He was the spokesman for Gregorio now, as he had once been the spokesman for the company. He watched Nicholas bring his mind to bear again.

Nicholas said, 'I have been waiting for Gelis to come. She has to come, to hear what we tell the Senate tomorrow.' He paused for breath. 'You are saying I can find the child *myself*?'

Tobie said, 'Have you not even noticed Gregorio? I am saying that Margot has gone in the hopes of bringing him to Venice. The box you were given at St Catherine's was made in Florence, of our African gold. Squarcialupi recognised it at once. Zacco told him to tell me. Gelis stayed last year in Florence. She made some arrangements. Added to what Margot knows, it seems highly probable – she thinks certain – that the child and his nurse have been placed there. If so, Margot has the best chance of finding him. She knows what he looks like.'

'So he exists,' Nicholas said.

Tobie sat where he was, his hands locked together. He said, 'Did they not even give you that hope?'

'Oh, they have always given me hope,' Nicholas said. Then he said, 'But Gelis made her promise never to tell. Why should Margot help me now?'

'Because I told Gregorio what they forced you to endure at Famagusta,' Tobie said. 'To my mind, and Margot's, and his, it cancelled all promises. Margot was eager to try, and Gregorio let her. It isn't only for you. It is because the child himself has turned into a pawn. When he comes, you shall not only see him, we will hold him for you.'

He waited. *They have always given me hope.* He would not tell Nicholas, now, the nature of Margot's particular skills, or how she came by them.

'He may not be in Florence,' Nicholas said.

Tobie said, 'Margot left fifteen days ago. Five days to reach Florence, and ten for the search and a gentle return. We meet the Senate tomorrow. Gelis has to be here to hear the result. I have spent the last eight months cursing the person who showed you that you were a diviner, but it is the only thing that is going to help us all now. Track the child. And track Gelis.'

'She persuades others to carry her ring,' Nicholas said. 'It confuses things.' It sounded plaintive, because his voice was operating on thoughts he had forgotten about already.

'But you will know when she comes into Venice. You must,' said Tobie. 'And if you have no sense of the child, you can trace Margot. Gregorio will bring you possessions, and maps. I'm here to supply whatever else you may need. With the proviso that none of this is any use if you are not going to survive it.'

Nicholas had blocked his lips with the back of his hand. He took his hand away. 'Oh, I shall survive it,' he said. 'Other people may not.' Then he said, 'I had better see Gregorio, and thank him. I am sorry. I should have noticed.'

Chapter 48

SUNDAY ENDED. As usual, the evening mist fingered its way into the Piazza San Marco, forming a nebulous tide like the water which now and then surged over the steps of the Piazzetta, and sent everyone splashing and rollicking home.

Jan Adorne, following a trailing cloak between the wrought iron gates of a palazzo, found himself in a paved garden where sweet, mocking laughter led him between fountain and orange trees, and into the arms of a girl made of marble. He recoiled, and heard through the mist a sprinkle of notes from a lute. Following, he found himself entering a tunnel made of grapevines and trellis.

There was a cloaked form at the end of it. Running towards it, he found himself swathed in a billow of warm, scented silk, and a hand touched his cheek while another caressed him.

The caress, in its experimental delicacy, was almost more than he could endure. When she vanished, and every door proved to be bolted save the one that had given him entrance, he plunged into the mist, and took himself to the nearest whorehouse that he knew of.

Simon de St Pol was there, on his way from one grand house to another, and in acrimonious mood. He relented in time, when assured once again of Jan's eager support; when convinced that their plan was unassailable. St Pol hated the Banco di Niccolò even more than did Jan and his father. He also loathed his own parent, de Ribérac. Jan wondered if the vicomte his father went whoring, or had his own supply of Venetian ladies.

Antonio Cavalli, diligent in his service to the elderly guest of his family, recollected his French and reported. 'Nothing has happened as yet. Master Gregorio spends his time watching for boats from Chioggia.'

He did not say, because he did not know, that Master Gregorio had gone without telling anyone to call on Katelijne Sersanders while her uncle and cousin were absent.

Her chamber was a mess: the nuns at Haddington would never have countenanced it for a moment. Entering, Gregorio made it clear at the outset that he wanted no secrets: only to know if she had heard any news of Gelis van Borselen. She had not. She had not even known that Gelis was expected in Venice. He felt a pang of guilt for having told her at all. When she asked after Margot he saw that she knew nothing of her movements either. They finished by talking of Scotland.

She missed it, he gathered. If the Princess Mary was ever allowed back with her babes – assuming the second was born – Katelijne would not mind returning with her. She missed Whistle Willie and Betha Sinclair and dear Phemie Dunbar.

'Do you ever hear from them?' Gregorio asked.

She had smiled. 'Phemie writes. She sends poems. They are meant for me, but I rather think she likes my uncle to see them. He sends her back commentaries sometimes.' She turned aside and began to show him some music.

He made some sort of response. He had wondered, hearing nothing, but assumed that communication from a priory was difficult. He began to think back.

The girl said, 'You must rest before Tuesday. You are all so busy, my uncle too. What are you wearing for the last day of the Carnival? My uncle won't go. Jan is to be dressed as a cockerel.'

Gregorio said, 'I don't know. Something very ordinary, I'm afraid. Julius is going to parade as a Venetian Senator, and Tobie as a fisherman, or so he says.'

Native caution, even at this moment, warned him not to mention the disguise he thought Nicholas might have chosen. Nicholas had thanked him for allowing Margot to depart.

Gregorio took his leave of Katelijne Sersanders and, instead of going back to the Casa, walked to the quay to which the boats from Chioggia usually came.

Monday arrived, and the solemn meeting in the Doge's Palace between the Senate and the Persian Envoys, attended by delegations from the House of Niccolò and from the Knights Hospitaller of St John of Rhodes, represented by Tobias Lomellini. The magnifico Marco Corner spoke for the interests of Cyprus and Venice. And, of course, of the prince Uzum Hasan, to whom his wife was related.

It was noted that the Bank had pledged itself to supply, at the stated prices, a reduced quantity of artillery, ammunition, handguns and other offensive weapons, together with four trained artillery officers, as per the lists the lords had placed before them.

It was noted that the Bank, contrary to the trend of the preliminary discussions, was providing no shipping, and no band of mercenaries. Further, to the distress of the Signory and the Ambassadors, it had notified its intention of lodging a claim against the Knights Hospitaller for the very sum of money which the Knights had proposed to devote to the purchase of most of these items for the war against the Grand Turk.

The Senate expressed its disappointment at this move by the Bank at a juncture so important to the welfare of all those present, and was only partly reconciled by the news that the way was not closed (were the money to be returned to the Bank), for a grant to be made to the alliance at a later date.

There was some vigorous discussion, and resolutions were taken which did not, however, change M. de Fleury's attitude or affect the final result. Impasse being reached, the Senate assembled a final accounting of the aid the alliance was being currently promised, presented it to the Envoys of the lord Uzum Hasan, and received their somewhat modified gratitude. In a buzz of angry conversation, the meeting broke up.

Outside: 'I regret,' said the lord Hadji Mehmet. 'You have, of course, a duty to Burgundy. Your worth as a merchant and an ally has been known to the prince Uzum Hasan, and he cannot but feel severe disappointment. There may, perhaps, be other occasions when your freedom is less circumscribed. The prince would like to see you in Tabriz. He will welcome meantime what help you have been able to give.'

They were speaking in Turcoman Arabic, but could not be sure of privacy even then. In any case, they were practised, Mehmet and Nicholas de Fleury, in communicating with their eyes. Nicholas said, 'If they are wise, Venice will appoint someone of worth. And perhaps, one day, I may come.'

Marco Corner, father of the Queen of Cyprus, was less gracious. 'I am afraid, Ser Niccolò, that you will look in vain for your concessions on the Tyrolean border – or may not find them quite what you hoped.' He was flushed.

'That depends,' Nicholas said, 'on what success my lords the Envoys have with the Holy Father in Rome. I gather the Patriarch of Antioch is to join them there. You may find me, in the end, as generous as the Order with the possessions of others.'

Tobias Lomellini, Genoese Treasurer of the Order, walked with

him to the wharf. 'I cannot begin to describe my disgust. On a
caprice, you have reversed all we talked of on Rhodes. You have
betrayed the Religion and, of course, the offer made by the
Patriarch is withdrawn.'

'You stole my money,' said Nicholas. 'I was going to forgive
you, but my company showed me I was wrong. What powers do
you possess to withdraw the Patriarch's offer?'

'The fullest powers,' said the Genoese. 'I have the papers of
authority, should you doubt me. A note of my decision will be
prepared for your wife, who I believe was involved. She can
obtain it from any clerk of the Order. Or I shall present it to her at
the banquet. I suppose, in spite of everything, the Signoria has
summoned you to the official banquet?'

'I'm on the list,' Nicholas said. 'And I do lend them large sums
of money.' The gold from the *Ghost*, he imagined, would long
since have been melted into bullion. Perhaps it had already gone.
At the very least, the Knights would now quietly use it to buy what
they needed, no doubt some of it from him. But they were answer-
able at law for what they had done. However worthy the cause,
they had no right to support it by piracy. Although of course, the
litigation would take years. Ochoa was in their power. He would
say whatever they told him.

'And your lady wife will be there?' Lomellini repeated.

'Nothing would please her better,' Nicholas said. 'If she arrives
in time.'

The banquet for the Persian Envoys was one of the better ones,
and Julius enjoyed it. Calling above the roar of conversation he
said to Tobie, 'I thought his wife was going to be here?' And,
observing Nicholas had overheard: 'The Sersanders girl said Gelis
was going to be here? When are you going to tell her you're setting
up family life in Bruges, and not Persia?'

'You've got it all wrong,' Nicholas said. 'I'd practically settled
on Innsbruck. No, she isn't here. She may come later.'

'You'd think she would enjoy all this,' Julius said. 'And the
child. Isn't she bringing the child? I thought she must be, because
Margot isn't here. Poor Gregorio. He hates it so when Margot isn't
here.'

'I don't suppose for a moment that she is bringing the child,'
Nicholas said. 'Venice, in Carnival-time? It would grow up
depraved.'

The Baron Cortachy, Envoy of the most noble, the most high and most powerful prince, the lord Charles, Duke of Burgundy (and counsellor of James, King of Scotland), conducted himself at table with all the address of one accustomed to the ceremonial of Brussels.

To Tobias Lomellini he said, 'I, too, am dismayed, although as a merchant I shall benefit. M. de Fleury has forfeited the right to act as exclusive purchasing agent for arms. I am told the Patriarch of Antioch has been in Caffa, consolidating Genoese privileges in order to placate the Order in Rhodes. It could have been worse.'

It could have been worse. The words, Adorne's own, stayed engraved in his mind as his name was engraved on a block of stone; on a wall. Was that to be the epitaph of this pilgrimage, this journey which circumstance had forced on him and his son, and which, at another time in his life, could have been glorious?

He should have come for his soul's sake alone. The sufferings and the rewards: the solitudes and silence of Sinai, the exaltation of the spirit he had experienced over and over in the Holy Land should have been sufficient. The jars and phials, the trinkets and the indulgences brought so far with such pains should have been acquired for those dear to his heart, and less for those from whom he or his Duke desired favours. And some of his party were dead.

Yet he served two princes, and was loyal to them, and had worked in their interest. And for his family, too, he had worked – this immense, growing family with which Margriet had blessed him; and which meant that he could not ignore the opportunities or the dangers which the future might offer his investments and his trade.

And likewise, he could not ignore his competitors. He wished de Fleury had not come, and that the child Kathi had not encumbered him, dear though she was. He wished he did not know, as now he did, that Jan was not of the stuff of which great statesmen are made. But the lad's future was safe, with a Pope who favoured Genoa, and the Adornes.

Jan had shown himself a good son, and in this interim should be permitted some frivolity, although his father could wish he were absent less often, and were seeing less of Simon de St Pol whose life he, Adorne, had saved in the salt-houses in Scotland. Splendid jouster though St Pol was, he had the name of a profligate. It was a tragedy, too, to see developed in Nicholas de Fleury what had seemed, long ago, merely the irresponsibility and lightness of youth. Now added to that was the sin of impiety. And what St Pol lacked: a chilling mastery of manipulation in business which others, too, had begun to identify as a threat.

With a fortitude supplied him by God, Anselm Adorne confronted an eventual return to his home and an untangling of the ludicrous situation precipitated by these poor, warring monarchs of England. Unrecognised for months by the Duke, the Yorkist King of England had been skulking in Holland as a house-guest of Louis de Gruuthuse. At the same time, thanks to Nicholas de Fleury, the Scots traitor Boyd, Earl of Arran, was raising a family in the Baron's own household.

Adorne owed allegiance to the Scots King who had condemned Boyd to death. His own daughter served the English King's mother. He could extract himself from the predicament with some honour, but it was de Fleury he blamed, and de Fleury on whom his thoughts constantly dwelled. It seemed the man was not going East, but had just confirmed his stake in the West: in Flanders, Burgundy, perhaps even in Scotland. But there, of course, the Baron Cortachy had already forestalled him. And now there were others. In future, Nicholas Fleury would find his opposition of a different calibre. He would face a coalition.

The pendulum gave him nothing. He sat finally by the light of one guttering candle, gazing at the lines on map after map; concentrating his being on Gelis, on Margot.

Nothing worked. Unless he had lost his mind, they were not in Florence, nor in Venice. He could not be sure of the sea: perhaps the boat with Margot in it was already sailing in from the mainland. Perhaps the faint shocks that sometimes touched him from this road or that village were traces of the passing of Gelis, or of the persons to whom she had given her kerchief, her cloak, her gold ring. She was shrewd. She had studied his power, in order to learn how to counter it.

The child, of course, he could not reach, knowing nothing of it. All he knew was that it was his, and alive, and a son. Two years ago, he would have perjured his soul for that knowledge. Now he could hardly assimilate it, his anxiety was so great. He had broken his pact with the Patriarch. He had been wrong.

At some hour during the night, Tobie thumped his shoulders. 'Sit up. You'll set your hair alight, and burn your papers all over again.'

He had brought a cup. After a certain argument they had had, the cup was strictly regulated, to yield so much sleep and no more. There was no time to waste. Margot had not come, and could not be found. Neither could Gelis. And the next day was Tuesday the twenty-sixth day of February. Martedi Grasso, the last, the most joyous day of the Carnival, when the lords of the night watch are blind, and nothing is outlawed but grief.

He was nowhere near his maps, in the end, when the power struck as suddenly and as sickeningly as it had that first time in the Tyrol, when he had been thrown to the ground amid images of water and fire. On this occasion it drew fewer eyes, occurring when, after a morning of festival ritual, the guests of the Doge and the Signoria had crowded into the Senate Hall to witness a spectacle. Miniature castles had been built on the floor and a score of scarlet-clad Senators were attacking them. Nicholas abruptly ceased watching.

Tobie, nearest to Nicholas, saw the shock run through his body. He rose. Gregorio, not far away, noticed and began to come over. The men about them, jovial in liquor, cheering on the performance, paid no attention. Tobie said, 'What?' and touched Nicholas on the shoulder. He was shaking, and had buried his head in his hands.

Tobie said, 'Come,' and put a hand under his arm. Then Nicholas straightened and, guided by Tobie, got out of the room. Gregorio, following, saw that both John le Grant and Father Moriz had noticed: he shook his head at them, and they stayed. Julius had observed nothing.

Outside, Nicholas said, 'I am sorry.' The Piazzetta milled with men as richly dressed as themselves; even his pallor was not unremarkable in a city where, for the moment, licence ruled and dissipation was the norm. Nicholas said clearly, 'They are both here,' and turned to Gregorio. 'Gelis, and Margot. But not to-gether.'

Until he saw Gregorio's face, even Tobie had not understood the extent of his anguish. Now Gregorio said, 'How can you know? Nicholas? How can you know?'

'Look at him,' was all Tobie said. He let Nicholas go. 'What do you want us to do?'

'I am sorry,' said Nicholas again. His eyes were still on Gregorio. 'I have to go back to the Casa.'

'To use your maps?' Tobie said. 'Or one of them is there?'

'I don't know,' Nicholas said. 'But Gelis is nearer.' Unexpect-edly, he caught both of Gregorio's hands and set them violently on his own shoulders, covering them with his palms. Gregorio's eyes were alarmed. Nicholas said, 'I need to know Margot as well as you do. Can you transmit anything, or take anything from me?' He was becoming whiter and whiter.

Gregorio pulled his hands away. He said, 'No. You are losing too much. If you can reach Gelis, that's enough.' He was almost as

pale as Nicholas. He repeated Tobie's words. 'What do you want
us to do?'

'Don't ask,' Tobie said. 'I was wrong. The boat will be quickest.'
The crowd was so thick that it took an effort to push through to
the landing-stage. He had thought at first that Nicholas was going
to faint, and then saw that he had given himself some sort of
respite; as if he had had the sense to detach himself somehow from
whatever had him in its grip. He waited patiently until they found
the *barchetta*, and then took his place without speaking.

The Canal was packed with boats and laughter and streamers.
The Casa, when they reached it, was silent, all its staff freed for the
revels save for the porter, sitting inside the double doors in his
black and white unicorn livery, consoling himself with watered
wine and bread and salami. It quite alarmed him when the padrone
appeared, all out of the blue, instead of being at the Palace with the
rest of them. The doctor said something as he passed, but Master
Gregorio looked straight ahead.

The porter jumped up. He said, 'Padrone! Your honoured lady
insisted! She said she would wait in the salon!'

Halfway up the double staircase, Nicholas stopped. Then he
turned, and ran up. Gregorio hesitated, but followed. Tobie was
running already. 'Do you think this is a lovers' meeting?' he said
over his shoulder. Ahead, Nicholas had opened the door of the
salon.

It was a beautiful room, running the full depth of the house and
fronting the Canal with a balcony. The girl facing Nicholas was
Gelis van Borselen, strands of fair hair coiling below the fine
headdress and back veil, her velvet travelling gown stained, as
when she had come to the deathbed of Godscalc. She said, 'What
have you done with him?' She looked only at Nicholas.

He moved forward and stopped. 'With whom?'

She said, 'Jordan. Jordan has gone. Where have you put him?'

Gregorio moved. Tobie grasped him hard by the arm. Nicholas
said, 'I suppose I don't need to ask which you mean. I have not
touched the child. I have never seen him.'

Gelis said, 'He was in Florence. They were to bring him. I
expected to find him in Venice. They say the house in Florence
was empty. Someone stole the child and his nurse, and the rest ran
away. Your doing. It must be your doing.'

Nicholas sat down. He said, 'Do I look as if I have won
something today?'

Then she looked round at the others. Tobie said, 'We none of us
know where your child is. Nicholas divined that you were here.'

He remembered, now, the severity of the brows, the coldness of the blue eyes. He held their gaze until, releasing him, they returned to Nicholas. She said, 'I am not wearing the ring.'

'You came an hour ago,' Nicholas said.

She sat then herself. Holding Gregorio still, Tobie moved quietly past them both to a ledge by the balcony, where he leaned, and Gregorio sank into a seat. Gelis said, 'Then you could divine where he is?'

'No,' Nicholas said. 'Or I would not have thought I should find him in Famagusta.'

Her face tightened. She said, 'The child was not to blame.'

'I understand that,' he said. 'If I knew him, I could find him.'

Tobie spoke. 'You could find him if you had something of his.'

'Nail clippings?' Nicholas said. You could see him watch her whiten.

Then she said, 'I could bring you something.'

Up till then, Tobie thought, Nicholas had refused to allow himself to believe. Even yet, you could see him torn by the need to protect himself. Nicholas, who never gave anything away. He said, 'A garment. Something that touches ... Or something he ... knows.'

'I will bring it,' she said, and got up.

Tobie said, 'Let us come with you,' but she shook her head and began to move to the door.

Nicholas stood. She said, 'It will be quicker. You could find me anyway.'

She left, and he let her go. Then he said, 'The maps are in my room. Gregorio, sit with me.'

There was no one to serve them. Tobie waited some moments in silence, watching the great map of Venice spread out on the desk, with every house, every rio carefully marked, and the little jewel swaying over it. Then he went first to his own room, and after that to the kitchens, where he mixed draughts and loaded a tray. He had done it often enough in a long and exhausting campaign. Something to keep a man going and useful, without burning him out before time. When he got back and put the tray down, they were talking.

Gregorio broke off and looked up. 'She is here. The jewel says so. But Nicholas says she is moving.'

Of course, he was speaking of Margot. Tobie said, 'Do you think the child is with her?'

'I don't know,' Nicholas said. 'And I don't think Gelis needs to know that Margot is involved unless and until we find Margot and the ... and Jordan together. It *would* be Carnival-time.'

'Easier to hide,' Tobie said. 'You say Simon is here. Perhaps even his father. The sooner we find that child and Margot, the better. You should change out of that. If we have to go out, we should all be in masquerade. You want to keep your son this time.'

He had got himself a fisherman's costume. He was going to look a fool, and didn't care. He saw Nicholas take some of his drink, and went off to dress. Gregorio had no disguise, but could wear a black cloak and mask. And Nicholas at least would be in black.

They were all in the salon again by the time that Gelis returned. Her cloak was fresh; she wore a plain gown underneath it. She stopped a moment and then moved forward, scanning them all. Her eyes rested on Nicholas.

He had not wanted to change. Tobie had had to persuade him that it was not irrelevant, and he had flung on the clothes, making his way quickly back, listening ceaselessly. Then she was there before him, her smile openly mocking. 'Alichino?' she said.

The narrow pourpoint and hose, the single garland, the black diabolical mask in his hand with its soft fur and incipient horns were unmistakable. She said, 'The devil-buffoon. How appropriate.'

'I knew you would think so,' he answered. He had some colour, and the worth of some hours of vitality, Tobie thought, depending on how much he was now going to expend. He said, 'Did you bring something?'

She brought it out from under her cloak: a little whistle on a silk cord. Tobie saw Gregorio swallow. Nicholas himself just said, 'Bring it,' and walked out of the room to his chamber. The girl, following, bit her lip, frowning at his back. When he sat down at the desk, she held back.

He looked up. 'Then give me it,' he said. The whistle changed hands. He was going to use it, Tobie realised, as his pendulum.

She had never seen it done before, Tobie guessed. He stood back with Gregorio, watching her move a step closer, then another, her eyes on his hand with the cord. The other, the left, was moving slowly over the paper. For a long time, she watched the glints and swings of the whistle. Then she caught sight of the diviner's face and stood very still, her eyes on it.

You would suppose that, in all the time they had spent together, she had seen something of this order of concentration. It occurred, in flickers, when Nicholas was calculating, or preparing a plan. Sometimes, devising some mechanical marvel with John, Tobie had seen them both like this, for odd moments. John thought of Nicholas, Tobie knew, as a master technician with no need for the softer emotions. In his heart, John thought that Nicholas was the same kind of man that he was. The trouble was, they all did.

Tobie said, 'If you are not getting results, you should stop.'

Sometimes, he didn't hear. It was Gelis's voice saying, '*Stop!*' that made him look up. The cord had inflamed the chafed part of his finger, but that was all. It had never been roused to full swing on this search.

Nicholas said, 'There are so many people. And he is being moved all the time. Is that possible?'

She said, 'You can't tell who has him? Or why?' She sounded distracted. 'Or if he is lost?'

'I can't tell,' he said. 'I need to be there. Will you let me keep the whistle?'

She said, 'What will you do?' Her eyes were on his face again, searching it.

'Walk about,' Nicholas said.

'Then I'll come with you,' said Gelis.

'We'll all come,' Tobie said. 'Nicholas. You need ten minutes' rest. Gelis will wait.'

He had expected her to object, but she left the room quietly. Gregorio said, 'Well?'

Nicholas had threaded the cord through his hands and was looking down at the whistle, lying flat on his palm. He said, 'They aren't together. The signs for the whistle are in different places from the signs for Margot.'

'What in God's name –' burst out Gregorio.

Nicholas looked up. 'She's clever, your Margot. She doesn't want to lead anyone to the baby until she's sure it is safe. She probably knows who is here. When Gelis has gone, Margot will find us.'

It brought Gregorio comfort but it was not, Tobie thought, necessarily true. The child might be missing, and Margot might be trying to find it. Or Nicholas, spent, was mistaken, and neither the child nor Gregorio's lover was in Venice at all.

He took Gregorio away, and left Nicholas to rest if he could. When he went back ten minutes later, he had gone.

One by one, the masqueraders took to the streets after dinner: in couples, in companies. Katelijne Sersanders, called for by friends, received her uncle's permission to leave. Her uncle also departed, bidden to celebrate with the Knights of the Order. Jan, attired in cocks' feathers, had already met with his friends in some tavern. Katelijne saw a play in an adjacent Campo and then, pleading indisposition, excused herself and made her way home. There, she changed quietly and went out again, feeling loose-limbed and free, as in Egypt. Unhappily, by then the lie had come true. She did feel sick.

Simon de St Pol, in ravishing costume, attended several parties and began, with a small group of acquaintances, to rove through the lanes and squares of the city. His father, for the nonce, stayed at home.

Julius, dressed as a Senator, introduced himself into a number of illustrious homes and began to enjoy himself greatly. Cefo went off to the rooms of a young woman acquaintance. Tobie took Gregorio by the arm and propelled him outdoors in high anger. As well as Nicholas, Gelis had gone. Tobie had no doubt the two were together, and he proposed to discover them both before – as the Franciscan had hinted – they killed each other.

Gelis said, 'You can still occasionally surprise me. I thought you would have demanded your nursemaids.'

There were fatigue-hollows under her eyes and she wore no mask and no elaborate headgear; only a netted cap into which her hair had been rolled and pleated with ribbon. Contradicting the simplicity, her cloak was a conspicuous one of white satin. You would say she was seeking a child, and wished to be easily visible. Or perhaps you would say that.

She had been ready, of course, to come with him. If he found anything, she did not want Tobie or Gregorio present. And neither did Nicholas. He wore the whistle hung from his neck, where it rested in the swathe of his cowl, and over the black needlework of his tunic. The black hood bound his head, and the black brimmed hat was pressed, slanting over it. Between hood, hat and mask nothing human appeared. He saw and breathed through cut eyes and cut nostrils. He was not dressed for children.

In his divining hand he carried his *batocio*, the small scrolled stick of the underworld being he represented, and three-quarters of his conscious mind clung to it. The stick was uneasy, stirring this way and that, but only a little. Never the heart-thumping blow he had experienced in the ducal Palace. He knew Gelis was glancing at him, for he was usually talkative enough, God knew. She didn't press for an answer. She walked a fraction behind, and let him lead her.

He had identified, now, the true impediment to his art, to his sorcery. Preoccupied since his arrival, he had failed to visualise that on this, the last day of the revels, the city would fill like a cornucopia with people. Tomorrow was Mercoledì delle Ceneri. Tonight at midnight began the time for abstinence, penitence, when last year's palm fronds became cinders.

Today the palm branches were green, and these could be flowers or people who slowly flowed, cheek to cheek, through the paved lanes and the narrow canals between the tall marble palaces; or spanned each bridge like the fringe of a fan. People garlanded roof-tops and balconies and clustered in every piazza: round the bull-baiting in San Geremia; below the stages in the Campo della Salute where the actors stalked through their dramas; around the Campo Santo Stefano where the human pyramid formed and re-formed and men wrestled naked, and artists sang and played carnival ballads to fiddle and lute; in the Campo San Polo where the Castellani and the Nicolotti staged a mock battle, and there was a bear and an ostrich and a live marionette, revolving to the sound of a musical box.

The mild February sun glittered on everything. It glowed upon the drifting headdresses of chiffon, feathers and fur; upon the grandiloquent hats burgeoning aloft into tall sheaves of plumes; upon globes and hoops and castles of saye; whorls of satin, winged fantasies sparkling with sequins. It flashed upon foil and wire and ribbons of silver and gold; turned a wand of white gauze in-candescent and played the shadows of giants and angels upon the silken white membranes of tents.

The noise echoed under the blue slots of sky in the alleys and expanded into the air of the piazzas: the roar of talking and laughter, the surge of music, the patter of drums. And scent and colour jostled together, strident as noise: musk and ultramarine and magenta, turquoise and amber, iris, cedar and emerald, frangipani and violet and rose.

Gelis said, 'You can't do it, can you? He's gone.'

It was not, for once, the voice of challenge, of scorn. Nicholas said, 'I am going to try.' Then he said, 'Why do you care?' A child passed, asleep on someone's shoulder, its garland cock-eyed. There had been a group of small boys on a bridge, being helped to pelt one another with rose-water eggs: the fallen shells conducted a long swaying dance in the water. There were children everywhere, winged like angels, padded like elves. But he felt nothing; nothing.

She said, 'I care because he is mine.'

'And I don't?' She had sent him to Cyprus.

She said, 'I don't know, Nicholas, what you want him for. I hope I never find out.'

They were in a crowded, shadowy lane. At the end, brilliant in sunshine, a masked youth leaned on the base of a pillar, one hand at the pipe in his mouth, the other tapping the little tambour which hung at his waist. As they came near he leaped down and led the way dancing, drawing the column of people behind him like an enchanter to the next play. From the curve of a bridge a tambourine suddenly rattled, and the strings of a guitar summoned, beckoned. The *batocio* stirred and flickered and turned but gave him no news. There were too many people. Holding his concentration, his senses sickened and swam. She put her hand surprisingly on his wrist and said, 'Stop.'

There was a great panelled door at his side, and he stumbled and leaned back against it. She released his wrist and stopped, too. The crowd continued to pass: cloaks, sleeves, trains of damask and silver; fans and muffs. Beyond an arch was the thunder of noise from the Piazza San Marco: its rows of stages, its thousands of people; the basilica with its mosaics like wrinkled gold skin at the end. He kept his eyes open.

She said, 'I could go on, but you can't. Later, the crowds may be less. I have rooms here.'

He looked where she indicated. It was not the doorway he occupied, but a more modest one opposite. There was a small balcony up above, bound with ivy. She said, 'I stayed here before I sailed, in the spring. David de Salmeton arranged it for me.'

His eyes had closed. He said, 'Are you not afraid that I shall stop, when you say that?'

'No,' she said.

'Or walk away?'

'I am fresher than you are. I am not offering you my bed or my sympathy,' Gelis said. 'Only the opportunity to recover so that you can do what I want you to do.'

'And after that?' Nicholas said. He merely wished to hear what she would say.

'According to my information, you did not keep your part of the bargain,' she said. 'The child is still mine.'

He wondered what made her think that. Being the devil, he was equipped with a dagger. It was a real one. It occurred to him that he wouldn't mind if David de Salmeton were in Gelis's house.

In fact he was not. The rooms he climbed to were empty. She went to fetch him some wine, and he pulled off his hat and the mask, and pushed back the cowl. His hair clung wet round his neck. He let his lids close, because it was quiet and he felt rather ill, and he knew that whatever occurred, for a while he was perfectly safe.

Down below in the alley, a page in a moretta mask and striped hose occupied the grand doorway he had just left and began, absently, to play with a jew's trump.

Chapter 49

GREGORIO SAID, 'THERE'S going to be fog. We'll never find them. We ought to go back to the Casa.' They had been back twice already, in case Margot had sent a message or come.

It was an hour to sunset and mist, like white smoke, had already drifted in from the sea and was filling the Piazzetta, so that the stalls of the butchers and the salami-sellers started to vanish, and the Doge's Palace dimmed, arch by arch. The haze searched through the Piazza until only the bell-tower soared clear, a finger of rose against the fading Basilica. The final wan rays of the sun lit the Lion of St Mark, and the angels' wings, and rested on the dull gold below, and then were extinguished.

Tobie said, 'I think the crowds are causing the trouble. No one can move. And Nicholas can't fine tune unless he has peace. I hope to God that girl keeps her head.'

The latter part of the pronouncement represented his doubts about Gelis. The first was, as ever, to keep Gregorio calm.

What Tobie could not understand, himself, was how the first, violent intimation had managed to penetrate to Nicholas through crowds just as great. It had seemed to come, he remembered, most clearly from Gelis; and had registered, perhaps, the height of her despair.

He had found it hard, himself, to keep his equanimity in this harsh, brilliant atmosphere of festival, sliding now, as the light waned, towards something darker, less innocent. Now the prostitutes were coming out in greater numbers, men as women, women as men; nursemaids with broad shoulders and thick calves pushing carts loaded with full-grown, lumbering babies, drooling, chanting, clawing at skirts with both hands as they passed. Every dark archway and porch seemed to be filling with rustling figures.

The real children had gone; or he thought so until, his breath caught in his throat, he saw an imploring masked figure before him, a limp child in her arms, its golden hair lifelessly drifting.

Tobie blundered towards her: she turned. He saw that the mask was two-faced; the figure that of a man; and the child in its grasp an effigy fixed to the stuff of his costume. Sickened, Tobie had hurried past.

He got Gregorio to agree to go back to the Casa, and to meet him later at the Rialto. Their boat would be there. He counted on Nicholas to remember that, if all else failed.

Nicholas woke up in darkness, suddenly. He had been asleep in a chair whose high back was comfortably padded, and which faced a small window whose panes glimmered white. He rose abruptly.

A voice said, 'The mist came down, but it is still very crowded.'

Gelis. He could make out the outline of a bed, and then her shape, lying watching him. He wondered how visible he had been against the light, and if she had or had not guessed what wakened him. He said, 'Do you have any particular resources for casual visitors?'

There was a stand of candles by the bed. She struck tinder and started to light them. Her fingers were steady. Without moving, he saw that his dagger had gone. She said, 'Through that door. There is no other way out: you will have to come back here.'

She had been watching him, then. He departed in any case, and found her standing when he came back, combing and pinning her hair. The line of her body had not changed. She said, 'It shook you awake. A real sign this time. So where did it come from?'

He walked into the room and stood looking at her. Behind his back was the other door which led outwards. He said, 'Somewhere in Venice. This time, that is all I can tell you.'

She finished what she was doing and sat down. She had regained all her composure. She said, 'You mean that is all you will tell me. I offended you. I remember.'

'In what way?' he said. He stood, no less at ease, his back to the door. 'My various mishaps in Cairo were not your doing. You even sent me your ring. As for Mount Sinai – I have to thank you, I gather, for rescuing me. That is, Father Ludovico did that, but you and he, I now see, are interchangeable.'

He lifted his brows. She said, 'He would never have forgiven me if you had died.'

Her voice was calm. The pulse that had wakened him beat. He could find the child. It didn't matter, now, what she said, except that the calmness in itself was an affront. He said, 'Remind me. In Africa, when you thought Father Godscalc and I were both lost, did you feel nothing?'

There was a little silence. Then she said, 'Recently, you had cause to think me dead. I felt what you felt.'

'I see,' he said. 'Certainly, it was annoying. All those plans gone to waste. Why did you go to wait for me at St Catherine's? There was no gold. Or perhaps you didn't know that?'

'Does it make any difference?' she said. 'I wanted to see what you would do. So did the Patriarch. And he didn't want you on Cyprus too early. On the other hand, I didn't mind when you went. Did you go to Katelina's tomb? I hope you did that much, at least.'

Your sister was a sweet lover, and urgent as you are, and wilful as you are, but never, never . . .

Nicholas said, 'Shall I please you? For whatever rage, whatever hatred you feel against Katelina or me, you obtained revenge in full measure on Cyprus. Nothing would have taken me there but the hope of my son, and you and Father Ludovico between you saw that I had it. Yes, I prayed in the Cathedral. Yes, I left the Cathedral and went to the Franciscans', and yes, I found there what you left for me. You are avenged. But in return, you cannot expect me to lead you to the child. And possessing the child, I shall need no others.'

She had grown very pale. She said, 'That will suit the Greek.' It sounded sardonic.

'The Greek?' he said, but she didn't reply, shaking her head with impatience.

Then she said, 'I suppose, then, I am pleased, to a degree. Better pleased than the Patriarch, who hoped to see you face East. We are not, perhaps, as interchangeable as you think. He may even expect us to part, honour satisfied.'

'*Honour!*' Nicholas said.

She jumped to her feet. 'A meaningless word, isn't it, between you and me? I use the same tricks that you do. We both cheat. I believed, finally, that Katelina came to you, and that you were kind to her, and that it was her own will to marry Simon and claim your child as his. I knew what she was like. But it wasn't like that, was it?'

Because of the fog, it was very quiet. Or perhaps it was quiet for other reasons. His heart beat, and the other pulse, and he felt shaken again between the two, as he had, looking down on the gold. He said, 'It *was* like that.'

'Not under the waterfall,' she said. And as he did not answer, she went on. 'Your words in Africa. You were so amused: had you forgotten? *I took her under a waterfall, as I remember.*'

He had forgotten. It had been idiotic of him to say it. Gelis had desired him to make love to her, as he had to her sister. And eventually, it had happened. And yet –

He said, 'How can it matter so much?'

She stared at him. Then she said, 'How can I explain it? One might forgive a passing affair, with sad consequences. But to commit the act twice: to take the same woman, now a mother, now married, and make her your lover – that is not ignorance. Not on your part or hers.'

He stood, shaken by pressures and tried to think. He said, 'There are different kinds of love, Gelis.'

'I am eager to learn,' Gelis said. 'So what kind of love seduced the wife of Simon de St Pol? Was it guilt that made you try to kill him in Scotland? What kind of love made you marry a courtesan and turn your back on Katelina? And what kind of love did she have, that she died in Famagusta when there was no need for her to have gone there at all? Did you never ask yourself that?'

She was not composed now. Her eyes shone as if full of tears, and her lips set hard as she ended. He felt suddenly incapable of going on. He said, 'I hardly need to. I'm sure you have all the answers. Just now, I think that is sufficient.'

He watched her collect herself. A tear had escaped. He watched it run over her cheekbone and down to her lips. She said, 'You don't want to know, do you? You really don't want to know. I wonder what instinct you are going by, and what you will do when the day comes when you are forced to hear it all, Nicholas. But not today, you are right.'

He prepared to move. As if she knew it, she spoke again. 'Shall I tell you something else? Your charming, untroubled sleep at this juncture confirmed another idea of mine. You have some fears for the child, but not many. I think you know who took him. Should I be right?'

Nicholas said, 'I didn't know he was alive. I do now. I don't know who has him.' If he had been overcome by something other than sleep, he didn't want her especially to know. It became important to leave before she began thinking of Margot. Turning at last, he jerked the door open.

Three men were standing outside. 'My bodyguard,' Gelis observed. 'I thought your brains were going to revive some time. Now you know where to go, I really should prefer not to be left behind. Shall we leave?'

It was difficult to do anything else. He found he did not really care. He hadn't been wrong. Something was going to succeed. And, of course, he was going to mislead them.

Unfortunately, she grasped his stick and threw it away, so that he was forced to resort to the flashing, eloquent whistle, which began to shudder as soon as he touched it. By then they had replaced his mask by a plain one. Gelis, too, had altered her cloak and her hood. This time, whatever he found, she wanted no witnesses. It should have troubled him. Instead the whistle throbbed, and his sense of elation kept growing even when the three soldiers manhandled him downstairs, and the crowds pressed about his senses again.

An hour before midnight, the mist dissolved to a haze and St Mark, had he looked down from his pickled pork, would have seen that his Republic's prince, elders, and priests were assembling outside the Basilica in his Piazza; that the stages and scaffolding had all gone, and that the Carnival, in a last blaze of glory, was withdrawing its revellers to the tall wooden bridge at the Rialto.

Singing, eating, drinking, embracing, merry-makers and artists alike crowded on the streamer-hung bridge and occupied either bank of the Grand Canal, thick and lively as lobsters. The water was covered with gondolas, glowing like insects in amber, upon which lounged the nobility, the effigies whose beringed white-gloved hands were decked with real diamonds; whose extravagant headdresses and masks had been manufactured by goldsmiths.

The boats were carved and gilded and mounded with ivy and flowers. Dishes gleamed under candlelit awnings while servants stepped up and down, and musicians competed. The flotilla swayed, awaiting the signal to sail.

In the first rank was the beautiful twelve-oar *bissona* of the Banco di Niccolò, with its unicorn crest. To it, one by one through the evening, had come everyone but its master. Julius, exalted, dragging Cristoffels, who had been reluctant to leave. John le Grant, subdued, with Father Moriz. Tobie, bringing with him Gregorio, induced to walk the few steps from the Ca' Niccolò by a combination of guarantees and assurances. The sail in procession down the Canal to the Basin would only take half an hour. Less, for everyone to be in position by midnight. And Nicholas would come to the boat.

So far he had not. Others were there, however, who could be recognised – by their coats of arms, by the liveries of their oarsmen and servants.

To the right, the flag of Corner and the lion banner of Lusignan stirred over the lantern-hung vessel of Marco Corner, his wife and his daughter Catherine, Queen Consort of Cyprus; and scent and music floated across from its cabin. The Canal was not very broad, and there was only one darkened boat between the gondola of the Queen and that of the Banco di Niccolò. Tobie, gazing across it, glimpsed Zacco's stout little bride, and two exotic figures he thought might be the princesses of Naxos.

There was a third, remarkable for its beauty, which twice came to the rail to survey the boats pressed flank to flank all about her. Black within its black cowl, her satin mask was edged with diamanté, and the parted, sensual lips were thickset with diamonds. Below one almond eye was sewn a single, sparkling tear. Over it all she bore a coronet of silver roses from which soared a spray of five black and white plumes. In time, she observed Tobie watching her, and vanished below.

No Nicholas. Behind the grand boats of ceremony, the flotilla of gondolas had lengthened, jostling seven, eight, nine abreast under the shadows of the Rialto and far beyond the curve of the Canal. Not all were occupied. Turning his back on Marco Corner and his neighbour, Tobie was met by the dazzle of lamps as the splendid boat on their other side roused to life and welcomed its owners. A moment later, the flag of the Knights of St John broke out aloft.

Tobie drew back to the shadows, and watched. The Knights' guests were all there, as he hoped. Anselm Adorne, emerging smiling from the splendid deck-cabin to stand at talk with his hosts, surveying the gaiety on the banks and the bridge. And – he sighed – a glimpse of Katelijne, unmasked, in a red gown with a garland and veil to conceal her cropped hair. He perceived, lurking beside her, a bundle of cock's feathers which he guessed, without difficulty, to be Jan Adorne. The youth seemed, from his movements, to be tipsy. Tobie was sorry, for a moment, for his father the Baron Cortachy, but the moment soon passed.

He scanned the fleet all around him, but saw nothing of Nicholas or of Gelis. He didn't expect, by now, to see Margot, although he wouldn't have said so to Gregorio. He noticed that the boat to his right was now lit, but didn't observe, of the smaller vessels behind him, that one was quite dark, although there were several people on board. Nor could he know that Gelis van Borselen was one of them, or that the master of the Banco di Niccolò, silenced and under duress, was another.

A roar came from the north, as the Serenissima's trumpets began to mount to the crest of the bridge for their fanfare. The noise, from thousands of throats, rose like a blizzard and levelled. Julius appeared, wine in hand. 'Where has the stupid man got to? We'll have to set off without him.'

Gregorio said, 'I'm going ashore.' It was perfectly possible, stepping from boat to boat.

John le Grant, also appearing, said, 'Why not wait until we get to the Basin? He can catch us then, during the fireworks.' Gregorio turned back abruptly.

The trumpets blared. It was a long and elaborate fanfare, and those hearers acquainted with Scotland found coming to mind certain strictures of an earthy, a whistling character. They were reminded, immediately, that in Venice all commonplace standards are useless. The fanfare ended. As if struck by the finger of heaven, a hedge of four thousand torches sprang alight on each side of the water. Hidden drums beat, and music blossomed like shrubs on each bank. The packed boats trembled and stirred and, moving, set off in consort on the last, glorious voyage back to the Piazza.

By now, such was the beat of the signal that the noise didn't matter. Pressed down in the little hired boat, concealed by its hood, Nicholas was not much aware even of Gelis, close to him, watching. His three captors leaned at his shoulders, their eyes, too, on the silver thing spinning. He could not have disguised it. He could not even have controlled the stick, very likely. All he knew, and they didn't, was that the force was coming from two people, close to one another. One of them he now knew was Margot. The other must be the child. And they were going towards it.

Once, he remembered the cruel hoax of Cyprus and the *dumm*, the deep summons he had seemed to experience then. But this time, he had not been thinking of gold; and Gelis was with him, her hands clenched white one on the other.

Once, he thought of something that he had been told about Margot, and that he thought sometimes that Tobie also knew.

It did not matter.

The flotilla moved down the crowd-lined Canal, passing the palaces of Bembo and Loredano and Cavalli; passing the Ca' Niccolò, beflagged and garlanded like the others; servants crowding its balcony; all its torches ablaze. No arrow crossed the water tonight.

On either bank, lamps strung along jetties threw blooms of peacock colour into the water. Streamers of mist veiled and unveiled the tinted window-lights studding the darkness: the gilded mooring posts faded and glinted and overhead the fireworks, when they began, seemed to hang behind films.

Katelijne watched them from under the flag of the Knights, and collected her thoughts, which kept straying. At the time of the Abundance in Cairo, every mosque and palace and tower was swagged and massy with light, and boats of joy moved like this through the water, bells tinkling, music rising, while fireworks flowered and spat. She remembered fireworks and the Unicorn knighthood, and the unobtrusive, deft actions by which Nicholas de Fleury had exiled two people, and caused her uncle to suffer the consequences.

Fireworks. Catherine wheels. What had she learned from her pilgrimage? She didn't know; or not yet. Her uncle had brought back literal catherine wheels, or their models. They were to decorate his magnificent house in another city built on canals. Everyone celebrated water. In Venice they married the sea. After the disaster at Negroponte, the Turks had laughed at the Venetian Envoy: 'You can leave off wedding the sea. It is our turn, now.'

Jan bumped into her, knocking the jew's trump out of her hand. She picked it up. He said, 'What do you want that for?' Without waiting for an answer, he walked unsteadily to the other side of the boat, the side next to the beautiful vessel she was pretending nonchalantly to ignore. The *bissona* flying the unicorn flag of the Banco di Niccolò.

Apprehension gripped her, turning to horror as she saw him lift one unsteady knee to the rail. She said quickly, 'M. de Fleury isn't there. What are you doing?' He was dressed, pathetically, in cock's feathers, with glass eyes and a stiff golden beak and a great ruff of iridescent blue and green plumage.

He paid no attention but continued to climb with the evident intention of crossing to the next boat. She wished they were not so close, or moving so slowly. For a young man, even when drunk, it was easy. Infuriatingly, all the people she knew – M. le Grant, Master Gregorio – seemed as yet unaware. Then she saw Dr Tobias step forward and hold a hand out to steady and stop him. There was an argument. Heads turned. She saw Dr Tobias shake his head and step back, while Jan fell inside the Bank's boat and, righting himself, began to walk forwards. Dr Tobias glanced towards her, and she knew he had seen her, but he didn't approach. A few feathers stuck to the gunwale.

She thought it was the end, but it wasn't. Far from wishing to join Dr Tobias, Jan had merely used his boat as a bridge. Reaching the opposite rail, he clambered over and dropped out of sight. Feathers rose, and he reappeared giggling. Kathi saw he was in the boat next to the Bank's. Once in darkness, it was now lit and raucous with laughter. The voices seemed to belong mostly to women. A man emerged, his golden tunic adorned with a panther skin, and a wreath of ivy and vines in his hair. The costume exhibited the splendid symmetry of his body, but when he helped Jan aboard, you could see that the bare, cross-gartered leg was not that of a young man at all.

She realised suddenly whose boat it was. This time, Jan was staying aboard. When he disappeared under the awning, there was an outburst of feminine laughter.

Her uncle had not seen.

The fleet moved round the loop of the Canal, passing the Ca' Foscari, the Palazzo Justinian. The loggias were full, the roof-tops crowded. Music fought against music from one house to the next, obliterated sometimes by drunken singing within. The heat from the massed torches warmed the dank night air of February; seagulls dipped and rose into fog. Their whining, thought Tobie fancifully, sounded like the souls of the dead; the shrill voice of the mask, of the *larva*, of the ghost from beyond.

The boat flying the Lusignan flag was filled with such phantoms. Chiefly he hated those masks which were white. A human back turned, and there was the oval, inhuman face, the pursed lips, the slender, classical nose, the ceramic cheekbones, down which a thread of silver or gold had been lazily drawn. The lightless eyes and cut nostrils above the beautiful gown; the shy, timorous gestures. The girl wearing the black diamanté mask had come forward again, and was gazing down at the boat with Jan in it.

Tobie had seen who was in the next boat. He had tried to stop Jan from climbing over. He knew Simon de St Pol had befriended Adorne's son. He knew the girls in St Pol's cabin were harlots, masked and costumed as men. The only mercy was that Jan also was masked, and the journey was short. Nothing much could occur in ten minutes.

Two minutes later, the curtains in the next boat flew apart and Dionysus emerged, dragging an indignant cockerel by the wrist. It was not apparent what they were arguing about. Then the argument suddenly stopped, as the eye of the cockerel fell on the Corner boat beyond, and the girl in the black mask who stood there.

Slowly she raised one gloved hand and allowed something to float from it: a kerchief. Jan leaned out and caught it. Then, shaking off the man at his side, he placed a precarious foot on the gunwale and offered his hands to the girl who began, with slow, ineffable grace, to step from her boat to his. Simon de St Pol made to move to prevent her.

Tobie called John's name, without making it urgent, while he himself scanned the Knights' boat. Adorne, to his relief, was not visible, but he could see Kathi's red gown, and where her gaze was directed. She saw him. He could feel her question, but do nothing about it. By the time John pushed to his side, the drunken cockerel and Simon were fighting in the next boat while the exquisite girl stood, one ringed hand arrayed at her breast, her mask sloping. The single tear glistened. The curtains of the deck-salon were open, and the entrance crowded with plumpish young gentlemen.

Simon was not a man of great patience. Perhaps only Jan was surprised when the golden god lifted his arm and caught his feathered disciple an efficient blow to the chin. Jan staggered back, stumbled and fell. The girl made no effort to save him. Instead she lifted her head and put first one gloved hand, then the other on Dionysus's near golden shoulder. The cockerel scrambled to its feet. Simon glanced at him, then turned his golden mask to the girl. She leaned on him, her white fingers folded, and he put a muscular arm round her waist.

Jan exploded between them.

By now, every boat within reach was alerted, and people were scrambling to watch. Tobie stood grimly at his own rail, with John and then the others crowding beside him. Father Moriz said something in disgust and walked away; Gregorio followed.

It was never a contest. Jan was the son of a jouster but not the champion that Simon was. He gripped the boy by the shoulders and spoke to him. When the boy continued to fight, he spoke louder. Last of all, Simon de St Pol twisted back the cockerel's arms and, pinning him down, leaned to draw the girl closer.

She came, in a glint of jewels and a rustle of taffeta. She came within an inch of them both. The eye spaces devoured, the diamanté lips hung; the spark of a tear lent its wistfulness to the virginal face. Then Simon wrenched off the mask and the headgear.

Nerio of Trebizond laughed and said, 'Oh! Oh! How cruel!' and rubbed the bare skin of Dionysus's chest with his finger. Then, leaning forward, he plucked a feather from the motionless cockerel's cap and stuck it in his own well-cut, masculine hair. 'Now who will ever teach him the difference?'

Laughter spread. The boy, freed by St Pol, stumbled to the side of the boat, where Tobie and John were already leaning to rescue him. Behind the mask, he was retching. Between them, the two

men lifted him over and set him shivering on the deck of the
Bank's boat. Below the mask, he was green. Tobie took him inside.
In the boat of the Knights, Katelijne Sersanders obtained leave
from her uncle to see to his son, taken sick in the neighbouring
vessel. Her uncle agreed, since Dr Tobias was there and M. de
Fleury (she could assure him) was not.

She crossed. Dr Tobias said, 'Thank God you're here. Hold the
bowl. I've got to see what Simon is up to.'

'I can tell you,' said Kathi.

Now they were close to the Basin; the deep-water anchorage off the
Doge's Palace and the Piazzetta. The young man Nerio, having
kissed all the whores, replaced his mask and swung himself laughing
back aboard his own boat from which, in a moment, the Queen of
Cyprus and her mother and aunts sent across a casket of sweetmeats. Simon's ladies fell on them. Simon ignored them. He
might be deprived of his partner, but that wasn't going to stop his
glorious plan.

He knew where the vessel was, because he had arranged for its
hiring. He knew who would be in it, because three of them were in
his employment as well. Having an office in Genoa, he had not
found it difficult to discover where Gelis van Borselen was going to
stay, or to forestall her when she wanted armed help. She would
not have heard his name mentioned. That is, she might not have
minded, but one could never be sure.

He had to admit, too, that his father had helped. It was awkward,
because his father and he had quite different ideas about what to
do with Gelis's son.

He fastened his panther skin a little more securely and began,
with confidence, to jump from boat to boat.

It had come to Nicholas some time before, that Gelis was frightened.
It did not mean much, in the curious place where he was. He
assumed she was afraid that he would somehow perish before he
had found what she wanted. When he could not concentrate any
more, he said, having obtained permission to speak, 'Do you think
I could see where we are?' They would not let him into the open,
but they drew back the curtain a little so that he could see how
close they were to the Basin and the end of their journey.

The end of his journey. Ahead was the terminus, the space of
water lit by the flood of torchlight from the Piazzetta where all the
regatta would finally come to rest. The place was marked by a
group of objects at anchor: the broad barge upon which, earlier,

the stilt-walkers and acrobats had performed, and the fire-swallowers had sent their columns of flame into the air; the raft with the windlass from which rose the double rope joining palace to campanile, up which the tightrope artists had walked; the floating sea-monster which by day delighted and terrorised children from canal to canal. And within the rectangle they described, a vessel he could not yet see, from which came the summons he felt.

He did not need the whistle any more; the desecrated whistle. He let it swing to its furthest extent from his lacerated finger, and loosed it to hurtle ahead, accurate as a date stone, through the curtain and into the water. Gelis started. The soldier behind struck his arm. Then he saw the golden figure leaping towards him, spanning the widening gap between boats. He had no doubt who it was.

He thought at first, naturally, that Gelis had planned it. He was surprised when she gave an order to her three hirelings beside him. 'Send that man away.'

He said nothing. If she did not recognise Simon de St Pol, it was not for him to tell her. Then he heard her repeat sharply, 'Stop that man from coming aboard!' and realised that she knew who it was. And, further, that the men also knew who it was, and were not going to do as she said.

Nicholas said, 'They are Simon's, not yours,' and watched, almost with pity, as understanding came to her face.

The boat slowed. The cluster of moored vessels ahead was very close. His own boat, just in front, would be among the first to drop anchor. Oddly, above the strange, dispersed clamour all about him, the music, the laughter, the subdued roar that rose like a thunder-cloud from the land, there came from ahead the sound of a jew's trump, playing a tune. A nursery tune: the notes he had built for a mechanical bird, once, to sing.

He looked at Gelis, and saw that she had unmasked. Her face in the dim light was white. He lifted his hands and, since no one objected, bared his face as well to the air. His hand throbbed. The trump, like a bee in his thoughts, had strayed into a different jingle. Simon arrived: in fur, and cloth of gold, and the glorious conviction of triumph. He threw his mask on the floor, walking to Gelis. 'Well, my dear. You have brought him to look at our son?' And bending, kissed her.

In front of Nicholas, he had clearly expected her to respond. When she did not, he put it down to shyness, perhaps, and was rougher the second time, so that she pulled away, gasping. Nicholas did nothing to help her. Only when Simon frowned and, looking up, jerked his head to dismiss the three men from the cabin did

Nicholas say, when they were alone, 'It is not your son, but mine.'

Dionysus turned, his panther-skin ruffled, his arm gripping the girl's shoulder. He said, 'She told you that?' He was smiling.

'Hardly,' Nicholas said. 'She wasn't trying to please me. But it wasn't difficult to make sure. You can't sire children now, can you? Although – poor Dionysus – you've been attempting for years. It must have been fun, at least, trying.'

'I have children,' Simon said, astonished. He let Gelis go. 'Bastards, I don't mind admitting, but if you took the trouble to ask, you'd find I was, forgive me, sufficiently adequate. Or am I supporting them out of philanthropy?'

'Do you want an answer?' Nicholas said. 'I did take trouble. No one has taken more trouble than I have. I found every girl you slept with in Scotland, and bedded them all. Some, I must say, are better than others. None of their children is yours. They're quite ready to swear it.' Outside, there was a scuffle. He kept his eyes on his wife, and on Dionysus, who was making no move now to embrace her. She had started to tremble.

Simon said, 'I suppose it makes sense. You try to murder me. You kill my sister. And now you are attempting to discount even my natural sons. It will be Henry's turn next.' He was breathing hard. He said, 'I have children. Your wife's child is mine.'

'Then come and see him,' said a voice.

Margot.

Nicholas swallowed. Simon frowned and Gelis, beside him, suddenly put out a hand to support herself. Margot, standing holding the curtain, looked worn, and a little stern. Behind her was Tobie.

Tobie said, 'We've got rid of the soldiers. Kathi followed you, Nicholas. We shouldn't have found you without her. The boat is over there. We can all go there in the *bissona*. Dionysus may as well see what there is to see.'

Margot came to Nicholas and said, 'There is no need to wait any more. Come.' And after a moment, when Simon and Gelis had left, 'Isn't this what you wanted?'

He had no original words. 'I feel,' he said, 'as if heaven lay close upon earth, and I between the two, breathing through the eye of a needle.'

'That is a man on the point of death,' Margot said. 'Not of life. I have done this for you. Don't belittle it.'

'*Belittle it!*' he said. And then, 'What of Gregorio?'

And she said, 'I am not afraid now. Not of anything.'

*

The little boat lay low between the moored vessels, its oars at rest, and the candle under the awning threw a single squat shadow, cloaked and hooded, which might have been that of a man or a woman. Then it altered a little, showing that the one figure sheltered another.

The *bissona* with the unicorn crest came up very slowly, and touched, its lights out. Margot did not step down, but waited until Nicholas stirred, and then let himself down, his head bent, from the one boat to the other. They saw him move to the awning and wait. Then he spoke, and someone answered inside, so that he parted the curtain and sank to his knees. The voice had been that of a woman, and Scots. They saw his shadow, quite still on the canvas.

On the bigger boat, Margot suddenly moved, and Gregorio's arms closed about her. 'Don't leave me,' he said.

There were tears on his cheeks. She looked up at him and said, 'I will do better than that.'

Then the curtain moved again, and Nicholas came out.

There was a child in his arms. Perfect in body, brown of hair, grey of eye – even by torchlight there was little doubt whose son he was. Then he smiled, and there was no doubt at all.

Across his head, the eyes of Nicholas held those of Gelis. Someone uttered an obscenity: Simon de St Pol, swinging round on her so that she flinched. Then he turned on his heel. His own boat lay just behind. The women had gone, but someone stood very still at the rail; a large man, wearing the mask of an owl. Then he vanished.

In the midst of the clangour about them they floated in silence. Trumpets stuttered. Fireworks crackled like distant artillery. Gelis suddenly held out her arms, her face running with tears, her gaze fixed on the child. He lay and smiled, but did not stir, who had known so many kind hands.

The bell of the Basilica spoke: a flat, harsh clang that deepened into a toll. The sound sank through the sparks in the air, down the walls with their torches; down the lamplit boats and the spiralling water, and wiped it all dark.

By due command of the bell, every light in Venice was extinguished, and all the noise stopped. The Serenissima lay plunged into darkness. Then, dimly, her other bells started to sound, hunting up, hunting down as they rang through their changes. Midnight had come, and brought a new order.

It was Julius who found a lantern, and tinder, and brought the light up on deck to where the others stood still. He walked to the side, to help Nicholas back. Where the little vessel had been, the water swirled, black and empty. The boat, the child, the woman and Nicholas, all had gone.

Canst thou bind the Unicorn with his band in the furrow?

Tomorrow. Tomorrow, when the apricots are here.

A NOTE ABOUT THE AUTHOR

Dorothy Dunnett was born in Dunfermline, Scotland, in 1923.
She is the author of the Francis Crawford of Lymond novels, a historical
sequence set in the sixteenth century; seven mystery novels; *King Hereafter,*
an epic novel about Macbeth; *The Scottish Highlands,* a book of
photographs by David Paterson, for which she wrote the text in
collaboration with her husband, Alastair Dunnett; and three earlier
Niccolò novels. In 1992, Queen Elizabeth appointed her an Officer of the
Order of the British Empire. Mrs. Dunnett lives with
her husband in Edinburgh, Scotland.

A NOTE ON THE TYPE

The text of this book was set in a digitized version of Imprint,
a Monotype face originally cut in 1913 for the periodical of the same name.
It was modeled on Caslon, but has a larger x-height and different
italics, which harmonize better with the roman.

Composed in Great Britain

Orkney

NORWAY

SWEDE

SCOTLAND

DENMARK

Edinburgh
Berwick

Zeeland

Newcastle

IRELAND

Lancaster

York

Lubeck
Hamburg
Bremen

ENGLAND

HOLY

Bristol

London

Antwerp

Cologne

BOHE

K
o

Southampton

Bruges
Brussels

Liege

ROMAN

Calais

EMPIRE

Atlantic Ocean
(Sea of Obscurity)

Seine

Brittany

Paris

Loire

Dijon

Ulm

Salzburg

Innsbruck

ARCHI
o

AUS

BURGUNDY

SWISS
CONFEDER-
ATION

FRANCE

Bay of
Biscay

Lyons

Savoy

Milan

Turin

Venic

Marseilles

Bologna

KINGDOM
OF NAVARRE

Bordeaux

Rhône

Pisa

Florence

Genoa

Siena

Pamplona

KINGDOM OF

Corsica
(to Genoa)

Rom

Valladolid

KINGDOM
OF

ARAGON

LEON &

Barcelona

Naples

Lisbon

Toledo

KING

Valencia

o

KDM. OF PORTUGAL

CASTILE

Balearic Is.
(to Aragon)

Sardinia
(to Aragon)

NAP

Lagos

Seville

Granada

SICILY
(to Aragon)

KINGDOM of
GRANADA

Tunis

Sousa

Ma

Monastir

BARBARY

Fez

Cairo

Nile

0   100   200 miles

Monastery
of St. Anthony

Gulf of Suez

Monastery of
St. Catherine

Gebel
Musa
(Mt Sinai)

Gebel
Katherina

Tor

Peter McClure
1993

0   80

Miles